A Dream Come True:

An Entertaining Way for Students To Learn Greek Mythology

Bill Hiatt

George Donnelly, editor

Julie Nicholls, cover designer

Bill Hiatt Publishing
Culver City, California

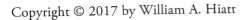

For every student who ever struggled to learn Greek mythology

Intended Audience for This Book

I wrote this book for students learning Greek mythology in a specific course at a specific high school. If you are in that course, this book is for you! If you are a student at another school, please keep in mind that there are many different versions of most myths and that there are too many myths for any general survey to include them all. Consequently, the mythological content of this book will be somewhat different from your regular text. There is no harm in using this book as a supplement, but you should not try to use it as a replacement for your assigned reading.

If you are an adult who enjoys mythology and wants to learn more about it, you may also find this book useful. However, it is not intended to be a substitute for more scholarly treatments of the subject. (If you're curious about the way in which the book approaches mythology, you can find an explanation in Appendix A.)

If you are interested in finding additional mythology resources, be sure to look at the suggestions in Appendix E.

Table of Contents

Chapter 1: Prologue

The last thing Keisha Henry could remember was being in a very long, very tedious study session for tomorrow's mythology test. She had never fallen asleep in a study group before, but she must have this time because she was alone and surrounded by fog so thick she couldn't see a thing through it. She had to be dreaming.

The fog didn't bother her—except that it was cold, so cold she shivered. She couldn't remember ever having a dream before in which she could feel something that intensely. For that matter, she couldn't remember knowing she was dreaming while she was still asleep.

Wandering in the fog was boring at first but rapidly became unnerving. Keisha knew dreams were supposed to be shaped by the subconscious mind, and as incoherent as they seemed, they often had some psychological purpose. What could her subconscious possibly be trying to tell her with a bleak and unchanging landscape?

She hoped it wasn't a suggestion that her life was going nowhere. There were days when she felt like that, times when she wondered if all the honors and AP classes, all the extracurricular activities, all the efforts to create a perfect transcript so she could get into the perfect college would really pay off. One of her sister's friends had done everything right and still not gotten into the school of her choice. Another had gotten into Harvard and then been unhappy there.

Keisha tried not to obsess over the future, but there were days when she wondered whether she was making progress or just wandering in a figurative fog—much like the dream fog that now surrounded her.

Just when she thought she could no longer stand the monotony, she saw a flash of brownish red in the fog. That had to be the hair of Patrick O'Riley, one of the guys in the study group.

"Patrick!" she called. He was far from being her favorite person. Actually, he was pretty close to being her least favorite—but at this point, she would have hung out with her worst enemy in preference to being alone.

"Keisha?" he asked as he blundered in her direction. He had a big smile on his face when he finally emerged.

"It is you. I was beginning to think I was alone here. Where are we?"

Keisha was tempted to point out their surroundings were just something her subconscious dredged up, but what would be the point of telling a character in her dream that?

"I don't know. I've never seen anything quite this unvarying before. Meeting you is the first break in the monotony I've had in what seems like hours."

"Think the rest of the study group is here?" asked Patrick, looking around and squinting at the fog as if he would find a way to see through it.

"If you and I are, it's a good bet they are, too," replied Keisha. Since the subconscious often used recent memories as raw material, she wouldn't be surprised to see more of the people she had been with when she fell asleep.

Sure enough, one by one her study buddies came staggering out of the fog: Yong Choi, Yasmin Sassani, Mateo Reyes, Fatima Hadad, and Thanos Logios.

At first, they were overjoyed to see each other, but that feeling only lasted until they remembered they still had no idea where they were or how they had gotten there.

"This has to be a dream," muttered Yong, staring into the swirling fog.

Keisha was surprised again. She'd never before had a character in a dream allude to the fact that it was a dream. Perhaps getting very little sleep over several days was having more of an impact on her than she cared to admit.

"I've never had such a dream that felt so real," said Fatima in her usual quiet voice.

"Real, maybe, but not realistic," Mateo pointed out. "Endless fog? Where in the real world would you find something like that?"

"There's no light source," added Yasmin. "I mean, obviously there's light, but where's it coming from? It's...it's as if the fog itself is glowing."

Then a long, mournful howl made all of them jump, even the usually stoic Yong. Keisha shivered again, but this time not from the cold.

Clearly, they were not alone.

They did not have to wonder too long what was sharing this foggy wilderness with them, because an enormous black wolf leaped out of the fog, fangs bared, eyes flashing. Everyone had the same reflex: turn and run. However, what were the odds any of them could outrun a wolf? Probably not much better than the odds of beating a wolf in a fight. Perhaps they could gang up on the wolf—but what if there were more wolves hiding in the fog?

"Phobetor!" shouted a stern voice from somewhere nearby. "Leave them alone!"

The wolf growled in the general direction from which the voice had come, but then, much to the students' surprise, it turned and trotted away.

"That was…anticlimactic," said Patrick. Keisha figured none of the guys were going to admit that they had been just as scared as the girls.

"Hello!" called Mateo. "Who's out there?" Aside from a distant echo of his own voice, he got no answer.

"Great! We don't have to worry about the wolf, just about a disembodied voice," said Yong.

"I know where we are," announced Thanos.

"Well," prompted Yasmin. "Don't keep us in suspense."

"This is the land of dreams—Demos Oneiroi the Greeks called it—in the Underworld," Thanos said, as if he were describing the weather.

"The what?" asked Patrick. "You mean, like the Greek mythological Underworld? That's the dumbest thing I've ever heard."

"Because there are so many much more rational explanations for a never-ending fog bank populated by enormous wolves?" asked Mateo, his voice dripping with sarcasm.

"It's a dream, genius!" snapped Patrick. "Just like Yong said. Isn't that obvious?"

Yong looked a little surprised. He and Patrick didn't normally get along, let alone agree with each other.

"How can we all be having the same dream, though?" asked Yasmin. "I've never heard of that."

"I'm dreaming, and the rest of you are just characters in my dream," replied Patrick, echoing what Keisha had been thinking only minutes before. Hearing him say it made her question her original assumption, though. If all these people were conjured up by her subconscious, how could they act so exactly as they did in real life? She'd never had a dream experience with so much real-world detail.

"I'm not in *your* dream," said Yasmin.

"You have been before," said Patrick, flashing her his most mischievous grin. "You weren't wearing quite as much, though."

Fatima looked disgusted, and Mateo smacked Patrick in the arm. "Don't be such a pig, man! Anyway, this is no time for flirting."

"I wouldn't call it flirting," muttered Yasmin, still glaring at Patrick.

"Sorry," said Patrick, raising his hands, though he didn't sound that sorry. "I was just joking."

"Getting back to the real question," said Keisha loudly enough to get their attention, "something weird is happening. I'm not saying we're really in the Underworld—"

"I just meant we were dreaming about being there, not that we were there," Thanos said quickly.

Keisha shook her head impatiently. "Yeah, I knew that's what you meant. So could we all be sharing a dream of the Underworld? Most scientists would say no, we couldn't share the same dream, but there are a small number of cases in which mutual dreaming may have occurred. Before right now I would have said it was impossible, but it's the explanation that best fits the facts."

"How is such a thing possible?" asked Yong.

"I don't know," Keisha replied, playing with her hair as she spoke. "I've never liked the evidence for extrasensory perception, but hypothetically that might be the answer. We were all really close together when we dozed off. We were sitting around a table, right? And we were all thinking about the same thing. If a telepathic connection is possible at all, the conditions would have been good for it."

Patrick snorted. "Seriously?"

"Perhaps a mutual dream would also be a more vivid one, because it's generated by the minds of several people, not just one," suggested Yong.

"Who cares? If this is a dream, I just want to wake up," said Fatima. She looked a little panicked and sounded as if she were about to hyperventilate.

"In ancient times people believed that dreams were a message from the gods—" started Thanos.

"So now the Greek gods are real?" asked Patrick, looking as if he was readying another joke.

Thanos looked at him with obvious annoyance. "Of course not. But maybe someone who does exist is trying to tell us something."

"That we should actually have read the material?" asked Mateo. He seemed to be trying hard not to laugh, but to Keisha it wasn't funny. She had been irritated that only three of them had done all the reading.

She looked carefully at Thanos, who, whatever else could be said about him, *had* done the assigned reading—and considerably more. From his contributions to the study group, she could tell he had read everything about ancient Greece he could get his hands on, including many of the ancient Greek texts from which the myths came, though she had only realized how knowledgeable he was during the group meetings. Nobody else in the group had really known him that well before, either. All she really knew about him was that he was very good at math. Frankly, he had ended up in the group mostly because he was an exchange student from Greece, and some of the others had the stereotypic idea that he must, therefore, know about Greek mythology. Actually, Patrick had thought Greeks still worshiped the ancient gods, but Keisha tried hard not to think about that—it made her grind her teeth too much.

"Thanos, why do you think we're here?" she asked finally.

"I wish I knew," he replied. "If we're here for a reason, though, we should find out what it is, right?"

"What makes you think this is the Underworld?" asked Yong. "I don't remember anything in the book about the Underworld being filled with fog."

"The descriptions in ancient texts vary," Thanos replied, "and the Underworld wasn't described as being necessarily the same throughout. That the land of dreams could be all foggy makes a certain amount of sense. What got me thinking this was the Demos Oneiroi, though, is that Phobetor is the name of the god of nightmares. He often assumes the form of animals—and the voice called the wolf Phobetor."

"Under that theory, whose voice did we hear?" asked Yong.

"Morpheus, the god of dreams," answered Thanos as if it was obvious. "He'd be the one in charge here."

"I don't remember that part at all," said Fatima, sounding less panicked than before but still a little worried. Dream or no dream, the test was still tomorrow, and the idea of sleeping through their review time seemed to be getting on her nerves.

"Morpheus and Phobetor were two of the children of Hypnos, god of sleep," Thanos explained. "There were others as well, called Oneiroi, who together were responsible for all dreams. They entered the mortal world through two gates. False dreams entered through the gate of ivory, while true ones, particularly those inspired by the gods, entered through the gate of horn."

"I'm reminded of how much I need to review," said Fatima. "I really need to wake up." She still spoke softly, but much more emphatically than usual.

"I've been trying to wake up for several minutes," said Yong. "I just can't. I don't think it's that easy. If it were, being charged by the wolf would have caused at least some of us to wake up."

"We need to figure out why we're here," said Thanos with a certainty that baffled Keisha. How could he possibly know that?

"We need to understand what whoever put us here wants us to know," he continued. "Then we'll wake up."

"How do we do that?" asked Yasmin, waving her hand at the fog. "There's nothing here. How do we learn anything from this dismal place?"

As is she had conjured it up, a black swirl formed in the fog, becoming larger and larger until it was an enormous doorway. No, not exactly a doorway. Yong investigated a little and discovered there was some kind of barrier, smooth as glass, that prevented anyone from walking through.

It was a window! But a window looking out on what?

Thanos, still Mr. Certainty, pointed at the enormous window, through which they could now see only darkness, but with something moving through it, like an image barely glimpsed from the corner of one's eye.

"There. We will find the answers there."

Chapter 2: Creation

"What are we looking at?" Mateo asked Thanos. Keisha prided herself on being well read, but she had to admit Thanos was probably the most likely to know the answer in this case.

Thanos stared for a minute at the blur they could see through the window, a fuzziness so indistinct it made their eyes hurt to look at it. Though no light came from it, it somehow stood out against the surrounding darkness "In the beginning was Chaos."

"I thought Chaos was a jumble of matter and energy," said Yong, squinting at the blur.

"Later Roman writers like Ovid describe it that way, but early Greeks like Hesiod portray something more like what we're seeing. *Chaos* originally meant chasm or void rather than confusion," Thanos replied. "That's why it's so hard for us to look at—you can't really see a void."

"There are other things out there," said Fatima, pointing at the window. "Unless I'm imagining them. It's so hard to tell."

"No, you're right," said Thanos. "That's Gaia, the Earth." He pointed to a large mass, gray and lifeless. "That one's Tartarus." He indicated a huge, dark pit, hard to see against the surrounding blackness. "Those two are Nyx and Erebus, night and darkness personified." He waved his right hand in the general direction of two black masses, even harder to see than Tartarus.

"I must not have gotten this far in the book," said Patrick, scratching his head.

"The creation story was in one of the first chapters," said Mateo. Patrick ignored him.

A sudden flash caught them by surprise. It was so bright, especially in contrast to the preceding darkness, that it momentarily blinded them.

"Was that the sun being born?" asked Yasmin.

"No," said Thanos, when their eyes had begun to recover. "Look more closely."

For the first time, they could see a human figure. Well, sort of human, anyway. He was the most handsome guy Keisha had ever seen, and she could tell from the expressions on the other girls' faces that they would not have argued the point. Of course, anyone would probably have looked good compared to chaos, darkness, and bottomless pits. Still, this newcomer drew her eyes like boy band concerts drew preteen girls.

"That's Eros," said Thanos, breaking the awkward silence. "You know, love," he added in response to Patrick's puzzled expression.

"Like Cupid?" asked Patrick.

"That's the Roman name," Yong pointed out.

"But I thought Cupid was a little baby," Patrick said, scratching his head again.

Thanos smiled a little. "Eros was always portrayed as what we would think of as a teenager in early myths and art, I guess because that's the age people tend to experience romantic love for the first time. It wasn't until later that he was pictured as a baby, to show the irrationality of love."

Keisha, usually a very attentive student, missed most of Thanos's explanation, as did Yasmin and Fatima, each of whom looked as if she was thinking about being held tightly in Eros's arms.

Thanos snickered and said something like, "fairest among the deathless gods, who unnerves the limbs and overcomes the mind and wise counsels of all gods and all men." Keisha realized he was quoting the Greek poet, Hesiod— and that he had caught the girls with their eyes riveted to Eros.

"Everything is…different," said Yasmin, perhaps trying to cover her embarrassment.

"Love changes everything," said Thanos.

The glowing Eros was now echoed by light from other sources.

"Erebus and Nyx just became the parents of Aether (the upper air) and Hemera (day)," Thanos said, pointing to something like a sunrise, but without the sun.

"Still no light sources," said Yasmin.

"Not very scientific," said Yong, scowling a little. "Light just comes from nowhere."

"Light comes from love," suggested Thanos. "Early Greeks didn't make much distinction between the physical and the spiritual. Later Greeks often used the physical to represent the spiritual."

"Earth is different now," said Mateo.

Sure enough, the Earth, which had been gray only moments before, was now green, and above it hung a recognizable sky, dotted with stars.

"Gaia brought forth Uranus, the sky," explained Thanos.

"Not mine," said Patrick. "That must be your..."

"Grow up!" snapped Yong. Patrick frowned at him and clenched his fists, but Mateo moved between them—a not very subtle hint to Patrick to leave Yong alone.

"Just as Mother Earth brought forth Father Sky, she also brought forth Pontus, the sea," added Thanos quickly, being careful not to say *Uranus* again, just in case. Looking more closely, Keisha noticed the shimmering water forming on part of the earth's surface.

"Then earth and sky made love, and from their union came many children, including the Titans," Thanos continued.

As if on cue, the view through the window shifted, so that the earth was much closer, and upon the green surface they could now see a group of godlike beings.

"The most important of the early Titans were Cronus and Rhea, who married and became the parents of the first Olympian gods," said Thanos. He pointed to a female Titan who looked somehow comforting and maternal— hardly a match for the male Titan standing next to her, handsome but hard-featured. Rhea looked like someone you might want to have for a mother, but Cronus was far from being anyone's ideal father.

"But weren't they brother and sister?" asked Mateo. "The ancient Greek believed in incest?"

"Not among people," said Keisha. "Like every other society, they had a strong incest taboo. However, early Greeks viewed the gods as being above human morality. Remember that the Greeks didn't understand genetics and had no idea what consequences inbreeding would have."

"Cronus and Rhea weren't the only brother-sister marriage, either," said Thanos. "Hyperion and Theia married and became the parents of Eos, the dawn; Helios, the sun; and Selene, the moon."

"Light sources—finally!" said Yong.

For a while, they watched the radiant Helios and Selene alternately driving their chariots across the sky while Eos glowed rosily on the eastern horizon.

"The ancient Greeks thought the world was flat?" asked Fatima.

"Yeah, most ancient people did in the beginning," Keisha replied.

They had already seen water on part of the earth's surface as Pontus had come forth, but now they also noticed water completely encircling the earth.

"That's Oceanus, another Titan," said Thanos. "He married his sister, Tethys, and they fathered the Oceanids, nymphs of the outer sea, as well as the Potamoi, river gods."

"So they had a god of the sea *and* a god of the ocean?" asked Yasmin. "That seems weird."

"Early Greeks probably thought of Pontus as being the Mediterranean Sea and Oceanus as being the larger body of water they had heard was beyond the Straits of Gibraltar—what we would think of as the Atlantic Ocean," Thanos explained. "Originally, those were the only two large bodies of water they knew about."

"There are a lot of other overlaps like that in Greek mythology," Keisha said. Some scholars think the early Greeks were a combination of many smaller groups. Each group had its own gods and goddesses, and when the groups came together, some duplicates may have been merged, but others were left as separate gods, even though they represented the same thing or had the same function.

"It's also possible that the same god might have been known by different names in different places, and over time people began to treat each name as a separate being."

"Boring!" announced Patrick after faking a very loud yawn. "Boring, and probably not on the test."

"Another Titan brother-sister combination was Coeus and Phoebe," said Thanos, probably figuring the best way to deal with Patrick might be to ignore him. "They became the parents of Asteria, goddess of falling stars, or comets, as we would say; and Leto, who later became the mother of Apollo and Artemis."

"Iapetus, however, did not marry his sister," continued Thanos.

"Well, it's nice *someone* didn't," said Mateo.

"He married Clymene, an Oceanid and therefore his niece, though," Thanos pointed out. "Their children were Atlas, Prometheus, and Epimetheus, names that will probably sound familiar."

"Nope!" said Patrick, though he was looking more and more worried as the flood of names kept coming.

Keisha was happy her reading enabled her to distinguish those siblings by their looks. Atlas was bulging with muscle but had a vacant expression on his face—a little like Patrick, actually. Prometheus looked thoughtful as he stared off into the distance. Epimetheus, by contrast, didn't seem to be paying much attention to what was happening around him, foreshadowing the trouble Keisha knew he would get into later.

"Crius married Eurybia, a daughter of Gaia and Pontus, and they became the parents of Perses, the destroyer; Pallas, Titan of warcraft; and Astraeus, the Titan of dusk and balance for Eos, the dawn."

"I wish I had something to take notes on," said Fatima, looking around unhappily.

"It's a dream," Mateo pointed out. "It's not as if you'll have them when you wake up."

Keisha was beginning to wonder how something so complicated could possibly be a dream, but she kept the doubts to herself.

"Are any of those last guys really important?" asked Patrick impatiently.

Thanos sighed. "We know them mostly because of their children. Perses married Asteria, his cousin, and they became the parents of Hecate."

"Never heard of her," said Patrick.

Keisha and Yong shared disgusted glances, but both refrained from saying what they were thinking.

"She was a versatile goddess, one who had power in the sky, on the earth, and in the sea," Thanos explained. "No one knows why she was so powerful, but later, when Zeus took over, she was the only Titan to retain all of her earlier authority.

"No one knows why her reputation changed, either, but slowly she became a goddess of the dark phase of the moon, of witchcraft and of evil. Instead of being revered, she was feared by all.

"Pallas had a more varied group of kids. He married Styx, nymph of one of the Underworld rivers, and became the father of Zelus (glory), Nike (victory), Cratus (strength), and Bia (force). Astraeus, the dusk, married Eos, the dawn, and they became the parents of the four winds, as well as the stars and planets the ancient Greeks knew about. The planets were named after other gods, but they were also gods themselves."

"That's hardly confusing at all," said Mateo.

"It's no different from anything else about Greek mythology," muttered Patrick.

"Some of the Titan women don't seem to have husbands," said Fatima.

"Some of the brothers married someone other than a sister," said Yong. "I wonder if the ones left over were lonely."

"Mnemosyne, the personification of memory, seemed content to study, but she was not alone forever," Thanos explained. "Eventually Zeus made her the mother of the nine Muses, for all the arts and sciences ultimately depended on memory."

"Zeus was a total player," said Patrick, actually right for once.

"Themis, the personification of divine order and law, was likewise eventually loved by Zeus and became the mother of the Horae, or seasons."

"That doesn't make sense," objected Mateo.

"It doesn't have to make sense; it's mythology," said Patrick gloomily.

"Why would an abstraction give birth to an aspect of nature like that? Wouldn't it make more sense if Gaia had given birth to the seasons?" Mateo asked.

"Perhaps the original storytellers were thinking about the fact that the seasons were part of the natural *order*," suggested Yong. "They might not have been making the same kind of distinction between nature and human society we would."

"Some stories also make the Morae (Fates), children of Zeus and Themis, again a blend of the natural—life and death—with the overall order of the universe," Thanos continued. "However, different storytellers made different associations, and in their view, the Fates were among the gloomy children of Nyx, I suppose because of how much people fear death."

"Night and Darkness had a lot of kids?" asked Mateo. "I wouldn't have expected them to be thought of as sources of life."

"A lot of people have sex in the dark," Patrick said. Keisha didn't admit it out loud, but that wasn't a completely stupid idea about how early people might have thought about darkness. Maybe Patrick wouldn't be completely hopeless—if he actually did his work.

"So who else did Nyx and Erebus give birth to?" asked Yasmin.

"Actually, Nyx by herself," replied Thanos. "Nemesis, the grim goddess of retribution; Moros (doom); Ker (destruction); the Keres (goddesses of violent death) Thanatos (death in general when he's by himself, but peaceful death when he appears with the Keres); Momus (blame); Oziys (pain); Apate (deceit); Geras (old age); and, worst of all, Eris (discord), the opposite of Eros. Eros brings together, but Eris pulls apart."

"But you said earlier that Erebus and Nyx were the parents of Aether and Day, both positive," said Yong.

"It's true that their children are a little more of a mixed bag," agreed Thanos. "Hidden away in the grim mob are also the Hesperides (nymphs of sunset); Hypnos (sleep, and our current host); and Philotes (friendship)."

"I don't get it," said Mateo. "There's no logic to that at all. Why would they have such different children?"

Thanos shrugged. "Haven't you ever seen siblings who were different from each other? I think you may be confusing the Greek concept with later religions that had a tendency to split everything into good and evil. Think about Christianity, for example, with the clear line between God and Satan, angels and demons. In early Greek thinking, there is no such split. Day and night don't represent good and evil. Even death isn't evil exactly; it just is. Remember that ancient Greeks had no devil."

Fatima shuddered and took a step back from the window. "Something weird is happening," she whispered. "I...I feel it."

Thanos squinted at the window, which had darkened noticeably. "The early gods and Titans lived together peacefully for a while, but eventually conflicts developed."

"How could that be, since they were all one family?" asked Mateo.

"Family members sometimes have fights," Keisha pointed out.

"Hopefully, not as bad as these, though," said Thanos. "These led to murder—and to war."

"Finally, we're getting to the good part!" said Patrick. "At last they'll be some gore!"

Fatima shuddered again, harder this time.

Chapter 3: Wars among the Gods

"Why would gods fight against other gods?" asked Yasmin, staring into the growing darkness. "You were just saying the Greeks didn't make a sharp division between good and evil the way a lot of modern religions do. What did they have to fight over?"

"The same things people have to fight over," Thanos replied. "Remember that the Greeks, like most ancient people, didn't conceive of the kind of infinite God that Judaism, Christianity, and Islam visualize. Instead, their gods were anthropomorphic."

"Anthropowhatic?" asked Patrick.

"Human in form," said Keisha tiredly. "They had greater abilities than humans, but they also had human flaws."

"So what was the fight about?" asked Mateo.

"Cronus hated his father. I don't think the myths ever explain why," replied Keisha.

"He was kind of like a rebellious teenager—only in a very dysfunctional family," said Yong. "Instead of just acting out, he turned to violence."

"He went Menendez brothers on his father?" asked Patrick, suddenly more interested.

"He had more motivation that just anger at his father, though," Thanos pointed out. "His mother, Gaia, was angry because Uranus had imprisoned some of her children."

"He kept his own children captive?" asked Fatima, sounding as if she couldn't believe it.

"Yeah," answered Thanos, "but only the ones that weren't physically perfect in his judgment. That meant the Cyclopes, because they had only one eye in the center of their forehead, and the Hecatoncheires, because each one had one hundred arms and fifty heads."

"So he had a bias against people with disabilities?" asked Fatima, even more incredulous than before. "And...and they were his own children?"

"The ultimate dysfunctional family," said Mateo.

"The really odd thing is that Uranus felt that way even though the children who disappointed him were actually better than average in everything except appearance. The Cyclopes were very clever and good with their hands when given half a chance, and the Hecatoncheires were mighty warriors. Hesiod says they were the 'most terrible'—in other words, the fiercest in battle.

"Anyway, Gaia, who always seemed to love her children, turned to Cronus for help. Since he hated his father anyway, he was more than willing."

"I can't see what's happening anymore," said Yasmin. Their window had gone completely black, darker even than the primal emptiness before the emergence of Eros. Not only that, but the ground shook beneath their feet.

"Earthquake?" asked Patrick, looking around worriedly.

"More like a dreamquake," replied Yong, though he too looked a little anxious.

"Perhaps Gaia trembled at Cronus's horrendous attack on his father, even though she put him up to it," suggested Thanos.

At that moment they heard a scream so loud that the surface of their window cracked a little. Several seconds passed before anyone could move.

"What was that?" Fatima finally managed to ask.

"Cronus must have just attacked Uranus," replied Thanos. He used a stone sickle his mother had given him to castrate his own father.

"What's castrate?" asked Patrick.

"Trust me, man, you so do not want to know," said Mateo.

"It's a kind of mutilation that renders a man incapable of having sex," said Keisha, trying to be clinical, though she had to admit she enjoyed Patrick's wince just a little.

They heard no more screams, though the ground continued to vibrate under their feet, a bit unnerving for people who grew up in California.

"Strangely, Cronus's violence brought forth new life," said Thanos, though even he sounded a little shaky. "Where his blood fell on the ground, the Erinyes, or Furies, were born—fitting, since they punished certain crimes against family members."

By now the darkness had cleared, and they could watch the grim Erinyes marching around, their eyes constantly searching for a crime to punish. Those eyes had no pity in them, and their faces had no more humanity than those of statues.

"Giants also came from the blood of Uranus," Thanos mentioned, and sure enough, they actually saw enormous drops of blood strike the earth. Then the gory ground exploded, and when the dust cleared, they could see an army of fully armored giants, each with a spear as long as the tallest tree.

"The giants, born from violence and blood, naturally loved war," continued Thanos, "and eventually they fought against the gods themselves. However, the blood of Uranus also created the Meliae, nymphs of the ash tree."

Coming forth more gently than the giants had, the nymphs, every bit as beautiful as the Erinyes were frightening, rose and sought out the trees they would claim as their own.

"Something's happening over there, in the sea," said Mateo, pointing at a large glob of foam.

"The flesh of Uranus—the part Cronus removed—the conquering Titan threw into the sea, and over time, Aphrodite, goddess of love, was born."

Keisha had to snicker. She and other girls had embarrassed themselves by getting hot and bothered over Eros, but now it was the guys' turn. As Aphrodite emerged from the sea foam, looking even more lovely than Botticelli had painted her, the guys' eyes focused unblinkingly at the window. Keisha was sure if she took their pulses, they would be racing faster than horses in the Kentucky Derby.

"Isn't Aphrodite the daughter of Zeus?" asked Yasmin.

Figuring Thanos was not going to answer, Keisha said, "That's one of the spots where the myths are inconsistent. Hesiod tells the story we've just seen, but there are other origin stories which make Aphrodite the daughter of Zeus and Dione, one of the daughters of Oceanus. The same thing happened with Eros. Hesiod has him as one of the primal forces emerging from chaos, while later stories make him the son of Aphrodite, with the father sometimes being Zeus and sometimes Ares."

"Why aren't they more consistent?" asked Yasmin.

"I'd guess it could have something to do with the differences among the groups that eventually formed Greek society, as we discussed earlier. It could also be that, because transportation and communication were much slower than they are today, people who lived some distance apart had less contact and might more easily develop different stories. Some scholars believe ancient people may not have cared much about the details, anyway, at least not enough to try to standardize the tales."

"The rule of Cronus is another example," said Thanos. He and the other guys had unglued themselves from the window, so Keisha figured Aphrodite must be offstage for the moment.

"Some writers describe the time he and Rhea were king and queen of the gods as a golden age of peace and prosperity. It's hard to visualize Cronus as a good ruler, though, because in some ways he seems even worse than Uranus.

"How so?" asked Mateo.

"First, Cronus betrayed his mother by keeping the Cyclopes and Hecatoncheires imprisoned. Even worse, though, Uranus had cursed Cronus for attacking him, and Gaia predicted that Cronus would be overthrown by his own son just as Cronus had overthrown his own father. Rather than risk that, Cronus took his children from Rhea as they were born and ate them."

"He was a cannibal?" asked Mateo, clearly shocked. "And he ate his own children?"

"Sort of," said Thanos. "As it turns out, he didn't actually digest them, perhaps because they were immortal. Essentially, he kept them prisoner in his stomach."

"Except for the fact that his victims didn't die, he was basically a serial killer. So, yeah, how he could have ruled over a golden age I don't know," added Yong.

"If he wasn't technically a serial killer, he was definitely a serial child abuser," said Yasmin. "And he did it all just to keep power."

"I'm guessing that didn't sit well with the women," said Mateo.

"That's right," said Keisha, though she thought that if he'd done the reading, he wouldn't need to guess. "Rhea was constantly grieving for her swallowed children, and Gaia remained angry over her children that Cronus had left imprisoned. When Rhea came for help to Gaia and Uranus, who wasn't exactly a member of the Cronus fan club either, they were willing enough to aid their daughter. They devised a plan in which Rhea gave birth to her next child, Zeus, on Crete, and Gaia took care of him and hid him away underground until he had time to grow up. Meanwhile, Rhea gave Cronus a stone wrapped up like a baby, and the distracted Titan swallowed it without realizing it wasn't really a child."

"Not very observant of him," said Mateo.

"The ancient Greeks weren't always interested in details like that, but I would bet Rhea was clever about presenting the stone," said Thanos. "Much later, when Zeus was grown and ready, Rhea and Gaia somehow got Cronus to vomit up his other children (Poseidon, Hades, Hera, Demeter, and Hestia) who then escaped while their father was recovering and naturally joined Zeus. Zeus had other allies as well, because he released the Hecatoncheires and Cyclopes from prison. The Hecatoncheires were formidable fighters, and the Cyclopes, who were great craftsmen, fashioned weapons appropriate for such an important battle. For Zeus they made his signature thunderbolts that could destroy anything they hit. For Poseidon they made a trident that could create earthquakes when it struck the earth or tidal waves when it struck the ocean. For Hades they made a vaguely described weapon, perhaps a kind of staff, which could also shake the earth and which had a touch deadly to any living thing—and probably at least painful to an immortal."

Hearing the rumbling of distant thunder, they gathered around the window to watch the battle, which Thanos told them was called the Titanomachy. Cronus and some of the Titans fought fiercely against the younger gods, but even their best efforts failed. Thunderbolts crackled from Zeus's hands one by one in rapid succession, searing the Titans and keeping them from getting close enough to fight the children of Cronus hand to hand. The earth shook as Poseidon and Hades struck it again and again, making the very ground beneath the Titans' feet unreliable and opening chasms that led to the Underworld itself. With Cronus and his allies so thoroughly battered, they were easy prey for the Hecatoncheires, and for Zeus's siblings. Once the Titans had been subdued, most of them were hurled by Zeus straight down to Tartarus, which became their prison, guarded by the very Hecatoncheires Cronus had kept as prisoners for so long.

"Was there peace then?" asked Fatima.

"Eventually," said Thanos, "but the gods had one more challenge first. Look!"

What Thanos was pointing at was not hard to see. It was a monster of some kind, a giant, but with the heads of a hundred serpents growing from his shoulders, each breathing fire like a dragon, and each uttering a different kind of animal cry.

"Where did that…that thing come from?" asked Mateo, looking glad that they were a safe distance away from it.

"Gaia was still not satisfied, for though Zeus had freed her children whom Cronus imprisoned, he had now imprisoned the Titans."

"Who seem as if they deserved it," Yasmin pointed out.

"I guess we could say Gaia wanted all her children free regardless of what they had done," Thanos replied. "Through Tartarus she became mother to Typhoeus, the monster you see advancing on Olympus."

"How did she have sex with a pit?" asked Patrick. "That is what Tartarus is, right?"

Keisha tried to conceal her shock that Patrick had actually been listening. "The Greeks must have assumed that even the abstract gods or those who represented geographical features also had human forms to use—or maybe they just didn't think it through."

"Zeus is coming down to face him…but why is he alone?" asked Yasmin.

"Typhoeus frightened the others away," suggested Thanos. "Don't worry, though. Some time had passed since the war with the Titans, and Zeus was much surer of his power."

Typhoeus took an incredible amount of damage and stayed on his feet. However, by the time the scent of burning flesh filled the air like a cloud around him, and all of the hundred heads had burned away, he could fight no longer. He finally fell with a crash so loud the crack in the window was joined by several others, and the ground beneath the students' feet shook again, even more violently than before.

Zeus threw what was left of Typhoeus into Tartarus and looked around, surveying the damage. The long battle had bathed the earth in fire and lightning, scorching a great part of it and boiling away most of the sea. Standing in the middle of the devastation, the king of the gods looked smaller than he had before.

"Is Gaia going to lay off now?" asked Mateo. "Will there be peace?"

Thanos nodded. "Long enough for earth and sea to heal, but this was not the last major challenge Zeus had to face.

"You see, Zeus himself was destined to be overthrown."

Chapter 4: Prometheus and Pandora

"Wait, you mean Zeus gets overthrown too?" asked Yasmin.

"Not in any surviving myth," Keisha replied. "The Greeks assumed the overthrow of Zeus would happen at some point in the future. However, he lived under the threat of overthrow, never knowing when it would happen or who would be involved."

"Well, he did have one clue," said Thanos. "He knew he would be overthrown by his own son."

"That makes sense," said Yong. "After all, he overthrew his father, and his father overthrew his grandfather."

"Zeus had a lot of sons, though, didn't he?" asked Mateo. "Oh, that's why he doesn't know who will bring him down."

"Exactly," agreed Keisha. "Well, at least he didn't try to eat all his sons like Cronus did."

"By all accounts, he was a better ruler, and many stories comment on his justice and wisdom," said Thanos.

"His wisdom sometimes took a back seat, though," Yong pointed out. "That's how he had so many sons; if he saw a beautiful goddess or even a mortal woman, he seems to have been unable to avoid having sex with her."

"He was a guy," said Patrick, as if all guys had sex with everyone in sight.

"Womanizing aside, he generally seemed to govern well," Thanos pointed out. "There was, however, one glaring exception in which he sounded a lot more like Cronus than himself: Prometheus."

"Prometheus was one of the second-generation Titans, right?" asked Mateo.

"Yes," said Keisha, "and because he was one of the gods who could foretell the future, he knew that Zeus would win and sided with him in the war between Zeus and Cronus.

"The problem was that Prometheus, who in some stories created the human race, disagreed with Zeus on how humans should be treated. Zeus wanted a larger portion of the sacrificial animals to be given to the gods than Prometheus thought was reasonable, so Prometheus met with Zeus at Mecone and offered a compromise that was really a trick involving two piles of ox meat that were not what they seemed.

"First, Prometheus took the animal's bones and wrapped them in fat. Keep in mind ancient people didn't know about the health risks of fat. To them it was the best part of the meat, so when Zeus saw the white fat glistening in the sun, it would have been appealing to him.

"Next, Prometheus took the ox's stomach and stuffed all remaining meat into it. When he offered Zeus a choice, the king of the gods momentarily forgot his wisdom and quickly picked the fat, which in fact had nothing edible within it, rather than the meat-filled stomach."

"I bet Zeus wasn't happy when he realized the truth," said Mateo.

"No, he was furious," replied Thanos. "However, having already made his decision final, he couldn't go back on it. Instead, he took his wrath out on human beings, refusing to give them fire. Prometheus, once again coming to the aid of the humans, stole fire and gave it to them despite Zeus's command.

"Zeus was so enraged by Prometheus's continued defiance that he punished him horribly."

"Like Cronus did with his father?" asked Patrick, unconsciously crossing his legs.

"No," said Thanos, "but in this case the punishment might have been even worse, because it was meant to last forever. Zeus ordered that Prometheus be chained to a mountain in the Caucasus. Then Zeus sent an eagle down to devour Prometheus's liver. The enormous bird ate it completely every day, but Prometheus, being immortal, didn't die. Instead, his liver grew back every night so that the eagle could eat it again the next day."

"Zeus sounds like a total psycho," said Yasmin. "Why do we have to read this stuff?"

"It's true that by modern standards, what Zeus is portrayed as doing was terrible," said Yong. "However, you have to keep in mind that a lot of these stories developed during very primitive times in a society whose morality was considerably different from our own. Hesiod can tell this story but still say that Zeus has everlasting wisdom."

"Put yourself in the place of a king in primitive times," suggested Keisha. "After all, kings and their war leaders were the first audience for a lot of Greek literature, like the epic poems of Homer. An ancient king would have little patience with someone who defied his orders; he would have seen that person as a danger to himself and to public order. The same king would be likely to see someone who defied the king of the gods as a threat to the whole universe."

"I get that," said Yasmin, "but that doesn't answer my original question. Why do we have to read material that expresses all these primitive values?"

"That's my question too," added Patrick. Keisha doubted he'd ever have thought of that without Yasmin but decided against saying that.

"Even primitive stories can have a decent moral message," Yong pointed out. "We can't think of it just in terms of Zeus. Prometheus is a good example of someone being willing to take chances for others, a real hero. He suffers for his choice, but in no version of the story does he seem to regret making it. His example could inspire people to care more about others.

"Anyway, the fact that you read a piece of literature doesn't mean you need to agree with its values. Questioning ideas you don't agree with is an important part of developing your analytical thinking ability."

"Greek values also evolved as time went on," Thanos said. "Hesiod may side with Zeus—though even Hesiod refers to Prometheus as kindly—but Aeschylus in *Prometheus Bound* tells the story from Prometheus's point of view and makes clear that Zeus is behaving like a tyrant. That supports Yong's point that the stories can be read in several different ways."

"As time went on, the Greeks were more and more likely to regard the myths as symbolic," said Keisha. "For example, because the name *Cronus* is very similar to the Greek word for time, some writers argued that Cronus devouring his children was symbolic of the way time devours us all."

"OK, so the stories aren't necessarily intended to glorify serial killers and dictators," said Fatima. "I'm still not sure why it's so important to read them."

"Cultural literacy," said Yong. "The Bible is the single biggest influence on Western culture, but Greek literature is certainly the second biggest. We can see its influence in Chaucer's *Canterbury Tales* and in Shakespeare's *Midsummer Night's Dream*—"

"Boring!" announced Patrick. Keisha was surprised it had taken him that long.

"Well, I want to hear the rest of Yong's answer to my question," said Yasmin, glaring at Patrick. Somewhat to Keisha's surprise, he scowled but said nothing else.

"Another of Shakespeare's plays, *Romeo and Juliet*, is ultimately based on Pyramus and Thisbe, an ancient Greek story, and Hecate appears as a character in *Macbeth*. That's only a few of the possible examples. There is a long list of other authors we could cite, including Dante, Ariosto, Milton, Shelley, Keats, Tennyson, Pope, Shaw, Joyce, Hawthorne, T.S. Eliot, Updike—"

"You weren't kidding when you said the list was long!" said Patrick. "But what do a lot of dead guys have to do with us?"

"It's not just dead guys," Mateo protested. "I read all of Rick Riordan's *Percy Jackson* books when I was in middle school. They're based on Greek mythology. Actually, if you look at modern fantasy books, many of them have a mythological basis."

"Fantasy books?" Patrick asked with a sneer on his face. "So if I don't read fantasy, it's all irrelevant to my life."

"How about astronomy?" asked Yong. "All the planets and moons in our solar system are named after Greek gods, though often using their Roman names."

"There was a god named Moon?" asked Patrick.

"No," said Yong, who seemed to be struggling not to make a joke at Patrick's expense. "*Sun* and *moon* are English equivalents. That reminds me that our names for days of the week have roots in Greek mythology too, though in switching from Greek to Latin to Norse and Old English, a lot of those connections got buried. One day, though, is still pretty close to its Roman form: Saturday, which was once the Latin equivalent of Saturn's day—Cronus's day to the Greeks."

"All kinds of other words come from mythology as well," said Keisha. "Like *erotic* comes from Eros, *aphrodisiac* from Aphrodite—"

"What?" asked Patrick, suddenly more attentive.

"I thought that would get your attention," she said with a smile. "Mythological words and phrases are spread all through our language. *Narcissist*—"

"What's that?" asked Patrick. Keisha thought that he, of all people, should have known.

"It's a term for someone who has too big an ego and gets wrapped up in himself or herself. It comes from Narcissus, a handsome guy who cared only about himself and was cruel to everyone else. The goddess Nemesis punished him by causing him to fall in love with his own reflection.

"A lot of other psychological terms come from Greek myths. For example, *Oedipus complex*, comes from Oedipus, king of Thebes. *Phobia* comes from Phobos, or fear, the son of Ares.

"Of course, the influence of myths isn't confined to psychology, either. As I said earlier, it pops up all over the place. *Adonis*, a term for a handsome young man, comes from the name of one of Aphrodite's lovers. *Herculean*, an adjective to describe some epically difficult feat—"

"OK, OK," said Patrick. "A lot of words come from mythology. I get it."

"We could also mention mythology's opera, the visual arts, architecture—" began Thanos.

"Let's not and say we did," said Patrick quickly.

"USC Trojans!" said Mateo happily. "What kind of shoes are you wearing, by the way?" he asked Patrick.

"Nikes," said Patrick. "Oh—"

"Yeah, oh," said Keisha, who was getting more tired of him by the minute. However, realizing his shoes were named after a Greek goddess caused Patrick to stop and think—or, if not actually think, at least keep his mouth shut for a while.

"OK," said Yasmin. "Now I really get it. There are a lot of things I'll miss in other literature and art—and game-show questions—if I don't know mythology."

"That's about the size of it," said Yong.

"I'm sorry to interrupt, but I've got a question about what we were talking about earlier," said Fatima.

"Ask away," said Thanos. "I think we're done."

"All right then, how could an ancient Greek have called the king of the gods a tyrant the way Aeschylus did?" she asked. "Wouldn't he have been afraid of being struck by lightning or something?"

"There are different theories on that," said Thanos. "A lot of myths are stories about people being punished for disrespecting the gods, so clearly the Greeks thought it could happen. Writers do seem to have believed they enjoyed a certain amount of latitude. Aristophanes and other writers of Greek comedy even made fun of the gods—except Poseidon. He was notoriously bad tempered, so they left him alone.

"When people are punished in the myths, it's usually because they did something overt, like Erysichthon chopping down Demeter's sacred grove or Actaeon accidentally seeing Artemis naked. Sometimes it's also long-term, like Hippolytus getting on Aphrodite's nerves by rejecting love and only worshiping Artemis. I guess the ancient Greeks probably believed the offense had to be serious or prolonged to merit the attention of the gods."

"That makes sense," said Fatima.

"To get back to our original story, the wrath of Zeus didn't end with torturing Prometheus. The king of the gods also wanted to punish the human race, so he had the other gods create the first woman, Pandora," said Thanos.

"The first woman was intended as a punishment for men?" asked Yasmin, frowning.

"Let me finish the story first. then you can tear it apart if you want.

"Prometheus had made the first men, but Zeus obviously couldn't ask him, so he turned to Hephaestus, the blacksmith of the gods, who molded Pandora from clay, making her a woman so beautiful even the gods were stunned by her."

"How would he have known what a beautiful woman would look like if she was the first?" asked Mateo.

"He had the goddesses as models," suggested Keisha.

"Probably," agreed Thanos. "In any case, Hephaestus was not the only one who contributed to her development. Aphrodite gave her grace, to make her as alluring as possible. Athena taught her needlework, so she would seem useful outside the bedroom. Hermes gave her the power of speech, so she could communicate well, but he also gave her 'a shameless mind and a deceitful nature,' as Hesiod puts it.

"Beauty is only skin deep," said Mateo. "Pandora was beautiful, but she wasn't a good person."

"Exactly," said Thanos. "Zeus was ready to trick Prometheus's brother, for whom Pandora was intended, in somewhat the same way Zeus had been tricked by Prometheus himself. Prometheus disguised the worse portion of the sacrifice to look more attractive. Zeus had the gods disguise a deceitful woman to be irresistible.

"Just to be sure, the beautiful woman was dressed magnificently. Athena gave her a gown the goddess had made herself. The Graces, attendants of Aphrodite, gave her a golden necklace. The Seasons crowned her with spring flowers. Then Pandora was ready for Epimetheus."

"The poor guy never stood a chance," said Yong.

Thanos nodded. "Prometheus had warned Epimetheus not to accept gifts from Zeus, but Epimetheus was not much of a thinker and wanted the beautiful woman for his wife as soon as he saw her. Also, the fact that Hermes presented her to him as a gift from Zeus made it seem undiplomatic to refuse.

"Zeus had given Pandora a jar—"

"I thought it was a box," interrupted Yasmin.

"It is in some later stories," agreed Thanos, "but in the earliest version, it's a jar. Anyway, the jar was supposed to be a wedding gift. However, when Pandora opened it, diseases and other kinds of evils flew out of it to plague the human race. Only hope, also trapped in the jar, remained behind. That last part could mean that humans were left without hope, which was trapped in the jar, or it could mean that hope was preserved to comfort humans later."

"So it's a question of whether the jar is half empty or half full," said Yasmin, smiling.

"Yeah," said Yong, "the pessimist would see this as a myth in which there is no hope, but the optimist would see it as an example of how hope can help us survive anything."

"I read this myth as a little kid," said Yasmin, "but the details were different. Pandora wasn't deceitful, just curious. She was told not to open the box but did so anyway."

"The myth probably existed in several different versions," said Thanos. "As far as I know, though, the curiosity part doesn't appear in any early Greek version. I think that was an attempt to give the story a different message. Hesiod used it to support the idea that there is no way to avoid the will of Zeus, but later on, especially after the rise of Christianity, when Zeus was no longer worshiped, someone probably wanted to give the tale a message more relevant to a different audience."

"Yeah, societies often adapt literature to their changing needs," said Yong. "I've seen some of the episodes of that '90s show, *Hercules: The Legendary Journeys,* and they're a perfect example. The Hercules in the original myths was someone who slept with practically every woman he encountered, just like his father, Zeus. He had so many children that the sons of Hercules eventually formed an army."

"Impressive!" said Patrick.

"Appalling!" countered Yasmin.

"Anyway, the Hercules character in the series didn't believe in sex outside of marriage. The original Hercules—Heracles in Greek—drank enough to dissolve the average human liver; the '90s Hercules never touched a drop. The original Hercules killed people, sometimes in war but sometimes with far less provocation. The '90s Hercules hardly ever killed anyone. The original Hercules had a fairly good relationship with the gods, except for Hera. The '90s Hercules was sort of a freedom fighter, standing up for humans against the gods on a pretty regular basis."

"Like Perseus in the *Clash of the Titans* remake," said Keisha. "He also fought the gods on behalf of humans and conformed better to modern morality than his mythic original."

"Yeah, that's what I'm saying happened to the Pandora story over the years," said Thanos. "People adapted it to fit new audiences."

"What's that?" asked Fatima. Everyone looked in the direction she was pointing and noticed that their foggy, unvarying surroundings, broken only by their "window" now had one other break in the monotony: a large jar, almost as high as some of them were tall, covered with Greek-style vase paintings.

"I wonder what's inside," said Patrick, striding over to it and grabbing the lid.

"Don't!" commanded Keisha, who was worried about the obvious connection to the Pandora story. "We don't know—"

She was too late. Patrick had already pulled the lid off.

Chapter 5: Hermes

The jar vibrated so hard it looked as if it were going to explode. Then out of the top flew an athletic looking, blond teenager wearing winged sandals, a bright white toga, a traveler's gray cloak, and a round hat that also had a small, golden wing on each side. In one hand, he carried a short staff, the caduceus, around which two snakes twined, and just above them were two wings, with a small sphere centered between them. In the other hand, he carried a golden lyre.

"Hermes?" asked Yong, not sure exactly what to do next. It was one thing to watch the myths happening through the "window," but confronting one of the characters in person was a completely different experience—especially where the temperamental Greek gods were concerned.

"I am indeed," replied Hermes. To Patrick he added, "Beware of opening random jars. You never know who—or what—might pop out of them."

"How did you happen to end up in one?" asked Keisha. Like Yong, she was uncertain how to approach the situation. Since this was a dream—she hoped—it probably shouldn't matter, but she felt uncomfortable anyway.

"I wanted to see your expressions when I popped out," said Hermes, smiling. "I'm sure you know my reputation for tricks. The day I was born I got out of my cradle on Olympus, walked all the way to Pieria (about forty-three of your miles), and noticed the cattle my big brother Apollo was herding. I thought it would be a good trick to steal some while he wasn't looking, so I picked out a few to take—well, more than a few, to be honest. I covered their hooves with boots so that they would leave no tracks and led them to Pylos, over four hundred and thirty-four of your miles away."

"I can see how someone like you could cover that distance," said Mateo, "but how did you get the cattle to walk that far, especially since they had to do it fast enough for Apollo not to notice?"

"The human storytellers do not say," replied Hermes, "but it must have been magic, don't you think?" He waved his caduceus, and the air sparkled around it.

"When I got the cattle to Pylos," he continued, "I sacrificed a couple to my fellow gods, eating a little of the meat myself. The rest I kept at Pylos.

"Not a bad prank for a day-old infant, you must admit," he said, clearly still proud of what he had done.

"Apollo couldn't have been happy with that," said Fatima.

Hermes chuckled. "Oh, indeed he wasn't. He used his prophetic gifts to find me, and he demanded I return the cattle. Naturally, I denied everything, my defense being that as a baby, I could scarcely have committed the crime. However, since I was a talking baby, he didn't believe me, and so eventually I had to lead him back to the cattle."

"So you lost everything?" asked Patrick. Clearly, he'd been hoping for pointers on how to get away with things and was disappointed Hermes had been caught.

"Not quite," said Hermes, smiling again. "You see, after sacrificing the cattle, I used some of the guts to make strings for a lyre just like this one. When I played it for Apollo, who had always appreciated music, he wanted the new instrument, and without hesitation, he traded the cattle for it. Later I made another for myself, and much later one for Orpheus, who was among other things a favorite music student of Apollo. By then Apollo had long since forgiven me, and we had become as close as brothers should be."

"I didn't realize the Greeks had a god of pranks," said Patrick, who, much to everyone's surprise, seemed genuinely interested. Probably he was contemplating some pranks of his own.

Hermes chuckled again. "I wasn't really the god of pranks, though I certainly enjoyed them. My chief role was as the messenger of the gods, because of my speed." He flew around a little to demonstrate, and there was no question—he was fast.

"Given my skills, I was also the god of thieves—and merchants, which gives you a good idea of how the ancient Greeks thought of merchants. Perhaps, though, my association with merchants came from the fact that I am also the god of travelers and of roads. Merchants typically had to travel, or at least hire someone else to, and a good deal of this travel required roads.

"I am also sometimes associated with athletes. Some artists considered me an example of the ideal male adolescent form—though I think Big Brother Apollo might have disputed that claim."

"How can you be a teenager when you're so old?" asked Patrick.

"The gods can appear as they wish," replied Hermes. With a wave of his staff he was a shriveled old man, then a baby, and then an identical copy of Patrick, who laughed loudly at the imitation. Finally, Hermes returned to his original form and gave a little bow. Everyone applauded since that seemed to be what he was waiting for.

"You know, all this talk of cattle has made me eager for sacrifices," he said as soon as the applause was over. "Where are the animals you have brought me?"

They all froze, even though they kept telling themselves they were just dreaming. Hermes looked so positive that they were about to offer him a sacrifice. The whole situation had gone from fun to awkward in less than sixty seconds. Not only did they have no animals with them, but none of them except the agnostic Patrick belonged to a religious tradition in which sacrificing to Hermes would have been acceptable even if they had an animal and were willing to kill it.

Hermes stood there expectantly, letting them fret silently for almost a full minute. Then he started laughing so hard he nearly fell over.

"Ah, the looks on your faces!" he said. "Even after our short time together, you should surely be able to recognize a joke when you hear one.

"I can plainly see that you have no sacrificial animals with you. Besides that, I know enough about you and your society to know that much has changed in the mortal realm and that none of you worship me or my kin—nor could you, without violating your own principles."

"Back in the day, you and your kind did care, though," said Mateo.

"Yes, as you say, 'back in the day' the stories told of gods who expected to be worshiped and harshly punished those who did not. So that I will not confuse you, I tell you plainly that I am not quite the Hermes of the storytellers. If I were, I could not be of much use to you."

"Use to us?" asked Yasmin, looking worried about when the next joke was going to hit.

"I may be inspired by what the original storytellers wrote, but I am in *your* heads now, not theirs, am I not? And were you not just a short time ago talking about how each society adapts myths to its own purpose?"

Again, Keisha was unsettled by a dream character referring to the fact that it was a dream. However, what Hermes was saying made sense to her.

"So we can deal with you without fear of being smited if we do the wrong thing?" she asked.

Hermes chuckled yet again. "Smiting was always more Zeus's area than mine, but yes, you may interact with me and the others without fear of being killed, cursed, transformed or generally made miserable. You may be pranked on occasion, though. You have been warned." He said the last part so solemnly that some of them started to worry about what he had in mind.

"You will, however, be told the stories just as the ancient Greeks first heard them," added the messenger of the gods. "Otherwise, you might become confused during your essay on the subject."

Keisha was amazed Hermes was actually concerned about their upcoming essay, but something else caught her attention even more.

"The others?" she asked.

"I think you have spent enough time just watching events unfold," said Hermes. "It is time for you to hear from those who participated. A few of the stories are mine, but many are not, and you would best hear those from the gods and humans who were the more closely involved.

"I will be your guide if you will have me, for I can take you anywhere very quickly, and the other function I did not mention was the guide of souls to the Underworld. There is no place I cannot go.

"Do you accept my offer?"

"Yes," said Thanos. No one else objected.

By this point they were all ready to get out of the perpetual fog—and how does one really say no to someone who can show you the whole ancient Greek universe?

"In that case, let us go to Olympus," said Hermes. He waved his staff, and before any of the students had time to think, they were in a marble throne room with two very imposing deities staring down at them from golden thrones.

Chapter 6: Zeus and Hera

Keisha knew they had to be in the presence of Zeus and Hera, the king and queen of the gods. She had to keep reminding herself she was dreaming to avoid feeling overwhelmed.

Both Zeus and Hera looked more mature than Hermes and made the group feel much more intimidated. Zeus's lightning bolts (thunderbolts as the Greeks called them) glittered and crackled threateningly in a quiver next to his throne. The large eagle perched nearby and eying them as if they were dinner made Keisha wonder if it was the same one that had eaten Prometheus's liver.

Zeus himself wore a bright white robe, a purple cloak, and a crown of olive leaves. His expression was neutral at the moment, which was just as well—none of them would have wanted to face him when he was angry.

Hera, wearing a golden crown and holding a lotus-tipped scepter, was no less imposing, though at least the peacock strutting near her throne was not as scary as Zeus's eagle. Unlike Zeus's eyes, her eyes looked sad, as if something was bothering her, but she was doing her best to cover whatever it was.

"Father," I bring you guests!" said Hermes, who then bowed. The rest of them stood awkwardly, not quite sure whether bowing themselves could be construed as an act of worship.

"Be at your ease, friends," said Zeus in a voice loud as distant thunder, but warmer. "You may bow to us as a sign of respect, the way you would to any earthly ruler. We expect no worship from you."

Relieved, they all did their best to bow to Zeus and Hera, who nodded in acknowledgment.

"Husband," said Hera in a softer voice, "perhaps refreshments should be provided to our guests."

Zeus looked annoyed. "Wife, you know how seldom we have human guests these days. We have nothing suitable, just the nectar and ambrosia reserved for the gods."

"If we ate that, would we be trapped here?" asked Yong.

Zeus laughed heartily. "No, it is not like the food of the Underworld that binds someone there forever. The problem with nectar and ambrosia is that too much would make you immortal—and immortality is something we offer very rarely, if at all."

"Why is that?" asked Fatima. "Didn't you have loyal followers that you wanted to reward?"

"We see a great deal, but we do not see everything," replied Zeus. "Mortals we think were worthy sometimes turn out not to be. Even our own kin cannot always be trusted.

"Consider the case of Tantalus, my own son."

Hera squirmed a little on her throne but said nothing. Keisha recalled the amount of pain Zeus gave Hera through his numerous affairs.

"His mother was Pluto, a nymph whose father was said to be Cronus."

"So she was your half-sister?" asked Mateo.

"I am his full sister," said Hera in a tone that suggested Mateo had wandered into dangerous territory. The queen of the gods might be trying to restrain herself from bickering with Zeus in the presence of guests, but she might not be reluctant to take issue with one of the guests if he offended her.

"Such relationships are forbidden to mortals," explained Zeus, "but among the gods, they are accepted. In any case, as my son, Tantalus was welcomed to Olympus and dined with us frequently. He betrayed that trust." Now it was Zeus's turn to look sad. Clearly, he still remembered how his son had let him down.

"Tantalus revealed some of our secrets to mortals," said Zeus after an uncomfortably long pause. "Even worse, he stole nectar and ambrosia to give to them. Think of it—completely unworthy mortals might have become as the gods are."

Given the faults the gods had, Keisha wondered if adding a few "unworthy" mortals would have made that much difference, but, not being Patrick, she kept that thought to herself.

"Even so, those were not his worst crimes," Zeus continued. "Not satisfied with being our guest, Tantalus wanted to prove to himself that he was our equal. He chose to test the limits of our knowledge. When we came to visit him, also an honor we bestowed upon few mortals, he killed his own son, Pelops, chopped up his body, cooked him and served him to us."

"Gross!" said Patrick, looking thoroughly disgusted.

"It was indeed," said Zeus. "Thus he became not just a doubter of the gods but a murderer of his own son. We realized what he had done, of course. Only poor Demeter, then looking for her lost daughter, Persephone, was too distracted to notice at first and ate a part of the boy's shoulder before she realized the truth."

"For such vile acts, Tantalus was condemned to suffer in the Underworld," replied Zeus, his eyes looking off into the distance as if he could actually see Tantalus enduring his punishment. "He is doomed to hunger and thirst forever and never be satisfied. Though the branches of a fruit tree hang almost right over his head, they pull back if he tries to pluck fruit from them. Similarly, he stands in a pool of water from which he should easily be able to drink, but it recedes from him whenever he tries."

"Tantalus may have been the worst example of a trusted mortal betraying that trust, but he was not the only one," said Hera. "Ixion owed us more, yet still betrayed us.

"Ixion was king of the Lapiths. His parents are variously named in different stories, though the theory that his father was Ares rings true to me. Ares is our son, but even we cannot deny he is overly violent, and so, alas, was Ixion."

Zeus frowned. "Yes, Ares has always been something of a problem."

"Why was he so...difficult?" asked Patrick, oddly sounding as if he cared about Ares. Keisha figured they were both jerks, so that made sense.

"He is a bully," said Hera, looking at the floor. "War may sometimes be necessary, but Ares delights in it. However, he is only happy when facing foes he can easily defeat. Confronted by someone who is his better, he quickly runs away."

"Yeah," muttered Yong, "definitely a bully." Yong's tone made Keisha think that he must have had some experience with bullies.

"Like his presumed father, Ixion was too willing to use violence when it was not needed. He married Dia, the daughter of Deioneus. In those days it was customary for the husband to pay his father-in-law a bride price, but Ixion failed to do so. When Deioneus demanded what was owed him, Ixion invited him to a feast, but instead of honoring his father-in-law, Ixion threw him into a fire pit and burned him to death.

"Like Tantalus's murder of Pelops, Ixion's murder of Deioneus was made more heinous because the victim was a family member. Also like Tantalus's crime, Ixion's was a violation of the sacred host-guest relationship, though the exact details were different. Tantalus fed us, his guests, the flesh of his murdered son; Ixion murdered his guest, Deioneus."

"At the very least, Ixion needed to be purified of his blood guilt," said Zeus, "but his crime was so horrendous that none of his fellow kings would even consider cleansing him. Taking pity on him, I purified him and invited him to Olympus."

The group was a little stunned by that revelation, even though the three who had the book already knew of it. It seemed out of character for Zeus to show such mercy, especially to someone whose crimes were so enormous.

"Having been saved by Zeus, one would have expected Ixion to be grateful, but instead he treated us as badly as he had treated his own family," said Hera. "Such was his ego that he dared to cast lustful eyes upon me, the goddess of marriage, as if I would ever betray my vows for anyone, let alone such a notorious sinner."

"And so again Ixion, this time as our guest, violated the host-guest relationship," said Zeus. "His act was made all the viler by the fact that he owed me everything. However, as yet he had not actually done anything, merely thought about it, so I resolved to give him one last chance. If he could resist the temptation to pursue his lust, then perhaps he could be forgiven for his sinful thoughts.

"To test him I made a woman, Nephele, from the clouds and gave her the appearance of Hera. I hoped that Ixion might repent before it was too late. Once again, I was wrong."

"Instead of resisting temptation, Ixion gave into it," said Hera. "We knew this not only because Nephele told us, but through the inescapable truth of her pregnancy, for by Ixion she became the mother of Centaurus, ancestor the centaurs. With such plain proof of Ixion's sin, there could be no further mercy, only punishment."

"Ixion was bound to a fiery wheel, a reminder of the flames which had killed Deioneus as well as the flames of his own lust," said Zeus. "The wheel was ever turning, spinning at first through the sky, but eventually in the Underworld, putting Ixion as far away from Olympus, the place whose hospitality he had violated, as possible. There he will remain forever.

"Can you now see why we do not bestow immortality casually on mortals?" asked Zeus. "Even those who are related to us and have received our special favors cannot be relied on to be loyal to us and to observe even the most basic morality."

Before anyone could answer, a handsome young man that Keisha thought was probably Ganymede, Zeus's cupbearer, rushed into the room.

"Forgive the intrusion, Majesties, but something strange is happening that requires your attention."

"Pardon us for a moment," said Zeus. Without another word, he, Hera, and Hermes left them alone in the intimidatingly large throne room.

"I wonder what could be happening," said Fatima. "Not knowing makes me nervous."

"We mustn't lose sight of the fact that we are dreaming," said Yong. "There is no real threat here."

"Can you explain what's happening, then?" asked Matteo.

"I do have a theory," said Yong.

"You would," said Patrick. Everyone else ignored him.

"Wasn't it Sherlock Holmes who said, "Once you eliminate the impossible, whatever remains, no matter how improbable, must be the truth'? I'm not any more of a fan of the evidence for shared dreams than Keisha is, but that or some other psychic phenomenon is the best theory we have.

"We can all agree the gods aren't real right?" Everyone nodded. "Well, then we have to find some reason we are all interacting with beings who don't exist. A shared dream whose details are so vivid because all of us are somehow creating it together is the only theory I can't immediately rule out."

"It still sounds like a stretch to me," said Mateo.

"Think about it," replied Yong. "The gods do act as we—well, those of us who read the book, anyway—would expect, but with some odd differences that work to our advantage. If Hermes were real, would he be a tour guide? Would Zeus and Hera be happy with those tours going through Olympus? That part doesn't make sense at all—unless we are creating them from our imagination, in which case it makes perfect sense. Because we're interested in doing well on our test, they're interested in reviewing the material with us. The gods we've read about wouldn't give us the time of day for something like that unless we offered them a really good sacrifice, were related to them, or were appealing enough that one or more of them wanted to make love to some or all or us."

"I could live with that last one," said Patrick.

Before anyone even had time to properly ignore Patrick, Hera returned.

"Ganymede was reporting some trouble in Thrace, but it was just Ares—again. Zeus will have the situation resolved and be back in just a few minutes."

Although the news seemed good, Hera continued to look unhappy.

"Why are you so sad?" asked Fatima, so moved by Hera's obvious distress that she managed to overcome her normal shyness.

"Ordinarily, it would not be dignified for me to tell you, but under the circumstances, perhaps I should." The goddess sat on her throne and looked off into the distance for a moment.

Just as Fatima began to think that Hera had forgotten about them, the goddess said, "Once Zeus was my hero. After all, he had led the fight against our cruel father Cronus and won it, making us safe. Shortly after that, I made my home far to the west, in the garden of the Hesperides, the nymphs of sunset. Zeus, already in love with me, followed me there, but he did not know how to approach me. He changed himself into a cuckoo and pretended to be cold outside. Taking pity on the bird, I took it into my home, at which point Zeus immediately transformed back into his magnificent godly presence and made love to me right then and there.

"We were married shortly afterward, the happiest day of my entire life—which has been thousands of years long, so that is saying quite a bit. Zeus, already king of the gods, made me his queen. I loved him with all my heart, and he loved me—or so I thought.

"Gaia gave me a marvelous tree as a wedding present. It produced golden apples that some stories said could grant immortality, though, since I planted it in the garden of the Hesperides, which no mortal could reach, their power has never been put to the test. I loved the tree for its beauty—and for the memories of that one happy day. I will never see another tree like that one, nor live another day like that one."

"Why not?" asked Fatima. Thanos, Keisha, and Yong cringed, for they all knew the answer already.

"Zeus still claims to love me, but he has never been faithful to me. Epic was his wisdom, epic was his power—and equally epic was his infidelity. He claims he betrayed our marriage vows to father the many gods and heroes who have contributed so much to the universe, and I cannot deny their contributions, but…"

Hera seemed unable to finish the thought.

"But you could tell that was just an excuse," said Keisha gently.

Hera nodded. "He could have produced nothing but monsters—something our brother Poseidon has done occasionally—and he would still have kept right on having sex with every attractive female he could reach. As king of the gods, if he could see someone, he could reach them.

"Your guide, Hermes, is the child of one such relationship, in that case between Zeus and the Titaness Maia. He also slept with the Titaness Leto and fathered the twins, Apollo and Artemis, as well as with the Oceanid Dione who some say was the mother of Aphrodite. With Dione's sister, Metis, he is said to have fathered Athena, though others say he was Athena's only parent, as she sprung full grown from his head."

To the people who hadn't read the book, that was confusing, but none of them had the nerve to interrupt, except for Patrick, who would certainly have interrupted if he hadn't been so mesmerized by the sheer number of Zeus's sexual exploits.

Noticing their confusion, Hera said, "Athena can tell that story better than I can. In any case, since Zeus and I had Ares and Hephaestus, among other children, and Zeus fathered Dionysus with Semele, a mortal woman, he was the father of all the principal gods of the younger generation.

"You would think that would have been enough for him, but no. He made love to our sister Demeter and fathered Persephone. He made love to Aphrodite and is said by some to be the father of Eros, though others say the love god really existed from the beginning. He made love to the Titaness Mnemosyne and fathered the nine Muses. He made love to the Titaness Themis and fathered among other Dike (justice)—ironic, given how little justice *I* received."

"What a stud," whispered Patrick admiringly.

"Even the repugnant Eris, goddess of discord, was not unpleasant enough to deter Zeus, who slept with her and fathered Limos, the very personification of starvation."

"When you need sex badly enough, it doesn't really matter if the girl's ugly," said Patrick, this time loudly enough that Hera couldn't avoid overhearing him.

"Am I to understand that you side with my husband in this matter?" the queen of the gods asked in a tone cold enough to freeze an inferno. "Do you think to justify what he did?"

Anyone with an ounce of common sense would have backpedaled at this point. Unfortunately for Patrick, he was the one member of the group who most clearly lacked common sense.

"Well, that's just the way guys are," he said with a shrug.

If only he had read the mythology book, he would have known about Hera's terrible temper. Unfortunately, he hadn't gotten past page one, and now he was going to pay for his negligence.

Hera cursed him in Greek, each syllable vibrating with rage. Then she waved her arm at Patrick, and suddenly he was gone. In his place was a small, red-haired Irish setter.

Hera had turned him into a dog!

The others were too stunned to react at first. Hermes had guaranteed nothing like this would happen. Of course, Hermes was not yet back—and Patrick had been asking for it. Still, his fellow group members couldn't help but feel sympathy for him.

"Yet even all those goddesses were not enough to satisfy him," Hera said, picking up the earlier conversation as if nothing unusual had happened. "Of the Greek heroes whose father was a god, that god was Zeus more than half the time. Heracles, whom you might know as Hercules, was the most famous, but he was certainly not the only one."

Patrick lay down on the floor and started whining, but Hera ignored him.

"The three judges of the Underworld were all once mortal kings and sons of Zeus. So was the heroic Perseus, the traitorous Tantalus, the beautiful Helen of Troy, and so many others, some of whom you will doubtless meet later. That most of them did much good in the world, I cannot deny—but knowing their contributions did nothing to decrease my pain."

Keisha could hardly believe that she was thinking of ways to get Hera to show Patrick some mercy. She was relieved that Zeus and Hermes had just returned. Surely they would do something.

"Wife, what have you been telling our guests?" asked Zeus, his tone nearly as cold as hers had been with Patrick.

"And what have you been doing to them?" asked Hermes, pointing at the dog that had formerly been Patrick.

Zeus looked in Patrick's direction. "How can we expect mortals to respect the host-guest relationship if we do not? Reverse this transformation at once!"

"He has given great offense," said Hera, glancing at the dog, who whimpered and back further away. "I will not undo what I have done."

Keisha was even more worried now. She had read somewhere that what was done by one god could not be undone by another. Zeus could punish Hera for disobeying him, but he couldn't change Patrick back unless she agreed to it.

"As your king, I command you to undo the damage," insisted Zeus. Was it Keisha's imagination, or was he edging closer to his thunderbolts?

No, she wasn't imagining it. She could tell that Hera had seen the movement as well.

"Oh, very well," the queen of the gods said. "I shall do it—if you do something for me in return."

"I am not in the mood to bargain," replied Zeus, one hand on a thunderbolt. "Do what I have ordered. When you are done, I will hear your *request*."

Keisha got the feeling that Hera might have continued her defiance if any other gods had been around to back her up, but aside from Zeus, only Hermes was present, and the messenger of the gods didn't look any happier with her than Zeus was.

"As you wish, dear husband," she said mockingly. She turned in Patrick's direction—and froze.

The dog Patrick had become was gone.

Hera recovered quickly from her surprise. "It appears the dog has left of his own accord. I cannot take back my curse if I cannot see the animal."

"If this is some trick—" began Zeus, lifting a thunderbolt.

"You have been staring at me the whole time," protested Hera. "How could I have spirited the dog away without your seeing something?"

"That is true," admitted Zeus. "Still, someone must have taken the dog. He is your friend," he said to the group. "Certainly, one of you must have seen something."

"I…think we were all watching you and Hera," said Yong. "I know I was."

"Someone who can move very fast must have done this, for our conversation has not been long," said Zeus, looking suspiciously at Hermes.

"I've been standing right next to you the whole time, Majesty," said Hermes. "Had I hidden the dog and returned, you would certainly have noticed something. Anyway, I pledged to our guests no harm would come to them."

"Iris is said to be able to move fast, is she not?" asked Thanos.

"Iris?" asked Fatima, looking puzzled.

"The first messenger of the gods," replied Hermes. "She is more ancient than I. Gaia and Pontus had a son, Thaumas, who married Electra, the Oceanid. Iris is one of their children. She flies along the rainbows on her golden wings and is almost as fast as I am."

"More to the point," said Zeus, "after she was replaced by Hermes as the primary messenger, she still flew occasional missions—particularly for Hera, as I recall."

"I had no opportunity to summon her," said Hera. "Again, you were watching me this whole time."

"Perhaps she acted on her own," said Zeus. "Her twin sister, Arce, was a traitor—you'll recall she served as a messenger for the Titans. Perhaps Iris would enjoy losing her wings and joining her sister in Tartarus."

"Don't be ridiculous," snapped Hera. "Iris has never been anything but loyal. If, as you think, she took the dog, you had not ordered her not to. You can hardly call what she did treason, then."

Instead of responding to her, Zeus turned to Hermes. "If Iris is involved, she could hardly have gotten in and out in broad daylight without Helios seeing her. Go at once to him and ask if he can tell us where she went."

"Helios, the sun, is all-seeing," Zeus explained to the group. "If Iris has taken your friend, he will have seen something."

Hermes left so fast he seemed to vanish. Unfortunately, he returned just as quickly, looking unhappy.

"Helios told me there is too much cloud cover around Olympus at the moment. If Iris came and went, he would not have seen her."

"Did you think to ask if he saw the dog?" asked Zeus.

"Yes, I did, but he cannot help us there. He can see millions of dogs. Telling which one used to be a human being? That he cannot do from so far up in the sky."

"Which means the poor soul could be anywhere," said Zeus, glaring at Hera.

"I am willing to take an oath on the River Styx that I had nothing to do with this," said Hera. *Hera probably isn't guilty*

Again ignoring her, Zeus turned to the group. "Never fear! I will not rest until I find your friend." *emphasizes Hera's anger with Zeus*

"Or at least until you find another woman with whom you can amuse yourself," muttered Hera. Zeus reached again for the thunderbolts and Hera, realizing she had pushed as far as she could at this point, left the throne room without a word.

"What exactly did the boy say that so angered her?" Zeus asked as soon as he was certain she couldn't hear.

"I believe he said something about how men, in general, react to sexual temptation," said Thanos. *Other gods will help them*

Zeus chuckled, "Ah, yes, that would have invited her wrath. Hermes, go and find Apollo. As the god of prophecy, among other things, he may be able to see what it would take us months to seek out."

Hermes bowed and vanished again. *worried about speaking*

"May I ask a question?" said Mateo, clearly nervous. *after what happened to Patrick*

"That depends upon what you wish to be changed into," replied Zeus, his face totally expressionless. Then he chuckled again. *Zeus is not all serious and makes jokes*

"I'd like to think my temper is a bit more in control than Hera's. You may speak freely."

"I don't understand why you and Hera have stayed married for so long. It seems as if you hate each other."

Everyone else was surprised Mateo had ventured into that kind of territory, but Zeus did not seem offended.

"Despite appearances, we do love each other," said Zeus. Keisha thought this had to be the most dysfunctional example of love she had ever seen, but, not wanting to join Patrick, she kept her mouth shut.

"Our relationship is...complicated, however. Once she even rebelled against me, helped by Poseidon and Apollo. The cowards bound me while I slept, intending to keep me prisoner while one of them ruled Olympus. Fortunately for me, they could not agree which of them should rule, and while they bickered, Thetis, daughter of Nereus, the son of Pontus and Gaia; and the Oceanid, Doris, sneaked in Briareus, one of the Hecatoncheires I had freed from imprisonment after the fall of Cronus. He easily freed me from my bonds, and, once free, he and I were more than a match for all the Olympians combined.

"Hera I punished by hanging her from the sky, with great anvils attached to her ankles. Eventually the other Olympians persuaded me to have mercy on her. Apollo and Poseidon I condemned to one year of servitude under King Laomedon, for whom they built the walls of Troy."

Yeah, thought Keisha, *nothing says love like imprisonment, torture, and slavery. What a family!*

"Hera and the others did rebel, remember?" said Zeus in response to their facial expressions. "Disloyalty such as that could make the world dissolve into anarchy. I had no choice but to punish them. Unlike Cronus, though, I did not try to kill them or imprison them forever in Tartarus. Their punishments were mild in comparison."

"I guess everything is relative," said Yong, looking immediately as if he were sorry he said anything at all.

"It would perhaps have been better if I had not made love to so many goddesses and women, but you must remember ancient Greek society was far different from yours. Though society did not believe in polygamy, kings were permitted to have relations with women other than their wives, and some such women even had a position in the household, though not as high a one as the wife did. Looked at from the that society's viewpoint, it was Hera who was in breach of social custom, not I."

Since Patrick wasn't around, there was no one in the group who agreed with that kind of double standard—women obviously didn't have the same latitude to sleep with multiple men. However, Thanos, who had studied early cultures quite a bit, had to admit that acceptable behavior in one society was often quite different from acceptable behavior in another. Most ancient Greeks would have seen Zeus as being at least partly right.

"I may have made love a bit too often," said Zeus, which the girls thought was a masterpiece of understatement. "However, Hera made war, inflicting savage vengeance upon my lovers and occasionally even their children. One of the cruelest examples was Semele."

Zeus had a faraway look in his eyes, just as Hera had when she spoke of their wedding—but Zeus's mind was a long way from Hera at this point.

"Semele, called both dark eyed and white armed, was one of the most beautiful women of her generation. She was the daughter of Cadmus, the first king of Thebes, and Harmonia, a daughter of Ares and Aphrodite just as lovely as her mother. Fearing the wrath of her husband, Hephaestus, Aphrodite gave Harmonia to mortals to raise. Eventually Harmonia took her place on Olympus as a goddess of marital harmony, though she had many misadventures in her mortal life before she ascended.

"Unfortunately, Semele's life followed a pattern similar to her mother's. She was unquestionably mortal but so beautiful that I could not help loving her. I came to her disguised as a mortal man, though I told her I was Zeus. All went well until Hera found out. Once she knew, she came in disguise and convinced Semele I was not really Zeus but was just bragging. When I returned, Semele asked for a favor, and I swore an oath on the River Styx to give her whatever she wanted."

Zeus looked almost as if he was about to cry.

"An oath sworn on the Styx is irrevocable, and so I was trapped when Semele asked to see me in my full glory, a sight no mortal can endure. I begged her to ask for something else, but she refused to listen. In the end, I had to do as she asked, and the sight of me caused her to burst into flames. I could not save her, but I managed to shield her unborn child from the inferno. I sewed him up in my thigh until he was ready to be born—and so came into being Dionysus, god of wine, no thanks to Hera, who would happily have killed the baby with his mother.

"Now I ask you, who was the more to blame: me for loving Semele or Hera for killing her?"

Keisha prayed that was a rhetorical question. Yes, Hera acted like a total psychopath, and Keisha knew that was only one of several times. However, she didn't want to give Zeus a completely free pass. If he had been faithful, Hera would have behaved very differently.

"It is not for us mere mortals to judge," said Thanos, who Keisha thought had quite a future as a diplomat.

"That's not quite the end of the story, though, is it?" asked Yong.

"No," replied Zeus. "Dionysus was eventually allowed to venture to the Underworld, free Semele, and bring her to Olympus as the goddess Thyone. Hades was not happy with that decision, for he lost a subject, and Hera was unhappy as well, for she had not killed a woman to make her a goddess. Nonetheless, most of Olympus rejoiced that Dionysus was reunited with his mother."

"If I may interrupt for a moment, Majesty, we are all concerned about our friend, Patrick," Thanos continued.

"I know you are," said Zeus. "As soon as Hermes returns with more news, I will act as swiftly as lightning."

Unfortunately, Zeus was almost immediately handed another problem, for at that moment an enraged Ares, god of war, stormed into the room.

Chapter 7: Ares

The god of war would have been handsome if his face had not been twisted in rage and covered in blood. Whatever he had been up to in Thrace must have been more violent that any of the students really wanted to think about.

"Zeus, why have you interfered in Thrace?" he shouted, shaking his spear. "That is my land, to do with as I please."

"You are its patron," replied Zeus, "but it is yours to protect, not to destroy."

"Toughening up people for war is helping them survive, not destroying them!" shouted Ares, making a sweeping gesture with his spear. The god was not paying any attention to anyone except Zeus, and his spear accidentally smacked Yong, knocking him to the floor.

All the other students froze, wanting to see if Yong was all right but not wanting to get caught by another one of Ares's wild gestures. Yong, fueled by adrenaline and surprise, didn't freeze, though it would have been better if he had.

"Watch it!" he snapped, still lying on the floor.

Ares looked at him, shocked and angry. "Mortal, who are you to speak a warning to me?"

"A guest," said Zeus quickly. "As such, he is entitled to be safe from your ill-advised moves, Ares. You must apologize at once if you do not wish to dishonor the hospitality of Olympus."

Ares bowed stiffly to Yong. "I beg your pardon, fragile mortal, unable to endure even the slightest blow. I took you for a man, but I see I was wrong. You are only a boy...or perhaps even a girl."

Yong was on his feet and looking almost as angry as Ares had only moments before. Keisha could see he was about to speak and would have given anything to be able to stop him, but she was too far away.

"That's not much of an apology," said Yong.

"Indeed, it is not," agreed Zeus. "Ares, you can certainly do better."

"Yes, I can. "Forgive me, weak and—"

"I'm not weak!" Yong almost shouted.

"Then prove it," said Ares. "Challenge me to single combat. We'll see how much of a man you are then."

"I challenge you," said Yong fast enough that Zeus had no chance to intervene.

Shocked as the students were by Yong's challenge, they still jumped when Hermes appeared right in front of them. The swift god was breathing heavily, as if he had somehow become aware of Yong's peril and raced back.

"Father—" began Hermes, looking worried for the first time since the students had met him.

"He challenged me, and I have a right to answer," insisted Ares. "Guest or no guest."

"You speak the truth," admitted Zeus, "but Ares, no good can come from this. Though by right you may answer his challenge, I ask you instead to allow him to withdraw it, for surely he spoke rashly and did not mean what he said."

"If in truth, he is not a man, then he is welcome to withdraw the challenge," said Ares, sneering at Yong.

Yong looked pale and shaky now, but he said, "I will not withdraw it."

"Father—" began Hermes again.

"It saddens me to say this, but the mortal has made his choice," replied Zeus. "Foolish as it is, it is his to make."

"Choice of weapons is my right," said Ares. "I choose swords."

"The mortal has no sword," said Hermes, perhaps looking for a loophole.

"He can use any one of mine," replied Ares. "I shall bring them back, and he may have his pick." Without waiting for a reply, Ares turned and almost ran from the throne room.

The other students rushed over to where Yong was standing. He looked as if he was beginning to realize what he had just done to himself.

"What's wrong with you?" asked Keisha, who resisted the urge to shake him. "You're usually so logical. Why would you challenge the god of war to a fight?"

"I just can't stand bullies," said Yong, looking down at the floor.

"We can put that on your tombstone," said Mateo.

"Aren't we forgetting this is a dream?" asked Yasmin. "Nothing is really going to happen to Yong."

"That's kind of what I figured," said Yong, though he sounded less convinced.

"We don't know what it is," said Keisha. "Yeah, it's a dream, but apparently an unprecedented shared dream, maybe more powerful than normal, more able to affect our physical bodies. I don't believe that old wives' tale about dying if you die in a dream, but this situation could be different. What if Yong dies in this battle, and the shock stops his heart? We just don't know what you're dealing with."

"There must be some way out of this," said Thanos. He looked at Hermes, who had just come over.

"If so, I don't know what it is," admitted Hermes. "Your friend might have withdrawn the challenge before Ares accepted it, and Ares even offered him that chance, however, mockingly, but your friend didn't take it, and now that Ares has accepted, he has the right to insist the challenge be completed."

"All right, then how can he beat Ares?" asked Mateo. "There must be some way."

Hermes shook his head sadly. "We gods are not all-powerful, but we are invariably more powerful than mortals. Whenever a mortal has challenged any of us, it has ended badly for that mortal. The idea that a mortal could do anything as well as a god is one manifestation of *hubris*, the excessive pride that inevitably leads to harsh punishment."

"Heracles won a fight with Ares, though, didn't he?" asked Thanos.

"Yes, there was a time," conceded Hermes. "Ares had a son, Cycnus, who became a bandit and frequently robbed pilgrims on their way to the oracle at Delphi. Apollo asked Heracles to deal with the criminal, and Heracles killed Ares's son. The war god sought vengeance, and Heracles wounded him in a fight. Since gods can't be killed, the wound was the best result Heracles could have hoped for. Is your friend the equal of Heracles, then? Because if he is not, I don't see how that story helps us."

No one wanted to say the truth aloud, but Yong, far from being Heracles, was the least athletic of the guys. Not only wasn't he Heracles, but he wouldn't have been a match for a human bully, let alone an enraged war god.

"Heracles won partly because Athena helped him, right?" asked Thanos, though he already knew the answer.

Hermes thought for a moment. "Yes, that is true—and it might just be a way out for your friend…uh—"

"Yong," said Thanos.

"Yes, it might just be a way out for Yong," continued Hermes. "Something similar happened during the Trojan War when Athena guided Diomedes's spear to strike gods more than once. In theory, gods can offer such help invisibly, and if Ares isn't paying attention, he might not notice. The problem is that Athena isn't here at the moment, and she is the only one I know of, aside from elder Olympians like Zeus and Poseidon, who could beat Ares, let alone help a mortal to do so."

"You could help, though, couldn't you?" asked Yasmin, putting a hand gently on the god's shoulder.

Hermes sighed. "The most I could do in a fight with Ares is run away."

"Could you make Yong faster?" asked Thanos. "Speed is your specialty. Maybe if Yong evades Ares long enough, Ares will tire of battle."

"Ares never tires of battle," replied Hermes. "As for speeding up Yong, I can try, but you know the myths well enough to know I have never attempted something like that."

To Yong, Hermes added, "Evasion alone will not be enough. Even if I can guide your limbs to make them faster, you're going to have to strike well enough with a sword to wound him. That is the only way he'll ever be willing to end the fight—without killing you."

"What about magic?" asked Thanos. "All Olympians can perform some feats we'd think of as magical or miraculous, like becoming invisible and changing shape, but the myths suggest you have more versatile magic."

"The later stories may exaggerate a bit," said Hermes. "I can go places no one else can easily go, and I can put even divine beings to sleep, though I doubt I could do that with Ares in the middle of combat. The rest of the abilities I'm supposed to have come from people confusing me with the Egyptian god, Thoth."

"Hermes Trismegistus," said Yong. "Hermes Thrice-Greatest. I read about that somewhere. Greeks living in Egypt after the time of Alexander the Great worshiped you as a giver of all kinds of hidden knowledge, including magical and astrological lore. Later on, medieval alchemists invoked you as a source of their knowledge, though they no longer saw you as a god."

Hermes shrugged. "Stories change over time, as you know. Some give me too much credit. Nonetheless, I will see if I can think of any magic that might be helpful."

At this point Ares returned, accompanied by two grim looking twins, their arms loaded with swords of various types.

"Who are those others?" whispered Fatima.

"Twin sons of Ares and Aphrodite," Hermes whispered back. "Deimos and Phobos—fear and flight."

"Cheating?" asked Mateo suspiciously.

Hermes winked. "No more than we plan to. Actually, they are probably just here to carry the swords. Ares is many things, but he isn't someone who would cheat in single combat."

"Mortal, come pick your weapon!" commanded Ares, his tone lacking even a trace of humanity. Yong, trying to keep from trembling, walked over with Hermes close behind.

"He picks, not you!" Ares told Hermes.

Hermes gave his half-brother a little bow, then said, "I am merely here to advise him. The choice is his."

Ares didn't look happy, but he clearly didn't want to look too concerned about a fight with a mortal, either, so he gestured in the direction of the weapons and backed away.

"Have you any training with a sword?" whispered Hermes.

"No," Yong admitted.

"Then take that one," suggested Hermes, pointing to a short, slender blade. "It's called a *xiphos*. It's lighter and therefore easier for an inexperienced arm to swing."

"Wouldn't a longer blade be better for keeping an opponent at a distance?" asked Yong, pointed to a longer one.

"The *kopis* would do that, but you don't look as if you have the arm muscle to wield it effectively." Yong felt his cheeks redden.

"Anyway, if you're moving fast enough, the length of the blade will be less relevant," Hermes added. "If Ares gets close enough to even make contact with your blade, whatever its length, you will have already lost."

"Hurry up!" snapped Ares. "I will await you in the courtyard—unless, of course, you succumb to your cowardice."

"Is that an option?" muttered Yong.

"No, it's too late for that," said Hermes, his tone lacking its usual lightness.

A door at the back of the throne room led out into a large, rectangular courtyard. The outer perimeter was walled and shaded by a roof supported by classical columns. It was also lined with several different kinds of trees, but the ones Yong noticed were the cypresses, because they were also said to grow in the Underworld—where he might soon be.

He kept telling himself he was just dreaming, that at worst he would awaken if something really bad happened, but the details were so realistic. He could feel the sun on his skin, hear the breeze rustling in the trees, and feel the cold metal of the borrowed sword as he clutched its hilt in his sweaty hand. How had he gotten himself into such a mess?

The audience was not huge, though Zeus and Hera were both there. Yong noticed that Zeus's seat was flanked by two burly winged figures whom he took to be Cratus and Bia, the same two who had chained Prometheus to the mountain. Evidently, Zeus was anticipating some kind of problem and wanted some muscle on hand just in case.

Yong cursed himself for reacting so impulsively. Evidently, he should have found some constructive way to deal with the bullies he'd encountered instead of just hiding the fact that he was being bullied and bottling up all the feelings he had about them. It was that seething accumulation of negative emotions that had gotten him into this mess.

Ares smiled at Yong like a predator about to rip its prey's throat out. Yong heard Zeus announce the beginning of the single combat as if Zeus were far, far away. The student worried he was about to faint. He managed to keep his awkward grip on his sword, but he couldn't seem to raise it. Ares could finish him off in seconds.

Then he felt the invisible presence of Hermes somewhere nearby, felt the god's hands clutch him around the waist and raise him into the air so that the charging Ares missed him.

Hermes did his best to make the maneuver look like a jump that had Yong end up behind Ares. Unfortunately, the war god realized immediately what was happening.

"Hermes! Stop helping the mortal."

There was no sound except the wind in the trees. Yong figured Hermes must be trying to hide.

"Father!" roared Ares. "Command Hermes to leave the field."

"Hermes, the rules of single combat require that the combatants must use only *their own resources*. You cannot aid the mortal in this way."

Again, there was no response.

"Hermes, I command you," said Zeus. "Leave the field of battle, or face my wrath." The king of the gods didn't sound wrathful. If anything, he sounded reluctant. Nonetheless, Hermes appeared and flew quickly from the center of the courtyard to where Zeus and Hera were sitting.

"Now, mortal, prepare to die!" yelled Ares, charging again.

This time Yong made some effort to raise his sword, though it would not have been enough if some kind of magic had not at that moment enveloped him.

Yong thought being lifted by Hermes had felt strange, but that sensation was nothing compared to this one. He felt his body expanding, stretching, growing a layer of thick, heavy scales. He dropped the sword as his arms and legs merged into his ever-lengthening body.

Seconds ago, he had been a regular guy. Now he was an enormous serpent. No, not just a serpent—a Greek-style dragon! He opened his mouth, revealing sharp fangs and a darting tongue. Then he sprayed fire in Ares's direction. The war god jumped out of the way and then howled in protest.

"Father, Hermes is defying your will. He must have helped the mortal again!"

"Hermes?" asked Zeus, looking suspiciously but not angrily at the messenger of the gods.

"You said yourself combatants had to rely on their own resources," explained Hermes. "Yes, I changed his shape, but only to reveal his true nature, for inside he is as strong as a dragon. Were he not, I could never have caused such a rapid metamorphosis."

"Nonsense!" shouted Ares. "Your magic changed him. He could never have done that himself."

"He could never have made himself a sword, either, yet you gave him one,

Brother," Hermes pointed out. "Was that a breach of the rules also?"

"Making sure each combatant has a weapon of the correct type is allowed by tradition," said Zeus. "By what tradition is changing a combatant's shape permitted?"

"It is well known by those who have studied magic lore that names have power, is it not?" asked Hermes.

"It is, but the combatant comes from a culture in which there is no hidden, true name that can be invoked magically if it is learned," said Zeus.

"True," conceded Hermes, "but I contend their names can still reveal something about them. In the Korean language spoken by Yong's ancestors, *Yong* is one of the words that can be translated as *dragon*."

Zeus smiled. "In that case, I will allow it."

"You must be joking," said Ares.

"I am completely serious," replied Zeus. "If Yong in fact, has a dragon within, then can releasing it be any different than arming a man for battle? Let the combat proceed."

Ares looked contemptuously at Yong. "Hide behind Hermes if you must. Dragons, unlike gods, can die. This trick will avail you nothing.

"Come to think of it," Ares continued, "Hermes has outwitted himself. He forgets that serpents and dragons have a special bond with me. I have often used them as guards and can control them—as I will now control you!"

Ares pointed his sword at Yong, who immediately felt an explosion of pressure in his head, like a migraine on steroids. He began to feel an irresistible urge to lie down before the war god and let that bloodthirsty deity cut him open and spill his guts on the ground of the courtyard.

Yong saw Hermes dash away and knew the clever god was implementing yet another plan. He had to hold out until Hermes could do whatever he was doing.

Yong focused every ounce of willpower he had on resisting Ares.

"Fight him!" he heard Mateo yell. "You can do it!" The other students quickly joined in, and Yong felt stronger, if only for a moment.

"I...will...not...obey!" he gasped, though really the sound was more like a hiss than a gasp.

Ares looked surprised, but he kept up his efforts to compel Yong.

However, he began to sweat, and his sword shook in his hand as if the effort was getting harder to sustain.

Yong managed another blast of flame, which Ares had to dodge, but the war god kept up his effort to make Yong obey him.

Finally, Yong felt the pressure ease, and he surged forward, spraying flame fast enough to burn Ares, who swore bloody vengeance on him.

Yong hesitated for a moment, sickened by the smell of burned flesh. He wanted to beat the bully. He wanted that so badly he could taste it on his serpent tongue. He just wasn't sure he wanted to do it by using the bully's methods.

"Father! What are you doing?" asked an unfamiliar voice.

Yong looked up. Above the makeshift battleground, Hermes floated with a fully-armed warrior whose face bore a striking resemblance to Ares's face.

Instinctively, Yong knew that the warrior was dead. Hermes had taken a quick trip to the Underworld, making good use of his authority as a guide of dead souls.

"Ascalaphus?" asked Ares, forgetting his burns and his anger for a moment.

Yong remembered the name. Ascalaphus was a son of Ares and Astyoche, which explained why he looked like Ares. The warrior had been king of Orchomenus, an Argonaut, a suitor of Helen, and a Greek commander during the Trojan War. When he fell in battle, Ares had been so overcome by grief that he had almost risked the wrath of Zeus to seek revenge after Zeus had expressly forbidden it.

That was the one story Yong could remember, aside from some versions of tales about Ares and Aphrodite, in which the war god had acted like something other than a bloodthirsty maniac.

"Father, you fight someone with the heart of a true warrior because he had the courage to stand up to you. Where is the justice in such an action?"

"Mortals must learn to know their place," insisted Ares, a little of his anger returning. "He disrespected me—"

"He objected to your knocking him down for no reason and insulting him," said Ascalaphus. "Does that really merit death? Should you not rather praise him for his valor?"

The air was heavy with silence for a moment. Then, much to Yong's surprise, Ares said, "If it is what you wish, my son, I will agree to his withdrawal of the challenge."

"I agree," Yong managed to say, hoping Ares could correctly interpret his hissing.

"Then let it be so," said Ares, with one eye on Ascalaphus. The war god seemed almost like a completely different person.

Yong, suddenly back in human form, staggered a little, then managed an awkward bow to Ares, whose attention was still so fixed on his long-lost son that he barely noticed Yong anymore.

Trying not to look as shaken up as he felt, Yong walked over and rejoined his friends. Hermes was still there, which gave Yong the opportunity to thank him.

"It was the least I could do," said Hermes. "I never expected any of you to be in so much danger."

"Is everything you said to Zeus really true?" asked Yong. It was an impolite question, but he had to know.

"Actually, you have an expression. What is it? Steer manure?" asked Hermes.

"Close enough," said Mateo, smirking.

"Well, it was steer manure," admitted Hermes. "Zeus only let me get away with that because he wanted to keep Ares from dishonoring the hospitality of Olympus but didn't want to overthrow tradition to make that happen. I gave him a plausible excuse for what I was doing, so he grabbed it and ruled in my favor."

"Then none of it was true?" asked Yong, visibly disappointed.

"Is there really a dragon inside you? If so, it wouldn't be that kind," said Hermes. "Dragons in Asian mythology have legs and don't breathe fire, among other things. I was pressed for time and had to use the kind of dragon that exists in Greek mythology.

"However, at least in the figurative sense, you do have a dragon within you," Hermes continued.

"Huh?" said Yong. For once, even he was having difficulty keeping up.

"Remember when Ares sought to control you, and you fought back?"

"How could I forget that?"

"Well, that was all you," said Hermes.   "I gave you a stronger physical shape but left your mind alone. You broke out of a god's control all by yourself."

"What does that mean?" asked Yong, still struggling with how fast the world kept changing around him.

"It means there are other kinds of strength than that which the muscles in your arms provide. You could never have beaten Ares physically, but you have the courage and the determination to face him mentally—and win. Be more confident in yourself, for few mortals could have done the same."

Yong had never thought about himself as lacking in confidence, but as Hermes spoke, he realized the truth. That was why he was having difficulty even talking about his bully problems, because he had thought getting bullied was somehow his fault. Now he could accept that whatever fault there was lay with them, not him.

"Who is that?" asked Yasmin, pointing to a white-robed man who looked as if he was putting some kind of salve on Ares's burns.

"Asclepius, our healer and someone with a very interesting past," said Hermes.

"How so?" asked Mateo.

"He started out as a mortal," Hermes explained. "He was the son of Apollo and a mortal woman, Coronis. Apollo loved her deeply, but she never trusted that love. When she found out she was pregnant, she became fearful that Apollo would abandon her, and so she agreed to marry Ischys.

"Little did she know that Apollo had a raven watching over her, and when the bird saw her betraying Apollo with Ischys, it flew at once to tell him. Heartbroken, the god cursed the poor bird, and its feathers, once the purest white, turned as black as Apollo's heart when the god of light had heard of Coronis's betrayal.

"Apollo could not bear to face Coronis again, so he sent his sister, Artemis, who killed both her and Ischys with her pitiless arrows."

Keisha cringed inwardly. She got the brokenhearted part, but killing the former lover? Any way she looked at it, it still appeared to be psychotic.

"However, when Coronis started burning on the funeral pyre, Apollo, remembering she was pregnant, saved the unborn child, Asclepius, and, once he was ready to travel, had me take him to Cheiron, the ancient centaur who was a son of Cronus. Cheiron trained many heroes, but to Asclepius he taught the healing arts.

"The boy proved a quick learner, and it was not long before he became the greatest healer in all Greece. All would have been well, but Asclepius discovered a very dangerous secret: the art of bringing the dead back to life.

"Some say he used the blood of Medusa, others that he found an herb in the mouth of a snake who was bringing its mate back to life (hence the presence of the serpent that still coils around his staff). Whatever the case, when he started raising the dead, he very soon got into trouble, for some gods considered it an act of hubris for a man, even the son of a god, to usurp a power that belonged only to the gods. Hades was said to have been very upset to have souls stolen from him, and Zeus was concerned that Asclepius might raise so many from death that he would unbalance the universe. Others say it was not until Asclepius accepted gold for raising the dead that the gods became angry. Whatever caused the problem, Zeus struck Asclepius down with a thunderbolt, reducing him to ashes in one stroke.

"However, Apollo did not want to give up his son so easily. First, he got Zeus to place his image in the stars, and eventually even to bring Asclepius back as a god. After that, Asclepius became one of the most popular gods among human worshipers, and his fellow Olympians praised Zeus for his wisdom in restoring such a useful fellow to life."

"I wonder if Ares wishes Ascalaphus could become a god," said Fatima, staring out across the courtyard to where Ares stood, still talking to his long-dead son.

"I'm sure he does, but Zeus seldom allows men to become gods," said Hermes. "As it is, I shall have to return Ascalaphus to the Underworld—and be fast about it if I want to avoid the wrath of Ares."

"You have one duty to perform first," said Zeus, surprising even Hermes by his sudden arrival right behind them.

"Yes, Majesty, I am at your service," said Hermes, making a deep bow.

"It is your mortal friends who require your service," said Zeus. "They are far too fragile to continue their journey unprotected, as recent events have demonstrated all too clearly. Take them to the forge of Hephaestus and tell him I wish them to be given suitable protective gear."

"Yes, Majesty, I shall attend to that at once," replied Hermes. "I will also follow your earlier order to seek wisdom from Apollo. I had to interrupt my earlier trip because of the...complication with Ares."

"Very good. My young friends," he said, turning to the students, "be cautious. Once you leave Olympus, I can no longer offer you protection under the host-guest relationship. It might also be wise, if a god offends you, to let the offense pass."

He was looking straight at Yong as he spoke the last sentence. Yong bowed but did not reply. From a practical standpoint, Zeus was giving good advice, but Yong wasn't in the mood to agree to just give any bully a free pass—even if that bully was a god.

Zeus said his goodbyes and then walked back to rejoin Hera. They seemed to be on better terms, but Keisha had doubts their reconciliation would last long.

"Well, my friends, let us go to Hephaestus," said Hermes. "It may take him some time to supply all of you, and I know you are anxious to rescue your transformed friend."

Yasmin thought it was funny to hear Patrick referred to over and over as their friend, when actually none of them could stand him. It was even stranger, though, that she actually found herself missing him. Even if he had been a friend, she had to admit that she didn't usually spend too much time worrying about her friends. For her, having friends was less about deep emotional connection and more about convenience. She enjoyed being with certain people, particularly ones with common interests, so she could have some fun with them, but she wasn't the kind of person who visualized having her closest high school friends for the rest of her life.

So why did she care about what happened to Patrick? She honestly wasn't sure, but she did want to find him.

Once, locating Patrick had seemed like an easy job. After all, everything around her was just a dream, so finding Patrick could be as fast as thought. However, feeling time stop when she was scared to death Yong was going to be chopped into little pieces right in front of her had given her a different perspective. Finding Patrick could be difficult—and dangerous.

Chapter 8: Hephaestus

"Where is the forge of Hephaestus?" asked Mateo.

"He has a kind of workshop on Olympus itself," said Hermes, "but he does much of his work under Mount Etna. The ancient Greeks assumed that was why Etna was a volcano, though some stories also attribute the eruptions to the idea that the monster Typhoeus, whom Zeus defeated, was buried under it."

"Is it far from here?" asked Fatima.

"Not for me," said Hermes. His smile and the Olympian background blurred away, and in what seemed like just a few seconds, they stood in a much darker, hotter place. Flickering torches provided the only light. In the distance, they could hear the echoes of what sounded like hammers striking metal.

"Wait here," said Hermes. "I thought it best not to bring you into Hephaestus's workspace—too many hazards. I will go and speak with him, and see what he can do for you."

Hermes vanished down a long, dark corridor, leaving them alone—and worried.

"The longer we're here, the less I like this," said Mateo. "I know it has to be a dream—but it just doesn't seem like one anymore."

"No, it doesn't," agreed Yong, "but since none of us believe the Greek gods are real, all these experiences have to be happening in our head somehow. Just to be safe, though, let's assume that getting hurt here might cause us some kind of injury in the real world. That'll keep us from doing risky things—"

"You mean like getting in the god of war's face and refusing to back down?" asked Mateo.

Yong's cheeks reddened. "Yeah, that's exactly what I mean."

"And rescuing Patrick," said Yasmin. "If this were just a dream, then it wouldn't matter what happened to him, but we have to assume that remaining a dog for very long might…hurt him somehow."

"I think we all agree on that," said Keisha. "There is something that's bothering me, though. If all of this is somehow being created from our subconscious minds, what does it say about us that it's so violent, that Patrick became a dog and Yong nearly got killed?"

"So it's more like a nightmare than a dream," said Mateo. "That doesn't mean we're psychos. Anyway, it's not our fault that the gods are so violent and unpredictable. That's exactly how they were in the myths. Our minds are just playing back variations of what we've read."

"What some of us have read," said Yong. "You're right, though. Aside from their concern about our mythology test and a few other odd bits, they're all pretty much who I would have expected them to be from reading about them. Come to think of it, though, there is another exception: Hermes hanging out with us for so long. Does that seem odd to any of the rest of you?"

"Not to me," said Yasmin. "It just seems consistent with the fact that this is *our* dream. Naturally, we're more central to it than mortals would be in a normal myth."

"Individual mortals were sometimes important to gods," Thanos pointed out.

"Yeah, their children occasionally," said Yasmin, thinking about Ares and Ascalaphus.

"Well, none of us believe ourselves to be descended from Olympians, so we can rule that out in this case," said Yong.

"We can't rule out romantic interests," said Mateo. The girls all shuddered.

"You mean...you think Hermes has...a crush on one of us?" asked Yasmin.

"I doubt that," said Yong. "He'd have made a move by now. The myths make it pretty clear the gods didn't waste much time on the preliminaries. Instead of worrying unnecessarily, let's just assume Hermes is being a nice guy. He had his faults in the myths, too, but there aren't that many stories about him lashing out violently."

"By the time some Greeks had started to believe in reincarnation, a story developed that Hermes had a son who kept reincarnating—" began Thanos, but at that moment Hermes returned, followed by a Hephaestus and his helpers.

Thanos, Keisha, and Yong had no difficulty picking out Hephaestus. Less handsome than the other Olympians and covered with soot from the forge, he was also easily recognizable from his limp, which some stories called a birth defect and others assumed had resulted from Zeus throwing him off Olympus and causing him to crash to earth when he had dared to support Hera in an argument. However the limp had come about, it slowed him down but did not prevent him from walking with determination, his cane hitting the stone floor hard with each step he took.

Behind him lumbered the three enormous Cyclopes who helped him at the forge, the same ones who had created the thunderbolts of Zeus, the trident of Poseidon, and the staff of Hades long before Hephaestus had even been born. They were gigantic in stature and could just barely fit in the tunnel, big as it was. Each one had a single eye in his forehead, and each of those eyes peered curiously at the students, for mortal guests were unheard of beneath Mount Etna.

As this group approached, two more figures became visible: a man and a dog. No, *not* a man and a dog, but mechanical creations of Hephaestus. Thanos thought about how amazing it was that, centuries before robotics, the ancient Greeks had visualized mechanical beings and believed Hephaestus had the ingenuity to build them. Both man and dog were fashioned from well-polished bronze and moved somewhat stiffly, their metal feet and paws clattering on the stone beneath them with every step.

"Greetings," said Hephaestus, with a little bow which the students returned. "Hermes has told me you need protection." Then, noticing some of the students staring at the Cyclopes, he added, "But not from them, I assure you. They are not like the savage cyclopean sons of Poseidon who live on an island far to the west and devour unwary travelers. No, my Cyclopes are civilized and gentle. Their names are Brontes, Steropes, and Arges."

The three Cyclopes bowed awkwardly, and again the students returned the bow.

"I suggest that, since none of you are combat trained, armor would be better than weapons," said Hermes.

"However, if they are not combat-trained, they may have difficulty moving in armor, even as light as I can make it," said Hephaestus. "That, too, is an acquired skill. I would suggest a linothorax might be a good choice."

"We don't know that term," said Matteo.

"That's like upper body protection made from several layers of linen, isn't it?" asked Thanos.

"Very good!" said Hephaestus. "The mortal variety could be as many as twenty layers glued together with animal fat. Properly prepared, it was tough enough to prevent an arrow from penetrating, yet it was far more cool, lightweight, and comfortable than metal armor. There hasn't been much demand for an Olympian equivalent; the gods have almost always wanted metal armor, but I do believe I could fashion something appropriate with the help of Athena. That will take time, however. Hermes, perhaps you and I can seek out our sister. The Cyclopes are not experienced in conversation, especially not with mortals, but my mechanical friend here has been built with all the social skills. His name is Ardalos, after my son who invented the flute and built a shrine for the Muses in Troezen.

"You may also find my smaller mechanical friend entertaining," said Hephaestus, pointing to the dog. "His name is Patricius."

"You named him—after our friend?" asked Thanos.

"He is newly forged, and I had been just about to name him when Hermes arrived. I thought perhaps he would make you less lonely for your absent friend until you can find him again."

"Thank you," said Thanos. "We are touched by your kindness."

"You are welcome. Now, Hermes, we have no time to waste, have we?"

"No, indeed," said Hermes. "Farewell, my friends. We shall return as soon as we can."

Hermes swept Hephaestus away in the way the messenger of the gods always did. The Cyclopes bowed again and went back to work at the forge.

"How may I entertain you?" asked Ardalos in a voice that sounded emotionless, yet more musical than a human voice. "Shall I play the flute for you?"

"Perhaps later," said Yasmin. "Since we found ourselves here in the first place because we needed to learn the myths, it might be better if you told us stories."

While that conversation was going on, Fatima knelt next to the dog. "May I pet you?" she asked, reaching out with her hand.

"You may do whatever pleases you," replied Patricius. His voice sounded like a bark, but the words were perfectly understandable. Fatima jumped back in surprise.

"You…you can talk!" she said, taking another step back.

"Hephaestus thought I might be more useful that way," said Patricius, looking at her sideways. "Why should that be so surprising?"

"I don't remember any myths about talking dogs, mechanical or living," said Keisha.

"Really early Greeks believed that animals had the ability to speak but that we couldn't understand their language. Remember the story of Melampus?" asked Thanos.

"I do," said Ardalos. "Melampus came from an ancient and illustrious family. His father, Amythaon, was on both his mother's and father's side descended from Hellen, the first Greek, son of Deucalion and Pyrrha, the only human couple that survived the flood, themselves the children of the Titans Prometheus and Epimetheus, respectively. Nor was that the only way in which the family was related to the Titans, for Hellen's wife, Orseis the nymph, was probably the daughter of Oceanus and Tethys."

Keisha began to miss Patrick. He would have interrupted this genealogy lesson. Everyone else was too polite to yell "Boring!" in this kind of situation, even though Ardalos probably didn't have feelings that could be hurt.

"Amythaon's and Melampus's mother, Idomene was descended from both Zeus and Poseidon by—"

"Pardon us poor mortals, Ardalos, for we have trouble absorbing so much information at once," said Thanos. "Besides, we were thinking about talking animals, and we have trouble switching subjects so quickly."

Again Keisha was reminded Thanos would make a great diplomat.

"I apologize for not being aware of your limitations," said Ardalos. "Yes, the story of Melampus shows the Greeks believed animals had the gift of speech. When Melampus was young, he came upon a sad sight: a mother snake that had been crushed by a wheel of a cart, leaving two infant snakes orphaned. Instead of just ignoring them or tormenting them, as young boys might do, Melampus buried their mother and raised the snakes himself. When they were old enough, the snakes licked out his ears to thank him, and from that day on, Melampus could understand the languages of animals, birds, fish, and even insects—every nonhuman living thing."

"*Aesop's Fables* also features talking animals," Thanos added.

"And Hephaestus made gold and silver guard dogs for the palace of Alcinous in Phaeacia," said Yong. "If animals can talk, and if Hephaestus can make animals, there's really no reason why he couldn't make talking ones."

"Was there ever a question he could?" asked Patricius. "Am I not here before you? What more proof would you have needed?"

"None," said Fatima, petting him on the head.

"Ardalos, would you please tell us about Hephaestus, your maker?" asked Mateo.

Surprisingly, the automaton actually sighed, or at least made a noise that sounded like a sigh.

"My maker is a most admirable god, skilled in many ways, master of fire and of metallurgy, able to fashion objects both mundane and magical. Also, he is a master architect, builder of the palaces of Olympus themselves—yet he is unappreciated."

Keisha suspected Ardalos didn't have built-in emotions, and his words were toneless, but she couldn't escape the feeling that there was emotion behind those words.

"Who doesn't appreciate him?" asked Mateo.

"His fellow gods. They treat him more like a servant than an equal. He is the first person they run to when they need something, but often the last person they will welcome with friendship.

"How did he get that limp?" asked Ardalos rhetorically. "He was injured trying to defend his own mother, Hera, from Zeus. Despite the facts being well-known, his fellow gods spread the malicious story that he is the deformed product of an effort by Hera to give birth to a child without the aid of Zeus, supposedly in retaliation for Zeus's creation of Athena without a mother. That motive makes no sense, for everyone knows Athena has a mother, Metis, the Oceanid, even though Zeus swallowed her before Athena's birth."

"What?" asked Fatima. "I thought only Cronus swallowed family members."

"Zeus only did it that once," said Ardalos, as if the number of times someone had eaten relatives or lovers made a big difference. "You know of the prophecy that Zeus will one day father a son that will overthrow him?"

Everyone nodded quickly.

"Well, there was a prophecy about Metis, too—that if she had a son, he would be more powerful than his father. Zeus didn't really consider that when he first made love to her."

"Big surprise," muttered Mateo.

"The more he thought about it, however, the more he knew he could not take the chance of having Metis conceive a child. Rather than risk his own downfall, Zeus tricked Metis into playing a shape-changing game with him, and when she turned into a fly, he swallowed her."

"Why couldn't he just stop having sex with her?" asked Keisha in an angry tone.

"The defenders of Zeus would say the prophecy might have created problems if she had conceived a child from any powerful father," replied Ardalos in a way that suggested he didn't believe that excuse. "What he didn't know when he imprisoned her inside his own body was that she was already pregnant.

"Metis, being the type of goddess to make the most of a bad situation, prepared for her child's birth by making weapons and armor for the child to grow into. That's actually one trick even Hephaestus would have had trouble recreating. However, all that hammering inside gave Zeus a terrible headache, which got worse and worse."

"How did she get from his stomach to his head?" asked Yasmin.

"She was basically prudence incarnate," explained Ardalos. "Perhaps she naturally gravitated toward Zeus's brain. In any case, when the pain became completely unendurable, Zeus asked Hephaestus to split his skull open in hopes of releasing the pressure—which proves my point. Hephaestus was born before Athena; hence, Hera couldn't have conceived him in retaliation."

Since Hephaestus had been the one who "programmed" Ardalos, Keisha had to wonder whether his version was the true one, but she knew it would be unwise to raise that issue, so she kept quiet.

"My maker split Zeus's skull with an ax, and out sprung Athena, fully grown and fully equipped. Despite his earlier reservations about children of Metis, Zeus embraced his new daughter—presumably after his head grew back together—and by some accounts she is even his favorite."

"What happened to Metis?" asked Yasmin. "Was she all right?"

"She could have jumped out when Zeus's skull was split, but she did not. No one knows why. Perhaps she had decided that even a small risk of another great war among the gods was too much to take and stayed voluntarily within Zeus. The stories all agree that she stayed in his head and gave him the benefit of her wise counsel. It must have helped, too, because he hasn't had to eat anyone to avoid his prophecy since then. His mistreatment of Prometheus was also something he did much earlier, before Metis had become a part of him.

"Maybe he'll even gain the wisdom to appreciate my maker one day," finished Ardalos. Unlike his earlier plunge into family trees, he seemed to have lost his interest in continuing. Again Keisha suspected emotions lurked behind that metal face and toneless voice, though there was no way to be certain.

Fortunately, Hephaestus and Hermes returned at that point, carrying several linothoraxes that glowed just a bit in the relatively gloomy chamber.

"You're going to like these. Athena, the best seamstress among the gods, herself sewed the linen from which they are made. They could stop the arrows of Apollo and Artemis themselves, at least for a time. They won't stop something like Ares's sword strokes very long—for that you'd need metal—"

"Which is why he's giving you the spare caps of invisibility," interrupted Hermes, unable to contain his enthusiasm for the idea.

"Really we both are," said Hephaestus, "for I made them, but it was Hermes who retrieved them from the Underworld just now."

"Isn't there only one of those?" asked Thanos. "I thought Hades had it."

"Hades isn't exactly the type to lend things out, yet invisibility caps appear in several other stories, used by Athena, by me, even by the mortal Perseus. How could there not be more than one?" asked Hephaestus. "Hades's original cap, created for him by the Cyclopes, is slightly more powerful, creating completely impenetrable invisibility, but the ones I will give you will work in most cases even against my fellow gods. It would take a colossal effort for someone to see you.

"The idea is that the linothoraxes will guard you against surprise attacks from a distance," said Hermes. "If you have any kind of warning, just put on your cap and vanish. Even a god cannot effectively fight what he cannot see."

"Aren't there ways—" started Thanos.

"Yes, there are ways to detect the invisible, clever boy," interrupted Hermes. "The caps should keep you safe, though, until I can act. Remember that I will be with you most of the time."

"As will I," added Ardalos.

"And I," barked Patricius.

"You're giving us the wonderful…beings you've created?" asked Fatima, astounded.

"Lending," corrected Hephaestus. "The armor and the caps are but loans as well. Hermes will collect them before you return to your world. However, you may use them as long as you are here and still need them."

"I don't mean to be rude, especially when you're being so generous with us, but why would we need a mechanical man or dog?" asked Mateo.

"You never know when you might need a skilled musician or storyteller," replied Ardalos.

"Or a faithful dog," added Patricius.

"If nothing else, Ardalos is durable," said Hephaestus. "In the event of an attack, he would make an admirable shield." Keisha thought Ardalos looked displeased by that—or was she just reading too much into facial expressions she could barely see in such low light?

"As for Patricius, his body is constructed like that of a guard dog—very handy in a fight. Those metal teeth will cut through flesh as well as even my best daggers, should the need arise. Even if he never has to fight, I have given him a sense of smell equivalent to the best hunting dog—if that dog had been a pup of old Cerberus himself."

"You mean he can sniff out Patrick?" asked Yong. "What's he going to get the scent from?"

Hermes held up a few hairs. "The dog version of Patrick was shedding a little on Olympus. I picked up the hairs, figuring we could need them at some point." The messenger god held the hairs under Patricius's nose.

"I have the scent," said Patricius after only a few seconds.

"Can you…find him wherever he is?" asked Mateo.

"If he's in the Underworld or at the bottom of the sea, I couldn't smell him from Olympus," explained Patricius. "He needs to be closer than that, but if we find a place where he's been recently, I should be able to follow the scent."

"We know he was on Olympus," said Fatima. "Why don't we just go back there?"

"No one could have just walked away with him," said Hermes. "Helios would have seen them at some point. Whether Iris or some other god spirited him away, he or she moved too fast, possibly even by air, to leave much of a trail. We will have to seek him out elsewhere. Fortunately, while we were gone, Zeus sent me a message. Helios has caught glimpses of Patrick several times. Surely Patricius can pick up his scent at one of those spots."

It took only a few minutes for the students to put their invisibility caps in their pockets and buckle on their linothoraxes, which they noticed had been decorated with the image of Athena, spear raised, ready to strike a blow.

"Someone is certainly proud," said Ardalos, who sounded disapproving. Keisha wondered if Athena was one of the Olympians he had mentioned earlier who didn't properly appreciate Hephaestus.

They all thanked Hephaestus for his many gifts, and then Hermes led them to their next stop—which they all prayed would eventually lead to finding Patrick.

Chapter 9: Aphrodite

"Where are we?" asked Mateo, looking up and down a beach much different from the ones he was used to in Southern California. Rather than being an expanse of white sand, this one was hilly and rocky, with one particularly big boulder jutting out of the rough sea in front of them.

"This is Cyprus," answered Hermes. "This is the most recent spot Helios saw Patrick."

"My family and I used to vacation in Cyprus when I was little," said Thanos, staring at the rock. "Things are pretty different, now, but that's Aphrodite's Rock, isn't it? Ancient Cypriots used to tell tourists that was the spot from which Aphrodite first emerged from the sea."

"Aphrodite?" asked Ardalos. "Let us be quick, then. No good can ever come from dealing with her."

"I don't mean to be rude, but what would you know about love?" asked Yasmin. "You don't...I mean, you can't—"

"I know of love only from what I have seen and heard," replied the automaton. "Aphrodite is my maker's wife, but loving her has brought him nothing but grief."

"To be fair, I wasn't asked if I wanted to marry him," said a sweetly musical voice surprisingly close behind them. Turning quickly, they found themselves face to face with the goddess of love.

The sight had nearly overwhelmed the guys when they had beheld her from a great distance through their "window" in the land of dreams. Now, standing close enough to touch her, all of their thought processes burned away in a hormonal inferno.

"We...we come on a mission...of the highest importance," Hermes managed to say. Apparently his godly status did not make him immune to Aphrodite's charms.

"Let us go then and discuss this...mission," said Aphrodite softly, taking his hand and leading him away. Once she was out of sight, the guys reverted to something like normal.

"Well, that was...informative," said Keisha, poking Yong in the ribs.

"You girls would have reacted the same way if Eros were here," said

Thanos.

"What happened to Hermes?" asked Mateo.

"He is doubtless making love to my maker's wife," said Ardalos in his usual toneless voice Keisha could swear was still giving off an emotional vibe.

"Aphrodite and Hermes?" asked Fatima.

"Hermes was a pretty versatile god," said Thanos. "Among other things he was sometimes used as the ideal for male sexuality, just as Aphrodite was the ideal for female sexuality. When you think about their connection that way, it makes perfect sense."

"Nothing about Aphrodite makes sense—and it is not as if Hermes was the only one with whom she cheated," said Ardalos. "Yes, she slept with Hermes and became the mother of Hermaphroditus, but—"

"Excuse me," said Mateo, "but does that myth have anything to do with hermaphrodites?"

"What's a hermaphrodite?" asked Fatima.

"Technically, a person with sexual characteristics of both genders," replied Thanos. He was trying to sound as clinical and detached as he could, but Fatima blushed anyway.

"The story goes that he was a handsome young man," said Yong. "No big surprise, given who his parents were. Anyway, when he was about our age, he made the mistake of bathing in a pond belonging to the water nymph Salmacis. She tried to seduce him, he resisted, and she prayed to the gods that she could be with Hermaphroditus forever. One of them granted her prayer…sort of. She and Hermaphroditus merged into one being."

"Myths are often used by early people to explain things," said Thanos. "Those that do so are referred to as etiological. This one could have been a way of explaining why some people were hermaphrodites. At the end of the story, Hermaphroditus asked the gods to transform anyone who bathed in that pond in the same way that he had been transformed."

"It doesn't sound as if he was very happy with the situation," said Keisha, "but Salmacis couldn't have been that pleased either. The story's a good illustration of the old saying, 'Be careful what you wish for because you might get it.'"

"It also has another possible message as well," said Yong. "There are no myths about Hermaphroditus after that point, though he's represented a few times in art. However, he was worshiped as a god, not only here on Cyprus, but even in Athens, where he had a temple at one time—and not as a vengeful, angry god, as you might expect from his misfortune, but as a gentle god of fertility. He was even sometimes used as a symbol for marriage, a physical image of the spiritual union between man and woman. His...unusual physical form didn't keep him from playing a positive role."

"So you're saying the story was intended to give hope to hermaphrodites?" asked Mateo, raising an eyebrow.

Yong chuckled. "I doubt that. The condition is very rare, after all. Hermaphroditus was also associated with effeminate males, those who didn't fit the ancient macho stereotype.

"The ancient Greeks might have been primitive by our standards in many ways, but their myths show a surprising tolerance for people who are different from the accepted standard. Hermaphroditus was still a god even though he combined both genders. Athena and Artemis were goddesses even though they rejected the traditional female roles. Hephaestus was a god despite having a physical disability," he added with a nod toward Ardalos.

"Oh, I see where you're going," said Keisha. "The myths could also be read as an argument against stereotyping. The centaurs, in general, are brutal and uncivilized, but Cheiron, the first centaur, was caring and wise, and over time he became the teacher of many great heroes."

"In the same way, the Cyclopes look like monsters by human standards, but the ones who work with Hephaestus are good, intelligent, and clever," said Thanos. "Yeah, I can see how someone who felt different, for whatever reason, could take some comfort from those stories."

"If I may finish what I was saying," interrupted Ardalos, who had been making an increasingly loud clicking noise for some time, "Aphrodite has had many lovers over the centuries, not just Hermes." His emotionless voice sounded colder than the nearby ocean. "She made love to Ares and became the mother of the terrifying Deimos and Phobos, who took after their father, as well as Anteros, the god of unrequited love, and Harmonia, who eventually became the goddess of marital and social harmony. She made love to Dionysus and became the mother of Priapus, a rustic fertility god. She made love to

Poseidon and became the mother of Rhode, who gave her name to the island of Rhodes. Of course, she also made love to Zeus.

"Nor did she confine herself to gods. She slept with Anchises, a Trojan prince, and became the mother of Aeneas, who would lead the Trojan survivors off to Italy, where his descendants eventually founded Rome. He was her most remembered mortal descendant, though there were many, many others."

"We all understand why Hephaestus would be hurt by Aphrodite's behavior," said Fatima, "but is what she said true? Was she really not given a choice about marrying him?"

"No choice at all," said Aphrodite, once again walking up behind them so quietly that none of them were aware she was back. She was still beautiful, but this time the guys managed to retain some of their thought processes, perhaps because she wasn't trying to draw their attention. Hermes, looking somewhat flushed, was only a couple of steps behind her.

"That was…quick," said Mateo, raising an eyebrow at Hermes.

"Our urgent need to find Patrick allowed only a little time," said Hermes in a mock-grave tone.

Ardalos focused on Aphrodite. "The marriage was legal and sanctioned by the king of the gods himself."

Aphrodite laughed. "When I first came to Olympus, Zeus was worried my presence would lead to conflict if I wasn't married and handed me to Hephaestus like so much property. The fact that arranged marriage was common did not make it right."

"Did being unfaithful improve your situation?" asked Ardalos.

"Did it improve his?" countered Aphrodite. "Was not he married to Aglaea, daughter of Zeus and Eurynome, one of the Graces who became my attendants? Did Hephaestus not have four daughters with her, before casting her aside when I came along?"

"Lies told by foolish storytellers," replied Ardalos.

"Surely Homer and Hesiod can't both be fools," muttered Thanos. Both Aphrodite and Ardalos ignored him.

"And what of the Ardalos for whom you are named?" asked the goddess. "Was he not a son of Hephaestus by a mortal woman—after Hephaestus was married to me? What of the various Italian and Greek kings who claim descent from him?

"It is not that I begrudge him such pleasure as he can find in the arms of other goddesses or mortal women. It is that I do not see why a woman is disloyal if she finds comfort outside of marriage, but a man can do the same thing, and not a single voice is raised in criticism."

"He would have been loyal to you if you had been loyal to him," replied Ardalos.

"I fear not," said Aphrodite, "for I see no example of marital fidelity among the gods, whether their wives are loyal or not. I do not ask for any, either, but only to be treated as the gods are treated, rather than being treated like the gods' property."

Ardalos clicked for a moment, then said, "My maker has never thought of you as property."

"Yet he follows the patriarchal custom of regarding women as such and always has. What of the story that when Zeus had flung Hephaestus from Olympus, and then he finally came limping back, Zeus offered him any goddess of his choice as a wife. What did your maker do? He asked for Athena, who had pledged herself to virginity. Hephaestus cared nothing more for her wishes than he did for mine, and Zeus granted him her hand. Fortunately, Athena was able to resist your maker by force when he tried to claim her, and in the end, he yielded to her wishes. He did so not out of respect for them but from the certain knowledge that Zeus would not risk the incredible discord Athena would bring to Olympus if she were forced to abandon her virginity."

"More lies," said Ardalos, "I have heard that story, too, but in three different, inconsistent versions. Athena herself would not agree with any of them. She and my maker are friends."

"She may have forgiven him," said Aphrodite, "but that does not mean he never tried to force her into marriage—or worse. Perhaps she is too embarrassed to admit what really happened. It is said, though, that her protection of Erichthonius, king of Athens, comes from the fact that the king was somehow the product of Hephaestus's failed attempt to force himself upon Athena—a child whose father was Hephaestus but who had no true mother. Athena took the child under her protection, not for the sake of his father, but for his own sake, since he was blameless."

"Again, nothing but lies and misrepresentations," said Ardalos. "Erichthonius was, in fact, the son of Hephaestus, but his mother was Atthis, daughter of Cranaus, the second Athenian king. His family also had some connection to Gaia, but his birth had absolutely nothing to do with any imagined assault by Hephaestus upon Athena."

Despite Ardalos's emotionless voice, the argument had become heated enough that the students backed away a little, partly to avoid getting in the way and partly so that they could talk without fear of being changed into something if Aphrodite didn't like what they had to say.

"I don't know what to think," said Yasmin. "At first Hephaestus seemed like one of the good guys. Now Aphrodite is making him sound like a total male chauvinist who thinks women are property, and it sounds to me as if he tried to rape Athena, at least by modern standards."

"What we're hearing is like the two sides to the story of a breakup," said Mateo. "Haven't you ever noticed the guy usually blames the girl and vice versa?"

"We're also dealing with different versions by different storytellers," said Thanos. "We could find versions of the myths that back up what Ardalos is saying and others that support Aphrodite's argument."

"In general, the surviving Greek myths are pretty patriarchal," said Keisha. "They reflect classical Greek culture, in which women *were* property, just as they were to some extent in almost every ancient culture."

"Yeah, the amazing thing isn't that women are portrayed as under the control of men, but that there are any stories that treat women differently," said Thanos. "Oppressive as the society was by our standards, in most myths the women still emerge as diverse characters, sometimes with real strength and intelligence. Occasionally, they win. Hephaestus couldn't have Athena, even though he wanted her."

"I've read that the conflicts among the gods in the stories may reflect conflicts among the different early cultures that eventually merged into classical Greek culture," Yong said. "Some scholars believe one group had a male-dominated pantheon, while another worshiped the Great Mother Goddess. The male group won the conflict, but one still sees echoes of it in the myths. Think about Gaia's conspiring to overthrow Uranus, then Cronus, and then even Zeus. There's also the long-running battle between Zeus and Hera."

Their conversation was interrupted by Aphrodite's voice getting suddenly louder. "What do you mean I can't love? I am the goddess of love. No one feels the emotion as truly as I do!"

"You feel sexual desire, but I see no evidence you feel love," replied Ardalos. "Forget about my maker for a moment. You obviously didn't love him. But who among the gods and men you chose to sleep with did you love? You never stayed with any of them, though some of them were unmarried."

"I did love a man once," replied Aphrodite, her voice much quieter and softer. "Would you like to hear the story?"   she asked, ignoring Ardalos and focusing on the students.

"Yes, please," said Fatima. "We would love to hear the story."

"It is hard for me to tell, but perhaps it will convince the tin man of my sincerity."

"Bronze," said Ardalos. "I am made of bronze." She ignored him.

"To tell the story properly, I must begin with my love's great-grandfather, Pygmalion, king of Cyprus, for he nearly prevented my love from ever being born.

"Pygmalion, disgusted by the actions of some Cypriot prostitutes, convinced himself that women were all immoral. Lost in his own misogyny, he decided never to marry—an awkward resolve for a king, whose duty it was to father an heir, but he persisted in his narrow-minded rejection of half the human race.

"However, it was not his fate to remain unmarried, and destiny will always have its way. In addition to being king, Pygmalion was a gifted sculptor, and though he professed to despise women, he kept sculpting them. Finally, he created an ivory statue of a woman so beautiful that he fell in love with it.

"After his slander against the entire female gender, it would have served the man right to remain in hopeless love with an unfeeling statue. However, at my festival he prayed to me for a wife 'like his ivory girl,' for he was too embarrassed to admit even in prayer that he loved a statue. Because he had turned to me for help, I decided to be merciful, and, knowing what he meant, I made the flames upon my altar flare three times in answer to his prayer. Racing home, he kissed the statue, whose lips were warm. Barely believing what he felt, he caressed her newly softened skin, saw the blush upon her cheek, and met her now living eyes.

"I took pleasure in attending the wedding I had helped to bring about, and Pygmalion, his hatred of women long-forgotten, had many happy years with 'his ivory girl,' who took the name Galatea.

"Together they had a son, Paphos, who became king and had and eventually fathered a son of his own, Cinyras.

"King Cinyras of Cyprus was both handsome and musically gifted, so much so that some whispered he was really Apollo's son. It was clear to all that he was far above the human norm."

"Unfortunately, life often mingles the bitter and the sweet. Pygmalion's life moved from bitter to sweet, but it was Cinyras's fate to have his life move from sweet to bitter because of his wife, Cenchreis, beautiful as Galatea, but fatally flawed.

"You have heard of hubris, have you not?" the goddess asked. "The disastrous pride that, among other things, leads men and women to compare themselves with the gods?"

"Yes, we have," said Thanos. The others nodded.

"People who are afflicted with hubris carry their vanity to insane lengths. In Cenchreis's case, she dared to say that Myrrha, her daughter, was more beautiful than I. Such presumption could not be left unpunished, and so Myrrha was overwhelmed by an incestuous passion for her own father—"

"What?" asked Yasmin, stunned. Her fellow students froze. Would Aphrodite take offense?

"I know that to you punishing people for comparing themselves to the gods must seem arrogant on our part, but, if left unpunished, hubris could do incalculable harm," said Aphrodite. "When mortals are allowed to think that they are as good as—or better than—the gods, they tend not to value their fellow men, nor be concerned with their welfare. The most miserable tyrants of all time may not have compared themselves to gods out loud, but they thought of themselves as gods, and untold millions have died because of such arrogance."

"I...did not think of it quite like that," said Yasmin, looking nervous.

"Nonetheless, that is the truth, especially for those who rule over their fellow men." said Aphrodite.

"I know many people believe that I was the one who contrived the punishment," replied Aphrodite, glancing at Ardalos as if daring him to comment. "I admit to having punished people at times by causing them to fall in love with the wrong person, but I never inspired an incestuous passion when there was any chance of such a hateful lust being fulfilled. In the case of Cinyras, the poet Ovid speaks the truth—Myrrha's unnatural passion, too horrible for me or Eros to contemplate, came from one of the Erinyes, who brought forth the curse from the Underworld itself."

Ardalos clicked loudly but said nothing. The students didn't say anything, either, and the silence became awkward.

"Don't you believe me?" asked Aphrodite.

"I think they are wondering why Cinyras and Myrrha were punished as well as Cenchreis," said Hermes.

"Cinyras should have reprimanded his wife for her presumption and did not," said Aphrodite. "Instead, he did nothing. As for Myrrha, she accepted her mother's excessive praise as well. The girl developed an exaggerated sense of her own importance, a feeling of entitlement that made her more vulnerable to the unnatural passion once it started to gnaw at her.

"It didn't take long for Myrrha to decide there was nothing wrong with her feelings. It was not conscience but practicality that drove her to despair, for she could see no way to satisfy her desire. As a result, she tried to kill herself, but her old nurse prevented her from doing so. The woman's desire to save the life of a girl she had cared for from infancy was understandable—but then the nurse went too far.

"Instead of trying to convince Myrrha to restrain her passion, the nurse schemed to help her to satisfy it by tricking Cinyras.

"Myrrha managed to sleep with her father for twelve nights without being discovered—Cinyras thought he was sleeping with his wife. On the thirteenth night, when he discovered the terrible truth, he pursued his daughter with a sword. She prayed to the gods to be removed from the sight of men, and I took pity on her, turning her into a myrrh tree."

"How is that pity?" asked Mateo.

"It spared her further shame, and it also spared her from being killed by her own father. She was able to find peace as a tree."

Mateo couldn't help being skeptical, but he had no desire to become a tree himself, so he didn't ask any follow-up questions.

"Nine months later, the trunk of the tree opened, revealing a beautiful baby who I could tell was destined to grow into the most handsome young man I had ever seen—and that is saying something, considering how many centuries I've lived. Fearful of the jealousy of the other goddesses, I locked the baby away in a magic chest and gave it to Persephone for safekeeping in the Underworld."

"That seems like an odd place to keep a baby," said Fatima.

"The chest protected him from all harm," said Aphrodite, "and no one in the Underworld crosses Persephone, for fear of the wrath of Hades. Unfortunately, Persephone opened the chest, fell in love with who the baby would become, and claimed him for herself. She is lonely in her loveless marriage with Hades, so I could hardly blame her, but I had seen Adonis's destiny first and was not about to lose him. I appealed to Zeus, who eventually ruled that Adonis spend one-third of the year in the Underworld, one-third with me, and choose who he spent the remaining third with."

"A baby had to choose?" asked Yasmin.

"No, the dispute went on so long that he was a young man by the time Zeus ruled," replied Aphrodite. "Adonis chose to spend his time with me, and my life was bliss—for a while.

"Adonis loved me with all his heart, but he also loved the hunt. I warned him to be careful, and he promised he would be, but one day he sought to kill an enormous wild boar, and it killed him instead.

"I came as soon as I realized he was in danger, but I was too late. I sensed the hand of a god in Adonis's death, but I never found out which one. Some say it was a jealous Ares, others that Artemis killed him to get revenge for the death of her favorite, Hippolytus, still others that Apollo struck him down because I had blinded Erymanthus, Apollo's son, for spying on Adonis and me during our lovemaking. Some would even argue that the male gods have an informal agreement to punish any mortal man who loves a goddess."

"No such agreement exists," said Hermes immediately.

"It matters not," said Aphrodite, as tears started to roll down her cheeks. "It only matters that I lost him, and lost him forever. The only piece of him I had left was the red rose that sprouted from his blood, and our daughter Beroe, though she too was mortal like her father, so eventually I lost her as well. Then the rose was all that was left to me—the rose, and my memories, immortal as I am. I would not forget, but like the thorns on the rose, the memories give me pain."

She sobbed then, and Hermes took her in his arms. She stayed there for a while, and he whispered to her what comforting words he could muster.

Then Aphrodite became aware of the students again, pulled away from Hermes a little bit, and made an attempt to smile.

"I am sorry! For a moment I forgot all about your search for your friend. I sent a dove to find him, and I anticipate hearing something anytime."

Just as she finished talking, a white dove sailed down from the sky, landed gently on her shoulder, and whispered in her ear.

"Good news!" said the goddess. "He has followed the dove back and will join us in a moment.

They heard rustling in the bushes, and in a minute or two Patrick came bounding onto the beach—the human version, not the dog one.

"Patrick, you're human again," said Thanos. "How did that happen?"

"I don't remember much," said Patrick, his voice almost as emotionless as Ardalos's. "I've been here for a while. That's really all I know."

"Unfortunate," said Hermes. "I hoped to learn from you who was responsible for your abduction. I'm sure Zeus will want to know."

"He could not tell you anything," said Patricius, who had been quiet for so long that the students had almost forgotten he was there. "He is not Patrick."

"How do you know that?"

"Smell," said Patricius, twitching his nose.

"We gave you hair from his dog form," said Keisha. "Maybe dog Patrick smells different from human Patrick."

"'Human Patrick' doesn't really smell like anything," said Patricius. "Rain, maybe."

Patrick just stood there, glassy-eyed, his mouth hanging open as if he had started to say something and then forgotten what.

"This is the longest I've ever seen him go without saying something sarcastic," said Mateo.

"Hmmm…Rain, you say?" asked Hermes. He waved his caduceus, which emitted a soft glow. Patrick glowed the same way—and then vanished, quite literally in a puff of smoke.

"I've seen this magic before," Hermes explained. "It's like what Zeus did to create a double of Hera with which to test Ixion. The only difference is that Zeus did it more skillfully. Whoever created this false Patrick evidently wasn't able to give it his personality."

"Or didn't want to," suggested Thanos. "Maybe the kidnapper didn't intend the deception to fool us for long. This could just be a way of toying with us."

"Perhaps," conceded Hermes. "As I think about it, anyone sophisticated enough to work that kind of magic in the first place could have made a more convincing copy than that."

"This means all of Helios's sightings are useless to us, doesn't it?" asked Yong.

Hermes nodded. "Since this one was false, they could all be. Unfortunately, we have no choice but to check them, anyway. In truth, we have no other clues. Your friend could literally be anywhere in the universe. Fast as I am, it would take a mortal lifetime for me to search every conceivable spot that a god could have taken him—and that assumes he's visible. It would take even longer if he is hidden somehow by magic."

"Where are my manners?" said Aphrodite. "Before you leave on what promises to be a long journey, I should be a proper hostess and entertain you." The guys could feel Aphrodite's irresistibility ratchet up a few notches. The air crackled with sexual electricity.

Then Aphrodite gave a little shriek, and the moment passed.

"Your dog bit me!" she said, pointing accusingly at Patricius.

"I beg your pardon, mistress, but my master bade me to do all in my power to aid these visitors on their quest. Letting them be enthralled here by you for days isn't likely to help them find their friend."

Aphrodite looked a little less angry. It was tough to be too enraged with a cute little dog, even if it was mechanical—and had her blood on its teeth.

"I suppose, given who your master is, I'm lucky I didn't lose the leg," she said, attempting a smile but not quite making it.

"I know you all should go now. Depart with my blessing, then. I'm off to the nearest lake to clean my wound."

They said their goodbyes, and Aphrodite left them, though the scent of rose petals lingered in the air.

"You know, we could have spared a couple of days," said Mateo, looking in the direction she had gone.

"And leave Patrick a dog any longer than necessary?" asked Keisha. "I don't think so."

"Well, where are we going now?" Yasmin asked Hermes.

"The land of the Hyperboreans, a place in the far north where the sun always shines, and the people live in happiness. Apollo visits in the winter and should be there now. That's good news, because he may be able to use his prophetic gifts to help us find Patrick if what Helios saw there was also false."

In seconds they sped off, all filled with mounting anxiety, and the guys with questions about what might have been.

Chapter 10: Apollo

Hermes ran into some turbulence on the way to Hyperborea, so unlike their other trips with him, the students were actually able to see some of the scenery. It was a good thing none of them had a fear of heights, because Hermes was levitating them far above the clouds, through which they could see glimpses of the earth below. It would have been an awe-inspiring view—had there been something beneath their feet, and a nice guard rail to prevent them from falling.

At least the delay gave them a chance to take about their recent experiences. Doing so while Aphrodite might have overheard would have been foolish.

"After all, even if she isn't responsible for poor Myrrha, she sometimes punishes people by making them fall in love with the wrong person," said Yasmin. "If I'd said something she didn't like, she might have made me fall in love with Patrick."

"The dog or the person?" asked Mateo, grinning.

"I'm not sure which would be worse," replied Yasmin.

"That's not very nice!" said Fatima, much more loudly than she usually spoke. "Patrick isn't the nicest person himself, but he's in bad trouble, so we shouldn't be making fun of him."

"He'd be making fun of any of us if the situations were reversed," said Keisha, "but you're right, Fatima, our focus should be rescuing him, not taking cheap shots at him."

Yasmin didn't usually pay much attention to Fatima, who was too quiet to really be much fun, but Yasmin couldn't help but be impressed by the other girl's willingness to stick up for somebody she didn't even like.

"I'm sorry," Yasmin said. "I was just kidding."

"Yeah, it was just a joke," said Mateo. "No one deserves to become a dog—not even Patrick."

"No one deserves to be forced to fall in love with her own father, either," said Yasmin. "I can't understand how the gods could allow such a thing. I get what Aphrodite said about the dangers of hubris, but why not punish the mother, who seems more responsible, rather than her daughter and husband?"

"It does seem like a lot of collateral damage," agreed Keisha.

"We have to keep in mind that the Greeks, like a lot of ancient people, believed in a kind of group responsibility," said Thanos. "If a ruler sinned, they didn't see anything wrong with the whole kingdom suffering. If a parent sinned, they saw nothing wrong with the children suffering."

"That's cruel," said Fatima.

"Early Greeks formed their religious attitudes based on the way they saw the world working," said Yong. "Leaving the supernatural aside, if a kingdom had a bad ruler, the people of that kingdom would suffer. If kids had bad parents, those kids would suffer. It wouldn't take much imagination to assume that suffering was the punishment of the ruler or the parent's sin by some god."

"That doesn't make sense," said Mateo.

"Of course it doesn't," agreed Yong. "Early myths aren't the product of logic. They're much more the results of emotion, intuition, creative connections, maybe even dreams, which remember ancient people often thought were communications from higher powers.

"Ancient people took the world as they experienced it and drew conclusions about the powers that were running that world. Remember that in general people were much more vulnerable than we are. If a drought happens in California, our lawns die. If a drought happened in early Greece, people starved. We can easily cure diseases that would have been fatal to the early Greeks, and people died all the time of what to them were mysterious causes.

"In other words, the world must have seemed like a very cruel place. Is it any wonder that they thought of the gods as cruel? The wonder is that they ever portrayed them as kind. Zeus brought disaster on mortal women by sleeping with them, but he also sent the rain that watered the crops. Aphrodite might sometimes punish people by making them love the wrong person, but she also brought people what even we would think of as true love. Bleak as their world was compared to ours, the Greeks could still see hope in it, and they expressed the hope in the myths as well as the bleakness."

"I understand better why the Greeks would have imagined gods behaving this way," said Yasmin. "That doesn't mean I have to like it."

"You can appreciate literature without having to agree with everything in it," said Keisha. "You can also repurpose it, as we talked about before. Today we can see the myths as illustrations of how bad arbitrary rulers are, or the importance of having consideration for other people. After all, the gods were sometimes harsh with people, but they were equally harsh with each other. Aphrodite's one true love was killed by one of her fellow deities, after all, and Zeus and Hera seem to make each other miserable more than anything else."

"We have arrived," said Hermes, not that the students could have missed the rapid plunge through the clouds. Despite the speed of the drop, the landing on solid ground was surprisingly gentle.

The land of the Hyperboreans was so far north that in the real world it would have been somewhere in the Arctic, but in this mythic world it was as the ancient Greeks had imagined it: a sort of idealized Greece in which there was no night, for the sun shone perpetually, and it was always spring. The scent of all the blooming flowers was nearly overwhelming.

Hermes had brought them down practically right next to Apollo, who looked quite at home in such a bright setting. Young and handsome as Hermes, Apollo also had an added glow. Yong recalled Apollo was among other things the god of light, and he certainly looked the part.

"Brother, I regret the need to disturb your winter retreat, but these young visitors from the mortal world have lost a friend of theirs." Apollo raised an eyebrow. "He was abducted, not just lost, and the clues we thought we had may all be false. Only someone with your prophetic gift could possibly help us."

"Greetings, new friends," said Apollo. "I will do what I can to find your companion for you. Hermes, tell me what you know of this mortal's disappearance."

"He was with the others, enjoying the hospitality of Olympus. There was an…incident with Hera that resulted in his transformation into a dog."

Apollo chuckled. "Said something undiplomatic, I take it."

"Indeed," agreed Hermes. "However, Hera relented and was about to change him back when we discovered he was gone."

"A trick by Hera?" asked Apollo.

"I did consider that," said Hermes, "but the only way it could have been managed would have been if Iris spirited him away, and since she travels by rainbow, it is hard for her to come and go inconspicuously. In this case, it would have been possible, for there was cloud cover around Olympus that prevented Helios from seeing clearly, but she would have had to dive almost straight down to avoid being seen. Unless she burrowed into the earth right at the base of Olympus, Helios would have seen something."

"The same would also be true of anyone else unless they flew invisibly enough to fool Helios," Apollo pointed out. "That would take someone with a great deal of magical ability." *Dealing w.th Someone powerful*

"Exactly what I thought," agreed Hermes. "There is other evidence the abductor was someone of considerable magical skill. Whoever it was made at least one magical copy of the victim, using something like the spell Zeus once used to make a copy of Hera from the clouds. Helios sighted the victim several times in widely separated spots, including here, but we now think they were probably all just copies."

"I've seen no dogs today, and certainly I could tell if I saw one who had once been human," said Apollo. "However, Hyperborea is a vast place, far larger than Greece itself, and mostly forest. The person—or dog, as the case may be—could be hidden beneath the trees so that Helios could not see."

"He could be hidden in any number of places, and these mortals will be long-dead in the time it would take me to search them all. That is why I seek your aid."

"Wise, dear Brother, very wise," said Apollo, nodding. "Be warned, though, that even I cannot know everything, and someone as adept at magic as this perpetrator may be able to hide even from my prophetic eye. Still, I will do what I can. Let us go to a quiet place where I can properly concentrate."

The students had been so focused on Apollo that they had not really noticed the large number of Hyperboreans milling around. None had interrupted, but when Apollo stopped talking, those who were nearby all greeted him. Every single one of them looked happy—almost too happy, Keisha thought. She had to admit, though, that they looked the way she *wanted* to feel.

"They have nothing to be unhappy about," Apollo answered when she asked about them. "They are all direct descendants of Gaia, and the earth produces regular harvests here without requiring much work on their part. As a result, they have no fear of famine. Disease is unknown to them as well, and they are so long-lived that even death is a rare occurrence. If they wish, they can prevent it altogether."

"How can they do that?" asked Mateo.

(margin note) It won't be easy to find him

(margin note) something bad might happen

"They plunge themselves into the Eridanus river, the same one into which Phaethon fell, and when they emerge, they have been transformed into white swans," Apollo replied.

"Why would they want to be swans?" asked Yasmin.

"No mortal wants to die," said Hermes. "I've guided enough mortals to the Underworld to know. To remain as a part of nature, particularly in a place like Hyperborea, where nature is in such perfect harmony, would be preferable to many.

"At the beginning, their fears were justified, for the Underworld was indeed a grim place. Initially, it was the fate of almost all mortals to exist as bodiless shadows of their former selves, unable to speak or even think, except under very specific circumstances—and when they could think, they spent most of their time lamenting their lost lives. In those days, mortals might easily have preferred being animals or even plants if such a transformation could enable them to evade death.

"However, as time went on, the gods made exceptions, first for those mortals they felt deserved special punishment for grievous sins and for those mortals they wanted to reward. Initially, most of those rewarded were direct descendants of gods, and the Elysian Fields were created for them. Then a certain number of other heroes were admitted. Eventually, judges were appointed to determine the fate of all mortals, sending all the virtuous ones to the Elysium and all the sinful ones to a place of punishment.   Somewhat later, souls were also allowed to reincarnate in the mortal world, sometimes because they missed the human world, sometimes as a way of becoming more virtuous and thus improving their afterlife. If I recall correctly, it was one of my sons who was the first to be allowed to reincarnate."

"I never thought of it as a progression that way," said Thanos. "I did notice that storytellers gave very different impressions of the Underworld. The earliest ones painted the gloomiest picture, while the later ones made it look better and better. I guess assuming the gods gradually made changes in the Underworld would be the only way to reconcile those diverse images."

"Didn't gods occasionally remove mortals from the Underworld completely to make those mortals divine?" asked Mateo. "Zeus said something about the mother of Dionysus."

[handwritten in left margin: for unmade?]

"Ah, yes," said Apollo. "Some humans were granted immortality so that they would be spared death completely. Others were raised from the Underworld to become gods after their death—though Hades has never been particularly happy with that course of action."

"You mentioned Phaethon a while ago," Yasmin said to Apollo. "Who was he?"

"Ah, Phaethon, proof that even the sons of gods may not live happy lives. He was the son of Helios, the sun god, and Clymene, an Oceanid who had married Merops, the king of Aethiopia.

"One might have expected Merops to be angry about Clymene bearing a child that was not his, but, knowing Phaethon to be the child of a god, Merops took the unusually wise course of raising Phaethon as if he were his own son.

"Being the son of a king was no small thing, and Phaethon should have been happy to be a prince, but unfortunately Clymene told him who his true father was, and Phaethon, hubris growing inside him, bragged incessantly about being the son of a god. Inevitably the other young boys were annoyed by his constant boasting, and eventually one of them announced loudly that the story was a lie.

"Phaethon went crying to his mother, who affirmed the truth of the story and sent him on a journey to meet his true father. How he got there no one knows. The Aethiopia of myth is not like the Ethiopia of reality, though. The real one is south of Egypt. The mythic one is supposed to be south of Egypt as well, but somehow simultaneously in the extreme east and west, near to sunrise and sunset, and hence close to the palace of Helios.

"In any case, Phaethon found his way to the palace, with its unmistakable golden walls and gleaming ivory roofs. Helios was so overjoyed to see Phaethon that the god not only welcomed him but swore on the Styx to grant him whatever his heart desired.

"The arrogant Phaethon asked to drive the chariot of the sun the next day. Helios, knowing that most gods could not do that, let alone a mortal, did his best to talk Phaethon out of his request, but the boy would not budge, and so the god had no choice but to let him.

"Unfortunately, the next day Phaethon quickly lost control of the horses, who ran far off-course, sometimes too high and sometimes too low. These low moments were particularly disastrous, burning the earth and boiling the sea, threatening to destroy all life if left unchecked.

"Zeus had no choice but to destroy the chariot with a thunderbolt. Plunging the earth into darkness until Helios could mount another chariot was better than allowing an inferno to destroy all life. In the same way, it was better for Phaethon to die than for all of humanity to die, though Helios wept for him anyway.

"His sisters, the Heliades, also wept for Phaethon, for in one version of the story they had encouraged him in his insane request. Eventually, Zeus pitied their grief and transformed them into poplar trees, but even in that form they wept, and their tears became the first amber.

"Alas, they were not the only ones who wept. King Cycnus of Liguria, a great musician with whom I was good friends, had also been a good friend of Phaethon's—too good, as it turned out. Cycnus was a fine human being, a man of much potential, but he was so overwhelmed with grief that he threw himself off a cliff rather than continue to endure it. I gave him what mercy I could by making him a swan—the first swan of Hyperborea."

Apollo was so visibly moved by his own tale that the party walked on for a while in silence, leaving it to him to decide when to continue the conversation.

"Eventually, I got Zeus's permission to commemorate him in the stars—through the constellation Cygnus, the swan."

"I...I don't want to sound stupid," said Fatima, "but I thought you were the sun god."

Apollo managed a chuckle. "It is a common misconception. Helios is the sun god, but by the end of the classical period, we tended to be identified with each other. My sister, Artemis, also became identified with his sister, Selene, the moon goddess."

"Who are they?" asked Yasmin, pointing to three gigantic figures in the distance.

"Ah, those are my priests, the three co-rulers of Hyperborea. They are the sons of Boreas, the North Wind, and Chione, the goddess of snow—ironic, since there is no snow here. However, there is in the Rhipaean Mountains where Boreas lives, just to the south of here. It is those tall, frozen peaks that make invasion impossible and thus keep the Hyperboreans safe from any threat of war, for, aside from being difficult to climb, they are inhabited by griffins, determined in defense of their gold against the fierce, one-eyed Arimaspoi, who constantly make war on them. Together, these two groups make the mountains impassable. No traveler could pass without being attacked by one group or the other, let alone any army, which would probably be attacked by both groups. Besides, the mountains themselves are virtually impossible to reach. To their south lies Pterophoros, a land of winter as eternal as spring is here."

"Then how do the Hyperboreans trade with the rest of the world?" asked Thanos. "I seem to recall them sending gifts to your shrine at Delphi, as well as selling their amber."

"The way in which they get in and out is a secret," said Apollo. "As they say in your world, I could tell you, but then I'd have to kill you."

The students were pretty sure Apollo was joking, but with Greeks gods, one could never be sure, so no one pressed the question.

Before long they reached a large marble structure. Its east-facing entrance was typical of ancient Greek temples. Since the carvings in the triangular area above the doorway and below the roof (the pediment) depicted Apollo killing Python, the fierce dragon from whom he had taken control of Delphi, this had to be Apollo's temple.

"Excuse me for a moment," said Apollo. "I can unlock the secrets of the universe more easily if I am alone." He turned away from them and entered the temple.

"What is Apollo the god of?" Yasmin asked Hermes.

"Actually, his duties are almost as diverse as mine," said Hermes, "though he shares most of them to some extent with other gods. He is associated with light, truth, healing, both vocal and instrumental music, the protection of cattle, the founding and regulation of cities—it is said he gave the Hyperboreans their laws—archery, and of course prophecy. Like most of us, he has an occasional dark side; he is the bringer of plague as well as healing, though he conjures up illness, much as he enters battle, partly to fight against the evils of the world."

"Why are all those trees here?" asked Mateo, pointing to the ring of trees planted around the temple. "The soil is very rocky; someone must have gone to a lot of trouble to get trees to grow right here."

"It isn't that hard in Hyperborea," said Hermes, "but even had it been much harder, someone would have made the effort. Those are laurel trees, sacred to Apollo. Which one of you can tell me why?"

"Because of Daphne," said Keisha.

"Who is Daphne?' asked Yasmin.

Hermes sighed. "Despite his looks, Apollo has not been lucky in love. The sad tale of Coronis you have already heard. That of Daphne is not much happier.

"She was a mountain nymph, the daughter of the river god, Peneus, and she stayed close to the gods her entire life. Not only did she become a priestess of Gaia, but she joined a band of nymphs who pledged themselves to follow the way of Artemis, Apollo's sister. They hunted by night, just as the goddess did, and pledged themselves to remain virgins, just as the goddess had.

"That last resolve was not pleasing to men, for Daphne was exceedingly beautiful, even though most men caught only the slightest glimpse of her, lit by shimmering moonlight, as she roamed through the forest in search of game. Still, many desired her.

"One such man, an exceedingly foolish one named Leucippus, decided to get close to Daphne by disguising himself as a girl and joining her hunting party."

"I've seen that premise in modern movies, usually comedies," said Mateo. "There are a lot of plots in which a guy disguises himself as a girl or vice versa."

"The same thing happens quite often in Shakespearean comedy," added Yong.

"Unfortunately, in this case, the results were not comic," replied Hermes. "Those women and goddesses who pledge themselves to virginity take the issue very seriously—and dire will be the fate of any man who tries to compromise them.

"Apollo found out through his prophetic gifts what Leucippus was up to, and, whether because Apollo resented the boy's affection for Daphne, or because he was offended by his intrusion into their virginal group, the god advised the nymphs to bathe naked. They discovered Leucippus's deception, and they tore him to pieces."

"Literally?" asked Mateo.

"And bloodily," said Hermes. "However, in one of the bitter ironies with which the world is full, the very fate Apollo wrought for Leucippus fell also upon his own grandson, Actaeon. I will wait to tell you of him until I have finished the story of Daphne, though.

"Having eliminated Leucippus as a rival, Apollo made his feelings for Daphne clear. However, she was not willing to give up her virginity, not even for a god. Unfortunately, Apollo would not take no for an answer, and he pursued her, certain that if he just kept pleading with her, he could, in the end, change her mind.

"When Apollo was about to catch her, Daphne cried out for help, some say to her river god father, others say to Gaia, whose priestess she was. Either way, just when Apollo was about to reach her, she appeared to become a tree—a laurel tree. I say "appeared" because later storytellers sometimes said that Gaia had actually whisked her away to Crete and left the laurel tree in her place as consolation for Apollo.

"Either way, the god had lost the woman he loved. To console himself, he pledged that henceforth the laurel tree would be sacred to him and that victors in athletic competitions would ever after be crowned with its leaves."

"You mentioned Actaeon a few minutes ago," said Mateo.

"Ah, yes," said Hermes. "That story begins more happily, though it does not end so. One day Apollo happened to see the Lapith princess, Cyrene, fighting with a lion to protect her father's flock of sheep. Impressed by the woman's valor and strength, Apollo immediately fell in love with her and carried her away to North Africa. Their relationship worked out better than most of Apollo's. Cyrene, ever busy, founded the city in Libya that is named after her, but she consented to concern herself with the traditional wife's role long enough to bear Apollo two sons, one of whom was Aristaeus. Apollo saw the child's potential for greatness, and so the god fed him on nectar and ambrosia, using that and the blessing of Gaia to make him immortal. Aristaeus became a useful god, just as Apollo had foreseen, and taught men cheesemaking, beekeeping, the fermentation of honey that produces mead, the extraction of olive oil from olives, the use of traps in hunting, and many other things as well. Apollo also transformed Cyrene into a nymph to make her immortal, and all should have been well—but, as you might guess, it was not.

"Cyrene, restless of spirit, eventually left Apollo despite the immortality he had bestowed on her and had an affair with Ares, the result of which was the cruel king, Diomedes of Thrace, who brought much suffering into the world.

"As for Aristaeus, he married the Theban princess, Autonoe, the beautiful daughter of Cadmus and Harmonia. She bore him two children, one of whom was the ill-fated Actaeon.

"Interested like his father in the hunt, Actaeon was out hunting one night when he came upon the goddess Artemis bathing in a pond. Actaeon should have averted his eyes and fled, but he was paralyzed by the goddess's beauty. Unfortunately, she saw him staring at her, and in her fury, she changed him into a stag, after which his own hounds tore him to pieces.

"Thus it was that Apollo's own grandson met as dark an end as that which he had contrived for Leucippus. That was also the end of Aristaeus's happiness, for Autonoe, consumed by grief over the death of her son, left her husband and soon died."

At that moment, Apollo came out of the temple and gestured quickly for Hermes to join him.

"Is it just me, or does Apollo seem drawn to women just like his sister? How many of them were virgin huntresses?" asked Yong as soon as Hermes left them.

"Cyrene wasn't sworn to virginity," said Thanos. "Apollo does seem to like strong, independent women, though."

"Just not enough to respect their wishes," said Keisha. "I know back in the day—or even much more recently—it was considered romantic for a guy to keep persisting no matter what. Now it usually ends up being sexual harassment or stalking. Think about it: Daphne would rather have been a tree, or at least leave her entire life behind, just to get away from Apollo, all because he couldn't accept her decision."

"To be continued later," said Thanos, hinting at Apollo's approach.

"Hermes has gone to fetch a few things, but while he does that, I will tell you what I have learned," said Apollo. "Though I do not yet know for certain who has your friend, I have more than once seen the dark of the moon in my visions. It is one of the symbols of Hecate, so I believe she must either have your friend or know who does."

"Has Hermes gone to question her?" asked Thanos.

"No, for the situation is more complicated than that," replied Apollo. "Hecate is elusive, not apt to be found unless she wants to be—which she does not seem to at the moment."

"She is very powerful, is she not?" asked Thanos.

Apollo nodded. "Truly, she is an exceptional case. "My mother Leto's sister Asteria is her mother. The Titan Perses, the destroyer, is her father. Her parents fought on the side of the Titans and are now prisoners in Tartarus, but she is not, for she foresaw Zeus's victory and fought for him.

"Zeus honored her for her wise choice, confirming her power in the sky, on the earth, and the sea. No other god has direct power in all three of those realms, and so you may be sure there were some who questioned such a sweeping grant of privilege.

"Nor is that the extent of her power. Always interested in magic, she has greater knowledge of it even than Hermes. Make no mistake, Hecate is formidable. If she has your friend and wants to keep him, it will be no easy task to recover him. Even if she is not the one keeping him prisoner and merely knows where he is, getting such information from her will be no simple thing unless she chooses to reveal it to you."

"Won't Zeus help?" asked Thanos. "Patrick was a guest of Olympus when he was taken."

"Even Zeus has his limits," said Apollo. "Hecate would be hard for him to enforce an order upon, because of where she is. You see, Hecate was once a friend of Demeter and joined poor Persephone in the Underworld during the girl's first imprisonment there. Hecate more or less stayed there, gaining authority even in that gloomy realm, while at the same time deepening—and darkening—her magic."

"She's evil?" asked Yasmin.

"There are some who would say yes. Certainly, the witches who claim to draw their power from her sometimes are, yet if she were truly evil, she would certainly have made more trouble than she has. Let us call her...difficult, rather than evil."

Considering that Apollo himself, one of the more virtuous gods, seemed to have no problem killing people who got in his way, the students didn't find the fact that he was calling Hecate "difficult" encouraging.

"Before you can face her, however, what I can unravel of fate suggests that you must first meet several gods, each of whom will have advice or a gift that could aid you in your quest. You must also meet several heroes in the Underworld and ask them to tell their stories. I have foreseen that within each of their tales will be a vital clue. By listening carefully enough, you should be able to discern whether Hecate or someone even more carefully hidden is behind your friend's disappearance. By then you will also have the power to find out where your friend is imprisoned—if you use wisely all the gifts and information you have been given."

"Isn't there a simpler way?" asked Yasmin. None of them knew how much time they had in this dream world—or what would happen to Patrick if time ran out before they found him.

"This is a puzzle of many pieces," replied Apollo. "You will need to put them all together to have a chance of rescuing your friend."

"In that case, whom do we need to seek out?" asked Thanos.

"Athena, my half-sister, who is in Athens; my twin sister, Artemis, who I believe is hunting in the area of Calydon; Pan, the son of Hermes, who is probably in Arcadia; Demeter, my aunt, who is in Eleusis; Poseidon, my uncle, who is in his palace deep beneath the sea; Dionysus, my half-brother, who is said to be somewhere near Thebes; Hades and Persephone, whom you can see in the Underworld on your way to visit the heroes. Hermes can find all of them fairly quickly for you, and he can also guide you through the Underworld. I have already given him a list of the heroes you must visit. Ah, here he is now."

Hermes landed right next to them, pulling from his bag several amulets and handing one to each of the students.

"This is beautiful," said Fatima. Each amulet was a necklace composed of an enormous piece of amber attached to a golden chain. Into the amber had been expertly carved an image of Helios, the sun god.

"The amber is from right here in Hyperborea, so it is genuinely the tears of the Heliades," explained Apollo. "The gold Hephaestus forged from the gold dust in Pactolus, the river in which King Midas washed away the ill-considered gift of the golden touch, given to him by Dionysus. Hephaestus also carved the image of Helios into the amber.

"Since we know someone's magic was involved in the disappearance of your friend, even if it were not Hecate's, it would be unwise to let you venture further without protection against magic. Normally, amber is a decent protection against evil spells in general. Mingled with the specific blessing of Helios, and the handiwork of Hephaestus, whose ability to endow objects with magic is unmatched, and that protection is considerably stronger. Enhanced by the wild energy of Dionysus, it will protect against a somewhat broader array of evils.

"Be warned, however, that this protection will not stand up against the magic of a hostile god for very long if that god is determined to do you harm. Like your light armor and invisibility caps, it is intended to protect you long enough to give you time to flee or for Hermes to bring more help."

"As is this," said Hermes, pulling out of his bag a large herb with a midnight black root and white flowers. "It is called moly, and only a god can pick it. It will provide specific protection against shape changes—which, as you well know, we gods are all too fond of inflicting on mortals. It served well to protect Odysseus from the evil wiles of Circe."

"Thus warded, and accompanied not only by Hermes but by Hephaestus's trusty mechanical man and loyal mechanical dog, you will be as well protected as you can be," said Apollo. "Just remember not to take unnecessary risks—such as needlessly offending gods or confronting monsters, for example."

"Will there be monsters on the way?" asked Fatima. "I thought the heroes had killed all of them."

Apollo looked at her grimly. "There are always monsters. Heroes kill what they can, but more rise to take their place. Is it not so in your world?"

"Yes," said Yong, thinking about everything from dictators to serial killers. Each generation had some. Idealists wanted to make a better world but had yet to achieve it.

"Then be not surprised that it is so here. Be on your guard, stay close to Hermes and the automatons, and watch each other's backs."

If only they had been doing that in the beginning, Keisha thought to herself, they would not be in this mess.

Chapter 11: Athena

As someone who had considered becoming an architect, Thanos was fascinated by the Parthenon as it had been in ancient times. He had seen it in its current ruined condition, but nothing could quite compare with viewing it in its full glory—even if he was only dreaming it.

Unfortunately for the speed of the quest, Thanos's obvious enthusiasm led Athena to give them a tour of the structure, which was absolutely the last thing any of them except Thanos wanted. Even Hermes looked impatient at the delay, though he seemed unwilling to say anything.

It was easy to see why he might have hesitated. Even when standing before the enormous gold and ivory statue of herself sculpted by Phidias, the goddess was far more formidable than her gigantic image. Like the other goddesses the students had met, Athena was beautiful, but she was also intimidating. Her gray eyes seemed as if they could look right into one's soul, and her face, even at rest, suggested she would tolerate no nonsense from anyone. It was perhaps a good thing Patrick wasn't with them, for Athena looked as if she could make being turned into a dog seem like summer vacation.

Adding to her imposing presence was the fact that, since Athens was expecting a possible attack from Thrace, instigated by Ares, Athena was fully armed. She wore an impressive helmet and carried a spear, both doubtless crafted by Hephaestus, and she wore the breastplate of Zeus, the aegis. Its surface looked like golden snake scales, and snake heads projected out from its edges.

"That's really impressive armor," said Mateo. "Did Hephaestus make it for you?"

"Actually, it was originally the skin of the giant, fire-breathing serpent Aex, a daughter of Helios," replied Athena. "After I defeated the monster, I used her skin to make this breastplate. I gave it as a gift to Zeus, my father, but he normally lets me use it, his thunderbolts being more than enough for him. When I charge into battle, it makes a noise like a roaring dragon, causes thunder to shake the heavens, and strikes fear into the hearts of men. Only a god can resist its influence.

"I would normally have the head of Medusa, which Perseus gave me as an offering, right there in the center, but I only add that at the last moment. I don't want to risk changing any of my own people to stone, not to mention my guests."

"Wow!" was the most Mateo could come up with in response.

"It's easy to see why you do so well in battle," said Yong.

"Battle is not just about force, though my foolish brother Ares has never quite learned that lesson," Athena replied. "War is also about strategy, about making the most of what resources one has. It is for that reason I am celebrated as the goddess of wisdom as well as victory in battle. It is also why Ares, despite his savage strength, has never beaten me."

At that point, Athena remembered the image of the Gigantomachy, the battle between gods and giants, which was on part of the Parthenon's eastern frieze (the band of sculpture just below roof level) and the tour continued.

"The giants were sons of Gaia incited by their mother to attempt the overthrow of Zeus, and they pressed us hard," said Athena, pointing to the space right above the Parthenon's eastern entrance. "There I am, with Nike, victory incarnate. It was in this battle I slew the giants Enceladus and Pallas single-handedly. My greatest act during the battle, however, took place after the giants threw a dragon at me. I threw it back so hard it ended up in the sky as the constellation Draco."

"Sister, we face no battle with giants, but a puzzle fit only for your wits," said Hermes, finally manning up enough to interrupt. "Please allow me to explain."

Athena listened patiently while Hermes filled her in on the details, looking increasingly concerned as the story progressed.

When Hermes was finally done, Athena said, "These are grave tidings indeed. If Apollo thinks Hecate, or, if not her, someone of equal magical power, is bold enough to violate the hospitality of Olympus itself, this could be the prologue to a much more serious threat. I know exactly what gift I can offer our guests to make their journey easier. Before I go, though, I must ask if you have anything belonging to your friend."

Since Patricius already had the scent, Hermes passed the dog hairs to Athena, who hurried off as soon as she had them, leaving the rest of the group standing at the east side of the Parthenon.

"She's impressive," said Keisha. Somehow, the word seemed inadequate, but more intense choices made Keisha feel too much like a fangirl.

Hermes nodded vigorous agreement. "She could probably be overcome by Zeus, Poseidon, or Hades, but I'd bet heavily on her to beat any of us younger Olympians in battle. However, she is as clever as she is strong. She taught humans to make chariots—invaluable for war—but it was also she who taught humans to create plows, rakes, and ox-yokes, making agriculture much more practical. She also taught pottery making, weaving, cooking, and other civilized arts."

"Much as my maker taught humans metal working in general and the forging of weapons and armor in particular," added Ardalos.

"Should we...should we ask Athena the truth about that Hephaestus story?" asked Yasmin.

"I have told you that truth already," said Ardalos, managing to sound offended despite his tonelessness.

"I think it might be...undiplomatic to ask," replied Hermes. "Hephaestus and Athena often work together in seeming friendliness, so whatever happened in the past, she seems to have forgiven and forgotten it."

Hermes looked at the students closely and could tell they were not satisfied.

"Well, rather than having you risk the wrath of Athena, I can add one more detail. I have heard Hephaestus did indeed make an attempt on Athena—but only as the result of a trick."

"My maker would never—"

"Hear me out," insisted Hermes. "Poseidon has long been hostile to Athena. Hearing of Hephaestus's infatuation for her, he saw a way to make trouble. If the story I've heard is right, Hephaestus really had been given permission to marry Athena by Zeus, but the blacksmith god did not know much about women, which helps explain his disastrous marriage with Aphrodite. In any case, Poseidon convinced him that Athena liked rough sex, expected it in fact, and that was truly the way to win her over. Hephaestus is certainly no rapist, but he went after Athena thinking he had, not just Zeus's consent, but her active interest as well. If that version is correct, it explains both Hephaestus's actions and why Athena was so forgiving of them."

Before Ardalos could begin his inevitable protest, Mateo asked why Poseidon seemed like such a troublemaker.

"He can be calm or wild, just as the sea he rules is—but I fear the wild side predominates," said Hermes. "He has never quite gotten over the fact that Athena was picked over him as the patron of Athens."

"The Athenians had a choice?" asked Fatima, shocked that mortals would even have had the opportunity to choose between two gods.

Hermes smiled. "No, the gods themselves served as arbiters, though Cecrops, first king of Athens, was involved to some extent. When the two gods could not resolve their disagreement, Cecrops proposed a race to the Acropolis. He was allowed to referee because of his own supernatural origins, for he was a son of Gaia and was half man and half serpent.

"Because the race was on land and not in the sea, Athena had the advantage. She reached the Acropolis first and planted an olive tree to signal her victory. Poseidon arrived seconds later and struck the rock of the Acropolis with his trident, producing a salt-water pool.

"He was too late, but he refused to acknowledge the fact or to accept the decision of Cecrops. As a consequence, the other gods agreed to arbitrate and sat in judgment at the Areopagus, right here in Athens, somewhat to the west of where we stand now. Based on the evidence provided by Cecrops, they declared Athena the victor."

"Did he accept the decision?" asked Mateo.

"No, actually he flooded the nearby land in protest," said Hermes. "Aside from Ares, few gods have a more violent temper."

"So Athena and Poseidon are still at odds with each other?" asked Fatima.

"To some extent," said Hermes. "They also disputed the patronage of Troezen, but there Althepus, one of Poseidon's sons, was king. He managed to work out an agreement in which Athena and Poseidon shared the city, and for a while, it seemed as if the two gods might finally be at peace.

"Unfortunately, it was not long after that Halirrhothius, another son of Poseidon, and wild, as his sons often are, raped Alcippe, a daughter of Ares by an Athenian princess. Ares killed Halirrhothius for his crime, and Poseidon demanded that the gods try Ares for murder.

"The gods convened again on the Areopagus—which coincidentally means Rock of Ares—and ruled in favor of the war god, for he could prove Halirrhothius had raped his daughter.

"Poseidon predictably blamed Athena for the outcome, and though Zeus has managed to enforce civility between them, the sea god has neither forgiven nor forgotten."

"It seems as if Poseidon gets away with quite a bit," said Mateo. "I'm surprised Zeus is so patient with actions like flooding the land when a decision of the other gods goes against him."

Hermes grinned a little at that. "Zeus is a little bit like what you would call a politician, particularly where Hades and Poseidon are concerned. Yes, he is king of the gods, but he prefers not to use force against the other two if he can help it.

"Partly his reasons are military. Yes, his thunderbolts are stronger than the trident of Poseidon or the staff of Hades. Nonetheless, if Poseidon plunges into the depths of the sea or Hades stays in the depths of the Underworld, Zeus cannot easily reach either one without boiling the sea or blasting the earth wide open. Neither course would be good for the earth or for humankind.

"Then there is also a personal reason. Zeus still has to deal with the prophecy of a son overthrowing him. If someone made the attempt, having Poseidon and Hades on his side, as when they fought together against Cronus, would be far better than having them as enemies. Yes, there are times when Zeus has laid down the law, but within reason he will do what it takes to keep his brothers as allies rather than make them enemies. To a limited extent, the same is true of his sisters."

"Then I suppose the other gods are fortunate they ever win an argument with any of Zeus's siblings," said Mateo.

"The situation is complicated," admitted Hermes. "Zeus doesn't want to lose Poseidon and Hades, but he can't afford to lose the support of we younger gods, either. Someone like Athena could be critical in the event of a revolt. She's more even-tempered than most, but even she can be pushed too far—and Zeus knows that."

"Someone so formidable might have little reason to rein in her anger," said Thanos.

"And yet she does quite often," the messenger of the gods replied. "Even with mortals, she is generally patient—but not always.

"Take, for example, the case of Arachne. The girl was a Lydian weaver of exceptional talent. Unfortunately, her hubris led her to challenge the goddess to a weaving contest. Miraculously, she managed to equal the goddess in craftsmanship, and Athena might have agreed to a tie, except that Arachne's subject matter was sacrilegious. Athena had portrayed the gods enthroned in all their splendor. Arachne, by contrast, had chosen to portray the gods having affairs with mortal women."

"I don't mean to interrupt, but the gods did have affairs with mortal women," said Mateo, who immediately realized he shouldn't have said anything. Fortunately, Hermes was not offended.

"I think it was partly the way in which she portrayed them, making them look foolish, that truly offended Athena," replied Hermes. Mateo stopped himself from pointing out that they were sometimes foolish.

"In any case, Athena tore the tapestry to shreds and hit Arachne with the loom. That might have been the only penalty, but Arachne could not reconcile her pride-bloated view of herself with what had happened. Instead of accepting that she had erred and making a graceful effort to get what she still could from life, she hanged herself.

"Athena arrived in time to undo the rope, but, further angered by Arachne's behavior, she changed her into a spider and the rope into a spider's web. That was a harsh fate, though Arachne had brought it on herself, and at least she could still spin beautifully."

Keisha knew Arachne had been incredibly proud and stupid, but she couldn't help sympathizing with her. Like Mateo, though, she was wise enough to keep her feelings to herself.

"Even I have felt the sting of Athena's wrath—indirectly," added Hermes. The students instantly focused even more intently on him. They felt they knew Hermes better than the others, and his willingness to get quite that personal touched them.

"You recall the story of Erichthonius, the result of an accidental union between Hephaestus and Gaia after Athena had driven him off?" asked Hermes.

The students were aching to ask how an "accidental union" was possible but thought it better not to ask.

"Yes, we remember," said Keisha.

"Well, Erichthonius, earth-born like Cecrops, had the upper body of a human and the lower body of a snake. Athena became his foster mother and soon learned of a threat to his safety—I forget exactly what. Since she was the patron of Athens, she figured that would be a safe place to bring him. She used a magic chest like the one Aphrodite kept Adonis in, and she brought it to the three daughters of Cecrops, two of whom were Agraulos and Herse. She instructed them to keep the chest safe and never open it.

"Meanwhile, I had fallen in love with Herse, and I wished to make my feelings known to her. I would have taken her as my wife, as Apollo did with Cyrene, even made her immortal if she had said yes. Much to my surprise, when I came to propose to her, Agraulos barred my way, insolently demanding to know what I wanted, then asking for a large sum in gold to allow me access—me, a god! It was the ultimate act of hubris, but as she was the sister of my intended bride, I decided to humor her. Leaving for the moment, I decided to return later, when I hoped she would be more reasonable. The gold was a small matter to me, but I saw no reason why any lover should pay for access to his love, let alone a god.

"What I did not know was that Agraulos was also inordinately curious. She opened the chest in which Erichthonius lay, and when she saw the half human, half snake baby, she denounced it as a product of Athena's lust.

"Athena, knowing that Agraulos had already gotten on my bad side, encouraged envy to blossom greenly in the girl's heart. When I returned, Agraulos insisted I should not see her sister, saying something about not moving until I was driven away. Since I had no intention of being driven away, I took her at her word and turned her to stone, then and there. It was my act, but Athena had planned to make sure it happened.

Even without Athena's little manipulation, you cannot deny that Agraulos was much at fault: she defied Athena's order and insulted her, and she selfishly barred my way to her sister, when she should have been happy her sibling would have such a marriage."

The students all thought to themselves that Agraulos sounded like a thoroughly rotten person, but again the punishment seemed harsh to them. All of them were, however, smart enough not to say that.

"If I may ask, what happened with Herse?" said Mateo.

"Knowing how evil her sister had been, Herse forgave me for turning her into stone, and together we had Cephalus, a son so handsome he was loved by Eos, goddess of the dawn. I kept my promise to Herse—she became immortal, and afterward the Athenians worshiped her as a minor goddess. All worked out well in the end."

Except for Agraulos, thought Keisha, but again she knew voicing that opinion would be most unwise.

"I see Athena has returned," said Hermes, who noticed her before the distracted students did.

"I have, and with just the right gift," said Athena, holding up a small piece of wood that looked singularly unimpressive.

"Which of you knows of my contribution to that great ship, the Argo, that took Jason and his comrades on the quest for the golden fleece?" she asked.

"You provided a piece of oak from the sacred grove at Dodona that was used in the prow of the ship. It was able to speak and give advice," said Thanos.

"Very good," said Athena. "However, this particular piece of prophetic oak has been polished with the hairs Hermes gave me. You would not need it to give advice, for you have Hermes for that. What it will do is enable you to communicate with your friend."

"He can't speak at the moment," said Yong.

"Ah, but he can bark, and I understand dog language," said Patricius.

"Very good," said Athena, handing the wood to Thanos for safekeeping. "When you wish to hear your friend's voice, just hold the wood and think of him. He may be able to give you clues about his location.

"I wish I could travel with you," she added, "but I cannot leave now in case the Thracians attack."

"That's all right," said Keisha. "What you have done already will help us greatly."

They said their good-byes, and Athena hurried off to inspect the outer defenses of the city.

"Shall we try to reach him now?" asked Thanos.

"Why not?" asked Yong. "Let's do it."

Unfortunately, all Thanos's concentration produced from the wood was the sound of slow, heavy breathing.

"He's asleep," said Yasmin.

"Well, at least he isn't suffering too badly," said Fatima.

"I think it best to let him sleep for the moment," said Thanos. "Apollo has already told us we need to visit all the gods and heroes he has specified to have a chance to rescue Patrick. He may as well sleep now. Later, when we have whatever information and tools we can get, we will have more need to talk to him."

The students quickly agreed, and before they knew it, they were on their way to Calydon to find Artemis.

Chapter 12: Artemis

Hermes had little difficulty finding Artemis, even though it was night by then, for she was hunting in the woods near Calydon, just as Apollo had predicted. As usual, the goddess was accompanied by a large hunting party that included both nymphs and women.

Though Artemis was Apollo's twin, the students could see little resemblance, except that they both were as good-looking as Olympians usually seemed to be. Apollo was blond, but Artemis's hair was midnight black. He loved the sunlight, while she preferred moonlight. Aside from his association with cattle, he was more of a city god, a giver of laws, a teacher of music. She preferred the wilderness and the exhilaration of the hunt.

Artemis greeted Hermes, the girls, and the automatons, then asked, "What are these boys doing here?"

"They are my guests, every bit as much as the girls are," Hermes explained. "Together, we are on a quest to find their lost friend, a quest your brother thinks you could help with."

Hermes explained the situation, and Artemis relented—a little. It was clear she would have preferred to be dealing with an all-female party.

"When I was three years old, Zeus asked me what I wanted, and the first thing I requested was to remain a virgin always. Men are usually a distraction at best, a menace at worst."

"But what about love?" asked Fatima without thinking.

"What about it?" countered Artemis. "Has it made Hera happier? Did it make my mother, Leto, happier? Because she had once loved Zeus, she was persecuted mercilessly by Hera, who tried to prevent her from giving birth to us. Hera kept Ilithyia, her daughter and the goddess of childbirth, from coming to my mother. Not content with such a callous act, which would have made my mother's situation hard enough, Hera sent Ares and Iris out into the world to threaten any land where my mother tried to stay, so that everyone would drive her away. Just to make sure she found no rest, Hera also sent the great serpent Python after her.

"Did Zeus come to her rescue? No, he did not lift a finger, though they had made *love*. If not for my Aunt Asteria, I don't know what my mother would have done.

"Asteria had been desired by Zeus, too, but she had the good sense to run away, finally changing herself into a quail and diving into the ocean to escape. At that point, Zeus gave up the chase, not wishing to offend Poseidon by entering his domain unannounced.

"At the exact point at which Asteria entered the water, the island of Ortygia emerged, and as Leto fled toward it, Asteria called out to her, offering her sanctuary.

"Hera reined in Python and the others at that point out of respect for Asteria, who had worked so hard to avoid Zeus. The queen of the gods was sure that my mother would still be condemned to perpetual labor, but then a miracle occurred, and my mother was able to give birth to me."

"Zeus's way of helping, perhaps," suggested Hermes gently.

"Or so he liked to claim long after—when it was safe to do so," said Artemis, sneering. "In any case, I had the same power to facilitate childbirth as Ilithyia did, and I would have helped deliver my brother Apollo right then and there. However, his prophetic gifts already working, he yelled from Leto's womb that Delos would be better. It was another newly arisen island nearby, floating freely at that time and so technically still part of Poseidon's domain. Asteria and I helped Leto across the sea to it, and then I helped bring my brother out into the light of day."

"I'm surprised you were able to get along with Hera or Zeus after that," said Keisha.

Artemis shrugged. "Eternity is a long time to hold a grudge, and like most gods, I am practical. Hera might have tried to stop Apollo and me from being born, but she never carries vendettas against Zeus's children by other women beyond birth if those children are gods. She did nothing to prevent Apollo and me from joining the others on Olympus—nor for that matter your guide, Hermes, nor Dionysus, nor any of the others born of Zeus's myriad affairs.

"Apollo and I decided there was nothing to be gained by continuing a fight we couldn't win, anyway. Zeus and Hera were too powerful for us. Better to take our rightful places and Zeus's guilt gifts than end up in exile—or worse."

"You almost make Zeus out to be evil," said Hermes. "He has his faults, but—"

"This is an old argument, Hermes, and one I do not care to revisit. Your mother, Maia, the daughter of Atlas and Pleione, did not suffer as mine did. Because she preferred solitude and lived in a cave on Mount Cyllene, Hera did not find out Zeus loved her until you were already born. Even so, did loving Zeus make her happy? Aside from getting you as a son, I doubt she got anything out of that relationship at all.

"Forget about Zeus, though, if you want to make apologies for him. Forget about Hera. What other gods are really happily married? Poseidon and Amphitrite? He is as unfaithful as his brother. Hephaestus and Aphrodite? In that case, she is the unfaithful one, but the result is the same. Few other gods even call themselves married, but they end up no better. Apollo is constantly miserable over one woman or another.

"The truth is that love is fleeting, not eternal. No wonder gods cannot stay loyal to each other forever. It is even worse when gods try to love mortals, or even to become close friends with them.

"Twice I broke my general rule of having only female companions, and twice I regretted it.

"The first was with Orion, handsomest of giants, not quite a god, but close. His father was Poseidon; his mother, Euryale, was the daughter of King Minos of Crete, and hence granddaughter of Zeus himself. Orion's father had given him the gift of walking on water as easily as on land, so he could freely move among the Greek islands.

"When I met him on Crete, his passion for the hunt was as great as mine, his skill nearly as great, and so including him in my party seemed natural.

"Ah, had I but known of his background, I would have realized what a bad idea getting close to him truly was. You see, long before he met me, he had been on Chios, and there met Princess Merope and fell in love—or so his defenders would afterward say. He raped her, though all the usual male excuses were given—he was drunk; her father, Oenopion, had promised her to Orion and then delayed time after time in honoring the agreement; there were too many more to recite them all.

"Oenopion obtained the help of Dionysus to blind Orion as punishment for his crime, but the giant was not so easily penalized. Wandering from island to island, he met Hephaestus on Lemnos, and the blacksmith god took pity on him—why I don't know—and gave him a guide, Cedalion, who rode on his shoulders and directed him.

"Eventually, Orion wandered far to the east, where he met Helios, and the sun god restored his sight."

"Perhaps Helios thought he had suffered enough," suggested Hermes.

"Well, I would not have, and I would not have made him a member of my hunting party—if I had known," said Artemis. "I did not. I took Orion for what he seemed to be, not knowing what he truly was. I still shudder when I think about it. A virgin goddess befriending a rapist!

"The horrible part was that I actually enjoyed his company. Even my mother, who was hunting with me at the time, approved of him. We could have remained close friends. Perhaps in time I would have made him immortal, and we could have hunted together for all eternity.

"Unfortunately, Orion had other…ideas about our relationship."

"He didn't—" started Keisha.

"No," said Artemis. "Even he was not foolish enough to attempt to rape me. I do believe, though, that he began to get ideas about marrying me. Later there were rumors, even some that I killed him for asking for my hand in marriage, or that Apollo did, but the truth was a little more complicated than that.

"Instead of asking me right away, Orion did everything he could to impress me. Unfortunately, his hubris got the better of him, and he once bragged that he would hunt down and kill every beast on the face of the earth.

"I reprimanded him at once. Though I am a hunter, I understand the importance of balance. Killing too many beasts would eventually lead to having no beasts to hunt. It is for the same reason I am the guardian of all young creatures. For the hunt to endure, the animals upon which it depends must endure as well.

"Orion acted suitably repentant, and I forgot all about the incident. Unfortunately, someone else had heard who did not so easily forget: Gaia.

"Fearful that Orion would carry out his threat, Gaia sent a gigantic scorpion to sting him, and he died before I could help him, though I slew the scorpion in revenge.

"Still not knowing the truth about Orion, my mother and I persuaded

Zeus to honor him with a constellation. Zeus agreed but insisted on also including the scorpion. Later, when I found out the truth about Orion, I came to see the wisdom in that, for in truth the scorpion was only defending the natural order against a brute who pretended to be civilized but was underneath it all no better than a beast himself.

"I should have learned my lesson from that debacle, but eventually I encountered yet another male whose passion for the hunt matched mine, and again I allowed him to join my party.

"I was more careful this time and made sure I knew the background of my new friend. He was Hippolytus, the son of Theseus and thus the grandson of Poseidon, but unlike Orion, neither Theseus nor Hippolytus had inherited Poseidon's savage nature. Instead, Hippolytus was a model of self-discipline who rejected love just as firmly as I did. Perhaps that had something to do with the fact that his mother was Antiope, the Amazon queen.

"Amazons, as you may have heard, have an all-female society, like my hunting band but on a larger scale. They made no room for love in their warlike lives and used sex merely to perpetuate their civilization, keeping the girl children and sending the boys back to their fathers. Though male, Hippolytus embraced their rejection of love. He seemed in every way the perfect hunting companion—and he was."

"Then why did you regret choosing him?" asked Fatima.

"Because I lost him," said Artemis, sadly enough to make the guys wonder if she had rejected love as fully as she claimed.

"You see, Hippolytus's rejection of love drew the attention of Aphrodite, who was not in the least pleased with it. She might have let that pass, however, except for the fact that he stopped worshiping her. In fact, some say that eventually he only worshiped me.

"Mortals were expected to give appropriate honor to all of the gods. I should have counseled him on a wiser course, but carelessly, I did not, and eventually Aphrodite decided that Hippolytus must be punished.

"Instead of attacking him directly, the goddess used his stepmother, Phaedra, as her instrument, filling her with an unnatural passion for her stepson. Phaedra tried to resist but failed.

"Encouraged by her elderly nurse, Phaedra attempted to seduce

Hippolytus, who naturally rejected her, not only because he had vowed to remain celibate but because she was his stepmother.

"Plagued by a mixture of shame at what she had proposed and anger at Hippolytus for rejecting her, Phaedra hanged herself, unfortunately leaving behind a suicide note that accused Hippolytus of trying to rape her. Theseus refused to believe his son's protests of innocence and exiled him.

"Alas, that was not the only penalty. In Theseus's grief, he invoked one of the wishes granted him by his father, Poseidon, to kill Hippolytus. As my hunting companion drove his chariot near the beach, a great sea monster rose from the ocean and frightened the horses. They ran wild, throwing Hippolytus to the ground. Tangled in the reins, he was dragged by the horses until he was nearly dead.

"I arrived too late to save him. All I could do was tell Theseus the shattering truth and say goodbye to Hippolytus, who then died."

"That's horrible," said Fatima.

"Better followed—and worse. In my grief I went to Asclepius, then still a mortal man, and begged him to raise Hippolytus from the dead, even offering him a great sum of gold to do so. Knowing what I asked was a violation of the natural order of things, Asclepius did it anyway. He thus earned the wrath of Hades, and Zeus was forced to blast Asclepius with a thunderbolt, as a warning to mortals that the boundary between life and death must not be broken.

"My affection for Hippolytus cost my nephew his life. Apollo, usually much more even-tempered, was so enraged by Zeus's decision that he tried to kill the Cyclopes in retaliation. Stories say he succeeded, but as they were immortal, he could not. He did injure them grievously, however, and bring upon himself the wrath of Zeus.

"Apollo could have ended up in Tartarus, but Zeus had pity on him, sentencing him instead to a year's enslavement to King Admetus of Pherae. Even I have to admit Zeus's wisdom and generosity in that case. Not only did he grant Apollo considerable mercy, but he eventually heeded Apollo's request to restore Asclepius's life and even make him a god."

"What happened to Hippolytus?" asked Fatima. "You said he was restored to life."

"He was—but I had to say goodbye to him. Keeping him with me would have been putting him at too much risk. Too many gods were angry with him and me at that point.

"I spirited him away to the grove of Aricia in Italy. I saw him only once more, when I came to make him immortal. Even then, we agreed it would be unwise for us to go back to our old relationship. Instead, Hippolytus remained in Italy, eventually being worshiped by the Romans under the name Virbius."

"So the story ended well enough," said Hermes.

"But it could have ended far worse. My nephew could have stayed dead, and my brother could have been imprisoned forever—and all because I befriended a mortal man. Never again will I make that mistake."

"I hesitate to press you after you have just relived such difficult times," said Hermes. "However, our need is urgent, and Apollo was sure you would have some gift or word of advice to help our mortal guests in their quest."

Artemis frowned. "Alas, I can think of nothing that would help. I would offer you one of my hounds for tracking, but it appears you are already well served in that way."

"Yes, very!" said Patricius.

"I fear you lack imagination," said a voice behind them.

Turning quickly, the students saw a goddess in white robes, crowned with a silver crescent moon.

Chapter 13: Selene

"Excuse me for asking," said Yong, "but how can you be here? Aren't you...up there?" he asked, pointing at the moon.

Selene smiled at him. "How do you think I managed such a trick?"

The question was probably rhetorical, but before Selene could continue, Thanos answered it. "Some of the myths show Helios interacting with people during the day or you doing the same during the night. Ancient Greeks didn't have a word for bilocation, but you must be capable of doing something like that."

"Something like that," Selene agreed. "I can make myself seen and felt anywhere the moon is shining, even as I drive it across the sky."

"A better question would be why you chose to appear here," said Artemis. Her tone was not exactly hostile, but it wasn't welcoming, either.

"Apollo told Helios of the visitors' quest, and he told me," replied Selene. "I wanted to offer my help—but hearing what you told them, I also wanted to correct the impression you are creating, for love is not always a bad thing. Neither is sex."

"Amen," said Mateo quietly.

"You don't understand any better than Hermes," said Artemis, waving her hand dismissively. "You are remote enough that Hera didn't find out about Zeus's affair with you until after you gave birth to his daughters, Ersa, goddess of the dew, and Pandia, who celebrates by the light of the full moon."

"I wasn't referring to Zeus," said Selene. "I'll admit I didn't love him—but Endymion was another matter."

Artemis snorted derisively. "I think that story proves my point better than yours."

"Then let me tell it, and our guests can judge," replied Selene. "Endymion was incredibly handsome, the equal of Adonis if you ask me, but don't tell Aphrodite I said so."

"There is little danger of that," muttered Artemis.

"Endymion was the second king of Elis. His father, Aethlius, was a son of Zeus, and, on his mother's side, a great-grandson of Prometheus. His mother, Calyce, was the daughter of the wind god Aeolus and therefore a granddaughter of Poseidon.

"Thus, it was no surprise Endymion was an exceptional young man. He had three sons by a wife who subsequently passed away, after which Endymion became lonely and was unable to find another woman with whom to fall in love.

"Though he was a king, he used to enjoy going out to tend the flocks by night; in those days kings were not averse to performing what later came to be thought of as menial tasks. He also loved to watch the night sky, gradually becoming the first astronomer in Greece.

"Looking down from the sky, I could not avoid seeing him night after night, looking back up at me. At first I feared as you did, Artemis, that nothing good could come from loving a mortal, but finally I could no longer resist him.

"I visited him so often while he served as a shepherd that we had fifty daughters, the Menae, goddesses representing the fifty lunar months in an Olympiad."

"The sheep got quite a show," said Mateo quietly. Again, the goddess fortunately didn't hear him.

"It was shortly after that I learned Endymion was fated to die young, almost immediately in fact. The will of the three Fates, Clotho, Lachesis, and Atropos, is hard to contravene, for as long as there have been humans, one sews the thread of each life, one measures it to determine how long the person will live, and one cuts it, at which point the life ends.

"There are, however, ways around the end of a mortal life if the person can be made immortal. Endymion was too close to his time for me to manage that transformation, but I knew Zeus could do it, and since Endymion was his grandson, I was confident the king of the gods would help, if not for me, then certainly for him. Unfortunately, I made one mistake.

"I told Endymion the story of my sister Eos, the dawn, and her love for Tithonus. She had asked for eternal life for Tithonus but forgot to ask for eternal youth, and so Tithonus lived but shriveled away until he became a cricket that Eos was forced to keep in a jar.

"I told him the story so that he would ask for eternal life *and* youth. I suppose I should have just instructed him exactly what to say, but he had common sense.

"Zeus not only heard his prayers but swept him up to Olympus for a visit. I had also told Zeus of my love for Endymion, so I thought nothing could go wrong.

"Zeus asked Endymion what gift he desired. That was the moment. All Endymion had to say was "eternal life and youth," but he was nervous by all accounts, and perhaps afraid life and youth would be two wishes rather than one. Whatever may have been going through his mind, he asked to remain eternally the way he would be at the stroke of midnight. In his mind that was a wish for both eternal life and eternal youth, for he expected to be both young and alive at midnight. He also expected to be with me as he generally was at that time.

"Unfortunately, whether by chance or by the trickery of a jealous god, the cloud cover was heavy that night over Elis, and I could not visit him. That should not have been a problem, except that without me there, Endymion fell asleep. He was still sleeping at midnight, and so his ill-worded wish made him sleep forever.

"When I reached him an hour or so later, I was already too late. I took him away to a secret cave on Mount Latmus, where he still lies to this day, forever young, but forever asleep. I do what I can. I hold his hand, I embrace him, I kiss him, I tell him what is happening in the mortal world—but he never squeezes that hand, returns that embrace or that kiss, or gives me one word in answer."

"How sad!" said Fatima.

"I don't see how you think that proves your point," said Artemis. "Your love is as tragic as my friendship with Orion or Hippolytus, almost as tragic as Aphrodite's love for Adonis."

"Tragedy is only where one makes it," said Selene. "I knew true love for many months, and I had many beautiful daughters from it. It didn't last forever, but what does—except us? My error was not in loving but in expecting an eternity of it.

"I will tell you all this: cherish those moments of love when you can grab them. Those who avoid love for fear of heartbreak end up breaking their own hearts."

"My heart is *not* broken," said Artemis.

"I suppose we are too different to agree," said Selene, sighing. "We are both goddesses who love the night—and there our similarity ends."

"You said you came partly to offer help," prompted Hermes.

"Oh, yes," agreed Selene. "I have a sense that love will help somehow, but I also have more practical advice. If the abductor of your friend is, in fact, Hecate, I know a way in which she can be defeated."

"It seems unwise to try," said Hermes, "for she is surely more powerful than all three of us put together. Stealth seems a better option. If she is the culprit, we find a way to sneak in and rescue the lost visitor."

"I know how powerful Hecate is," conceded Selene. "Her Thessalian witches sometimes try the ritual of drawing down the moon, whereby they think to steal some of my blood for their magical purposes. Because of such attacks, I have studied magic—not as much as you, Hermes, but enough to stumble across some interesting ideas.

"In the later stories about us sometimes mortals confuse us gods with each other or even deliberately identify us with each other."

"Yes, so I have read," agreed Hermes. "What of it?"

"You also know how Hecate is often referred to as triple Hecate, perhaps because of the grant of power Zeus gave her in the sky, on the earth, and in the sea."

"Yes," said Hermes, but how does that help us?"

"In some ancient Greek works on magic, her triple nature is laid out in more detail. She is said to be Selene in the sky, Artemis on the earth, and Persephone in the Underworld. It stands to reason if she is somehow magically linked to the three of us, that if the three of us stand together against her, we should have the combined power to defeat her."

"An interesting thought," admitted Hermes, "but even if you have such power in theory, would any of you know how to use it?"

"I would," said Selene.

"I would not," said Artemis. "I've had little use for magic before. A good bow and arrow always served my purpose."

"It would not be a hard thing for me to teach you," said Selene. "As for Persephone, you know her stay in the Underworld has given her an affinity for certain kinds of magical forces."

"But what about the sea?" asked Hermes. "She has power there as well."

"She is identified with Crateis, whom we know as Ceto, goddess of the ocean's dangers, mother of monsters. They are linked, just as Hecate is linked to Artemis, Persephone, and me.

"If you ask for Persephone's cooperation, I will obtain Ceto's."

"Hades won't be happy with other gods entering the Underworld," said Hermes. "I can get in, probably with our human guests, since I have what amounts to a pass from Zeus for them, but I can't bring all of you in with me."

"Which is why we will invoke her somewhere else," said Selene. "You know as well as I do she can be raised at any place where three roads meet. We pick such a crossroads where the moon is shining, so I can come, and near the sea, so Ceto can easily join us. Hecate is too confident in her strength not to appear, and once she is before us, we will use our varying powers and our connection to neutralize hers."

"I don't like the idea," said Hermes. "It sounds as if it would require practice if it could work at all, and all four of you are not going to be able to be in the same place very often. Come to think of it, how do you practice such a combination without using it on Hecate?"

"We test it on some of her witches," said Selene.

"In which case, she is bound to find out what you're up to," Hermes pointed out.

"Do you have a better plan?" asked Selene.

"Yes," said Hermes. "My plan is to know what I'm doing before I do it. We aren't even sure Hecate *is* the culprit in the first place. It will do us no good to provoke a confrontation in which we can't prevail—but it might be worse in some ways to prevail only to discover that Hecate is innocent, after all."

"I see your point," said Selene, though she sounded reluctant. "Just remember my offer if you do discover Hecate is at fault."

"I will certainly take it into consideration," said Hermes. "Ladies, if there is nothing else, we must leave quickly. The time to complete this quest grows ever shorter."

"Wait!" said Artemis. "I just remembered something that might prove useful."

From her pack, she pulled a pair of men's sandals.

"Poseidon gave me these after Orion's death," said Artemis. "They have the same gift Orion had; their wearer can walk on water as if it were land."

Hermes looked almost as skeptical as he had been over Selene's plan. "I thank you, sister, but—"

"No, I can't think of any specific use for them on this quest either," said Artemis, "but Apollo must have sent you here for a reason, even if he didn't know what it was himself. Perhaps the lost visitor is surrounded by water, and one of the mortals can use these to rescue him."

"I suppose anything is possible," said Hermes, transferring them to his own bag. "Thank you again."

"Do you hear that?" asked Artemis. Right after she spoke, they could all hear her hunting dogs doing a chorus of barking, howling, and whining. The combination was very unsettling.

"We should—" began Hermes.

"Don't leave yet," said Artemis, making it sound more like a command than a request. "The hounds *never* act this way. It has to mean something."

Artemis raced over to where her hunting party was, then returned almost as fast.

"I can't tell what's wrong with them, but the reactions of animals are not to be lightly discounted. Their various responses are an omen of some kind. Without my brother's prophetic gift, I cannot be sure, but I think whatever they are sensing is related to our visitors' quest. There is nothing in the woods nearby that could account for their behavior.

"I now realize there is something else I can give you," continued Artemis. "I can accompany you on this quest. The other hunters can take care of the hounds, and as long as I hear no distressed cries from the young creatures I protect, I should be able to stay with you for a while."

Hermes looked as if he would have much preferred a similar offer from Aphrodite. The other guys looked as if they had just found out that their least favorite maiden aunt was going to be chaperoning them on a date with the girl of their dreams. Nonetheless, Hermes seemed unable to think of any way to decline.

"We would be honored to have you," he said, fake-smiling at the divine huntress.

"I would join as well if I could," said Selene, "but I suspect you may have to go places moonlight cannot follow—to say nothing of traveling during the day. I will watch you when I can, though, and help you if I can."

We appreciate your aid as well. Now we are off to find Pan."

Artemis rolled her eyes. "I really can't imagine he'll be easy to find—or much use for this kind of quest when we do."

"Everyone has a use," said Hermes, sounding a little offended. "It just requires patience to figure out what it is."

Chapter 14: Pan

It was still night, and now even darker, for clouds had covered the moon. The group had reached the deep woods of Arcadia, further in than most people ever got, looking for the elusive Pan. Hermes and Artemis were conferring a distance away, which gave the students a chance to talk.

"OK, I'm just going to come right out and say it—I don't like Artemis being here," said Mateo.

"Have a problem with independent women?" asked Keisha.

"Well, *I* don't have a problem with independent women," said Yong. "There's a difference between being independent and being isolated, though. Artemis is isolated. Athena was more like the model independent woman."

"Not exactly, at least not in the way we'd think of it," said Thanos. "Athena isn't subordinate to any man, that's for sure, but she is kind of a one-of-the-guys type. In the *Eumenides*, Aeschylus gives her a speech before the Areopagus, in which she is defending Orestes, who murdered his mother, Clytemnestra. He killed her to avenge his father, whom she killed. In Athena's speech, she clearly states that she is for the male and entirely on the father's side. It's almost as if she would rather have been born a man."

"You make her sound transgender," said Yong. "I don't think the Greeks had that concept, but if they had, Athena could have resolved the situation much more easily than a transgender person today. All she would have had to do was transform herself into a guy."

"So clearly, she doesn't actually want to be a man," Thanos agreed. "Maybe a better analogy would be a girl raised by a single father in a house full of brothers. Either way, she clearly likes men—except sexually. Artemis just as clearly dislikes them, perhaps because she's had bad experiences befriending them. She's close to Apollo, but other than that, I think she wouldn't complain too much if everyone of the male gender vanished."

"Also, Athena chose to be a virgin herself, but doesn't care if anyone else marries," said Yong. "Artemis actively encourages other women not to marry and even punishes anyone in her hunting band who does. Both goddesses play nontraditional roles for women in ancient Greek society, but other than that, they're really not that similar."

"Can we stop head-shrinking the gods?" asked Yasmin, looking around nervously. "Artemis is pretty close—"

At that moment, a blood-curdling shriek echoed through the forest around them, causing all of them to jump. Hermes and Artemis were at their sides in an instant.

"Don't worry," said Hermes. "That's just Pan showing his playful side. He likes to frighten travelers with his eerie screams."

"Oh, yeah," said Keisha. "That's where the English word *panic* comes from."

"Pan, come out!" shouted Hermes. "These are our guests, and they have enough to worry about without your adding to their troubles."

Nearby leaves rustled, twigs snapped, and Pan emerged in the clearing in which they were standing. Thanos, Keisha, and Yong, who had done the reading, knew what to expect, but Mateo, Fatima, and Yasmin, who had not, jumped at the sight.

Pan was a hybrid creature identical to the satyrs. He had a human head, but goat horns sprouted from his brow. His torso, though atypically hairy, was basically human. Below the waist he was all goat, though he walked upright.

"Well, there you are," said Hermes. "These mortals are on a quest with which you can help." Hermes again explained the quest, while Pan listened with surprising interest.

"Well, if my dear Aunt Artemis can spare time from the hunt, I surely can spare time from watching over shepherds to accompany these mortals on their journey."

"Aunt Artemis?" asked Yasmin.

"Pan is my son," Hermes explained. "He is the child I had with the nymph, Dryope."

"And what a father Hermes was!" said Pan, his rough face lit by a big smile. "My nurse drew away from me in horror when she saw me, but Hermes, delighted rather than horrified, picked me up in his arms, hugged me tenderly, wrapped me up in wool to keep me warm, and flew me up to Olympus, where he presented me to all the other gods. He didn't care that I wasn't the usual, physically perfect Olympian. He was proud of me anyway—just as a father should be."

Hermes was also smiling now. "Pan has always brought me great joy. He was happy from the moment he was born—as everyone should be. Even someone like Ares smiled to see him."

"Hermes, can I speak to you for a moment?" asked Artemis. She was noticeably not smiling about Pan.

As soon as Hermes and Artemis had moved away, Pan turned to the students and said, "A moment with her can turn out to be much longer. Perhaps you would like a tune to pass the time?" He pulled out an instrument composed of several tubes of different lengths.

"Panpipes!" said Thanos, who had read about them but never seen them.

"Exactly!" agreed Pan, who immediately began to play them. Worried as they were, the students could not help but feel happier as they listened.

"That was very good," said Yasmin as soon as he had finished.

"Shepherds watching their flocks for long periods need to do something to pass the time," said Pan. "Music helps with that, so as the god of shepherds, it is no surprise that I play. Unfortunately, not everyone appreciates my playing. Apollo, in particular, is not a fan."

"Really?" asked Mateo. "I would have thought Apollo would enjoy all good music."

"He certainly enjoys all the music he plays himself," said Pan with a wink. "That doesn't mean he appreciates anyone else's." Then he chuckled.

"No, he really isn't that arrogant—but he doesn't like my style. Too informal, too unpredictable. He's much more an enthusiast of structure, of order. Improvisation is not something he thinks belongs in music. To him music is a study, a discipline, an outgrowth of the intellect. To me, it is something one feels in one's heart, an outgrowth of the emotions.

"Actually, the creation of the panpipes was inspired by an emotion: unrequited love. I really wanted the nymph Syrinx, but she, influenced by Artemis's ideals, had sworn herself to chastity—or perhaps she found my goatish self a little intimidating. In either case, she ran from me. I chased her clear from Mount Lycaeum to the River Ladon. As soon as her feet touched the soft soil of the riverbank, she rooted herself in it and became a reed. Her rejection hurt me, but I wanted to remember her anyway, so I cut parts from some of the reeds to make the panpipes, and when I play it, I think of my love for her.

"Soon after I first created the instrument, I decided to challenge Apollo to a music contest. We selected Tmolus, the mountain, as our judge, for he was old and therefore wise, or so we hoped. A large audience gathered to watch our competition. I played my new panpipes, and Apollo played the lyre Father had made for him so long before.

"When I played, everyone became happy. Birds came down from the sky and squirrels from their trees to listen. When Apollo played, the audience was struck silent from sheer awe.

"Tmolus declared Apollo the winner, and almost the entire audience agreed. The one exception was the unfortunate Midas, who never did have good judgment. I was happy that he thought my playing was better than Apollo's, but even I knew it was unwise of Midas to announce his opinion publicly. Apollo was so angry that he turned Midas's ears into donkey ears.

"Poor Midas tried to hide the change by wearing a Phrygian cap, whose long flaps concealed his ears. Unfortunately, his barber found out the truth. Feeling he would burst if he could not tell someone, the barber dug a hole in the ground, whispered the secret into the hole, and then filled in the hole, burying the secret forever—or so he thought.

"A reed, just like the ones from which I made my panpipes, grew up from the ground where the hole had been, and it whispered the truth into the breeze, which carried it all over, so everyone knew the truth.

"The moral," continued Pan, looking around to make sure they were still paying attention, "is that mortals should best stay away from disputes and contests between gods. No matter which side the mortal takes, disaster inevitably follows. It is better to take the humble course and decline to be involved."

Pan looked around and scratched his head. "The moment grows long, even for Artemis. As I understand the situation, we should be moving faster than this. I'll go and see what's keeping them."

As soon as he was gone, Yasmin said, "Am I the only one who noticed Artemis doesn't want Pan to come with us? Why would she care?"

"I don't know how to put this in mixed company," said Thanos.

"We're big girls," said Yasmin. "We can handle whatever you have to say."

"Well, Pan represents everything Artemis opposes: she embodies restraint of sexual desire; Pan symbolizes giving into it. You probably don't know this, but the ancient Greeks considered the goat as a symbol of lust. Pan may have lost Syrinx, but...well, that didn't stop him from having sex at every opportunity. One myth even says he had sex with every one of Dionysus's maenads—and there were by one count hundreds of them then—during one night."

"Wow," said Mateo. "I don't know what else to say. He's living out every male's fantasy."

"Are you saying every guy wants nothing more than to have sex with every single girl he can get his hands on?" asked Keisha, preparing to be offended.

"Keisha, you know me well enough to know I'd never do that," said Mateo, a little offended himself. "There's a difference between fantasy and reality. I actually want to find a woman I can love and marry. That doesn't mean the kind of thing Pan gets away with doesn't make a nice...daydream."

"I understand now why he makes Artemis uncomfortable," said Yasmin. "She represents one kind of excess, and he represents its opposite. I don't think either one of them really has the right idea."

"Despite the myths, many ancient writers would have agreed with you," Thanos pointed out. "I think it was the Roman playwright Terence who first wrote, 'Moderation in all things.' Aristotle attributed a similar saying to Chilo, one of the seven sages of Athens. There was also a related quote, 'Nothing in excess,' inscribed on the temple of Apollo at Delphi."

"I don't get one thing, though," said Mateo. "Why do the myths say one thing, and the philosophers sometimes say something else?"

"I think it's a mistake to assume Greeks took the myths the same way modern people would take their sacred texts," said Thanos. "Ancient Greek religion creates a very different impression than the mythology does. Remember that the myths were mostly transmitted, not by prophets and priests, but by storytellers and poets. Sometimes the myths were closely connected with religion. Other times they were for different purposes, even entertainment. Different writers frequently rearranged the details, something that wouldn't happen as easily with a text people already regarded as holy.

"Sometimes the myths are intended to embody moral principles, but even then the Greeks didn't normally assume they were supposed to do what the gods were doing in the stories.

Keisha nodded her head in agreement. "Yeah, remember that, at least past really early times, the Greeks increasingly didn't believe in the stories even though they still believed in the gods. Later versions of the stories tend to tone down the more outrageous behaviors of the gods or just interpret the whole story allegorically."

"At the risk of sounding like Patrick, allewhatically?" asked Mateo.

No one would have openly admitted to it, but the mention of Patrick gave all of them a pang. Like it or not, they were worried about him.

"An allegory is a story in which the characters and events are symbolic. For instance, someone might take the story of the affair between Ares and Aphrodite and interpret it as love overcoming hate or war. A lot of Renaissance painters used the story that way. Their imagery makes Ares look as if he's been tamed or overcome by Aphrodite."

"I think that's one of the reasons the Greek myths survived," said Yong. "Certainly not because of their initial moral message—or lack of one in some cases. It was because they stimulated the imagination. Later philosophers, writers, and artists were able to achieve greatness by evolving those myths into something far greater than just the bare words with which they started. Maybe the earliest versions were the result of primitive people trying to make sense of a universe that made no sense to them—and their efforts make little sense to us. What those myths produced, though, was more, so much more."

"I'm still a little skeptical about that," said Yasmin. "It feels to me like, because someone ages ago pronounced the myths classics, we have to keep thrashing around to find some way of justifying that assessment. I admit being in the middle of them like this has given me a different perspective, and yeah, I think they're entertaining, but I'm not sure they've stimulated me to think some great thought."

"We aren't all going to have the same reaction to them, and that's OK," said Keisha. "Let me give you an example of what I think Yong is talking about, though.

"A Roman writer named Apuleius wrote a book called *Metamorphoses*, which includes a story about Cupid and Psyche, Cupid being the Roman name for Eros. It's not an early myth. In fact, most critics believe Apuleius created it himself, and that he wrote it as an allegory.

"Psyche is a girl who is so beautiful that men worship her. She doesn't encourage that worship, but it happens anyway. Unfortunately, as men worship Psyche, they stop worshiping Aphrodite, who, as you might expect, is angry that a mortal is stealing devotion from her, even if unintentionally.

"Psyche already has a rough life because, beautiful as she is, worshiped as she is, not a single man has proposed to her."

"I sort of get that," said Mateo. "Each one probably thinks he doesn't have a shot with her, because of all the other guys who want her. Everyone thinks the same thing, and so she ends up alone. I've seen something like that happen in real life to pretty girls a couple of times."

Keisha chuckled. "Yeah, I can see how it would. Anyway, Psyche's two much less beautiful sisters married princes, but Psyche herself was still alone.

"Not content with that, Aphrodite sent Eros to make Psyche fall hopelessly in love with some unworthy man. Apuleius was using the tradition in which Eros is Aphrodite's son. Anyway, Eros scratched himself with one of his own arrows and fell in love with Psyche, so he left her without fulfilling Aphrodite's command. Instead, he began to plot how to make Psyche his wife.

"Meanwhile, Psyche's parents had begun to suspect that they had somehow displeased the gods. They consulted the oracle of Delphi, who made a horrifying pronouncement: Psyche was destined to wed no mortal lover, but to be the bride of a monster whom neither men nor gods could resist. Not only that, but the girl must be led soon to a nearby mountain, at whose top her husband waited for her.

"Psyche's parents interpreted the command to marry their daughter to a monster as a death sentence, and the people who had admired Psyche's looks so much lamented her fate as well. Only Psyche accepted her fate, for she blamed herself for all the excessive praise bestowed upon her."

"She sounds a little too good to be true," said Fatima.

Keisha smiled. "You have to admit, though, she's a refreshing change from characters cheating on their spouses, inflicting drastically harsh punishments, or even eating their own children. Anyway, when the time came, a marriage procession—which ended up being more like a funeral procession—took

Psyche up to the summit of the mountain, where Psyche's parents and all of her friends said their good-byes, then reluctantly left her to her fate.

"Psyche was surprised when gentle Zephyrus, the west wind, lifted her gently from the mountain and set her down carefully in a place filled with blooming flowers. Apprehensive at first, Psyche expected a monster to pop out and devour her at any moment, but none did. Eventually, she went to sleep.

"When she woke up the next day, she found a large grove of trees. In the middle of the grove was an enormous fountain, and right behind it a palace so magnificent Psyche knew no mortal hands could have created it. She went inside and discovered that the interior was equally amazing, but the architecture was not really what surprised her.

"Voices called out to her and told her that they were her servants. They were apparently invisible, but they must have kept the enormous castle clean, and they prepared the best meals she had ever eaten, while invisible musicians played the best music she had ever heard.

"The best part, however, was the arrival of her husband, who was not the monster she had been expecting. Kind and loving, he made it clear he would do whatever he could to make her happy.

"Psyche *was* happy—except for one thing. Her husband wouldn't let her see him. He visited her only at night, kept the palace dark while he was there, and then left before she awoke at dawn."

"That sounds suspicious," said Mateo. "Was he a monster after all?"

"Sorry, no spoilers," said Keisha. "You'll know soon enough. Anyway, Psyche accepted her husband's wish at first, because she really did love him. However, over time she became a little lonely. After all, during the day, when her husband was gone, she had only the company of invisible servants.

"Eventually, she began to miss her sisters, and she asked her husband to allow them to come for a visit. Her husband thought the idea a bad one, but he had promised to make her happy, and so he yielded to her desire.

"Zephyrus soon brought her sisters, and Psyche was overjoyed to see them. Good fortune is always better when there is someone to share it with, and Psyche delighted in showing her sisters around the palace. Even though they were princesses, what Psyche had was vastly superior to what they had, and they became jealous.

"Questioning Psyche, her sisters eventually pried out of her that she had never actually seen her husband. That was all they needed to start picking away at her happiness, which they so resented.

"They pointed out how suspicious it was that her husband would not allow her to see him. What reason could he possibly have for such a demand? In the cloud of suspicion her sisters conjured up, there could only be one.

"They reminded her that the oracle had predicted her husband would be a monster, feared by gods and men alike. Surely, the oracle must have been right. That, and only that, could possibly explain her husband's strange behavior.

"Once the sisters had planted a seed of doubt in Psyche's mind, they told her she must find out the truth, for if her husband really was a monster, he no doubt planned to eat her or kill her sooner or later. They suggested waiting until he was asleep, then slipping out of bed to get an oil lamp and a knife. She could use the lamp to see who—or what—her husband truly was, and if, as seemed likely, he was a monster, she could use the knife to cut off his head.

"After her sisters had left, Psyche thought about what they had said. She wanted to believe in her husband, but what her sisters said did make sense. Eventually, she convinced herself that it could do no real harm if she got one brief glimpse of her husband. The next night, when she was sure he was sleeping deeply, she quietly got out of bed, lit the lamp, grabbed the knife, and took a forbidden glance at her husband.

"Instead of seeing a horrifying monster, she saw a man so handsome she knew he had to be a god. Unfortunately, instead of being satisfied and quickly extinguishing the lamp, she came closer to get a better look, and as she bent over him, a single drop of oil fell on him and burned his shoulder.

"He awakened immediately, and when he realized that Psyche had broken the one promise he had asked of her, he jumped out of bed, spread his white wings, and flew out the window.

"Psyche realized he intended to leave her forever, and she tried to follow him out the window. Of course, without wings she could not, and she fell to the ground with a thud.

"Hearing the sound, Eros spun around in midair and looked down on her. Sadly, he told her how foolish she had been. He had defied his mother to marry her, asking only one thing of her, and that one simple thing she had failed at. Love and suspicion can never coexist, and so he had to go. He urged her to rejoin her sisters, whose words she heeded more than his own, and then he flew away."

"I don't understand why he was so angry," said Yasmin. "What he asked of her was weird. How could he blame her for being suspicious?"

"Maybe he wanted to see if she would love him for himself and not because he was a god," suggested Fatima. "If she had seen him, she would have known."

"I don't think that's it," said Yong. "If he wanted to, he could have looked like an ordinary man. Besides, having the west wind carry her to a golden palace that could only have been the work of divine hands was sort of a dead giveaway, wasn't it? How could she have thought her husband was anyone but a god?"

"It doesn't seem as if being a god and being a monster are that mutually exclusive in Greek mythology," said Mateo. "Didn't Athena tell us about Helios having a dragon daughter? Didn't Gaia have children who were half human and half snake? The fact that the guy was living in an unnaturally great palace wouldn't necessarily rule out his being a monster. I don't think the point is that Psyche is being stupid; it's that she's being disobedient. Wives were supposed to obey their husbands without question.

"Not that I'm saying that's the way it should be," he added quickly in response to stares of doom from all three girls. "That's the way ancient people thought about it, though, right?"

"It is," Thanos agreed, "but I don't think that's all that's happening here. Most societies have stories about people being tested by the gods. They're given some rule to obey, usually one that doesn't have an obvious reason, but as long as they obey it, all is well. If they disobey it, though, terrible disasters happen. Often the story is set up in the context of marriage, but sometimes it's the husband who has a rule to follow, rather than the wife. That's why I think the story is more about humans obeying gods than wives obeying husbands. Psyche was tested by the gods, and she failed."

"The story isn't over yet," Keisha reminded them. "You need to hear the ending to really know what the story's about.

"By the time Psyche pulled herself together enough to look around, the palace was gone, and she found herself at a place not far from where her sisters lived. She went to them and told them what had happened.

"They pretended to share her grief, but each was secretly delighted because each one imagined that Eros might now choose her. As in so many stories, their egos were their downfalls. Each one went up the mountain from which Psyche had first been taken and asked Zephyrus to take her to Eros. Each one then foolishly jumped—but Zephyrus was not there to hold her up, and so each fell to her death on the hard stone below.

"Psyche wandered the earth, looking futilely for Eros. Once she saw an impressive temple on a mountaintop and thought that he might be there.

"She spent a long time climbing, but when she reached the summit, she discovered the temple was not a temple of Eros at all, but one for Demeter instead.

"Psyche noticed disorderly heaps of grain and farm implements. Rather than leave them in confusion, she put everything back in order. In the process, she pleased Demeter, who appeared to her and gave advice.

"The harvest goddess told her the key to winning back her husband would be to seek out Aphrodite and submit humbly to the goddess of love. If Psyche could gain Aphrodite's forgiveness, then surely Eros would forgive her as well.

"Psyche had wandered into a land with which she was not familiar, but it wasn't hard to find a temple of Aphrodite anywhere, and so she quickly found one in which she made a prayerful submission.

"Aphrodite angrily appeared to her, told her she was worthless, and pointed out that Eros still suffered from the wound Psyche had given him—literally the burn on his shoulder, but figuratively his broken heart.

"Despite how she felt, Aphrodite did not entirely reject Psyche but decided to test her, though, as if often the case in myths like this one, the tests were rigged against the person to whom they were given.

"First Aphrodite wanted her to sort the grain in the temple storeroom. For some reason, there was a much bigger, less organized pile than in Demeter's temple, and Aphrodite wanted the whole job done by sunset.

"Psyche stared at the enormous task and became despondent, for the job seemed far too big for her to do. Still, she loved Eros so much she tried, even though there was no hope of finishing.

"Watching from a distance, Eros took pity on her and inspired ants to help. They got each grain sorted by type with no mistakes by the deadline.

"Aphrodite knew Psyche could not possibly have done the job on her own, so the next day she gave her a second task: to cross the river and find a flock of sheep with golden wool, some of which she was to gather and bring it to Aphrodite.

"The job seemed simple enough, but when Psyche got to the river, the river god warned her that the task was too dangerous to do in the morning, for the rams, burning with power from the rising sun, itched to destroy mortals with their sharp horns and hard teeth. If, however, she waited until afternoon, the rams would be resting beneath the shade of trees, and Psyche could safely gather some of the wool from the branches against which they scraped earlier in the day.

"Psyche successfully gathered the wool as the river god had suggested, but again Aphrodite was not impressed because she knew Psyche must have had help. Consequently, she assigned Psyche a third task: to go down the Underworld with a box Aphrodite gave her and ask Persephone to put some of her own beauty in the box so that Aphrodite could adorn herself with it for a meeting with the other gods."

"That doesn't make any sense," said Mateo. "Why would Aphrodite, already the most beautiful goddess, need to borrow beauty from somebody else? And why would Persephone want to give her any?"

"Spoiler alert: Aphrodite was tricking Psyche," said Keisha. "Anyway, at first Psyche couldn't imagine any way she could get to the Underworld without dying. Desperate enough to risk anything, even death, for the slightest chance to be reunited with Eros, Psyche went to the top of the highest tower she could find and prepared to jump.

"A voice from inside the tower—Apuleius doesn't say whose voice, but I would bet Eros's—asked her why she doubted she would have help to reach the Underworld, considering a miracle had happened on each of her other tests. The voice pointed her to a cave that would lead her to the Underworld and told her how to get past Cerberus, the fierce, three-headed guard dog, as well as Charon, the cranky ferryman who would normally only take the dead across the river to the Underworld.

"Doing as the voice suggested, Psyche was able to reach Persephone, who received her kindly, filled the box for her, and sent her back to Aphrodite.

"However, the voice had given Psyche one other piece of advice: under no circumstances should she open the box, for it would be a grave error to give into curiosity. Unfortunately, on the long way back to Aphrodite, Psyche did indeed become curious. She also wondered if a little divine beauty would help her win back Eros.

"Finally, the temptation became too great, and Psyche opened the box. Inside was not some of Persephone's beauty, as she had been led to believe, but only sleep so deep no mortal could ever awaken from it. It engulfed her, and she fell into a sleep that might have been eternal.

"At this point Eros, recovered from his wound, managed to slip away from Aphrodite, find Psyche, gather the sleep back into the box, and awaken her with a gentle touch of one of his arrows.

"Eros told her to complete the errand his mother had given her and let him attend to everything else. Leaving her, he flew to Olympus and begged Zeus to help him convince Aphrodite of Psyche's worth. Moved by what Eros told him, the king of the gods persuaded Aphrodite to accept Psyche.

"Eros, who had already forgiven her, flew her up to Olympus, where Zeus made Psyche immortal, and where Eros and Psyche were married with the blessing of Aphrodite. Their daughter, Hedone, was as beautiful as her mother and became the goddess of sensual pleasure. Then they—"

"All lived happily ever after," said Mateo. "The story sounds more like a fairy tale than a myth."

"Western fairy tales are in many cases adapted from Greek and Roman myths," Yong pointed out. "Faeries and similar beings are portrayed in a way very similar to the gods: they have abilities greater than humans, and they are usually better looking, but their behavior is often unpredictable. They can be good but are also capable of great evil—just like the gods."

"Earlier you were talking about…what was it? Oh, yeah, allegory," said Mateo.

"I was," said Keisha. "The literal story does sound like a fairy tale love story, but most critics think that Apuleius had more than that in mind. The name *Psyche* actually means *soul*, and Apuleius may have intended Psyche's quest to represent the soul's attempt to seek out and win divine love. The journey would be hard, but not impossible for those willing to persist at it."

"That sounds weirdly modern," said Yong.

"By the end of the classical period, the Greeks had become a lot more philosophical and spiritual than the early Greeks had been," said Thanos.

"Which is why the view of the gods was changing," said Keisha. "Apuleius was supposed to have been a religious man, a priest of Asclepius in fact, but he doesn't seem to have been a believer in the old myths. He used the mythic gods as literary characters and probably believed the actual gods were quite different."

"Speaking of gods, since Pan, Hermes and Artemis are evidently still talking, maybe we should check on Patrick," suggested Fatima. "I know we can't rescue him yet, but if he's awake, maybe we can reassure him."

Thanos pulled out the wood Athena had given them and concentrated. In a moment, doglike whimpering came from the wood.

"I will translate," said Patricius. "He is asking what is happening."

"Can he understand us if we talk back to him?" asked Yong.

"Dogs can always understand," said Patricius. "Sometimes they pretend not to."

They are able to communicate with

"Patrick, it's Yong. How are you doing?" *Patrick*

Loud barking shook the piece of wood in Thanos's hands. "I'm a *dog*! How do you think I'm doing?" Patricius's translation only confirmed their worries.

"We're going to rescue you," said Mateo. "The gods are helping. Can you tell us where you are?"

"Dark. I'm in a dark place. That's all I know."

"Do you know who took you?" asked Yong.

"No clue. Can you just…just get me out of heeeeeeeere?" The barks turned to a howl.

"We'll get there as soon as we can," said Mateo.

"We'd better go now," said Thanos. "Whoever is holding you prisoner might hear you talking to us."

"OK," said Patrick, his howl back to a more normal bark. "OK, but hurry up, please! I…I'm afraid."

Patricius didn't do justice to the emotions behind the words, but the students could pick them up oddly well from Patrick's dog sounds. Fatima

he's still sarcastic

looked as if she wanted to cry, and the others were not too far behind her.

Something about the usually cocky Patrick being afraid made the situation even more alarming than they had thought. They had to rescue him sooner rather than later.

Unfortunately, at that point they heard the gods returning, their voices raised in anger.

"I am tired of your antics," Artemis said to Pan. "I will not continue on this quest if you join the party."

"I don't see why you are so hostile to me," Pan protested. "I gave you a gift of some very fine hounds once." *The gods are always fighting*

"And then you chased my poor companion Syrinx until she had to become a reed just to escape from you," replied Artemis, glaring at him.

"Perhaps if you had more reasonable rules, she would not have had to run from me," said Pan, his face reddening, though his voice was calm. "Why must they all be virgins? It is unnatural."

"My companions make that choice of their own free will," said Artemis. "They know well enough that men would be but a needless complication in their lives. Do you really think if they had husbands that those husbands would be content to allow them to continue to hunt with me as they wish? It would, however, be easier if the gods stopped trying to seduce any of them who are even remotely beautiful."

"Aha!" said Pan. "Your problem is not truly with me, but with gods in general. I drove only Syrinx, whom I truly loved, from your band. Ares, Zeus, and even your own brother, Apollo, were responsible for the other losses you've suffered, yet you criticize none of them as you do me. In truth, you should not criticize any of us, merely for following our natural inclinations." *Similar to w how Patrick*

The students were again reminded of Patrick, who might have said much the same thing, though in a much less sophisticated way. *Said*

"Am I not right, friends?" Pan asked, turning to the students.

"Let's leave them out of this," said Hermes, sliding quickly between the students and the other two gods. "You both know how badly it goes when humans get caught in the middle of quarrels among the gods."

"Hippolytus," whispered Artemis, looking teary-eyed for a moment.

"Aunt, you are not alone in suffering losses when the gods contend with each other, and mortals get in the way. You know Arcadia here is my land, and I know well how much a mess your meddling made of its royal house—particularly the Princess Callisto."

"That was not my fault!" snapped Artemis. "As with so many other things, it was Zeus's. Callisto joined me freely and was happy to be a member of my company. Zeus, wanting to make love to her but knowing she would never allow him close without calling for my aid, disguised himself as me in order to approach her. He gave her the impression that I was willing to set aside her vow so that Zeus could make her the mother of a great son. Then he returned as himself, and Callisto, thinking she had my permission, reluctantly lay with him. Later, when I discovered she was pregnant, she claimed that I had told her to make love with Zeus. Naturally enough, I thought she was lying—and blaspheming in the process—and turned her into a bear. When I learned the truth, I turned her back immediately, for she was blameless.

"The only problem was that Hera had also learned the truth. She turned Callisto back into a bear and then...my hands still tremble to remember it...tricked me into shooting at her. Since I never miss, she fell down dead—another woman whose life was destroyed by a man."

"Interesting that you blame Zeus, when it was Hera who engineered the death," said Pan. "Yes, it was wrong of Zeus to trick Callisto, but was it not more wrong for Hera to trick you into killing her? Why must the man always be the only villain in the way you tell every story?"

"Every man is not a villain—all the time, anyway," Artemis said, though she sounded a little grudging. "Zeus did what he could to save the child, sending Hermes to rescue the yet unborn baby from the body of Callisto and give him to his own mother, Maia, to care for. Of course, the babe would not have been in danger in the first place if not for Zeus." I agree with Pan

"The babe would not have existed at all if not for Zeus," countered Pan. "And that child grew up to be Arcas, the great king who gave his name to Arcadia."

Artemis nodded. "Arcas was a great hunter as well, but he almost died before becoming either hunter or king—because of yet another man."

Pan rolled his eyes. "Zeus protected Arcas, if you'll recall."

"And yet the man who threatened Arcas, his own grandfather, Lycaon, was the product of another one of Zeus's countless seductions."

"Men cannot be blamed for doing what comes naturally," said Pan.

Now it was Artemis's turn to redden with anger. Turning to the students, she said, "You, who want my help on your quest, shall be the judge of whether Pan or I am right about who should be blamed."

"As I said before, leave them out of this," said Hermes, sounding a little angry himself. "If you must have a judge, let it be me."

"You are his father!" Artemis protested.

"As I am your brother, of whom you have never had reason to complain," Hermes replied.

"There will be no judge, at least not now, but I will tell my story anyway," said Artemis, glaring at both Hermes and Pan, as if daring them to contradict her.

"Lycaon was poisoned by hubris almost from the cradle because he could not handle his own exalted ancestry. Zeus had long before seduced Niobe, daughter of Phoroneus, who had a child, Pelasgus. Once he grew up, he married the Oceanid Meliboea. Their son was Lycaon, who was thus grandson both of Zeus and of the Titan Oceanus, as well as being related in various ways, through Phoroneus, to the kings of places as far-flung as Argos, Thebes, Crete, Phoenicia and even Libya.

"A man might accept such ancestry humbly, but not Lycaon. He reveled in it, coming with time to believe himself equal to, or even superior to, the gods.

"At first he seemed a good king, a civilizing influence like his father, but as his hubris gradually ate away at his better impulses, he became more and more arrogant, a trait he passed on to his fifty sons, all but one of whom had a reputation for being unruly and impious. Their father, who should have shown them the right path, actually encouraged them in their slide toward ruin.

"Lycaon hated his grandson, Arcas, presumably because he had disapproved of Callisto's role as one of my companions. He also hated his one good son, Nyctimus, hated him passionately. The horrible day came when Lycaon, driven insane by his own delusion of godhood, tried to strike a blow at his hated son and grandson, as well as Zeus himself.

"Lycaon had invited Zeus to a banquet, which the king of the gods chose to attend. Shortly before Zeus was to arrive, Lycaon dragged his son into the temple of Zeus Lycaeus, which the king had built himself, and murdered that son upon the altar, calling him a sacrifice to Zeus.

"Leaving the mangled corpse upon the blood-drenched altar, Lycaon went to the banquet as if nothing had happened, or so it seemed, but looks can be deceiving. Earlier Lycaon had murdered Arcas, and, in imitation of the crime of Tantalus, served his cooked flesh at the banquet to test the omniscience of Zeus.

"Zeus, already enraged by the defilement of his temple with a human sacrifice, came to the banquet to pass sentence upon Lycaon. His outrage became even greater when he saw what was being served.

"Lycaon stood before Zeus with a sneer on his face, ready to defy him. Worse, all forty-nine surviving sons smirked at the king of the gods, clearly in on the joke, perhaps thinking Zeus was not strong enough to take on all forty-nine of them.

"Needless to say, they were wrong. With a thunderbolt or two, Zeus reduced Lycaon's wicked sons to ashes. The king, horrified but unrepentant, challenged Zeus, who had just destroyed the king's sons, to make his own son whole again.

"Without a moment's hesitation, Zeus turned Lycaon into a wolf, for men who acted liked beasts should be beasts—and for once I could not doubt his justice, except that no true beast would ever have behaved as badly as Lycaon.

"Then, with loving care, Zeus made Arcas whole and restored his life, doing the same for Nyctimus. The latter ruled a short time, and Arcas followed him, both ruling far more wisely than Lycaon.

"Yet the evils Lycaon committed echoed long after his time. Some say Zeus decided to flood the earth in part because of him. Others say that the temple of Zeus Lycaeus was cursed for the rest of eternity, and that each time a sacrifice to Zeus was offered there, a man would become a wolf. If that new-made wolf abstained from human flesh for nine years, he would be restored to human form; if he failed to restrain himself, he would be a wolf until his dying day."

"Is that the origin of the later folklore about werewolves?" asked Yong.

"Maybe," said Pan, "but Artemis is using it as a demonstration that all men are evil. It is not true, Aunt, and you know it. That Lycaon was evil, we all agree. Surely, though, you can see he was a horrendous exception."

"All men have a kind of beast within," said Artemis. "Some restrain it, some do not. Some wear it visibly," she added, looking down at Pan's goat legs.

"Artemis, that's—" began Hermes, ready to respond to the obvious insult to his son.

"Father, I shall handle this myself," said Pan. Turning to Artemis, he said. "You forget yourself, Aunt, for I am more than just your humble nephew. I am the great god Pan."

As he spoke, he seemed to grow larger, until he was a giant towering over all of them, and his gentle voice had become a deafening roar.

Artemis, not to be intimidated, drew her bow and readied an arrow.

Hermes, who clearly did not lack guts, got between them and persuaded them both to stand down. Then he pulled them aside to see if they could work out some kind of agreement.

"That was...scary," said Mateo. "But what was that? I was getting the impression Pan was a fuzzy little protector of shepherds who was...sexually active. How did he become so threatening so fast?"

"You remember the differing descriptions of Eros, one of which makes him a primal force that helped bring the universe into being, the other of which makes him the son of Aphrodite?" asked Thanos.

Mateo nodded, though he looked a little blank.

"Well, Pan also has two very different natures, depending on which tradition one is looking at. He is the humble protector of shepherds that we saw first, but he is also sometimes seen as the powerful embodiment of the all of nature. Later storytellers occasionally tried to explain the difference by saying there were two Pans, one the son of Cronus and thus on the same power level as Zeus, Poseidon, and Hades, and one the much less imposing son of Hermes. Apparently, our dream Pan can manifest as either one."

"I'm beginning to think we shouldn't have both Artemis and Pan with us if they can't get along any better than that," said Keisha.

"Yeah, we need to get our clues and equipment together and go get Patrick," said Mateo. "He's miserable right now."

"OK, but how do we disinvite a god—and if there is a way, which one should go?"

The students spent a little time debating how to get themselves out of this mess, but in the meantime, Hermes somehow got Pan and Artemis to make peace.

"We have agreed to disagree," said Pan, trying to cover a smirk.

"Artemis has agreed to make no more sweeping attacks on the male gender," said Hermes, glaring at Pan. "Pan has agreed to make no more unwarranted criticisms of women who choose to remain virgins."

"We both love nature, after all," said Artemis, sounding as if she were reading from a script. "Our similarities are much greater than our differences."

"Well, then, let us be off to visit Demeter," said Hermes.

"Perhaps we should visit Dionysus first, suggested Pan. He's closer." Turning to the students, he stage-whispered, "It's been too long since I visited the maenads—nearly a week in fact!"

Hermes looked horrified. Artemis looked annoyed but just rolled her eyes rather than exploding.

"It's Demeter next," said Hermes firmly. "We will stick to the order Apollo gave us."

Chapter 15: Demeter

They found Demeter on the porch of the Telesterion, her temple in Eleusis, just northwest of Athens. The goddess, though beautiful as the other Olympians, appeared as an older woman than her niece, Artemis. In her long and flowing brown hair, she wore a crown of small white flowers. In one hand she held a cornucopia, the traditional horn of plenty, with wheat stalks sticking from its end, and in another a torch. She looked almost as if she were posing for a painting.

As before, Thanos was fascinated by seeing the structure as it had been in ancient times, and Demeter responded, once again delaying their mission.

"There was a temple here almost as long ago as Homer wrote the *Iliad* and the *Odyssey*," said Demeter. "Let me see, that would be about twenty-seven hundred years ago, give or take. Two hundred years later, Iktinos, the same architect who designed the Parthenon, built the first Telesterion, a temple large enough to hold thousands, for the Eleusinia, celebrated here every fall, was one of the largest religious ceremonies in Greece. Construction continued on and off for years after that.

"The Persians destroyed the Telesterion when they conquered Attica, but once they were driven out, Pericles had it rebuilt. Later a tribe called the Costoboci destroyed it while raiding Eleusis, but the Roman Emperor Marcus Aurelius rebuilt it. The last time it was destroyed by the forces of Alaric the Visigoth, few worshiped us Olympians anymore, and the Telesterion was not rebuilt—then or ever." Demeter looked very sad. She did not elaborate, but they all knew she was talking about the triumph of Christianity in the Roman world.

Hermes explained the quest to her, and she looked sympathetic, but she also said she did not know how she could help.

"I could offer you what Persephone has told me about the geography of the Underworld, but if what Apollo says is true, you will be able to ask her yourself, and in any case, Hermes knows the place quite well.

"I must, however, disagree with Apollo. I doubt your friend is there at all."

That simple statement caught the students off-guard. Could Apollo be wrong?

"I cannot imagine Hecate would be party to such a kidnapping," Demeter continued. "I do not share the same skepticism about her some of the gods seem to have."

"Her patronage of witchcraft—" Hermes began.

"I don't doubt that some of her worshipers have used the power they got from her for dark purposes," Demeter interrupted, waving her hand dismissively. "Mortals will do crazy and even evil things in the name of the gods. Who is at fault in such a case, the mortal or the god?"

"Should not the god stop such abuses?" asked Hermes.

"Hecate helped me through the darkest time in my life," replied Demeter, "and I will not say a word against her, no matter how hard you press me."

"The darkest time in your life?" asked Fatima, her concern evident in her voice.

"When my daughter, Persephone, was stolen from me. You see, she was so beautiful that Hades had heard of her even in the dark depths of the Underworld, and he asked Zeus for her hand in marriage. Zeus should have just said no, but he always goes out of his way to avoid angering Poseidon or Hades. On the other hand, he didn't want to anger me, either, so he couldn't very well openly give his consent, even though he was Persephone's father as well as our king, and thus could have claimed the legal right to wed her to whomever he pleased."

Artemis began muttering under her breath, though she stopped when Hermes glared at her.

"Trying to satisfy Hades without offending me, Zeus privately consented to the match without letting me know. Such sneaking about did not trouble Hades, for he wanted Persephone, not the ceremony or feasting that was part of a normal marriage."

"Typical!" said Artemis, rolling her eyes. She would have said more, but another stern glance from Hermes reminded her of their agreement.

"Not long after, Persephone was out gathering flowers when she saw an unusually large and beautiful one that she did not recognize—odd, considering her connection with nature. She reached over to pick it, but it was a trap, and as soon as she was close enough, the earth split open, and Hades rose up from the Underworld, grabbed her, and dragged her down into his dark kingdom.

Hecate heard her cries but did not see what had happened. Nor could she find Persephone, though she looked.

"When I realized my daughter was missing, I set out to look for her, but I had no luck. Neither men nor gods could tell me what had befallen her, for it is hard for anyone except one of the inhabitants of the Underworld to know what happens there."

It occurred to Keisha that was an excellent reason to suspect that was where Patrick was being held, but she knew better than to interrupt the goddess.

"After nine days," Demeter continued, "I found Hecate, who had been looking for me. She told me she had heard Persephone's cry and knew that my daughter had been kidnapped. Together, we asked Helios what he had seen, and he was able to tell us that Hades was the one who had abducted Persephone. The sun god also told me that Zeus had given his consent and tried to comfort me, pointing out that by marrying Hades, Persephone would become queen of the Underworld.

"If even someone like the radiant Helios, though sympathetic, was clearly not willing to offer me any real aid against the schemings of Zeus and Hades, I knew that no one else was likely to, and so I left Olympian society and wandered the earth disguised as an old woman. I behaved almost as if I thought Helios had lied and was still hoping somehow to find the missing Persephone, though I knew perfectly well I never would—unless I took a more active role.

"Much as the gods would like to keep us goddesses in secondary roles, they are not as all-powerful as they like to pretend. Zeus is the one who brings down the rain to water the crops, but through the grace of Gaia, they can never grow and ripen without my touch, and that touch I withheld as long as Persephone was a prisoner in the Underworld. Zeus could strike me with a thunderbolt or exile me to Tartarus—but he could not make the grain grow without me. Nor could Hades. The king of the gods sent Iris to deliver his order for me to return to my duties, but I refused, and Zeus knew better than to try to compel me, though he was no doubt trying to work some scheme to force my hand.

"When I came to Eleusis, still in my old woman disguise, the daughters of King Celeus greeted me kindly. As a test of their hospitality, I told them I had been kidnapped and sold into slavery by Cretan pirates, but I had escaped my master and was looking only for such work as a woman of my years could do, such as taking care of a baby.

"The princesses treated me well and brought me to the palace itself, where there was a newborn prince, Demophoon, to be tended.

"When I met Queen Metaneira, she welcomed me as warmly as had her daughters, for she had caught a glimpse of my divine radiance and knew in her heart that there was something special about me. When I said I had methods to protect her child against witchcraft, she believed me and gave me the responsibility of tending the baby.

"I know it may seem strange, but the child comforted me a little, though he did not compensate for my loss of Persephone. Still, he was a good babe, and his family treated me well, so I resolved to make him immortal. That would have annoyed Zeus, who doesn't like mortals to be given that gift without his blessing, but frankly, by that point annoying Zeus was just another reason to do it.

"Every day I secretly anointed Demophoon with ambrosia to develop his immortal body, and every night I buried him in the hearth, where the flames of the hearth fire would burn his mortal part away.

"Metaneira could see he was growing faster than an ordinary baby under my care. She could also see he had begun to look like the gods, so she should have known she was witnessing a miracle and been satisfied. Instead, she came one night to spy on me, and seeing the child in the flames, she screamed, ruining what I had planned to do.

"I revealed myself to her then and scolded her for her lack of faith. I could not complete the process of making Demophoon immortal, but I did predict he would always be honored, and so it came to pass, for every year a mock battle was performed at Eleusis in his honor.

"Meanwhile, Zeus kept sending gods to me with rich gifts as bribes to get me to withdraw my curse upon the crops, but none of them could sway me, for what mother would casually leave her own daughter to such a fate?

"Finally, fearful that famine would eventually destroy the human race, Zeus was forced to yield to me. He sent Hermes to tell Hades that Persephone would have to be released from the Underworld.

"Unfortunately, Hades had one last trick. He knew what Persephone did not—that by ancient law anyone who eats in the Underworld is forever bound to it. Persephone had been refusing to eat, but just before she was to leave, he gave her a pomegranate, thinking its bright red color would entice her.

"Even then, she didn't eat much—just six seeds, in fact, but that would have been enough to keep her forever in the Underworld.

"Zeus, however, knew he could not allow that law to stand unchallenged if it meant that the earth would never be fruitful again. With Hermes as a negotiator, Zeus got Hades to agree to a compromise: six months of each year (one for each seed), Persephone must remain in the Underworld; the other six months she was free to walk the earth with me. I accepted that agreement reluctantly, knowing it was probably the best deal I was going to get, but during the fall and winter, when Persephone is with Hades, the earth becomes less fruitful, though all growth does not stop as it did when Persephone was first captive in the Underworld.

"To help the mortals recover from the loss of the previous year's crop, I gave Triptolemus, another son of Celeus and Metaneira, an ample supply of seed and a chariot of dragons to fly it throughout the world and to teach all the peoples of the world how to grow their crops in the best possible way.

"The Eleusinians, already grateful to me, built this temple in my honor, and I taught to them the rites that are now called the Eleusinian Mysteries, whereby the initiates might win their way to a better afterlife.

"Before that, aside from a few favored children of the gods, who dwelt after death in the Elysian Fields, the most mortals could hope for was a shadowy existence in which they could neither speak nor even really think, floating aimlessly and pointlessly through a sunless realm.

"However, Persephone, as women often must, made the most of her forced marriage with Hades, and through her ties to the lord of the Underworld, she was able to offer mortals a better fate. Henceforth morality and faith would play a role, as they should have all along.

"Hades and Persephone's daughter Macaria, the goddess of a blessed death, represents some of that change, for she is the protector of those who courageously fight for a cause in which they believe."

"Is Persephone…happy with Hades now?" asked Fatima.

"She is…not miserable," replied Demeter, "and even I must agree some good has come from her misfortune, though I refuse to give Zeus credit for wisdom in that case. If you ask me, it was a lucky accident.

"To get back to my original point, it was Hecate alone who helped me find out the truth of Persephone's abduction, and later it was Hecate who agreed to accompany Persephone to the Underworld, both to keep her company and to guarantee that Hades would release her each year when the time came.

"If she is darker than some would like, it is because she dwells in that dark place."

"The same might well be said of Hades," suggested Hermes quietly.

Demeter looked at him intently. "Hades need not remain there all the time; he chooses to stay away from the light."

"And so does Hecate these days," the messenger of the gods pointed out. "She is Persephone's companion during the fall and winter, but unlike your daughter, she does not emerge when spring begins, but chooses to stay there."

"She is keeping an eye on Hades," insisted Demeter, though she did not sound completely certain.

Hermes raised an eyebrow. "Perhaps more than just an eye. Hades must be awfully lonely for those six months without a wife."

The students cringed a little, expecting Demeter might take offense, but she just laughed, then looked at their shocked faces.

"Jokes are a part of the rituals of Eleusis," said Demeter. "Even sexually suggestive ones. Nothing young Hermes can say is likely to upset me. Besides, I've heard much more credible rumors that it is he, and not Hades, who from time to time has shared a bed with Hecate."

"Nonsense!" snapped Hermes, blushing a little.

Demeter smiled, clearly enjoying herself. "You are worshiped as her consort at Pherae in Thessaly, and even here in Eleusis, it is sometimes said the great hero Eleusis for whom the city is named, your son by the Oceanid Daeira, is really your son by Hecate. Pausanias and Propertius both tell similar tales."

"Idle gossip," insisted Hermes. "We are both associated with the Underworld—and that is as far as our connection goes."

"In truth, Hecate is, like me, a virgin," said Artemis, giving Hermes and Demeter both stern looks.

"Yet there was one time—" began Hermes.

"Enough!" snapped Artemis. "I may not place quite the same faith in Hecate that Demeter does, yet I will not stand by and listen to a woman's virginity be questioned, particularly not by an uninformed man."

Hermes seemed to want to respond, but, conscious of the time, he said to Demeter, "Perhaps Hecate is not the abductor; Apollo could not be sure. What he was sure of was that the trail led to the Underworld, and so there we must go. If you can think of no way to assist us in this quest, we will bid you good-bye and be on our way, for time is short."

"If Apollo thought I had something to contribute, then I must," said Demeter. "I don't really know, though—oh, wait, I do have a thought.

"Hermes, I know you can gain entry to the Underworld and that you have Zeus's permission to bring the mortals with you, but you don't have the approval of Hades, whom I do not trust. He has the nasty habit of wanting things that do not belong to him, and I would not put it past him to try to keep these mortals once they enter his domain."

Hermes looked shocked. "Surely he would not defy the will of Zeus himself."

"You know as well as I do that he has never been happy with the division of realms after the defeat of Cronus. Recall that when your father and uncles drew lots to see who would get which part of the world for his share, Zeus drew the sky, Poseidon the sea, and Hades the Underworld. From the beginning, Hades felt cheated to have been given such a domain. If someone from the Underworld kidnapped the hapless mortal for whom you search, Hades is a much more likely culprit than Hecate. He is no stranger to kidnapping, after all. Perhaps abducting someone under Zeus's protection is the first step in a scheme to undermine the king of the gods."

"I had not thought of that," said Hermes. "But if that is the case, how can I protect the mortals in my charge? I am no equal to Hades if it comes to a fight in the Underworld."

"I recall something from the adventures of Aphrodite's son, Aeneas, that might prove useful," said Demeter. "He was advised by the Sibyl of Cumae, Apollo's prophet in Italy, to take with him a golden bough, a metal branch that could only be plucked from one rare tree that grows in the woods outside the sibyl's cave. The bough enables mortals to pass by certain menaces unharmed and enter certain areas from which they might otherwise be barred. It also enables them to return. Like the rule about eating food in the Underworld, the power of the golden bough cannot be defied—even by Hades himself."

"An excellent thought," agreed Hermes. "I will at once fly to Cumae and retrieve the branch."

"You cannot," said Demeter. "Take the leader of the mortals with you. The bough can only be plucked by one who is destined to enter the Underworld alive. As a god, you don't count."

"Who is your leader?" Hermes asked the students.

"We…don't really have one," said Keisha. "But if we need one, I nominate Thanos, who knows what's going on better than the rest of us."

Though each of them would have liked to see what Italy looked like in this dream world, no one could fault Keisha's logic, so they quickly voted to elect Thanos their leader. Hermes whisked him off to Italy equally quickly, leaving Demeter, Artemis, and Pan to keep the students company until he returned. However, Pan, sensing he was now outnumbered and not wanting to start another fight that might imperil the quest, pretended to study the nearby architecture while Artemis and Demeter talked.

"Well, now at least we don't have to listen to Hermes make excuses for Zeus or even Hades all the time," said Artemis.

"We cannot really fault him for defending his own father," said Demeter. "Anyway, I set aside my hatred for Zeus long ago. He may serve his own interests and play the politician too often for his own good—and ours—but in the end, even I have to admit the universe is in better hands with him than with either Uranus or Cronus."

"I'm surprised to hear you say that after the way he treated Iasion," said Artemis.

Demeter's expression darkened, but only for a moment. "Zeus acted poorly in that case, though all worked out well in the end."

Turning to the students, most of whom looked puzzled, she said, "The storytellers have that one wrong. Because they assumed Iasion was mortal, they thought Zeus killed him. He was the son of Zeus and the Oceanid Electra, so how could he have been mortal? The fact that he is worshiped as my consort in Samothrace ought to have given them a clue."

"Even so, Zeus hurt him for no reason," said Artemis.

"He did act without thinking," conceded Demeter. "I met Iasion at the wedding of Cadmus and Harmonia, at which many of the gods were guests. For us it was love at first sight—and not because of that pesky Eros, I promise you. Iasion and I were meant for each other. You would say we were soul mates.

"I've been with other gods. Zeus—well, let us face it, everyone's been with Zeus—and from that I got Persephone, that priceless gift, but I never loved the king of the gods nor envied Hera, not even for a moment.

"Poseidon, true to his violent nature, approached me when I had first lost Persephone—not to offer help, but to demand sexual gratification. I refused and fled from him when he was having difficulty accepting my refusal, eventually transforming myself into a mare and concealing myself among a large herd of horses in Arcadia. In that moment, I forgot Poseidon's affinity for horses. He picked me out with no trouble and tricked me by becoming a horse himself. Though I had refused him as a god, my horse form found him attractive as a horse. Together we became the parents of the divine horse Arion—a most difficult labor, I can tell you—and a beautiful daughter named Despoine, who became a fertility goddess in Arcadia, worshiped there in the mystery cult of Acacesium, along with me, Persephone, and Artemis. As with Zeus, I was thankful for the children, but I had no love for the man, who, though he had not exactly forced me, had certainly tricked me.

"With Iasion it was different. We lay together in a well-ploughed field and became the parents of twins: Plutus, the god of wealth, particularly the wealth from the fruitful earth; and Philomelus, the inventor of the wagon and the plow, whom I afterward remembered in the stars as the constellation Bootes.

"Zeus claimed later that he thought Iasion had tried to rape me, though how he could have thought that I'll never know. Other goddesses theorized that the gods don't like it when one of us makes love to a mortal, though Iasion wasn't mortal. In any case, the gods, who have mortal women all the time, could not reasonably complain of such a thing.

"Whatever Zeus was thinking—or more likely, not thinking—he blasted Iasion with a thunderbolt. Afterward, he was sufficiently repentant to help me restore Iasion, whose immortal nature enabled him to survive Zeus's attack."

"Still, I would not so easily have forgiven such a thing," said Artemis.

"I did not exactly forgive, easily or otherwise," said Demeter. "I simply make peace with what I cannot change—and so do you, for as much as you complain of the way Zeus treated your mother, you still accept his gifts."

Artemis looked angry, but Demeter pushed forward anyway.

"That much can be said for Zeus as well. He forgave your brother Apollo's attack on the Cyclopes, and he even forgave Apollo, Poseidon, and Hera for rebelling against him—after suitable punishment. Particularly since Apollo is his son, and thus fits the prophecy of his overthrow, that incident could have gone very differently if Zeus had wanted it to."

"I think you are going soft, Aunt," said Artemis, who sounded as if she was having difficulty controlling her temper. "You are too willing to excuse the evils of men."

"I excuse nothing when I have the power to administer justice," said Demeter. "Have you forgotten how I handled Erysichthon when he and twenty companions invaded my sacred grove and started cutting down the trees to get wood for a new banquet hall? I gave him a chance to change his course, appearing to him as my own priestess and ordering him to stop. Instead of stopping, he threatened me with the ax, at which point I showed him my true form, which caused his friends to flee in terror and left him alone to face me.

"For valuing a banquet hall so much he was willing to violate a sacred space, I cursed him with an insatiable hunger and sent him home to banquet—endlessly. The more he ate, the hungrier and the thinner he got. His parents, trying to save him, spent all their wealth to feed him, but in vain. Eventually, he became a beggar on the streets, eating garbage and rats. Ovid, who always did like gruesome details, also mentions that finally he ran out of anything else to eat and ate himself."

At that moment, they heard what sounded like screams in the distance.

"What could that be?" asked Demeter, looking around.

"We should investigate at once," said Artemis, drawing her bow.

Demeter, Artemis, and Pan raced in the direction from which the uproar was coming.

"That story about Erysichthon sounds like something out of Stephen King," said Mateo.

"Well, at least the guy was clearly evil," said Yong. "He even threatened to kill someone he thought was a priestess."

"What about Demeter threatening to kill the whole human race to get her daughter free? Isn't that carrying maternal instinct a little too far?" asked Yasmin.

"She knew she wouldn't actually have to do that," said Ardalos in his usual toneless way. "Zeus and the other gods would never have allowed the situation to go that far—and they didn't."

"I'm a little more concerned with the sexual conduct," said Keisha. "Demeter being tricked into sex makes me feel uncomfortable. I felt the same way about the Zeus and Callisto story, and there are other myths that work the same way. I know the ancient Greeks wouldn't have worried about that kind of situation, and since we don't have shapeshifters in real life, no woman has to face such a trick, but isn't what Poseidon and Zeus did wrong?"

"Guys do sometimes trick girls into having sex in our society," said Mateo. "When a guy tells a girl he loves her and doesn't really mean it, for instance. That's pretty low. I don't think what the gods are doing in the myths is any better—a different lie, but still a lie."

"Since we don't believe in arranged marriages, what happened to Persephone is just as bad," Yasmin pointed out. "She wasn't tricked in the same way—but she wasn't given a choice, either. That's even worse, as far as I'm concerned."

"The stories reflect the brutality of the times," said Yong. "We've talked about this kind of thing before. We don't have to embrace the brutality. We could just as easily repurpose those stories as cautionary tales. The gods get away with things that in some cases they wouldn't tolerate humans doing. They get away with them because they can. On some level, aren't these really stories about the corruption of power? What would a human being do if he or she had enough power to ignore the constraints of society? That's why so many modern retellings of the myths make the gods the villains. Now we even have revisionist interpretations of superheroes."

"I suppose you're right," said Keisha. "The stories also pose the question of whether or not doing whatever you want really makes you happy? Can Zeus really be happy with all the chaos he causes, particularly knowing that his fellow gods may not always have his back? There is that prophecy that he is doomed to fall, and it haunts him throughout the myths. Is Poseidon any happier? I doubt it."

"Maybe we'll get to find out since we're meeting him," said Mateo.

At that point, Mateo's linothorax proved its usefulness by deflecting an arrow that would otherwise have pierced his heart.

Chapter 16: Dionysus

Looking in the direction from which the arrow had come, the students saw at least twenty centaurs galloping toward them and simultaneously readying arrows.

"Invisibility caps!" yelled Mateo, not that anyone really needed to be prompted. In seconds, they were all invisible. Hermes would have been proud of their quick response.

Ardalos and Patricius had no way to conceal themselves, but the centaurs at first seemed uninterested in them. Nor were the centaurs as surprised as they should have been when their prey disappeared. They weren't even startled enough to slow their pace. Instead, they surrounded the area where they had last seen the students and started firing arrows as fast as they could. As with Mateo, the linothoraxes protected the other students' torsos, but with so many arrows flying into their general area at close range, it might only be seconds before an arrow struck some unprotected spot. Once somebody did get hit, for all they knew, the arrow or the blood might be visible, showing the centaurs exactly where that person was.

Ardalos and Patricius, as aware of the danger as the students were, did what they could to interfere with the attack, with varying results.

Ardalos wasn't designed for combat. He got himself in the line of fire, and, since he was the work of Hephaestus, the arrows just bounced off him. However, the centaurs were numerous enough to trample him to the ground, and with a couple of them standing on him, he wasn't going to be getting up anytime soon.

Patricius had somewhat better luck, both because he could maneuver faster and because he could bite. Against one centaur, he might have done well. Against several, though, he too was overcome quickly. Like Ardalos, Patricius couldn't be destroyed by the centaurs, but once they had him under their hooves, he was no longer much of a threat to them.

However, Ardalos and Patricius had distracted the centaurs long enough for the students to attempt escape. Running away was not an option since the centaurs had them almost surrounded. Fortunately, they were close to the temple entrance, and the centaur encirclement hadn't closed them off from that side, so they stumbled back through the closest doorway, hoping the centaurs wouldn't hear and follow.

"Scatter!" ordered Mateo as soon as they were in the temple. Unlike most Greek temples, which were home to the statues of the gods but not the location most of the ceremonies occurred, this one was designed to house the rituals of the Eleusinian Mysteries, which, being secret, could not be held at outdoor altars. Consequently, the temple's main room was huge, with ample space to spread out in, large columns to hide behind, and eight ascending tiers of stone stands along each wall, like in an amphitheater but too narrow for sitting down. The centaurs could not easily climb up such stands. Their horse legs could handle sloping hills but not stonework that ascended at right angles. Getting to the top rows at least limited how close those equine archers could get to their targets.

The students heard hooves clattering against the floor and knew the centaurs had followed them in. In a moment, the first of them entered, and the rest soon joined them. They moved more cautiously now that they were not sure where their targets were located.

The students were invisible but not inaudible, and the centaurs seemed to have sharp hearing. Consequently, the students tried to stay as still as they could, but sooner or later the centaurs would find them. Yes, the area was large, but it was finite, and there were seventeen centaurs searching it, the other three presumably remaining outside to keep Ardalos and Patricius down.

When Hermes had worked out the invisibility strategy for them, he had intended it to be temporary protection until he could whisk them away, not a long-term strategy. He hadn't gotten back yet from his mission with Thanos, though, and the other gods were still out chasing the original combat sounds.

Mateo was thinking hard about a way out of this mess. He couldn't even see where the other students were; they were as invisible to each other as they were to the centaurs. If they tried to talk to each other, they would give away at least some of their positions. That meant concerted action of any kind was impossible.

Mateo decided the best plan was to sneak out and try to find help. He knew the odds were against him. Once he started moving, he'd be more likely to make noise and get himself caught—and killed. Even if he got outside, he wasn't sure where Demeter, Pan, and Artemis were now, and he could easily walk into the middle of a battle. On the other hand, if he did nothing, he and everybody else would probably die. Considering they were dreaming, how serious that was he didn't know—but he didn't want to find out, either.

Walking across the floor in shoes would make more noise than walking barefoot would, so Mateo slipped out of his shoes, which he left on one of the seats. Then he cautiously stepped down toward floor level.

He couldn't hear much noise as he took a few steps on the cold mosaic floor, but one of the centaurs seemed to be moving in his direction. It could be coincidence, or the centaur might have heard something.

It took every ounce of willpower Mateo had to avoid running in panic for the nearest exit. Instead, he crept as quietly as he could toward a doorway that seemed miles away. It took more time than he wanted it to, but he made it to the door without being caught. However, his friends couldn't possibly have long before one of them was found.

Once outside, Mateo saw Ardalos and Patricius, still held helpless beneath centaur hooves. Ardalos struggled, and Patricius was barking as loudly as he could, but neither one was going to be escaping any time soon. If they had not been made by Hephaestus, they would already have been crushed beneath those same hooves, so at least that was something.

Mateo listened as well as he could over Patricius's barking. He could hear sounds of battle, but either there were a lot of echoes, or the battle was all around them now. Either way, he couldn't tell in which direction he might find any of the gods.

He looked back. Patricius could probably smell his way to at least one of them, but Patricius was stuck where he was—unless Mateo did something to free him.

At this point, that would be a much higher-risk proposition than going off alone to find one of the gods, even with a battle of some kind going on, but what choice did Mateo really have? He didn't have the luxury of searching the whole city.

Ardalos was pinned by two centaurs, but the smaller Patricius had only one on him at this point. The mechanical dog still appeared to be intact, so if the centaur could be forced to move enough to free Patricius, he should be able to run and find help. The question was, how could Mateo get something as big as a centaur to move?

Mateo looked at the ground, littered with arrows from earlier. An arrow would be a crude weapon for hand-to-hand combat, but it might be a decent way of surprising the centaur.

Picking one of the arrows up, Mateo crept over and rammed it into the centaur's arm as hard as he could. He had no idea how to make his attack effective, and the centaur probably wasn't hurt that badly, but the beast shouted and swung at the spot where Mateo was standing, knocking him backward with such force that he ended up on the ground.

He also shifted his hooves just enough for Patricius to get free.

"Patricius, run and get help!" Mateo yelled, knowing he was giving all three centaurs his exact position.

The dog took off faster than any flesh-and-blood animal ever could have. Mateo doubted if even the centaurs could outrun him.

Of course, they weren't trying to. All three of them were aiming arrows in the direction from which his voice had come.

Two of the arrows bounced off his linothorax, but the third scratched his arm. By then Mateo had scrambled off the ground and staggered in the general direction Patricius had gone.

The centaur who had been holding Patricius took off in pursuit. He could easily outrun Mateo, but he still couldn't see him, so he was moving slowly enough for Mateo to keep ahead of him—but only for a while. Barefoot, Mateo felt the roughness of the paving stones in what passed for a road and knew that he wasn't going to be able to run even as fast as normal.

Then he saw his blood on the ground and knew that the centaur could track him easily using his blood trail. Covering the wound with his hand to slow the blood flow, Mateo did what little he could to run faster. Every step scraped his feet, but he hoped not enough to make him bleed. All he needed now was a second blood trail.

The centaur was gaining on him and had readied another arrow. Even if it bounced off the linothorax again, it would verify his position.

Just as Mateo was sure his luck had failed him, Patricius came bounding around the corner, with Demeter following close behind.

"How dare you intrude upon my holy city?" she demanded. The centaur, brave enough when he was only facing high school students, was visibly shaken by the sudden appearance of a goddess.

"I meant no offense," he said with surprising humility.

"Yet you invaded my city, and even my temple," the goddess said. "How could that not be offensive?"

With a wave of her hand, she transformed the centaur into an ordinary horse. "If you would act like an animal, at least be a useful one.

"Take off your cap so I can find you easily," Demeter said to Mateo. Patricius must have realized Mateo was near and prompted her.

Much to Mateo's surprise, as soon as his cap was off, Demeter swept him up in her arms and started running with him. Patricius barked along behind.

"I can walk," Mateo muttered, embarrassed to be carried like a baby.

"Not fast enough," said Demeter. Though not as fast as Hermes, she was certainly running faster than Mateo could.

Demeter reached the temple just in time, turning each centaur into a horse as she went. By the time they reached the others, Yasmin and Keisha had both suffered wounds, but no one was seriously injured. Demeter waited for Artemis and Pan to join them, then rushed off to get appropriate salve for their wounds.

While she was gone, the others made Mateo tell his story. He didn't like to brag, so they had to drag it out of him, but eventually, they got most of it.

"You are very brave...for a man," said Artemis.

"For someone of any gender," said Pan. For once, Artemis did not seem to mind being corrected.

Demeter returned with a salve that smelled like honey and caused the students' various wounds to heal almost instantly, leaving no scar.

"What is that?" asked Yong, looking at the almost-glowing ointment.

"It is a compound made from ambrosia, the food of gods," said Demeter as simply as if she were giving him a recipe for brownies.

"Does that mean...we'll become like you?" asked Mateo.

"From what I'm told, it sounds as if you're already braver than some of us," said Demeter, making Mateo blush. "To answer your question, no, not without a great deal of special preparation, as I tried to do with Demophoon. Though you might prove worthy of such a gift, you must soon leave us, must you not? I doubt any change I wrought here would follow you back."

"Which reminds me, we've lost a lot of time we could have spent on our quest for Patrick," said Yong.

"I know—and in a most suspicious way," agreed Demeter. "Little of what just happened makes sense."

"What do you mean?" asked Yasmin.

"Except for old, wise Cheiron, who comes from different stock, being a son of Cronus, centaurs are wild and unruly at best. Their actions would not surprise me were it not for the circumstances. Normally, they stick to the wild and hardly ever attack cities. Not only that, but, ignorant as they are, they know this is a holy place. They have enough sense of self-preservation not to attack temples and similar sites, yet in this case, they showed not a moment's hesitation in doing so."

"They clearly had encouragement from someone with a lot of magic," said Artemis. "Aside from the ones you saw, there were a few others, but not enough to create all the noise we heard. Someone invisible even to us was creating battle noise to confuse us. Not only that, but the centaurs we found were fortified by magic. We had a much harder time besting them than we should have."

"It could be the work of Ares," suggested Pan. "I hear he has a grudge against one of our guests, and battle noises are one of his specialties."

Demeter shook her head. "He would never attack so near Athens for fear of the wrath of Athena, and I've never known him to use centaurs as troops."

"The location from which they seem to have come provides a clue," said Artemis. "We cannot be sure, but at least one witness saw them emerge from the Pluotonion."

Seeing the puzzled looks from the students, Demeter explained. "The Pluotonion is a temple somewhat to the east of here. Since the rise of Eleusinian mysteries, it has been a place of worship for my son, Plutus, the god of living wealth grown from the soil. However, it was originally dedicated to Pluto, or Hades as you know him, the god of dead wealth—the gold, silver, and gems that lie in the ground and all belong to him. More to the point, there is an entrance to the Underworld within it."

"You mean—" began Keisha.

"Yes, this more or less proves that Hades is involved," Demeter said.

"It doesn't prove that at all," said Pan. "Hades has never used centaurs, either. Nor does he have an obvious motive."

"That we know of," said Demeter. "The fact we do not know of it doesn't mean there isn't one. Before he kidnapped Persephone, I had no idea he even knew she existed, much less desired her for a wife."

"One thing seems certain," said Artemis. "Our visitors are in more danger than we imagined. I am not the strategist Athena is, but even I can tell you the other party of centaurs, who were raging off in the direction of my own temple, were just a distraction. They seemed to have no obvious purpose other than to wreak very loud and visible havoc, exactly the kind of thing that would draw us off to investigate. That left the other group free to try to capture the visitors— or worse."

"In that case, why were the ones that came after us not also magically reinforced?" asked Yong.

"I'm guessing whoever sent them was not expecting them to have so much trouble taking you," said Artemis. "Whatever god is responsible knew you were accompanied by other gods but underestimated how resourceful you would be in resisting capture."

"One part of that bothers me," said Keisha. "The centaurs weren't surprised when we became invisible, so they must have known we could. If a god supercharged the centaurs you fought, wouldn't he have at least given the ones he sent after us the ability to see through invisibility?"

Artemis shrugged. "Not being Apollo, I don't have all the answers. I'm still inclined to think that whoever is behind this simply underestimated you."

"A more interesting question is why would anyone take the trouble to attack a few visitors to our world?" asked Pan. "What possible reason could anyone with that much power have to fear mere mortals?"

"An excellent question," said Hermes, striding into the room. Thanos followed him, carrying a golden branch that glittered in the lamplight of the sanctuary.

"Perhaps the attack was a distraction to keep us from seeing something else," the messenger of the gods suggested. "The Thracian attack Athena was expecting seems to have been a false rumor, though I suppose one could yet come. Even the kidnapping of a mortal from Olympus could be a way to divert our attention. There may be a deeper design here than we have yet guessed."

"Perhaps we need to visit my brother again," suggested Artemis.

"Time is short for these mortals to find their friend, so I do not think we dare journey all the way to Hyperborea again. After all, we have no guarantee that Apollo will have been able to discern more than he did the first time. I think instead we should visit Poseidon, the next god Apollo suggested could help us."

Demeter shook her head. "I would not visit Poseidon. How can we be sure he is not in some way involved in whatever conspiracy is afoot?"

Hermes pondered for a moment, then said, "It is true that visiting him has its dangers, especially if, as Apollo told us, he is still in his palace beneath the sea. If something goes wrong, even Zeus would have a hard time rescuing us. Yet we must brave even worse danger in the Underworld, and Apollo did say Poseidon had a way to help us."

"All right," said Demeter grudgingly, "but at least take the time to think of a strategy. Why not go to Dionysus first? He is much less likely to be involved in this plot."

"At times, he has centaurs in his entourage," said Pan. "He can beguile beasts as well as men. It is true, however, that he has never joined any conspiracy I know of."

"His encouragement of unrestrained excess concerns me," said Artemis, "but it is not as if we have to swim out of an ocean of wine to be free of him; escape would be relatively easy if something went wrong."

"If someone is after our mortal guests for some reason, changing our itinerary might spoil their plans," Pan pointed out. "They could be readying an undersea ambush even now."

Hermes seemed reluctant to deviate from Apollo's instructions, but he had to admit Demeter, Artemis, and Pan all made good points, so in the end, he agreed.

"Dionysus is not yet where Apollo said he would be, though," Hermes pointed out. "Apollo suggested Thebes, but he is still on Naxos—not that that matters, for the extra trip will not be long for me."

"I need to stay here and watch over the harvest," said Demeter, "but as I do, I will listen for any unusual events that may shed light on this conspiracy."

"Thank you, Aunt. Your help has been invaluable," said Hermes.

They all said their goodbyes, and then Hermes swirled the group off to Naxos. Just as he said, the slightly longer distance made very little difference.

They found Dionysus celebrating in the Melanes Valley, a place whose dark soil Hermes said had been much blessed by Demeter, who also had a temple on the island. Aside from grapevines, which apparently tended to sprout wherever the wine god held court, the place was green with olive trees, lemon trees, and too many other types of vegetation to count.

They wouldn't have needed a nose as good as Patricius's to find the god, for the closer they got to him, the heavier the air became with the scent of wine.

When they first caught sight of Dionysus himself, he was seated on a surprisingly tame looking panther. He looked even younger than Hermes, and his features were softer, almost feminine, though there was power in his eyes, which seemed at first to be as gentle as his face but became more intense the longer one looked into them, almost as if one could see clear into eternity through them.

He was crowned with a wreath of ivy leaves and wore a long robe. In one hand, he held a thyrsus, a long staff tipped with a pine cone, and in the other, he held a golden goblet filled with wine. In contrast to the restless energy Hermes projected, Dionysus put out a come-and-stay-awhile vibe.

Next to the god sat a beautiful woman wearing a small gold crown and a dress that reminded Thanos of the images of women in Minoan art he had seen, with elaborate patterns in reddish brown, off-white, and golden yellow. The only difference was that the woman's breasts were not exposed. Thanos sighed but figured that was probably for the best under the circumstances.

If this couple was hard to take one's eyes off of, their companions nonetheless demanded attention. The group was dominated by satyrs—goat men much like Pan—some playing panpipes and some dancing wildly with beautiful nymphs, their body language suggesting that later they would do far more than just dance. There were also a couple of centaurs, as Pan had predicted, though they were not at the moment dancing. Completing the group were women who must have been maenads. They were dancing in elaborate patterns, though their eyes had a trance-like stare. Pan stared back at them and the nymphs with particular appreciation, and it was not hard for Thanos to guess why he had voted to visit Dionysus before Poseidon.

Dionysus waved his thyrsus, and the dancers parted to allow the students and their accompanying gods to move close enough to speak.

"Welcome, family and guests!" said Dionysus, raising his goblet to them. "I'm sure you could use some wine after your long journey,"

"Thank you, brother, but our haste is urgent," said Hermes quickly, after which he explained the nature of their quest. Keisha wondered how tired he was of having to do that all the time.

Predictably, instead of knowing immediately what they needed and just giving it to them, Dionysus noticed Artemis scowling at the cavorting satyrs.

"Honestly, sister, you need to learn how to relax," said the god of wine. "You spend all day every day in a state of tremendous tension. Sooner or later it will snap you like a twig."

"Just because I have self-discipline and purpose in my life does not mean I am tense," said Artemis, looking tense—and looking as if she would like nothing better than to put an arrow right between Dionysus's mocking eyes.

"Sometimes one needs to forget one's purpose for just a little while," said Dionysus, taking a sip of his wine. Turning to the students, he said, "Is not the thinking among your world's physicians that stress is harmful? Without joy in one's life, how can there not be stress?"

"I have the joy of the hunt and many others you could not appreciate in your drunken stupor, *little* brother," said Artemis.

Dionysus stiffened, and his smile faded.

"Younger than you I am, but not, therefore, less wise." Turning to the students again, he asked, "Do not your psychologists often argue that bottling up emotions is not a good thing? Will not those feelings eventually burst forth, doing harm not only to the person but to those around her? I ask, for I know of no god who strangles her emotions more than my judgmental sister."

"You lie!" shouted Artemis.

Yong was reminded of Shakespeare's line about protesting too much, but he knew better than to say anything.

"Dionysus, we should—" began Hermes.

"Too late, brother," said Dionysus, "for our sister has insulted me and must be answered. I am no liar, merely someone who tells her truths she would not hear. Let our guests judge, then, sister, which of us is in the right. What will they think, I wonder, when they hear the tale of the Calydonian Boar?"

Both Artemis and Hermes started to protest, but something dark in Dionysus's eyes stopped them. He was determined to tell his story, and they could see it.

"I knew King Oeneus of Calydon well, for he had welcomed me into his home and acknowledged me as a god—not something everyone did, for as my sister points out, I was the youngest of the great gods, and I had to struggle for recognition at first. Oeneus, however, opened his eyes and knew me for who I was, and I rewarded him by teaching him wine-making, which knowledge, in turn, he spread throughout his kingdom. He was a good man, a pious man— but Artemis sought vengeance against him for the most frivolous reason."

"It was not frivolous," insisted Artemis.

"We will let our visitors decide," said Dionysus. "It was the custom throughout Aetolia to make sacrifices to all the major gods at the beginning of every harvest. One time Oeneus forgot the sacrifice to Artemis—"

"He did not forget. It was a deliberate insult, an expression of his hubris," Artemis insisted. "The altar was right there—how could he have missed it?"

"Nonetheless, every writer agrees that he did," said Dionysus calmly. "And what did you do? You sent an enormous boar to ravage the countryside."

"He could have done the righteous thing and begged for my forgiveness," said Artemis. "Instead, he recruited warriors to kill it."

"He tried to appease you, but you refused to heed his prayers," said Dionysus. "In any case, it was during the Calydonian Boar hunt that a great many good men died—and not just from the boar.

"Oeneus and his wife Althaea had a son, Meleager, a warrior so excellent some men whispered he must really be the son of Ares. In any case, on the seventh day after his birth, Althaea received a visit from the three Fates, though whether in dream or reality no one knows.

"Clotho said that Meleager would be brave, and Lachesis said he would be noble—but Atropos, the Fate who cuts the thread of life, said that Meleager would live only until a particular log burned up completely in the fire. Hearing that prophecy, Althaea snatched the log out of the fire and hid it in a chest."

"I'm sorry to interrupt, but how could those prophecies all be true?" asked

Yasmin.

"Something must have become snarled in the weaving of the Fates," said Dionysus. "That would explain why they appeared to Althaea, for they hardly ever directly reveal destiny to any mortal. They needed to do it that time so that Althaea would save her son and reconcile the incompatible prophecies.

"Meleager led the hunting party, which included a number of great heroes who had also been part of the crew of the *Argo,* the group that brought back the golden fleece. Among them was Atalanta, one of Artemis's favorites, a girl abandoned by her father because he was disappointed she was not a boy. Left to die in the wilderness, Atalanta would surely have perished, but a she-bear found her and nursed her. Later, some hunters found her and raised her as their own. Atalanta did bond with the hunters, but when she learned how her own father had rejected her, she vowed to remain a virgin and eventually became part of Artemis's hunting party, one of its most skillful members, in fact.

"She left Artemis's band to sail with the *Argo,* distinguishing herself then and later by being more skillful than many of the men."

"She was in all things exemplary," said Artemis. "How does that in any way prove your point?"

"It makes me wonder how you could risk such a one by allowing her so near the monster you had created—but Atalanta is not actually my evidence; she is merely background our friends will need to know. You see, Meleager had at some point fallen in love with Atalanta, as men often become enamored of women they can never have."

"Blame Aphrodite or Eros, for that, but not me," said Artemis. "Or blame the foolish men for wanting what they *know* they cannot have."

"Let me finish," snapped Dionysus. "Their love is not your fault, either. Unfortunately, it did lead to Meleager's downfall.

"Atalanta's presence caused friction from the first. Her fellow Arcadians initially refused to hunt with a woman, until Meleager announced on behalf of his father that the hunt would be canceled if the bickering continued. How Oeneus could actually do that and just leave the boar on the loose I don't know, but Meleager got what he wanted—Atalanta in the hunt and grateful to him.

"The hunt itself was largely a catastrophe. Two centaurs who had joined the party decided to rape Atalanta, and she had to kill both of them before proceeding with the hunt—"

"Men—" began Artemis.

"Stop interrupting me!" demanded Dionysus, and for a moment they all felt a moment of disorientation.

"Dionysus, remember our guests," said Hermes.

Dionysus, who had momentarily seemed much larger and fiercer, as well as more wild-eyed, bowed apologetically, but then he immediately pressed on with the story before Artemis could jump in again.

"Ancaeus, one of the very hunters who at first refused to hunt with Atalanta and then mocked her hunting technique even though she had drawn first blood, was mauled by the boar and died. Several other hunters perished, some at the hands of the boar, some at each other's hands through accident. The death toll could have been much worse, with even heroes like the fathers of Achilles and Ajax, dying as well, but Amphiarus, co-king of Argos, managed to get off a shot that blinded the boar, and Meleager dealt the boar a death blow with his spear.

"Oeneus had promised the boar's hide to the hunter who killed it, and most men thought that honor should have been Meleager's. However, still hopelessly infatuated with Atalanta, Meleager argued that the hide should be given to her, that the wound she inflicted would have been fatal in time.

"Meleager's maternal uncles objected to this, the eldest, Plexippus, arguing that the prize belonged by right to Meleager, but that, if he would not take it, it should go to Plexippus himself, by virtue of his being Oeneus's senior male relative. Meleager awarded it to Atalanta anyway, at which point the uncles tried to seize it from her, and in the ensuing scuffle, Meleager killed them both.

"Nor was that the end of the bloodshed, for the Curetes, the people ruled by another one of Meleager's uncles, declared war on Calydon, demanding that the boar's hide be given to Iphicles, another uncle whom it was falsely claimed had actually drawn first blood.

"The Calydonian forces should have been able to hold their own, but Meleager, after his mother had cursed him for killing some of her brothers, refused to fight, and the Calydonians suffered heavy losses.

"Finally, Meleager's wife, forgotten earlier in his passion for Atalanta, reminded him of how much the people of Calydon would suffer if the city fell, and at last he re-entered the battle. Protected by the fact that the fatal log had never finished burning, Meleager could not be killed, not even by an arrow from Apollo, and he eventually won the battle.

"Unfortunately, in the process of winning, he had killed all his remaining uncles, making his mother mad with grief. Afterward, she took out the log, threw it in the fire, and watched it burn. He died, of course, seemingly of his battle wounds but really of the fact that the Fates' condition for his death had been fulfilled.

"Althaea, regretting what she had done, hanged herself, as did Meleager's unfortunate wife. Altogether, hundreds of people died—and all because a virtuous man neglected by accident to make one sacrifice. If that isn't an example of pent-up emotions leading to excess, I don't know what is. Every drop of that blood, Artemis, is on your hands."

"I admit to sending the boar, as was my right," said Artemis, "but even the way you tell the story, the rest sounds like foolish mortals doing foolish things."

"All of those foolish things came about because of the stupid boar," insisted Dionysus. "Good men and even a few good women died, through no fault of their own."

Artemis smiled coldly. "On the contrary, most of the deaths seem to flow from the inability of men to accept a woman as an equal, even if she proves herself to be their equal or even their superior. Before our guests decide—"

"Our guests never agreed to judge and will not," said Hermes, eager to keep mortals out of the crossfire.

"Be that as it may," said Artemis, "they are entitled to hear the full story of our host, who pretends to be the bringer of joy when he is, in fact, the bringer of pain. He is no saver of sanity but rather a giver of madness.

"When King Lycurgus of the Edonians refused to accept Dionysus as a god and attacked his party with terrifying force, Dionysus threw himself into the sea to escape, allowing his followers to be captured. Why he didn't display his power as a god and save them right away, he alone can explain. Later he drove Lycurgus mad, and the king, thinking he was chopping down a grape vine, dismembered his own son.

"The crops died then, and, after the land had remained barren and starvation threatened, the Edonians sent a message to the oracle of Delphi, and

Apollo answered that only the death of Lycurgus would bring fertility back to the soil. When they heard that, the Edonians had Lycurgus tied to wild horses and torn apart."

Dionysus took a big swallow of wine and laughed. "So your argument is that your persecution of a good man for a small omission is somehow justified, whereas my just punishment of a man for blasphemously and brutally attacking me and my followers is not."

"You made him chop up his own son—"

"I did no such thing. I inflicted madness upon him, but he was a violent man. His nature determined the form his madness took. On other occasions when I punished people with madness, such as the Argive women after Acrisius banned me from Argos, they simply wandered in the wilderness like beasts.

"No, Lycurgus brought about his own destruction, sanctioned by the other gods, including your own brother."

"You say madness is given its form by the afflicted themselves, but it is odd that those afflicted by you so often express that madness through violence to themselves or others," Artemis pointed out. "After some shepherds killed one of the first winemakers, Icarius, the Athenian women you struck mad hanged themselves, one by one, until the shepherds appeased you."

"The madness brought out that which was already within them," insisted Dionysus. "Yet again, you do not consider the seriousness of the offenses, either, for those shepherds committed murder, rather than merely omitting to sacrifice."

"Then what of Pentheus, king of Thebes, your mother's city, whom you had torn apart by his own frenzied mother and aunts?" asked Artemis, looking smug.

"What of him, indeed? A man who not only denied my divinity but sought to arrest my followers and boasted he would cut off my head—what god would tolerate such offenses? Certainly, you would not, *dear* Artemis. Again, the crimes were greater than that of Oeneus, and the death toll far less than inflicted by your boar.

"In fact, it surprises me you do not see that one of the objections to my worship was the liberating effect it had on women, called on to participate in religion not controlled by their fathers, husbands, or sons."

"I have little use for the rule of men," conceded Artemis, "but I inspire women to avoid men, not to kill them. Besides, men are not your only targets, for when the daughters of Minyas denied your divinity and devoted themselves to weaving, the work of Athena, during your festival, did you not turn them into bats?"

"You keep repeating the same weak argument," insisted Dionysus. "Over and over you give examples in which the offense is greater than that of Oeneus and punishment less severe. If some of the people struck with madness acted violently, it was because they had tried to bury violent emotions within them and paid the price for it.

"I also wonder why you do not mention the Tyrrhenian pirates in your tedious list of my offenses. They mistook me for a human boy and captured me, intending to rape me and then sell me into slavery. Their helmsmen, who looked with his eyes of spirit as well as flesh, could see I was a god and warned the master and the crew, but no one believed him.

"Then the men heard the hissing of snakes and saw grape vines growing up from nowhere, twining around the masts, dyeing the sales wine purple with their juice, and they began to doubt their evil course, but it was already too late.

"I turned myself into a roaring lion, frightening the pirates so much that they dove overboard. Rather than letting them drown, I changed them into dolphins. To the helmsman I showed both mercy and favor, for he alone had acted righteously, and I forgave him his past piratical acts."

"Even I would not say you acted too harshly in that case," said Artemis, sounding humble for a moment. Then she added, her tone sounding progressively more and more confident, "Let us speak, though, of your treatment of Orpheus—for that, surely even you can find no excuse.

"Orpheus was the greatest mortal musician who ever lived, the son of King Oeagrus of Thrace and Calliope, the muse of eloquence and epic poetry. Raised by his mother at Pimpleia, practically in the shadow of Mount Olympus itself, Orpheus had Apollo as his music tutor. So fond was my brother of Orpheus that Apollo gave him as a gift one of the three original lyres fashioned by Hermes.

"Dionysus, can you deny how much joy Orpheus brought into the world with his music?"

"I completely agree," said Dionysus. "Indeed, if Apollo and I agree on one thing, it is on the excellence of Orpheus."

"Music was not his only contribution, either, for in his travels he brought civilization to savages, even teaching cannibals to live entirely on fruit."

"Again I agree," said Dionysus. "And again I wonder what the story of Orpheus has to do with our argument."

"It is necessary for our guests to understand the context," Artemis insisted. "Orpheus broke new ground in another area, for he was the only man the Greeks called a hero who was not a warrior. The *Argo* could never have succeeded in its mission without him, for only he could counteract the song of the Sirens and enable the crew to get past them."

"I'm still agreeing, for I too believe the early definition of heroism to be too narrow," said Dionysus.

"Yet you tried to copy that old heroic ideal when you fought wars against the Amazons and against the kingdoms of India," Artemis pointed out. "You made war in the east so much it was said your exploits inspired the eastern conquests of Alexander the Great."

"I confess that when I was younger, I feared to be thought too feminine," admitted Dionysus. "In my divine adolescence, I tried to prove my manhood by feats of arms. I have learned since the folly of such posturing, for violence does not make someone a man. However, it does not make someone a woman, either, and the Amazons needed a lesson in humility. As for the Indians, I made peace with them and taught them the secrets of winemaking when I realized how wrong I had been."

Artemis was frowning, probably over Dionysus's criticism of the Amazons, but instead of responding, she pushed forward with the story of Orpheus.

"For all his ability, Orpheus was not immune to tragedy, for his beautiful bride, Eurydice, accidentally stepped on a snake and died on the very day of their wedding.

"Unable to bear such a loss, Orpheus did what few mortals have dared, and only one, Heracles, have ever done successfully—he invaded the Underworld. However, unlike Heracles, he did not do it with violence, but with the power of music. He had long had the ability to charm even the beasts with his music, and then he demonstrated that even magical beasts like

Cerberus, the Underworld's three-headed guard dog. Even Underworld gods like Charon, the ferryman, were not immune to that compelling power.

"Arriving safely at the court of Hades and Persephone, Orpheus moved even them with his playing—or perhaps Hades was only pretending his stony heart had been moved. No one really knows. What we do know is that Hades, from whose fingers the souls of the dead are nearly impossible to pry, offered Orpheus a chance to bring Eurydice back to the land of the living. All Orpheus had to do was not look back as Eurydice followed him, and if they completed the journey out of the Underworld that way, Eurydice would be returned to life.

"The task seemed simple enough, but the trip was long, and Orpheus began to wonder if Hades had tricked him. He became more and more impatient to know the truth, and just before he reached the cave mouth through which he would re-enter the world, he finally could stand the wait no longer and glanced back.

"Eurydice was indeed right behind him, but as soon as he looked back, she was gone. He tried to sing his way back into the Underworld but found the way blocked. Hades had, as our visitors would say in their world, improved his security.

"After that, Orpheus was never the same. He still played, but sadly now, and even the animals wept to hear him. You would have thought he had suffered enough, but apparently not, for it was then that Dionysus killed him!"

"I certainly did not!" snapped Dionysus.

"Your maenads tore him to pieces for neglecting your worship and that of the other gods in favor of Apollo's."

"I've heard that ridiculous gossip, too, but that makes no sense, and you know it," Dionysus insisted. "That Orpheus revered Apollo is beyond dispute, but he never worshiped him exclusively nor neglected his duties to me—and I can't imagine why his loss would have caused such a reaction. That he might have slighted Hades or even Persephone I could have understood, but why would he have blamed me?

"You need to remember that Orpheus spread more than just music; he spread religion as well. It was he who started the cult of Hecate in Aegina—"

"Hecate? I had forgotten that," said Hermes, suddenly looking more worried.

"Yes, Hecate, and it was he who helped popularize the worship of Demeter and Persephone in Laconia as well. He was so associated with Demeter's worship at one point that at Taygetus the priests kept a wooden statue of him in Demeter's temple. Would he have abandoned her worship as well—and if so, why was his statue still seen in her temple centuries later? An even better question would be why you do not blame Demeter or any of the other gods for his death? If he stopped worshiping all of them except Apollo, certainly I would not have been the only one who had a grievance. You yourself would be as good a suspect as I—better, in fact, since Orpheus believed in love and was far closer to my philosophy than to yours."

"I would never have acted against someone so close to my brother," said Artemis, "and if I had, he would have fallen by one of my silver arrows, not by the claws of your maenads."

"Ah, a good point," conceded Dionysus, "but you forget the most important piece of evidence—Orpheus's obvious dedication to my worship, even more than that of Demeter. He is often credited with encouraging my inclusion in the Eleusinian Mysteries, and who was at the center of his own Orphic Mysteries? I was."

"Those texts may not even be by him, or be earlier than the death of Eurydice," Artemis pointed out.

"The ancients thought they were by him, and what did they think gave Orpheus his unique insight into the afterlife? His journey to the Underworld, after which they claimed he studied so diligently that he unearthed the secrets of the gods themselves.

"Personally, I'd rather believe that Orpheus, though deep in sorrow over the death of Eurydice, turned his pain into the energy to help others toward a better afterlife. Perhaps he was searching in the beginning for a way to restore Eurydice to life, but if so he found something else instead.

"Pardon me for interrupting, but I'm confused," said Yasmin. "I know you're the god of wine, but how are you connected with the afterlife?"

"The Orphic literature gives me a different background, one impossible to reconcile with the traditional story—unless one believes in reincarnation, which some later Greeks did," Dionysus explained.

"Anyway, the Orphic story goes that I was born originally under the name of Zagreus and that I was the child of Zeus and Persephone. Moreover, it asserts that Zeus had intended me to be his heir."

"You are arrogant to believe that nonsense," said Artemis.

"You only say so because you are convinced that if anything happens to Zeus, Apollo will take over," said Dionysus. "In any case, Hera, who in the traditional story was responsible for the death of my mother, in this version heard about Zeus's plan. Desiring to secure the throne of heaven for one of her own children, she convinced the Titans, some of whom were still roaming around loose in the Orphic version, to kill me. I was just a child at that point, so they were able to trick me into letting them get close enough to grab me, after which they tore me apart and ate me in an attempt to get around my immortality.

"Athena saw what was happening and rescued my heart, carrying it to Zeus on Olympus. Zeus was able to use the heart to enable me to be reborn through Semele, but when he learned what the Titans had done, he blasted them with thunderbolts and reduced them to ashes.

"The Orphic literature goes on to say that from these ashes the human race arose. That was an attempt to explain why humans were capable of both good and evil: the good came from the soul, which was derived from Zagreus, while the evil came from the body, which was derived from the Titans.

"According to the literature, that was the secret that Orpheus discovered: the Titan part of the human heritage was holding them back, keeping them in darkness in the Underworld, then forcing them to reincarnate over and over. The key to achieving a blessed afterlife was to, as our visitors would say, 'get in touch' with their Zagreus part by living the right kind of life to break the cycle."

"Very like Buddhism in some ways," said Yong.

"Most likely copied from Buddhism centuries after Orpheus lived," said Artemis, sneering at Dionysus. "Brother, you can't possibly believe any of that."

"I like to think there is a little bit of me in everyone," he replied, matching her sneer with a smirk. "But whether Orpheus really became a great mystic and religious teacher after the death of Eurydice or not, people in later generations believed he had—a belief that could hardly have taken root if they remembered him as a worshiper of Apollo alone."

Artemis shook her head. "None of that explains why your maenads killed him."

"No, it doesn't, but there is a reason for that. Filled with grief, poor Orpheus swore to never love another woman. Unfortunately, many of the women of Thrace loved him—and some of them were maenads. When he rejected them, they mingled their anger with their maenad frenzy, and they came after him, intending to kill him. The sticks and stones they threw fell to the ground, unable to do violence when confronted with the music of Orpheus. Unfortunately, the maenads themselves made enough noise to keep the music from reaching their ears. Orpheus did not even try to escape, and they tore him to pieces—the same way Zagreus died in the Orphic myths.

"His head floated down the Hebrus and out to sea, still singing, until it finally drifted ashore on Lesbos, where the people gave it burial and where an oracle arose in his honor, the only one connected to a mortal rather than a god, and it became famous as far east as Babylon. The Muses lovingly gathered up the rest of his body and buried it, and they also memorialized his lyre in the stars, so that as long as men looked skyward, they would remember the music of Orpheus."

Fatima realized tears were running down her cheeks and wiped them off as fast as she could. Artemis, however, was not moved.

"So women whose love of Orpheus turned to hatred by rejection were responsible? I think you fabricated that story yourself with the aim of convincing me you were innocent, since you know how little respect I have for love."

"Yes, if you're going to blame anyone, blame Aphrodite," said Dionysus, though it was clear from his expression he was joking. "But I did not invent the story just now. It is at least as old as Ovid, who wrote more than two thousand years ago.

"For that matter, the maenads are not the only ones who may have felt the sting of unrequited love because of Orpheus. There is a cryptic story in Orphic literature about Orpheus charming the goddess Hecate into giving special privileges to Orphic initiates. How did he charm her, I wonder? Might he have overdone it and actually caused her to fall in love with him? It is also sometimes said it was Hecate who sent the snake that cut short Eurydice's life. It seems to me the goddess has a far better motive for hating Orpheus than I do."

"Ridiculous!" Artemis snapped.

"Haven't we had enough of this pointless argument?" asked the woman sitting next to Dionysus. "If not, I, Ariadne, the wife of Dionysus, demand to be heard. *She is able to insult her*

"Artemis, you are cold and unfeeling," began Ariadne. Some of the students gasped inwardly, but Artemis did not immediately respond.

not every woman agrees with Artemis

"Be a solitary hunter if you must, but do not look with such scorn upon we women who would find life cold without love. Do not look so judgmentally upon my husband, either, for I know he is not capable of the crime against Orpheus that you allege.

"I grew up as a princess in Crete, only barely mortal. My father, King Minos, was the son of Zeus and Europa, a Phoenician princess. My mother, Pasiphae, was the daughter of the sun god, Helios and the Oceanid, Perseis, and thus a minor goddess in her own right. You would have thought that with such ancestry I would have lived a joyous life, but even the gods are not always happy, and certainly their children are not.

"As a young woman, I had found no one to love, though I had many suitors, for at that time Crete was a powerful kingdom and controlled much of mainland Greece. Sadly, I fell in love with the handsome son of Poseidon, Theseus, even betraying my father by helping Theseus with his quest and then getting him off Crete alive.

"Deprived of my family, I took comfort from the fact that I would be the wife of Theseus, but such was not my destiny. When we stopped at Naxos, I fell asleep, and when I awakened, Theseus and his crew were gone. At the time, I thought he had abandoned me, only finding out much later that he was under the influence of a spell and came back for me after the spell faded.

"I was not there, however, for in the meantime Dionysus found me, dried my tears, and fell in love with me. Soon after he made me his wife, and then he made me immortal so that we might be together for all eternity. In the years since, we have become the proud parents of many sons: kings, lords, and Argonauts—great sons of a great father.

"In all the time since we wed, he has never given me one reason to complain, but has been ever the perfect husband, though I know you, Artemis,

Not all gods have unhappy marriages

would deny that such a thing is possible."

"Let us say it is...rare, at least in my experience," said Artemis with surprising tact.

"Well then, he is one in a million," said Ariadne, "and I would swear he is no murderer. The mortals he has punished well deserved it, and Orpheus clearly did not."

"I am still not convinced," Artemis admitted, "but it does seem pointless to pursue the argument further, particularly as I have committed myself to a quest."

"Speaking of which," said Hermes, seizing the opportunity, "Dionysus, have you thought of a way in which you might fulfill Apollo's prophecy by aiding our party?"

"I have indeed," said Dionysus, "for I have heard you must yet visit my uncle, Poseidon, and he is temperamental enough to make Artemis seem agreeable by comparison."

Artemis scowled at that but refused to be baited.

"However, he is fond of certain wines, and one, in particular, that is rare in this region." Dionysus waved his thyrsus, and a couple of satyrs carried out a large oak cask.

"This vintage is made from the fruit of the horsewood tree and is called sea grape wine," Dionysus explained. "The tree grows only in the Caribbean, but Poseidon somehow developed a taste for this particular wine. I suppose it was fated to be so, given the association with sea and horses, both of which he loves. If you bring this cask to him as a gift, he may be better disposed toward you—though I make no guarantees."

"I am sure he will appreciate such a gift," said Hermes. "Thank you, brother, and now we shall be...wait, where's Pan?"

"Can you not guess?" said Artemis, nodding toward the bushes behind which Pan had doubtless led some maenad or nymph—or perhaps more than one. "I shall bring him back."

"You've had enough...stress for one day," said Hermes. "I will retrieve him, and then we shall be on our way."

Chapter 17: Poseidon

The students and their divine escorts walked down to the coast, where the weather had taken a sudden turn for the worse. The sky was gray, and the waves crashed against the sand as if they were trying to drill into the earth.

"I need to ask Poseidon's permission to bring you down," said Hermes, who then turned and dived into the rough sea. *the meeting may not go well*

"Poseidon is angry," said Artemis, looking worriedly at the surf.

"Poseidon is always angry," said Pan, still sulking over being forced to leave his maenad.

"This is a sudden change in mood, though," said Artemis. "It bodes no good."

Neither Pan nor Artemis acted as if they felt like talking much. Artemis seemed as if she was thinking about Orion. After a while she walked down the beach a short distance and stared out to sea, as if expecting him to come striding back over the waves and apologize for the wrongs he had done her—or perhaps convincingly deny their truth and rejoin her on the hunt.

Pan wandered in the other direction, though he was more likely scouting for willing nymphs than remembering some lost love.

Both gods clearly wanted to be alone, but, mindful of the earlier centaur attack, neither ever got out of sight of the students. However, they were far enough away that the students felt comfortable talking among themselves.

"So, what do you think?" asked Mateo. "Is Artemis right, or is Dionysus?"

"I'm not sure the situation is as simple as that," said Keisha.

"Yeah, neither one is entirely right," said Yong. "I'm not willing to let Dionysus completely off the hook when he drives someone mad, and they commit heinous crimes. How do we really know he didn't push them in a particular direction?"

"On the other hand, people often use being drunk as an excuse for things," said Yasmin. "Alcohol lowers people's inhibitions, but it doesn't turn them into different people. What they do under the influence is still something they wanted to do."

"Madness is more than just ordinary drunkenness, though," said Fatima. "Lycurgus was actually hallucinating."

"Dionysus's psychological point is well taken—within limits," said Keisha. "Yeah, it's probably unhealthy to bottle up emotions instead of dealing with them, but that doesn't mean people should all do exactly what they want. Anybody remember Freud's theory about the id?" *Talking more to reader thu[s] to Mateo and Yasmin*

Thanos, Yong, and Fatima all nodded. Mateo and Yasmin looked blank.

"Just so we're all on the same page, Freud theorized that there were three parts to the human personality: the id, the ego, and the superego. The id is the instinct, the basic drives. The superego is the social constraint, the moral sense, and is sort of at war with the id, trying to restrain it, while the id is constantly trying to break free. The ego is the force that attempts to balance the two competing pressures."

"OK, that makes sense," said Mateo. "I don't know what it has to do with Greek mythology, though."

"Freud thought that our psychology found ways to express itself indirectly, both in dreams and myths. A Freudian literary critic might see Dionysus as more of an advocate for the id, while someone like Artemis, if we leave out the occasional bursts of temper all the gods seem to have, is more of an advocate for the superego."

"OK, and from that we get—what exactly?" asked Mateo. "I can't see where you're going with this."

"Freudians tend to argue that a good psychological balance is somewhere in between the two extremes. Someone who locks away all those id-based desires is going to be unhappy and unhealthy. Someone who gives into them all the time is going to end up being a rapist or a serial killer."

"I'm not a rapist or a serial killer—and I don't want to be!" insisted Mateo. "But I don't have to go around all day trying to restrain myself from killing someone."

"Calm down, I'm not saying you are," said Keisha. "All of us have antisocial impulses, but we aren't always that conscious of them because the superego checks them. We don't have to fight consciously to avoid killing someone.

"I am saying we need some superego restraint, or eventually we'd go over the deep end. The joy that comes from the freedom Dionysus represents is good—in moderation. Freedom with no restraint, though, becomes anarchy, chaos. It becomes Lycurgus chopping up his own son."

"Dionysus doesn't seem to me to just represent the id," said Mateo. "OK, so his followers look kind of like an orgy waiting to happen, but he's a happily married god himself, in that way more restrained than some we've met."

"I don't think Artemis is all superego, either," said Yasmin. "Dionysus and Pan both think she's wound a little too tightly, but I think she's doing exactly what she wants to do. It's just different from what most women in the time period wanted to do, so the men around her don't understand it.

"You know," Yasmin continued slowly, as if choosing every word carefully, "I was the one most vocal about thinking Greek mythology was bad to read in the beginning, but I'm changing my mind.

"Because it grew out of ancient Greek religion, I guess I was thinking of it as a threat to our own religious values, but I'm realizing it doesn't have to be read that way at all. These 'gods' aren't like God or Allah at all. They're more like humans, and it helps to think of them that way. They are much more powerful, sure—and they do all the good, and all the evil, that someone with superpowers might do. They're sort of like superheroes and supervillains combined."

"That's a good point," said Yong. "If we think of them as people, and ask what we can learn from their adventures, we can see things to do—and not to do—just as we can with the human characters. A while ago, Keisha mentioned abuse of power as something the example of Greek gods teaches us to avoid. Let's not also forget the bad results of vengeance. In really early times, private justice was common. If someone hurt a family member, for example, it was the responsibility of the other family members to get justice—though what they thought of as justice would look more like revenge to us. Homer lived in that kind of world, and a lot of the myths are shaped by that. The gods often react just as vengefully as mortals. The myths also show the evolution of a better way, though: the development of courts, the replacement of private justice with the rule of law, as we see in the formation of the Areopagus."

"I agree," said Thanos. "Think about the myths as part of a search, not a finished product. The early storytellers make it clear that not even the gods have all the answers.

"Think about how the way in which the gods are portrayed changes with time. Demeter starts out as a simple agricultural goddess, a bringer of harvests, and Persephone's abduction is just an etiological myth, an explanation of why we have seasons. Generations later, Demeter and Persephone star in the Eleusinian Mysteries, in which their experiences serve as a guide to the initiates, a way to achieve a better afterlife."

"Like the Orphic image of Dionysus?" asked Keisha.

"Exactly!" agreed Thanos. "Dionysus starts out as the god of wine and ends up as a savior figure, a dying god who rises again and shows the way for his followers to rise again after death. That's a lot more sophisticated way to look at him, a move from the earthly to the spiritual. Orphics ended up preaching an aesthetic lifestyle, not the pleasure-loving hedonism that the god represented in the beginning."

"And he just kept on changing with time," said Yong. "We talked before about how each society adapts stories to its own needs and values. The ancient Greeks didn't really see Apollo and Dionysus as contrasting characters, but some later societies cast them that way. I think I've read it was Nietzsche who set up the terms *Apollonian* and *Dionysian* that a lot of later literary critics and sociologists made use of. For him it was a contrast between rigidly logical, which he saw as life-denying, and creative, which he saw as life affirming. Later writers sometimes used the same terms for exactly opposite purposes. For instance, Paglia argued that all social progress in Western societies came from the revolt of Apollonian reason against Dionysian emotionalism."

"My brain hurts," said Mateo. "I need to talk about something more relaxing for a while."

Unfortunately, Mateo's wish would not be granted. Just at that moment, a soggy Hermes shot out of the waves and landed somewhat awkwardly on the shore.

"I can't get all the way down," he said. "Poseidon is blocking me."

"He dares block the messenger of Zeus?" asked Artemis. "Surely this is evidence of his involvement in whatever plot is now in motion."

"If that were true, why would Apollo send us to him?" asked Hermes. "I think there must be some other explanation."

"Poseidon needs no reason to be difficult," said Pan. "He just is. Remember, he has rebelled against Zeus before, and he might again. If he's smart enough to stay in the water this time, there wouldn't be much Zeus could do about it, short of hitting the ocean with enough thunderbolts to boil it away, killing humanity in the process."

"So you agree with Artemis that Poseidon is involved in a conspiracy?" asked Hermes.

"I hardly ever agree with Artemis," said Pan. "I don't think he is involved in the conspiracy that concerns our visitors, but who knows what he's planning?"

"Perhaps I can help," said a gentle, female voice behind them. Turning, they saw a goddess as beautiful as Aphrodite, but somewhat more aquatic. Her hair was held in a gold net, and on her brow sat a crown shaped liked golden crab claws. Her dress was blue as the sea, as were her eyes.

"I am Amphitrite," she said for the benefit of the students. "I am the wife of Poseidon, and queen of the sea, though my title is in some ways older than my marriage. My grandparents were Pontus, the sea himself, and Gaia, the earth herself, who became parents to my father, Nereus, the old man of the sea. My other grandparents were Oceanus, the great ocean that circles the earth, and Tethys, parents to my mother, Doris. Doris and Nereus became parents to the Nereids, of whom I am the eldest. No one of my generation is more attuned to the salt water parts of the world than I am."

"It sounds as if you are the perfect wife for Poseidon," said Fatima, who meant it as a compliment. However, the sorrow in Amphitrite's eyes told Fatima it might have been the wrong thing to say.

"One would have thought so," said Amphitrite, "but I always had my doubts. In fact, I fled from him at first, swimming clear out almost to where doomed Atlas upholds the sky and staying there.

"Perhaps I should have remained where I was," said Amphitrite, glancing out to sea. "When Poseidon sent Delphinus, god of dolphins, to beg me for my hand in marriage, I weakened and said yes, for who that loves sea creatures could possibly resist a dolphin?"

"Are...are you happy?" asked Fatima. It seemed like a dangerous question, but in this dream world Hera had answered, so why not Amphitrite?

Amphitrite looked out to sea again. "Poseidon is a magnificent warrior, and he commands the waves as if he was born to do exactly that. Second only to Zeus himself, he is exactly what any woman who wanted a powerful husband would want. Not only that, but all the wealth in the sea is his. Any woman who desired material things would want him as well.

"As for me, I wanted not power, nor position, nor wealth, but only a husband who would love me—or failing that, the freedom to roam the seas, dancing with my sisters and playing with the creatures of the sea, as I used to do before my marriage."

"Surely Poseidon loves someone as beautiful as you," said Mateo, surprising himself as much as anybody. He wasn't normally one for flowery compliments, but Amphitrite looked so sad that he couldn't help wanting to cheer her up.

Amphitrite smiled, but her smile was bitter, not bright.

"Perhaps he loved me. Perhaps he loves me still. Or perhaps his desire to marry me was simply because it was his way of asserting his dominion over the ocean."

"But wasn't he already king?" asked Yasmin.

"Early Greeks practiced matrilineal inheritance, which means they passed property through the women," said Thanos. "In historical times it was different, but early on, kings ruled by right of marriage, not in their own right. Some of the myths echo that earlier pattern."

"Yes, Poseidon may have been thinking in those terms. One of my grandfathers, Pontus, was the sea; my other grandfather, Oceanus, the great surrounding ocean. What better way to lay a claim to both than by marrying me, the eldest goddess related to both aquatic families?

"He said then and still says now that he loves me, but I was not his first choice. I think he always wanted Demeter, perhaps to assert his power over land as well as water. You know of the absurd way he threw himself at her while she sought Persephone. Before that, he sought the hand of Hestia, giving up only when Zeus honored her request to remain a virgin. She is the goddess of the sacred hearth, the center of the home. Marriage to her would have given Poseidon a place of honor in every single civilized dwelling.

"I would like to think he courted me for love, but to me, it seems more likely that when his two efforts to expand his empire to the land aborted, he sought me out to make sure that at least his hold on the sea was uncontested.

"You know of his petty contests with other gods to become the patron of various cities and how, after Athena had won Athens, he flooded the nearby plain. He did the same when Hera won Argos.

"I fear what he wants is not me, but power. Now that he has it, his love affairs rival in number even those of Zeus himself. Aside from Demeter, he has also loved Aphrodite. That last I might have forgiven, for what god has not loved Aphrodite at least once? But then there was some unnamed nymph, whose son was the great shapeshifter, Proteus, whom Poseidon made his seal herder. Then there was Halia, a sea goddess whose six sons still haunt the caverns of Rhodes. Then there was Gaia herself, who through Poseidon became the mother of Antaeus, a giant so fierce he made himself king of Libya by force and used the skulls of his slain enemies as a ghastly roof for Poseidon's temple."

The students noticed Hermes fidgeting, which made them more nervous. This conversation was not getting them any closer to rescuing Patrick, but having accidentally provoked Amphitrite to pour out her heart, none of them could see a polite way of interrupting.

"That was the thing about Poseidon's children," said Amphitrite. "They too often inherited their father's violent nature, making them as a group even more bloodthirsty than the children of Ares. Oh, there were exceptions, of course. Proteus is as gentle as any inhabitant of the sea. Aeolus, the god of the winds, can be gentler than his father, though he can also raise just as great a storm if he puts his mind into it. Bellerophon, Neleus, and Theseus were fine heroes, and Ancaeus made a more excellent pilot for the *Argo* than any other man living could have done. Among his sons were also some good kings in Greece as well as places as far away as North Africa and Italy.

"Unfortunately, far too many of Poseidon's sons turned their abilities to evil, for when a son of Poseidon went wrong, he went very wrong. For instance, the king of the sea produced a race of brutal Cyclopes, the opposite of those useful fellows who were blacksmiths before Hephaestus learned his craft. These ones violated the rules of hospitality by killing and eating passing travelers, all the while mocking the gods. Then there was Laestrygon, the founder of another race of flesh-eating giants. Less gigantic but not much more civilized, Busiris, an Egyptian, sacrificed visitors to the gods, though such worship has always been abhorrent to us.

"Even those sons who started out well did not always end so. Unfortunately, even the best people can be spoiled by bad parenting. Violent as he can be with others, Poseidon is the very worst of over-indulgent fathers, sometimes showering his sons and daughters with so many gifts that he unintentionally corrupts them.

"The ten kings of Atlantis, his sons, by Cleito, were among those he spoiled until their very souls rotted away.

"Poseidon made their land an island, impregnable to attack, and he brought unprecedented prosperity to it so that his sons' subjects would want for nothing.

"Those sons had been good men in the beginning, but over time they forgot that it was not their own excellence, but the blessing of Poseidon, that had brought them unprecedented levels of wealth and power. Worse, now that their egos were the size of their father's ocean, they became unsatisfied with what they had, craving more and more. As their desires increased, their morality slowly rotted away, until it was gone, and only the desire remained.

"Devoured by hubris, these kings, who had besides Atlantis itself already some lands in Libya and in Italy, would settle for nothing less than the conquest and enslavement of the entire world. They cared not about the number of people who would be killed in their war, nor the countless more who would be made miserable by its outcome.

"Poseidon should much earlier have tried to change their course, but he did not, and in the end, Zeus and the other gods would not tolerate the horror the Atlanteans were inflicting on the rest of the world. Their continent was smashed by earthquakes and sunk into the deepest parts of the ocean so that humans would learn the folly of such uncontrolled ambition—though later generations unfortunately did not always remember that lesson."

By now the students were feeling exhausted by the sheer magnitude of what Poseidon's sons had done—but Amphitrite was not quite finished.

"You might have thought that no one could be worse than the kings of Atlantis, but even more terrible were Otus and Ephialtes, giant sons of Poseidon by Iphimedeia, the wife of his own son, Aeolus. Their doubly adulterous conception led to the one of the greatest threats not only humankind, but the gods themselves, had ever faced."

"Why couldn't Zeus just blast them with thunderbolts or have the Hecatoncheires throw boulders at them?" asked Yong. "He'd defeated tougher adversaries that way."

"Ah, but not quite like these," said Amphitrite. "You see, there was a prophecy that the giant brothers could not be killed by gods or men. Even the thunderbolts could not have overcome the shield of destiny itself. That was what made the brothers so dangerous."

"How could they have become invulnerable?" asked Mateo. "That wasn't very common among mortals, was it?"

"No, not common at all," agreed Amphitrite. "Unfortunately, I do not know how such a miracle occurred. There is a weird story that Iphimedeia was really the goddess Hecate, which would suggest she used her witchcraft to make them invulnerable, but that has always seemed ridiculous to me, though the waters of the River Styx in the Underworld will make a human's skin impenetrable, as my sister Thetis proved with Achilles. It is possible that Iphimedeia was a priestess of Hecate and somehow brought the goddess's power to bear on her sons, but even that seems unlikely.

"However, I have always believed that the fault was Poseidon's, for he has shown the power to give humans the same kind of invulnerability the River Styx conveys.

"Once Poseidon loved the beautiful Lapith woman, Caenis. Some storytellers say he raped her, though I have difficulty believing even he would descend to that level, and he does seem to have loved her."

Amphitrite paused for a moment, quivering a little.

"He loved her enough to grant her a wish, which he hardly ever does, and she, evidently not as in love with him as he was with her, and tired of being a woman, wished to become a man.

"Not only did Poseidon grant her that wish, but he made her skin impenetrable by any weapon as well—again not like him, for it was the only time I ever knew him to grant more than a mortal had requested, particularly odd since she had just rejected him.

"Caenis soon changed her…uh, his name to Caeneus and became a great Lapith hero. Unfortunately, in the war between Lapiths and centaurs, the centaurs realized they couldn't wound Caeneus and solved their problem by getting the strongest of them to beat him into the ground, after which he suffocated."

"So he wasn't invulnerable the way we think of it?" asked Yasmin.

"No, he could be killed, just like Achilles, but such men were much harder to kill than most people because nothing could pierce their skin. Still, Poseidon would have to have done more than that to make his sons immune to anything that gods or men could do. It would have been just like him, though. I have told you how he led the Atlanteans to their downfall. He could have done the same with Otus and Ephialtes, granting them such a dangerous gift without thinking twice about it.

"However their invulnerability came about, it led them inexorably toward hubris, for what man could resist the temptation posed by being so mighty he was beyond the reach of justice, human or divine. They wasted no time using it, testing it and their strength by going to Thrace and capturing Ares, whom they held prisoner in a jar for thirteen months, during which they terrorized the other Olympians. Though the others were clever enough not to be caught, they quickly learned that Otus and Ephialtes were not easily killed.

"By that point, the giants were so overwhelmed by hubris that no outrage was too great for them. They piled Mount Pelion on Mount Ossa in an attempt to create a peak as tall as Mount Olympus. It would have been simpler to just climb Olympus, but that would not have caused as much disruption and misery. They even turned on their own father, threatening to throw mountains into the Aegean Sea until it became dry land.

"Even that was not enough to satisfy their arrogance. Ephialtes demanded sex with Hera, while Otus demanded sex with Artemis."

"How well I remember that," said Artemis. "It was one of the very few times I sympathized with Hera, since we were in the same predicament. Though the giants were not that intelligent, or else they would simply have stormed Olympus instead of trying to build a rival peak, even they would eventually have figured out that they could take us by force unless we could find a way to defeat them.

"With most of the gods uncertain what to do, Apollo and I worked out a plan. I distracted the brothers by agreeing to come here to Naxos and let Otus have me if he and his brother would stop besieging Olympus and leave the rest of the world in peace.

"That got the brothers angry with each other and off-balance. Ephialtes, who had not received a similar offer from Hera, insisted that he should have me before Otus did, and they both came to Naxos, bickering all the way. After they had arrived, I turned myself into a white doe and ran between them so fast that, if they hadn't been so stupid and so unfocused, they would have realized I was moving faster than any mortal animal could have.

"Instead of thinking, each seized his javelin, intent on proving himself a better hunter than the other. It was not hard for me to manipulate them enough that they pierced each other with their weapons and died.

"You see, Apollo had perceived a loophole in the prophecy. The brothers could not be killed by either gods or men, but as they were unique, not precisely either one, they could kill each other."

"Thus ended a serious threat to the rule of Zeus," said Amphitrite. "Unfortunately, Poseidon did not learn the lesson he should have.

"Zeus may sometimes be cruel, even paranoid, over the prophecy that one of his sons will overthrow him, but at least he has learned the truth that the son of a powerful father may be a powerful threat. Poseidon, however, fathers children everywhere he goes without a second thought. Enough of them have been monsters, whether physically or mentally, that by now he should have learned greater caution— or at least better parenting."

"You see?" Artemis asked the group. "You see how little self-control men have, and how marriage is just a device by which they exploit women?"

Amphitrite managed a genuine smile. "Dear niece, I cannot quite agree. Poseidon may have married me for his own reasons, but by that marriage I have been able to moderate his violence, much as poor Persephone has done with Hades. Many prayers Poseidon would have left unanswered I have managed to fulfill. Many times have I diluted his wrath. Though it is not the life I would have chosen, I can still see a purpose in what has happened.

"The marriage also gave me children I would not otherwise have had, not monsters as Poseidon breeds with other women, but good sons and daughters raised under my watchful eyes.

"Fish-tailed and green-skinned Triton was our firstborn. He became his father's herald, and by blowing on his conch, he can calm even the roughest sea. Cymopoleia, goddess of the stormy wave was next, and she became the worthy wife of Briareus, one of the Hecatoncheires. Last was Benthesicyme, lady of the deep swells, who married Enalus, king of Aethiopia; she a good wife for him and a good queen for the country."

Artemis looked as if she wanted to say something about the marriage point, but Hermes cut her off.

"I believe you came to offer your help in our quest."

"That I did," said Amphitrite. "The sea grape wine will help, but more is needed. Poseidon is hearing whispers from the depths that there is a plot to replace him as ruler of the sea."

Hermes looked shocked. "How would such a thing even be possible? The old sea gods, including your grandfathers, seem content to let Poseidon rule. Who does he think covets that honor?"

"Aphrodite," replied Amphitrite.

Hermes could not help laughing. "How can he think that? Aphrodite has never shown the slightest interest in commanding the waves."

"She was born from the waves before Poseidon even existed," explained Amphitrite. "She was even named from *aphros*, the sea foam. What really worries him, though, is that she sprung from the sea after Cronus had cast Uranus's severed flesh into it. In a sense, that makes Aphrodite a kind of daughter of Uranus, a former king of the universe, and thus perhaps more powerful than she appears. She is of an elder generation, more like a Titan than an Olympian in terms of age."

"Even so, the Olympians beat the Titans," Hermes pointed out. "Anyway, how could Aphrodite harm him in the depths of the ocean?"

"He thinks she has help. You, for one."

"What?" asked Hermes, looking worried. "What reason has he to suspect me?"

"You just visited Aphrodite, did you not?" asked Amphitrite.

"Only to help these visitors find their friend," replied Hermes. "It is for the same reason I am here now." Then he frowned. "This lie was concocted by someone to keep me from seeing him! I must speak to him at once."

"And so you may," said Amphitrite, "for I have convinced him to give you a chance to explain. However, he will not allow Artemis and Pan to accompany you, for if there is a conspiracy, they could be your allies in it. Also, you may bring only one of the visitors—who, by the way, he also suspects. He finds their arrival too coincidental."

"They are all—" began Hermes.

"He has heard of the quest, but if the story is true, only one of them needs to talk to him and receive what aid he can give, not all. I would suggest the Aethiopian, for we all know how partial he is to them. Since the sinking of Atlantis, they have been his favorite civilization. If anyone can persuade him to help, it will be she."

Keisha felt suddenly queasy. "My ancestors did come from Africa, but I have no idea whether any of them were from Ethiopia or not."

Amphitrite smiled reassuringly. "It matters not. Some ancient geographers thought of everything south of Egypt as Aethiopia. If you can advocate well, he is more likely to listen to you than to any other member of your party."

The situation had been scary before, but at least Keisha had been with the rest of the group. What if Poseidon didn't believe, or she accidentally offended him? She could end up changed into an eel or something and locked in an undersea dungeon, maybe in even worse shape than Patrick.

Patrick—that was the problem. If Apollo was right, they needed help from Poseidon to save Patrick. If she was the only one Poseidon would listen to, then she had to make the attempt.

"I'll...I'll do it," she said, hoping she wouldn't regret her choice.

Hermes looked quickly around. "Artemis, Pan, please keep watch on the rest of our visitors to keep them safe."

"I will as well," said Patricius.

"And I," agreed Ardalos.

"Dionysus, Ariadne, and their party aren't far away, either," said Pan. "If we need more help, I'll let out one of my shrieks, and they will surely come to see what's happening. In the short time you'll be gone, I think the visitors will be safe enough."

"All right," said Hermes, not sounding as if he really thought it was. "How are we to get down? The sea is too choppy for me to navigate."

"Triton will help you," said Amphitrite. "Poseidon still trusts him and me, so he can still calm the waves, and I can enable the Aethiopian visitor to breathe under water."

At an unseen signal from Amphitrite, Triton, green and fishtailed as his mother had said, emerged, blew loudly but resonantly on his conch, and calmed the sea. At the same time, Amphitrite gestured around Keisha, and she felt different.

"You can now breathe water as if it were air, and your body will be immune to forces like undersea pressure as well," said the queen of the sea.

Keisha wasn't completely reassured, but when Hermes whisked her underwater, it was indeed more like being in air than she could have imagined. Even the cold didn't really reach her.

She did notice Hermes was moving more slowly than he did when he was flying through the sky. She didn't think about that too much, though, because being surrounded by Amphitrite, Triton, and a contingent of dolphins made her feel oddly like a performer at Sea World rather than a teenager trapped in a weirdly real dream. It was a relief to get away from that, if only for a few minutes.

Before long, Keisha and her escort arrived at Poseidon's palace, which was resting at the very bottom of the Aegean Sea. It should have been pretty dark down there, but Poseidon somehow kept the palace's golden walls glowing to provide an eerie kind of illumination for the place. As Keisha got closer, she realized much of the bluish green light was coming from thousands of bio-luminescent sea creatures. She didn't think any of the myths described Poseidon's palace being lit that way, but she recalled reading somewhere that the ancient Greeks had recorded sightings of bio-luminescence in the sea.

When they swam into the courtyard, landscaped with seaweed and decorated with coral sculptures, they saw Poseidon immediately. He looked superficially like Zeus, with the same muscular body type beneath his robes and the same distinguished beard. However, Poseidon's face was rigid with suppressed anger, hard as the basalt throne on which he sat, and his eyes were dark as the depths of the sea. He held his trident, that great weapon that could bring tidal waves when it struck the sea and earthquakes when it struck the land, and he was gripping it so hard his knuckles were white.

Keisha had known this would not be easy, but, looking into those dark eyes, she wondered if it was going to be impossible.

"Uncle, I have come to put your mind at rest," said Hermes. "I am not part of any plot against you." Keisha had expected to hear voices in an oddly distorted way, but evidently Amphitrite's spell allowed her to hear voices as she would if she were in air rather than water.

"Hermes," said Poseidon in a deep voice that reminded Keisha of the roar of the ocean, "you have always been a trickster."

"In fun, perhaps, but never in malice," replied Hermes. "I swear by the Styx I am part of no conspiracy against you."

"Normally, such an oath would be absolute," Poseidon conceded, "but I am not sure I trust it any longer. "I have heard there are ways to avoid the force of that pledge now. Even if there were not, could not someone as clever as you mentally withdraw yourself from the conspiracy, swear the oath you just swore, and then reenter the conspiracy?"

"Propose the words yourself, and I will swear to them," said Hermes. "As for the first part, not even once has any god escaped this oath. The power of Zeus himself constrains all gods to fulfill what they have sworn, and if somehow a god still manages to resist, the penalty for breaking the oath remains in force: one year of unconsciousness, and nine years cut off from all interaction with the other gods. Even that may not be the end of the penalty, for surely such an oath breaker would never be trusted again."

"But how do we truly know that happens?" asked Poseidon. "Since no one has ever broken such an oath, can we be sure that the decree of Zeus will be fulfilled? Even if it is, can we know how? Would the offender fall unconscious the moment he broke the oath, or would the penalty only befall him if he were caught?"

"Do you doubt the power of Zeus to enforce his own decrees?" asked Hermes, careful to keep his tone neutral, though the question was a kind of challenge.

"I do not doubt Zeus," said Poseidon, "but even his power has its limits, and we both know the day will come when he is overthrown. That which is not absolute can be overcome by one with sufficient power and guile."

"And you think that is me? Aphrodite? Uncle, neither of us has that kind of magic."

"You may not be the only ones involved," said Poseidon. "Someone in the

Underworld may be as well, for I have heard that the dog-headed, fish-finned Telchines have been released from Tartarus, and no one knows the full extent of their power."

"The Telchines?" said Hermes, incredulous. "Surely no one, no matter how much he or she wished you ill, would risk unleashing them again, for who could control them once they were out? That would be like releasing the Titans."

"Aye, they are powerful," agreed Poseidon. "They learned magic and the art of metalworking long ago, when the Cyclopes were held in Tartarus, and they it was who created the sickle Cronus used to mutilate his father.

"The makers of a weapon that could so harm a god would be a formidable menace indeed, all the more so since Cronus favored them, not realizing that the force that helped him to the throne could help him off of it or even take it for themselves.

"Sensing Cronus would be defeated by Zeus, they did not take a side, but hid away at Rhodes, gathering more and more power. When the day came that their ability to control the weather began to rival even that of Zeus, he managed, but only with great difficulty, to defeat them before their plans could reach fruition.

"Tartarus is well fortified and well-guarded, but remember that the Telchines' parentage is unknown. Some say they are children of Gaia and Pontus, but others that they are in fact the spawn of Tartarus himself and Nemesis. Ask yourself, then, who would be better at finding a way out of Tartarus than the children of Tartarus?

"Then ask yourself how safe the oath on the Styx is when sorcerers who know how to use its water in their magic are free to do as they will. Have you forgotten how they sprinkled the water of the Styx on Rhodes to make it sterile?"

"This is nothing but wild speculation," Hermes protested. "Besides, even if they could get out of Tartarus, they couldn't get past its guardians."

"Shapeshifters said to be good enough to fool even other gods?" asked Poseidon. "If anyone could get past those guardians, it would be they.

"However, bandying words back and forth with you is pointless. I value action over words, even the words of an oath. If you want to prove the purity of your intent, nephew, go investigate my fears yourself.

"Fly to the Underworld right now and check with Hades to make sure the Telchines are still held prisoner. Prove my fears groundless, and I will accept your claim of innocence, even without an oath."

"I intend to go to the Underworld with these visitors as soon as—" Hermes began.

"Now," said Poseidon. "You will go now, this very second, or you will make me even more suspicious."

Keisha found herself trembling. Facing Poseidon would have been hard enough with Hermes at her side, but how was she supposed to talk to such a formidable—and ill-tempered—god without anyone around who had her back?

Hermes must have thought the same thing, considering how reluctant he looked.

"Why—"

"Do not question me, Nephew, just go. My suspicion mounts."

"The visitor I have brought is under Zeus's protection, and I was charged—"

"Surely you do not mean to suggest that the visitor needs to fear any harm from me?" asked Poseidon. "Or perhaps you think I cannot defend guests in my own palace?"

"She is your guest, then, and under your protection?" asked Hermes.

"So I have said. Now go, Nephew, faster than the wind. The sooner I can be convinced the Telchines are not behind some sinister plot against me, the better."

Hermes attempted a reassuring smile for Keisha, did not quite succeed, and then flew off.

Keisha wondered if she was going to end up like Patrick. If Poseidon decided he didn't like her, he could change her into pretty much anything he wanted and hide her anywhere in the sea. There was no way her friends would ever find her if that happened.

"Now then," said Poseidon, turning his icy eyes upon her, "you are an Aethiopian, are you not?"

"From...I'm from another world," said Keisha. "In that world, my ancestors came from…Aethiopia."

"You do not seem very sure," said Poseidon.

"The names are different where I come from," said Keisha.

"You come here seeking my help?" asked Poseidon, looking her over.

"Yes…your majesty." Keisha wasn't sure what to call him, but as he was the king of the sea, *majesty* seemed like a safe choice.

"Our friend was abducted, and Apollo named you as one of the gods we needed to visit for help," Keisha continued.

"I have never denied help to an Aethiopian who asked, but you must make your request in the proper way. Pray to me, and I will answer your prayer."

Keisha froze. Hermes had told them that the gods all knew that Keisha and her friends could not worship them and would not ask them to, but now here was Poseidon, making exactly that request.

The last thing Keisha wanted to do was let Patrick down, but every part of her Baptist soul rebelled against the idea of giving in to Poseidon's demand. Surely there had to be a better solution than violating her own principles.

"Hermes said all the gods knew our own religious principles would prevent us from worshiping them and would not expect it of us," she said, hoping the statement wouldn't get her turned into a sea slug.

"I do not *expect* it of you," Poseidon replied. "However, if you want my help, you will have to. If not, you are free to go. Amphitrite and Triton will escort you back to the land."

"Husband—" began Amphitrite.

"I have spoken!" roared Poseidon with surprising force. "I have spoken, and my word is law here. She may pray and receive what she needs, or she may go."

"Please, Majesty—" began Keisha.

"Prayer or go," the sea god told her harshly. "I will listen to nothing but a prayer now."

Keisha, who, for some odd reason, didn't want Poseidon to see her cry, turned to Amphitrite. "Please take me back. I'll…"

She was going to say she would find another way to save her friend, but the words wouldn't come out.

If Apollo was right, there was no other way.

Then Poseidon's rigid face cracked a little, and he smiled.

"So, you are not part of some plot after all," he said, taking Keisha completely by surprise.

"What do you mean?" she asked, conscious that wasn't much of a response, but not knowing what else to say.

"Of course I knew that you visitors from another world could not worship us as a matter of principle. If you were not really such a visitor, but part of some plot against me, your being here would have been part of that plot, and you would have done whatever I asked to keep from being sent away. Because you were ready to uphold your principles rather than pray to me, I know you are innocent."

"Thank you," said Keisha, not knowing what else to do, but glad not to be a sea slug.

"I am still not sure about Hermes, though," Poseidon said, staring at her as if he expected her to come up with some kind of evidence.

"We have been with Hermes for...some time," said Keisha, suddenly realizing that she had lost track of time in this dream world. Had it been hours—or days?

"We haven't seen him do anything suspicious," Keisha continued.

Poseidon leaned forward in his throne. "And were you truly with him every minute?"

"He did take Pan and Artemis aside to mediate their argument," Keisha admitted. "There was also a time, with Aphrodite..." She blushed when she remembered what Hermes had been doing with her.

"So you weren't actually with him all the time?" asked Poseidon. "He could have conspired with Aphrodite, with Pan and Artemis, or even with all of them?"

Keisha tried to get control of her fears enough for her brain to function properly.

"If I remember my myths correctly, Pan had almost no interaction with you, so no opportunity to form a grudge. Artemis doesn't seem that happy with any of the male gods, but she seems much angrier with Zeus than with you, and two of the few men she ever trusted were your son, Orion, and your grandson, Hippolytus."

"Not entirely reassuring, since she felt Orion let her down, and I killed Hippolytus, though only in fulfillment of his father's wish—another cursed oath on the Styx!" said Poseidon.

"She told us both stories, but in neither case did she sound critical of you," said Keisha. "She doesn't seem…to be someone who keeps her opinions to herself."

Poseidon actually chuckled at that. "No, indeed, she does not, and that would make her a poor conspirator. Still, we were on opposite sides in the Trojan War and have occasionally been at odds since then. I cannot entirely rule her out.

"However, aside from the Telchines, whose powers would explain a great deal, I most distrust Aphrodite, who is more than capable of turning Hermes inside out if the mood strikes her."

"She is hardly a close friend of mine," said Amphitrite, "but she could turn you inside out as well—and has. Do you remember that line from Sophocles, something like 'Aphrodite immortal works her will upon all?' If she were interested in power, the woman could take over all of Olympus in days at most. For that matter, she could have been the queen of the gods to begin with if she had wanted. She would have had no difficulty getting Zeus to marry her instead of Hera. The fact that she didn't tells me she was content to play a less conspicuous role. Why would she suddenly want something she had every opportunity to get and did not take? Besides, if she wanted to recruit someone for a conspiracy, would not Ares be her first recruit? Is there any sign of that?"

"No," admitted Poseidon, "but I have reason to distrust her—and so do you. Do you not remember the fate of Nerites?

Turning to Keisha, he said, "Nerites was the brother of my queen and the only son of Nereus. He was as handsome as Amphitrite is beautiful, and in her early days, during the reign of Cronus, when Aphrodite was often in the sea, he caught her eye. In the end, she loved him as intensely as she later loved Adonis, but he did not share her feelings."

"If we're being honest," said Amphitrite, "my brother only really loved himself."

"He was a bit cocky," admitted Poseidon, "but he was also a good person. After I was made lord of the sea, I selected Nerites as my charioteer, and we spent hours riding the waves together. Though he was older than I, he always chose a younger form, and it was hard for me not to think of him as a friend, or even as a son.

"Unfortunately, Aphrodite remained convinced that he would eventually love her and join her in her new home on Olympus. She did not try to compel him, as she probably could have, but when she finally lost hope, she became angry with him and turned him into the shellfish that bears his name, the one with the beautiful spiral shell."

"I can understand how a mortal could be changed that way, but how could a god be?" asked Keisha.

"My point exactly," said Poseidon. "Aphrodite has more power than any of us suspect."

"Or you have the story wrong," said Amphitrite. "Yes, she loved him once, but I suspect she forgot him eventually, for on Olympus, aside from her poor husband, she had Ares, Hermes, and Dionysus to choose from—and even Zeus, occasionally.

"No, husband, you cannot see it, for you were too fond of Nerites, but it was his arrogance that doomed him, not his lack of love for Aphrodite. He gloated too much about his being able to speed away with you, leaving even his nephew and your actual son, Triton, far behind. It is said he had the audacity to challenge Helios to a chariot race, and his transformation was the result of losing that ill-considered race. Notice that shellfish, though beautiful, is extremely slow-moving."

"Helios is no friend of mine," Poseidon conceded. "Not since we fought over who should be patron of Rhodes, but he denies it was he who changed Nerites, or that such a race ever occurred."

"He may have been lying to keep the peace, or it may just be that some other sea god, jealous of your favor for Nerites, worked this change upon him. Aside from you, there were not many who truly liked him."

"Would you speak so of your own brother?" asked Poseidon, face hardening again.

"Because he was my brother, I know his faults," said Amphitrite. "Because you saw him as a son, you refuse to know them."

"Someday I will find a way to restore him," said Poseidon, "and then we will find out the truth of it." Turning to Keisha, he asked, "Have you seen anything on your journey that might be suspicious?"

Keisha had already been thinking about it, and so without hesitation she was able to say, "I think someone is trying to create conflict among the gods."

Poseidon raised an eyebrow. "Really? What would make you think that?"

"The kidnapping of our friend created tension between Hera and Zeus. He'd gotten in trouble with Hera already, and so Zeus believed she engineered the abduction. It was timed so Helios could not see what was happening."

"Alas, it is not hard to stir strife between Zeus and Hera," said Poseidon. "However, I cannot think of why any god would feel the need to kidnap your friend for any other reason. Is there more?"

"When we visited Athena, she was getting ready for an attack from Thrace that she thought Ares was instigating, but apparently that was a false rumor."

"Ares and Athena seldom get along, so they would be logical targets for someone trying to make trouble," said Poseidon, nodding his head. "Is there more?"

"When we visited Demeter, someone attacked Eleusis. Apparently, it was someone with a lot of magic, someone who could weave illusions that at first confused even the gods. Demeter, Hermes, Pan, and Artemis rushed off to deal with what they thought was a huge battle, and as soon as they were gone, centaurs tried to capture us. We were saved, but just barely. The whole mess caused more conflict, though, because Demeter was sure the centaurs had come up from the Underworld, which in her mind implicated Hades, but Pan argued against that theory. Forgive me for saying this, but Demeter also thought we should not come visit you."

Poseidon frowned at that. "She blames me still for something that happened centuries ago, and she blames Hades still for marrying Persephone."

"The centaurs did seem to come from a spot where Demeter said there is an entrance to the Underworld, so it could have been someone trying to make Hades look guilty."

"What of Artemis and Hermes?" asked Poseidon. "What do they think?"

"Artemis seems to agree something is happening, but she doesn't favor a particular theory about who is behind it, at least not that I remember. Hermes was almost certain at one point that Hecate was doing the plotting, but

Demeter defended her quite vigorously."

"Hecate is powerful," said Poseidon slowly, "and many suspect her of wanting vengeance on the other gods. Also, she has freedom of movement within the Underworld. If I am right about either the Telchines being freed or the oath on the River Styx being undermined, she could have been in a position to do either or even both. She could also have brought centaurs into the Underworld and then sent them up again, making it look as if Hades was the guilty one."

"You don't think it could be Hades?" asked Keisha.

"My brother has never been happy with the results of our little lottery to divide the world among us, yet, for the most part, he seems content to govern his share and seldom leaves it. He could have a second residence on Olympus, as I do, but he has never bothered. It doesn't seem as if he has any interest in expanding into my realm or Zeus's."

"Has Hecate?" asked Keisha.

"Come to think of it, even though Zeus granted her wide powers—a course of action of which I did not approve, by the way—since she first entered the Underworld as Persephone's companion, she has not much bothered with the sky, the sea, or the earth. She is more active among humankind than Hades and comes out more often, but again, she shows little sign of seeking more power than she already has."

"So everyone looks somewhat guilty, but no one really is," said Triton.

"Someone is trying to stir up trouble," said Poseidon. "Too much has happened to be coincidental. Perhaps whoever is behind this is also behind your arrival in this world," he added to Keisha. "The appearance of strangers such as you is unique. In all these centuries, no one like you has ever appeared here."

"I wish I knew why we did," said Keisha, "but my friends and I have no idea."

"If, as you say, you came in through the Demos Oneiroi, perhaps the answer lies there. Few of us gods know either Hypnos or Morpheus, for they keep mostly to themselves, but conceivably they could be involved or at least provide another clue. What else did Apollo tell you to do?"

"After we had visited you, we were supposed to return to the Underworld and talk to Hades and Persephone," said Keisha. "Then we were to question some of the human heroes there, at least one of whom is supposed to have a critical clue."

"Perhaps that is how I can help," said Poseidon. "Hermes has better knowledge of the Underworld than I, but I was talking not long ago to Mnemosyne, the goddess of memory and mother of the nine Muses. You know about the River Lethe in the Underworld?"

"Isn't that the one that wipes the memory of whoever drinks from it?" asked Keisha.

"The very same," said Poseidon. "Dead souls drink from it to forget their former lives, in the beginning to become mindless shadows, later on to prepare for reincarnation.

"Lethe's power is antithetical to Mnemosyne's, and it is also at odds with the teachings of the Orphics, who want initiates to be able to retain certain mystic information from one life to the next rather than entering each new life completely blank. Since Mnemosyne inherently distrusts forgetting, and since she much loved Orpheus, her grandson, she badgered Hades for centuries about giving the dead an alternative to Lethe.

"Hades is not exactly known for his willingness to accept advice, but with Mnemosyne's gentle prodding, supported by Persephone's pleas, he eventually allowed Mnemosyne to create a spring in the Underworld near Lethe. If drunk after Lethe, it can reverse Lethe's effects. If drunk without having drunk from Lethe, it amplifies the memory in strange and wonderful ways.

"Have each member of your party drink from the spring, and all of you will become incredibly good, not only at recalling what they have heard but in visualizing it. Each story you hear will become like your own memory. If there is any important detail in any of them, one of you will be much more likely to find it that way."

"Thank you so much!" said Keisha. "That sounds like exactly what we need."

"I am glad I could be of help," said Poseidon, "for I now believe resolving your quest may unmask the conspirators as well, solving our problem as well as yours."

At that moment Hermes returned, looking grim.

"Uncle, the Telchines are still in Tartarus," said Hermes. "However,

Hades is uneasy. He shares your concern that someone may try to liberate them, and he is increasing his precautions to prevent such an attempt, but he also fears he may be wrong and that the Telchine rumor may be a distraction from some other threat."

"I have never known Hades to be that uncertain," said Poseidon. "That is almost the most troubling thing I have yet heard."

"The air is thicker than usual with magic in his realm," Hermes explained. "I can feel it myself. As master of that realm, Hades should be able to bar whatever that strange force is, but so far he has been unable to."

"Anyone who could steal a mortal right out from under Zeus's nose on Olympus could probably find ways to infiltrate the Underworld without Hades's knowledge I suppose," said Poseidon. "However, the more I think of the possibilities, the more ominous they become. You know what this could be?"

"The emergence of the long-prophesied son of Zeus who will overthrow his father?" asked Hermes.

"I fear it," said Poseidon, "and I fear this son has allies among us. This mortal suggests there is an active effort to turn us against each other, and I think that she is right.

"I am sorry I delayed your quest, Hermes. Hurry with the visitors to the Underworld.

"We may only have days—or hours—before this threat changes our world forever."

Chapter 18: Hades and Persephone

At first the trip back was smooth, but it became increasingly turbulent as they neared the surface, and neither Triton nor Amphitrite seemed to be able to do much to calm the waters this time.

"This is not Poseidon's doing," said Amphitrite. "I sense...another."

When Hermes and Keisha finally made it back to the beach, they could see that the other students looked frightened. Artemis and Pan both looked worried, and Dionysus, who had come down to the beach, looked angry enough to inflict madness on someone—anyone.

"Why has your husband done this?" the wine god yelled at Amphitrite. "Why has he attacked Naxos with an earthquake?"

"He has done no such thing," said Amphitrite. "We were even now in his palace, and his only concern was to get Hermes and the visitors back on their way."

"Who else can bring about earthquakes?" demanded Dionysus. "It was not Gaia; I asked her already."

"Hecate has power over the earth," Hermes pointed out. "And over the sea," he added to Amphitrite.

"And no motive to attack me," Dionysus replied.

"Neither has my husband," said Amphitrite.

At that moment, Poseidon himself burst out of the ocean, looking around frantically.

"Someone is interfering with the sea!" he said, looking at the other gods as if expecting an explanation.

"Why have you sent an earthquake against me?" asked Dionysus, pointing his thyrsus at Poseidon.

The sea god looked shocked. "I sent no earthquake. Whoever is agitating the sea is doing the same with the earth as well."

Poseidon stepped on to the beach, intending to reason with Dionysus, but as soon as his feet touched the ground, grape vines sprung up all around him and wrapped themselves around his arms and legs.

"You shall not trespass upon the island that you tried to sink," said Dionysus, eyes glistening with something that looked a lot like madness.

Poseidon, whose conversation with Keisha had calmed him, shifted back into anger faster than Hermes could fly. With a shout that shook the earth, he flexed his muscles and tore the grape vines out of the ground. In a few seconds, he shredded them off his arms and legs, after which he tossed the mangled bits and pieces of vine in Dionysus's face.

"Save these tricks for mortals, little boy! They will not work on me."

"How about this one?" asked Dionysus, sending madness out from himself in waves. The students would have been driven hopelessly insane at that point if Apollo had not given them the amber charms, but even with that protection, they felt as if someone was pumping drugs into their systems so fast their hearts might explode. They were not going to be able to hold out long. Even the other gods looked shaky.

Poseidon, already filled with wrath before Dionysus had tried to demolish his mental balance, struck the earth once with his trident, this time really causing an earthquake.

"Cease this attack, or I will sink this miserable rock," he screamed. Storm winds hit the beach so hard they sprayed sand in every direction, and an ominous swell started forming in the sea.

"Protect the visitors!" yelled Hermes to Pan and Artemis as he threw himself between Poseidon and Dionysus.

What Artemis and Pan could do against a tidal wave wasn't clear, though the huntress raised her bow, uncertain whether to open fire at Dionysus or Poseidon, and Pan, after morphing into Great God Pan, shrieked loudly enough to be heard on the other side of the Aegean. Amphitrite, however, had a more immediate solution, standing in front of the students and using her own control over the sea and storm to shield them as much as she could.

"Uncle, Brother, end your quarrel with reason, not with force!" Hermes shouted. Had he not been able to move so fast, he would have tasted Poseidon's trident at that point. Other than that, Dionysus and Poseidon reacted as if he wasn't there. Each, frustrated that his first attacks had failed, rapidly escalated.

The ocean looked darker and more menacing with every second, and the clamor Dionysus was creating in each of their heads became harder and harder to tune out.

Not only that, but each god's allies began to arrive. A small army of satyrs, centaurs, and maenads formed behind Dionysus, even as the waves behind Poseidon bulged with sharks and other menacing sea creatures, and the shadow of an enormous sea monster fell across the beach. Rising further and further out of the water, the thing looked skyscraper tall, bulkier than the largest ship the ancients had, and more than capable of swallowing all the students in one big gulp.

"My money's on Poseidon," muttered Mateo, though no one except Keisha could hear him over the wind.

To Keisha, this looked a little like an impending nuclear war. How could either side win? Sure, Poseidon was a more powerful god, even though his advantage might be diluted a little by fighting out of the water, and on Dionysus's own turf, but even if Poseidon killed the wine god's whole army and sunk his island, what then? He couldn't kill Dionysus, and gods like Demeter, who already mistrusted Poseidon, would probably throw themselves into the battle against him. Poseidon would have, not victory, but an endless civil war against his fellow gods.

All things considered, that was probably exactly what whoever had caused the original earthquake wanted.

Hermes's caduceus glowed brightly as he tried to charm the combatants to sleep—or at least to saner moods—but he was making little headway. Poseidon was poised to strike the ground with his trident again, even as Dionysus's troops charged in his direction, and a forest of grape vines sprouted beneath the sea god's feet.

Then there was a blinding flash as a thunderbolt struck midway between the two warring gods, tearing a gaping hole in the ground and filling the air with static electricity.

"Zeus wishes an end to this violent fray!" Hermes shouted into the momentary silence that followed the painfully obvious display of Zeus's displeasure. "For god to fight against god in this way is forbidden."

Poseidon's trident hung in midair but did not strike. Dionysus's madness coiled around him like a giant snake but did not poise itself to attack.

Keisha had hoped this pause might lead to conversation, to a realization by the two gods that someone was pitting them against each other, but that wasn't what happened.

Poseidon turned without a word and flung himself into the sea, which calmed rapidly and emptied of its load of hostile marine life. Dionysus likewise turned without a word and led his troops away.

"Not exactly a permanent peace, but right now I'll take it," said Hermes, looking weary from his efforts.

"Is it over?" asked Yasmin, looking first in the direction Dionysus had gone, then back out to sea.

"Knowing my husband, it has only just begun," said Amphitrite. "I will follow him and try to calm him, and I will send word to Ariadne, who I know will do the same with Dionysus, especially once she realizes the truth—some outsider wants Dionysus and Poseidon at each other's throats."

"I'm sure Zeus won't let anything more happen," said Mateo.

Hermes sighed. "You should know by now that matters are never so simple. Zeus is still going to be reluctant to offend Poseidon, but unless Zeus can prove Poseidon didn't cause that first earthquake, he can't just ignore Dionysus's claims, especially since Dionysus is one of his favorite sons. That means he isn't likely to force either to make peace. They may not attack each other directly, but if they start going after each other's mortal favorites, the situation is only going to get worse."

"What does that mean for our efforts to save Patrick?" asked Fatima.

"It means they are even more urgent," replied Hermes. "The riddle of where Patrick is and the riddle of who is pitting the gods against each other are one. If we find the answer to either, we find the answer to both."

"Then it's time to head to the Underworld?" asked Thanos.

"It is," replied Hermes, "and in that one respect, we are in luck. I don't know if Zeus intended this, but that pit he created where the thunderbolt struck narrows to a crack that goes all the way down to the Underworld. That saves us a trip to the nearest entrance, for now we have our own."

After thanking and saying goodbye to Amphitrite, the group walked closer to the pit, from which sulfurous vapors were pouring. With a wave of his caduceus, Hermes banished the foul stench.

"That's a good sign," said Hermes. "Noxious vapors usually indicate a way to the Underworld."

"What about what it does to all the people who live here?" said Mateo, thinking about environmental hazards.

"Depending upon how the quest turns out, perhaps they will build a Pluotonion over it," said Hermes. "If they wish, I will fill it in for them.

"Is everyone ready?"

"How do you know this ends up in the right place?" asked Artemis, looking skeptically into the gloomy depths. She was a goddess who loved the forest and the night sky, not one who wanted to burrow underground.

"There are caves and chasms in many places," said Hermes. "I know not how it works, but they all open in exactly the same spot, near where Charon runs his ferry."

"Maybe they're all really some kind of fold in the space-time continuum," said Yong. "Never mind," he added when Hermes looked blank. This world obviously ran on what the students would think of as magic much more than on science.

After asking again if everyone was ready, Hermes waved the caduceus, easing their descent through the enormous gap in the earth. As it narrowed, somehow Hermes kept magicking them through it in complete defiance of the laws of physics—which, Yong had to keep reminding himself, did not apply here.

After a much slower trip than most of those with Hermes, they found themselves in a gloomy cavern. It was not completely dark, though they couldn't tell where the weak illumination was coming from. Hermes used the caduceus to give them a little more light.

In the distance, they could hear the sound of running water.

"Is that the River Styx?" asked Yasmin.

"The Styx is only portrayed as the first river in Homer's *Iliad* and Virgil's *Aeneid*," said Hermes. "In every other work, it was the Acheron that people had to cross in Charon's ferry."

They had to walk only a short distance to reach the riverbank. Standing nearby and eying them curiously was Charon.

He would have been hard to miss under any circumstances. Most gods chose to look young, or at least middle-aged but vigorous. Charon looked old, as if he had been standing in the same spot since the dawn of time. His face looked worn, almost skeletal, though part of it was covered by a long and unruly white beard. His clothes were filthy rags, making it clear he could care less about his appearance.

However, he was far from being the ancient, worn-out peasant whose appearance he had chosen to wear. Out of his pale face glowed eyes red as flame, and a feeling of strength radiated from him, reinforced by the enormous hammer that hung at his belt. He might be doing what a lot of ancient Greeks would have thought of as a menial job, but he was clearly not someone whose authority could be easily questioned.

"He is an ancient power," Hermes said in response to Yasmin's whispered question. "Nominally servant to Hades, he has been here since long before Hades was even born, for he is the son of Nyx and perhaps Erebus, spawned from utter darkness when the world was young."

Charon attempted to block their path before Hermes even had a chance to speak.

"Living humans may not pass," he said in a voice that reminded one of bone scraping on stone.

Hermes withdrew the golden bough from his pack and handed it to Thanos, who waved it at Charon. The ferryman gave them a threatening frown.

"Why do you have so little respect for the ancient ways?" Charon asked Hermes.

Hermes sighed. "The golden bough is an exception allowed by those ancient ways, Charon. Anyone who bears it may pass."

"Only one of them carries it," Charon pointed out. "*He* may pass; the rest must stay behind."

"They are all members of one party," protested Hermes.

"They may be joined as tightly as Hermaphroditus and Salmacis for all I care," said Charon. "If you wish to invoke an exception, well and good—but the exception covers only he whose hand touches the branch, not everyone he would bring in with him."

"Aeneas and the Sibyl both got in with only one golden bough between them," Hermes pointed out.

"Indeed, but the Sibyl had performed certain rituals beforehand," replied Charon.

"What rituals?" asked the messenger of the gods.

"I will not say," said Charon.

Having listened to Charon's exact words earlier, the students all touched the branch at the same time, but the ferryman refused to budge.

"Only one person can be the holder of each branch, no matter how many hands are laid upon it," said Charon.

"I invoke my right to enter as the messenger of Zeus," said Hermes.

"You may enter. You could have done that to begin with," said Charon. "You may not, however, bring any living mortals in with you."

Frustrated, Hermes pulled the others back to talk to them.

"I could take him," said Artemis, glancing back at Charon.

"He is tougher than he looks," said Hermes. "Perhaps you, Pan and I together could defeat him. No one has ever tried, because the ferry will not leave the dock without him, and crossing the River Acheron by any other means is impossible, at least for the mortals.

"Acheron, unlike most rivers, was not born of Oceanus and Tethys, but of Gaia and Helios, bright among gods. Acheron might have had a destiny equally bright, but he quenched the thirst of the Titans during the war against Zeus, and after Zeus had won, he condemned Acheron to guard the entrance to the Underworld and never again feel the soft touch of his mother or the warmth of his father.

"That is why Acheron is the river of pain, for he remembers all he has lost and is tortured by those memories. It is said those who try to cross without the ferry become overwhelmed by a sense of loss and drown before they can reach the opposite bank.

"Why not let Thanos go in with you and find the necessary clues?" asked Keisha. "You took only me to visit Poseidon, and that worked."

"You do not understand," said Hermes. "Thanos could find the clues by himself, but that could take more time—time we do not have. It is only a matter of time before conflict breaks out above: Zeus vs. Hera, Athena vs. Ares, earth gods vs. sea gods, or some other combination. Possibly too much will happen at once for Zeus to suppress it all, and the very fabric of the world itself will be torn by the violence. We have to solve this mystery before that can happen.

"Not only that, but I suspect you cannot return to your own world except the way you came, the Demos Oneiroi. Unless you want to be trapped here, we have to get you in. I will try something else."

Hermes walked back to Charon. "These mortals have the express permission of Zeus to enter the Underworld."

"If that were true, you would not have bothered to obtain the golden bough," said Charon. "Of course, if you wish to return with written orders from Zeus—"

"Our quest is urgent," insisted Hermes. "The very fate of the world—"

Charon sighed, a sound like air escaping from a corpse. "Everyone says that. The world survived the fall of Uranus, and then the fall of Cronus. It will survive the fall of Zeus as well, or even of all the gods, for new ones will arise to take their places. So it was, and so it will always be."

Hermes walked back to the group, his hands clenched into fists.

"I have no doubt if I had time to explain the matter to Zeus, I could get the orders, but who knows how rapidly I could see him at this point—or even if he still trusts me. Whoever is behind this plot tried to turn Poseidon against me and could easily do the same with Zeus. The risk is too great."

"What about Hades?" asked Thanos. "Surely he would give permission. Wouldn't that be good enough?"

"Hades is...distracted. I trust Apollo's prophecy enough to believe that if we all get in, he will help, but I have no way of knowing what will happen if just I or I and Thanos go in to get him to give permission. Only if we are all there can we be sure of success."

"Doesn't the golden bough regrow each time it is harvested?" asked Yong. "Why not just go back and pick enough of them for all of us?"

"Even with my aid, that would be too slow a process. I suppose if there is no alternative—no, wait, I have it!"

Hermes dashed over and whispered something to Charon, who smiled— or made the closest approximation he could—and then motioned for everyone to get on the ferry.

"What did you say to him?" whispered Thanos as the boat moved away from the shore.

"Charon's unbending commitment to rules loosens up for only one cause: greed."

"Is that why each dead soul must pay one obolos to cross?" asked Yong.

"It is," agreed Hermes. "Strange, for Charon has no real use for money, but he wants it anyway. It is the said the spirit of avarice lives in a cave nearby, and his constant presence has poisoned Charon's mind.

"Luckily, as the god of thieves, I have much to offer. As you would say in your world, I made Charon an offer he couldn't refuse."

They all laughed at that, but Charon, eyes locked on the opposite bank of the river, did not react at all.

Just as they landed, Cerberus, the enormous guard dog of the Underworld, spawn of the monsters Typhoeus and Echidna, bounded over to confront them. Intimidating as Charon was, Cerberus was several times worse.

He had an enormous body, more like a horse's than a dog's, and from it sprouted three gigantic, snarling heads. As if that were not enough, his tail was a long, vicious snake, and fifty more snakes sprouted out around his heads like a living collar.

He would let the dead enter, but not leave. He did not seem inclined to let the living enter or leave, and Charon either did not have any control over him or simply didn't care what happened to them.

In seconds, any one of them could be a chew toy.

Then, anticlimactically, Hermes tossed Cerberus a honey cake, which the terrifying hound plopped down and devoured right then, wagging his tail—his snake—vigorously.

"That's all it took?" asked Yong.

"Music would have done it also, but it might have taken longer," said Hermes. "Of course, if you thought that was too easy, I'm happy to let you go back and see if you can outrun him or beat him in a fight. Heracles subdued him once."

"That's OK," said Yong. "I was just wondering."

"Yes, so was Pandora," said Hermes, grinning.

From the grim cavern where Cerberus roamed, it was only a short walk to the Asphodel Fields, so-called because the ground was covered with asphodel plants, with their grayish leaves and pale white flowers.

"Who are they?" asked Yasmin, pointing to figures even paler than the flowers. They wandered aimlessly around the shadowy plain, looking almost like characters from a scene in a zombie apocalypse movie.

"The recently dead," said Hermes, who chuckled when the students flinched away.

"They cannot hurt you, for they are like shadows of who they were in life. If you look closely, you can see who they were, but they retain little of their past selves, having drunk from the waters of Lethe."

"What happens to them?" asked Fatima. "They look so…sad."

"Just beyond these fields is a place of judgment, presided over by three judges appointed by Zeus and Hades: Minos, former king of Crete, son of Zeus and Europa; Rhadamanthus, his brother; and Aeacus, son of Zeus and Aegina."

"Why are they all sons of Zeus?" asked Mateo. "Why not Hades, since they are officials in his kingdom?"

"Grim Hades has no known mortal son," said Hermes. "No sons of any kind, really, and only one daughter, Macaria, as Demeter told us."

"His brothers have so many," said Fatima. "I don't understand why he doesn't."

"Mortals worship him, but they also fear him, even more than the temperamental Poseidon," Hermes replied. "It would be a rare woman indeed who would choose Hades as a lover. Everyone fears his touch means death."

"Women aren't always given a choice, though, are they?" asked Keisha. "Persephone wasn't."

"Hades tried such an abduction once before, with the Oceanid Leuce. Immortal though she should have been, she died and became a white poplar. Persephone, despite her youth and comparative innocence, managed to survive life in the Underworld, but Hades did not try again, and he never tried with a mortal—or if he did, the unhappy woman did not survive.

"The only woman who ever wanted to be with Hades was the nymph Minthe. All would have been well, but, as so often happens, though she loved Hades, he did not love her. When Hades brought Persephone to the Underworld, Minthe made the mistake of boasting that she was far more beautiful and would soon win Hades back. Persephone, or perhaps Demeter, changed her into a mint plant for her presumption."

"I would have thought she would have hoped Hades would love Minthe and let Persephone go," said Yasmin.

"I have never asked, but I assume Persephone knew Hades would never

210 A Dream Come True

release her of his own free will, whether he loved her or not. No one knows whether Hades even can love. If he can, he already had Minthe before he abducted Persephone. Either there wasn't any possibility of his loving Minthe, or he wanted someone of greater standing to be his queen. Zeus had Hera, after all, and Poseidon had Amphitrite, in both cases children of former rulers of their respective realms. Even Hades showed no desire to marry a daughter of someone like Tartarus, Erebus, or Nyx, so the best he could do would be someone from the Cronian line. Hestia was pledged to virginity, and Demeter could have defended herself too vigorously, so her daughter by Zeus, Persephone, would be the best choice if what Hades wanted was prestige."

"Then he doesn't even love her?" Fatima asked.

"I was merely speculating," said Hermes. "I don't know it was a question of family background—but if had been, Minthe could never have competed, and Persephone would have known that.

"I think Persephone knew she might be with Hades forever, and, if that were the case, she wanted to make the best of her situation, which may be why she survived when Leuce didn't. Part of making the best of it would be having a faithful husband, and that she got."

"I don't think we finished talking about the judgment," said Keisha.

"Actually, I already told you much about the afterlife that follows the judgment when we were with Apollo," said Hermes. "Just to be clear, those souls who have led a good life are sent to the Elysian Fields, a place that is like an idealized Earth, a little like Hyperborea, but even better. Those who have led an evil life are assigned suitable punishment. Those who have led an indifferent life remain here forever, or perhaps only until they reincarnate. The reincarnation part is, as you know, a later addition, and writers didn't agree on exactly how it worked."

"It would be better to think they reincarnated," said Fatima. "Imagine what it would be like to just drift aimlessly forever."

"It is best not to dwell on that, and we should be on our way to the palace of Hades," said Hermes.

They moved relatively quickly past the solemn judges, who would have objected to their presence had Thanos not raised the golden bough for them to see. Just beyond them flowed Lethe, shaded by a white cypress, and a small pool, shaded by a white poplar—Leuce, presumably.

"That's the pool of Mnemosyne," said Keisha. "Poseidon told me we should all drink from it to supercharge the way our memories operate, so we'd be more likely to spot clues about Patrick."

"Then do so," said Hermes, "but quickly. I sense Hades nearby and want to be sure we catch him before he moves to a different part of the Underworld."

Each one of the students drank, and all of them felt tingly, but none of them experienced any difference in their memories.

"The effect may take time," Hermes cautioned. "If Poseidon got his information from Mnemosyne herself, it must be good."

Hermes rushed them in the direction of a towering structure with a highly polished black marble facade, standing in a grove of poplars and willows, but with cypresses lining each side of the building.

"More landscaping than I'd expect," said Yong.

"It is said little grew here before Persephone came to live in the palace," said Hermes. "It is also said Hades planted the grove to cheer her, though it did not have much effect."

As they came out of the trees in front of the entrance to the palace, they all froze. Even Hermes, more familiar with the Underworld than any of them, looked shocked.

Arms and legs extended, chained tightly between two columns, was a pale and handsome god, his eyes closed. To his left stood another god with similar features but midnight black skin and an expressionless face. In between them stood a goddess, half white-skinned and half black, wearing a dark saffron robe, her face twisted in an expression that made Dionysus at his most frenzied look stable by comparison.

"What...what is the meaning of this?" asked Hermes, his caduceus raised protectively in front of him.

"Hades has sent us to greet you," said the black god, his voice deep but toneless as Ardalos's.

"He wishes us to bring you to him," said the goddess, her voice soft but oddly pitched.

Addressing the god, Hermes asked, "What of your brother? Why is he chained that way?"

"Hades has decreed it," said the black god.

"But why?" said Hermes. Artemis drew her bow, and Pan crouched, ready for battle. They were even less happy than Hermes.

"I did not ask," the black god replied. "Come with us now."

Hermes looked conflicted. "This is not the welcome I expected. Before we enter, I must have assurances that the visitors are considered guests of Hades."

"We have been given no such assurances," the black god replied. He showed no emotion, but the goddess looked impatient and fidgety.

"Come now," she said, "and do not further waste our time."

"One moment," said Hermes, after which he pulled the students back a little into the trees, with Artemis and Pan following close behind. Ardalos and Patricius stayed behind to eye the grim reception committee suspiciously.

"I am not sure it is safe to enter," Hermes told them. "Were it not for Apollo's prophecy, I would suggest immediate flight. Even as it is, I am tempted."

"Why?" asked Mateo. "Those guys are creepy, but isn't that the way the Underworld is supposed to be?"

"Who are they?" added Fatima.

"To answer your questions, no, the Underworld is not supposed to be quite as 'creepy' as that, and the black one is Thanatos—death you would call him. The white one is Hypnos, sleep, his twin brother, obviously now a prisoner of Hades, though what possible reason Hades could have for that I know not. The one of mixed color is Melinoe, whose origin is uncertain."

"Her story is late…Orphic, I think, isn't it?" asked Thanos.

"Yes, and Orphics, as you know, view the world quite differently from earlier storytellers. In Orphic belief, Melinoe is an obstacle to reaching a good afterlife, someone initiates are taught how to deal with. However, she is sometimes also portrayed as leaving the Underworld to roam during the night, bringing hauntings and madness to unwary mortals.

"Just as Orphics saw Dionysus as Zeus's successor, they saw Persephone as his true bride, like what you would think of as a soul mate. In their version of the relationship, Zeus found Persephone more beautiful than Aphrodite, loved her more than Hera, and would do anything to be with her. Their lovemaking was even described as a marriage, probably to emphasize that

Dionysus was the rightful heir of Zeus."

"If that was how they thought Zeus felt, how did they explain his allowing Hades to marry Persephone?" asked Fatima.

"They didn't," said Hermes. "Perhaps they believed Persephone was fated to spend half the year in the Underworld and that Zeus was merely bowing to the inevitable; perhaps they thought her imprisonment served some greater purpose. Orphic literature never says he agreed to allow her kidnapping, and, as you heard, even Demeter concedes that Persephone has been able to make the Underworld a better place."

"What does any of that have to do with Melinoe?" asked Yasmin.

"That is where the storytellers do not agree. Some say that Zeus made love to Persephone once again, this time when she was already married to Hades. Zeus disguised himself as the Underworld king, which would have allowed him to slip into the Underworld while Hades was away. It was during their second lovemaking that Melinoe was conceived."

"What?" asked Keisha. She had thought she was past being shocked by anything in the myths, but evidently, she was wrong. "Zeus lets Persephone be imprisoned for half of each year. He claims not to be able to do anything about it—but he finds ways to get into her prison and have sex with her."

"It may not be that simple, though," said Hermes.

"With Zeus it is always that simple," replied Artemis.

"No, it isn't!" snapped Hermes, looking more irritated than the students had ever seen him. "The Orphics believed Zeus and Hades were separate beings, just as other Greeks did, but they also identified them in some ways. Orphic writers often called Hades Cthonic Zeus."

"That's just another term for Hades, not an attempt to identify him with Zeus," said Artemis.

"Maybe not," replied Hermes. "Orphic writers sometimes refer to me as Cthonic Hermes, but there is only one of me—at least as far as I know. Anyway, Melinoe's mixed skin coloring was said to come from the mingling of the darkness of Hades with the light of Zeus—almost as if somehow they were both her father, as if Zeus was more than just disguised as Hades but was somehow one with him at that time. That would also explain why later writers sometimes call Hades Melinoe's father."

Artemis snorted. "Hermes, once again you are too willing to relieve Zeus from blame. He slept with his brother's wife—and in his brother's form, to trick poor Persephone. No other explanation makes sense.

"Maybe Hades really is her father," suggested Pan. "Perhaps the darkness is from Hades and the light from Persephone."

"It might be better for us to agree to disagree rather than keep arguing," said Hermes, glancing nervously in the direction of Thanatos and Melinoe. "Whether the Orphics are right or not, Hades never accepted Melinoe as his daughter, and she became a goddess to be feared and appeased, but never really loved. Perhaps she seeks to torment mortals in recompense for the torment inflicted upon her by her ambiguous circumstances. However she came to be who she is, Hades's use of her to greet us fills me with dread, for he has never employed her before."

"Indeed, being greeted by Madness—and Death—seems an evil omen," agreed Artemis, glancing at the menacing envoys.

The goddess's willingness to drop her argument with Hermes so abruptly chilled Keisha. It was just one more reminder of how dire their situation was.

"Should we leave?" asked Pan.

"Apollo said we must visit Hades and Persephone, as well as some of the dead in the Elysian Fields. If we leave now, we may never have the information to rescue your friend—who, if I am right about Hecate, could easily be a prisoner here in the Underworld."

"It begins to look as if Hades, not Hecate, could be behind all this," said Artemis. "How else can we explain this bizarre greeting or his imprisonment of a fellow god?"

"Perhaps he is behind it, or perhaps someone else has convinced him that we are," said Hermes. "When I visited him while Keisha was with Poseidon, it was clear he was far more agitated than normal. Someone was using magic to affect the Underworld as they have also affected earth and sea. If someone penetrated that far, the same person could have poisoned Hades against us."

"In either case, what likelihood is there we can get Hades's help now?" Artemis asked. "I say we leave here and head back to Hyperborea to get further advice from Apollo."

Hermes looked at the students. "We are here on your behalf. If we go forward, we risk facing the wrath of Hades. If we leave, we risk losing your friend and your only way home. What would you have us do?"

"What choice is there?" asked Keisha. "We can't just leave without Patrick. We have to at least try."

The others nodded, some more quickly than others. *Yong couldn't live with himself if he left Patrick behind*

"Neither alternative is great, but I'm going to take the one that allows me to look at myself in the mirror," said Yong.

After the decision had been made, Mateo said, "We have three gods with us. How much danger can we be in?"

"If Hades really is hostile, he has the advantage here," said Hermes. "An escort of ten gods might not be sufficient, unless two of them were Zeus and Poseidon. Still, you have made your brave choice, and those of us who are with you will do what we can to protect you."

"We are ready," Hermes told the "welcoming" committee. Thanatos bowed slightly, Melinoe sneered, and Hypnos gently snored. The first two turned and led them into the courtyard, both moving with silent steps. Those of Thanatos were measured and regular, those of Melinoe twitching and flickering as if she was not fully there. *wants to please Persephone*

The courtyard was large and nicely landscaped, probably to please Persephone again, though the ironic pomegranate trees were certainly a mistake in that case. There was also quite a bit of mint planted around the edges of the courtyard. Thanos couldn't help but wonder if that was Persephone's counter to the pomegranates; if she had to be reminded of the fruit that trapped her all the time, she was determined to remind Hades of the woman who actually loved him, the one he threw away to chase Persephone. Thanos supposed it was equally possible both were ironic gestures by Hades toward Persephone—just another dysfunctional relationship, this one expressed through gardening.

Then Thanos noticed their guides had slowed. At the same time, he noticed that their group was not alone in the courtyard. Moving out of a shadowy corner was a beautiful woman, her pale skin lit by the moonlight-like glow in the courtyard, her gleaming eyes focused on him. *Persephone?*

Thanos found himself drifting away from the others and toward this woman. She was putting out the same vibe as Aphrodite, though this time it was directed exclusively at him.

It was suddenly easy to forget that he was in the Underworld, and he longed to creep away, to vanish into the shadows with this woman, to—

"Son, watch out!" said Hermes, who had clamped a strong hand on his shoulder. *It's a trap*

To the woman, Hermes shouted, "Begone!" and waved the glowing caduceus at her. Suddenly, she was no longer beautiful—or human. The upper part of her body was pale human flesh, but the lower part was an enormous snake body with gray skin. Confronted by the power of Hermes, the thing shrieked and vanished back into the shadows.

Hermes pulled Thanos around to face him. "You must be more careful here. All is seldom what it seems."

"Why not just let him have his fun?" asked Melinoe, licking her lips. "He clearly wants to."

"Who...what...was that?" asked Thanos, still a little groggy.

"That was a lamia, a daemon who seduces young men so that she can drink their blood and eat their flesh," said Hermes. "There would have been little 'fun' involved." *10/10 Spelling*

"An object lesson in how sexual desires can be destructive," said Artemis, though her tone was not unkind.

"Leave the boy alone," said Pan. "It's not as if every woman he meets is going to want to kill him. Aunt, if you had your way, the human race would quickly become extinct."

"I thought Lamia was a Libyan queen loved by Zeus. Didn't she go mad when Hera stole her children and eventually became a spirit who hunted and ate other people's kids?" asked Yong.

"True, but what you just saw is a different kind of creature whose origin is less certain," said Hermes. "Sadly, there are many of them, the lamiae, and sometimes they escape into the world above with Melinoe or Hecate. When they do, no young man is safe from them."

"Dude, you really know how to pick them," said Mateo, poking the blushing Thanos in the ribs.

"Hades awaits," said Thanatos, perhaps impatient with the conversation, though his toneless voice gave no definite clue.

From the courtyard, Thanatos and Melinoe led them into a large, high-

Shows that they're brothers

ceilinged room—clearly the throne room.

Two figures, who had to be Hades and Persephone, were seated upon the ebony thrones. The man resembled Zeus and Poseidon, though his pale skin looked gray and bloodless enough to have been carved from stone, and his dark eyes were deeper and more frightening than Poseidon's. The sea god's eyes let one glimpse into the depths of the ocean, but Hades's revealed only the darkest corner of Erebus, absolute blackness without any hope that there would ever be light. His staff somehow looked as menacing as the trident of Poseidon, though it was not as clearly a weapon. The only touch that made him look a little less like some fierce guardian statue was the crown of white poplar leaves on his head, and even that seemed almost ready to wilt.

Persephone looked almost as grim but more human. Long-haired and beautiful, but made less lovely by her joyless face, she wore a crown of white asphodel flowers, but barely visible within it was a smaller golden circlet. Looking more closely, they could see how much of Hades's wealth gleamed from her. In the moonlike light, it was hard to tell the gold from the silver, or the emeralds from the sapphires, but it was clear that her husband had draped her with every precious gem and chain he could find.

Yes, she did look lovely that way—lovely and imprisoned, weighed down by her jewelry, a trophy wife in more ways than one.

Just looking at her made Keisha sad. The queen looked so alone, even sitting right next to the husband. Neither Amphitrite nor even Hera had looked so silently miserable.

At least they had agreed to marry their husbands. Persephone had not had even that opportunity.

Hermes bowed to the king and queen of the Underworld, and everyone else followed his lead.

"Nephew, I had not thought to see you again so soon," said Hades in a voice as deep as a bottomless pit.

"Uncle, I believe I mentioned the quest of our visitors here, a quest with which Apollo said you could offer help."

"Ah, yes, the mysterious visitors whose arrival so conveniently coincides with disruptions all across the universe," said Hades.

"Visitors we are proud to welcome as our guests," said Persephone quickly.

The way Hades glared at her suggested that he had not intended to extend the protection of the host-guest relationship to them, but he could not disavow her invitation.

"Before I offer you help, I have questions," Hades said to the students.

"We will happily answer any question to which we know the answer," said Thanos.

"Let us begin, then, with how you came to be here. Hypnos, who should have known, was unable to tell me. As you can see from his current condition, I am most anxious to learn the truth."

"Uncle, none of us know that truth, not these visitors, nor the god of sleep, nor even Apollo and Zeus," said Hermes.

"I was not asking you," replied Hades. "We may not know why strangers came from another world, but surely they know."

"Majesty, I'm afraid we don't," said Thanos. "We fell asleep in our world and woke up here. We assume this is all a dream, at least it is for us. That's all we know. As soon as we can, we will leave."

"Uncle, they are just ordinary mortals, no threat to you at all," added Hermes.

"Why would you think I would feel threatened by them—unless you know they are more of a threat than you say?" asked Hades, leaning forward. "I do not usually know much of what passes in the other realms unless a mortal pounds on the ground to invoke me, but when strange magic stirred here, I made a point of finding out what was happening elsewhere.

"Doesn't this one have a dragon within him?" asked Hades, pointing to Yong. "Did he not burn Ares with his breath? Did he not resist the war god's control over ordinary dragons? No mere mortal could do that."

"He had a little help from my magic," explained Hermes.

"Yet you told Zeus himself that all you were doing was displaying what the mortal had within him. Were you lying to the king of the gods?"

"I was…giving him an opportunity to preserve the sanctity of guest rights upon Olympus," said Hermes.

"This one," said Hades, pointing to Mateo, "seemed to be able to overcome centaurs, even though he was unarmed."

"He was invisible—" began Hermes.

"Ah, yes, which brings us to the subject of my spare invisibility caps. Nephew, I'm having a hard time remembering your asking to borrow them."

"If you have an issue with me, let us deal with it—once *your* guests are safely returned to their home," said Hermes.

"Husband, I can find no fault with them," said Persephone. "They seem to be good people. My mother sent me word that they were trustworthy. Apparently, some other gods found them equally virtuous. After all, if they were not, none of them could have plucked the golden bough." She stopped and looked at Thanos.

"Oh, I nearly forgot," he said, laying the branch at Persephone's feet, "to ensure our safe return from here, I am supposed to present it to you, right?"

Persephone smiled for the first time, "Yes, you have done well, and the blessing of the golden bough does guarantee that you can leave here." She looked at Hades as if making sure he understood.

"It is true that only those whose destiny is to come here can pluck that bow from the tree," said Hades, "or so it has always been, yet such strange things are happening I wonder if they have found some way around that safeguard."

"Nonetheless, they are our guests, and they have the bough," said Persephone. "The time for questions is done."

Hades was not prone to the same sudden rages that Poseidon was, but clearly he wasn't happy Persephone was pushing on him so hard.

"What is it exactly that you expect of me?" he asked Hermes. "How am I supposed to aid these so-called mortals? Do you take me for Athena, who helps with every heroic quest that crosses her path?"

"Perhaps your blessing to speak to the departed heroes in the Elysian Fields would suffice. The golden bough will grant them access, but some heroes might be reluctant to speak. They are not like Aeneas, who came seeking his own father. None of those to whom they wish to speak will know who they are, and some perhaps will be no happier to see them than you are."

"Even if I wished to do such a thing, you know the Elysian Fields is not entirely under my rule," said Hades, wagging a finger at Hermes as if scolding him. "Cronus rules there."

"What?" asked Keisha. "I thought he was a prisoner in Tartarus."

Much to her surprise, Hades shrugged. "Strange, is it not? The storytellers cannot agree on that point—even with themselves. Hesiod both states that Cronus is in Tartarus *and* that he rules the Elysian Fields. Other assume that Zeus released him and the other Titans at some point, but they offer no explanation for Gaia's continued anger over their imprisonment. Nor does anyone try to explain how Zeus, eager to protect his rule at all costs, would allow his dethroned father to roam free. To add to the confusion, even those storytellers who say Cronus rules the Elysian Fields never have him appear in any stories involving the place. The Greeks had a few temples to Cronus, though, and the Romans made much of Saturn, whom they equated with Cronus.

"Here is what I think. Cronus is somehow in two places at once. What rules the Elysian Fields is some fragment of him, some shadow, incapable of threatening Zeus."

"Why would Zeus allow even that?" asked Thanos.

"Either as a gesture of forgiveness or as a way to annoy me," said Hades. "By rights, the Elysian Fields should be mine, yet somehow it isn't."

"The Elysian Fields did not exist when you, Zeus, and Poseidon drew your lots," said Hermes. "I can see how it came to be assigned to someone else, though it might have been wiser to give it to you.

"Having visited this Cronus who rules Elysium, I would say he is not really the same as the one who languishes in Tartarus, for you are right in thinking Zeus would never trust the original Cronus with power—or even freedom."

"There are two Cronuses?" asked Thanos. "I don't remember any myth suggesting that."

"Yet the idea is not without precedent," Hermes replied. "Homer portrays the mortal shadow of Heracles roaming around in the Underworld, but other writers say his mortal part burned away on the funeral pyre, leaving his divine part to join us on Olympus. Eros is both a primal force and the son of Aphrodite, perhaps through some divine reincarnation like the rebirth of Dionysus in Orphic belief. There are many other examples.

"Though no storyteller or even mythographer takes up the issue, I would say from having met the ruler of the Elysian Fields that he is the kind of king the original Cronus dreamed of being, or perhaps the one he wanted us to think he was: the benevolent ruler of a golden age, now reborn in the Elysian Fields.

"This Cronus also seems mixed with Chronos, time personified, whom some Orphics think emerged at the beginning of creation. Later storytellers often confused Cronus and Chronos. In any case, the ruler of Elysium seems to govern the only place where mortals no longer need to fear the ravages of time. If you look at him that way, Uncle, it is no insult to you that he rules Elysium, for is not time in some ways the master of us all, despite our immortality?"

Hades snorted derisively. "As always, you are the apologist for the way things are. You take harsh reality, coat it with some fairy tale from Zeus, and call it blessed."

"Perhaps I just accept what I cannot change," said Hermes. "I may not be the god of truth, like Apollo, but I always tell you the truth as I know it. Here is one such truth: you may not rule Elysium, but you are respected there enough that your wish would be sufficient to gain us the ear of those with whom we wish to speak."

"When a guest makes a reasonable request, is it not a host's duty to fulfill that request?" asked Persephone.

"Indeed, but these guests are not requesting something unconnected to my hospitality here. Instead, they ask for favors in a realm that is not really mine. Perhaps I should offer them instead a banquet to celebrate their visit?"

Persephone, who knew better than anyone the danger of eating food in the Underworld, looked horrified, but Thanos, quick on his feet, reacted before she could.

"Majesty, much as we appreciate your offer, our time here is short, and we have no idea what will happen to our friend if we cannot bring him back with us. We must reach the Elysian Fields soon if we want to find the clues we need."

Hades's mouth twitched a little, though it was hard to tell whether he was grimacing or smiling. "Very well, I will encourage the heroes in the Elysian Fields to speak with you—as soon as one of you passes my test."

"Test?" asked Hermes, sounding worried.

"To prove you are worthy of the heroes' time."

"The golden bough—" began Persephone.

"Gives them the right to enter, but it does not compel the inhabitants to give the visitors their time. For that I will require something more."

Hades scanned the group for a moment. Then he pointed at Fatima, who cringed visibly.

"You in the back, the quiet one, I will assign this task to you."

"Majesty, allow me—" began Yasmin, who surprised herself a little by interrupting.

"Did you not hear me?" asked Hades, his voice a little louder now. "I assigned the task to her already, and my word is law here. It is not for anyone else to question. She will do it, or no one will."

"I'll do it," said Fatima so quietly it was hard to hear her, even in the comparative silence of Hades's palace. However, the king of the Underworld did hear her, and this time his smile was unmistakable—but still sinister.

"The test has been accepted. Stand over there," he commanded, pointing again to Fatima. She moved to the spot Hades indicated, even though that forced her to stand all alone. No one could miss the fact that she was shaking a little.

Hades gestured, and Patrick appeared right next to her—human Patrick, not doggie Patrick.

"He was here all along?" asked Yasmin.

"Perhaps," said Hades.

"That's an illusion!" said Hermes.

The image of Patrick faded. Hades, though not as prone to angry outbursts as Poseidon, had ways of communicating his displeasure, such as the stare of doom he now bestowed on Hermes.

"Nephew, you have nearly ruined the test. If you speak again, I will declare that the visitors have forfeited the challenge, and they will receive no help from me.

"Now," he continued, scanning the students again, "you know that your friend is not here, so I will need one of you to play what would have been his role in the test."

"I volunteer," said Yasmin, stepping forward.

"You don't know what he's going to ask you to do," said Yong.

"Does it matter?" she asked. "Just hunting for Patrick instead of trying to find the fastest way home is a risk. Can this be any riskier? Besides, I can't stand seeing Fatima all by herself over there."

Yasmin surprised herself again. She and Fatima weren't enemies, but they'd never exactly been friends, either. Still, the other girl looked so isolated over there, so vulnerable. Yasmin would have felt like slime if she hadn't offered to help.

"Stand by your friend," commanded Hades, and Yasmin obeyed. "Thanatos, step over there with them."

"Uncle—" began Hermes.

"Silence!" snapped Hades. He barely raised his voice, but something about his tone sent chills down everyone's spine, even the other gods. "I have had enough of your interference." The king of the Underworld raised his staff. "Not quite as showy as Poseidon's trident, but it has its uses. It too can split the earth, but more important, a single touch will kill. It won't be fatal to a god, but your recovery may be quite long and difficult."

"Why are you so angry with him?" asked Persephone. "He only wishes to help the mortals under his care. No doubt he would anger Zeus if he failed them."

"I am not at all sure that is his only motive," said Hades. "For all we know, it could be he who is behind the disruptions."

"How could I be?" asked Hermes. "I have been with these mortals the whole time."

"Someone who moves as fast as you could easily slip away unnoticed," said Hades. "Someone who has the ability to travel anywhere could easily recruit allies. Someone who can assume the identity of 'Hermes Thrice-Greatest' could easily be responsible for such magic as we have seen.

"Even if I am wrong," continued Hades, raising a hand to forestall Hermes's protests of innocence, "he is interfering with the performance of a task I have requested and that the mortals have agreed to. I will not have my authority here undermined."

"He is family," protested Persephone.

Hades gave her another sinister smile. "Family? Well, I suppose. But a family in which son overthrows father, in which brothers conspire to cheat each other, steal each other's wives, belittle each other's authority."

It did not take a genius to realize that Hades had less than an ideal relationship with Zeus and Poseidon.

"So Hermes is family," agreed Hades. "Does he ever visit us? Only when

Zeus sends him here to deliver a message. And what of my huntress niece and furry grandnephew? Do they come to break bread with us? Have you ever seen them here in all these millenniums?"

Artemis started to protest, but Hades raised his hand again, and the room seemed to get darker. Without any physical change, Hades somehow seemed very large, and the other gods very small.

"The test happens now, or it never happens. Mortals, what say you?"

"Go ahead," said Yasmin. Fatima, too frightened to speak, nodded.

"Very well," said Hades. Thanatos is going to embrace one of you. Young lady—"

"Fatima," she whispered.

"Fatima, you will choose which one of you he embraces."

Fatima looked confused, so Thanos, knowing Hermes dared not speak again, took the risk of saying, "Thanatos is death, remember? Whomever he touches dies."

"My touch is gentle," said Thanatos in a voice now frightening in its lack of emotion.

"They are guests—" began Persephone loudly.

"Who have freely chosen my test," said Hades.

"It's only a dream," said Yasmin, trying to reassure Fatima, who looked as if she would die before she could make a decision.

"So you think, anyway," said Hades. Turning to everyone else, he said, "The next word any of you speak will condemn you to Tartarus. The choice is now hers, and no one else's."

That Hades could arbitrarily fling someone into Tartarus without the approval of Zeus seemed doubtful, but clearly, no one was willing to call his bluff. The large, echoing room was suddenly silent as a tomb.

"Well?" Hades asked, looking at Fatima with his piercing eyes. "Which one of you will receive the embrace?"

"I will," whispered Fatima, stepping forward.

Yasmin looked as if she might try to jump into Thanatos's arms herself, but Fatima beat her to it, flinging herself right into the embrace of death.

The girl too shy to open her mouth in class had just sacrificed herself for someone else.

Or at least, so it appeared at first. Thanatos became a swirl of shadows that engulfed Fatima—and then he faded away, leaving her stunned, but alive.

"Another illusion!" said Hermes, looking shocked but also very happy.

"Everyone is ready to believe me a monster," said Hades. "Your surprise that I am not hurts me, Nephew."

"I...I passed the test?" asked Fatima, still shaky.

"You did indeed," replied Hades. "I wanted to see if you would be willing to die for someone else, and you were. You are in harmony with my daughter, Macaria, who protects those willing to die for a good cause."

"Melinoe is gone," said Pan, looking around.

"Like Thanatos, she was an illusion," Hades explained. "The real Melinoe would be...an unpredictable envoy, and Thanatos is an elder power who comes when he is fated to come, not at my bidding."

Hades handed a ring to Fatima. "This is my signet. Show it to anyone in the Elysian Fields, and they will treat your request as they would mine."

"Take the golden bough also," said Persephone, "for you will need that to enter the Fields. Hermes will be able to show you where they are."

"Master, master!" shrieked a shrill voice behind them.

"Eurynomus, what's wrong?" asked Hades.

Turning, the students saw the small Eurynomus rushing forward. He was shorter than they were, and he had bluish-gray skin and an enormous vulture head too large for his body.

"Someone has broken Hypnos free!" the little creature shouted.

Hades narrowed his eyes. "I was just about to release him, since it is clear the visitors are not some plot of his against me—but that someone else would break him free before I made my decision troubles me deeply."

Turning to Persephone, he asked, "Is Heracles here? He does have the unfortunate habit of wanting to free prisoners of the gods."

"He always asks first, though," Persephone reminded him. "Besides, he is not exactly inconspicuous. If he were anywhere in the Underworld, you would surely know it."

"True," said Hades. "Eurynomus, is there any evidence of who did this deed?"

"Unbelievable evidence," said the little creature. "The chain was cut—not an easy thing to do. I asked Amphiarus, the oracle who lives underground at Oropus, to give his opinion, and he said he could not see who had done the deed. He added, though, that the magic felt Telchine."

"There it is again," said Hades. "The Telchines *are* still imprisoned in Tartarus, yet people keep seeing them, and now someone is feeling their unique magic. What could be the meaning of this?"

"I just had a thought," said Thanos. "Maybe this is the water from Mnemosyne's pool talking, but Majesty, didn't you say not long ago you thought Cronus could simultaneously be in Tartarus and in the Elysian Fields? If he can do it, why not the Telchines?"

"We know gods can be in two places at once," said Keisha. "Selene met with us at night, even though she was up in the sky in her lunar chariot."

"Those may be the most clever insights I've ever heard from a mortal," said Hades. "Yes, some gods can be in two places at once, and yes, that would explain Cronus. In his case, though, he would have to be doing it with Zeus's consent. I can't think of any reason for Zeus to give such consent to the Telchines—unless it is Zeus himself who is behind all of these disturbances."

"I am no admirer of Zeus," said Artemis. "Even so, I have a hard time imagining him unleashing that kind of menace."

"Yet it makes a horrible kind of sense," said Hades. "Perhaps Zeus is dissatisfied with the results of our long-ago lottery. Perhaps he seeks absolute mastery not only over the sky but over the sea and Underworld as well. Powerful as he is, he would have difficulty taking on Poseidon and me together. With Telchine help, though, he just might pull it off."

"At the risk of disrupting the entire universe in the process?" asked Hermes. "Say what you will about Zeus, he is more cautious than that."

"And more legalistic," added Persephone. "I have no reason to love him, either—"

"And yet you have," said Hades, a touch of bitterness in his voice. "Perhaps you still do."

"He is part of my family," said Persephone, dodging Hades's accusation. "He is part of yours as well, and you must admit this kind of trickery is not his style."

"No," said Hades, scowling at Hermes. "We know who our ultimate trickster is."

"This is getting us nowhere," said Pan. "Whoever is causing these strange events wants us to mistrust each other. So far I've heard mistrust for Hera, Iris, Ares, Hecate, Tartarus, Hermes, Dionysus, Poseidon, Zeus Hypnos, and even you, Granduncle. A case can be made for any of those, but clearly they cannot all be guilty.

"Perhaps we should consider Apate—treachery and deceit incarnate, secretive daughter of Nyx, sister to Hypnos, which would have given her a reason to free him if nothing else," suggested Hades. Despite naming another possible suspect, he kept staring at Hermes.

"If we want to accuse those primal abstractions, the way in which some of us receive misleading news suggests the fine hand of Pheme, rumor and gossip incarnate," said Persephone.

"Sometimes called the messenger of Zeus," said Hades, as if that proved his earlier point.

"I do not wish to be disrespectful," said Thanos, "but we should be on our way to the Elysian Fields soon."

"You have my permission to go," said Hades. "I will remain here and probe this matter further. All of you be warned—anyone, god or mortal, involved in this vile conspiracy shall pay for his or her crimes."

On that ominous note, Hades rose from his throne and quickly exited, with Eurynomus loping behind.

"I apologize for his treatment of you, my guests," Persephone said. "It was wrong of him to put you to the test."

"Everyone is on edge now," said Hermes. "I understand why he might be suspicious of strangers."

Persephone sighed. "I fear there is a darkness in him which recent events cannot excuse, for he has been that way as long as I have known him.

"He may not always have been as he is now, though. I have occasionally thought that cursed lottery doomed him. It is sometimes said that ruling over this gloomy place made him dark, just as ruling over the untamable sea made Poseidon wild. Perhaps the three brothers would have done better to rotate, but it is too late to worry about that now."

Hermes bowed to her. "Thank you, Sister, for your bravery in standing up to him."

Persephone smiled. "I do what I can to moderate his harshness. I only wish I could do more. Speaking of which, I should not leave him alone to brood too long. Who knows what rash accusation he may make next?"

After everyone else had thanked her and she had wished the party good luck, Persephone, who managed to get off the throne despite being weighed down by her jewels, slowly departed.

"Not a very practical way to dress," said Mateo.

"He gives her jewels to buy her love," said Fatima quietly. "He wants the one thing he can never have."

"Considering how he treated you, it's pretty generous of you to feel sorry for him," said Yasmin.

"Well, how do we get to the Elysian Fields?" Thanos asked Hermes.

"That's easy. We go back to the place of judgment, then take the right-hand path. It will lead us to the Elysian Fields—hopefully, the final part of your quest."

With Hermes leading the way, the trip was short, and before they knew it, they were on the correct path. It was winding and therefore a little hard to stay on, but none of the students worried—until a shadowy figure blocked their path.

They could not see it clearly, but it appeared to have the head of a dog and the fins of a fish.

"A Telchine," whispered Hermes fearfully.

Chapter 19: Deucalion and Pyrrha

Hermes waved his caduceus, spreading out what protection against magic he could. The students knew their amber amulets and the dose of moly they'd taken shielded them in some ways, but having heard so much about the unusual nature of Telchine magic, they weren't sure how well guarded they really were.

Just as they had done when earlier threats emerged, Artemis readied an arrow, and Pan poised himself to lunge at the Telchine. Ardalos and Patricius positioned themselves between the students and the Telchine. The mechanical dog bared its teeth and growled.

"Let me pass," said a voice halfway between human and dog that sounded as if it was coming up from the bottom of a well. "I have no quarrel with you."

"Foul Telchine, your malice is well known. Zeus in his wisdom imprisoned you in Tartarus, and back there shall you go. There is but one of you, and you face three Olympians, so you may as well surrender now."

The Telchine's laugh echoed through the cavern. "My brethren are nearby, but even alone, I think I am a match for an errand boy, a woman who thinks she's a man, a freak of nature, a couple of primitive automatons, and a few weak mortals. It took Zeus himself to defeat us before—and he only managed because he caught us by surprise."

"You must come with us," said Hermes. The Telchine was big enough to almost completely block the path ahead of them, and the caduceus, despite its glow, didn't look like much of a weapon against it.

"Consider carefully whom you face," said the Telchine, "for I mastered magic before any of you were born. When Gaia needed a weapon to give Cronus to use against the great Uranus, she came to us.

"Think about that. A weapon that could harm a god—a king of gods— beyond any hope of healing. Think what other weapons we might have dreamed of during our long imprisonment. Think of what I might be able to do to you right now."

Was the caduceus shaking a little? Was Hermes even more frightened than he had been when Death and Madness showed up to greet them? It certainly looked that way to the students.

"Your skill at weather working is well known," said Hermes finally, his voice surprisingly steady. "It is not, however, something you can use to full advantage in the Underworld."

The Telchine laughed again. "It is only one of my many gifts. Cold as the place is, fire works quite well down here."

A wall of flame erupted in front of the Telchine, making him completely invisible to them. Artemis shot her arrow, but it vanished into the fire without a trace. If it struck the Telchine, it made no sound when it did, unless that sound was lost in the crackling of the flames.

Then the fire surged in their direction, and the students thought they were doomed. They saw a flash, felt an instant of heat—and then the fire was gone. So was the Telchine, though the echo of his mocking laughter remained.

"It is not your time—yet," its voice whispered faintly, as if from a great distance away. Then even that far away voice fell silent.

"He escaped!" said Artemis, clearly enraged.

"If he was ever here at all," said Hermes.

"What do you mean?" asked Pan. "He certainly seemed to be here."

"I was braced to resist a major magical attack, but what hit us was...impressive looking, but not really all that strong.

"Perhaps long imprisonment has weakened him," said Artemis.

"Perhaps," conceded Hermes, "but why is he here? Having just escaped from Tartarus, would he not wish to be as far away from the Underworld as possible?"

"This isn't the worst place to hide from Zeus," said Pan.

"No, but it's a terrible place to hide from Hades," countered Hermes.

"How so?" asked Pan. "Someone certainly has the power to create...static, I think our mortal friends would call it. You told me Apollo was having more difficulty than usual giving you a direct answer, and Poseidon, Dionysus, and Hades all failed to discern the true source of the threats on their respective realms. If the Telchines have such a power, maybe they don't need to fear detection."

"No power is absolute," said Hermes. "The fact that many people have seen Telchines recently proves that—assuming they don't want to be seen. If they have the power to make it more difficult for us to see what they are up to, why not flee to a remote area the gods don't pay attention to and hide there?

Why stay in a realm Hades watches closely?

"And what would the Telchine be doing on the road to the Elysian Fields? Go forward, and he ends up at the entrance to the Fields, where he is much more likely to be detected. Go back, and he stands before the judges of the Underworld, not far from the palace of Hades. Again, he is much more likely to be detected. There is no place else he can go from here.

"Escape with an imperfect way of avoiding detection, then lurk near the prison? No, the Telchines are many things, but they are not stupid. They would have fled—which means we just saw an illusion."

"Aside from the weakness of the fire, he did seem real enough," said Artemis.

"And only a short time before, we were fooled by illusions of Thanatos and Melinoe," Hermes pointed out. "Hades can clearly craft illusions that will deceive even gods, and we already know Hecate can. Who else might be able to?"

"To what purpose?" asked Pan.

"It's part of the same strategy someone is using to turn us against each other," said Hermes. "If we can't trust our own senses, how can we tell what is real and what isn't?"

Yong thought to himself there was something ironic about a character in a dream saying that. He and his friends hadn't been able to trust their senses from the very beginning.

"At the moment, we have no way of testing your theory," Artemis pointed out. "However, if there are Telchines on the loose, we had better get our visitors to the Elysian Fields, where they will be much safer than they would be on this road."

At this point Hermes, Artemis, and Pan didn't agree on much, but they did agree the students would be safer once they reached their goal. No one except the gods, the blessed dead, and the occasional golden bough holder, had ever been able to enter Elysium, so it was safe to assume that if there were Telchines roaming around, they wouldn't be able to breach the place.

After a relatively short trip, they reached what looked like the entrance to another cavern, except that they could see sunlight through it.

"Is that magical illumination, like the moonlight in other parts of the

Underworld, or is it actually the sun?" asked Yong.

"That depends on who you believe," said Hermes with a wink. "Is this just a magical doorway to another part of the Underworld, or is it a portal to an island in the far west? The place seems to be above ground, but whether or not it actually is depends on who's telling the story."

"Is something wrong?" asked Yasmin, noticing Artemis and Pan were both looking nervously at the entrance.

"I must from time to time visit Elysium," said Hermes, "but most gods do not."

"Immortal as we are, something about death still disturbs us," said Pan. "That's one of the reasons Hades has so few visitors. The price of being immortal is to watch mortals you care about die until there is a seemingly endless line of them."

"I don't understand," said Yasmin. "Death isn't the end in your world. You can communicate with those who have passed on. Why wouldn't you want to?"

"Those who have led indifferent lives are little more than shadows, as you have seen," said Artemis. "Those who have led virtuous lives and are in Elysium are...I don't know how to describe it. It is as if there is a veil between them and us. We cannot truly communicate with them, either. Why else would there be so many stories of gods mourning those they have lost? Yes, the soul lives on, and yes, the gods know that those they loved are happy, but that's still different from being able to see them every day and share their experiences as they once did. I can no longer hunt with my companions, just as Aphrodite cannot make love to hers."

It was the first time any of the students had ever heard Artemis compare herself to Aphrodite, but evidently they did share a common sorrow.

"You mean you can't visit Elysium?" asked Fatima.

"We can be there physically, but for us, it's like watching someone from a great distance and knowing we can never move closer."

"I don't remember that in any of the stories," said Thanos.

"No surviving tale says that exactly," said Hermes, "but think about it. Is there any tale of the gods visiting Elysium? No. Would there be any reason for gods to mourn mortals who died if they could visit them anytime? No."

"Myths don't always make sense," muttered Mateo.

"No, they don't," agreed Hermes. "But later writers did try to make sense of them sometimes, so I can't help trying."

"Why not just make mortals you love gods?" asked Keisha. "That seems to work."

"It does not always," said Hermes, "though why it sometimes fails, no one really knows. What we do know is that Hades would oppose any mass conversions of mortals into gods. He resists even individual exceptions, and Zeus does not like to overrule him.

"For that matter, Zeus himself would forbid us the unrestrained creation of immortals. As he told you, the gift cannot be withdrawn once it is given, and he doubts that many are truly worthy.

"After all," Hermes added, "how many of us who were born gods are truly worthy?"

That was a question all of the students were wise enough not to answer. Hermes seemed friendly and very protective of them, but they couldn't be sure that he, like all the other gods they had met, didn't occasionally lose control of his temper.

"Some few there are who seem to transform into gods on their own," said Thanos. "Remember the story of Adonis? No storyteller ever suggested that Aphrodite found a way to make him immortal, yet he was worshiped wherever Greeks settled. He became one of the so-called dying gods."

"Oh, yeah," said Keisha. "The ones who die in the fall and rise in spring, representing the seasons the way Persephone does."

"Exactly," Hermes said, nodding. "Aphrodite still mourns him, though, for he, like the dead in Elysium, is not really ever with her as he was before, despite the periodic celebration of his resurrection. In some cities, their marriage is celebrated one day, and his death is mourned the very next, which may be close to the truth of how much contact between them there is now."

"Do you see the problem?" Pan asked the students. "A mortal can have an afterlife, maybe even become a kind of god, and still not be the companion the gods remember from his or her mortal life. That is why most of us forgo the pain of visiting Elysium."

"Now I'm worried," said Keisha. "If we can't communicate with the blessed dead—"

"Have no fear," said Hermes. "Sometimes mortals can do what gods cannot. In the presence of the golden bough, mortals can speak to the inhabitants of Elysium.

"However, it may be best to divide our party for a while. I will accompany you, for my role as guide of souls to the Underworld allows me to commune with the blessed dead more than most can. Artemis and Pan, however, cannot, and going in would only give them pain without advancing your quest in any way. Ardalos and Patricius will not be of much use in Elysium either. I would suggest those four conduct a thorough search of the Underworld since it is likely the place Patrick is being held prisoner."

Both Artemis and Pan look relieved, but Ardalos seemed offended.

"Our maker told us to aid the visitors," he said tonelessly. "How are we to do that if we are not with them?"

"Once the visitors have found whatever clues they can in Elysium, they may need to move fast," said Hermes. "The best way you can help now is by searching where they might have to search. Perhaps you will not discover where their friend is, but even ruling out some places will make the search easier."

"I still have his scent," said Patricius. "Should he be nearby, I will sniff him out."

Yong was about to object to the plan. If the search Hermes was proposing was so valuable, why hadn't Apollo suggested it in the first place? However, looking at Artemis's and Pan's faces, Yong decided to say nothing. Apparently, they really couldn't do much in Elysium themselves. Perhaps Hermes was giving them a job that would make them feel useful.

"After saying their good-byes, Artemis and Pan moved quickly back down the path, with Patricius trotting after them, and Ardalos dragging along behind. Despite his limited ability to convey—or even feel—emotion, it was clear he would rather have stayed with the students as he believed Hephaestus wanted.

Stepping from the gloom of the Underworld into the light of the Elysian Fields was almost too wonderful to describe. The scene that greeted them was like an idealized version of ancient Greece. The sun was bright, but not overly hot. The breeze was cool without being chilling. The air was perfumed with the scent of thousands of flowers that bloomed in patches dotting an earth so green with grass it looked like a modern lawn. Except for a few items in the Underworld, such as Persephone's jewels or Melinoe's saffron robe, the colors had seemed washed out, like the gray-leafed plants with their white flowers. Here the colors were vivid enough to hurt eyes used to the Underworld blend of shadow and paleness.

There were many people scattered around. Some just seemed to be walking around, enjoying the scenery. Others were competing in sports like boxing, wrestling, and archery in small arenas obviously set up for the purpose. Some performed plays for appreciative audiences in amphitheaters. Here and there one could see couples walking hand in hand and whispering to each other.

"How are we going to find anyone here?" asked Keisha.

Hermes smiled. "Remember that one of my jobs is to guide souls to the Underworld. I have a kind of affinity for the dead. Yes, this place is vast, but I can seek out any specific person you need without too much trouble. Apollo gave me a list of which ones might be most likely to give us the clue we need."

"They don't seem to notice us at all," said Yong. "Are visitors that common?"

"Not at all, but you are for all practical purposes invisible to them without the golden bough. Thanos, if you hold it up and concentrate, they will become aware of us. I see Apollodorus nearby, and we will want to speak to him first."

"Apollodorus is the one who wrote *Library*, that ancient summary of myths intended for students in his time?" asked Thanos.

"The very same," said Hermes. "As I think about, he is even more familiar with Elysium than I am, for he travels through it quite a bit to seek new stories. He may, therefore, show us the quickest way to reach the people we seek."

"The dude wrote the ancient equivalent of *Sparknotes*?" asked Mateo.

"Sort of," said Thanos. "His summary was intended for student use, but it was also a great literary work in its own right."

"Golden bough," Hermes prompted.

"Oh, right," said Thanos, holding it. The moment he did so, several people glanced in their direction, and Apollodorus, eyes focused on Hermes rather than on the students, walked in their direction.

"Greetings, my lord," he said, bowing to Hermes. "I see you have brought guests." His eyes widened. "By their appearance I would judge they are...not of this world."

"Indeed," said Hermes. "They are visitors from another world who urgently require our assistance. A friend of theirs has been abducted by dark forces, and they have very limited time to rescue him."

Apollodorus raised an eyebrow. "Dark forces? Could they have anything to do with the rumors we have been hearing? Normally, we get little news from the land of the living, but recently we have heard tales of dissension among the gods."

"Those tales are all too true," said Hermes. "We suspect the god or gods responsible for the growing tensions are also responsible for the disappearance of their companion.

"You can aid us, my friend, by helping us locate each of the blessed dead to whom Apollo directed us. He believes that somewhere in Elysium lies the final clue needed to resolve their quest."

"I will do whatever I can," said Apollodorus. "Whom do you seek first?"

"Deucalion and Pyrrha," said Hermes.

"Ah, yes, the survivors of the Great Flood," said Apollodorus. "Oddly, they seem to like to stroll along the seashore. You will likely find them along the western coast of the Elysian Fields."

"Then they should be easy enough to find," said Hermes. "Will you accompany us, Apollodorus? I would not trouble you, but we may need your help later on."

"It is no trouble. Visiting again with some of the heroes I wrote about so long ago would be a pleasure."

"Then let us be on our way," said Hermes, who magically whisked the whole group to a white, sandy beach, beyond which lay a gently rippling sea that sparkled with reflected sunlight.

"If this is all really underground, it's impossible to tell," said Yong.

Just as Apollodorus predicted, they found Deucalion and Pyrrha walking along the shore, their arms around each other.

"A marriage that lasted thousands of years," said Fatima, clearly in awe.

"One does see that from time to time in the Elysian Fields," said Apollodorus.

"It's too bad the gods can't seem to follow that example," muttered

Hermes.

Thanos again raised the golden bough, and Apollodorus introduced the students to Deucalion and Pyrrha, who were more than happy to help.

"I don't know whether the story of our lives is the one with the clue you need," said Deucalion. "However, you are more than welcome to hear our story.

"I am the son of the Titan Prometheus and the Oceanid Hesione, though for some reason I was born mortal, not divine. The lines were vaguer in those early days."

"I am the daughter of the Titan Epimetheus, Prometheus's brother, and Pandora," said Pyrrha.

"Beautiful as her mother, but not cursed as her mother was, to bring misery into the world," said Deucalion.

"Epimetheus stayed married to Pandora after...the incident?" asked Keisha.

"He loved her despite everything," said Pyrrha. "Zeus rules the universe, but Aphrodite rules our hearts."

"Pyrrha and I were happily married for many years. For a while I was king of Phthia. Then my father, who had realized that Zeus planned to flood part of the world in response to the evils of mortals, warned me what was to come. I built an ark, loaded it with provisions, and just before the rain started, Pyrrha and I climbed aboard.

"For nine days and nine nights the rains fell, but we floated safely to the top of Mount Parnassus, which remained above water, as did some of the other mountaintops."

"When the waters finally receded, Zeus sent Hermes to grant us whatever we desired. At the time I thought we were the only mortals left. As it turned out, the flood only affected part of Greece, and a number of mortals even in those areas managed to climb mountains fast enough to avoid drowning. However, unaware of that, we asked for the creation of a new race of people.

"Hermes told us that if we threw stones over our shoulders, we would create that new race."

"It seemed too good to believe," said Pyrrha, "but we knew better than to question the gods, so after we came down from the mountain, we did what Hermes had told us, and every stone I threw became a woman, while every stone Deucalion threw became a man. Together we created the Leleges, the new inhabitants of eastern Locris, where we settled and started a new life."

"The gods granted us wonderful sons," said Deucalion. "The first was Hellen, who became the ancestor of most Greek peoples. He settled in Thessaly, from whence Pyrrha and I had come. There he wed the nymph Oreis and had three sons. Each was excellent in his own way, but sadly there was discord among them. The first, Aeolus, became Hellen's heir, but the other two, Dorus and Xuthus, were made joint heirs of certain property.

"You would have thought that good brothers could have shared with each other in peace, but our grandsons often fought with each other. Xuthus was accused of stealing from the joint inheritance and exiled to Athens.

"There he wed King Erechtheus's daughter, Creusa, but perhaps Xuthus really had stolen from his brothers, for misfortune followed him to his new home. When Erechtheus died, the Athenians asked Xuthus to arbitrate the succession. He chose Cecrops as the next king, but the other Athenian princes were so angry over the decision that Xuthus had to leave Athens."

"Again Xuthus started over, this time in the city of Aegealus, where he was chosen king—and again misfortune found him," said Pyrrha. "You see, he and Creusa had no children, though Xuthus very much wanted one. To make matters more complicated, Creusa was loved by Apollo, and when she realized she was pregnant, her instincts told her it was Apollo's, not Xuthus's. She feared the wrath of Xuthus and planned to conceal her pregnancy, give birth in secret, and then abandon the infant, a common custom in early Greece."

"That's horrible!" said Fatima.

"Which is why, I suppose, the gods so often intervened to stop it," said Pyrrha. "In this case, Apollo was not about to let the princess make such a tragic mistake, particularly as his own son was involved. He sent Hermes to take the child from his cradle and bring him to Delphi to be raised by the priests there. Eventually, the oracle told Xuthus that the next person he would meet would be his son, and Apollo made sure Xuthus encountered Ion right after that. Xuthus was happy, for he believed Ion to be a long-lost son, fathered before Xuthus had met Creusa.

"Alas, the possibility of tragedy still hung over them, for Creusa did not know Ion was her son by Apollo. She and Xuthus had not yet had a son, but

Creusa feared Ion would become Xuthus's heir even if she gave Xuthus a son. The maternal instincts she struggled to overcome when she sought to abandon Apollo's child burned in her with renewed strength for her yet unconceived son, whose right to inherit could only be assured in one way—by killing Ion.

"Creusa tried to poison Ion to secure Xuthus's inheritance for her future son. However, alerted by an omen from Apollo, Ion avoided drinking the poisoned wine. He then threatened the servant who had brought him the wine and found out that Creusa was the one trying to kill him. Ion would have killed her, but Athena appeared and revealed the truth to both of them. She also told them not to reveal what she had said to Xuthus.

"That was the end of their misfortunes, for each got what he or she wanted. Xuthus went on thinking Ion was his own son. Though the truth is usually best, in this case, it would have crushed him. As for Ion and Creusa, they were reunited with each other."

"Did Xuthus and Creusa ever have a son?" asked Fatima.

"Yes, they had Achaeus shortly after," said Deucalion. "The younger prince, despite Creusa's earlier fears, became Xuthus's heir and was given Aegealus in the region later called Achaea, but he left it to Ion because he wanted to return to Thessaly and win back what he felt Xuthus had been unfairly deprived of in their original homeland. There he conquered a region that came to be known as Thessalian Achaea. Much later, his two sons returned to the original Achaea, where they married into the royal houses of Argos and Sparta, eventually becoming kings of both cities.

"Ion too had many adventures, fighting on the side of his mother's city, Athens, and eventually becoming its king. His descendants were the Ionians who ultimately settled many islands and towns along the western coast of Asia Minor.

"As for Xuthus's two brothers, they also prospered, for Aeolus become father to the Aeolians, while Dorus became father to the Dorians. In a few generations, it was hard to find a Greek people that were not related in some way to the sons of Hellen.

"We meant to repeople the world with our stone children, but ironically it was our flesh children who helped repeople Greece."

"Thank you for the story," said Thanos, bowing, "though if there is a clue to the location of our friend, I'm not smart enough to see it."

"Perhaps, like the jigsaw, you must have all the pieces," suggested Hermes. "Maybe we need to hear all the stories, for each has a piece of the clue."

"That would explain why Apollo wanted us to visit so many people," said Keisha. "It's too bad in some ways, though. Putting the clue together might be beyond us, especially with stories as…rich in detail as these."

"I could help you," said Apollodorus. "I studied all the myths extensively for months and have a better knowledge of them than any mortal—despite what Hyginus says."

Hermes smiled. "You may also be able to help yourselves more than you know. Remember that you all drank the water of Mnemosyne. Didn't it make a difference?"

"I…I can remember the whole story we just heard," said Mateo, clearly surprised. "I don't just mean the details. I mean exact words."

"Perhaps the clue is in the language, then," Apollodorus suggested. "If Apollo guided you well—and he has never failed anyone—then everything he wanted you to do must contribute in some way to your success."

"Apollo sent you to Poseidon, among others," said Hermes. "Poseidon told you about the waters of Mnemosyne, and they have given you the gift of total recall. That means Apollodorus is right. Somehow, that recall will help you discern the clue."

Suddenly they were almost knocked off their feet by an earthquake. It was mild by California standards, but the Elysians were alarmed by it.

"Earthquakes never happen here!" Apollodorus almost shouted. "Never!"

"This is an evil omen," said Deucalion.

"It is more than that," said Hermes. "It could be a sign the end of the world as we know it."

"What you do mean?" asked Pyrrha.

"Four of the most heavily defended places in our universe have been attacked in one way or another. A mortal protected by Zeus's hospitality was snatched from Olympus. The sea near Poseidon's palace was nearly torn from his control. The Underworld, so carefully policed by Hades, is now haunted by images of Telchines, and the air thickens with magic. Now this place, protected by some aspect of Cronus, filled with the greatest heroes of all time, and immune from the disasters that plague humans on earth, has an earthquake.

"As yet we have seen only minor displays of power, but they indicate someone strong enough to be a threat, someone fearless enough to challenge the most powerful gods directly. There would be no profit in making such a challenge unless whoever it is believes he or she can win.

"Hermes, these are grave matters indeed," said Deucalion. "Perhaps Zeus will need you now."

"He has not summoned me," said Hermes, "and helping the visitors find their friend will almost certainly lead us to whoever is causing these disturbances."

"In that case, let us hasten to the next person Apollo suggested," said Apollodorus, looking at an unusually agitated Elysian sea.

"Yes, for time may be running out," said Pyrrha, looking up at clouds that had subtly darkened in the last few minutes.

Keisha hoped she was imagining it, but she thought she heard the echo of mocking Telchine laughter in the distance.

Chapter 20: Io and Her Family

Hermes squinted at the list Apollo had given him. "This can't be right. The next name is Io, but she is a nymph, not one of the blessed dead."

"Some say that her parents were mortal," said Apollodorus.

"She lived with mortals and may have had mortal foster parents," said Hermes, "but her father was the river god Inachus, and her mother, the Oceanid Melia."

"As Deucalion said, the boundaries were a little less clear in those days," Apollodorus replied. "Besides, her brothers, Phoroneus and Aegialeus, were mortal."

"Or at least pretended to be," said a voice behind them.

Turning, they saw a beautiful woman with a headdress that made her look as if she had two horns sprouting from her head. Her gown looked to Thanos more like what one saw in ancient Egyptian art than in ancient Greek. As he looked more closely, the garment looked almost like cowhide, and it seemed to change from white to dark red to black as he watched.

"Io," said Hermes, bowing to her, "I had not thought to find you here."

"I come here sometimes to view my family," said Io. "Word of your arrival with such…unusual guests have already spread all over Elysium, so I came to you because I owe you a long-ago favor. I thought I might be able to help in some way."

"Indeed you may, for we are on a critical quest, and you are one of the people to whom Apollo sent us. He was sure that a clue, or part of one, is buried somewhere within your story."

Io smiled. "You could tell part of that story quite well yourself, but if you need my version, I am happy to tell it.

"I grew up in Argos, the city of which Phoroneus, my brother, was first king and founder. Actually, he ruled the whole Peloponnese, and that was not his only achievement, for he was one of the first men to make use of the fire Prometheus had stolen. He also introduced the worship of Hera in the region, and I, as his dutiful sister, became Hera's priestess.

"Unfortunately for me, I was not to continue long in that role, for Zeus saw me and fell in love with me, bringing discord and misery into my life."

Hermes looked uncomfortable but did not interrupt.

"Caught by Hera, Zeus quickly changed me into a cow to conceal his adultery, but Hera was not fooled. Pretending to believe Zeus, she commented on what a beautiful cow I was and asked him to give her the wonderful animal as a gift. In early times Hera was a goddess who looked after cattle as well as marriage, and Zeus couldn't think of a reason to refuse the seemingly reasonable request, so he gave me to his wife just as he would have given a real cow.

"While she decided what torment to inflict on me, Hera tied me to a tree near Nemea and had Argus, called Panoptes, which means all-seeing, stand guard over me.

"She could hardly have chosen better. Argus was a son of Gaia, and, though he was mortal, he was incredibly strong, having already defeated a fierce bull, a warrior satyr, and even a band of murderers.

"However, his best characteristic as a watchman was that he had eyes all over his body, and only a few of them closed in sleep at any one time, so that he was able to keep watch perpetually."

"How did you manage to escape?" asked Yasmin. "Did Zeus save you?"

"Not personally," said Io. "Zeus seldom directly stood up to Hera—no matter how miserable his wife was making the other women in his life. Had it been up to him, I might still be chained to that tree."

"That's not fair—" began Hermes.

"I know, I know, he sent you to rescue me," said Io, "and I am grateful for your help, which is why I am here. What I do not understand…what I never will understand, is why the king of the gods cannot keep his own wife in line— or, failing that, why he cannot honor his own marriage vows."

"Hera is powerful, just as all the children of Cronus are," said Hermes. "Zeus does what he can to avoid strife among them, for when the gods are at odds with each other, the whole universe suffers. Humankind suffers. As for his vows, perhaps he was unwise to make them. Perhaps formal marriage should never have been instituted among the gods. Sometimes I think it would have been better to allow the gods to make love to whom they will—"

"As they do anyway," Io pointed out.

"Are not the children born from those unions a blessing to the world? Would you argue that the world would have been better off without your son,

Epaphus, and his illustrious line?"

"Ever ready to defend your father," said Io. "I suppose I cannot fault you for that, and you know I love Epaphus more than anyone in the world. However, the argument that the gods' sexual desires are justified by the children they produce is an old and tired one, and frankly unworthy of you."

"Yet it is one that is well-supported by many storytellers," replied Hermes. "Is it not true that Zeus commanded the sun and moon to cease their movements to extend his night of lovemaking with Alcmena to three nights, all to produce an extraordinary son, one whom he intended to be the ruler of all Greece?"

"You do realize there is another explanation for Zeus reordering the universe to suit himself?" asked Io.

"The goddesses are no different," replied Hermes. "For is it not said that Demeter lay in the field with Iasion to ensure Thebes a good harvest as her wedding gift to Cadmus and Harmonia? Is it not also said that Aphrodite loved Anchises because she knew their son, Aeneas, would rule the Trojans who survived the Trojan War and that their descendants would eventually found the Roman Empire?"

Io didn't respond directly. Instead she said, "Since you feel so much like talking, why don't you tell the part you played in the story?"

"As you wish," said Hermes, looking mildly irritated. "Zeus, worried for your safety, sent me to rescue you from Argus. I flew in disguised as a woodpecker to see what I could do. Master thief though I am, I could never have stolen you away from a watchman some of whose eyes are always awake. Becoming a shepherd, I lulled Argus to sleep with my music, and when his last eye had closed, I cut off his head."

Despite herself, Fatima jumped a little.

"It was the only choice I had," said Hermes. "Once Argus awakened, he would have pursued Io to the ends of the earth. I feared he was too strong for me to defeat in battle, and some would say that putting him into eternal sleep would not have been much better than killing him outright."

"Zeus could have rescued me without killing Argus—if he had cared enough to do so," said Io.

"I'm not so sure," said Hermes. "Argus would have fought even Zeus to follow Hera's instructions. No, once Hera placed you in his custody, she sealed his fate—and she well knew it. All this show of grief, and placing Argus's eyes on the tail of the peacock as an eternal reminder of his death, was just her way of twisting the knife in Zeus, and in me as well."

Io sighed. "You need feel no guilt, Hermes, but if you do, it is unfair of you to try to cast that guilt onto Hera. Zeus could have avoided a direct confrontation with Argus and still saved me if he had taken the time to figure out how. No, the whole sorry mess was Zeus's fault from beginning to end."

"I could argue that point further, Io, but our quest grows more urgent by the second, and we have many heroes to speak with before we can be sure we have the clue we need. I will forgo the argument if you will finish."

"I said I wanted to help, and I meant it," said Io. "After you had freed me, I thought I could escape, but Hera sent a gadfly to sting me incessantly, making me wild. On and on I ran—or sometimes swam. On those rare moments when I eluded the gadfly, I was still haunted by the staring, accusing eyes of Argus. I found Prometheus chained in the Caucasus Mountains, and he and I briefly discussed the different kinds of misery inflicted on us by Zeus. Then the gadfly found me again, and I ran as far as India. Then I doubled back, reaching Arabia, from which I swam across to Aethiopia. From there, I went north to Egypt, and at last, I was safe. Either the gadfly died, or Hera had newer lovers to torment. The one thing I know for sure is circumstance, not Zeus, ultimately came to my rescue.

"He did change me back into human form, though—that, and only that, will I give him credit for. At long last, I gave birth to my son, Epaphus."

"After which you must admit that things went well for you and your family," said Hermes.

Io gave the divine messenger a thin-lipped smile. "My family did well for itself, though for that I can give little credit to Zeus, nor do I give much to any other god, although Zeus and others did interfere a great deal.

"Epaphus, aided by his ability to transform into a bull, became Apis, the sacred bull of Egypt, and afterward its king. He married Memphis, a daughter of the Nile River, and together they founded the city that bears her name.

"They had a beautiful daughter, Libya, who had the misfortune to be loved by Poseidon, though at least Amphitrite didn't spend years torturing her. She did have excellent twin sons, though, Belus and Agenor.

"Belus married Achiroe, like his grandmother a daughter of the Nile, and in his turn had twins, Danaus and Aegyptus. They could have accomplished so much, but instead discord entered their lives and poisoned their relationship, making them enemies whose foolishness ultimately destroyed most of both their families.

"It was the desire for power that put both of them on the road to destruction. While Belus lived, he ruled Egypt himself, bestowing Arabia on Aegyptus and Libya on Danaus. That arrangement worked well enough until Belus's death, at which point Danaus and Aegyptus could not agree who would inherit the throne of Egypt.

"In an attempt to settle the issue, Aegyptus proposed that his fifty sons marry Danaus's fifty daughters. Danaus was suspicious of this arrangement, which would have given the family of Aegyptus a decisive advantage when the two brothers were both dead. When his suspicions were confirmed by an oracle, who told him Aegyptus planned to kill all of his daughters, Danaus fled from Egypt with the help of Athena.

"Aegyptus could have let the matter rest, for he had Egypt and could probably have taken Libya if he wanted it, but he was uneasy. Each of Danaus's daughters could theoretically marry into a different royal house, potentially giving Aegyptus fifty foreign enemies to fight at some future point. Instead of trying to make peace some other way, he sent his fifty sons after Danaus with an army, instructing them to capture the Danaids and return with them.

"Danaus fled with his daughters to Greece, coming eventually to Argos, then ruled by Pelasgus, one of Phoroneus's sons, who offered him and his family sanctuary.

"That proved to be a big mistake on Pelasgus's part because Danaus soon claimed the throne of Argos. Pelasgus, as the son of the prior king, might have been viewed as the rightful holder of the throne, but in those days the idea of direct hereditary descent wasn't always followed. Danaus was less closely related to Phoroneus, but he was a direct descendant of Inachus, as well as being able to claim descent from Zeus and Poseidon, which Pelasgus could not."

Hermes looked as if he wanted to make the obvious point, but if so, he restrained himself.

"The Argives saw both claims had merit and could not make a decision right away. That night a wolf attacked a bull, the leader of the Argive herd, and the wolf emerged victorious. The Argives saw the bull as King Pelasgus and the wolf as Danaus, and they offered Danaus the throne, a ruling to which Pelasgus gracefully yielded.

"Thus, when Aegyptus's fifty sons arrived with their army, Danaus had an army at his disposal. However, Argos was not well prepared to resist a siege, and a battle would have cost many lives on both sides. Danaus had an idea that was both less and more bloody than all-out war. He pretended to agree to the long-postponed marriages, but he told his daughters to murder their husbands on their wedding night.

"Forty-nine of the daughters did as their father wished. Only one, Hypermenestra, refused to kill her husband, Lynceus. Lynceus had declined to force himself on his unwilling bride, and Artemis appeared to her and told her to spare his life.

"Danaus, furious, prosecuted his daughter in the Argive court for disobeying her father—and her king. Only the timely intervention of Aphrodite saved her."

"What happened to Danaus?" asked Mateo. "He prosecuted Hypermenestra, but what about his own conspiracy to murder his sons-in-law?"

"Those were primitive times, and the laws somewhat unclear," said Io. "On the one hand, Aegyptus's sons would have used force to carry away the Danaids, and many lives would have been lost. Aegyptus had no legal right to control the marriage of his brother's daughters and had sinister motives for wanting to do so. On the other hand, Danaus had agreed to the marriages, so technically his daughters were murdering their lawful husbands."

"The daughters could have faced grave consequences, as could their father as well, since the Argives might have deposed him and tried him for murder. Neither the people nor the court went that far, partly because of the intervention of Zeus—and yes, Hermes, he tried to do good there, however belatedly and ineptly. With his permission, you and Athena purified the daughters in the lake at Lerna, absolving them of the blood guilt, so that the Argive court was satisfied.

"Soon after Aegyptus learned of the deaths of almost all of his sons, he died as well, perhaps of grief. To lose one son is terrible, but to lose forty-nine must be almost unbearable.

"Danaus seemed to have emerged as the victor, but no one ever truly wins when family members shed each other's blood. Not long after Aegyptus died, Lynceus returned and killed Danaus to avenge the deaths of his brothers. He would have killed the other daughters as well, but the Argives refused to allow that kind of mass revenge, since the girls had been cleansed of the blood guilt, and Lynceus accepted the decision.

"Perhaps he knew that justice would prevail in the end, for after the girls died, the judges of the dead, their distant kin, refused to accept their earthly purification, even though it was sanctioned by Zeus himself. Instead, they demanded one in the Underworld—an eternal one, as it turned out, for the girls were sent to carry water for their purification bath but were given only leaking vessels, so they could never succeed in bringing enough water for the purpose.

"Lynceus and Hypermenestra became king and queen of Argos, so that their descendants, the future kings, would have the blood of both Aegyptus and Danaus—exactly what would have happened in a number of kingdoms if the brothers had been willing to share. As it was, Egypt, Arabia, and Libya all ended up in other hands."

"That family did far more than just govern Argos, though," said Hermes. "From them descended both Perseus and Heracles."

"Ah, more heroes," said Io, looking sad. "Both sons of Zeus, too, for he could not seem to leave my family alone. Yes, Hermes, they did great things, but so have some mortals whose father wasn't Zeus. Perseus lived a happy life, I must admit, but Heracles lived a miserable one, despite all his great achievements."

"In the end, Heracles became a god, though," Hermes reminded her. "What more could a mortal ask? I'll also point out that it was Hera, not Zeus, who was responsible for his misery, as she was for yours. Those tales might also be valuable for our visitors, but I think it will be someone else's place to tell them."

"I am content with that," said Io, "for this argument grows tiresome, and I know you would and I could argue forever about Heracles."

"What happened to Belus's brother?" asked Mateo.

"When Belus inherited Egypt, Agenor went to find his fortune elsewhere. He married Telephassa, who seemed to be the daughter of a river god, though there is some difference of opinion as to which one, and settled in Tyre, where they became king and queen and had many children, among them Cadmus, Phoenix, Cilix, and Europa.

"Unlike Aegyptus and Danaus, these siblings knew how to share, and they might have been happy if only the gods had left them alone.

"Unfortunately, Europa was cursed with the same beauty that seems to run in the family, and she caught the eye of Zeus. Waiting until she was near the seashore, Zeus became a beautiful white bull. Frightened at first, Europa was won over by the bull's apparent tameness and his breath that smelled of roses, even hanging garlands of flowers from his horns."

"Much as I hate to interrupt," said Hermes, "you cannot blame their love on Zeus. Europa was surely not stupid enough to think she had found a tame bull, let alone one roaming wild, and with breath like roses. She must have known she was in the presence of a god. Those flower garlands sound like flirtation to me."

"She was an innocent girl," snapped Io. "If you are going to insult her, I will leave the rest of the story untold."

"I mean no offense," said Hermes. "Please continue…for the sake of the visitors."

Io turned to the students. "What do you think? Is Hermes right, or am I?"

"It is not fair—" began Hermes.

"If they want the rest of the story, told by me, they will give me an answer—and it had better be an honest one!"

That left the students with a dilemma. They knew getting involved in arguments between gods never went well, but they had no idea whether they had already heard the significant detail in Io's story or not. If they were lucky, perhaps Io wasn't far enough up the divine food chain to change them into something unpleasant. If the moly Hermes had given them was still working, they ought to be immune from that kind of transformation, anyway.

"If I'm being honest," said Mateo, "it sounds as if Europa must have known what she was getting herself into."

"On the other hand," said Keisha. "Europa lived in a world where there were many wondrous things. The bull was clearly extraordinary, and bulls were sacred to Zeus and Poseidon, but surely every unusual bull didn't need to be one of those two gods."

"We can't really know what was in her mind at that moment," said Thanos. "Maybe she knew she was dealing with a god, maybe not."

"Please," said Fatima, "we can't all honestly agree with you, but our friend's life may depend on something you haven't said yet."

"Never fear, child," said Io gently. "Your companions gave me answers that were both truthful and diplomatic. I will finish the story, though whether or not it will help I cannot say.

"Finally, Europa was so charmed by the bull that she playfully got on its back—exactly what Zeus had wanted. He rode away, taking the terrified Europa with him across the sea. Some say he swam, others that he ran across the surface of the water as if it were land.

"He took her clear to Crete, where he made love to her. She fared both better and worse than many of Zeus's lovers. She became no goddess, unlike Semele; she received no worship, unlike Alcmena. On the other hand, Hera never caught on, though how she could miss a supernatural bull running halfway across the Mediterranean, I can't imagine. In any case, Europa did not suffer her wrath as I did. Zeus even found a unique way to honor her, for the whole continent of Europe bears her name.

"Even more important, Zeus managed to give her a normal mortal life. Rather than being an unwed mother earning the laughter of all those around her for claiming that the father of her children was Zeus, she became the wife of Asterion, king of Crete. He was a wise enough man to know he would be blessed if he raised the children of Zeus as his own, and so he was.

"The three children were Minos and Rhadamanthus, whom you met in their role as judges of the dead, and Sarpedon, all three of whom led long and successful lives. Minos succeeded his stepfather as king of Crete, becoming the most powerful ruler of his time. He ruled so long he met Heracles, a distant cousin of his some eight generations later. As a result, some later writers assumed that there were two kings named Minos, the second a grandson of the first, though I think the sons of Zeus sometimes live much longer than the norm. Minos's brothers are also credited with being far beyond a normal lifespan. Rhadamanthus is said to have married Heracles's widowed mother, Alcmena, and to have tutored Heracles as a boy. Sarpedon is even said to have fought in the Trojan War a generation later, though some writers say that was his grandson, another son of Zeus.

"Minos began as a good ruler, so good it was thought he received from Zeus himself the numerous laws he published. Unfortunately, he was also proud, and, like his true father and some of the other members of my family, a little too suspicious of threats against his own power. Imagining his brothers to be threats, he found excuses to banish both of them.

"Fortunately, they took their exile well, each making their mark in the world without feeling the need to seek revenge against Minos. Rhadamanthus traveled through the islands of the Aegean, gaining a reputation for integrity that ultimately earned him a spot as a judge of the dead. Sarpedon stayed for a while with his uncle, Cilix, though eventually he conquered the Mylians and founded a kingdom of his own, Lycia, in Asia Minor."

"Cilix? Oh, yeah," said Yasmin. "What happened to Europa's brothers?"

"Agenor sent them to search for Europa, but he made the mistake of telling them they could never come back unless they brought her. He should have known better. Since no one had any idea where she had gone, he was sending the rest of his family out an impossible errand, for three brothers by themselves could never search the whole world.

"Cilix ended up in Asia Minor, where he eventually gave up the search and founded the kingdom of Cilicia. Phoenix traveled further away, to North Africa, where he spent time with the Punics near the eventual site of Carthage. After hearing of his father's death, he returned to take over his kingdom, which was renamed Phoenicia in his honor.

"As for Cadmus—"

"He is on our list," said Hermes. "To be sure we get whatever clue Apollo thought would be there, we must hear the story from him."

"Very well," said Io. "You can find him nearby, in a place that looks not unlike ancient Thebes."

Hermes looked worriedly up at the darkening skies. "Perhaps I should speak with Cronus about what's happening in Elysium, but I am reluctant to delay the quest. Io, can you see the visitors safely to Cadmus?"

"It would be my pleasure."

No sooner had she spoken than Hermes flitted away, leaving the students feeling vaguely abandoned. He had been with them almost constantly since early in their journey.

Not so long ago, they had been escorted by three Olympians and two automatons. Now they were left with one minor goddess. She seemed benevolent, but she just wasn't Hermes. Elysium should be safe enough, but the darkening sky suggested a coming storm—in a land that was supposed to have none.

Then there was the fact that Hermes hadn't wanted to check in with Zeus because he'd been afraid Zeus might have been turned against him. What if Cronus had been turned against him—and he never came back?

Io was already marching in the direction of Cadmus and beckoning for them to follow her.

"Should we go with her?" asked Yasmin. "I'd almost rather wait for Hermes."

"I don't think we have a choice," said Thanos. "Our time *is* limited, though I don't know how much. Anyway, Hermes said he'd be back soon. If he is, we have no worries. If not...well, then we have bigger problems, but waiting here for him would be pointless, anyway."

"Onward, then," said Keisha, sounding more pessimistic than any of them could ever remember her being.

Chapter 21: Cadmus, His Family and His In-laws

Traveling with Io was slower than traveling with Hermes, but eventually they saw what looked like a city wall in the distance.

"Why would there be a duplicate of Thebes here?" asked Keisha.

"There is no need for cities as such," said Io, "but sometimes the blessed dead get nostalgic about the places that meant something to them when they were alive. If they want to see a place badly enough, it comes into being here. The Elysian Fields are mostly open spaces such as you saw when you first entered, with the occasional sporting arena or theater, but they are also dotted with cities built from the memories of the dead."

When they got close enough, they could see Cadmus standing in front of the wall, looking at the gray sky. One wave from the golden bough got his attention.

Since Io, unlike Hermes, couldn't make herself visible to the blessed dead, Apollodorus handled the introductions.

"Visitors are rare...but all the more welcome," Cadmus said.

"Does the wall have seven gates?" asked Thanos.

"Ah, you know the stories," said Cadmus. "It does indeed, and if we went within, I could show you the Cadmeia, the fortress I was responsible for building, as well as the Ampheion, the great funeral mound in which are buried Amphion and Zethus...pointless, I know, since their bodies are back in the real Ampheion, but having the mound does make the place feel more like home somehow, even though it and the wall were both added after my time. There are a great many other sights as well, but you sound as if what you need is my story rather than a tour."

The other students, not sharing Thanos's excitement over tours of ancient sites, breathed a silent sigh of relief.

"Like my brothers, I went out searching for Europa, though I had no better luck than they did. I sailed to Rhodes, where I made offerings to Athena, hoping for her guidance. I also built a temple to Poseidon and endowed a priesthood for it, for when traveling the seas, it is always wise to keep Poseidon on your good side.

"Eventually, my men and I made our way to Delphi, hoping to consult with the oracle. Unfortunately, she told us to give up our search for Europa, and at that moment I knew we were fated not to find her.

"Instead, the oracle told us to follow a cow until it fell from exhaustion and then to build a city where it fell. Knowing I could not return home without Europa, I had little to lose, and anyway it would be risky not to do as the oracle commanded, so we bought a cow.

"The creatures wandered eastward across Boeotia, finally falling on the spot on which I later built Thebes. I wanted to sacrifice the cow to Athena, and I sent my men to draw water for the ceremony.

"Unfortunately, I didn't know that the nearest spring was guarded by a fierce dragon. Even worse, the dragon was no ordinary dragon, but the child of Ares by one of the Erinyes. My unsuspecting men did not stand a chance.

"When I realized what had happened, I vengefully attacked the dragon. I should have died, too, but Athena must have protected me. I was able to stab the dragon, then crush its head with a boulder I should not have been able to lift.

"I had honored my men's memory by killing their killer, but now I was alone. Fortunately, Athena appeared to me, praised what I had done, and told me to sow the dragon's teeth in the soil.

"I did as she commanded, and from those teeth rapidly grew the Spartoi, the Sown Men. They were warlike and fought each other until only five remained. Finally seeing the folly of killing each other, these five resolved to follow a more peaceful path. When they learned it was I who had sown the dragon's teeth, they accepted me as their leader, and with their help I began to build Thebes.

"However, though Athena was pleased by what I had done, Ares was not. He initially demanded blood for blood and would have killed me, but it is said Zeus restrained him.

"Zeus knew, though, that Ares could not be denied some kind of restitution for his loss. In the end, I had to serve the war god for a Great Year, which is the equivalent of eight ordinary years. He put me to hard labor, but I patiently endured, and at the then of my term I was free—from the labor, though not entirely from Ares. He still bore a grudge against me, even though he could not at first openly pursue it.

"Aside from Ares, the gods favored me, so much in fact that Zeus arranged my marriage to Harmonia, the daughter of Ares and Aphrodite. Though some goddesses from time to time made love with mortal men, few men were granted the right to actually marry one, and of those few, only I was happily married. To add to this singular honor, the gods themselves attended the ceremony and gave us many rich gifts. Some might say too rich, for a couple of them, the necklace from Hephaestus and the robe from Athena, were later coveted and brought much misery to those who possessed them.

"Harmonia and I had several daughters: Agave, Autonoe, Ino, and Semele. One would have thought that women descended in different ways from so many gods and fathered by someone favored by them would have led blessed lives, but each of them had much misery. Our only son, Polydorus, alone was spared any great disasters in life.

"Agave married Echion, one of the Sown Men, and became the proud mother of Pentheus, who as my eldest grandson, was designated my heir. I shall have more to say of him in a minute.

"Autonoe married Aristaeus, Apollo's beekeeping son. She gave birth to the unfortunate Actaeon, whose death at the hands of Artemis I understand you have already heard. As the wife of a god, Autonoe might have hoped for better. She might also have expected to become a goddess, just like Cyrene, Aristaeus's mother, but the marriage did not last—and that was not the worst of the tragedies Autonoe would face.

"If only the gods would just leave my family alone," muttered Io. Cadmus, who couldn't hear her, continued as if there had been no interruption.

"Semele's story you already know. Loved by Zeus, she was destroyed by Hera's jealous wrath, though Zeus managed to save the unborn Dionysus, and eventually he got permission to make Semele a goddess and bring her to Olympus to live. It's hard to complain about the outcome, but what a miserable journey she had to reach it!

"Ino's life too was a mixture of happiness and sorrow. She became the lover and then unofficial wife of King Athamas of Boeotia, one of the sons of Aeolus. Unfortunately, the sons seldom became as virtuous as their father."

"I would have objected to the match had it not at first been kept secret, for Athamas's family, though distinguished by descent from Deucalion and

Pyrrha, was surrounded by disasters of its own making. I will tell you of the sad fate of his brothers later.

"Athamas himself had a bizarre first marriage, for at Hera's request he wed Nephele, Hera's double fashioned from clouds to deceive Ixion. The problem was that Nephele, once made, could not easily be unmade. You would think someone with the beauty of Hera could have made a satisfactory life for herself, but she was very unhappy, being a goddess of sorts but having no real role to play on Olympus.

"Hera, either moved by Nephele's plight or worried about a twin of herself roaming around Olympus, arranged a marriage for her as a solution to both problems, but it did not bring happiness to Nephele. She and Athamas had two fine children, Phrixus and Helle, but Nephele, thinking she should have been the bride of a god, not a mere mortal, remained dissatisfied.

"Finally worn out by his wife's contempt for him, Athamas lured Ino into a secret affair which produced two sons, Learchus and Melicertes. Some say the swine married her later, though it was difficult to see how, since he never really divorced Nephele.

"Nephele eventually found out, and, though she would rather not have been married to Athamas, she resented his disloyalty and went running to Hera. Hera vowed eternal vengeance against Athamas and his family, but then she seemingly did nothing, perhaps taking time to consider her different options.

"It was at around this time that my poor Ino began to fret about the status of her own sons. Phrixus was older than they were and born to Athamas's actual wife, so neither of her sons would have any kind of hope of inheriting the kingdom. Determined that one of them should succeed Athamas, she hatched a vile plan—though I would like to think that Hera was somehow involved.

"Ino roasted the seed corn so that it would not grow, and when the newly planted crops failed to sprout, Athamas sent messengers to the oracle at Delphi to find out what was wrong. Ino bribed them to return with the false report that Zeus was angry and that only the sacrifice of Phrixus and Helle would appease him.

"Athamas didn't want to sacrifice his own children, but the people demanded that sacrifice, and so he reluctantly agreed. It is also said that Phrixus was willing to sacrifice himself to save the citizens from starvation.

"Nephele might not have been much of a wife, but she was a devoted mother and searched for a way to save her children. She went to the ever-helpful Hermes, who gave her a miraculous golden ram that could both talk and fly.

"When it was nearly time for Phrixus and Helle to be sacrificed, the ram flew down from Olympus, ordered them to get on its back, and then flew away with them.

"Unfortunately, as they left Europe behind, Helle's grip weakened, and she fell into the Hellespont, which was named after her. Phrixus believed she died, though some say Poseidon saved her. Grief-stricken, Phrixus flew on, landing safely in Colchis, on the far side of the Black Sea. There is much more to say about the ram's golden fleece, but I suspect you will want to hear that part from Jason himself.

"Nephele demanded justice for her nearly sacrificed children, and Hera obliged, partly feeling obligated to help Nephele, and partly for another reason. You see, before the failure of the harvest, Hermes had secretly brought to Athamas and Ino Ino's nephew, the infant Dionysus, with instructions to raise him as a girl and thus prevent Hera from finding him. Unfortunately, Hera had figured out he was with Athamas and Ino, and she picked this moment to strike them down.

"Hera drove both of them mad. Athamas shot Learchus with an arrow because the king thought his own son was a stag he was hunting. He would have killed Melicertes the same way, but the infant Dionysus temporarily blinded him. Ino fled with Melicertes, seemingly to protect him from Athamas, but, being mad herself, she hurled herself into the sea, taking the child with her."

"That's...horrible," said Fatima, struggling for words.

"It would have been," said Cadmus, "but Zeus took pity on Ino and Melicertes. He forgave my daughter the evil she had attempted to do to Phrixus and Helle. Whatever Ino's faults, she had protected Dionysus, and for that Zeus made her the sea goddess Leucothea. Melicertes too became a god named Palaemon, who rode on a dolphin clear to the Isthmus of Corinth, where the people worshiped him.

"Say what you will about Zeus—and my ancestor Io had plenty to say, I'm told—it is hard to criticize his role in my life. More than once he has saved members of my family."

Io grumbled that Zeus just helped Ino to spite Nephele, who was after all Hera's ally. However, since it was Cadmus, not Hermes, who made the argument, she did not attempt to press the point.

"Wow! It doesn't sound as if Athamas's brothers could have fared much worse than he did," said Mateo.

"In fact, they had even worse fortune and did even more to bring it upon themselves," said Cadmus.

"Sisyphus started out well, founding the city of Ephyre, which was eventually called Corinth. Though not virtuous, he was at least clever, once outwitting Autolycus, the master thief.

"Autolycus was the twin brother of Philammon, and their mother was Chione, but each twin was the son of a different father. Philammon's father was Apollo, and he grew up to be a master musician, composer, and singer. Autolycus's father was Hermes, and he grew up to be a master thief. Not only was he clever and agile, but he had the power to change the appearance of what he stole, making the theft virtually impossible to detect.

"Sisyphus could not help noticing that his herd of cattle kept getting smaller, while Autolycus's kept getting bigger. To test his theory that Autolycus was somehow stealing cattle, Sisyphus marked one hoof on each beast with a phrase like, 'Autolycus stole me.' The next time Sisyphus noticed his herd shrinking, he checked Autolycus's herd and discovered the missing animals. Autolycus could probably have removed the markings, but he didn't know they were there, and so he was exposed for the thief he was.

"Alas, cleverness does not always walk hand-in-hand with morality, and so it was with Sisyphus, who showed himself time and again to be far more unscrupulous than the thief he had outwitted.

"When his father Aeolus died, Sisyphus should have become his heir, but Salmoneus usurped the throne instead. Sisyphus went to the oracle of Delphi for advice, and received the odd prophecy that, if he fathered sons by his niece, Tyro, those sons would avenge him."

"Wait!" said Mateo. "The gods told him to have sex with his niece?"

"I know that seems odd," said Cadmus, "for incest was forbidden among mortals, though it is true that early Greeks sometimes defined incest rather narrowly, applying it only to parent-child and sibling relationships. Defined in that way, the restriction would not prevent an uncle-niece relationship. Since the storytellers pass over that problem in silence, I can't be sure what they were thinking, but I have always thought the prophecy was a kind of test. The gods love to test people, after all, and the oracle did not tell Sisyphus to sleep with his niece; she only told him what would happen if he did.

"Whether one views the relationship as incestuous or not, everyone would agree that Sisyphus should have valued the innocence of a young girl more than the throne, but he did not. Without a moment's hesitation, he seduced his own niece, who gave birth to two of his sons.

"The poor girl thought her uncle loved her. When she found out that his motive was not love of her but hatred of her father, she went mad and killed the two boys.

"Far from being grief-stricken at this turn of events, Sisyphus at once realized how to take advantage of it. He took the two bodies to the marketplace and falsely accused Salmoneus of their incestuous begetting and their murder. Outraged, the people drove Salmoneus from Thessaly and hailed Sisyphus as their king. *he was framed*

"Salmoneus, the usurper, was hardly a model of proper morality, but even he didn't deserve such vile treatment, and Tyro certainly did not. Because of Sisyphus, both of their lives were destroyed.

"At first it seemed that Salmoneus might pull his life together. He went to Elis, where he founded the city of Salmonia and became its king. Unfortunately, his new subjects soon discovered the sad truth: the earlier false accusation and exile had taken their toll on Salmoneus, who was now completely insane.

"The mad king proclaimed himself Zeus, demanding that people sacrifice to him and worship him. He dragged cauldrons wrapped in animal hide behind his chariot to make a sound like thunder, and he threw flaming torches into the air and said they were lightning.

"His people hated him, for he was a terrible tyrant as well as being a blasphemer, and, since the city was new anyway, many left—a good thing for them, since the thunderbolts Zeus hurled at him destroyed the city right along with him."

different from our society

"Didn't Zeus take into consideration that he was crazy?" asked Fatima.

"In our society, we have the idea that someone can be not guilty by reason of insanity," said Thanos, "but that wasn't true in ancient Greece, was it?"

"No, we had no such belief," said Cadmus. "It was the act that mattered, not what may have brought the act about.

"As for poor Tyro, Salmoneus had brought her with him, not because he still loved his daughter but because he didn't want to give Sisyphus the satisfaction of killing her. However, he blamed her for his exile, as did Tyro's stepmother, Sidero, who treated her cruelly.

"Tyro never seems to have mourned her two murdered children, another sign that, though she did not claim to be divine as her father did, she was still very much insane.

"Searching for some way to fill the gaping hole Sisyphus had ripped in her heart, she thought what she needed was a lover, and she shamelessly pursued the river god Enipeus. Surprisingly, given the way gods often behaved, Enipeus wasn't interested.

"The same could not be said, however, for Poseidon, who, disguised as the river god, slept with Tyro. Disturbed by the deception, Tyro was even more disturbed when she discovered she was pregnant. Knowing the wrath she would face from Sidero, Tyro kept the pregnancy secret, and when she give birth to two fine sons, she exposed them in the wilderness."

"Exposed them?" asked Yasmin.

"Oh, like what Creusa was thinking about doing with Ion," said Mateo.

"Yes, it was a sadly common practice, a way of avoiding the blood guilt for killing an innocent child," replied Cadmus. "An exposed infant was left alone in some wild place, the theory being that if he died, it was the fault of the gods, for they could have saved him, and not the fault of the parent who exposed him."

this is necessary

"I'm sorry, but that's just crazy," said Yasmin.

Cadmus nodded. "No good ever came of such a practice, which was still murder, and in a sense blasphemous, for it blamed the gods for a mortal's wrongdoing." *Considered blasphemous*

"The gods had more than enough of their own wrongdoing to account for," muttered Io. "Poseidon took a bad situation and made it even worse."

"However, it may be that Tyro hoped the boys' father would save them, for instead of leaving them on the ground, she floated them down the Enipeus River in a chest. Sure enough, Poseidon spotted them and protected them from harm until they were found by a horse-herd, who rescued them and took them to be raised by his wife.

"The two boys grew up to be the one bright spot in Tyro's life. Pelias and Neleus they were called, and when they found out who their mother was, and how cruelly she had been treated, they wanted to avenge her."

"Even though she'd abandoned them?" asked Mateo.

"She was still their mother, though, and somehow they felt a bond with her. Most people viewed exposure differently in those days, and I suppose they must have as well," replied Cadmus. "Salmoneus was long dead by then, but they sought out Sidero. She took refuge in the temple of Hera, and Pelias made the mistake of killing her, even though she had claimed the right of sanctuary and died clutching the altar.

"Hera did not react right away, but she never forgave Pelias for the sacrilege and looked for ways to punish him in the future."

"I thought you said the sons became a bright spot," said Fatima.

"Well, as bright as anything could be in that gloom-ridden life," said Cadmus. "They were loving sons, or at least they tried.

"Tyro ended up married to Cretheus, whom the storytellers all say was her uncle—"

"So Cretheus was one who believed an uncle-niece relationship was not incestuous?" asked Mateo.

"I think the storytellers got the marriage part wrong," said Cadmus slowly. Cretheus had been appointed Tyro's guardian, some said by Zeus himself. As a guardian, his relationship to Tyro would have been more like that of a father than that of an uncle, so the prohibition on incest should have applied. Cretheus was by all accounts a good man, certainly far better than Sisyphus and Salmoneus, so I doubt he would have consciously broken the law of the gods, nor risked dethronement and exile if the truth came out. I have never found a polite way to ask him myself, but I believe there were two men of that name, for such situations often confuse the storytellers. After all, they did make a complete mess of the three Aeoluses. If we assume Uncle Cretheus had a son named after him, Tyro could have married that son, for marriages between cousins were definitely not regarded as incestuous, even if the cousin was the son of her guardian. Not only that, but such a marriage would have been a good way for Uncle Cretheus to ensure the future of his niece and her children, for Cousin Cretheus would have been the heir to the throne of Iolcus, which Uncle Cretheus had founded.

"Whatever may have happened, Tyro found what happiness she could. She and the man I think was Cousin Cretheus had several children, including Aeson, the father of Jason, whom I imagine you will meet later. Cretheus also adopted Pelias and Neleus, treating them as his own sons.

"As for Sisyphus, ruining the lives of his brother and making his niece miserable for many years was not the end of his evil. When Zeus was running off with the nymph Aegina, her father, the river god Asopus, was pursuing them. I should mention that river gods, though theoretically on a much lower level than someone like Zeus, are tough combatants, and fighting him would have been disastrous regardless of what happened. Zeus was without his thunderbolts, but even if he had won, he would have risked alienating Aegina. In this instance, avoiding conflict would have been the best policy."

"Not stealing girls from their fathers would have been even better policy," muttered Io, looking as if she was near the end of her patience.

"Sisyphus knew where Zeus had taken Aegina. It would have been one thing to tell Asopus out of a sense of moral responsibility or empathy for the outraged father, but Sisyphus decided to sell the information instead, letting Asopus know that the king would tell all he knew in exchange for the creation of a spring in Corinth. Asopus gave Sisyphus what he wanted and almost caught up with Zeus. Needless to say, the king of the gods became profoundly unhappy with Sisyphus.

"Given all the disasters for which Sisyphus was now responsible, Zeus wasted no time in sending Thanatos, Death himself, to take Sisyphus down to the Underworld. Unfortunately, Sisyphus had acquired powerful magic from somewhere that would enable him to bind Thanatos, and he tricked the god into allowing himself to be bound.

"With Thanatos imprisoned, no one could die, which would quickly create pain and eventually social chaos. Ares was not usually the first to worry about either pain or chaos, but he was worried about the absence of death on the battlefield, so he rushed to unbind Thanatos, who was then able to take Sisyphus down to the Underworld.

"However, Sisyphus had one last trick. Anticipating just such a situation, he told his wife not to bury his body if he died. Since he was unburied, he could not enter the Underworld itself. Normally, such a state would be a terrible one, but in this case, it kept Sisyphus away from the torture he suspected would be in store for him.

"Under these circumstances, Thanatos was uncharacteristically unsure what to do. Sisyphus managed to persuade Persephone, who had come to see what was wrong to return him to the mortal world to remind his wife of her duties. Once he got there, he became material enough to function, and he planned to stay in the world of the living, leaving the body unburied.

"That was perhaps not his best trick, for there was no way the gods were going to miss his continued absence from the Underworld, though a couple of storytellers say they did. What really happened was that Hermes showed up in a very short time, arranged for proper burial of the body, and then dragged Sisyphus back with him to the Underworld. Once there, Sisyphus was doomed to the endless task of rolling a stone up a hill, only to have it rolled back as soon as he reached the top with it. In some ways, it was a milder punishment than he deserved."

"I think you were going to tell us about Pentheus, your grandson," said Thanos.

"Oh, yes. Over time I had begun to feel the continuing displeasure of Ares hovering over me like a dark cloud. Fearing that he might punish the whole city, as gods often do when they find fault with a king, I abdicated the throne, passing it to my grandson Pentheus, the child of my eldest daughter.

"I could hardly have chosen worse. Though Pentheus did not seem overly proud as a young man, once he became king, the signs of hubris were plain. I hear you have already visited Dionysus, so you have probably heard the sad tale from him. Pentheus was one of the rulers who tried to oppose the spread of the religion of Dionysus, with disastrous consequences.

"I was still in the city at the time, and I tried to warn him. Teiresias, the blind prophet who speaks by the inspiration of the gods, also tried to warn him.

He would not listen to either of us, and he ended up being torn apart by his own mother and aunt who were too lost in their Dionysian frenzy to know what they were doing.

"With Pentheus gone, the wrath of Dionysus was easily appeased by the establishment of his worship in Thebes. However, Ares still remained an issue. Though I had no evidence, I feared that Ares might have led Pentheus astray and that the whole mess was my fault. Dionysus, while not confirming that theory, told me it would be better both for me and for Thebes if I left. At that point, I could hardly have argued with him, even if I wanted to.

"Leaving the throne in the hands of Polydorus, my only son, Harmonia and I departed, traveling to the area that later became Illyria—and right into the middle of a war.

"The Encheleans were fighting for survival against other inhabitants of the area, but they had received word from an oracle that they would be victorious if they accepted as their leader the man who arrived in a chariot pulled by two oxen. Shortly afterward, Harmonia and I arrived in exactly the kind of transportation predicted by the oracle.

"The Encheleans promptly offered me the throne. I took their oracle as the will of the gods and so accepted the throne gladly, after which I led them to victory.

"While living among them, Harmonia and I had one more son, Illyrius, who became the ancestor of their royal family and gave his name to the region. Though Harmonia and I missed Thebes and our remaining family there, we were happy in our new Illyrian home.

"Ares, however, took one last slap at us, changing us into serpents as further punishment for my long-ago murder of his dragon son. Fortunately, the other gods would not permit his spiteful act to stand. Instead, our souls were transferred here, leaving the snakes behind to guard our tomb."

"Harmonia died?" asked Yasmin. "I thought she was a goddess."

"She was, but she had long ago decided to share my fate, something gods can do but seldom choose to. However, once we were in the Elysian Fields, Aphrodite persuaded her to resume her divine duties, and I was happy to see her do it, for she brings happiness to many married couples. She still visits me, and I can still commune with her in a way we dead usually cannot interact with gods."

"So your story has a happy ending?" asked Fatima. "So many don't."

"My personal story does, but alas, my departure did not spare my family further tragedy."

"Polydorus, though otherwise happy, died relatively young, and his son, Labdacus, was still an infant at the time. Fortunately, there was someone who could serve as regent. Chthonius, one of the Sown Men, had a son, Nycteus, who in turn had two daughters, Nyceis and Antiope. Nyceis had become Polydorus's queen, and thus Labdacus's mother. Since that made Nycteus the king's grandfather and closest male relative, he became the logical choice for the regency.

"Unfortunately, Nycteus and his brother Lycus proved to be less than ideal leaders. Nycteus's other daughter, Antiope, was loved by Zeus and became pregnant, but either Nycteus refused to believe her, or he was arrogant enough to believe that, king of the gods or not, Zeus should have sought his permission."

"Zeus ruined someone's life again," said Io. "By this time, I'm sure none of you are surprised."

"I don't understand why Nycteus was angry," said Yasmin.

Cadmus smiled indulgently. "In your world things are different. Some people are more willing to accept the idea of an unmarried woman making love to a man of her choice, but in my society daughters were expected to preserve themselves for their husbands."

"Many women still believe in that even in our world," said Keisha. "They just wish men would meet the same standard."

Cadmus chuckled. "Even in my society, there were people who criticized the double standard that allowed men to do things that would be frowned upon if women did them. However, the two genders were even further separated than in your world. In ancient Greece it was fathers, not their daughters, who made the important decisions about their daughters' futures—including marriage. A daughter who was not a virgin was a daughter who would be harder to arrange a marriage for, so fathers often severely punished daughters who made love to someone before they were married.

"To avoid such punishment, Antiope fled to Sicyon, whose king, Epopeus,

266 A Dream Come True

agreed to marry her and even to raise the sons of Zeus as his own. He was a wise man who understood that being loved by a god brings honor, not dishonor, to a woman."

"How can you spout such nonsense?" said Io, clenching her fists, but of course Cadmus couldn't hear her.

"Antiope's father should have accepted her marriage to a king, but again hubris got in his way," said Cadmus. "He refused to accept his daughter's honorable marriage because he had not been the one who arranged it. Instead, he went to Sicyon with an army, intending to carry Antiope back to Thebes by force. Epopeus resisted this invasion, and in the resulting battle, Nycteus was killed.

"Bent on revenge, Lycus, who succeeded Nycteus as regent of Thebes, took another army to Sicyon, this time successfully. Much blood was shed on both sides, including that of Epopeus, and in the end, Lycus won the battle and dragged Antiope back with him to Thebes.

"On the way, she gave birth to twin sons, Amphion and Zethus, giving Lycus a chance to do the right thing. Like Nycteus, he made the wrong choice, exposing the newborns on Mount Cithaeron and giving Antiope to his wife, Dirce, who treated her as cruelly as Sidero had treated Tyro, but for far less reason.

"Of course, his foolishness would eventually be his undoing. Whatever others thought, I always believed the exposing of infants to be no better than murder, and attempting to murder the sons of the king of the gods was bound to bring evil upon the family of Lycus sooner or later, and so it did.

"Amphion and Zethus did not die, for they were rescued by cattlemen, who raised them near the same mountain on which they were meant to perish. Zeus watched over them, at one point sending Hermes to give Amphion, who had shown an aptitude for music, a lyre.

"Back in Thebes, Labdacus reached adulthood and became king, though Lycus continued to play an important role in the city. Unfortunately, Labdacus had poor judgment, and he got himself into an unwinnable war with Athens that resulted in his own death and left Lycus once again as regent, this time for Labdacus's son, Laius.

"It was at this point that Antiope escaped from Dirce. Perhaps with Zeus's help, though the stories do not say, she managed to find her sons, and she even managed to convince them that she was their mother.

"Alas, the loving reunion was soured by revenge, for Amphion and Zethus decided that Dirce must be punished for her evil treatment of their mother. They hunted the woman down and killed her, some say by having her trampled by a bull.

"Unfortunately—I know, I use that word a lot, but misfortune still seemed to follow in the footsteps, not only of my family but of anyone related by marriage—Dirce, whatever her faults, was a devout worshiper of Dionysus. The god, not wishing to attack the sons of Zeus directly, inflicted madness on poor Antiope, who one would have thought had already suffered enough. She wandered through Greece until Phocus, a grandson of Sisyphus, was permitted by Dionysus to cure her. He then married Antiope, and she finally had a little happiness after so many years of misery.

"Back in Thebes, Lycus's poor choices finally caught up with him, for Amphion and Zethus killed him in battle. They also drove Laius, the legitimate king of Thebes away, claiming the throne for themselves.

"In doing so, they had gone beyond even the demands of vengeance, robbing Laius, who had nothing to do with their mother's suffering, of his rightful crown. Normally, such an act would displease the gods, but, perhaps because they were sons of Zeus, or perhaps because Ares still bore a grudge against my family, the twins were permitted to retain the throne they had stolen."

"Let me guess," said Mateo. "One of them had a daughter who was loved by Zeus, or they ended up fighting over the throne and killed each other."

"Actually, the brothers cooperated well with each other," said Cadmus. "Much as I hate to admit it, they were even good kings in the beginning. I had already built the upper city, but they did a good job building what became the lower city, including the wall you now see behind me. The city had grown too big to be defended by the Cadmeia alone, and, having conquered the city themselves, they well knew how much it needed a wall.

"Zethus had frequently made fun of Amphion for his interest in music, but in this case, it paid off. Like Orpheus, Amphion was able to charm the stones from which the walls were made to move into position just by playing his lyre and singing. This is the kind of thing one might expect when a son of Zeus plays a lyre of Hermes.

"Alas, they did not marry well, picking women for their beauty and not for their character. I was fortunate indeed, for Harmonia had both, but it is not always so.

"Amphion married Niobe, a daughter of the blasphemous Tantalus. Zethus married Aedon, a daughter of Tantalus's friend, Pandareus, who stole the golden dog made by Hephaestus from the temple of Zeus on Crete and was afterward turned to stone. Though children do not always inherit the sinful tendencies of their fathers, in this case, the women were at the very least haunted by their cursed backgrounds. The first proved to be ruled by hubris, just like her father; the other was possessed by jealousy.

"Zethus and Aedon had two children, Itylus and Nais. Zethus loved his children dearly, even more than his own life, but Aedon's love for them was overshadowed by her jealousy of Niobe, who had seven sons and seven daughters. What an utterly ridiculous thing to care about, and yet this envy poisoned Aedon completely, partly because Niobe incessantly bragged about her own children.

"One day Aedon, devoured by her jealousy to the point that it was nearly all that was left of her, tried to kill one of the sons of Amphion, but her clumsy plot instead killed her own son, Itylus. As tragedy so often breeds tragedy, so did this senseless killing, for Zethus died of grief for his son. As for Aedon, Zeus sent Poine, vengeance incarnate, to deal with her. Aedon, however, prayed for mercy, and Zeus, for reasons known only to himself, changed her into a nightingale, whose sweet song was really Aedon's lament for her lost son.

"If Niobe had possessed even an ounce of wisdom, she might have learned from her father's fate or even from the unfortunate Aedon's to cherish what she had, but with proper humility. Unfortunately, humility was as absent from her nature as wisdom.

"Niobe also had reason to know how swift to punish hubris Artemis was. She had before her the example of the Chione I mentioned some time ago, the lover of both Hermes and Apollo, who had bragged so incessantly about how beautiful she must be to win the affection of two gods in one night. Artemis finally took one of her arrows and shot the girl right through the tongue. Even if Niobe had somehow missed that obvious example, any fool could tell you that Artemis and Apollo are fiercely protective of their long-suffering mother, Leto.

"So what does Niobe do? She boasts about her superiority to Leto, because Leto only had two children, while she had fourteen. Greater stupidity could hardly be imagined.

"It was not long before Artemis shot six of the daughters and Apollo six of the sons. Some said that two were spared to leave Niobe the same number of children as Leto, but, in fact, one son and one daughter prayed to Leto for deliverance and were spared because of that plea. Had all of Niobe's children had the wit to do that, they might all have survived their mother's bloated ego.

"Niobe, at first refusing to accept the truth, or perhaps expecting the gods to resurrect her children, refused to let them be buried for nine days. The gods themselves finally arranged for the burial, after which Niobe fled to Mount Sipylus, where she wept perpetually. Eventually, someone—the storytellers differ as to who—turned her to stone, though it is a stone on which water still forms, for Niobe has never stopped her weeping.

"One might have expected Amphion, always the more sensitive brother, to have died of grief like Zethus. Instead he flew into a rage and vengefully attacked the temple of Apollo. Foolish as revenge normally is, it is doubly so when a man seeks revenge against a god. Apollo shot him down. Even Amphion's own father, Zeus, could not allow such sacrilege."

"All of that is so…depressing," said Fatima. "It makes me sad."

"Despite the fact that Amphion and Zethus usurped the throne that should have belonged to my family, the story fills me with sorrow as well. They were good men who deserved a better fate, and Thebes mourned much after their deaths."

"Well, now at least your family must have regained control of Thebes," said Mateo.

"Would that they had not!" said Cadmus, speaking so forcefully that the students jumped. "This next part of the tale fills me with shame, and I could not bring myself to tell it, except that perhaps the clue you seek lies within it.

"Yes, Laius did regain the throne, but were there any justice in the world, he would not have, for his sins were already great.

"During his exile, he had taken refuge in Elis, specifically in Pisa, where Pelops, the resurrected son of Tantalus, ruled. Possessing some of the virtue his father and sister lacked, Pelops treated Laius as an honored guest; indeed, since Laius stayed so long, he became almost like a family member.

"Pelops had two legitimate sons, but his conspicuous favorite was an illegitimate son named Chrysippus. While teaching the boy chariot-riding, Laius was filled with lust for him.

"Many might have overlooked Laius's infidelity to his wife, Jocasta, though even that was a sin—I had my faults, but I was always loyal to my Harmonia. However, Laius put himself beyond anyone's sympathy when he kidnapped the boy with the intention of raping him—a triple sin, for it encompassed not only the rape itself, but also the violation of the bond between tutor and pupil, as well the obligations of a guest under the sacred host-guest relationship.

"Thank the gods Chrysippus had spirit. Though younger and less experienced than Laius, he fought him off and managed to escape, running back to his father's court so swiftly he might have been mistaken for a son of Hermes.

"Laius might well have received the punishment his crimes deserved right then, but while he was contemplating where to flee, he received a message from Thebes that Amphion and Zethus were dead, and that he was now free to return as king. Fetching his wife, Jocasta, who knew nothing of his crimes, he rode away as hastily as he could, pretending his speed was eagerness to return to his homeland now that it was safe.

"He need not have sped so fast. Chrysippus should have denounced Laius at once to his father, but he fell into the error of many victims and believed himself somehow to blame. Ashamed of what had happened, he said nothing, planning to find some excuse to stay away from Laius in the future. What a sigh of relief he must have breathed when he learned Laius had returned to Thebes."

"How…how could Laius live with himself after that?" asked Yasmin.

"I don't know," said Cadmus. "As you have noticed, men were often more savage in my time than in yours, but even by the standards of my time, Laius was a villain beyond any hope of excuse. Amazing it is that the gods did not at once strike him down, but sometimes the gods wait for the right moment to strike, and this was one of those times.

"Laius got more happiness than he deserved, living with Jocasta as king of Thebes, but one problem nagged at him—he had no children, not even one son to succeed him. He consulted the oracle at Delphi, who told him he would indeed have a son, but that son was destined to kill his father and marry his mother.

"This would have been a moment for Laius to beg forgiveness from the gods, but, oblivious to his own sins, he set about trying to cheat fate in the way so many mortals do. He resolved to never have sex with Jocasta. However, the first time he became drunk, his lust got the better of him, and Jocasta became pregnant.

"Again Laius might have prayed for mercy, but again he didn't. Instead, he decided to expose the child. Jocasta might have objected, but, having been told the prophecy, she didn't, thereby dooming herself as well."

"Wouldn't she have been doomed anyway?" asked Yong. "After all, Laius had already learned her fate from the oracle."

"Ah, what a question," said Cadmus, "and one no mortal can truly answer. Even the gods sometimes seem uncertain.

"There are those, such as Sophocles, who believe that fate is shaped by our character and actions, not fixed from the beginning of time. Under that theory, Laius brought his own fate upon himself by his many crimes, and Jocasta, while not as guilty, by not objecting to what he did, earned a dire fate of her own.

"In any case, Laius, sure he could beat his fate, not through repentance but through cleverness, made his preparations to murder his own son. As if worried that the baby would somehow crawl to safety, Laius drove a spike through its feet. Then he handed it to a shepherd to expose on Mount Cithaeron. However, the shepherd, far more moral than his king, could not bring himself to let an infant die. Instead, he gave the child to a shepherd from Sicyon. Sophocles says it was Corinth, but he was wrong. Anyway, the shepherd ultimately took the child to King Polybus of Sicyon, who had wanted a child, but he and his wife, Merope, had none. They took the child and raised him as their own, giving him the name Oedipus, or Swell-foot. They considered him theirs to the point that, even when he came of age, they did not tell him he was adopted.

"This Polybus, the son of Hermes and Cythonophle, daughter of the Sicyon for whom the city was named, was a wise and virtuous man, ironically the sort of father Oedipus should have had, just as Merope would have been a better mother than Jocasta. Their one fault, though they did not know it, was not telling Oedipus of his adoption.

"One day a drunken youth insulted Oedipus's parentage by claiming he was really not a son of the king and queen at all. Oedipus should have asked his parents, but instead he went to the oracle at Delphi, who, instead of answering his question about who his parents were, announced that he would kill his father and marry his mother.

"Forgetting his earlier question, the horrified Oedipus fled. Though not by any means as great a sinner as his true father, Oedipus made one similar mistake. Instead of trying to obtain mercy from the gods, he attempted to prevent his fate on his own.

"He reasoned that if got far away from his parents, he would never fulfill either part of the prophecy. Not knowing Polybus and Merope were not truly his parents, he intended to get as far away from them as he could.

"If only he had left his fate in the hands of the gods, it would never have come to pass, for he would never have encountered Laius and Jocasta. In much the same way, if Laius and Jocasta, accepting what the gods had planned for them, had raised Oedipus as their son, they too could have avoided their fate, for Oedipus was too good a person to have knowingly killed his father or married his mother.

"While Oedipus was fleeing Sicyon, Laius was also on the road, heading back to Delphi to ask the oracle for advice about a new crisis. The Sphinx, a creature with the head of a woman, the body of a lion, the tail of a serpent, and the wings of an eagle, flew from as far away as Aethiopia. After settling near Thebes, it posed a riddle to all passing travelers, devouring all who failed to answer correctly. Since no one could figure out the riddle, that meant in practice that Thebes was largely cut off from the outside world, because it took a great deal of maneuvering to bypass the creature.

"Not knowing that Hera had sent the creature as punishment for Laius's treatment of Chrysippus, Laius and five attendants managed to get around it and reach the main road. However, when they got to a place where three roads met, they encountered Oedipus, whom they tried to shove rudely out of the way.

"Oedipus might have borne this insult with patience, but I know few princes who would have. Neither side would yield, but Oedipus proved to be a better warrior, killing Laius and all his men. Oedipus continued down the road, not knowing he had just fulfilled the first part of the prophecy.

"As Oedipus approached Thebes, he encountered the Sphinx, who asked him its dreaded riddle: what walks on four feet in the morning, two in the afternoon, and three in the evening? Oedipus gave the correct answer, man, for a man crawls as a baby, walks upright as a young man, and walks with a cane as an old one.

"Defeated, the Sphinx flung itself onto the jagged rocks below and died. As a result, when Oedipus arrived at Thebes, he was hailed as a hero. When Laius was found dead somewhat later, the citizens wanted to make Oedipus their king. Not knowing he was really Laius's heir by blood, the Thebans tried to figure out how to give Oedipus a legitimate claim to the throne on which they so urgently desired to place him. In the end, they decided to marry Jocasta to Oedipus. Not only was she the previous queen, but she was the daughter of Menoceus, one of the sown men, and therefore a woman of some importance in her own right."

"They expected a recently widowed woman to marry some stranger?" asked Fatima.

"Yes, they put the city's need for a king ahead of Jocasta's feelings," said Cadmus. "Fortunately for them—and unfortunately for her and Oedipus—she agreed, inadvertently helping to fulfill the second part of the prophecy and sealing her own doom in the process.

"For ten years Oedipus governed Thebes well. He and Jocasta were happily married and had two sons, Eteocles and Polynices, and two daughters, Antigone and Ismene.

"Only then did the inexorable end to their tragedy begin to unfold. A plague struck Thebes, and Oedipus sent Creon, brother of Jocasta, to seek the counsel of the Delphic oracle. Creon returned with a very specific prediction: the plague would end once the city expelled the murderer of Laius, who was living within its walls.

"Not realizing what he was doing, Oedipus laid a curse on the murderer of Laius and swore that he would be driven from the city. He then proceeded to investigate.

"Unfortunately for him, the truth was not hard to discover once someone really started looking for it. Piece by piece, he assembled the truth, just as you try to assemble your clues.

"It was during that time Oedipus was visited by Teiresias, the same blind prophet who had earlier warned Pentheus about Dionysus. The stories about how Teiresias became both blind and a prophet vary, but they agree on three things. First, he had been granted a long life by the gods, some say as long as seven generations. Second, he was from an illustrious family and thus worthy of trust. His father was Everes, a son of Gaia. His mother was the nymph Chariclo, a companion of Athena as well as being related to both Udaeus, one of the Sown Men, and the god Apollo, whom you may remember is the god of prophecy. Third, when he spoke from the inspiration of the gods, he was never wrong, an even more certain guarantee that when he spoke, mortals would be well advised to listen.

"Teiresias revealed the truth about the murder of Laius, but Oedipus refused to accept it. However, not content with just rejecting the prophet's advice, he accused the prophet of being involved in a conspiracy against him, an imaginary plot that Oedipus thought included Creon as well.

"Jocasta soon after realized the truth and begged Oedipus to stop looking, but he would not, partly because of his duty to the city, but a little because of his own hubris. He had already figured out that he was not the son of Polybus and Merope, but he now believed himself to be the son of a god and wanted to verify his hunch, thus increasing his fame.

"He discovered the truth just minutes after the distraught Jocasta had killed herself. Oedipus, overcome by guilt, used the pins of Jocasta's brooches to blind himself, and, in fulfillment of his own oath, left Thebes forever. His daughter, Antigone, joined him as a guide.

"Alas, even that was not the end of my family's suffering. Creon, related by marriage to the royal house much as Nycteus had been, seemed a sensible candidate for regent. He served reasonably well until Eteocles and Polynices came of age, but it did not take long for the situation to deteriorate after that, for neither son was as noble as his father.

"Eteocles and Polynices agreed to share the throne, rotating control of it every year. However, Eteocles, who had the first turn, refused to relinquish the throne when the time came. Instead, he drove Polynices from the city.

"At first it seemed as if Eteocles would get away with breaking his agreement. The people of Thebes, perhaps unhappy with the idea of a rotating monarchy, generally accepted Eteocles as their king, and so Polynices could do little to oppose his brother. However, Polynices did not give up; instead, he waited for an opportunity to take back what he felt was rightfully his.

"In the meantime, Oedipus, purified by his intense suffering and by his own contrition, managed to overcome the consequences of this cruel fate. Once regarded as cursed, he came to be regarded as holy instead, blessed by the gods.

"Here was an opportunity for my family to overcome the curse Laius had brought upon it, for the blessing of Oedipus was a powerful thing. Perhaps it could have freed them. Instead, they selfishly squandered the opportunity, each fighting for his own advantage, not for the common good.

"Creon had received an oracle that the bones of Oedipus, who was nearing death, would protect the city of Thebes if they were buried there. However, if they were buried at Colonus, near Athens, where Oedipus now wished to be buried, then Athens would receive the protection, and Thebes would go into decline.

Creon, who had been eager to be rid of Oedipus, now wanted him back, though more for his own benefit than for that of Thebes, for a prosperous Thebes meant prosperity for Creon. Polynices and Eteocles each wanted their father's blessing to secure the throne. None of them thought much about the welfare of our family as a whole, let alone the welfare of Thebes, and that proved to be their undoing.

"Creon came to Colonus where, pretending to be concerned for Oedipus's welfare, he invited the former king to return to Thebes. Oedipus refused, and Creon resorted to force, first taking Oedipus's daughters hostage, then trying to violently drag Oedipus away. Theseus, king of Athens, saved both Oedipus and his daughters.

"Polynices also came and feigned concern for Oedipus, but Oedipus, who saw through his pretense as easily as he had seen through Creon's, gave his son a curse rather than a blessing. If Polynices had not been doomed before, he certainly was after.

"Very soon, Oedipus died, but his body just vanished before Theseus's eyes, swept up to Olympus in a rare gesture of acceptance by the gods themselves. Nonetheless, Theseus made a tomb for him, as Oedipus had asked, and the blessing of Oedipus, who had essentially become a god himself and to whom a shrine was dedicated, often came to the rescue of Athens after that.

"Thebes could have enjoyed that protection itself if only Oedipus's own family members had been able to see beyond their own selfish interests. They could not, and so they doomed themselves.

"Polynices went ahead with his invasion plans, having gained powerful allies in Argos."

"The Argives thought he had a right to the throne?" asked Mateo.

"Based on the original agreement between the two brothers, a case could have been made for the justice of Polynices's claim," said Cadmus. "Unfortunately, people often act from more personal motives than abstract right and wrong. King Adrastus of Argos would probably not have cared one way or the other about who had the right to the throne of Thebes. The issue only became important to him once Polynices had married into his family.

"You might think an exiled prince would not be regarded as a good candidate for an arranged marriage, but Adrastus ended up with not one, but two, exiled princes as sons-in-law.

"Adrastus had two beautiful daughters, and suitors came from all over Greece. Certainly, there were better choices than Polynices available, but Adrastus was afraid that picking two of the suitors would alienate the others, potentially leading to war.

"Adrastus asked the Delphic oracle for advice and received an odd reply from Apollo, something about marrying one daughter to a lion and another to a boar. He had no idea what to make of that suggestion, until a fight broke out between two of the suitors.

"One of the fighters was Polynices. The other was Tydeus of Calydon, exiled for the killing of his brother, though Tydeus claimed the death was accidental. On his shield, Polynices had the image of the Sphinx, with its lion body; on his, Tydeus had a boar, representing the Calydonian boar. Adrastus saw them as a symbolic fulfillment of the oracle's prophecy and arranged for their marriage to his daughters.

"Unfortunately, as part of the marriage contract, Adrastus agreed to help each of his new sons-in-law win the thrones of their respective countries.

"As Argos prepared for war, Eteocles invited Polynices to Thebes, and it looked as if war might be averted. Alas, the brothers could still not reach agreement, and Eteocles again exiled Polynices, condemning many good men to death in the process.

"Even then, it seemed as if disaster might be avoided. Adrastus assembled a large army and named seven champions to lead the assault. One of the men he selected, Amphiarus, his brother-in-law and by some accounts co-king, was a seer who knew that the war with Thebes would not only fail to win Polynices the throne but result in the death of many men, including all the champions except Adrastus. He at first refused to go and tried to convince others not to go as well.

"He might have saved many lives, but unfortunately one of his fellow Argives gave Polynices a strategy to outwit the seer. Years before Eriphyle, sister of Adrastus and wife of Amphiarus, had resolved an argument between them, and they had sworn solemn oaths to accept her judgment in any future quarrel. If Eriphyle sided with Adrastus, Amphiarus would have no choice but to accept her decision.

"Polynices had somehow gained possession of the much-coveted necklace of Harmonia, said to have the power to keep its wearer looking young. He offered it as a bribe to Eriphyle, and to her eternal shame, she took it and forced Amphiarus to follow Adrastus to war. The seer knew his own wife had betrayed him for a piece of jewelry, but, fearing to break his oath, he went anyway.

"Adrastus marched his army partway to Thebes, but then, perhaps worried by the earlier protests of Amphiarus, sent Tydeus on ahead to see if a peaceful settlement could be reached.

"Tydeus was a mighty man and a favorite of the goddess Athena, but he was no diplomat. He defeated all the Theban leaders in non-lethal single combat, but this tactic didn't convince them to make peace. It did anger them, though, and they treacherously sent fifty men out to ambush him. With the aid of Athena, Tydeus killed all of them but one, whom he spared at the request of

Zeus. He came back to the Argive army covered in glory—but having completely failed in his mission.

"Adrastus then had his army march to Thebes, where it readied for battle. It was then that Ares, still nursing his grudge, took one last stab at me.

"When Eteocles consulted Teiresias, the prophet told him that Thebes could only win if a member of the royal family sacrificed himself to Ares. The war god had doubtless thought that one of my kin would have to die, but to my shame none of them had the courage to sacrifice himself for the city. Instead, Creon's son, Menoceus, a member of the royal house through Jocasta's marriages, killed himself so that Thebes might live.

"At first the battle went badly despite Menoceus's brave death. The Thebans were driven from the field, and the Argives prepared to climb the walls. Then Canapeus, one of the seven champions, started to climb the wall using a scaling ladder, with other Argives ready to do the same. Unfortunately for the Argives, hubris got the better of Canapeus, who said something about being able to climb the wall and set fire to the city even if Zeus opposed him. The king of the gods struck the blasphemer with a thunderbolt, and the Argives abandoned the effort to scale the walls.

"Inspired by such a sign from the gods, the Thebans rushed back into battle, killing three more of the Argive champions and badly wounding Tydeus. However, Tydeus managed to kill his attacker, Melanippus, before falling from blood loss.

"Seeing her favorite wounded, Athena raced off to get a healing potion that could save him. Amphiarus, who hated Tydeus for having encouraged the Argives to shed their blood before Thebes, knew that Athena wanted to save Tydeus and suspected that she might even want to make him immortal. In an attempt to prevent that, Amphiarus cut off Melanippus's head and tossed it to Tydeus, inviting him to further abuse his slain foe's body.

"All Tydeus had to do was ignore this temptation, for the gods frown on the savage practice of dishonoring the dead, but he gave into his darker impulses. He cracked open his enemy's skull and started to eat his brains.

"Athena, who had just returned, was so shocked by what she saw that she poured out the healing potion on the ground and abandoned her former favorite, who soon died from his wound.

"At this point Polynices, fearing the Argives would lose, offered to settle the conflict with a fight to the death between himself and Eteocles. His brother accepted, not to save lives, but to have the satisfaction of killing Polynices himself.

"Eteocles got what he wanted—in a way. He did mortally wound Polynices, but Polynices did the same to him, and they both died on a field already drenched with blood that did not need to be shed.

"Nor was that the end of it. Creon, not trusting the Argives to fulfill their agreement, or perhaps because he wanted to avenge Menoceus, took command of the Theban troops and proceeded to slaughter every Argive who could not escape fast enough.

"Amphiarus had foreseen that he would end up in the Underworld before the end of the day, but Zeus fulfilled Amphiarus's fate in a way the seer had not anticipated. Just as Amphiarus was about to be captured and killed, Zeus split the ground with a thunderbolt, creating a chasm into which fell Amphiarus, his chariot, and his charioteer.

"Amphiarus ended up in the Underworld—alive. Subsequently, he was made immortal and became the seer of the Underworld.

"Of all the other Argive champions, Adrastus alone escaped. He was riding Arion, the horse child of Poseidon and Demeter, which no mortal steed could outrun. Most of his men, however, were not so lucky."

"So much death," said Fatima, looking pale.

"Would that this battle had been the end of it, but it was not," said Cadmus. "Creon was now king, but he proved to be a poor one, overcome by hubris almost from the first.

"He should have learned from the example of Tydeus that the gods do not sanction the desecration of the dead, but he refused to accept that simple lesson. Instead, his decree forbade the burial of any of those who fought against Thebes—but particularly Polynices. As far as I was concerned, the two brothers were both at fault, but Creon treated Eteocles like a hero and Polynices like the darkest villain imaginable.

"Seeing Creon's anger, the Thebans were afraid to defy him—all except one. Antigone, Polynices's sister, buried Polynices as the gods would have wanted. Even when Creon caught her, she refused to disavow what she had done.

"Ismene, who had been afraid to help her sister, came to Antigone's defense now. Creon's own son, Haemon, to whom Antigone was betrothed, defended her equally loudly, but to no avail. Even the blind prophet, Teiresias, had no luck when he offered Creon one last chance to change course. In his arrogance, Creon set his own judgment above that of the gods—and paid for it.

"Creon ordered Antigone sealed up in a tomb, intending to avoid the blood guilt by letting her starve instead of killing her outright. Haemon secretly tried to free her, but by the time he reached her, she had hanged herself. Distraught, Haemon threw himself on his own sword. Eurydice, his mother, killed herself when she heard the news, and thus Creon paid for his ego in his family's blood.

"Creon thought of suicide but was so shattered by these disasters that he could not even manage that. The stories differ at that point, but it seems unlikely to me that Creon ever truly ruled again. Some arrangement must have been made until Laodomas, the son of Eteocles, was old enough to rule.

"I do not know what kind of king Laodomas might have made, for soon after he took the throne, the Epigoni, the sons of the seven champions of Argos, raised an army to take revenge on Thebes. This time the city fell, though, thanks to Teiresias, a large part of the population evacuated before the attack. Teiresias knew he was fated to die as soon as Thebes was in Argive hands, so it would have been in his interest to have had the Thebans mount as spirited a defense as they could, but he chose their lives over his own. If only my worthless descendants had risen to that level.

"Laodomas did stay to fight, but it did him no good. He died at the hands of his cousin, Thersander, the son of Polynices, who became king.

"That at least ended my family's long plunge into evil, but it did not inaugurate a new era of heroism as I might have liked.

"Between the casualties of war and the losses from flight, the city was but a shadow of its former self. Thersander somehow raised an army to join the Greek attack on Troy, but he was killed before he ever got there. My family ruled for two more generations, after which another dynasty took over for three. The last king, Xanthus, was killed by the king of Athens—the city which had the blessing of Oedipus that Thebes might have had. After that, Thebes fell under the control of Athens. It did eventually rise again—but in spite of the legacy of my family, not because of it."

"Why do such things happen?" asked Fatima, so wrapped up that she forgot the stories were all myths.

Cadmus sighed. "That question no man can answer. The important thing is to avoid such disasters in the future. Arrogance, selfishness, and a host of other human weaknesses destroyed my family over time—and through the discord they caused, wrecked their city as well. Take care that the same does not happen to those you love."

"I see you have finished already," said Hermes, appearing suddenly behind them. "That is good, for I must take our visitors to see Cronus."

"He isn't on the list Apollo gave us," said Yong.

"No, but he requires your presence, and this is his realm."

"I have never seen Cronus summon anyone in all my time here," said Cadmus.

"Yes, but times are changing," said Hermes, pointing at the gray sky. "I'm afraid we must bid you goodbye and head to Cronus's tower at once."

"Wait," said a quiet but still commanding voice.

The students turned in that direction, and they saw someone who could only be the Teiresias they had heard so much about. He looked much as he must have at the end of his mortal life, with silver hair, blind eyes that somehow still seemed to look right at you, a wrinkled face, and a determined expression. He walked slowly but steadily, leaning on the same staff Thanos remembered Athena was supposed to have given him.

"Old friend, Hermes just told them they must hasten to Cronus," said Cadmus.

"That's just the thing," said Teiresias, pointing with his staff. "That isn't Hermes."

Chapter 22: Bellerophon and Perseus

"Of course I'm Hermes! Who else could I be?"

"One of the conspirators trying to start a war among the gods," said Teiresias in a tone so casual he could have been talking about the weather. "Your disguise is almost flawless, good enough to fool mortals, the blessed dead, even some of the gods—but not good enough to fool me. Actually, I foresaw that an impostor would show up in Hermes's place; that's why I came."

Hermes's face twisted with rage, and even the students could tell he was not the real Hermes.

Raising the caduceus, the impostor said, "Old man, do not attempt to stop me. You are no match for me; nor is the cow goddess over there. Certainly these mortals are not."

"Did you think I would be fool enough to come here alone?" asked Teiresias, and, as if on cue, Artemis, Pan, Ardalos, and Patricius all appeared. All four looked poised to attack, and Patricius did a good mechanical imitation of a growl and bared his bronze teeth.

The false Hermes gestured with his caduceus, and a wave of magic rolled in their direction. The students, despite what protection they had, staggered a little, but Pan charged, Artemis fired, and Patricius leaped. False Hermes would have a hard time stopping them all.

Unfortunately, the impostor was as fast as the real Hermes. In an eye blink, he was gone, leaving no trace behind. Artemis's arrow buried itself in a distant tree, and Pan and Patricius both flopped on the ground.

"Ouch, I should have known he'd do that," said Pan, pulling himself off the ground.

"Do you know which way he went?" Artemis asked Teiresias.

"Sadly, no. Even I cannot see all. Nor can I tell you who that was, for there is powerful magic at work here. I could tell that was not really Hermes, but I could not discern his true identity."

"Then we still don't know who is responsible for all this?" asked Thanos.

"Alas, no," replied Teiresias. "That is why your quest is so important. Just as Apollo and Hermes perceived, when you find your friend, you will find the god responsible for this dire threat."

"What of my father?" asked Pan. "Where is he?"

"Imprisoned," said Teiresias, "but where I do not know. My guess would be the same place in which the visitors' friend is being held."

"Do you know how much time we have to find him…them?" asked Yong. "We still don't know how long we have here."

"Nor do I," said Teiresias, "but I believe time is running out for you—and for Olympus. Thanks to Apollo, Zeus now knows there is a conspiracy and does what he can to prevent war among the gods. Eirene, peace incarnate, sends out her soothing energy, and Eros, both the primal force and his younger manifestation, work to reinforce the bonds of familial love among the gods—"

"Such as they are," said Artemis.

"Indeed, we are a contentious family at the best of times," admitted Io.

"Which is why someone is so easily able to play on your divisions," said Teiresias. "I fear Zeus's attempts to prevent all-out war can hold the gods together only a short time with this much force arrayed against them."

"That impostor did not seem so powerful—and he ran from us," said Artemis. "Would not someone capable of rending the gods asunder have stood and fought us?"

"There is more than one god involved," said Teiresias. "Too many different powers are being used for any single deity to be responsible. The one we just confronted was not the ringleader."

"It sounds as if we should move fast," said Keisha, "but how can we without Hermes? Will you be able to guide us?"

"Indeed I will," said the prophet, "but my knowledge of what is and what may be to come does not always give me the power that Hermes would have had to handle problems in the Underworld. That is why I have summoned other help. Ah, here she is now."

The students were surprised to see Persephone walking toward them.

"In fact, my authority here is second only to that of Hades, and he has given his blessing to my effort to aid you," said Persephone. "There is no door I cannot unlock, no citizen of the Underworld I cannot command. Even here in Elysium my authority is respected."

Teiresias, Cadmus, and Apollodorus bowed, and the students followed their example.

"With your permission, I would like to go and search for Hermes," said Io, "just as he searched for me long ago."

"I was about to suggest that very thing," said Teiresias.

"I have another suggestion," said Persephone, turning to Apollodorus. "Between Teiresias and me, we can guide our visitors, so your knowledge of the Underworld is no longer needed."

Apollodorus, who clearly wanted to tag along, looked downcast.

"However," continued Persephone, "I'm sure someone of your literary sense can tell that these events will merit an epic poem. Would you do me the favor of sorting that out with the poets? I trust no one to organize this important work as much as I trust you."

Apollodorus's mood visibly swung from sad to happy. "I will attend to it at once, my queen." With that, he hurried off, and Keisha could almost swear she heard him humming.

"You did not wish him to accompany you?" asked Cadmus, looking amused.

"He will be more use on the task to which I assigned him," said Persephone. "Asking for a new epic poem is like tossing the apple of discord among the poets. Each thinks he should be the one to write it. Homer and Virgil get into a fight over a new project every time. Apollodorus is far from being the greatest writer among them, but he is one of the best organizers. How else could he have pulled that unruly mess left by the storytellers into a reasonably coherent narrative?"

After saying goodbye to Cadmus and Io, the group headed for its next hero, Bellerophon, whom they were lucky enough to find with Perseus, who was right after him on the list.

They could not have been more different. Both were handsome, as one might have expected, since both were sons of gods, but there was a grimness about Bellerophon that contrasted sharply with Perseus's happiness.

"I do not even belong here," said Bellerophon. "It was my father's influence alone that brought me to the Elysian Fields."

"You are too hard on yourself, friend," said Perseus. "No resident of Elysium is without fault. Every single one of us did things in life which we have good reason to regret."

"The gods do not require perfection," Persephone added. "If they did, Elysium would be an empty field."

"Let our visitors hear my tale and see if they agree," said Bellerophon, looking sadly at the students.

"I was a member of the family of Sisyphus, so I started with much to live down. My grandfather was so terrible, in fact, that my grandmother was ashamed of him, and rather than refer to him as the founder of the city, the Corinthians made themselves look foolish by inventing a fictional founder, Corinthus, an alleged son of Zeus."

Keisha had to smile at the irony of a character in myth calling another character fictional, but as usual, she kept quiet about it.

"My father, Glaucus, was no model of virtue either, despite his divine ancestry—his mother had been Merope, daughter of Atlas. He became so obsessed with perfecting his horses, both for chariot racing and for war, that he fed them human flesh, an offense against the gods. He also offended Aphrodite in particular by refusing to allow his mares to breed. He was cursed by the gods to never father children, and eventually the horses he had tended so carefully turned on him and devoured him, some say after being maddened by Aphrodite."

"I don't understand," said Mateo. "If your father couldn't father anyone—"

"Glaucus was my *legal* father," replied Bellerophon, "but Poseidon, who once made love to Eurymede, my mother, was my true father.

"The one good thing I might have gotten from Glaucus would have been the throne of Corinth, but I ended up exiled—my own fault, for I killed my brother, Deliades, though I hadn't meant to. We got into a fight, and I killed him by accident. That was terrible enough, but since the people of Corinth knew of Glaucus's violent temper and strange practices, they judged me by him and assumed I had committed deliberate murder.

"Needing to be purified of the blood guilt, I went to Tiryns, where Proetus, Perseus's uncle, was king. He agreed to help with the necessary rituals and made me his guest.

"Unfortunately, I was a good-looking young man, if I do say so myself, and I caught the eye of Proetus's wife, Anteia, who secretly asked me to make love to her.

"I would never have offended against the laws of hospitality by sleeping with my host's wife, so I naturally refused. Anteia, angered by my rejection, told her husband it was I who had tried to seduce her.

"Proetus wanted to kill me, but he knew taking the life of a guest would offend the gods, so instead he found some excuse to send me to King Iobates of Lycia, bearing a sealed letter asking Iobates to kill me. The plot might well have succeeded, except that Iobates made me his honored guest before reading the letter, so he too was stuck with the restrictions of the host-guest relationship.

"Trying to get around the prohibition against killing me, Iobates asked me to accept a dangerous quest and kill the Chimera, a fire-breathing monster with the head of a lion, the body of a goat, and the tail of a serpent. The quest sounded suicidal, for at that point I had not yet realized my divine ancestry. However, I thought perhaps I was getting what I deserved for killing my brother, so I accepted the quest.

"Guilty as I was, though, I really didn't want to die, and so I went to see the seer, Polyeidus. He told me that I could defeat the Chimera—but to do so, I needed to tame Pegasus, the winged horse, and ride him into battle.

"I had always been good with horses, but how was I, a mere mortal, going to tame Pegasus? The seer couldn't say, but he suggested I spend the night in the temple of Athena. That night she came to me in a dream, told me that Poseidon was my true father, advised me to offer a sacrifice to him, and handed me a magic bridle I could use to tame Pegasus. When I awoke, I thought I had just had a foolish dream—but there was the bridle, clutched in my right hand.

"After making my sacrifice to Poseidon, I sought out Pegasus and threw the bridle over his head. Instantly, he became as docile as if I had raised him from birth, and I was able to mount him without trouble.

"Much later I learned that Pegasus was actually my half-brother, the child of Poseidon and Medusa. No wonder flying on him felt so natural!"

Bellerophon actually smiled as he remembered Pegasus and the dangers they had faced together. It hurt Fatima to realize how far his life must have gone downhill after that.

"With the ability to fly, I knew I could stay clear of the Chimera's claws, perhaps even its fiery breath, but I needed a plan. I decided to use arrow fire to put the beast on the defensive. That worked well, so that the monster was somewhat caught off-guard when it opened its mouth to breathe fire. Instead of flying higher at that point, as I had been doing, I plummeted in its direction, shoving at it a spear tipped with lead. Its fiery breath melted the lead, which flowed down its throat, searing and poisoning the creature.

"I was elated to have done so well, but Iobates was frustrated, for I had survived what he thought was an impossible mission. In vain he sent me out again, this time against the Solymians, and then against the Amazons, and finally against the Carian pirates. In each case I flew far above their heads and dropped boulders on them, making them scatter and flee the field.

"Iobates, still convinced I had tried to seduce Proetus's wife, decided he would have to kill me and sent the palace guard to ambush me when I returned.

"I could have avoided them by flying away, but, not knowing the cause for such ungrateful behavior, I was angry, and I made the rash decision to put my alleged descent from Poseidon to the test.

"I prayed to Poseidon to flood the plain behind me, and he did. The palace guards could see well enough that the gods were on my side, and they fled in the opposite direction. As I followed, the waves kept pace with me.

"By the time I reached the palace, Iobates tried diplomacy, but I refused to listen to his envoys, and step by step, I brought the sea closer and closer to the palace.

"The men having failed, the women decided to do what they could. They came out before me naked, all of them offering themselves to me if I would turn back the flood.

"Having never been with a woman, I was overwhelmed by that much attention, and I stammered a refusal to accept them under such circumstances, for what I wanted was a willing bride, not a mob of women who felt forced because they wanted to save their city. However, I did pray to Poseidon to end the flood, and the waters flowed back into the sea, where they belonged.

"Having watched the way I behaved, Iobates couldn't believe that a man who would reject all the women of the city could possibly have made such an improper attempt on a host's wife. Because of his new doubts, he revealed the contents of the letter and questioned me.

"When he learned the truth, he apologized—and did much more. He made me the husband of his daughter, Philonoe, and he made me his heir as well.

"I had everything a man could want: a loving wife, an honorable family, fine children, and the memory of my heroic deeds, with the promise of more yet to come. I even had a flying horse. What more could I have possibly desired?

"Yet it is all too often that people do not appreciate what they already have, and that was the trap into which I fell. Hubris took hold of me and began to gnaw at my soul. I was already hero and prince, but I wanted to become a god.

"One day I flew Pegasus toward Olympus, intending to join the gods without invitation. Zeus refrained from striking me down with a thunderbolt out of respect for my father, but he sent a gadfly to sting Pegasus. He reared, throwing me, and I fell to earth, landing in an enormous thorn bush.

"Blind, crippled, and filled with shame for what I had done, I wandered away from any place where men lived, preferring the solitude of the wilderness, in which I died."

"Hard on yourself much?" asked Mateo.

"Yeah, you made a mistake—a big one," conceded Yong. "That one mistake, however, doesn't cancel out all the good things you did."

"And you paid the price for that mistake, suffering much before your death," said Persephone. "You have already atoned. The days when you needed to feel guilty are long past. Had Zeus not forgiven you, you would never have been admitted to the Elysian Fields."

"And turning down all those women?" asked Mateo, clearly fascinated. "I would never have had that much will power."

"Nor I," added Pan. "Why, I would have—"

"We know what you would have done!" snapped Artemis.

"May I suggest that we hear the story of Perseus?" asked Teiresias. "Remember that time is short."

"Well, if my friend Bellerophon thinks he is the only one who sprung from a dishonorable family, he is much mistaken," said Perseus. "My grandfather, Acrisius, and his twin brother Proetus are said to have fought each other in the womb, and they continued to fight for the first many years of their lives. Like their ancestors, Danaus and Aegyptus, they could hardly have been worse brothers if they had tried.

"It was probably inevitable that they would fight over the throne of Argos when their father, Abas, died. Abas had wanted them to share the kingdom by serving as king alternately, but, of course, neither one wanted to share with the other, and war resulted.

"Acrisius drove Proetus out of the city, but Proetus was determined to win. He went off in search of allies, eventually finding one in Iobates, who was king of Lycia, as you know from Bellerophon's tale. A bloody war between Argos and Lycia was the fruit of this alliance, but neither side emerged victorious.

"Belatedly realizing the cost of their pride, the brothers agreed to divide power, though in a different way than Abas had decreed in his will. Acrisius took Argos and the area nearby, while Proetus took Tiryns and other cities to the east.

"Whether because they had offended the gods or for other reasons, neither man lived happily after that. I think when men spill that much blood in an effort to satisfy their pride, they cannot escape the consequences.

"In the case of Proetus, his three daughters went mad, some say because they offended Dionysus, others because they offended Hera. The seer Melampus offered to cure them in exchange for marriage to one of the daughters and a third of the kingdom. Proetus, ever mindful of his own power, said the price was too high, and Melampus went away, knowing Proetus would soon call him back.

"It was not long before the curse upon the daughters of Proetus spread to other Argive women, and Proetus again called for Melampus. However, by then the price had gone up: Melampus wanted a daughter and a third of the kingdom for himself and another daughter and a third for his brother, Bias. At that point Proetus had to agree, and Melampus succeeding in curing the king's daughters and all the other afflicted women. Proetus got what he needed—but he lost two-thirds of his kingdom in the process, and the heroes of subsequent generations, such as Amphiarus, would be remembered as descendants of Melampus and Bias, not of Proetus. The descendants of Proetus's only son, Megapenthes, did end up ruling in Argos for several generations, but eventually that line died out.

"As for Acrisius, he suffered even more. He longed for a son, but he had only one daughter, Danae. He asked the oracle at Delphi how he could obtain a son, and he was told he would never have a son, but only a grandson who would grow up to kill him.

"Horrified, Acrisius locked Danae in a bronze-walled chamber guarded by savage dogs. He felt certain that these cruel precautions would keep any man away from her.

"However, Acrisius did one humane thing for his daughter: he left part of the chamber open to the sky, so that she could have light and air. It was in that way that Zeus saw Danae and fell in love with her."

Artemis snorted, but, mindful of the limited time available, said nothing.

"Zeus came to Danae in a shower of golden rain, and she became pregnant with me. Because Acrisius never visited her, and because the servants delivered food only indirectly, she was able to keep my birth secret for a while. Unfortunately, when I was about three or four years of age, Acrisius heard me playing and discovered the truth—or at least the part of the truth that he was willing to accept.

"The evidence that I was the child of a god was plain enough, for what mortal man could have breached my mother's prison undetected? However, Acrisius wanted to kill me to prevent the prophecy from being fulfilled, and his men might have balked at the killing of a god's child, so he concocted the wild theory that the father was Proetus, who had entered by means of some vile magic. The story had a hint of credibility, for there had been rumors that Proetus had tried to force himself upon Danae, his niece, in the days before he was driven from Argos.

"Under such a theory, Acrisius could make it permissible to expose both me, the supposed product of incest, and my mother, perhaps the deluded co-conspirator in his brother's evil. Without a second thought, he ordered us put in a chest and cast out to sea.

"You have heard enough of our stories to know that leaving a child to die almost invariably backfires on the one who tries it, and so it was in this case, for my mother and I did not drown as he had hoped. Instead, protected by the blessing of Zeus, we drifted gently ashore on the small island of Seriphos.

"The chest in which we were trapped was found by Dictys, a noble man living in humble circumstances, though he was the son of Magnes, the son of

Aeolus. He was a fisherman, and the chest became tangled in his nets. He took us in and raised me as his own son, and all would have been well—if not for his brother.

"Though Dictys was a humble fisherman, his brother, Polydectes, was king of the island. It would have been better if their positions had been reversed, for Polydectes was as selfish as Dictys was selfless.

"The king saw my mother, who despite all of her ordeals, was still beautiful, and he wanted her for himself. However, she politely declined his overtures. He was determined to have her, with or without her consent, but I was a man by now, and instinctively he knew it would be unwise to try to take her by force with me around.

"Polydectes pretended that he had changed his mind and wanted to marry Hippodamia, the daughter of King Oenomaus of Pisa. Then he invited the leading men of the island, including me, to an *eranos*, a kind of party in which the guests are expected to make a contribution toward the bride price the host will need to pay as part of the marriage contract.

"When I asked Polydectes what an appropriate gift would be, he named a horse. Then he looked me disdainfully as if, being the foster son of a fisherman, I could not afford to bring such a gift. In fact, Dictys had prospered over the years and would certainly have given me a horse, but the king's attitude hurt my ego, just as he hoped, and I made a foolish gesture that might have been my death. I told him I could bring him anything he desired, even the head of Medusa, the gorgon.

"To my surprise, he accepted my offer immediately, claiming my words were the equivalent of a solemn oath. Dictys and my mother had both taught me to be honorable, so I did not immediately refuse, even though I knew that the promise I had accidentally made would be impossible to fulfill. After all, I could see no way for a mortal man to overcome such a powerful adversary as Medusa.

"Medusa had once been an incredibly beautiful woman—too beautiful for her own good. The admiration of so many men filled her with hubris, and she began to loudly proclaim her own beauty superior to that of the goddess Athena.

"At first Athena allowed this insolence to pass, perhaps hoping that

Medusa would see the error of her ways. Instead, Medusa became more and more arrogant, even allowing Poseidon to make love to her in Athena's own temple.

"That was too much even for a relatively patient goddess to endure. Athena couldn't punish Poseidon, but she could—and did—punish Medusa, making her face so ugly that one look at her would turn a man to stone, transforming her hair into snakes, and in every other way making her resemble the immortal gorgons, whom she was now forced to join as a mortal sister.

"However, Zeus was still watching over me, and to aid me he sent Hermes and Athena, doubly eager to come because of her own grudge against Medusa.

"Hermes provided me with an adamantine weapon called a *harpe*, a sword whose blade was rounded like that of a sickle—a perfect choice for lopping off Medusa's head. Athena gave me a highly-polished shield in which I could see Medusa's reflection and therefore avoid looking at her. However, they also told me I would need more than that to retrieve the head of Medusa.

"Through Athena's guidance and Hermes's magic, I reached the home of the Graeae, the gray women, so-called because they had been old since birth. It was they who knew the location of the Stygian nymphs from whom I could get the rest of my gear.

"These women had only one eye among them, so I waited, and when they started to exchange it, I snatched it away, threatening to destroy it unless they told me what I wanted to know. They threatened, they begged—but in the end, they told me where to find the nymphs.

"Again with Hermes's help, I reached the home of the nymphs, another place mortal men cannot normally reach. They happily gave me the other items I needed to fulfill my quest: a cap of invisibility, such as those you now carry; a magic bag that could contain whatever was put into it; winged sandals, enabling me to travel to the far west, where the gorgons were, without the aid of Hermes.

"Athena and Hermes had me time my arrival in such a way that the gorgons were all asleep. Athena had shown me the images of the gorgons earlier, so I knew which one was Medusa. Carefully and quietly, I approached her, being careful to look only at her reflection. With Athena guiding my hand, I was able to cut off her head in a single stroke, after which I hastily tucked it in the magic bag.

"I should have been able to fly away with no problem. However, even Athena had not realized one thing. Medusa was somehow still pregnant with her offspring by Poseidon. Instead of being born in the usual way, they flowed out with the blood from her severed neck.

"One was that very Pegasus who flew off and soon became Bellerophon's steed. The other was Chrysaor, a giant with a golden sword who made such a racket that the other gorgons awakened and nearly caught me. They were winged and could have flown after me, but luckily I was still invisible, making it harder for them to track me.

"Against all odds, I had achieved my goal—with huge amounts of help from Athena and Hermes. However, it was still a long way home, and one more adventure awaited me on the way.

"The quickest route would have been to fly over the ocean, but I'll admit that idea made me nervous. Out over the open sea, hours away from even the smallest island, what would happen if my winged sandals failed me? Not being a son of Poseidon like Bellerophon, I decided not to take the chance. Instead I took a longer route that kept me over land most of the time, flying across northern Africa, then north along the eastern shore of the Mediterranean, finally doubling back toward the west, across Asia Minor and back to Greece.

As I flew near the city of Joppa, I saw a beautiful woman chained to an offshore rock, and I could not help but love her."

"Like father, like son," muttered Artemis, but she smiled as she said it. Perseus had an undeniable charm, and like Bellerophon, he hadn't slept with every woman in sight the way his father did.

"I should have rescued her at once, but I flew inland instead. She could have been some monster in disguise, so I decided to learn her story first.

"I quickly learned that she was Andromeda, the daughter of King Cepheus and Queen Cassiopeia. One would have thought they were blessed by the gods, for Cepheus was supposed to be the son of Agenor and brother of Cadmus—which would have made him five generations older than I, yet he only looked old enough to be my father. During his wanderings in search of Europa, he had become not only king of Joppa but also of Aethiopia, whose princess, Cassiopeia, became his wife.

Yet their current grief suggested they were cursed, rather than blessed, by the gods. It was Cassiopeia's foolishness that had created the situation, for the queen had compared Andromeda's beauty to that of the Nereids, with the consequence that Poseidon sent a sea monster to destroy the city. The oracle of Ammon told the king that he would have to sacrifice his only daughter to the monster in order to appease Poseidon.

"I offered to rescue Andromeda, asking only that Cepheus allow me to marry her. He seemed oddly reluctant, but he finally agreed, and I flew to Andromeda's rescue.

"I arrived almost too late, for Cetus, the great sea monster, was already rising from the depths to devour the helpless girl. Yelling at her to cover her eyes, I took the gorgon's head from my bag, and the monster was instantly turned to stone. I understand people are still shown the huge rock that was once a monster.

"I flew Andromeda back to her parents, expecting to celebrate our marriage and then finish the trip home. However, Cepheus had failed to mention one thing: before I showed up, she was already betrothed to someone else—his brother, Phineus, if you can believe it.

"Phineus's men somehow heard that Andromeda had been rescued, and they came to the palace to escort her back to Thrace, where Phineus was king.

"I now realized that Cepheus had tricked me. Technically, he had no right to give me Andromeda in marriage, for she was already promised to someone else. Unfortunately, I was in love with her, and I did not intend to give her up so easily.

"I tried to reason with the envoys of Phineus. While acknowledging their master's prior claim, I pointed out that, if not for me, Andromeda would have died, and that since she was not actually married to Phineus, her father had the right to change his mind.

"Alas, Phineus had sent soldiers, not lawyers, to collect his bride, and his men decided it would be easier to just kill me than to argue with me. I had no choice but to show them the gorgon's head. I knew Cepheus would have to face an angry brother, but at least he now had an extremely realistic collection of statues.

"Wishing to avoid any further violence, I flew Andromeda back to Seriphos, where I planned to marry her—once I took care of my last piece of unfinished business.

"In my absence, Polydectes had planned a forced marriage. Dictys and my mother had delayed the inevitable by seeking sanctuary in the temple of Athena, but eventually Polydectes would have found a way to force them out.

"Arriving at his palace, I told him I had the gift he requested. He laughed and called me a liar—but his laughter died with him when he saw what I had in my bag. The friends and allies with him were no longer laughing, either.

"After that Seriphos could have been said to be mine by right of conquest, but I gave it to Dictys, who I knew would govern far better than his brother. My mother, who had been sure I was dead, wept for joy when she saw me again, and she wept even more when Dictys presided over my wedding to Andromeda.

"I presented the gorgon's head to Athena, for I feared it was too powerful for a mortal to have. I also returned the invisibility cap, winged sandals, and magic bag to Hermes, who returned them to the nymphs. The sword and shield they insisted I keep as their gifts, and I accepted them gratefully."

"And you all lived happily ever after," said Fatima quietly.

"Well, not quite, though I did have much happiness in the years that followed. However, though I had everything a man could want, one thing still troubled me: my grandfather."

"You wanted revenge?" asked Mateo.

"No. As I think you have already learned, no good comes of revenge. I wanted to find my grandfather and reassure him that I wished him no ill and would never kill him.

"Alas, he had heard that I was alive and looking for him, so he fled from Argos. I searched for him for many months, but I did not find him.

"When I reached Larissa, I decided to take a brief rest and participate in their games. Unfortunately, a discus I threw went wild, killing one of the onlookers. That was terrible enough, but imagine my horror when the onlooker turned out to be my grandfather in disguise."

"That was not your fault," said Persephone. "It was his, for trying to avoid his fate instead of leaving it in the hands of the gods. Had he raised you as his grandson instead of trying to kill you, he might never have died at your hand."

"Or I could have killed him accidentally, just as I did," said Perseus. "I didn't kill him purposely, but I felt responsible anyway.

"Because of my feelings of guilt, it did not seem right for me to take the throne of Argos, even though the people would have been happy to have me. Instead, I spoke with Cousin Megapenthes and traded kingdoms with him: he took Argos, and I got Tiryns. He was eager enough to do that, since his father's deal with Bias and Melampus had greatly reduced the area actually ruled from Tiryns, but I was content to rule a kingdom well and not worry about its size.

"During my reign, I fortified both Midea and a relatively small city I renamed Mycenae. The same Cyclopes who are said to have built the walls of Tiryns for Proetus built my walls as well. The new fortifications paid off, for in a few generations Mycenae became for a while the most important city in Greece, surpassing even the great Argos.

"Andromeda and I were blessed with many children, though sadly there was discord among some of them when they were grown. One way or another, though, my descendants ended up on the thrones of Mycenae, Elis, Sparta, Messenia, and even far away Persia."

"Persia?" asked Yasmin, shocked. "I read that the Greeks and the Persians were great enemies."

"So they were—long after my time," said Perseus. "That doesn't mean I was any less proud to count the royal family of Persia among my kin. Actually, that came about in part because in later life I reconciled with the deceitful Cepheus, who had never been blessed with a son. I allowed him to adopt one of my sons, Perses, as his heir. Unfortunately, Perses had other ideas—or perhaps the gods had other plans for him. In either case, instead of staying in Aethiopia or Joppa, he wandered much farther to the north and east. I was unhappy with him at the time, but I could hardly complain about the result."

"You can see why he's such an optimist," said Bellerophon. "Yes, he too had problems, but the end of his life wasn't dominated by them because he didn't stupidly try to become a god."

Struggling to overcome her shyness, Fatima patted Bellerophon on the shoulder. "You need to stop beating yourself up over that one thing. Perseus was a great hero—but so were you."

"On that, we can all agree," said Persephone.

"But now we must be going," said Teiresias, who had clearly become the group's self-appointed timekeeper.

The students said their thank-yous and good-byes, but they left with some reluctance. Bellerophon and Perseus had both seemed somehow more approachable than many of the people they'd met—both human and divine.

"I think it's because Bellerophon is willing to admit he's at fault, even if he overdoes it a bit," suggested Yong. "Most of them don't ever acknowledge they've done something wrong."

"Perseus also seems more conscious of his human failings, but in a different way," said Keisha. "How many of the people we've met would have given Athena the gorgon's head because they didn't want to misuse it? How many would take the smaller kingdom because it didn't seem right to take the bigger one? He's really the only one I can think of that would do either."

"Perhaps that's why he was one of the few heroes who died peacefully in his old age," added Thanos.

"You know, both of them cared about how women felt rather than just treating the women like property or only using them for pleasure," said Yasmin. "That's pretty unusual, at least from what we've seen."

Walking ahead, Teiresias and the gods were engaged in a somewhat grimmer discussion.

"The sky over Elysium hasn't gotten any worse, but it hasn't gotten any better," said Artemis, squinting at it.

"I'll take that as good news," said Pan. "It means Cronus is able to hold in check whatever magic is involved."

"Unless Cronus is one of the conspirators and is causing this problem in the first place," said Persephone.

"Hermes said this Cronus is benevolent, not really like the one in Tartarus," said Artemis.

"He could be wrong," said Persephone. "Notice that he rushed off to see Cronus—and then disappeared. Also, someone knew precisely where you were, just as Cronus would, and sent the fake Hermes to your exact location."

"Any seer might have managed that," replied Teiresias. "Nor do we know that Hermes was captured by Cronus. He could just as easily have been captured on the way.

"Such speculation is pointless. We simply do not know yet, and we may not until our visitors have all their clues."

Persephone looked back at them. "They are so young and so unused to our world. Do they really have the ability to solve this mystery?"

"We had better hope they do," said Teiresias. "They may be the only chance we have."

Chapter 23: Jason and the Argonauts

They found Jason sitting on the bank of what Teiresias told them looked just like the Anauros River in Thessaly. The bank on both sides was rocky and dotted here and there with poplar trees.

"I've seen the Anauros," said Thanos. "It's a much smaller stream than this."

"Ah, but it was much wider in ancient times," said Teiresias.

Jason already seemed to know who they were, but the prophet made the usual introductions anyway.

Jason chose to appear young, much as Perseus and Bellerophon had, but his eyes looked older and much more troubled, making him more like Bellerophon than Perseus.

"Are you...in pain?" asked Fatima, sounding worried.

"There is no pain here," said Jason. "Sometimes, though, I do think about all the harm I caused at the end of my life, and it troubles me. However, for your sake, I should begin my story from the beginning.

"From what Teiresias has told me about the people you have already visited, you will know about Aeolus, yes? And Cretheus?"

"Yes, we have heard of both," said Thanos.

"Then you probably heard Cretheus was king of Iolcus. His heir should have been Aeson, my father, but as you know, Cretheus remarried to the unfortunate Tyro and was even generous enough to adopt Pelias and Neleus, her sons by Poseidon.

"Cretheus had not intended to confuse the line of succession, but by adopting Tyro's sons without reference to their position relative to Aeson, Cretheus left room for an argument to be made that Pelias and Neleus were now elder sons and thus had a better claim than Aeson. Needless to say, upon Cretheus's death, Pelias made exactly that argument.

"Undoubtedly, Pelias was corrupted by the lust for power that ruins so many men, but he had a hidden motive to want the crown. An oracle had foretold that a descendant of Aeolus would kill Pelias, and easiest way to protect himself from his own family members would be to become king.

"With the power being king gave Pelias, he might have found a way to kill all of his relatives, but even he could not stoop quite that low. Had he killed his mother, Tyro, he would have faced popular revolt and possibly the wrath of the Erinyes as well, for matricide is one of the crimes they punish, so he settled for keeping a close eye on her. Had he killed his brother, Neleus, he would have faced his mother's wrath, so he settled for driving Neleus into exile instead.

"Pelias would have dearly loved to kill my father, Aeson, but Tyro, who had developed an affectionate relationship with him, pleaded with Pelias not to kill him, and so again Pelias relented, though he did keep my father a prisoner.

"My uncles, Pheres and Amythaon, would not have been spared, but they both fled before Pelias could have them arrested and executed.

"That left only me, and I would surely have died if not for the cleverness of my mother, Polymele. She was the daughter of the crafty Autolycus, the master thief, and she was good at keeping a cool head during a crisis. When I was born, she had her kinswomen mourn over me as if I were stillborn. Pelias, not half as smart as he thought he was, was fooled by her deception, and she was able to smuggle me to Mount Pelion, where I was raised by Cheiron, the centaur who trained so many other young heroes.

"When I reached manhood, I intended to claim the throne from my usurping uncle and liberate my father. On my way to Iolcus, I came to this river whose image you see before you—and my life changed forever.

"Looking back on it, I don't know what I was thinking. How was I, one young man, going to recover the throne from Pelias, who had the Iolcan army with which to fight me and was a son of Poseidon besides? I had not one single ally, and I was but a distant descendant of Prometheus and a great-grandson of Hermes. I didn't know it at the time, but I was being stupid.

"Fortunately, fate was kind to me that day. I saw an old woman standing at the river bank, asking passersby to carry her across, but no one would, and she was too feeble to walk to the nearest bridge. Touched by her plight, I offered to carry her across the river on my back, and she accepted.

"I had figured that such a frail old woman would be light and easy to carry, but I was wrong. As soon as we were in the river, she became heavier and heavier, until I feared her weight might sink us both and drown us.

"Some men would have thrown off the old woman to save themselves, but I kept on, and I just barely managed to drag us to the far bank. I had lost one of my sandals in the mud at the bottom of the river, but otherwise I was unscathed. *Gods test mortals*

"Imagine my surprise to discover that the old woman was Hera in disguise, testing mortals as gods often do. She blessed me and promised aid in my quest.

"I assumed she meant my quest for the crown, not knowing that she foresaw a much greater trial. I also didn't know at the time that she hated Pelias because he had dragged away Sidero, who had sought sanctuary in Hera's temple, and because he had afterward ignored the worship of Hera every time he could."

"So it wasn't just chance that Hera appeared that day," said Yong. "She wasn't just testing mortals in general; she was testing you, wasn't she?"

"I believe she was making sure I was worthy to be her instrument against Pelias. In any case, I was grateful to have a divine ally to counteract Pelias's relationship with Poseidon.

"That last point was especially important because the occasion on which I planned to confront him was the annual sacrifice to Poseidon. I picked the time because it was one of the few moments when I was sure to be able to catch him outside the palace and in sight of all the people, so he would not just be able to kill me secretly. *Smart and thoughtful*

"Unfortunately, I didn't have the element of surprise I thought I would have because an oracle had told Pelias to beware of a man wearing only one sandal. He spotted me easily and confronted me before I could confront him.

"When I revealed who I was and challenged his right to the throne, Pelias knew that I must be the Aeolian destined to kill him. However, he dared not kill me right then, nor even openly deny my claim, for the people, perhaps charmed in some way by Hera, looked at me as at a god or great hero come among them, and Pelias could clearly hear their muttering. Not only that, but either unbelievable luck or Hera herself had inspired my exiled uncles and their sons to ignore the potential danger from Pelias and attend the sacrifice to Poseidon. Perhaps they decided Pelias could not move against men of their stature, for Uncle Pheres was now king of Pherae, and Uncle Amythaon was now a close friend of King Neleus of Pylos, Pelias's own brother. Whatever their motivations behind appearing, they at once took my side, endorsing my demand that the throne be restored to me.

"Faced with popular pressure and the possibility of intervention from Pherae and Pylos, Pelias had no choice but to appear to agree to hand over the crown to me. However, he had one trick left to play.

"Pelias claimed to have been visited by the ghost of Phrixus, who told him that Iolcus and the other cities in the region would never prosper until Phrixus could be returned to Greece, along with the golden fleece from the ram on which Phrixus had flown to safety so long ago.

"Pleading old age, though he didn't look all that old to me, Pelias requested that I do as Phrixus had asked to lift the curse from Iolcus and the surrounding lands. I knew that such a long voyage would have many dangers, and that King Aeetes of Colchis would never relinquish the fleece without a fight, but, trusting in Hera, I agreed to fulfill the quest.

"Since Colchis was far away, I needed a sturdy ship to make the voyage, but I needn't have worried about that, since Hera persuaded Athena to get Argus, a shipbuilder the goddess of wisdom had trained herself, to build a mighty vessel with fifty sets of oars. Into the prow of the ship Athena herself placed wood from the sacred grove at Dodona—much like the piece of wood I hear you carry. It had the power to speak and even to aid us as a seer might. By such miracles was the mighty *Argo* created.

"A ship with fifty oars was a reminder this was a quest I could never complete alone, not even with Hera helping me. I sent messengers in all directions to find heroes willing to accompany me on the journey.

"There too Hera must have blessed me, for almost every hero of my generation answered my call. Even the heroes who fought before Troy were not a more distinguished company, if I do say so myself.

"One of the first to volunteer was Cousin Acastus, Pelias's son. The usurper must have been secretly horrified, for he assumed the voyage was a suicide mission, but he couldn't warn Acastus without giving away his plan to kill me. Rather than let me live, Pelias was willing to sacrifice his own son. If he had not already been doomed, that choice would surely have sealed his fate.

"I could hardly believe my good fortune when dozens of men I had learned about from the stories of Cheiron poured into Iolcus, all ready to take risks for glory—and for my sake.

"Nauplius, the incredibly long-lived son of Poseidon and Amymome,

very committed to killing him

became my navigator, and a better one could hardly be imagined, since the man had practically invented navigation. His presence and that of a few more of Poseidon's sons also helped ensured that Pelias could not simply pray to his father to sink us, which he might well have tried otherwise.

"For seers I had my pick: Amphiarus the Argive, who afterward became the seer of the Underworld; Idmon, son of Apollo, who came even though he knew he was to die on the expedition; Mopsus, a third-generation seer taught the art by Apollo himself; Orpheus, whose magical playing and voice saved us more than once.

"For heralds and diplomats, I had my choice of two sons of Hermes, Echion and Aethalides, the second so well-beloved by his father that he was given the gift of being able to remember all of his previous lives."

Like Bellerophon, Jason became more and more excited as he talked about his crew. Happiness for him might have been being able to forget the end of his life and remember only the amazing voyage of the *Argo*.

"For fighters I had such a group as had never assembled before and would never assemble again. The greatest, of course, was Heracles, the son of Zeus and the strongest man who ever lived. I also had Castor and Pollux, twin brothers the second of whom was also a son of Zeus; Caeneus the Lapith, whose lover, Poseidon, had blessed with a change in gender and an impenetrable skin; Butes the Athenian, beloved of Aphrodite; Ascalaphus, the favorite mortal son of Ares; Calais and Zetes, the winged sons of Boreas and Oreithyia, the Athenian princess; Euphemus, son of Poseidon and brother-in-law of Heracles, said to be able to walk on water like Orion, though I never saw the feat performed; Laertes, my uncle by marriage and father of Odysseus; King Neleus of Pylos and his son, Nestor; King Peleus of Aegina, grandson of Zeus and father of Achilles; his brother, Telamon, father of Ajax; and so many others we would be here all day if I told you of them all.

"I cannot help but wonder if Pelias realized I might actually succeed as he saw all these heroes assembling. If so, he betrayed no hint of his fears but pretended to be delighted by the power of my crew.

"He must have chuckled a little when the whole expedition almost came apart over a hasty decision I made. Atalanta, who had been hunting with Artemis, left the goddess to join my crew, but at first, I refused to allow her to accompany us. One woman alone with so many men on a long sea voyage! That seemed like asking for trouble, especially since if even one crew member made inappropriate advances to her, we might all face the wrath of Artemis.

"That decision was by no means universally popular, and Meleager of Calydon, already in love with Atalanta, was particularly strong in his demand that I reconsider. It was partially because I could see he was in love with her that I hesitated, for I feared he might be the one to approach Atalanta improperly. I finally gave in because I worried Artemis might also be offended by the implication that women were not as good as men."

"And so I would have been," said Artemis sternly, though Jason could not hear her.

"One more hitch came in the form of a unanimous demand by the crew for Heracles to be captain. He was the mightiest among us, and it would have been selfish of me to disagree, but secretly I felt hurt. After all, it was my quest. Much to my surprise, Heracles felt the same way, for he declined the captaincy, offering it to me instead. Naturally, I took it, and we were soon underway.

"In those days, a long ocean voyage required frequent stops to resupply, and our first stop was the island of Lemnos. There we encountered a strange situation, for all the men had disappeared.

"We first realized something was unusual when a group of armored women appeared on the beach to oppose our landing. Seeing them, we thought that perhaps Amazons had invaded and conquered the island, but Amazons are not known for seafaring, and Lemnos was far from any of their lands.

"Aethalides, our eloquent son of Hermes, convinced them of our peaceful intentions, and, after conferring for a while, they agreed to welcome us to their island—actually, more than welcome us.

"Hypsipyle, their queen, told me a sad tale of their oppression by their husbands, against whom the women had revolted, after which they exiled all the men to Thrace. After they had done so, however, they realized they needed men…better ones than the tyrants they had before."

"Were they lonely without men?" asked Mateo.

"Indeed, and there were also practical matters to consider. An island without men was doomed to be a wasteland eventually, for the women had no way to reproduce on their own. I'm surprised that concern didn't occur to them immediately. Perhaps they expected some goddess to come to their aid, but none did.

"In any case, Hypsipyle offered us the chance to be their replacement husbands, so that the women of Lemnos would not die one by one until the island was uninhabited. To me she made the best offer of all, for I was to marry her and become the king of Lemnos.

"We had before us a clear choice. We could do as duty required and try to complete our quest, though some or all of us might die in the attempt, or we could pursue safety, pleasure, and love on the island. I had to ask myself why I was striving so hard to win the throne of Iolcus when a far richer kingdom of Lemnos could be mine with no effort at all."

"I would have been tempted to take Lemnos," said Mateo.

"And so I was as well—but I chose the path of duty, politely declining the queen's offer. Accepting it would have left my father prisoner, and if Pelias's story of Phrixus was true, I would also have condemned my homeland to be under a curse. If my men had stayed, some of them would have left their lands without a king or without an heir to the throne. No, it was best to thank the Lemnian women and then be on our way.

"Alas, by the time I returned to the ship, many of the women of Lemnos had already arrived, showered my men with gifts, and made them Hypsipyle's offer. Like me, they had been reluctant to accept at first—but their wills weakened quickly."

"Under the circumstances you described, how could they possibly have accepted?" asked Keisha.

"They didn't exactly accept the offer to stay permanently on Lemnos as husbands of its women, but they did agree to accept the women's hospitality, and even I went along with the idea. Heracles, Atalanta, and a few others stayed with the ship, but the rest of us went for the feasting and such other entertainments as were offered to us."

"We all know what that means," said Pan, grinning broadly. Artemis predictably rolled her eyes.

"Why would you do that?" asked Yasmin. "It must have been obvious to you that the Lemnian women were just trying to get you to stay."

"It should have been obvious," said Jason, "but it wasn't. I didn't know this at the time, but Aphrodite was working against us. Well, not against us, exactly, but for the Lemnian women. You see, Lemnos was one of the islands of Hephaestus, and Aphrodite did not wish to see one of her husband's territories become deserted, so she worked a little magic on us to make us more…receptive."

"We *really* know what that means," said Pan. "I wish I had been there."

"Feel free to go visit now," said Artemis. "Not that you ever needed Aphrodite's help to be receptive."

"We might have ended up staying," admitted Jason, oblivious to both Pan and Artemis, "if not for Heracles. Somehow, he was strong-willed enough to fend off the goddess's manipulations, and he reminded us of our duty, perhaps with some help from Athena. We came to our senses and left as rapidly as we could, lest the Lemnian women again tempt us from our path.

"They let us go with their blessings, an ending we would not have expected—if we had known the whole truth. Much later we learned the real story behind the Lemnian women's dilemma.

"Hypsipyle had told me that Aphrodite, shocked by their husbands' frequent raids into Thrace, the land of Ares, her lover, had punished them by making them detest their own wives. However, the truth was quite different. The Lemnian men were warlike, but their sudden revulsion for their women was actually the result of the women neglecting the worship of Aphrodite, though perhaps the women did not know that.

"Either way, the men did treat their women horribly, throwing them out of their homes and replacing them with women captured in Thrace. However, the women did not exile them, as they told us. Instead, they murdered all of them.

"Perhaps the men deserved to die," said Artemis.

"They kept the truth from us, knowing that we would never have accepted their hospitality if we had known," said Jason. "Within each of us would have dwelt the nagging suspicion that sooner or later they would have treated us the same way they treated their first husbands."

"Why didn't the prow of the ship or any of the seers warn you?" asked Thanos.

"Ultimately, the secrets of the future are held by the gods," said Teiresias.

"Seers know only as much as the gods are willing to tell them. I would guess that since Aphrodite was trying to get the Argonauts to stay, the vision of their seers might have been clouded for a time."

"Exactly what I thought," said Jason. "Hera or Athena must have gotten Aphrodite to back down eventually, but the goddess of love got what she wanted. Enough of the Lemnian women became pregnant during our time with them that sufficient boys were born to save the island from eventual depopulation. Some years later, Euneus, my son by Hypsipyle, became king and finally purified the island of the blood guilt.

"It may well be that the gods intended for those events to happen," said Teiresias. "Your visit was the first step toward helping the Lemnian women achieve some kind of redemption."

Jason chuckled. "Orpheus said almost exactly the same thing—but he also had us stop over in Samothrace to be purified and to be initiated into the Samothracian mysteries. I think he feared possible lingering effects from whatever power had clouded our judgment on Lemnos.

"After a few more days of travel, we came to the kingdom of the Doliones, whose king, Cyzicus, welcomed us enthusiastically and bestowed upon us such hospitality as most guests can only dream of.

"Unfortunately, while we feasted, a tribe of savage, gigantic sons of Gaia, each with six arms, attacked the *Argo* and flung great stones into the harbor, attempting to block it. Heracles, who was on guard duty, as before, killed several of them with his bow, and his fellow guards also fought well, driving the giants back.

"However, the giants were not the worst thing we faced on that part of the trip, for after we had left, we were blown off course and had to land on an unknown shore in almost total darkness. We were immediately attacked, but we fought back, we won—and then we learned the truth.

"When dawn came, we saw to our horror that we had returned to the land of the Doliones, who, mistaking us for invaders, attacked us. Before us lay the dead Cyzicus, as well as several of his best warriors. Gladly would I have fought six-armed giants barehanded to avoid seeing that sight.

"The Doliones grieved for their fallen king and his comrades, but they did not blame us, for our accidental defense was brought on by their accidental attack. Together we held the funeral games in Cyzicus's honor.

"For a dozen days after, the weather was too rough for us to sail, and I worried that perhaps the killing of Cyzicus had lost us Hera's favor. I was not entirely wrong, though I misinterpreted which goddess was angry with us.

"Then a halcyon, bird of peace, hovered over my head for a minute, after which it landed on the prow of the ship. It sang, and Mopsus, who knew the language of birds, was able to interpret.

"Apparently, Cyzicus had angered the goddess Rhea, mother of Hera and the other elder Olympians, by hunting and killing her sacred lion. We Argonauts had also angered her by killing so many of her six-armed brethren. Since they attacked us, I thought she was being unreasonable, but one doesn't argue with goddesses. I also thought that being tricked into killing our friends was certainly enough of a price to pay, but the penalty she called for, raising a statue to her on the mountain, was mild, and I bowed to it, as did all the others.

"The clever Argus carved the statue from the wood of an ancient vine, and we carried it to the summit of Mount Dindymum, where I offered sacrifice as my men danced in full armor. The goddess accepted our devotion, sending miracles such as the creation of a spring, later called Jason's spring, nearby. After that, the weather remained calm, and we were able to depart the land of the still-grieving Doliones.

"Heracles, seeing that we could use some diversion, proposed a contest in rowing, the victor to be the one who could row the longest without stopping. We eagerly accepted, though it should have been obvious to any idiot that Heracles was bound to win such a contest.

"After all the rest of us fell from exhaustion, Heracles ended up rowing the *Argo* all by himself, only to have his oar break from the strain, forcing the least exhausted among us to help row the ship to shore. I've always wondered if Hera, annoyed by Heracles's overwhelming victory, had something to do with his oar breaking—especially since it led to his being separated from the quest.

"Heracles went ashore to find a suitable tree, an enormous pine tree which he uprooted singlehandedly and started to carry back with him. While he was doing that, his squire, Hylas, had gone to find water, a seemingly simple errand that had dire consequences.

"Long before Heracles had killed Theiodamas, king of the Dryopians, in battle, but when Zeus's son discovered Theiodamas had a son, Hylas, he felt pity for the fatherless boy and took him in, training him to be a warrior much as a father would have. As a result, Heracles had more of a bond with Hylas than with most people.

"When Hylas found a pool and bent over to fill the jug he had brought, the nymph of the pool saw him, and, charmed by his good looks, pulled him into the water to be with her. He cried out in surprise, and Polyphemus the Lapith, another Argonaut, heard him.

"Polyphemus was unable to find Hylas, but he did find Heracles and told him something had happened to his squire. Fearing the worst, Heracles rushed off to find Polyphemus, forgetting all about the need to get the tree back to the ship so that Argus could fashion him another oar. Polyphemus went with him, and the two searched all night, but in vain.

"Odd as it may seem, in the morning none of us noticed the absence of Heracles, Hylas, and Polyphemus. We sailed away, discovering that some of the crew members were missing some time later when we were far enough away to make going back difficult.

"The situation led to discord among the crew. Telamon was the loudest among those demanding to return and find Heracles and the others. Zetes and Calais were the most determined on the other side, and, facing such strong beliefs on both sides, I was at first reluctant to make a final decision.

"Fortunately, I was saved from having to alienate part of my crew by the timely arrival of Glaucus, who rose from the sea to greet us."

"The sudden appearance of Glaucus would have been more than enough to halt any argument and force people to stare at him in amazement. His skin and beard were green, and his lower body was that of an enormous fish. Even stranger than his appearance, though, was the story of how he came to be.

"Gods, in general, arose from one of the primal powers when the universe was young or were descended from those original gods. A few select mortals also became gods through the help of one or more divine patrons. Glaucus is the only known case of someone becoming a god by accident.

"Glaucus began life as a humble fisherman in Boeotia, but one day he observed that some of the fish he caught seemed to come back to life. Looking carefully, he realized it was the fish he had laid on a particular patch of grass.

Glaucus didn't know it, but he had stumbled upon a rare herb, first sown by Cronus and normally only grown on the sacred island of Helios.

"Out of curiosity, Glaucus tasted a little of the grass himself, but it affected him differently than it had affected the fish. He wasn't dead to begin with, so the magic that might have brought him back to life instead made him immortal. Perhaps because his fish had touched it first, it also made his form more fishlike."

"What did he say to the Argonauts?" asked Thanos.

"Oh, sorry," said Jason, "I forgot myself for a moment. Glaucus told us not to go back. Heracles, who had interrupted his labors to join our quest, was fated to complete those labors now. Polyphemus was destined to found a city in Mysia near where we had left him. As for Hylas, he had become husband to that water nymph who had pulled him into her pool. He was content, and even if he hadn't been, we would never have been able to find him."

"Hearing from a god, especially one known for prophecy, ended the argument, and we sailed on with mixed feelings. The more practically minded among us lamented the loss of Heracles, though those more motivated by their own pursuit of glory were not so sad. After all, just as Heracles had rowed the ship all by himself, he would have been powerful enough to defeat all of our later adversaries all by himself, leaving little for the rest of us to do."

"When I read Apollonius's *Argonautica*, I got the impression that Heracles was so upset over Hylas's disappearance because they were lovers," said Thanos.

Mateo was glad Patrick wasn't around at that point because if he hadn't already gotten himself changed into something, he would have undoubtedly said something at this point that would have brought down someone's wrath on him.

Jason looked surprised and didn't immediately answer, so Teiresias fielded the question instead.

"We know enough about your world to be aware that the issue of whether men should love other men and women should love other women is divisive, and I sense even within this group that there is division. We have not the time to resolve that issue now, nor is it likely all of you would be satisfied no matter how long we talked about it. Rather than arguing the underlying moral questions, I will try to give you a brief understanding of the history and let it go at that.

"Even in ancient Greece, the question was controversial. Long after my time, Plato seemed to praise what you would call gay love in *Symposium*, but then he argued against it in both *Republic* and *Laws*. The earliest versions of the myths typically don't include it, though the later ones, particularly the Roman ones, often do, sometimes to the point that any friendship between males was portrayed as sexual—as if the only feeling a man can have for another man is a sexual one.

"Look upon the issue as your conscience bids you. The wisdom of the Greeks casts little light on something like what you would call gay marriage, mostly because society was still struggling toward an understanding of sexual relationships in general—and the prevailing one was almost completely different from that of your society.

"You think of marriage as a union between two equals. Most ancient Greeks saw it as a property arrangement. The woman was the property of her father, who sold her to a particular man, who became her husband. She was then his property. That is where the term, 'bride price' comes from. Your society still preserves an echo of than in the father's giving away of the bride during the marriage ceremony."

"Some of the stories don't make it seem that way," said Keisha. "Orpheus risked everything for Eurydice. Was she really just property to him? There are lots of other love stories, too."

Teiresias smiled. "As I said, the ancient Greeks were struggling toward an understanding. Some of them felt more or less the same way you do about love being the foundation of marriage. That still wasn't the norm, though. And stop scowling at me, Artemis. I am explaining what *was*, not necessarily what I wanted. Remember I was at one time a woman myself.

"That's too long a story for now," he said, raising a hand to forestall the obvious question. "In any case, it's not surprising with a property-based idea of marriage that society didn't develop the idea of a gay loving relationship between equals, though a few existed. Mostly gay relationships were modeled on the marriages of the time, which meant they were expressions of the supremacy of one person over another. One partner was considered dominant, just as men were dominant in marriage. In real life, the subservient partner was very often a slave to or a social inferior of the dominant partner. The subservient one might also have been considered too young by the standards your society rightly maintains. In none of the cases I've mentioned was there a loving relationship between equals.

"In the myths, it was much the same. In most cases one partner is clearly dominant. The gods are portrayed as having that kind of relationship with mortals, like Apollo and Hyacinthus, Hermes and Crocus, or Dionysus and Ampelos, but where is the myth in which Hermes and Apollo have a relationship? There isn't even one.

"The Greeks made many great contributions to later society, but their understanding of relationships was not among them.

"Heracles and Hylas were clearly friends, and since Hylas was an orphan, Heracles was very protective of him. To me, that is what bonded them. The same is true of the other pairs I mentioned, all of which can be explained as friendships or as some other kind of nonsexual relationships. You can imagine them as sexual relationships if you like, just as the later poets often did, but it is the bond between the characters that is important, and that bond wasn't necessarily sexual."

"I wasn't really trying to start an argument," said Thanos apologetically. "I was just curious."

"It's not a bad question," said Teiresias. "Because your group is not in agreement about the related modern issues, I thought it best to elaborate a little. I agree with Apollo that clues to the location of your friend lie buried within these stories, and I didn't want you to be distracted from potential clues by a modern controversy. Speaking of which, we should let Jason finish, for his tale is not nearly done."

"Soon after we lost Heracles, we came to the land of the Bebrycians near Chalcedon," said Jason. "The king of that region, a son of Poseidon named Amycus, was inhospitable and violent. Instead of welcoming guests, he demanded that they face him in life-or-death boxing matches.

"Refusal would have meant having to fight all the Bebrycians and much bloodshed. Pollux was confident he could beat Amycus, so he accepted the challenge on our behalf.

"His confidence was justified, for, strong as Amycus was, he was not as skilled as Pollux, who eventually hit him with a mortal blow behind the ear. Unfortunately, Amycus's warriors were not willing to accept that outcome, and we ended up having to fight them all anyway, though by the grace of Hera and Athena, we made short work of them.

"Making our way toward the Bosphorus, we were blown off course and had to land in a part of Thrace then ruled by Phineus, the incredibly long-lived brother of Cadmus."

"Ah, yes, Phineus," said Teiresias. "Like me, he was a blind prophet, but he misused his gifts, with the result that he was tormented by the Harpies."

"That's right," agreed Jason. "The harpies were vile creatures with the heads of women and the bodies of birds. They flew down whenever Phineus was trying to eat, devouring most of his food themselves and soiling the rest.

"Phineus agreed to help us in our quest if we would help him with the harpies. Zetes and Calais flew after the creatures and would have killed them, but Iris appeared and warned them it was not the will of the gods for the harpies to die but guaranteeing the harpies would no longer torment Phineus.

"True to his word, Phineus gave us valuable advice, including how to avoid a menace at the northern end of the Bosphorus, the Symplegades...clashing rocks, you would say. No ship had ever before been able to avoid being crushed when those two massive cliffs came together, but Phineus advised us to release a dove, and if it flew through successfully, to try to copy what it did."

"How could the ship move as fast as a dove?" asked Yasmin.

"Lacking the equipment to haul a ship that big overland, we didn't have much choice," said Jason, smiling. "Remember that we had sons of Poseidon on board, as well as Athena's help. We managed to get through just in time, though we had to travel faster than any normal ship could have. Once we were through, whatever dark spell had animated the rocks was broken, and they became anchored in their open position, allowing free navigation from the Mediterranean to the Black Sea.

"From there we should have had clear sailing to Colchis, but even for those favored by the gods, life is never without incident, and even the pleasant times have their share of pain. During our brief stop in the land of King Lycus, as hospitable as Amycus had been inhospitable, we lost two crew members. Our helmsman, Tiphys, became ill and soon after that died. Not long after, Idmon, who had foreseen his own death, was gored by a boar while out hunting and perished quickly.

"We had one more stop before we reached Colchis: the island of Ares. There we had to face the birds of Ares, fierce avians who could shoot their feathers like arrows. Worse, we couldn't kill them without incurring the wrath of Ares.

"Fortunately, one of the crewmen was aware that Heracles had used noise to frighten away the Stymphalian birds, so we tried the same, yelling as loudly as we could and beating on our shields. Sure enough, the birds flew away as fast as they could.

"We had come to the island in the first place because Phineus had told us we would find useful allies, and sure enough, shortly after we drove away Ares's birds, we encountered the four sons of Phrixus. They had been shipwrecked on their way from Colchis to Greece to reclaim the throne of Athamas, their grandfather. Since the Argonauts had rescued them, and since their own grievance was not unlike mine, they were more than willing to help us.

"We would need all the help we could get, for King Aeetes of Colchis was mistrustful of strangers and fiercely protective of the fleece.

"The king was long-lived, being the son of Helios and the Oceanid Perseis. He was every bit as strong and mean-spirited as he had been when Phrixus first arrived. Then he would not have welcomed a stranger unable to give a gift like the golden fleece. Needless to say, we had no comparable gift to present to win his hospitality, much less the fleece. Even worse, though we didn't know this at first Aeetes had received a prophecy that someone of his own blood would betray him. Seeing the sons of Phrixus, whose mother was Chalciope, the king's own daughter, Aeetes was even more suspicious of us than he would have been ordinarily.

"The advantage we did have was Hera and Athena, who convinced Aphrodite to cause Medea, Aeetes's daughter, to fall hopelessly in love with me. We could not directly approach Medea, but the sons of Phrixus got their mother to do so, and Medea agreed at once to do whatever she could to help me.

"Not only was Medea a granddaughter of Helios, but she was also a priestess of Hecate and an expert in all forms of magic. She would be a powerful ally, whether we had to resort to force or to trickery.

"Aeetes would have liked nothing better than to kill us at once, but the Argonauts were a daunting group, so he used the same strategy as Pelias—trying to get rid of me by requiring the performance of an impossible task as the price of the fleece.

"Really this task was more like many tasks. First I had to yoke two fire-breathing bulls Aeetes had gotten from Hephaestus and plow the field of Ares. Then I had to sew some dragon teeth Aeetes had gotten from Athena; I hear they were leftovers from the ones Cadmus used. When men sprouted from them, I was supposed to defeat them all.

"Heracles could have done all of that with ease, but no one else would be likely to survive it. Despite that, I had no lack of volunteers: Peleus, Telamon, Idas, Castor, Pollux, and Meleager all offered to take the challenge, but I knew I couldn't ask any of them to do what I wouldn't do myself. I was the leader, and it must be my life that was at risk.

"Now was the moment to put Medea's willingness to help to the test. Again using Chalciope as an intermediary, I received Medea's agreement to meet before dawn at the temple of Hecate. There Medea offered to give me an ointment to protect me from fire and injury for a day, and she also offered advice on how to defeat the new crop of sown men—if I pledged to take her home as my wife.

"I had suspected my goddess allies were influencing Medea in some way, but I hadn't realized how completely in love with me she was. However, I wasn't bothered by her devotion. Unmarried and unbetrothed, I was free to accept her offer, and at the time I wanted to. Aside from being powerful, she was beautiful, with the golden glint in her eyes characteristic of all descendants of Helios, alabaster skin and midnight black hair.

"Using Medea's ointment, I was able to survive the fiery breath of the bulls long enough to yoke them, plow the field, and sow the dragon's teeth. Then, following her advice, I threw a stone among them, causing them to fight each other. Enough of them killed each other that I was able to dispatch the remainder with comparative ease.

"Aeetes was furious that I had completed the supposedly impossible tasks.

A wise man might have assumed from my triumph that it was the gods' will that I win the golden fleece, but Aeetes never interpreted the gods' will to be against his own interests.

"Rather than honorably fulfilling his bargain, the king of Colchis met with his advisers to plot the destruction of all of us. He might have succeeded if Medea had not slipped out and warned us. She did more than that, for it was she who charmed the dragon guarding the fleece in Ares's grove and made it possible for us to escape with the precious relic. Then we all boarded the *Argo* and sailed away as fast as we could.

"A safe distance away we stopped briefly to offer a sacrifice to Hecate and to plan our next move. Phineus had advised us not to return the same way we had come, but we knew of no other route that would get us back in a reasonable time—and without having to drag the *Argo* overland at least part of the way.

"Again Medea came to the rescue, this time offering a magical way to follow rivers that did not even exist in our world, a way that no one else could follow. Her plan involved entering the Danube from the Black Sea and sailing down it until we were among strangers no Greek had ever seen up to that time. Then Medea would guide us south down an otherworldly river that would get us back to the Adriatic. By that time, we would have eluded any possible pursuit and only needed to go south out of the Adriatic and west to return home.

"Unfortunately, Aeetes was faster to respond than we thought. When he discovered the fleece, Medea, and his unwanted guests were all gone, he immediately dispatched a large fleet under the command of Apsyrtus, Medea's brother.

"Unfortunately for us, Apsyrtus was quick-witted enough to realize we might not have gone the way we came. Instead of taking the whole fleet to the Bosphorus, he sent only part of it that way, sailing with the rest of it toward the Danube. Somehow he managed to get there before we did, despite the help Hera gave us to point us in the right direction. I have always suspected some other god of interfering, though if so, I have no idea which one. Worse, Apsyrtus was somehow able to follow Medea's magical route, so that when we reached the river's end at the Adriatic, the Colchian fleet had blocked our exit.

"Regardless of how the situation arose, it was a dire one. We were but one ship against a fleet blocking one of two possible exits. The only other way out would have required us to return to the Black Sea without knowing how many other ships Aeetes had or where they were. There was no way we could win a sea battle, and Apsyrtus was not about to let us fight a battle on land—unless he could be tricked into it somehow.

"Apsyrtus, far more honorable than his father, offered us generous terms. We could depart and even take the fleece, which I had fairly won, with us— but we had to leave Medea behind to stand trial for her treason against her father."

Jason paused for a moment and looked down at the ground. Then he continued, but very shakily. "I have no excuse for what I did next. I was in a bad situation, and I handled it badly."

"There was no honorable way out," said Teiresias. "You would have ended up committing some evil no matter which path you pursued."

Jason sighed. "Perhaps, but I wish with all my heart it had been otherwise."

"Having sworn a solemn oath to all the gods to marry Medea, I couldn't turn her over to Apsyrtus. On the other hand, I couldn't have asked all the Argonauts to die defending her, though if I had asked, they would have.

"Medea pointed out that there was a third option, though it involved outright treachery, as well as fratricide on her part: meet Apsyrtus under a truce, kill him, and escape.

"Would he have fallen for that?" asked Mateo.

"He trusted his sister," said Jason. "Too much, as it turned out. She convinced him to meet her secretly and alone, implying that she had realized how wrong she had been to betray her father and that she had a plan for stealing the fleece from me.

"They met on a small island sacred to Artemis in Kvarner Gulf. What Apsyrtus didn't know is that I was hiding there, and when his guard was down, I attacked that honorable man and killed him."

"He wasn't entirely honorable," said Teiresias. "He was willing to plot a way to get out of the terms he had offered."

"Even so, I have never felt right about killing him. In the moment, I thought about saving Medea. Later on, I wondered why she was so willing to lure her own brother to his death. I also wondered why someone with such powerful magic couldn't have found a better way to resolve the conflict."

"Because of course it's always the woman's fault," muttered Artemis.

"Once Apsyrtus was dead, Medea held up a torch as a signal to the Argonauts, who attacked Apsyrtus's ship and killed every man aboard. With no one left alive to warn the rest of the fleet, we were able to flee before any of the other Colchians realized what had happened.

"Needless to say, when they did find out, they would have pursued us, but Hera sent flashes of lightning to deter them from following us, and they took the hint.

"That was, however, the last help Hera was able to give us for a while. The *Argo's* talking prow told us that Zeus was angered by our failure to honor a truce and by our murder of Apsyrtus. Our only way to appease him was to be purified of the blood guilt by Circe, Medea's aunt.

"Circe lived on an island difficult to find without magic, but fortunately Medea had no trouble once Castor and Pollux had prayed to Zeus to allow our passage. Getting Circe to purify us was a little more complicated. After all, Apsyrtus was her nephew, but in the end, her affection for her living niece outweighed her outrage over her dead nephew, and she performed the necessary ceremonies. However, she also condemned Medea for what she had done and told her she would no longer be welcome as a guest, not only because of Medea's betrayal of her father and her murder of Apsyrtus, but also because she had joined herself to me, a foreigner. Our eyes averted from Circe in shame, and Medea's full of tears, we left her hall. Medea knew she would never be able to return again. Her path now lay with me, and only me.

"However, Zeus was not yet done with us. He ordered us to the island of the Phaeacians, knowing that many dangers lay between Circe's island and the Phaeacian kingdom.

"Fortunately, Hera had not forgotten us. Through Iris she sent word for Hephaestus to temporarily cease work on his forge so that the volcano beneath which the blacksmith god labored would not erupt as we passed by. Iris also carried a message to Aeolus, the wind god, to restrain all but the gentle breezes, so that we could reach the land of the Phaeacians without again being blown off course. Most importantly, Hera asked Thetis the Nereid, wife of Peleus, to organize her Nereid sisters to guide us through the dangerous straights guarded on one side by the many-headed monster Scylla, and on the other by the great whirlpool, Charybdis. Thetis was even then angry over having to marry a mortal against her wishes, but she did as Hera asked, or else we would certainly not have survived.

"There was one menace remaining—the alluring song of the Sirens that had drawn many sailors before us to shipwreck on the jagged rocks that lurked in the shallows just in front of the Sirens' perch. However, we were forewarned of that threat, and Orpheus was able to counter it by playing such loud and fast music that he drowned out the Sirens. Only Butes heard enough of their song to leap from the ship and swim in their direction, and he would have died, except that Aphrodite rescued him. We would have liked him returned, but the goddess of love swept him away with her to Sicily and made him her lover, an honor we could hardly begrudge him.

"Most of the Colchians had long since abandoned the pursuit, but, fearing the wrath of Aeetes, they had made new homes at various points along our route. Only one ship remained on our trail, and that one found us when we were on the island of the Phaeacians, enjoying the hospitality of the King Alcinous and Queen Arete. To these rulers the Colchians made their demand that Medea be turned over to them to face justice at home.

"Strictly speaking, Aeetes had a legal right to exact vengeance upon the murderers of his son as well as to have his daughter returned to him. It would have been quite possible for Alcinous to accept the Colchian demand, leaving me again with two equally bad choices: let Medea, to whom I was pledged, be taken or fight for her, in this case not only against the Colchians but against our hosts, who were descended from Poseidon and well-loved by him. Neither course of action would have been honorable, but to avoid both seemed impossible.

"Fortunately for me, Medea appealed to Queen Arete, who had real influence with her husband. As you would say, Medea pleaded insanity in taking the side of strangers against her own father, but she argued that her actions didn't merit condemnation.

"Arete, who knew well that not all fathers treated their daughters well, tried to convince Alcinous, who always took her advice seriously, not to hand Medea over. Though Alcinous accepted that Medea had followed Zeus's instructions to be cleansed of her misdeeds and that at least some of the gods seemed to be supporting my quest, he was still concerned about the fact that Medea had pledged to marry me without her father's consent. As a result, he wanted to send Medea back to Aeetes if she were still a virgin but to refuse to release her if she were already married to me.

"Arete warned us of the king's decision and advised us to get married at once, which we did. Thus I fulfilled my oath to all the gods, and thus Alcinous refused to give the Colchians Medea. Realizing the foolishness of making war on a people so well loved by Poseidon, the Colchians settled nearby as their comrades had done. Medea and I were no longer being hunted, at least for the moment.

"Yet, though it had not been the will of Zeus for Medea to fall into the hands of Aeetes, nor was it his will that we now return home easily, either, and this time he allowed Hera no way to give us aid. When we came within sight of Greece, a mighty wind blew us so far off course that we ended up in Libya. Even worse, the ship was pushed far inland during a flood, and, when the waters receded, it was trapped there. Even the helmsman Ancaeus, despite being a son of Poseidon, thought we were doomed for sure this time. Not only did we lack any obvious way to reach the sea, but the land around us was desert, with little or no fresh water and no apparent food supply.

"Our prayers at first went unanswered, and, despondent, I wandered away from the group and lay down in the sand, covering myself with the purple cloak Athena had given me at the start of the voyage.

"Perhaps Athena had guided my actions, for the cloak caught the eye of some passing nymphs, goddesses of Libya, who lifted the cloak to look upon me. Afraid of offending them, I piously averted my eyes, but they encouraged me to speak. After I had told my story, they gave me a riddle about Amphitrite unyoking Poseidon's horses and about bearing the mother who had borne me, assuring me that, once I understood it, I would find my way out.

"Overjoyed, I returned to my shipmates, who quickly shared my newfound optimism. Lynceus, who had amazing eyesight, spotted the distant hoof prints of a horse, presumably a member of Poseidon's team whose prints would lead us back to the ocean. Peleus identified the "mother" of the riddle as the *Argo*, who had borne us in her belly all these months, and who we must now bear on our backs, carrying her with us as we followed the prints.

"Without Heracles, such a task would not be easy, but somehow we managed it. For nine days, we followed the tracks with the Argo resting on our backs. Finally, we came to a spot where there was a lake...well, really more like a lagoon, at least from what we could see of it. It was deep enough for the *Argo* to float in it, and the water was salty, but we could find no connection to the sea. Of more immediate concern, we could see no fresh water anywhere nearby, and the long trek across the Libyan desert had exhausted our supply.

"Since our need for water was desperate, we expanded our search, but we found nothing. Then, whether through the art of Medea or the grace of the gods I know not, we found ourselves at the extreme west, the garden of the Hesperides.

"When we arrived, Heracles had only just left, having killed the guardian dragon and taken the golden apples of the Hesperides as one of his labors. His battle with the beast had happened so recently that the body of the dragon still twitched, and Lynceus thought he caught a distance glimpse of the great hero as the son of Zeus lumbered away.

"The three weeping nymphs complained much of Heracles when we found them, saying that *he* was the beast and that he had cruelly stolen the apples after slaughtering their guardian. However, they took pity on us and showed us the spring Heracles had created by striking the ground with his foot.

"Our thirst refreshed, we took the time to marvel at how fate had brought Heracles and us so close together. Volunteers went out to see if they could catch Heracles and ask him to rejoin us, but they could not overtake him, and one of them even died in a fight with one of the local inhabitants. Not even the fleet-footed Euphemus, the long-sighted Lynceus, nor the flying Boreads could catch up to him, and so eventually we gave up the search.

"The Hesperides did not know how to find an outlet to the sea, and so we headed back, intent on finding one ourselves. On that trip, we lost yet another comrade, for Mopsus the seer was bitten by one of the deadly snakes spawned by the blood of Medusa as Perseus flew over Libya with her head. We took the time to dig poor Mopsus a grave, for so honor required, but we held no funeral games because our water would soon run out again, and we couldn't keep traveling back to the garden of the Hesperides to get more.

"We sailed the *Argo* around the lagoon, but without finding any way out.

Orpheus suggested I take the tripod given to me by Apollo and use it as an offering to the local gods. After all, three local goddesses had appeared to me unbidden before, and they had been friendly, so I thought the suggestion a good one.

"When we came ashore and offered sacrifice, Poseidon's son, Triton, appeared to us in the form of a young man and offered us a dirt clod as a gift. It seemed an odd gift indeed, but Euphemus accepted it on our behalf, for it is unwise to turn down the gifts of the gods.

"To our amazement, Triton showed us a narrow way to the sea, one we had completely missed, despite all our rigorous searching. Even more, he adopted his natural, fish-tailed form and swam in front of us to guide us through the narrow passage and out into the bay. We built altars to Triton and to Poseidon on the shore, and the next day we again set sail.

"Traveling east, we needed to go ashore at Crete to renew our supplies, but we had not been able to make arrangements in advance, and so the dread bronze giant, Talos, blocked our way."

"My master's work," said Ardalos. Patricius barked his agreement.

"Yes, and, to our misfortune, extremely good work," said Jason. "Zeus had given Talos to Europa to protect the island, and the automaton was strong enough to rip loose huge boulders and hurl them at unknown ships that got too close.

"We should have gone somewhere else, but we were low on supplies, and Medea assured me she could get Talos out of our way. Not knowing what she meant, I allowed her to try—a choice I afterward regretted.

"Medea once again invoked the dark power of Hecate, and a shadow fell upon Talos. He had one weakness, a soft spot near his ankle where his otherwise invulnerable skin could be pierced. Under the evil effect of Medea's spell, he scratched that spot on a rock. Hephaestus had given him a real circulatory system, in which flowed the ichor of the gods, but when the bronze man's skin was broken, his ichor leaked out, and he fell to the earth, lifeless.

"I worried much about what Medea had done, for destroying a creation of the gods without praying for permission is at best extremely risky. Earlier, we had been forbidden to kill the harpies, after all, and Talos was as much an agent of Zeus as they were.

"That night we spent on Crete without incident, after which we built an altar to Athena before departing. The next night, however, was so black we might have been in the Underworld rather than on the high seas. Fearing the wrath of Zeus over the death of Talos, I prayed earnestly to Apollo to light our way.

"The bright god appeared before us, firing arrows of light that pierced the darkness of the night, leading us to a nearby island, which we named Anaphe—Revelation, you would say.

"While there Euphemus had a Hermes-inspired dream in which he made love to a woman who revealed herself as a daughter of Triton and future nurse of Euphemus's children.

"Based on an earlier oracle I had heard, I believed the dream was a sign that Euphemus should now make use of the clod of earth given to him by Triton. At my suggestion, Euphemus threw the clod into the sea, and where it hit the water, an island rose. He named it Calliste, but eventually it would be called Thera, and his descendants would indeed live there. Long afterward, one of those descendants also became the ruler of Libya, a sure proof of the good that comes from accepting a gift of the gods.

"By now the worst of our journey was over, and it was not long before we spotted the familiar Greek coastline. A few days later we were back in Iolcus, where I had the honor of presenting the golden fleece to Pelias. After that we took one last voyage on the *Argo*, which we left near Corinth after dedicating it as a shrine to Poseidon."

"What about Pelias?" asked Mateo. "Did he just give you the crown after that?"

"Sadly, no. In fact, I learned that Pelias had shown even more ill-will while we were gone. Thinking we would never return, he had felt safe in forcing my father to commit suicide. Overcome by grief, my mother also killed herself—but not before uttering a terrible curse on Pelias.

"Pelias had never intended to give me the throne; he assumed the quest would kill me. Now, with my parents' blood on his hands, he could hardly have given me the throne even if he wanted to, for he knew my vengeance would be swift."

"Did the Argonauts help you take the throne?" asked Yasmin.

"That was not what they had signed up for, and I did not try to press them, since they had already been away from home and suffered so much. In any case, I could hardly have expected Acastus to fight against his own father. No, if I was going to retake the throne, it would have to be on my own.

"It was then I made the worst mistake of my life—I let Medea guide me."

"Once again, it's the woman's fault," muttered Artemis.

"I should have known better," Jason continued. "There was something...wrong with the woman. I should have realized that when she used trickery to kill her own brother."

"Nothing was wrong with her!" snapped Artemis. "She was poisoned by the magic of Aphrodite."

"Or perhaps that magic uncovered a flaw in her," suggested Pan. "Not every woman whom the gods have fallen in love to serve a particular purpose ends up the way Medea did."

Artemis would have continued the argument, but Jason, who couldn't hear her or Pan, continued the story.

"Then she killed Talos, which was unnecessary and risky. No, I should have known better than to leave the fate of Pelias in her hands. My claim had popular support before, and now, having brought back the golden fleece, I had the even more enthusiastic support of the people and, thanks to Pelias's rash agreement, I had the law on my side as well. I might easily have led a successful revolt.

"However, Medea feared that the treacherous Pelias would find some way to kill me before I could beat him in battle, and certainly his past history supported the theory that he would try to use deceit to undo me. She insisted she had another way, and to my eternal shame, I listened.

"Given his public promise, Pelias had to pretend at first that he was making arrangements to transfer the crown to me, and Medea took advantage of that brief time to make friends with Pelias's daughters.

"She showed the girls her power, chopping up an old sheep and boiling it in a pot with certain herbs and secret spells, after which it leaped out, alive and now a young lamb. She offered to help them do the same for their own father.

"The gullible girls accepted her help—but she was tricking them. The daughters chopped up their own father and boiled him, but Medea didn't use the rejuvenating magic, so Pelias stayed dead.

"I was horrified when I learned what Medea had done. Killing Pelias was one thing; many would have said I had every right to take his life for taking the life of my father, and there was little doubt he would have killed me as soon as he had the chance. However, it was one thing to kill a man, quite another to make his innocent daughters the unwitting instruments of my vengeance.

"Needless to say, the people of Iolcus were equally horrified, and all their respect for me was burned to ashes as if it had been struck by a thunderbolt from Zeus. They now loathed Medea and me, and my former comrade, Acastus, who hated us no less, had no difficulty getting us exiled from the city.

"Just imagine it—I had undergone that whole quest for the sole purpose of retaking the throne of Iolcus and freeing my father. Now my father was dead, and I was never to see Iolcus again. Not only that, but the very gods who had supported me so much before now turned their backs on me."

To the students' surprise, tears started dripping down Jason's cheeks. Persephone looked worried.

"This isn't normal, I take it," said Pan.

"No," replied Persephone. "The blessed dead should not feel sorrow, however much they might have had to regret in life. If they are deemed worthy to be in the Elysian Fields, they are forgiven whatever their sins may have been, and that sorrow is lifted from them.

"I was concerned by Bellerophon's melancholy, but this is even worse. I should consult with Cronus at once."

"That's what Hermes was going to do right before he disappeared," said Pan. "It might not be safe."

"Are you all right?" Fatima asked Jason. "You don't need to continue if you don't want to."

Jason wiped his eyes. "If I understand your quest correctly, you need...my whole story to be sure you have the clues you need. I will try to continue.

"Medea and I went to Corinth after our exile, and there we were well received considering the disgrace into which we had fallen. Medea seemed stable enough as long as no one posed a threat to us. She was content to love me. I was anything but content, but I pretended for her sake. I should have been, for I was with the woman who had sacrificed everything for me, but I wasn't.

"In the beginning, I had wanted the crown of Iolcus as a matter of principle and a way to protect the rest of my family. Having lost that crown, I began to want power for more selfish reasons, and over the years that desire ate away at me.

"I knew well enough that the rulers of Corinth had taken me in partly in hopes that my status as Iolcus's rightful heir could somehow prove useful to them. They may even have hoped to use Medea's power for all I knew. As long as I was part of their schemes, I might yet rise to a higher position—or so I hoped.

"Ironically, my opportunity came, but not from the Sisyphids who had been ruling Corinth. Temporarily, Creon, the son of Lycaethus, assumed the throne, though I forget how."

"I thought I read somewhere that Creon ruled before Sisyphus," said Thanos.

Jason tried to smile but didn't quite make it. "Corinthian nonsense. They were always trying to pretend that Sisyphus was not their founder. Keep in mind that Sisyphus's grandson, Bellerophon, whom you met earlier, was a contemporary of Perseus—and Perseus was the great-grandfather of Heracles, who you know was my contemporary. How then could I have been in Corinth before Sisyphus, who lived about seven generations before me?"

"You couldn't have," said Thanos.

"Exactly! As I said, Corinthian nonsense. Anyway, Creon had a daughter, Glauce, but no son, and he needed a male heir if he wanted his family to hold onto the throne. Most of the socially prominent men in Corinth at the time had some connection to the family of Sisyphus—except me. Creon conceived the idea of marrying me to Glauce. I would eventually succeed to the throne of Corinth as his son-in-law, and then one day his grandson would rule. That plan was simple enough, but one obstacle stood in the way."

"Medea?" asked Yasmin.

"Yes, she was already my wife, and I could not take another without putting her aside. Had I been the man I had been when I was younger, I would have done what was right and stayed with Medea, who, whatever her faults, had been a loving wife to me for years and given me three fine sons.

"Unfortunately, that man had died within me long before," said Jason, starting to cry again. "I may still have cared a little for Medea, but I cared for power far more by then. I had even come to resent her for robbing me of my chance to rule Iolcus. What better way to satisfy that resentment than to replace her with another wife?

"I had forgotten the savagery of which Medea was capable, and I doubt Creon had known about it in the first place, for she had been a model wife and citizen for ten years. When I told her what I intended to do, she begged me to reconsider, but I refused. She pretended to accept my decision, but deep inside her, the obsessive love for me was turning into burning hatred.

"The first part of her revenge came in the form of two gifts, fine robes and an even finer tiara, which she sent two of our sons to deliver to Glauce as wedding presents. When the bride-to-be put them on, they burst into flames. Her screams attracted the attention of Creon, who attempted to rescue her, but she was already beyond saving, and all he managed to do was get himself burned to death as well. The blaze spread until it burned down the entire palace.

"Needless to say, my hopes of being king of Corinth burned that night as well. With Creon dead, the Sisyphids easily took over again—and as an ally of Creon's, I was far from being their favorite person. Another exile was the best I could possibly expect.

"If only Medea had been content to wreck my plans, but she was not. No, she would not be satisfied until I had been destroyed."

By now Jason was pale and shaking, and he could no longer look anyone in the eye. "Memerus and Pheres, the two sons who had delivered the fatal gifts, didn't suspect anything was wrong and returned to her. Knowing how much I loved them...she...she...killed them both. What mother would do such a thing? Yet she did.

"I know, I know. The fault was partly mine for being willing to abandon her in the first place. My sons would have lived if I had been a faithful husband."

"What happened to Medea?" asked Yasmin, almost whispering the question.

"She fled in a chariot drawn by dragons," said Jason slowly. "The storytellers insist Helios had given it to her, but that seems hard to believe, unless because the murder of his great-grandchildren happened inside, he did not yet know of it.

"Any love she had ever had for me was gone, but at first she tried to find love elsewhere—with Heracles, if you can believe such a thing. The son of Zeus had his father's weakness for women, but even he wouldn't stoop as low as Medea had now become, and even she didn't dare use her magic against someone as powerful as he was.

"Then, bizarrely mirroring my own quest for power, she decided to marry for advantage, not love. She succeeded in marrying Aegeus, the elderly king of Athens, and would eventually have succeeded in putting their son, Medus, on the Athenian throne if not for the arrival of Theseus, another son of Aegeus who had just come of age. That, however, is a story I will leave for Theseus to tell.

"What happened to Medea after her plans in Athens failed I don't know. The storytellers had her reconciled to her father, though knowing Aeetes I can't imagine that ever happening. Some even say she became queen of Elysium, but that I know is false.

"I had one consolation, for she had needed to flee before she found Thessalus, our last remaining son, so he survived.

"I should have taken him and gone somewhere else to live quietly, but grief over what I had lost blinded me to what I still had. Despairing, I walked to where the *Argo* still stood as a monument to Poseidon, and a lay down next to it, weeping for the lost days of my heroism.

"I was still lying there when a piece of wood broke away from the ship, hit me on the head, and killed me. Perhaps that was exactly the end I deserved— killed by my own rotting past.

"Had I lived, I could at least have seen my son achieve what I never could. You see, poor Acastus had an unworthy wife who embroiled him in war by accusing the noble Peleus of having tried to rape her. The gods alone know why she did such a thing, but the end result was a war in which Acastus lost his life. Peleus, remembering our good times together and my lawful claim to the throne of Iolcus, put Thessalus upon it, thereby at long last reversing the usurpation of Pelias that set all these dire events in motion."

Jason abruptly looked down at his hands, then looked up, horrified.

"Blood!" he screamed, holding up his perfect clean hands to show everyone. "Blood!"

"There is no blood," said Teiresias, sensing the truth he couldn't see.

"Yes," insisted Jason, "yes there is! It is the blood of Apsyrtus, of Talos, of Pelias, of my own sons! Can you not see it?"

"Has he gone mad?" asked Pan.

"The blessed dead cannot go mad," said Persephone, looking at Jason, a troubled expression on her face. "Yet somehow their minds are being poisoned as their past failings are forced back upon them. This cannot be happening— yet it is.

"Pan, Artemis, I must stay here and tend Jason. Please make sure our visitors complete their quest. I dread to think what will happen if we cannot find out what evil force is to blame for all of this."

Turning to the students, she added, "If it was not clear before, it must be now. You hold in your hands not only the fate of your friend, but all of ours as well."

Chapter 24: Theseus

They found Theseus in front of the image of the temple of Poseidon on Cape Sounion, the southernmost point in Attica. They got an unexpected bonus, for Heracles was with him. The two heroes looked somewhat similar, though Theseus appeared younger, and Heracles was considerably bigger and more muscular.

After Teiresias had made the introductions, Thanos asked Heracles how he happened to be there.

"At the end of your life, you became a god, right? So you aren't really one of the blessed dead?"

"Yes, after death I became the doorkeeper of Olympus, but gods who were once men can visit their former comrades in Elysium, and I find myself coming here frequently," replied Heracles.

"And well it is you chose today to do so," said Teiresias, "for you are on the list of people whose tale Apollo said our visitors would need to complete their quest. He must have foreseen you would be here when we needed you."

"What is this place?" asked Thanos.

"It is Cape Sounion, which hold a special place in my life, as you will soon learn from my tale," said Theseus. "It is the place I come to remember my mortal father, Aegeus. The temple to Poseidon was built centuries after my time, but it is appropriate, for Poseidon was my true father, though Aegeus never knew that.

"But I forget myself. Cousin, you are elder and mightier. Your tale should come first."

Heracles smiled. "You have already piqued our guest's curiosity, so, having started, you may as well finish."

"Very well, then," said Theseus. "Perhaps that is best, for my accomplishments will seem little compared to your epic achievements.

"My mortal father, Aegeus, came from a long line of Athenian kings that claimed descent from Hephaestus, and some say Gaia. Aegeus was the great-great-great-grandson of that Erichthonius who was the foster son of Athena.

"During that family's long history, the throne had been usurped more than once, including the overthrow of Pandion II, Aegeus's father, by Metion,

Pandion's own brother. After Pandion had died, Aegeus and his brothers (Nisus, Pallas, and Lycus) avenged their father by recapturing Athens. The brothers then decided to divide the Athenian territory among them. Aegeus kept Athens, Nisus took Megara, Pallas took Paralia, and Lycus took Euboea. However, Lycus quarreled with his brothers and ended up being exiled to Messenia.

"As you may know from the other tales you've heard, brothers seldom successfully share power, and for that reason and others, Aegeus became more and more fearful of being overthrown. Nisus and Pallas each had armies of their own, after all, and Lycus had made friends with Aphareus, king of Arene. Not only that, but some of the sons of Metion were still lurking around, plotting to recover the throne in their father's name.

"Most worrisome for Aegeus, though, was that, despite being married twice, he had no sons to succeed him. Men are less likely to uphold a king's right to the throne when the throne will inevitably end up in the hands of a brother or nephew anyway, and Aegeus knew that.

"Naturally, he went to the oracle of Delphi, who told him to avoid wine and to make love with the queen after returning to Athens. That sounds simple enough, but the oracle worded this advice like a riddle, and Aegeus failed to understand that if he avoided Dionysus's drink, his wife would soon bear him a son.

"Aegeus went to the wise Pittheus, king of Troezen, to ask for his help in interpreting the oracle. Unfortunately, Pittheus was tricky as well as wise. Perceiving that the son of Aegeus was destined for great things, Pittheus wanted to ensure that son would be his own grandson. Consequently, he got Aegeus drunk and placed him in bed with Pittheus's daughter, Aethra.

"However, it is what gods want that counts in the end, not what men want. Pittheus did not know that Aethra, guided by a dream from Athena, had also slept with Poseidon that same night and that she had become pregnant by the god. Aegeus didn't know that, either, and so when he discovered Aethra was pregnant, he naturally assumed the child was his.

"Glad as Aegeus was to have a son, he decided against taking me to Athens until I was a man. As a baby of a non-Athenian mother to whom Aegeus wasn't married, I would be a ripe target for resentment and assassination. As an adult hero, I would be far more likely to gain acceptance. Consequently, Aegeus buried a sword, a shield, and a pair of sandals underneath a large rock. He asked Aethra to raise me without revealing who my father was, but to send me to him when I could lift the stone and take from beneath it the gifts he had left for me. If I was strong enough to do that, he figured I would be strong enough to be a hero who could plausibly be acknowledged as his heir regardless of who my mother was.

"I first met Heracles when I was about seven. He had come to dine with Pittheus and had laid his lion-skin armor on the ground. When my friends and I came in, they fled in terror as soon as they saw what they thought was a living lion. However, I grabbed an ax from a guard and tried to attack the lion."

Heracles chuckled at that. "I didn't then know he was my cousin, but it was easy to see that he had the right spirit to become a hero, and I suspected even then that some god might really be his father, though I said nothing."

"Having met Heracles, about whom I had heard so much already, I decided I wanted to grow up to be just like him," said Theseus. "I didn't succeed at that, but I did the best I could."

"You may not have performed feats that were quite as dramatic," said Heracles, "but you avoided some of the mistakes I made along the way."

"Sadly, not all of them, as my tale will presently reveal," said Theseus. "Anyway, the time came when I tried to lift the stone and succeeded. Then my mother told me to seek out my father in Athens. She and everyone else suggested the easy sea route across the Saronic Gulf, but I chose the much more dangerous overland route because it offered more adventure. Lifting the rock didn't seem like that much of an achievement, and I wanted to prove to my father that I was worthy to be his son.

"In those days, there were a large number of bandits and even outright killers on the road, and I encountered a number of them on my trip to Athens. The fights are sometimes grouped together as the 'Labors of Theseus,' though they didn't compare to Heracles's labors.

"First I met Periphetes, a son of Hephaestus, but very unlike his father, for instead of being a great craftsman, Periphetes was a brute who used his club to crush the skulls of unwary travelers. I wrestled the club away from him and beat him to death with it.

"Next I encountered Sinis, a brutal son of Poseidon whom I would never have wanted to acknowledge as a brother. He bent down pine trees, tied passersby to them, and then let them fly upward, tearing those unfortunate travelers in half as the trees to which they were tied moved in different directions. I gave him the same treatment he had given so many others.

After that, I killed the sow of Krommyon, a beast that had ended many other lives. At least it had the excuse of being a beast. Skeiron had no such excuse for forcing travelers to wash his feet and then kicking them off a nearby cliff and into the sea as they did so. I pretended to obey him, then grabbed him by the feet and threw him off the same cliff. He died the same way his victims did, devoured by a giant turtle who lived nearby.

"You might have expected that Cercyon, king of Eleusis, would have been better than these cruel murderers, but he was not. Instead of welcoming guests as he should have done, he forced them to wrestle with him, killing each one in turn. He was strong, but I was stronger, and I killed him as he had killed so many others."

"Not only strong, but clever," added Heracles. "Theseus was the first to make wrestling a contest of skill rather than just a test of strength."

Theseus smiled at the compliment. "I'm not sure I'm the first, but I did realize that sports require brain as well as brawn. Anyway, after defeating Cercyon, I faced my final challenge before reaching Athens: Procrustes, who pretended to give strangers hospitality and offered to let them stay the night but then made them fit the bed, either by cutting them down or stretching them until they were the same length as the bed. Naturally, I did the same to him.

"Finally, I reached Athens, but, trying to figure out the best way to approach the father I had never met, I at first said nothing about being his son. However, word of my exploits had preceded me, and that was how Medea knew I was coming.

"After Medea had fled from Corinth, she came to Athens, and Aegeus married her because she convinced him she could use her magic to enable him to father a son.

"Aegeus had not forgotten about me, but he had begun to wonder if I had survived, and in any case having two sons would safeguard the succession better than having just one.

"Medea did indeed bear him a son, Medus. The boy was destined to travel east and found a royal line that would rule over the people named Medes after him. However, Medea, not knowing of her son's future Median empire, wanted him to inherit Athens from Aegeus. She recognized me as Aegeus's son even though he did not, and so she determined to get rid of me any way she could.

"Medea convinced Aegeus that I was a stranger who had come to overthrow him. Pretending to be impressed by my exploits, Aegeus asked me to defeat the bull of Marathon, who had been running wild to the northeast of the city. Much to Medea's disgust, I defeated the beast, which I then dragged back so that Aegeus and I could sacrifice it to Apollo.

"Aegeus then held a banquet in my honor at which Medea was supposed to poison me. Fortunately for me, right before I could drink the poisoned wine, Aegeus realized that the sword I was wearing was the very one he had left under the rock at Troezen so long ago, and he knocked the poisoned cup from my hand just in time.

"Now that Aegeus knew the truth, he turned on Medea at once. She had powerful magic, but even she couldn't have stood against the king and his army, so she fled, taking Medus with her. Immediately after, Aegeus acknowledged me as his son and heir.

"In some ways, being reunited with my human father was the high point of my life, at least as far as happiness was concerned."

"But you accomplished so much after that," Heracles protested. "You can't really think you peaked so early."

"No, it wasn't the most heroic point in my life," agreed Theseus. "You of all people will recall how difficult the life of a hero is, though. My early triumphs came without personal cost. My later ones, on the other hand, took a heavy toll.

"Long before I had come to Athens, the seeds of my next challenge had already been sown—by King Minos of Crete.

"Minos shouldn't have gotten himself into such a mess, but the once-wise man who had governed Crete so well had a long lifespan as children of gods often do, and he had been ruling for three generations or so. Over time, hubris began to eat away at his soul, as it did the souls of so many other great men.

"At one point Minos believed that some of his subjects were doubting his right to rule. The king, who had already demonstrated that he had the favor of Zeus, his father, decided that he needed to show that the other gods respected his rule as well. In order to do that, he prayed to Poseidon to send a bull up from the sea, promising in return to sacrifice the bull to the sea god.

Poseidon answered the prayer, and the people were duly amazed when a great bull rose from the sea. Unfortunately, Minos was so impressed by the beauty of the bull that he did not keep his bargain. Instead, he sacrificed a different bull.

"Much as I love my divine father, I must confess that he has a temper greater than most, and he was enraged that Minos would fail to keep his promise after Poseidon had shown him such singular favor. The lord of the sea looked around for some way in which to punish Minos, and then he thought of the king's wife, Pasiphae. The fact that she was a daughter of Helios, a god relatively hostile to Poseidon, made her an even more desirable target.

"Pasiphae was essentially a goddess living as a mortal, but the other gods did not come to her defense because, like her sister Circe, she was an accomplished witch whose magic had done much harm. Thus it was that Poseidon was able to persuade Aphrodite to inflict a horrible curse on Pasiphae, forcing her to fall in love with Poseidon's bull."

"Gross!" said Mateo.

"Indeed," Theseus agreed. "In any case, Aphrodite exerted herself to produce the maximum effect, so that even someone with Pasiphae's divine ancestry would be affected, and so she was. She became so overcome with passion for the bull that she could no longer control herself.

"It happened that a famous inventor taught by Athena herself, Daedalus, a son of Metion, the usurper, had fled from Athens to Crete after being accused of the murder of his nephew. Pasiphae tricked him into swearing an unbreakable oath to grant her what she desired, and then forced Daedalus to build a wooden cow in which she could approach the bull and consummate her desire."

"Even more gross," said Mateo. His fellow students nodded.

"Unfortunately for her, but completely in accord with Poseidon's plan, Pasiphae became pregnant and in due course gave birth to the Minotaur, a creature with a bull's head and a man's body.

"Disgusted as Minos was, not only by Pasiphae but by her half-human bastard, he dared not kill the creature, for it was apparent the king had already offended the gods, and he knew the monster was part of their plan. At the same time, he could not bear the shame of having the Minotaur in public view, so he got Daedalus to construct a labyrinth in which to hide the creature. The finished project was so elaborate that no one except Daedalus himself would have any hope of finding the way out, so it effectively trapped the Minotaur far from prying eyes.

"As so often happens, though, when great men try to cover their follies, others suffer. Minos locked Daedalus and the inventor's son, Icarus, in a tower to prevent Daedalus from revealing the secrets of the labyrinth to anyone. Daedalus, being the clever inventor he was, managed to fabricate wings for himself and his son, so that they could escape.

"Unfortunately, Icarus was young and impulsive. He failed to listen to his father's instructions not to fly too high or too low. Excited to be one of the first humans to fly, the boy soared too high and got too close to the sun, whose heat melted the wax holding the feathers on his wings. He fell into the sea from such a great height that the impact killed him: first blood for the Minotaur—but sadly not the last.

"You see, the Minotaur ate human flesh, and Minos, fearful of letting it starve, needed a supply of victims. Alas, he found one—in Athens.

"Minos's son, Androgeus, one of the greatest athletes at the time, traveled to Athens to take part in the Panathenaic games and won every single event in which he competed. It is said he was killed by jealous rivals. No one knows for sure, but he was dead, and Minos immediately declared war on Athens.

In the resulting conflict, Minos first conquered Megara, where Uncle Nisus ruled. He had a lock of purple hair that guaranteed the safety of the city as long as it remained in place, but his daughter, Scylla, having developed an obsession for Minos, pulled out the lock while her father slept, enabling Minos to capture the city and kill Nisus. Scylla did not profit from her betrayal, for even Minos was disgusted by it and ordered her thrown from his ship, after which she drowned. Unfortunately, she had already badly damaged the Athenian cause.

"Nonetheless, Aegeus led the Athenians to successfully resist the numerically superior army of Minos—until Minos prayed to Zeus, who sent a plague that broke the Athenian spirit and forced Aegeus to sue for peace.

"As reparation for his lost son, Minos demanded seven Athenian young men and seven Athenian young women each year. Aegeus had little choice but to agree, and he may have assumed that the youths sent as tribute would simply be enslaved, rather than suffering the fate for which Minos intended them—to be food for the Minotaur.

"When I learned of this custom, I insisted on being included among the tribute the next time it was collected. Aegeus at first refused, but I was so stubborn in my insistence that I could rescue the other Athenians and put an end to the vile custom that he eventually yielded. I think he thought I was being like Icarus, but I had already achieved quite a bit, so there was some evidence the gods were on my side. He asked me to exchange the black sails we would use on the trip to Crete for white ones if I had managed to come back unharmed, a request that showed he had at least some hope.

"As we came near Crete, we were approached by a Cretan ship, commanded by Minos himself, who insisted on boarding our vessel to inspect the tribute. In the process, the king, who, like his father, had a hard time resisting beautiful young women, made improper advances to one of them, and I demanded he leave her alone.

"I was being stupid, of course, for he could simply have had me killed on the spot for my insolence. I think he wanted to make me cower in front of my fellow Athenians first, so he declared himself a son of Zeus, and the king of the gods thundered to confirm his words. Nothing if not cocky at that age, I told him I was a son of Poseidon. The king laughed, threw a ring into the ocean, and demanded I bring it back to prove my words.

"I had never asked Poseidon for anything in the past, but I had no choice now but to try. I plunged into the sea and was met by dolphins and Nereids, who took me to the palace of Poseidon to see my father. He embraced me and returned Minos's ring to me. Amphitrite, Poseidon's queen, also gave me a purple robe and a golden crown Aphrodite had given her as wedding presents.

"When I swam back up with clear evidence I was Poseidon's son, Minos was embarrassed, to say the least. Worse, he couldn't just kill a son of Poseidon, and certainly not at sea. However, he still believed in the archaic notion that if he did not kill me directly, he could escape both blood guilt and retribution by Poseidon, so offering me to the Minotaur would still be an option. Just to make sure of my quick death, he designated me as the first to enter the labyrinth.

"I'm not sure whether luck was on my side, or whether Poseidon was helping me, but either way, the king's daughter, Ariadne, fell in love with me on sight and knew she had to do something to save me.

"She managed to get in to see Daedalus, who had not yet escaped. He told her I could find my way back out if I tied a ball of thread to the entry door and then unwound the ball as I went. Then all I would have to do would be to follow the thread back to where I had come.

Using her suggestion, I had no fear of entering the labyrinth, for I knew I would be able to get out. Killing the Minotaur while I was unarmed required more courage, but I knew that was the only way to save my fellow Athenians, and in the end, I managed to kill him with my fists alone.

"Once I had broken the lock, sneaking out of the labyrinth was no problem, for Minos, assuming no one could escape, let the guards leave once each victim's footsteps had become too faint to hear. Getting reunited with the other Athenians was more problematic, for even I couldn't fight the whole palace guard, but here again Ariadne came to our rescue, tricking the guards who watched over the Athenians and thus facilitating their quiet escape.

"She also had a ship waiting for us. Before we departed, I damaged all the Cretan ships to ensure we would not be followed, and then we set sail. Ariadne went with us, for I had promised to take her to Athens and make her my wife in exchange for her help.

"I thought the worst was over—but I was wrong. On the way back to Athens, we stopped at Naxos to resupply, and it was nice to have the opportunity to sleep on dry land. How was I to know what dire consequences would come from that shore leave?

"While I slept, Dionysus came to me in a dream and ordered me to leave Ariadne behind, for he had decided to make her his wife. When I awakened, I was reluctant to comply, since I had given Ariadne my solemn word to take her back to Athens. On the other hand, I knew defying the god would potentially put everyone on board at risk, so in the end, I did as Dionysus had demanded and left her behind.

"When she woke up and found me gone, she was heartbroken at first, but Dionysus came to her quickly with an offer of marriage. Though still in love with me at first, she knew it would be folly to turn down a god, so she accepted. If you've met her, you know she made the right choice, for Dionysus is very good to her.

"I was not so lucky. To ease my grief at parting from her, Dionysus caused me to forget all about her, though eventually I did remember her. Alas, his spell may have worked too well in the beginning, or perhaps my mind was still wrestling with the suppressed memory of deserting Ariadne. For whatever reason, I forgot to replace the black sails on the ship with white ones. Poor Aegeus saw the ship returning with black sails, and, thinking me dead, he threw himself from the very cliff I have recreated here. The earthly father I had only just barely started to know was lost to me forever.

"I became king then, but it was at first a hollow honor, tainted by the death of Aegeus."

"Your subjects would not have agreed," said Heracles. "Aside from ending the tribute to Crete, you unified the land, encouraged the settlement of foreigners who brought valuable skills, established a stable coinage, and even anticipated some features of later Athenian democracy. You are one of the few kings of the time remembered for more than just the wars you fought."

"I'm sorry to interrupt," said Keisha, "but I'm not sure I understand how you stopped the Cretan tribute. Wouldn't Minos have continued to demand Athenian youths as recompense for the death of his son? Wouldn't he have been angry Ariadne ran off with you?"

Theseus nodded. "If Minos had lived, he might indeed have gone to war with Athens again. I think that was his intention, but he was distracted by the escape of Daedalus. He didn't want to lose the inventor's services, and I think he suspected him of helping me escape.

"As it turned out, Minos would have fared better if he had just let Daedalus go, but he insisted on hunting him down instead. That plan backfired, because Daedalus managed to trap and kill Minos, after which the inventor fled so far away that the Cretans could never find him.

"Thus was the curse Minos had brought upon himself by breaking his deal with Poseidon finally ended. If not for that one bad choice, who knows how much longer Minos might have lived, how much more he might have achieved?

"Unfortunately, my own life did not work out as well as it might have, and, like Minos, the problems were largely of my own making. If I had governed my heart as well as I governed my city, I would have ended up much happier.

"Over time I remembered Ariadne, but there was no point in pining for her. She was Dionysus's wife, and nothing could change that. However, a king must have a queen, and so I began to contemplate whom I might choose. Still young and impulsive, I came up with a daring plan: I would marry an Amazon."

"So you weren't like some guys today who don't want a relationship with a strong woman?" asked Yasmin.

Theseus chuckled. "No, indeed! I wanted a partner, not a subordinate, and Amazon women were used to being independent. However, I would have been wiser had I sought a strong woman elsewhere.

"The Amazons did not marry. They had short-term sexual relationships with men from neighboring areas that ended in each case as soon as the Amazon became pregnant. The boys they sent back to their fathers; the girls they kept and raised to be the next generation of warriors. There was no room in their society for permanent relationships with men.

"I suppose knowing I couldn't have an Amazon made me want one even more—foolish, I know, but I would not be the first man whose desires were amplified by the barriers between him and his objective.

"In pursuit of my goal, I decided to try diplomacy first, for I had no real desire to win a wife through warfare, though in those days that was often exactly what kings did.

"The Amazons were not typically interested in negotiation, and they had no real reason to trust me, especially after Heracles's recent conflict with them. On the other hand, they respected heroic exploits, and my fame had reached even their homeland, a kingdom in northern Asia Minor, near the southern shore of the Black Sea. Consequently, they agreed to a meeting, though I think they might have rejected my request if they had known my purpose.

"I took a small group of soldiers with me, not enough to seem like an invasion, but enough to reinforce my status as a king, important in dealing with an Amazon queen whose permission would be necessary if my plan was to succeed. Mostly for moral support, I also took Pirithous, my best friend, who was king of the Lapiths.

"We sailed to the Black Sea and then rode inland to meet with the Amazon leaders. Unfortunately, their previous queen, Hippolyte, had some time ago been killed in a conflict between the Amazons and Heracles—"

"A story I'll share in due time," said the son of Zeus.

"In any case, her sister, Antiope, was now queen. When I learned that, I almost lost hope, for it was difficult to imagine a sister of Hippolyte agreeing to a request from a cousin of Heracles. However, I decided I had nothing to lose by making my request."

"In fact, Hippolyte fell in love with me," said Heracles. "The other Amazons just misunderstood and thought I meant to abduct their queen."

"Ironically, somewhat the same thing happened to me," said Theseus. "Antiope fell in love with me. Amazon culture may deny the importance of romance, for the Amazons are descended from Ares—but even Ares could not resist Aphrodite. As much as these warrior women deny any love for men, they are still women. If a man can love a woman and still be a warrior, why would a woman be any less a warrior because she loves a man?"

"Unfortunately, Amazons, in general, would not even listen to such an argument, and all of them wanted to reject my request. Antiope knew she could never persuade her people, but she was willing to run away with me, even though it would cost her the crown.

"Alas, as with Heracles and Hippolyte, the Amazons misunderstood the situation and thought I had abducted their queen. What started as a diplomatic mission ended up as a full-scale war, sometimes called the Attic War, in which the Amazons assembled all their forces and invaded Greece for the first time.

"During the months it took the Amazons to assemble their army and make their way to Athens, Antiope had become my wife and given me a son, named Hippolytus after her sister. She loved both her son and me breaking Amazon tradition on both counts, and she had no desire to return with her former sisters. Indeed, she armed herself and fought by my side.

"Seeing that Antiope was no captive might have ended the war, but in the confusion of battle, an Amazon named Molpadia killed her. Enraged, I killed

Molpadia and led the Athenians into battle so fiercely that even the daughters of Ares were shaken by my determined assault.

"We won the battle, and eventually the war, but to me, it was a hollow victory. Just as a triumph over the Minotaur cost me my human father, triumph over the Amazons cost me my wife."

"At least you had a son," said Fatima.

"Yes, and I loved Hippolytus dearly. Since his mother was gone, however, I felt the need to send him to Troezen to be raised by the only woman I trusted: Aethra, my own mother. Just as Aegeus had been reunited with me, I looked forward to a joyful reunion with Hippolytus when he came of age.

"I did not then know that his homecoming would be as tragic as mine, though for entirely different reasons.

"Not long after, I received an offer from Deucalion, son of Minos and now king of Crete, to normalize relations between our two kingdoms. Deucalion had no desire to invade Greece, so to him it was better to make Athens a friend than leave her as a potential enemy. As a goodwill gesture, he offered me Phaedra, Ariadne's sister, as a wife.

"Eager as I was for peace, I was even more eager for Phaedra. My heart ached from the fresh loss of Antiope, and I imagined that somehow Phaedra and I could have the love I missed with Ariadne. I said yes to the treaty and the marriage that sealed it—unaware that I was sealing my fate at the same time."

"Phaedra was not a good wife?" asked Mateo.

"At first she was an excellent wife," said Theseus. "I never had the nerve to ask how she felt about being married to a man who had loved her sister first, but if she cared about that, she never even hinted it. Instead, she seemed content to let the past be the past.

"She might have married me because her brother asked her to, but over time she grew to love me, or so I thought, and I was happier than I had been in years. When Hippolytus returned to me as a young man, I thought my happiness was now complete. I could hardly have been more wrong.

"Hippolytus was a fine son, but he was as different from me as I was from Poseidon. As you can tell, I wanted the love of a woman in my life, but Hippolytus devoted himself to Artemis and the hunt."

Theseus paused for a moment, and it looked as if he was going to have difficulty telling the story.

"Artemis told us what happened with Hippolytus—and Phaedra," said Yong.

Theseus looked relieved to be able to avoid reliving that painful memory, but it was clear from his expression that was not all the misfortune that had befallen him.

"After losing another wife and being responsible for the death of a son, I'm afraid I behaved very badly," Theseus said finally. "There is no excuse for what I did. I should have been the bringer of peace to my people, not discord. My grief was overwhelming, but as a king, I should have been able to master my feelings, and I was not.

"By this point I felt considerably older—and more bitter—than when I started my first trek to Athens, but something in me longed for the innocence of my youth. I had what your society would call a midlife crisis, even though I wasn't really that old as your society reckons such things.

"On a diplomatic mission to Sparta, I chanced to see Helen, the very same Helen over whom the Trojan War was fought a generation later. Longing for a love strong enough to banish my grief, how could I not be moved by the most beautiful girl I had ever seen? She was then only thirteen, too young to marry, but it was not uncommon in those days for marriages to be arranged before one or both of the parties was of age, though the actual marriage would not take place until both came of age. I approached her father, King Tyndareus, but he refused my request.

"The wisest course would have been to accept his answer, but Helen's beauty had so captured my heart that I decided to abduct her. It was a dishonorable course, but I was too wrapped up in my twisted emotions for my own good—or my city's, since abducting Helen was bound to mean war with Sparta.

"I did seek the advice of my best friend, Pirithous, but though he was a loyal and true friend, his advice was not the best. Far from trying to talk me out of kidnapping Helen, he enthusiastically agreed to help me, provided I swore an oath to help him obtain another daughter of Zeus as his bride. Foolishly, I swore the oath, and then together we kidnapped Helen from Sparta.

"Though young, the girl was not frightened, and I dared to hope that perhaps in time she might come to love me as much as I thought I loved her, despite our rough beginning. However, stupid as I was being in some ways, I knew better than to press her right away. Instead, I took her to Aphidnai, whose ruler, Aphidnos, I trusted to keep my secret. I left her in the care of Aethra, my mother, under whose loving attention Helen could grow up and hopefully become my willing bride.

"Then Pirithous called on me to live up to my oath, and I realized for the first time how rash I had been—for the daughter of Zeus Pirithous had in mind was none other than Persephone, wife of Hades!

"I did everything I could to talk him out of his blasphemous desire. It seemed likely we would accomplish nothing but getting ourselves killed. However, he was adamant about trying to take Persephone. I think he had misinterpreted the words of an oracle and believed he was actually fated to marry the goddess. He also believed himself a son of Zeus, who according to Pirithous had repaid the infamous Ixion's interest in Hera by sleeping with Ixion's wife, Dia.

"Even if he was, mortal sons of Zeus don't automatically get to marry goddesses," Heracles pointed out.

"I tried explaining that to him," said Theseus, "but he wouldn't listen to me. At first I thought he might be deterred by the difficulty of entering the Underworld, but we basically walked right in, something no mortal had ever before been able to do. This made Pirithous even more certain that he was destined to have Persephone. Even at the time, I wondered if Hades was just toying with us.

"We found our way to the palace of Hades, and, as politely as we could under the circumstances, made our request to him. He pretended to actually be considering the idea, but, of course, he wasn't.

"He offered us chairs, but as soon as we sat in them, we discovered we were trapped there. The king of the Underworld intended to keep us riveted to those chairs forever."

"Fortunately, I came through the Underworld during my labors, when I was supposed to capture Cerberus, and I visited Hades to gain his consent," said Heracles. "While in his palace, I saw Theseus and Pirithous, still gripped by their chairs. I was allowed to free Theseus, whose only sin was an ill-advised oath, for the gods themselves have been known to make that mistake. Pirithous, however, had to remain as the penalty for his unbelievable hubris."

"Yes, without Heracles, I would still be in that chair," agreed Theseus. "As it was, I got off lightly.

"I was afraid, having been gone for so long, that Sparta would long since have attacked Athens, but there too I was luckier than I should have been. Instead of waging all-out war against Athens, Tyndareus, who somehow found out where I was keeping Helen, sent her brothers, Castor and Pollux, to rescue her. They did so, taking my mother prisoner in the process."

"So you had to rescue your mother?" asked Thanos.

"I would have gone to war if I had needed to," replied Theseus. "However, she was treated honorably, not like an actual prisoner. What she really was was a hostage for my good behavior, a way of ensuring that I would not try to kidnap Helen again. Considering the circumstances, Tyndareus acted with surprising restraint.

"Was your mother unhappy?" asked Fatima.

"She was treated as a respected member of the Spartan royal household, and Helen liked her, so she ended up looking after the girl, much as she had been doing in Troezen. They developed a lifelong friendship—and my mother lived long enough to accompany Helen to Troy."

"Could you have competed for Helen's hand several years later?" asked Thanos. "I know practically all the kings in Greece did, but I don't recall that you did."

"I doubt Tyndareus would have received me as a suitor, and even if he had been willing, I was no longer king then. In fact, on their way back to Sparta, Castor and Pollux had stopped in Athens, where they denounced me for my gross violations of hospitality and other traditions and demanded my replacement. They helped install Menestheus, another descendant of Erechtheus, on the throne, and it was he who became a suitor for Helen.

"I might have fought to recover my throne, but, rightly ashamed of my recent conduct, I decided that accepting my dethronement and exile would be the only honorable course.

"I went to the island of Scyros, where I had inherited lands through some relative of my mother's. King Lycomedes pretended to be pleased to have me as one of his citizens, but secretly he feared I might try to displace him as king. While giving me a tour of the island, he threw me off a cliff, and I fell to my death."

"That's horrible!" said Yasmin.

"It was probably a just repayment for my sins," said Theseus. "However, as you can tell from my presence here, the gods eventually forgave me my faults. They even allowed Demophon, my son by Phaedra, to recover the throne of Athens after Menestheus died at Troy.

"Best of all, the gods allowed me to serve Athens one last time, for my spirit marched ahead of the Athenians at the battle against the Persians at Marathon, raising Athenian morale enough to contribute to their victory. After that, my bones were found with the help of the oracle at Delphi and returned to Athens at last."

"You deserved such an honorable end—and more," said Heracles. "I always thought you were too hard on yourself. You made mistakes, but what mortal man has not? On balance, you certainly did more good than harm."

Theseus smiled weakly. "You did far greater good."

"I also did far greater harm," said Heracles. "But I will let our guests judge that, for I know time is short, and my tale is long even at its most concise."

The ground shook so hard beneath their feet that all of them except for Heracles had to struggle to stay upright.

"You should begin at once," said Teiresias, "for time may be even shorter than we thought."

Chapter 25: Heracles

"It is often said that Zeus made love to mortal women for the express purpose of fathering heroes," Heracles began. "I have no idea whether that was true in general, but I know Zeus planned my birth. Without meaning to sound too full of hubris, it was Zeus's intent to father a son who would become the greatest hero Greece had ever seen. Most storytellers agree he succeeded, but the success became both a blessing and a curse to me."

"How could being a great hero be a curse?" asked Mateo.

"I would think you have already heard enough heroic stories to know," replied Heracles. "Heroes typically have greater abilities than ordinary mortals do, but they also face much greater challenges—sometimes of their own making. Theseus has told you of his overly ambitious marital plans, and how they caused his downfall. Much as he looks up to me, my failings were in fact much worse."

"You are always too hard on yourself," said Theseus.

"I am realistic about myself," insisted Heracles. "Yes, Zeus succeeded in endowing me with strength greater than any other man has ever had or will ever have—but being that far above the human norm made it hard to learn humility. After all, how could I avoid hubris when I could hold my own against some gods in single combat?"

"Under those circumstances, you did as well as could be expected," said Theseus. *too hard on himself*

"I did not do as well as I needed to," insisted Heracles. "I was too sensitive to any affront to my dignity, real or imagined. All too often, I got into conflict with others over trivial offenses that were better overlooked, even started wars because of them. Many good men died who would have lived if not for me."

"And far more people lived who would have died if not for you," said Theseus. "You were not perfect, but I still maintain you did more good than harm." *Theseus is supportive*

"As always, we will have to agree to disagree about that," replied Heracles. "However," he added, looking up at the sky as it darkened again, "I should begin the tale our guests have come such a long way to hear."

"My mother, Alcmena, was a granddaughter of Perseus and had a well-deserved reputation for virtue. She had much to endure, for her early life was filled with misfortune, despite her royal birth. She had nine brothers, but all nine of them were killed in war with the Teleboans, so even as a young girl, my mother was no stranger to grief. Nor was the loss of her siblings her only source of sorrow.

"Alcmena's father was Electryon, King of Mycenae, and as a princess, she was expected to marry someone of appropriate social rank. Her father's choice for her was her cousin, Amphitryon, a true hero as well as a prince, a man so noble that Alcmena quickly fell in love with him.

"Unfortunately, Amphitryon killed Electryon. Everyone agreed the death was accidental, but Sthenelus, Electryon's brother who succeeded to the throne, demanded Amphitryon's exile, and Amphitryon was too honorable to resist.

"Alcmena could have used her father's death as a reason to get out of the betrothal, but instead she went into exile with Amphitryon, leaving her childhood home behind forever. Partly she did that for love of Amphitryon, but partly she did it also for the sake of her brothers. Fearing that Sthenelus would not seek proper revenge, she insisted that Amphitryon seek vengeance on their behalf. After he had agreed, she married him—but she refused to consummate the marriage until he did as he had promised. Considering how much she loved him, she must have had considerable willpower to make this demand, but Amphitryon, who loved her as much as she loved him, willingly respected her demand.

"Creon, who was ruling Thebes at the time, purified Amphitryon of the blood guilt, but he was only willing to join Amphitryon in a campaign against the Teleboans if Amphitryon would first rid the Thebans of the Teumessian Fox, a large and fierce beast whose lair was in the nearby mountains."

"Couldn't the army of Thebes have taken care of one fox?" asked Mateo. "Why did Creon need Amphitryon?"

"The fox was a magical beast sent by the gods to torment Thebes, though I forget why. It was an especially difficult opponent because it was fated never to be caught. I have sometimes wondered if Creon proposed such a quest because he didn't want to help Amphitryon. How he could have expected Amphitryon to succeed is beyond me.

"However, Amphitryon had the wit to realize there might be one way.

Cephalus, who had just arrived in Thebes to be purified of blood guilt himself, had a magnificent hound, a gift from King Minos to Cephalus's wife, that was destined to always catch its prey. Amphitryon asked to borrow the hunting dog in exchange for a share in the future Teleboan plunder, and Cephalus readily agreed.

"As you might imagine, pitting a fox who could never be caught against a dog who would always catch its prey created a situation in which fate was too much in conflict with itself to be completely fulfilled, a paradox Zeus could not allow. Therefore, the king of the gods changed both animals into stone. Technically, the fox had never been caught, and the dog had never failed to catch, for Zeus acted before the dog began the hunt. *zeus is clever*

"With Theban aid secured, Amphitryon at once launched an attack against the Teleboans, leaving Alcmena alone, and it was then that Zeus acted.

"Though he found most women willing enough to sleep with the king of the gods, he knew Alcmena was too virtuous to betray her husband, even in a good cause. For that reason, Zeus approached her in the form of Amphitryon, supposedly back from avenging her brothers and ready to enjoy his much-delayed wedding night.

"To ensure that I was as mighty as possible, Zeus had Hermes arrange with Selene and Helios to make the night three times its normal length. Helios, in particular, was annoyed by such a breach of the natural order, but he did as Zeus had ordered him. Hypnos also did his part, keeping most mortals asleep so that they never noticed the difference.

"When the real Amphitryon returned the next night, he was surprised at Alcmena's relatively unenthusiastic reaction and at her statement that she had already greeted him after his return. From Teiresias he learned the truth, but, being a wise man, he didn't say a word about what had really happened to Alcmena. He knew she was innocent of any wrongdoing, and he also knew it was not for men to question the ways of Zeus. *very wise and forgiving*

"However, Amphitryon was not about to be robbed of his wedding night, so he made love to Alcmena, just as he had intended. The result was that nine months later Alcmena gave birth to twins: Iphicles, the son of Amphitryon, and me, the son of Zeus. Only later did Alcmena find out the truth, and then she took the sensible attitude that, since she had not knowingly slept with Zeus,

Not Suprising

she was not at fault. Nor did she blame Zeus for the deception, for deep in her heart she felt he had only done what was necessary to give me life."

Artemis looked very unhappy but didn't even mutter this time. After all, Zeus's trickery was the only reason Heracles had been born, and she may have suspected nothing she could say would convince him Zeus was in the wrong.

"However, Zeus's plan did not succeed entirely," Heracles continued. He had originally wanted to make me king of Mycenae, a position that by that time would have also made me high king of Greece. Unfortunately, he made the mistake of announcing on Olympus that the descendant of Perseus about to be born would be king of Mycenae. Hera, enraged that he would so honor yet another of the children of one of his adulterous unions, tricked him into swearing a solemn oath to that effect. Then she got her daughter, Ilithya, goddess of childbirth, to agree to prolong Alcmena's labor. While that was going on, Hera herself raced to Nicippe, the pregnant wife of Sthenelus, and caused her to give birth prematurely to Eurystheus. Because he was born before me, he, not I, became king of Mycenae. Zeus was furious, but under the terms of his oath, he could do nothing to undo Hera's trick. Perhaps it was just as well, for I would never have made as good a king as Theseus did in Athens, however much he might say otherwise.

"Hera, not satisfied with depriving me of my intended birthright, sent two serpents to kill me when I was an infant. They would have killed Iphicles as well, but I strangled both of them before they could do any harm. Teiresias took that opportunity to proclaim my future greatness.

"Amphitryon, who already knew that one of his sons was really the child of Zeus, now knew which one, not that it mattered to him, for that good man always treated me as his true son, anyway.

"He made sure I had the finest education. When I was old enough, I learned archery from Eurytus, a grandson of Apollo; wrestling from Autolycus, that tricky son of Hermes who had lived long enough to know every maneuver ever invented; military strategy from Castor, Helen's half-brother; charioteering from Amphitryon himself.

"Alas, Amphitryon also tried to give me musical training from the great Linus, said to be a brother of Orpheus, though I don't know that for certain. Impatient with my fumbling attempts, he struck me, and without thinking, I struck back, accidentally killing him.

"In truth, I have killed many men, but Linus is one of the ones who haunts me most, for he did not in any way deserve to die.

"Amazingly, I was never prosecuted for that killing, partly because I was still a child, partly because I had not meant to kill Linus, and partly because the fact that he struck first could make my reaction seem like self-defense. However, after that Amphitryon decided to end my musical education, sending me out instead to watch over the family herds.

"When I was eighteen, the lion of Cithaeron attacked the herd of Amphitryon and the nearby ones of King Thespius of Thespiai, so my mortal father asked me to hunt and kill the beast—no easy feat, since he was no ordinary lion. Amphitryon knew I was no ordinary herdsman, though, so he wasn't worried.

"During my pursuit of the creature, I ended up staying with Thespius for fifty nights. Impressed by my strength and perhaps by the prophecy of Teiresias, he decided he wanted his daughters to bear my sons, whom he hoped one day would grow up to become heroes like me. His strategy was the same one Pittheus would pursue later with Theseus's mother Aethra—except that this time, instead of one daughter, there were fifty."

"Fifty!" said Mateo in amazement. "How did you manage that?"

"Not as fast as Pan would have," said Heracles, winking at the goatish god. "I had fifty nights, remember, and there were only fifty daughters, so it wasn't really such an amazing feat.

"Actually, I didn't know at the time that I was making love to fifty different women. Perceiving that I was innocent in such matters and might be embarrassed by being expected to make love to all the sisters, Thespius persuaded them to all pretend to be the same girl, and in the darkness, I was fooled."

"Even if you thought you were only dealing with one girl, weren't you worried about how her father would react?" asked Yong.

"Thespius explicitly gave me permission, which I have to admit I thought was odd, especially since he made no mention of marriage. I was naive at the time, though, and I didn't realize he was using me for breeding purposes. I just thought he was exceptionally hospitable."

Thanos snorted a little at that, and Heracles raised an eyebrow.

"Even though I was eighteen, the education my stepfather provided had not extended to what parents in your society sometimes refer to as 'the birds and the bees,'" said Heracles. "I didn't know much about the social traditions involved, either. How many questions would you really ask if you were in that situation?"

"It's a pretty unlikely situation to be in today," said Thanos, looking down at the ground, "but I suppose I probably wouldn't ask too many questions, either."

"Then we agree. Anyway, I finally killed the lion, though it took me longer than I at first thought."

"And no wonder," muttered Mateo.

"Shortly after I returned from Thespius, I ran into some Minyans traveling to Thebes to collect the annual tribute to Orchomenus. Shortly after the war between the Thebans and the Teleboans, the king of that city had been killed in Thebes as the result of some stupid argument, and Erginus, his son, had defeated the Thebans in combat, after which he imposed a high tribute: a hundred cows a year for twenty years. I hadn't learned economics, but I had seen firsthand the difficulties such high tributes created for the common people of Thebes, who were not the ones responsible for the death of the king. Not only that, but Erginus had required that the Thebans largely disarm themselves, making them vulnerable to potential foreign attack.

"When I tried to speak to the envoys, they rebuffed me rudely, and their general arrogance offended me. Stupidly, I got into a fight with them, and they ended up dead.

"That would have been bad enough, but afterward Erginus spread a rumor that, rather than killing soldiers in a fight, I had mutilated heralds, diplomats under the protection of the gods, cutting off their ears, noses, and hands, and sending them back to Orchomenus with their severed parts tied around their necks."

"No one who knew Heracles at all would ever have believed such a thing," said Theseus.

"I admit to having sometimes struck in anger when I should have restrained myself, but never against unarmed men, particularly diplomats," said

Heracles. "However, at the time I was not as well-known as I afterward became, and so it was easy for Minyan propagandists to paint me as some kind of savage. They did so as a way to give Erginus an excuse to demand that Thebes surrender me to him.

"Creon did not wish to comply, but the rumors Erginus had spread made it difficult for him to refuse, since they made it unlikely that any other city would support Thebes if it refused to hand me over, and even some Thebans, remembering the death of poor Linus, doubted me. As if the adverse public opinion were not enough of a problem, there were also few weapons on hand to resist the Minyans, even if Creon had wanted to.

"Desperate, I addressed the people, particularly the young men, urging them to stand up and fight for the freedom of their city. However, my words alone were not enough. What I needed was some proof that the gods were on my side, which by implication would clear me of the charge of ignoring the sanctity of heralds. Then I needed weapons with which to arm the people.

"Athena, ever willing to help a hero, came to my rescue with an inspiration that solved both problems at once. She told me to take from the temples the weapons left as offerings for the gods. Such an act without divine permission could easily have gotten a mortal cursed or even killed. The fact that I accomplished the deed renewed people's faith in me—and gave me weapons, which Athena herself then distributed to such men as were willing to fight with me.

"With the help of the gods, I led the Thebans against the Minyans, and we were overwhelmingly victorious, so much so in fact that Orchomenus was forced to pay twice the tribute the Thebans had been paying, and it was never again a threat to Thebes."

"In my heart, the victory was overshadowed by the death of Amphitryon in battle. However, the citizens of Thebes rejoiced despite the loss of Amphitryon and others, for war is never without its casualties. Wanting to reward me for liberating the city, Creon gave me his eldest daughter, Megara, as my wife, and for a time I was actually happy. We lived in Thebes for some years and had several children. I also had a dear nephew, Iolaus, the son of Iphicles, though we were close enough I sometimes felt as if the boy were also my son.

"I might have remained quite contentedly where I was, for at that point I didn't feel the urge to seek out adventure, and the city was at peace. Ironically, it was Hera who put me back on the path of heroism—though at the cost of destroying the life I had built.

"For no reason except sheer malice, Hera drove me mad, so that I imagined myself in the middle of a battle instead of being in my own house. In that state, I shot my own sons down, thinking them enemies, and I would have done the same to Megara and Iolaus, except that Iphicles arrived in time to save them. He would ordinarily have been no match for me, but in my maddened state, I wasn't thinking very strategically, and so my brother managed to maneuver around me and rescue his son and my wife.

"It's hard even to describe the horror I felt when I recovered and realized what I had done."

"It wasn't your fault," said Theseus. "Men should not blame themselves when gods drive them mad. Whatever happened was Hera's responsibility, not yours."

"It is easy to say that," said Heracles, "and easy to agree that the idea is rational—but far, far harder to feel in your heart that you did no wrong when you see the bodies of your children lying in pools of their own blood, riddled with your own arrows.

"At least Megara was still alive, but she was lost to me forever. Like you, Theseus, she was willing to believe that what happened was not my fault, but when she looked at me, she couldn't help but see the murderer of her children rather than her loving husband. Nor did Iphicles ever again look at me the same way he had before. At least my mother didn't turn on me. Surprisingly, neither did Iolaus, even though I had tried to kill him. Still, the loss of so many family members was almost impossible to bear.

"I sent myself into voluntary exile, going to Thespius to be purified of the blood guilt, which he was eager enough to do. However, I knew that no mere ritual would ever be enough to assuage my guilt.

"Naturally, I went to the oracle at Delphi, and she at least gave me hope. She instructed me to go to Mycenae, where Eurystheus still held the throne that Zeus had intended for me. I was to perform ten labors for him, labors which would be both difficult and dangerous, but if I could complete them successfully, I would not only cleanse myself of guilt but achieve immortality. At that point, I wasn't even sure I wanted immortality—but being cleansed from guilt was what I desired most of all. I did as the oracle told me, reporting to Eurystheus in Mycenae as fast as I could.

"Despite the fact that Eurystheus had the crown, he persisted in seeing me as a rival. Perhaps Hera goaded him in that direction, but whether or not she did, he seized on the labors as a golden opportunity to belittle me or perhaps even kill me.

"The first labor was to kill the Nemean lion that had been terrorizing the people all around the hills of Nemea, where the creature lived. The task was far tougher than my earlier lion killing because the beast was invulnerable in the way we ancient Greeks understood the term: its hide could not be pierced by any weapon. However, it was not equally resistant to bludgeoning and pressure; my club could stun it. Once that was done, I was able to strangle it with my bare hands.

"It occurred to me that the beast's hide would make excellent armor if I could figure out how to skin it. Eventually, I discovered that the lion's own claws could penetrate the hide, so I used them to strip it away, after which fashioning it into armor, with the head part as a kind of helmet, was easy.

"Eurystheus was so frightened when I appeared in my lion armor, carrying the beast's bloody carcass, that he hid. Afterward, not wanting his cowardice to be exposed again, he ordered me to present my trophies at the city gate instead of in the palace, and from then on Copreus, the herald, gave me my instructions.

"Realizing that getting me killed would be harder than Eurystheus had first thought, he gave me an even more dangerous task for the second labor: to kill the Lernean Hydra, who lived in a swamp south of Argos.

"I knew the Hydra was a gigantic serpent whose breath and bite were both poisonous, but I wasn't worried, figuring I could kill it before it could poison me. I quickly learned, however, that I had been overconfident. Cutting off its head was indeed easy enough, but as soon as I did, two heads grew in its place.

"Even worse, Hera, determined to kill me this time, sent a gigantic crab after me at the same time I was trying to battle the Hydra. I managed to kill the crab, but I realized I needed a new plan, or the hydra would finish me.

"Iolaus had accompanied me on this mission as my charioteer, so I called on him to bring me torches. Each time I chopped off a head, Iolaus seared the neck so that no new heads could grow from it. In this way, we were able to kill the hydra. One of its heads proved to be immortal, but I solved that problem by burying the head under a rock too heavy for anyone else to lift. Then I dipped my arrows in its blood, making the slightest scratch from one deadly, and hauled the carcass back to Mycenae.

"Being certain that either the Nemean lion or the hydra would be bound to finish me, Hera was for the moment out of monsters, and the best Eurystheus could do for the third labor was to order me to defeat the Erymanthian boar, which was huge and fierce but lacked any special defenses or attacks. The one twist in this case was that I was ordered to bring it back alive. I did this by making enough noise to frighten it out of its cave, after which I netted it, threw it over my shoulder, and carried it back to Mycenae, where Eurystheus cowered at the sight of the creature.

"While I was out catching the Erymanthian boar, Eurystheus, probably with Hera's help, was plotting a fourth labor that he hoped would doom me.

"He had seen enough to know that a mere test of courage or strength wouldn't stop me, so this time he tried a different kind of challenge. Remembering my accidental killing of Linus and my temper in general, Eurystheus gave me a task that would bring the wrath of another goddess down upon me if I failed: I was to bring back the Cerynitian hind, recognizable by its gold horns. The beast was sacred to Artemis, so even injuring it slightly would earn me the goddess's anger.

"I could have easily shot the hind down from a distance, but catching it was much more difficult, for it was faster than I. However, showing a patience Eurystheus didn't realize I had, I tracked the hind for a full year. My speed might be less than the beast's, but my stamina was greater, and in the long run, my relentless pursuit wore it down. When it was finally exhausted, I was able to catch it with a net as I had the boar, only this time I carried my prey much more gently.

"On the way back to Mycenae, I encountered Apollo and Artemis, and the goddess questioned me quite closely."

"I did indeed," said Artemis.

"Fortunately, I was able to reassure her that I had done no harm to her sacred animal. Afterward, I finished the trip to Mycenae, making Eurystheus more frustrated than ever.

"For the fifth labor, the Mycenaean king picked something he thought would be impossible: to drive away the Stymphalian birds from the lake in northeastern Arcadia which was their current dwelling. Eurystheus was sure I would fail since I couldn't fly, and the birds were too numerous for me to shoot down all of them. Not only that, but they were able to shoot back, using their feathers like arrows. The sheer size of the task made it look impossible.

"However, I knew that birds could be easily frightened if one could find the right noise to startle them. Athena came to my rescue by giving me a bronze rattle made by Hephaestus. Sure enough, the loud noise it made caused the birds to fly away, just as I had hoped, and again Eurystheus didn't get what he wanted.

"For the sixth labor, Eurystheus tried a different approach. The job was meant to anger me because of its undignified nature and as a result, provoke me to some act of violence. My task was to clean the stables of King Augeias of Elis in a single day. The king, though a son of Helios and an owner of great herds of cattle, had oddly never bothered to have the stables cleaned.

"This labor, like the preceding one, wasn't likely to be solved by brute force, or so Eurystheus thought. I don't know why he persisted in thinking I lacked the brain power to solve such a problem, but I quickly figured out what to do.

Before I executed my plan, I naturally needed the permission of Augeias, and so I offered to clean his stables in a day in exchange for a tenth of the kingdom. Augeias, thinking the task impossible, readily agreed to my price on the assumption that he would never have to pay it.

"After the cattle were out of the stables, I diverted the Alpheus river through the area, and the stables were cleansed completely in a very short time—much to the disgust of Eurystheus and Augeias.

"The Elean king refused to pay me what he had promised, claiming at first that I should not have tried to charge him for a task I would have to have performed for Eurystheus anyway, then claiming that he had not made an agreement with me in the first place.

"I was angry, but I had learned better how to contain my temper, and I agreed to submit my claim to arbitration. Phyleus, the king's son, testified on my behalf, and it was clear that the tribunal was going to rule in my favor. Enraged, Augeias expelled me from the kingdom before the result could be announced and then banished his own son—for telling the truth.

"The offense against me I could perhaps have ignored, but that a man should treat his own son so badly offended me far more. Later, when my labors had been completed, I led an army to invade Elis, and the deceitful Augeias died in battle. I gave the kingdom to Phyleus without trying to claim my tenth, though he would happily have given it if I had asked.

"For the seventh labor, Eurystheus gave me the task of bringing back to Mycenae the Cretan bull, the very same one that had risen from the sea in response to the prayer of Minos and subsequently fathered the Minotaur.

"This was another mission in which the bull had to be brought back alive—no easy feat since it was both bigger and stronger than the Erymanthian boar. Not only that, but the attitude of the gods was problematic at best. Poseidon had originally intended the bull to be sacrificed, but since Minos had failed to do so, some people believed the god now viewed the bull as a sacred animal who should not be touched, much like the hind of Artemis.

"I went to Minos for advice and help, but the king, who had no desire to be reminded of the bull's existence or the humiliation it had inflicted on him, refused to help me, though he did give me permission to take the bull.

"As it turned out, Poseidon seemed more than willing to allow me to fulfill my labor. Not only was I able to subdue the beast, but after I had wrestled it to the ground, it actually became obedient to me, even going so far as to allow me to ride across the sea from Crete to Greece on its back.

"Eurystheus didn't hide from the creature I brought back this time. In fact, charmed by its magnificence as much as Minos had been, he decided to keep it. However, he made the mistake of dedicating it to Hera, who didn't want to be reminded of yet another one of my triumphs. She caused it to escape and wander off to Attica, where eventually Theseus defeated it.

"That episode suggested to me that Hera, who had once seen Eurystheus as her champion, was now tiring of him. He had been unable to destroy me so far, and it may have seemed to her that he would never succeed. In addition, his cowardice and self-absorbed attitude had begun to make him unpopular with his people, as a result of which he became a further embarrassment to Hera. She could not afford to let him be overthrown, though, because then I might have ended up with the Mycenaean throne.

"Eurystheus, despairing of finding a task I couldn't complete, sent me to retrieve the flesh-eating horses of Diomedes, king of the Bistones in Thrace for my eighth labor. Again there was the potential of getting on the wrong side of a god, for Diomedes was the son of Ares.

"Ironically, I did risk getting myself on the wrong side of a god, but not because of the labor. On the way to Thrace, I stopped at the court of a friend of mine, King Admetus of Pherae.

"Admetus was a favorite of the god Apollo, for it was he that Apollo had served as a herdsman when the god was being punished for his attempted murder of the Cyclopes. Admetus had treated Apollo well, and the god had favored him whenever he could—in one case arguably more than he should have.

"The Fates had decreed that Admetus should die relatively young, but Apollo wanted to save him. Like many of the elder gods, the Fates were impatient with younger gods who tried to interfere with their duties, but somehow Apollo succeeded in reaching an agreement with them. Some say he had the assistance of the eloquent Hermes; others go so far as to say he got the Fates drunk, which seems unlikely to me. In either case, the Fates agreed that Admetus could live beyond his ordained span if he could find someone else to take his place."

"Why couldn't Apollo just make Admetus immortal?" asked Keisha. "Wouldn't that have been easier?"

"Sometimes the gods are able to grant the gift of immortality, but sometimes not," replied Heracles. "Perhaps Apollo tried and failed in this instance. You'd have to ask him.

"In any case, Admetus was overjoyed when he heard what Apollo had done for him. The king was popular and assumed that someone was bound to be willing. He was wrong.

"Admetus asked everyone he knew, but they all refused. Even his elderly parents preferred to cling to what little life they had left than give it to their son.

"One person did eventually agree to give her life to Admetus—the one person he hadn't asked, his wife, Alcestis. To his eternal shame, Admetus accepted her offer. Almost immediately, he realized his mistake, for without Alcestis, his life suddenly seemed no longer worth living. By then, however, she was already dead.

"It was then that I arrived. Admetus tried to keep the truth from me, but I quickly found out and was furious with him. I was also determined to right that wrong by bringing Alcestis back to life.

"As she was so recently dead, I believed that Thanatos might not yet have claimed her. I prayed to Zeus to be able to see Thanatos when he came, and sure enough, as I watched, the dark one appeared at Alcestis's tomb, ready to take her.

"I'm not sure whether Zeus's gift of sight also enabled me to interact with Thanatos or whether he allowed me to speak himself, but I challenged him to wrestle for her spirit."

"How could you wrestle with Death?" asked Yong. "Was he as physical as the Olympians are portrayed as being?"

"Not normally," said Heracles. "Then again, he would have had no reason to accept my challenge, yet he did. I didn't think this at the time, but I afterward wondered if he became material enough for me to beat him on purpose. He may have been irked by Apollo's interference with the natural course of events and saw me as a good way of restoring what was meant to be. Whatever the reason, he did accept the challenge, and I did win, so Alcestis was restored to the world of the living.

"By comparison, the actual labor was easy to complete. The man-eating horses were beaten with little effort. I did kill Diomedes in the process, but when I think about how many people he killed to feed his infernal team, I cannot feel too much regret.

"I attached the horses to his chariot and drove them back to Mycenae. Eurystheus planned to make the best of a bad situation by keeping the horses for himself, but since they would eat nothing but human flesh, that plan proved impractical. As much contempt as I held for Eurystheus, even I must admit that there were lines he wouldn't cross. Instead of becoming a new Diomedes, he asked me to kill the twisted beasts, and I naturally did as he asked.

"Eurystheus's plan for the ninth labor showed some imagination. I was to obtain the belt of Hippolyte, queen of the Amazons. Since the belt was a symbol of her sovereignty, Eurystheus must have assumed that she would not give it up easily, and I assumed the same. As a result, I gathered some of my friends, including Telamon and Peleus, to travel with me in case my request led to war.

"That, of course, was what Eurystheus—and Hera—were hoping. If the Amazons killed me, the king and the goddess would have achieved what they wanted. If I somehow killed all of the Amazons, I might still have been doomed, for Ares would have been angered by the extermination of a culture he supported, and Artemis might possibly have taken offense as well.

"My men and I sailed to the Amazon kingdom, on the shore of the Black Sea. Though generally mistrustful of men, the Amazons respected heroic deeds, and so I was able to get an audience with the queen, who even came aboard my ship to confer with me.

"Somewhat like Thespius, Hippolyte may have wanted to have me father one of her daughters, for such a girl would surely have been an exceptional fighter. A motive like that would certainly explain the queen's willingness to negotiate with me, and she seemed willing enough to give me her belt.

"Unfortunately, Hera, fearful that I would succeed peacefully, stirred up the Amazons to think I was on the verge of abducting their queen. When they charged my ship, I wrongly believed that Hippolyte was trying to trap me. We fought, and I killed her, an act I much regretted when I later learned she had been innocent.

"Hera got part of her wish—bloodshed was required for me to get the belt. However, my men and I managed to defeat the Amazons without having to kill a huge number of them, and we succeeded in sailing away with the belt and without bringing down upon ourselves the wrath of any other gods.

"Ironically, a much larger danger greeted us on the return trip. We happened to dock at a coastal city near Troy for supplies, and as we were approaching land, we saw a beautiful woman chained to a rock in the harbor. I could not help but be reminded of the way in which Perseus found Andromeda, and I knew I had to help the woman if I could.

"It did not take much inquiry for me to learn that the woman was Princess

Hesione, the daughter of King Laomedon of Troy, and she was chained up for no fault of her own to be eaten by a sea monster, again just as Andromeda had been.

"After the revolt against Zeus, about which I think you have already heard, Poseidon and Apollo were sent to serve Laomedon as part of their punishment. The king had them build the walls of Troy, and for the most part, they served him well.

"However, both Poseidon and Apollo began to mistrust Laomedon. Though he claimed his intent was completely defensive, once he had a city protected by walls built by gods, it could never fall to any human enemy, a situation that Laomedon could exploit for offensive purposes. Apollo, the god of truth, believed Laomedon secretly planned an attack on Greece, so he and Poseidon ensured that the western wall was built entirely by men, and thus remained vulnerable. Had their suspicions proved wrong, they could always reinforce the wall later.

"Apollo's doubts were verified when their service ended. Laomedon had promised them the same wages given to day laborers, which was how Zeus intended them to serve, but Laomedon now refused to pay. Can you imagine a king trying to cheat two gods out of what was an insignificant amount of money to him? A man who would do such a thing might do far worse if given half a chance.

"Outraged by the king's behavior, Poseidon sent a sea monster, and Apollo sent a plague. Rather than humbling himself in an effort to make peace with the gods, Laomedon decided to sacrifice his own daughter to placate them, even though the gods hate human sacrifice."

"But didn't Poseidon command that Andromeda be sacrificed?" asked Thanos.

"When the gods do command such a thing, it is normally a test of character," said Heracles. "They do not intend it to actually be carried out. The fate of Tantalus proves clearly what the gods think of human offerings, as does that of Lycaon. Besides, in this case, the gods didn't ask for any such thing. Laomedon assumed that was what they wanted, so he had not even the excuse of divine command to justify his evil intent.

"Not fully understanding how the situation had come about, I hastened to Troy and offered to rescue Hesione. Remembering the story of Perseus just as well as I did, Laomedon eagerly agreed, promising us as a reward two horses as swift as the wind and able to run across water, animals given to King Tros by Zeus when the king of the gods made Ganymede, Tros's son, his cupbearer on Olympus. We would have rescued the woman regardless, but we gratefully accepted Laomedon's offer.

"We returned to the coast just as the monster was due to emerge, and when it rose from the sea, we slaughtered it without mercy. Then we unchained Hesione and returned her to the arms of her father.

"Unbelievably, rather than learning from his mistakes, Laomedon refused to give us the promised reward. We might have attempted to seize the horses by force, but I knew I needed to complete my labors and worried that if I spent too long in Troy, Eurystheus might try to deny credit for the ninth labor somehow. He had hinted at something similar earlier, when I had taken time out to play my ill-fated part in the expedition of the *Argo*. Instead of provoking an immediate conflict, therefore, we vowed to return once my labors were complete and take what was ours—by force, if necessary.

"Having sent me far to the north and east of Greece in the ninth labor, Eurystheus sent me to the far west for the tenth. I was to go to Erytheia, home of Geryon, a three-headed, six-limbed giant who had an enormous herd of cattle. I was to bring back the entire herd, no small feat in itself given the distance, but that would mean defeating not only Geryon, but also whoever he had guarding his herd.

"I traveled across the whole length of Libya, killing wild beasts as I went to make the land easier to settle later on. When I reached the far west, I set up pillars to commemorate my exploration, north and south of the place where the Mediterranean joins the great ocean.

"By that point I found the heat oppressive, and Helios, worried based on my jokingly pointing an arrow at the sun that I might try to shoot it down, sent Oceanus to give me a golden cup like the one in which the sun god traveled from west to east during the night. With such magical assistance, I was able to reach Erytheia much more easily than I could have otherwise.

"I found the herd without difficulty—they were purple, and thus hard to miss. Standing guard were Orthus, the two-headed dog, brother of Cerberus;

and Eurytion, the fierce herdsman. I clubbed the first, shot down the second, and began to herd the cattle away. Geryon tried to stop me, and he too died by my arrows.

"I would like to have taken the golden cup all the way back to Greece, but the cattle were subject to terrible seasickness, so I eventually had to land in what you would call Spain and then travel the rest of the way overland.

"Aside from the difficulty of controlling a herd that big, I had to contend with thieves attracted by such a large and valuable prize. My worst fight was against the Ligurians because they were so numerous that I ran out of arrows. Fortunately, Zeus answered my prayer, raining down pebbles I could throw at the Ligurians with devastating effect.

"Between thefts and cattle that wandered off, I spent months getting the cattle back, a large part of it in various regions of Italy. When I was finally back in the Balkans and moving south, Hera sent gadflies to sting the cattle, the same tactic she had used to drive Io mad, and the poor beasts ran far to the north and east, with me pursuing as rapidly as I could.

"I feared they would take me back to the kingdom of the Amazons, which was perhaps Hera's intent, but fortunately—or unfortunately, depending on how you look at it—they went across the Danube and even further north, far from where I had ever been before.

"During my stay, a strange woman, half human and half viper, stole my horses and insisted I sleep her with if I wanted them back. I was sure I could overcome her physically, but it was not my habit to kill women when I could avoid it. I would have avoided fighting even the Amazons if I could have done so. As a result, I slept with her instead, and the experience proved to be…quite positive for both of us. I stayed with her long enough for her to give birth to three sons.

"What about Eurystheus?" asked Yong. "Wasn't the reason you left Troy without getting what was due you the desire to avoid conflict with him?"

"Let us just say the serpent woman made the risk worthwhile," replied Heracles. "It was not as if Megara wanted me back," he added in response to glares from the girls. "I was at that point free of any real commitment to any woman."

"My, what a hard life you've led," said Pan, winking at him.

"That was obviously one of the easier parts," admitted Heracles. "Anyway, when at last I knew I had to leave, I left behind a bow, telling the woman—whose name I never learned—that the son who could properly draw the bow should be her heir. The youngest son, Scythes, was the only one able to do so, and so he became the leader of the people later known as Scythians when he came of age.

"When I finally returned, Eurystheus accepted the cattle, all of which he sacrificed to Hera—but he found a different way to cheat me. Complaining that Iolaus had helped me defeat the hydra and that I had charged Augeias a fee for cleaning his stables, Eurystheus claimed that neither of those labors should count. Using that standard, he might also have refused to accept the Stymphalian birds and the Amazons for being incorrectly completed as well, so rather than flying into a rage, I bore his decision patiently and accepted that I would have to complete two more labors.

"Bringing back Geryon's cattle had been difficult enough, but for the eleventh labor, Eurystheus sent me to fetch the golden apples from the garden of the Hesperides. Since the garden was Hera's, I could expect that it would be filled with traps for me, but the real problem was a logistical one: the garden was designed to be unreachable by mortals. Theoretically, it was in the west, not far from Geryon's land, but, though I didn't know it at the time, its entrance was not located in a fixed location in the mortal world, which explains the confusing references to the garden's location in various stories.

"My original plan had been to travel to Egypt, then west clear across Africa until I found the entrance to the garden. I had no difficulty reaching the far west, but I found no trace of an entrance to the garden.

Deciding I must somehow have missed the entrance, I worked my way eastward, this time encountering significant problems in Libya, where I met the despicable Antaeus, who challenged all passersby to wrestle with him and killed every one of them, using their skulls to roof a temple of Poseidon.

As a son of Poseidon, Antaeus had skin that could not be pierced by any weapon. In addition, he was also the son of Gaia, and from her he derived his great advantage as a wrestler, for he could not tire as long as he was touching the ground.

"It did not take me long to realize I couldn't defeat Antaeus with conventional wrestling tactics, so I lifted him off the ground to deny him the continual rejuvenation his mother provided. After that, it was a relatively simple matter to strangle him.

"Antaeus had two captive women whom he called wives, Iphinoe and Tinge, who wanted to show their gratitude at being liberated from their tyrannical master. By Iphinoe I became the father of Palaemon, a famous wrestler, and by Tinge I became the father of Sophax, the founder of Tangier and ancestor of the Mauritanian royal family."

"That was quite a lot of...gratitude," said Pan with a smirk.

"It was indeed," agreed Heracles. "I hoped the conflict with Antaeus would be the last. Unfortunately, in Egypt I made the mistake of passing through the territory of Busiris, an evil ruler who was said to be another son of Poseidon and who was in his own way as uncivilized as Antaeus. In particular, instead of honoring guests, he sacrificed them to Zeus, a custom my father abhorred. When trying to reason with the Egyptians failed, I allowed myself to be bound, but before I could be sacrificed, I broke my chains and killed Busiris and his son in the battle that followed.

"Egyptian troops blocked my way eastward, and I thought I could avoid more bloodshed by going south to Aethiopia and then east. Instead, I found myself at war with Emathion, son of Eos and Tithonus and king of Aethiopia. He launched an unprovoked attack on me, and I was forced to kill him, too.

"However, I did eventually reach the coast, after which Helios again lent me his golden cup, as well as opening for me a magic pathway that enabled me to pass from what you would call the Persian Gulf up to what is now known as the Caspian Sea."

"Why would you need to go to the Caspian?" asked Thanos.

"Helios advised me to seek the advice of Prometheus. From where I was, Helios's hidden route was faster than backtracking to the Mediterranean and then to the Black Sea, the only other way to get to the Caucasus Mountains, on one of which Prometheus was still chained by the will of my father.

"I prayed to Zeus for permission to liberate that long-suffering Titan, but Zeus told me I could only free Prometheus if I could find someone else who was willing to die so that Prometheus could go free.

"I was shocked, for the condition sounded almost like human sacrifice, but then I remembered the unfortunate Cheiron, the immortal centaur whom I had accidentally wounded with one of my arrows and who was now suffering pain from that wound, which, thanks to the Hydra venom on the arrow, could never heal. Cheiron had been longing for death, and now that he could die for such a good cause, he was more than willing. It took quite a while to obtain his agreement, but once that was done, Cheiron was able to die, and Prometheus was at last freed from his torment and able to rejoin the society of the gods.

"Grateful for what I had done, Prometheus showed me the way to reach the garden. As with the ungeographical path Helios gave me to the Caspian, I suspected magic was somehow involved to make it possible for me to reach the place, but I didn't care as long as I got where I was going.

"On the way, I almost lost everything through the trickery of Atlas. That Titan, whose penalty for siding against Zeus had been to support the sky on his shoulders, begged me to take his burden for just a few minutes so that he could pad his shoulders. Taking pity on him, I agreed.

"Then it became apparent that Atlas intended to walk away and leave me with his crushing burden forever. Fortunately for me, Atlas's plan was more desperate than well thought-out, and I was able to use his own trick on him, asking him if he could hold the sky again for just a little longer while I padded my shoulders. Needless to say, as soon as he had assumed his burden again, I left him and never looked back.

"When I finally reached the garden, I had to fight Ladon, the giant serpent coiled around the tree to guard it. The creature could have stopped almost anyone else, but I managed to strangle it, after which I had no difficulty picking some of the apples to bring back as proof to Eurystheus. That done, I gave them to Athena to return to where they belonged. The last thing I wanted was to give Hera one more reason to hate me.

"For the twelfth and final labor, Eurystheus asked me to do the seemingly impossible: to capture Cerberus and bring him back from Hades. I'm sure Eurystheus thought that even if I managed to survive a battle with Cerberus, I would surely not be able to survive the wrath of Hades. No doubt Hera thought the same.

"At least for this labor, finding my way down to the Underworld was easy enough. There were several known entrances, though it would have been

368 A Dream Come True

foolish for most people to use them. I picked the one in the cave at Cape Tanairon, very near the spot whose image you now see behind you.

"I expected to have trouble with Charon, but he yielded to me without argument and ferried me across the river. I never understood why an elder power would so willingly dismiss the rules, particularly one who was such a stickler for them normally, but I said a prayer of thanks to Zeus anyway. I had to think I had gotten some divine help, and indeed at times I felt the presence of Athena and Hermes, though they didn't reveal themselves.

"Cerberus too allowed me to pass, and I made no hostile move against him. Instead I went immediately to the palace of Hades to ask his permission to capture the beast. If Eurystheus had intended Hades to do his dirty work, I was not about to facilitate that plan.

"Luckily, Hades gave me permission, but with the requirement that I had to capture Cerberus without using any weapons—and the unspoken requirement that I not harm the creature. I was allowed to wear my Nemean lion armor, so part of me would be protected from Cerberus's teeth and claws, but even so, it would be a tough fight.

"Not only did Cerberus have three heads, but each one had a mane of snakes, and his tail was a snake as well. He was incredibly strong for a dog, but fortunately not too strong for a son of Zeus. It took me a long time, but eventually I succeeded in forcing the mighty hound to the ground so that I could chain it.

"Getting Cerberus back to Mycenae was quite a chore, and unfortunately I spread terror throughout the countryside, but eventually I did manage to deliver him to Eurystheus, who hid in the most distant part of the palace. I didn't care, though, because once I had returned Cerberus to his home, I was free. Eurystheus didn't try to quibble with the way any of the other labors had been performed, and so my servitude was at an end.

"The first thing I did when my life was finally mine again was to visit Megara in Thebes—not to attempt to mend our relationship, for I knew there was no hope of that, but to ensure she was well taken care of and legally free to marry if she chose. As it happens, she married Iphicles, with whom she had become friendly in my absence, and she offered me such forgiveness as she could.

"I would have been better off if I had decided to stay unmarried, but I wanted a family, even though I often think the pleasures of home life were never meant for men such as me. However, at that time I think I was trying to recapture the happiness I had experienced with Megara so long ago.

"At about that time, Eurytus, my former archery instructor who also happened to be king of Oechalia, held a contest to determine who would marry his daughter, Iole. She would be given to any man who could beat her father and all her brothers in an archery contest. Considering my skill as an archer, this seemed like a perfect opportunity, and so I took it.

"I easily prevailed in the contest, but then Eurytus refused to give me Iole's hand in marriage, arguing that I might kill her children as I had Megara's.

"I cannot easily describe how hurt I was that a former tutor would treat me in this way. It was even worse that all of Iole's brothers except Iphitus agreed with their father."

"I restrained myself with difficulty from trying to take Iole, who was rightfully mine, by force. Would that I had continued to maintain that restraint, but alas, I didn't.

"In a short time, Eurytus accused me of having stolen some of his cattle— a ridiculous charge. The cattle had really been stolen by Autolycus, and I thought—with some justice, I might add—that Eurytus was just looking for more excuses to deny me Iole.

"Many stories were invented later to blacken my name, particularly during the time when my descendants were conquering a large part of Greece. It was said, for example, that I invited Iphitus to be my guest when he came to investigate the theft and then killed him in cold blood. Sadly, I cannot deny killing him, but I acted not in cold blood, but in madness, for Hera, still determined to destroy me, drove me insane one final time.

"I was horrified when I realized what I had done, and I went at once to seek purification from Neleus, king of Pylos, who turned me down, claiming that his friendship with Eurytus prevented him from helping me. The real reason was that Neleus still resented me for catching him trying to steal some of Geryon's cattle, and I would not forget his petty attempt at revenge, though I should have.

"I found another king who purified me easily enough, but I became very ill and knew that the gods were not yet satisfied. I went to the oracle at Delphi, who, for the first time, at least as far as I know, refused to respond.

"I would be the first to admit that my faults were many, but I had not killed Iphitus on purpose, and I was outraged that the oracle would deny me her guidance. I took her sacred tripod and announced my intention to found my own oracle.

"This act was an example of the hubris I spoke of earlier. Whether the oracle's refusal to speak was fair or not, I should have accepted it, but instead I defied the oracle. Naturally, what I did brought Apollo's wrath upon me, and he appeared in person to take the tripod back. A terrible battle between us was averted only by the intervention of Zeus, who threw a thunderbolt between us to separate us before either could harm the other.

"I probably should have been punished for my theft of sacred property, but Zeus, realizing that Hera was manipulating circumstances again to put me in the worst possible situation, took pity on me and prevailed upon Apollo to show mercy as well. In exchange for returning the tripod, Apollo agreed to give the answer I wanted.

"I had feared I might be sent back to Eurystheus, but this time the gods demanded a punishment that was theoretically more humiliating: I was to be sold as a slave, the payment to be given to Eurytus as reparation for the death of his son. The one mitigation was that my slavery would last only a year, not my whole life.

"Hermes auctioned me off, and Omphale, the rich queen of Lydia, won the auction, paying a hundred times what a slave would normally be worth.

"At first, she did seem to want to humiliate me, forcing me to dress in women's clothing while she wore my armor and carried my club. However, as time went on, she fell in love with me, and we had a son together."

"And this was punishment?" asked Pan with another smirk.

Even Heracles could not help smiling a little. "Omphale realized that there were better ways to get her money's worth. Once she started sending me out to deal with various local bandits, she understood she could use me to bring order back to her more unruly provinces—a far better return on her investment than simply making fun of me.

"Omphale actually considered marrying me and making me her king, but in the end she didn't. Even though I loved her, I also loved Greece, and she knew it. I would never have been happy staying in Lydia, and when my term of service was up, she let me go, even though the parting pained both of us.

"Once back in Greece, I prayed to Zeus to prevent me from being driven mad again, and since I never was, I assume my prayer was answered. That problem taken care of, I got together with Telamon and Peleus to plan our revenge on Troy for cheating us.

"Laomedon would have been wiser to give us what was owed to us, but he still refused, confident in his god-built walls of Troy and in his large army, for the force we brought against him was small, nothing like what the Greeks would bring during the Trojan War."

"However, Laomedon didn't realize how powerful Heracles was," said Theseus. "By this point, he should have, and the mistake cost him dearly."

"It did indeed, though I had hoped he would not remain obstinate until the bitter end," said Heracles. "I suppose I should have expected that a man willing to risk cheating two gods wouldn't hesitate to cheat the son of a god.

"Laomedon tried and failed to burn our ships after we had landed, and he also failed to keep us away from the walls. I knew about the western weak spot, and our plan was to assault that area. It was a good plan, but it almost failed— because I nearly lost my temper. Even after all the suffering I had brought upon myself, I still had not mastered self-control.

"When we breached the walls, the honor of being first through the breach should have been mine, but Telamon charged through instead. Angered by my friend's presumption, I raised my sword to him and might have done worse but for his quick thinking.

"Gathering up stones from Troy's shattered wall, he stacked them and proclaimed the pile of rocks an altar to me in honor the victory. It was a small gesture, but it made me realize how foolish I was being.

"We went on to conquer the city, in the process killing Laomedon and all his sons except one, Podarces. To make amends to Telamon, I offered him Hesione, the woman we had rescued, as part of his share of the spoils."

"Women should never be *property*," muttered Artemis.

Heracles nodded. "War is cruel that way, but at least the women survive, and I for one always treated captive women with respect. So did Telamon, who offered to save any one person Hesione named.

She picked her one surviving brother—an unusual request, since the male members of the royal family of a conquered city are normally put to death. Telamon and I decided to grant her wish, provided she offered a ransom so that our enemies would not think us too soft-hearted. She offered one of her veils, and in honor of the occasion, Podarces became Priam, whose name sounds like one of the words for buying. The other leaders and I even agreed to allow Priam to assume the throne—as long as he agreed to keep the peace with us and with our families, and he agreed without hesitation.

"On the way back Hera managed to distract Zeus long enough to have a great wind blow us off course and force us to land on the island of Cos. The Coans, thinking us pirates, attacked, and sadly, many of them died, including the king. At that point, we managed to halt the slaughter and make peace with the Coans. There was even talk of my marrying Astyoche, the princess, and becoming king of the island, but, though I wanted peace, I didn't want to end up stuck on Cos. Ironically, though, my son with Astyoche eventually did sit on the throne."

"No doubt she was *grateful* that you spared the island," said Pan.

"Jealous?" asked Theseus, raising an eyebrow.

"I never set out to have children by so many women," said Heracles in answer to glares from the girls and Artemis. "I would have been perfectly happy to be the loyal husband of one woman if Hera had allowed me to. I was blissfully happy with Megara and likely would have remained so if the gods had left us alone.

"Once I returned from Troy, Athena asked me to help the gods in their battle with the giants, for a prophecy foretold that they could only win if I fought on their side. I was naturally willing to do what I could, and with my help, the gods prevailed. In some ways, that victory was my finest achievement, for if the gods had lost, the world would surely have descended into anarchy."

"Even I must admit that was well-done," said Artemis. "I have had my differences with Heracles, but no one could deny the good he did when he turned the tide of battle in our favor."

"Would that all my wars had worked out as well as that," said Heracles. "Once the giants had been defeated, I launched the campaign against Augeias which I mentioned earlier. After that, I made war on Neleus, king of Pylos—though in that case, I would have been wiser to forget his past wrongs.

"People afterward said I fought him only because he had refused to purify me of the blood guilt for the killing of Iphitus, but, as with so many stories about me, that was a malicious lie. In truth, Neleus, like his brother Pelias, had a fair number of crimes to his name, including the attempted theft of Geryon's cattle when I was trying to bring them back to Mycenae. In fact, the man was a usurper, having taken the city of Pylos from its founder, Pylas, much as Pelias took Iolcus from Aeson."

"Did that mean he deserved to die?" asked Fatima.

"Probably not by the standards of your society," conceded Heracles. "I would have been happy to accept reparations for his earlier bad conduct toward me, but he refused even to admit any wrong. Nonetheless, as I mentioned earlier, I have often wondered if I should have just let the offense pass.

"I had intended only a retaliatory raid of a kind that Neleus himself frequently conducted against people like the Epeians, but Neleus fought back furiously, changing what I had thought of as a punitive raid into an all-out war.

"Another lie told about that war is that I wounded Hades during it. The king of the Underworld never intervened in mortal wars and had no reason to this time. Another version that attempted to emphasize my hubris had me fighting not only against Hades, but also Poseidon, Hera, Ares, and Apollo—a combination I could never have prevailed against, even with Athena at my side. I don't deny being stupid at times—but I was never that stupid.

"Poseidon did in fact offer aid to Pylos, but he chose not to engage me directly in battle, and I certainly was not foolish enough to attempt to force him into one.

"It is also said I killed not only Neleus but eleven of his twelve sons in battle. I would gladly have spared the sons, but like their father, they stubbornly kept up the fight even after it was clearly lost—brave, but foolish. Even so, contrary to what some stories say, I spared Periclymenus, who had been granted the gift of shapeshifting by Poseidon. When this warrior, with whom I had served on the *Argo*, changed into an eagle to retreat, I could easily have shot him down, but I allowed him to escape, partly because of his valor and partly as a peace offering to Poseidon.

"Nestor, the youngest, who had been fostered among the Gerenians, took no part in the fighting. Never having intended a war of conquest, I confirmed Nestor as the new ruler of Pylos. He silently accepted my gift—though he never forgave me for the slaughter of his family. I cannot truly blame him, though it pained me that such a wise man would hate me so much.

"Despite that hatred, however, Nestor never tried to take revenge, though he had several opportunities to attack sons of mine during his long, god-favored life. I sometimes wished I had been able to let go of past wrongs as well as he did. The last years of my life would have been better if I had followed his example.

"I had an even graver wrong than those of Neleus to address before I could finally be at rest. Oeonus, my cousin, the grandson of Electryon, had been murdered in Sparta because he had killed a watchdog that was attacking him. Worse, it was the sons of Hippocoon, who was then usurping the throne of Sparta, who had murdered Oeonus. In those days, it was more or less the responsibility of the family to avenge family members, and so I hurried to Sparta, bringing with me Cepheus, king of Tegea and his sons to assist me in the fight against Hippocoon and his sons. My brother Iphicles also came along to lend his support, as he often did.

"I was victorious, but the victory was almost the costliest I had ever won. Not only did Cepheus and all his sons die in the fighting, but so did Iphicles, leaving Megara to grieve once again.

"There were those who wanted me to become king of Sparta at that point, but I had no wish to rule a city bought with my brother's blood, and in any case, Tyndareus was the rightful ruler, so I called him back to assume the crown again.

"At last I was free to marry and settle down—or so I allowed myself to dream for a while. During my trip to the Underworld, I had talked with the ghost of Meleager, who suggested I marry his sister, Deianeira. I now remembered that advice and gave it serious consideration.

"Deianeira was a spirited woman who in one case later fought at my side. She was also a woman of great intelligence, and her beauty was nearly legendary. Like me, she was said to be the child of a god. Just as men whispered her brother Meleager was actually the son of Ares, they said Deianeira was really the daughter of Dionysus.

"Unfortunately, by that point Deianeira also had another suitor: the river god Achelous, whom she found terrifying. I challenged him to wrestle me for her, and he agreed.

"Achelous put up a good fight, particularly since he could change himself into a bull at will. When I not only managed to wrestle him to the ground but broke off one of his horns, he finally conceded the victory to me.

"For seven years I lived happily with Deianeira in Calydon and had several children. I could not help but be reminded of my early days with Megara in Thebes. Was I really going to finally be allowed some happiness, or was Hera once again scheming my downfall?

"She didn't drive you mad again, did she?" asked Yasmin.

"Not this time. Either Zeus made sure Hera stayed away from me, or her own attitude was starting to mellow. Even she could not deny my service to the gods during the war with the giants, especially considering I had saved her from being raped during the battle. No, this time I had no one to blame but myself and my still untamed temper for the disaster that befell me.

"Angered by a servant's clumsiness, I accidentally killed him. By that point in my life, I should have been able to control my strength better. To make the situation even worse, the servant was a relative of King Oeneus, my father-in-law. At least I hadn't killed my own sons again—but I had killed, and justice demanded that there be consequences.

"Considering that the death was accidental, the boy's father was willing to forgive me, as was the king. I was amazed by their generosity, but I refused to accept it. Too often before I made this kind of foolish and fatal mistake. If I was to live up to the heroic title so many people thought I deserved, then I must do more than just kill monsters and win battles. I must also exemplify justice. With that in mind, I went voluntarily into exile.

Deianeira came with me, though I did not ask her to, and my children did as well, so at least I still had a family. I also had a new home, for my old friend, Ceux, king of Trachis, offered me a place as soon as he heard of my exile.

Alas, it was on the trip to Trachis that the seeds of my own death were sowed. At one point, we came to a river guarded by the centaur Nessus. He claimed to have been given the job of carrying travelers across the river by the gods themselves and offered to carry Deianeira across. Why I wasn't more suspicious, I don't know. I was well aware of the violent and uncivilized nature of most centaurs, but I had known centaurs such as Cheiron, and thinking Nessus to be similarly moral, I allowed him to carry Deianeira across.

"Her screams alerted me when Nessus reached the far bank and tried to gallop away with her. I shot Nessus with one of my arrows before he could get far—but that did not kill him fast enough to keep him from setting his revenge in motion.

"As he lay dying, Nessus whispered to Deianeira that his blood was a powerful love charm and that if ever I proved unfaithful, all she needed to do was smear one of my garments with his blood, and I would fall in love with her all over again.

"Why Deianeira would take advice from a creature who had been kidnapping her only moments before, I couldn't say, but she managed to save some of the blood.

"I can't blame her entirely for my eventual doom, for I too played a part. After settling in Trachis, where we were happy once again, I could have emulated Nestor and left well enough alone, but one wrong done to me still irked me, even years later: Eurytus's refusal to allow me to marry Iole.

"What was truly ridiculous about my feelings was that I loved Deianeira and had no desire to discard her in favor of Iole. Since Iole was considerably younger than I was, I actually thought about marrying her to Hyllus, one of my sons. However, most of all, I wanted Eurytus to acknowledge that he had wronged me. My hubris would not let the matter rest.

"Stubborn as Neleus had been, Eurytus refused to acknowledge the rightness of my cause, and the situation quickly degenerated into all-out war. Eurytus and his surviving sons all died, and I claimed Iole as part of the spoils of war, intending to take her back to Trachis with me.

"On the way back, I wanted to offer sacrifice to Zeus but did not have proper garments, so I sent Lichas, my herald, back to Trachis to bring me what I needed.

"Lichas went to Deianeira and asked for the clothing I needed. Unfortunately, he also told her about my returning with Iole.

"Deianeira remembered Iole's name and our shared past from my various stories, and she feared I intended to make Iole my new wife. Shocked, she recalled the words of Nessus, and she poured his blood over my robe before giving it to Lichas to bring back to me.

"What Deianeira didn't realize, but Nessus had, was that his blood would be mixed with the hydra poison from my arrow. When I put on the robe, the poison started burning into my skin, causing me unendurable pain as it did so. By the time I managed to tear the robe off, the poison had oozed deeply into my flesh. Before long it reached my bones, making the pain even worse.

"Some of my men managed to get me back to Trachis, but it was clear I wouldn't survive that torture for much longer. Poor Deianeira, realizing what she'd done, killed herself, which made my situation even worse. I now knew the only way to relieve the pain was to die, but doing so at this point would orphan my children. In some ways that was worse agony than the one the poison inflicted, but knowing I would eventually die of the poison anyway made the choice a simple one.

"Brave little Hyllus helped me get to the top of Mount Oeta and build a pyre, onto which I then climbed. The future great archer, Philoctetes, lit the pyre when Hyllus could not bring himself to do it and received my bow and arrows as a reward.

"I had expected to die. Some might even have thought that was exactly what I deserved. However, the gods led me to a better fate. Once the mortal part of me had burned away, Hermes whisked the divine part of me up to Olympus. There I was welcomed into the fellowship of the gods, all of whom rejoiced—even Hera, who had finally given up her grudge against me and even offered me her daughter Hebe, the goddess of eternal youth, as my divine bride.

"Unfortunately, the sons I left behind did not fare so well. The cowardly Eurystheus decided to attack them now that I was no longer around to protect them, and poor Ceux lacked the military might to stop him. My sons fled south to Athens with Eurystheus and his army close behind.

King Menestheus offered my sons sanctuary and refused to surrender them when Eurystheus demanded he do so. In the ensuing battle, Eurystheus was killed, proving once again that sometimes it is better to forget about the past— it certainly would've been in his case.

"Somehow, despite all the blood I had sprinkled on the situation, Hyllus and Iole fell in love and married. My other sons took wives as well and made preparations to go to war with the heirs of Eurystheus.

"During my stay at Trachis, I had made friends with the Dorians, whom I helped against the Lapiths. Remembering this aid, the Dorians became allies of my sons by Deianeira, as did some of my other sons from other parts of Greece. It took a few generations, but eventually the heirs of Eurystheus were overthrown everywhere, leaving my descendants in control of the bulk of Greece, including Mycenae, where Zeus had once intended me to rule. Hera had done nothing but delay the inevitable, creating needless discord in the process."

Keisha's head was swimming with all the details from Heracles's story as she tried to compare it to the others. If there was some common element that would provide the clue they needed to determine who was disrupting Olympus, she still couldn't see what it was.

She was still pondering when the earthquake that had been hinted at earlier finally struck, knocking her down and splitting the ground beneath her.

Chapter 26: Heroes of the Trojan War, Part 1

In one way or another, all the students thought about what would happen if they died in this strange dream world. *Still not sure if reality or dream*

A real earthquake would have been frightening enough, but the chaos surrounding them was more like a Hollywood-disaster movie earthquake, complete with cracks in the ground that widened until they were big enough for a person to fall into. The sky above no longer looked like sky, but like the ceiling of a cave, which is what it had probably been all along. From that ceiling, large chunks of black rock fell, hitting the stony ground with resounding crashes. One hit would probably be deadly. *have to be careful*

Only the quick thinking of the gods saved them. Pan and Artemis herded them together quickly, and grabbed Theseus and Teiresias as well, though since they were dead already, they were presumably at much less risk. Then Heracles raised the Nemean lion skin over them like a tent, with himself, Artemis, Pan, and Ardalos providing support for the makeshift covering. The lion skin could not be penetrated, and the gods were able to endure the impact as the rocks struck, though Keisha could swear she heard bones break once or twice.

When the earthquake finally subsided, the rocks had formed a mound over them that would have buried them alive had not Heracles been able to push the stones aside. *This book had a great editor*

"That was close!" said Mateo, looking around. The replica of Cape Sounion had been completed obliterated. The image of the sea had been replaced by jagged rock, the ground all around them was gray with fallen stone, and the temple of Poseidon lay in ruins.

"What could possibly have done this?" asked Theseus.

"I fear even I cannot tell," said Teiresias. "We still face the same problem—we need to know who is behind these disruptions in order to stop them. However, now I fear the time left before our universe comes apart completely may be too short to solve this mystery. Still, Apollo's plan remains our only hope." *Something very bad is happening*

"At least the Underworld gods have not lost control completely," said Heracles, pointing to the ceiling of the cave. Flickers of blue sky flowed across the rock surface like bad CGI. "Someone is trying to restore Elysium to normal."

"That will do us little good unless we can find some answers," said Teiresias. "I recommend we proceed at once to the final group of heroes. Luck is still with us in one respect, for they are all in one place. The earthquake brought them together, for they too seek answers."

"I fear I will just slow you down," said Artemis, pointing to a broken leg. "This is no great injury for a goddess, but only someone such as Asclepius or Apollo could heal it right away. I'm sure Hades has the proper salve at his palace, but I cannot make it there alone."

"I can help you get back," said Pan. "Teiresias, can we leave without putting our visitors in danger?"

"The distance is short," answered the seer. "With me to lead and with Heracles and Theseus to watch over us, I'm sure we can make it."

"Do not forget us," said Ardalos. "We too will protect our visitors in any way we can, however long their journey may be." Patricius barked his agreement.

"I can make that journey even shorter," said Hermes, who had suddenly appeared next to Teiresias. The swift god looked bruised and dusty, but otherwise unharmed.

"Where have you been?" asked Artemis, leaning on Pan for support.

"Held prisoner in the tower of Cronus—or so someone wanted me to believe, anyway. However, it's pretty hard to keep me prisoner anywhere in the Underworld, and when the earthquake began, I used the confusion to escape."

"Could Cronus be behind all this?" asked Heracles. If so—"

"No, I fear our quest will not be resolved so easily," said Hermes. "I never actually saw him, and even if I had, I'm not sure I would have believed my eyes. Whoever is behind this wants us gods to distrust each other."

"And that strategy has been successful," added Teiresias. "I sense Zeus still trying to keep the peace, but we are at most only hours away from a war among the gods. Such a conflict could destroy this world."

"Then allow me to take us at once to where the heroes of the Trojan War have gathered," said Hermes. "Pan, can you make sure Artemis gets help?"

"I will indeed," said Pan, who picked up Artemis in his hairy arms and carried her away. She protested loudly that she didn't need to be carried—

protests that echoed for some time after they were out of sight.

Hermes waved the caduceus, and in moments they stood before a scene out of a nightmare.

Since the messenger of the gods had mentioned Troy, Thanos assumed it was the flaming city before them. Screams echoed from it as if the city was just now falling. Above it, someone had managed to restore a sky image, but it was a cloudy night sky that allowed not even a hint of moonlight to penetrate. In fact, the only light came from the burning city. Then Thanos realized it was smoke, not clouds, that hid the moon.

Hermes made the caduceus glow, bathing the students and their escort in a friendlier light, then gestured for them to move forward, toward a group of men and women who seemed on the verge of fighting each other.

"Hermes," one of them said, "can you blot out this…this horror?" pointing to the Troy reenactment. "Our Greek 'friends' conjured it up to torture us."

"That's a lie!" one of the Greeks protested. "The Trojans did this to blacken our reputations."

"None of you did it," said Hermes quickly. "I will attempt to erase it while Teiresias explains our urgent need for your help."

The words of the god calmed the angry Greeks and Trojans a little, and by the time Teiresias had finished telling them what was happening, they all looked anxious and ready to cooperate.

By that time, Hermes had managed to mute the sounds of screaming and wrapped the sight of the burning city in deep fog.

"This is the best I can do for the moment," said Hermes. "Will it be enough?"

"It will indeed," said one of the Greeks, looking a little embarrassed. "We should have known better than to be fooled by such an evil trick."

"Zeus himself has been fooled more than once recently," said Hermes. "That is precisely why we need your help. If we cannot unravel this mystery, I fear we will all be doomed."

"Most willing we are to do what we can," said one of the Trojans, bowing. The others followed his example.

"Then let us begin with your early lives," said Teiresias. "Introduce yourselves, and tell our guests something of your life before the Trojan War."

"May I begin?" asked one of the Greeks. "I do not wish to give offense to my Trojan...friends."

"We have no time for such niceties," said Teiresias. Yes, begin—and be quick about it."

"Very well, Father Teiresias," said the Greek, stepping forward. He was a tall man with a very serious look and a conspicuous crown on his head. "I am Agamemnon, king of Mycenae and high king of the Greeks, leader of the expedition to Troy.

"Though I do not fault myself for making war on Troy—for we had ample cause—I fear my story is not an inspiring one, for I often made mistakes that got many people killed needlessly. My one defense is that at least I managed to rise above the level of my ancestors, who indeed brought down a curse upon my family.

"You have heard of Tantalus, who served his own son to the gods to test their omniscience? Well, he was my great-grandfather, and my family might have perished right then and there, but the gods reassembled and resurrected poor Pelops, Tantalus's son. That was all well and good, I suppose—but then they proceeded to spoil him rotten.

"By far the worst offender was Poseidon, who taught Pelops charioteering and even brought him to Olympus for a while, sending him back only because Zeus began to think the boy was too favored, and Zeus was right. How could Pelops not feel hubris when the gods themselves encouraged it?

"Back on earth, Pelops turned his thoughts toward marriage, and naturally he just had to have Hippodamia, the much sought-after daughter of King Oenomaus of Pisa.

"That the girl was beautiful no one would deny, but loving her was usually fatal, for Oenomaus had received a prophecy that his son-in-law would kill him.

"He could have just refused to allow her to marry, but, not wishing to seem a cruel and unreasonable father, he instead proposed to marry her to anyone who could beat him in a chariot race—the catch being that all suitors who lost the race would be put to death. The king had reason to be confident no one could beat him, for he was one of those odd cases in which a mortal has two divine parents, in this case Ares and Asterope, who was the daughter of

Atlas and Pleione. Not only that, but Ares had given him a team of immortal horses who should theoretically have been able to win any race. Eighteen men tried and failed to beat him, so at first his confidence seemed justified.

"Undeterred by such a seemingly impossible task, Pelops prayed to Poseidon, who once again extravagantly blessed him, this time with a golden chariot and a team of winged horses. So equipped, Pelops at least stood a chance.

"Pelops did suffer a setback before the race. His charioteer and friend, Cillus, died. Pelops buried him and built a temple of Apollo at the burial site, later also founding the city of Cilla nearby. Even this disaster in the long run worked in Pelops's favor, however, for the ghost of Cillus offered to frighten Oenomaus's horses during the race. Being immortal, they might not panic as normal horses would, but the appearance of a ghost was still bound to slow them down.

"Pelops should have been willing to settle for what seemed like an overwhelming advantage, but he was tempted to make the race a sure thing. The impulse was understandable, since losing meant dying, but the way in which he went about guaranteeing victory would bring misery upon his family for generations.

"Pelops approached Myrtilus, a son of Hermes and Oenomaus's charioteer, with the offer of a considerable bribe to betray his king: a share of the kingdom and a night in bed with Hippodamia. Myrtilus, who secretly loved Hippodamia himself, accepted the dishonorable bargain, figuring that one night with her was better than nothing."

"Seldom have any of my sons behaved so dishonorably," said Hermes sadly.

"How could Pelops offer Myrtilus a night with his own wife?" asked Yasmin. "That makes it sound as if he didn't really love her. She was just a possession to him."

"My theory is that Pelops never intended to honor his agreement," replied Agamemnon. "Let me get to that in a moment, though. Before the race, Myrtilus took the bronze linchpins out of the axles of Oenomaus's chariot, replacing them with wax. Naturally, such fake linchpins would not last long, and early in the race they broke, causing Oenomaus to be thrown from the chariot and killed, though Myrtilus, who knew what to expect, survived. Unfortunately for him, Oenomaus, who realized Myrtilus had betrayed him, cursed the charioteer with his dying breath, and Ares heard him.

"Shortly afterward, when Myrtilus was flying over the sea with Pelops in his chariot, Pelops pushed the traitorous charioteer out, and he fell to his death. Afterward, Pelops accused Myrtilus of trying to rape Hippodamia to justify the killing, but I don't believe a word of that. It was just an excuse not to meet his part of the agreement.

"Alas for Pelops, Myrtilus cursed him as the charioteer fell toward the sea, and Hermes heard the curse."

"I certainly did," said Hermes.

"It's like a chain reaction," said Yong.

"Exactly," said Agamemnon. "One bad deed or misfortune leads to another, on and on. At first, Pelops didn't suffer the effect of his betrayals, however. Not only did he marry Hippodamia, but he became king of Pisa. The Pisans, who had no love for the brutal Oenomaus, were perfectly willing to see Pelops take the throne, and if they knew of his treachery, they decided to overlook it. The fact that Hephaestus himself purified him of all blood guilt certainly didn't hurt, either.

"Oddly enough, Pelops even rose above his earlier treachery, for by all accounts he was a wise and just king, eventually becoming so influential that the Peloponnese was named for him after this death. He had many sons and daughters, who during his lifetime were mostly prosperous and well-connected. His son Pittheus became king of Troezen and grandfather of that Theseus whom you have beside you. His daughter Nicippe became queen of Mycenae and mother of Eurystheus. Another daughter, Astydaemeia, married another son of Perseus and became the grandmother of Alcmena, the mother of Heracles over there. One of his sons, Alcathous, became the maternal grandfather of Ajax, that bold warrior who fought by my side. Through other children Pelops extended his influence to many parts of Greece.

"However, the curse of Myrtilus would not lie forever dormant, and Pelops managed to awaken it with his excessive favor for his illegitimate son, Chrysippus."

"Loving his son was a bad thing?" asked Fatima.

"Loving a son is never a bad thing," replied Agamemnon, "but loving one son more than the others can be, especially when one is a king, and the designation of the heir to the throne is at stake. Two of Pelops's legitimate sons, Atreus and Thyestes, feared that Pelops would make Chrysippus his heir. Encouraged by Hippodamia, whose virtue was unfortunately not as great as her beauty, Atreus and Thyestes murdered poor Chrysippus and threw his body down a well.

"When Pelops discovered the truth, he expelled his murderous sons, adding another curse to the family legacy for good measure: that they and their descendants should perish in strife against each other. He planned to inflict some terrible punishment on Hippodamia, for his love for her had withered in his heart as soon as learned of her part in the plot. She preempted his revenge by committing suicide. Pelops, who spent the rest of his life grieving for Chrysippus, did not long survive her, and the kingdom of Pisa eventually fell victim to the avarice of its neighbors.

"Atreus and Thyestes ended up in Mycenae, then ruled by Sthenelus, their brother-in-law, who invited them to rule Midea in his name—a far better fate than they deserved. Much later, Eurystheus entrusted Atreus with Mycenae itself when he went on his foolish and fatal crusade against the Heraclids.

"After Eurystheus died in battle, the Mycenaeans received an oracle from Zeus ordering them to choose a son of Pelops as their king. Even though Atreus was my father, why Zeus would have favored him is beyond me. Neither he nor my uncle was worthy to wear a crown. Perhaps he wanted a cursed monarch whose disastrous fate would pave the way for the descendants of Heracles. Perhaps he simply wanted to fulfill one or both of the curses under which the brothers labored. Whatever motivated the king of the gods, his actions in this case make me doubt that success is a sign of the gods' blessing, for often they heap men with gifts as a prelude to destroying them.

"About that time, a sheep with golden fleece was born in Atreus's flock. He took it as a sign of Zeus's favor, and he was sure the people of Mycenae would see it the same way and choose him to be their king. However, Thyestes learned of the sheep's existence and knew he had to have it.

"It was then that Thyestes seduced my mother, Aerope, a granddaughter of Minos who behaved little like the princess she was. He used her to help him steal the golden sheep, after which he got Atreus to declare publicly that whoever had such a golden sheep should become the next king.

"Atreus was dumbfounded when he discovered that Thyestes had the sheep, but he could not stop him from becoming king of Mycenae. However, Atreus was not about to accept his brother as king without a fight—and once again Zeus intervened, this time in an even more exceptional way. He sent Hermes to tell Atreus that the following day the sun would rise in the west and set in the east.

"With such amazing inside information, Atreus was able to trick Thyestes into agreeing to abdicate in his favor if the sun rose in the west. Thyestes, taking the whole thing for an ill-tempered joke on Atreus's part, played along, I think to humiliate my father when the promised miracle did not appear.

"When the sun did in fact rise in the west, Thyestes had no choice but to relinquish the throne, and Atreus banished him from Mycenae forever. He would have done well to let the matter end there, but unfortunately, he discovered that Thyestes had gotten the sheep in the first place by seducing my mother.

"He drowned her for her betrayal, but for his brother, he planned an even worse fate. Pretending to want to make peace with Thyestes, he summoned him to Mycenae and invited him to a feast. What Thyestes didn't know was that he was dining on the flesh of his three sons. At the end of the meal, Atreus revealed the truth."

"How...how..." started Yong, who found himself unable to finish.

"Hatred had poisoned his soul," said Agamemnon. "It was a bitter irony that he selected a method so reminiscent of the crime of his grandfather, Tantalus. It was even more bitter that Atreus seemed to have forgotten how angry with Tantalus the gods were, and how thoroughly he lost the high regard in which they held him. I tell you this: if he was not already twice cursed, his horrible revenge would certainly have brought divine wrath down upon him. Thyestes had done much evil, but surely no man deserves to suffer as he did.

"What Atreus did not know was that Thyestes would soon have another son, a child he fathered by raping his own daughter, Pelopia, though the girl did not at the time realize it was her father who had assaulted her.

"How could any man do such a thing?" asked Yasmin.

"No man with even a shred of morality could have," said Agamemnon, "and no reason could possibly excuse such a deed, though Thyestes thought he had one. You see, Atreus made the mistake of letting him live after that unspeakable feast, probably because Atreus wanted to prolong his suffering. That gave Thyestes, now every bit as corrupted by hate as his brother was, a chance to consult an oracle about how best to get his revenge. The oracle told him that a son, born of his own daughter, would be the only one who could kill Atreus."

"Did she lose her...oracle license for that...or something?" asked Mateo.

"It was not the fault of the oracle, who spoke only what the gods told her," said Agamemnon. "Sometimes the gods give us tests, and I have always thought that was what they did in this case. Perhaps if Thyestes had recoiled in horror from an incestuous rape, he might have broken the curses on himself or least gotten some mercy from the gods. Instead, he showed that he now put revenge before everything else, even his poor daughter. As if to blacken his deed even further, he assaulted her right after she had participated in sacrifices to Artemis, showing how little he respected the gods.

"Pelopia didn't know it was her father her assaulted her, but she had managed to hide his sword, thinking she might use it as proof against her rapist later. Not knowing she was pregnant, she returned to the court of King Threspotus in Epirus, where her father had long ago sent her, ironically for safety. Thyestes, belatedly afraid that someone might discover his deed, fled to Asia Minor just in case.

"In the meantime, Atreus's vile acts had caused the crops to fail in Mycenae, and widespread famine threatened. Atreus consulted an oracle, who told him to bring Thyestes back into the kingdom to restore the land's fertility. As a result, Atreus went searching for his brother. He failed to find him, but while visiting Threspotus, his eye fell on Pelopia. Not knowing she was his own niece, he asked Threspotus for her hand in marriage. Threspotus agreed, though I don't know why. Pelopia agreed as well, which makes me wonder if she didn't know who Atreus was. In some Greek societies, marriage between an uncle and a niece was permissible, but that wouldn't explain her willingness to marry her father's archenemy.

"Perhaps by that point the poor girl had been driven insane as a result of the crime against her. That would certainly explain her subsequent behavior, for being the queen of Mycenae brought her no joy. When her child was born, she knew it was the child of the rapist and exposed it in the wilderness.

"However, she had not shared the story of her rape with Atreus—or anyone else, for that matter—so Atreus believed the child was his and sent out men to search for him. They found the boy, safe and sound. Atreus didn't punish Pelopia, but he ceased regarding her as his wife. He did, however, take great joy in raising her son, whom he called Aegisthus, as his own, little knowing how much harm the boy would grow up to do.

"Sometime later my brother Menelaus and I found Thyestes, who had returned to Greece to consult the oracle at Delphi. Knowing our father wanted him, we captured him and brought him back to Mycenae, unwittingly moving us all one step closer to disaster."

"Atreus might have interpreted the oracle's words as meaning he should try to reconcile with his brother, but instead he threw Thyestes into prison. Though the crops grew a little after that, it was clear the gods were still frowning on Mycenae. Atreus didn't consult the oracle again. Instead, over the years he convinced himself that the gods wanted Thyestes dead and that shedding his blood would restore prosperity to the land.

"By that time Aegisthus had come of age, and Atreus sent him to kill Thyestes. For a weapon, Atreus gave him the very sword Pelopia had taken from Thyestes so long ago. As a result, when Aegisthus arrived at Thyestes's cell, the captive recognized the sword and begged Aegisthus to tell him where he had gotten it.

"Aegisthus was the only person to whom Pelopia had told the story of her rape—omitting the fact that Aegisthus was a child of that rape—so he was able to repeat it to Thyestes, who realized that the man sent to kill him was his own son.

"Naturally, Aegisthus didn't believe Thyestes, but his father insisted that Pelopia be summoned, and in the spirit of honoring a dying man's last request, Aegisthus did so.

"When Pelopia saw her father and heard his tale, she realized for the first time that it was he who had raped her, and whatever little sanity she might have had fled from her. Asking to see the sword, she stabbed herself with it.

"Aegisthus should have been horrified by the fact that his father was also his grandfather and had raped his mother, but for some reason he wasn't. I had always thought there was something a little off about the boy, and evidently, I was right. Instead of damning his father as a rapist who was responsible for the death of his mother, he embraced that father and vowed to help him seek revenge on Atreus, whose only crime against Aegisthus had been raising him as a son.

"You can well imagine what happened next. Aegisthus returned to Atreus with the bloody sword, claiming to have killed Thyestes. At the first opportunity, he used that sword to kill Atreus in a cowardly surprise attack.

"My brother Menelaus and I were smuggled out of Mycenae by friends of our father. We hid at Calydon for a while but ultimately ended up in Sparta, where King Tyndareus treated us well and eventually equipped us to recover the throne of Mycenae, which we did.

"I tried at that point to break the curse on our family. Thyestes had sought sanctuary at the altar of Hera, and I knew spilling his blood there would only make us even more despised by the gods. Instead of killing him, my brother and I offered him more mercy than he had ever offered anyone, allowing him to depart for Cythera and promising never to come after him as long as he stayed there. The twisted Aegisthus went into hiding, and we did not pursue him, either.

"For a while we believed the curse on us had been lifted. The people of Mycenae accepted me as their king, and the city had an unprecedented period of prosperity. Tyndareus gave me his daughter, Clytemnestra, as my wife. He also, though I will leave that part for Helen to tell, gave Helen to Menelaus, and when Tyndareus died, Menelaus received the throne of Sparta.

"I was wrong, though. The curses were asleep, not dead, and the time would come when they would once again rise to plague us. However, that would happen during and after the war, so I will wait until later to reveal how they emerged once again."

"Is it my turn, then?" asked a woman so incredibly beautiful that the guys had no problem telling she must be Helen. They couldn't even find words to describe her.

"It is, and you had better start your tale at once," said Teiresias, who, being blind, was the one man in the group whose whole attention was not riveted to Helen's every move.

"Zeus came to my mother Leda in the form of a swan," said Helen. "She slept with Tyndareus and with Zeus in the same night, with the result that nine months later she gave birth to four children, two of whom, Castor and Clytemnestra, were the children of Tyndareus, and other two, Pollux and me, were children of Zeus. Some stories even suggest that, instead of giving birth in the normal way, my mother laid two eggs, but that part of the story makes no sense. I suppose the children of Zeus might have come from an egg, but why would the children of Tyndareus have done so? There was an early tradition that Zeus had mated with the goddess Nemesis when both were swans and fathered me that way, and I think the egg part comes from confusion with that earlier story. As far as I know, Leda was my mother, and she gave birth to me in the same way any mother would have.

"Tyndareus was a wise man, and though he knew Zeus had slept with my mother, he never faulted her for it. Nor did he treat any of us differently, but raised us all equally as his children.

"Clytemnestra and I were never particularly close, but Castor and Pollux remained inseparable, so much so that when they died, Pollux was offered a place on Olympus, but he decided to share immortality with his brother, so they both spent part of their time in the Underworld and part on Olympus. Eventually, men worshiped them as the Dioscuri, but to me they would always be my brothers and my protectors.

"Would that Atreus and Thyestes had been such brothers," said Agamemnon.

"I was fortunate that way," said Helen. "I had a wonderful childhood, well, except for—"

"An event I have never stopped regretting," said Theseus.

"I forgave you long ago," said Helen, "for I too made mistakes in the name of love, and at least yours did not lead to the greatest war ancient Greece ever knew.

"Tyndareus had no trouble marrying Clytemnestra to Agamemnon, but I posed a different problem, for virtually every king in Greece except the already married Agamemnon asked for my hand in marriage. Other fathers had needed to deal with more than one suitor, but my poor father was faced with a virtual army of suitors. Of the great men who fought at Troy, only Achilles was absent from the list. Some said he was too young, but there may be another reason, which I will leave to him to explain.

"Though women did not necessarily pick their husband in my time, Tyndareus and my brothers would certainly have listened to my wishes. However, I didn't know whom to pick. Faced with a selection that included young and handsome Diomedes, king of Argos; quick-witted and bold Odysseus, king of Ithaca; massive and fearless Ajax, prince of Salamis; kind and soothing Machaon, a physician as handsome as his grandfather, Apollo; Antilochus, a seafaring descendant of Poseidon and prince of Pylos; manly Ascalaphus, king of Orchomenus and son of Ares, I had no idea whom to choose. There were good arguments in favor of each man—but none of them held a special place in my heart. If only one of them had, much suffering might have been avoided.

"Tyndareus too could not find one man who obviously stood out from the others, for each had his own special excellence. However, my mortal father had another problem to consider. He could only choose one of the suitors. How would the others react? How could he avoid making at least some of them bitter enemies? With such fears, Tyndareus could not bring himself to decide among the suitors, but realistically, he could only keep them waiting so long without making enemies of all of them.

"Odysseus helped solved this problem. He had formally become a suitor, but he thought he had little chance of being chosen. Anyway, he decided he wanted to marry my cousin, Penelope. In exchange for Tyndareus's help to win Penelope's hand, Odysseus offered Tyndareus a solution to the suitor issue: have all the suitors swear an oath to defend whoever was chosen from attack by anyone else. Such an oath was unusual, but every one of the suitors, eager for my hand, all swore to it without hesitation.

"Thus freed from fear, Tyndareus proceeded to choose the man he had probably favored all along: Menelaus. Though not a king himself, Menelaus had the support of Agamemnon, and Tyndareus knew both men well and respected them. Besides, a solid link with Mycenae, which Agamemnon had already restored to wealth and power, was no small thing. From a political and strategic standpoint, Menelaus was the best choice.

"But what did you think of him?" asked Fatima.

"He had lived in Sparta long enough that I thought of him as I would my brothers. I had no passion for him, but I did feel comfortable with him, and I knew he was a good man. At the time, that was enough for me.

"Much to Tyndareus's relief, the suitors accepted the decision and returned home to look for other wives. Odysseus won the hand of Penelope, though in the end he still had to beat her father, Icarius, in a foot race in order to claim her, despite the prior assurances of Tyndareus. Nonetheless, Odysseus was happy, and he too sailed home.

"Not long after that, Castor and Pollux died in a conflict with two Messenian princes, Idas and Lynceus. Our whole family was heartbroken, but at least Tyndareus could make the trusted Menelaus his heir, and it was not long before my husband inherited the throne, and I became his queen.

"I thought I had a long, peaceful life to look forward to. How wrong I was!"

"At least most of your early life was peaceful," said a formidable looking man in golden armor. "All I can remember in my early life was turmoil."

"Speak on, Achilles," said Teiresias, "for the time has come to tell your tale."

"Speaking of suitors, my mother, Thetis, the Nereid, was courted by both Zeus and Poseidon. However, she knew both were already married and didn't want to be the lover of either one. Thetis was friendly with Hera and was a sister of Amphitrite, Poseidon's queen, and she had no desire to hurt either one of them.

"She did get her wish to be the lover of neither god—but not in the way she hoped.

"Zeus learned that Thetis was destined to give birth to a son greater than his father, so that her son by either Poseidon or Zeus could conceivably be a threat, and particularly a son by Zeus could be the very one destined to overthrow him. For that reason, he and Poseidon agreed that Thetis should be married to a mortal.

"Harmonia had taken her marriage to Cadmus well, but Thetis was not happy with that arrangement, even though Peleus, my father, was a great hero.

She bowed to the order of Zeus, but only on the condition that Peleus could prove his worth by capturing her.

"I suspect Zeus would have insisted on the marriage regardless, but Peleus proved both clever enough to find Thetis, and strong enough and determined enough to hold her, though she transformed herself into a wide variety of forms, including a lion and even fire.

"Their marriage was celebrated on Mount Pelion in the presence of all the gods—except one. Eris, the goddess of discord, was not invited, a costly mistake I will let my Trojan friends tell you about.

"Despite the grandeur of the wedding, Thetis remained unhappy at being married to a mortal. Determined to compensate herself by having a divine son, each time she gave birth, she attempted to make the child immortal. Some other power must have been working against her, though, because her efforts failed each time. Worse, they resulted in the deaths of the children. Though she had intended no such outcome and grieved much over their deaths, when Peleus discovered what was happening, he angrily forbade her from trying to immortalize a child again, and she left him, never to return.

"However, she was pregnant with me when she left, and when I was born, she made one last attempt. She did not succeed in making me immortal, but she didn't kill me in the attempt, either. In fact, by dipping me in the River Styx, she succeeded in making my skin impenetrable by any weapon. The only exception was my heel, by which she had held me during the ritual.

"Unable to keep me easily in the undersea realm from which she came, Thetis gave me to Peleus, but she gave me the assurance, which I was too young to understand at the time, that she would never be far from me—a promise she kept throughout my life. I think perhaps the love that she would have given to all my dead brothers she focused on me, for seldom has any goddess spent so much time protecting a mortal son.

"When I was old enough, Peleus sent me to Cheiron for training. Shortly after that training was complete, however, my mother reappeared, just as she had promised—but not in the way I would have wanted.

"Thetis had heard a prophecy that I had two possible destinies: I could live a long and insignificant life or a short and glorious one. Naturally, having been trained as a warrior, I wanted the short and glorious life, though Thetis insisted I was too young to realize what I was choosing.

"Knowing that the Trojan War was coming and that I would die if I went to Troy, Thetis insisted on hiding me and would not take no for an answer. I agreed because I had no real choice, but I was horrified when I found out the details of her plan.

"Thetis hid me at the court of King Lycomedes of Scyros—an ill-omened choice considering he was the very king who had murdered Theseus years before and would not hesitate to do the same to me if he knew who I was. Far worse, though, was the *way* in which Thetis concealed me. Without telling the king I was her son, she got his permission to disguise me as a girl named Pyrrha and hide me among his daughters as one of their servants. No one else knew, not even the girls themselves.

"That plan…seems as if it would be…tricky to implement," said Thanos.

"I believe a better word would be stupid," said Achilles. "Disguise a young man my age—about the same age you are now—as a girl and hide him among girls? In your society that would have the making of bad comedy, would it not? The very idea is laughable.

"Well, of course, I fell in love with Deidamia, one of the king's daughters, and eventually I made love to her—much to her surprise, for my disguise had been very good. Afterward, she was understandably worried, but I revealed to her who I was and reassured her that my mother would protect her if her father found out she had lost her virginity to me. I also pledged to be faithful to her, and I really meant it—at the time.

"As you might expect, given the way my luck was running, she became pregnant. It's hard to conceal that kind of thing in the women's quarters of a palace, but somehow we managed it. I'd like to think my mother was looking after us. Anyway, Deidamia gave birth to a son, Neoptolemus, whom we were able to hide among the numerous children of the servants. Thetis has to have helped with that because otherwise, I can't understand how an extra child could have gone unnoticed.

"Not too long after, Odysseus came looking for me."

"How did he know you even existed?" asked Yong.

"I'd trained with Cheiron, and those who trained at the same time still remembered me. Not only that, but there was a prophecy that the Greeks could not win the Trojan War without me, which is why Odysseus was hunting for me.

"By this time, I longed to be free of my female disguise and take my rightful place as a warrior. I was about to reveal myself, but a look from Deidamia stopped me. Clearly, she didn't want me to go to Troy any more than my mother did."

"When no one came forward, Odysseus pretended to accept that I was not there and presented gifts to the daughters of Lycomedes and their maids. While the girls were choosing, Odysseus caused a trumpet blast and a clash of swords outside. Fearing that the palace was under attack, I reflexively stripped to the waist to fight unencumbered and then grabbed the shield and spear which lay among the gifts.

"At that point, I had no choice but to reveal all, and Lycomedes was none too happy to discover I had slept with his daughter while being offered sanctuary in his house. However, knowing who I really was consoled him a little, for he now had a potentially heroic grandson. In any case, the fiercely protective Thetis guaranteed the safety of both mother and child, just as I had predicted she would.

"I was the only Greek leader who had not sworn the oath of Tyndareus, so I could have decided not to join the war. Since I was pretty sure I would die before the walls of Troy, I certainly had reason enough to refuse. However, I still wanted glory, not long life, and so I agreed to become part of the expedition.

"You haven't told us what started the war yet," said Mateo.

"In fairness, I will let our Trojan friends tell that part of the story. Hector, will you honor us with the tale?" asked Achilles.

Hector, a tall and imposing Trojan, stepped forward. "You've heard the details more directly from your mother; I know them much more indirectly. However, it is perhaps time a Trojan spoke, for otherwise, our visitors may forget all about us."

To the students he said, "I am the eldest son of Priam and Hecuba, and I would have inherited the throne—had there been one left to inherit. Much as I respected my father, if I had been king, there would have been no war, for I would have sent Helen back to the Greeks at their first demand, and that would have been an end to it."

"You didn't want to fight?" asked Mateo.

"Though we lived in savage times, we didn't all love war," replied Hector. "War may bring glory to us heroes, but in the end it brings misery to everyone. Unfortunately, the gods manipulated us for their own purposes—and not always good purposes, if you ask me.

"Some storytellers say that Gaia complained to Zeus that men were becoming too numerous and too impious, and the war was his way to thin out the human population and make men more righteous. He certainly accomplished the first goal, though I doubt he achieved the second."

"Suffering can make a man more righteous," said Heracles. "It is a hard path, but it is the one from which I learned. However, I don't believe Zeus planned the war. If he had, he would have arranged events differently, for the way the war came about made the gods look foolish. How did that encourage men to be more righteous?"

Hector shrugged. "I always did my duty to the gods and always will, but the destruction of Troy made me doubt their wisdom. For the sake of getting that part of the tale told, I will accept what you say rather than arguing with you. ~Eris is behind the war~

"I'm sure we all agree that it was Eris who sparked the war. Angered by not being invited to the wedding of Peleus and Thetis, she came anyway, bearing a golden apple, which she announced was for the fairest."

"Where did she get it?" asked Keisha. "That part of the myth always seemed random to me."

"No one knows," said Hector. "She could have stolen one of the apples of the Hesperides, for they presumably have some kind of magic, but wherever it came from, in her hands it became the apple of discord. Throwing it among the wedding guests created immediate conflict, for Hera, Athena, and Aphrodite each claimed to be the fairest, and all of them refused to stop arguing about their claims."

"That's never made sense to me," said Thanos. "Why would Aphrodite care about what other goddesses think? As for Hera, she has her faults, but no other story portrays vanity as being one of them. And Athena? She always acts as if she wants to be, as we would say, one of the guys. Now, out of nowhere, she wants to win a beauty contest? The whole story makes no sense."

"All I can think is that the apple warped their minds somehow," said Hector. "It would have taken powerful magic to get the goddesses to respond so out of character, especially Athena. However, no one really knows exactly how Eris created that conflict, only that she did. Even Zeus could not undo whatever spell she had cast, and there was no reasoning with the goddesses, so Zeus needed to find a way to resolve the issue.

"He could have chosen the fairest himself, but Zeus is nothing if not a politician, and the last thing he wanted was to alienate two of the goddesses unnecessarily. Keep in mind that one was his wife, one was among his favorite daughters, and one was in charge of a sphere of life he greatly valued, love—at least to judge by the number of goddesses and mortal women to whom he made love. No, Zeus couldn't afford to make the choice himself, and trying to force another god to choose would alienate that god. What the king of the gods needed was a mortal, and he knew just the one—Paris, my brother, though so unlike me that it was sometimes hard to believe we were kin.

"Shortly before Hecuba had given birth to Paris, she had a dream in which she saw herself giving birth to a flaming torch that burned down the whole city. She told Priam about it, and he consulted his seers, even though the meaning of the dream was obvious. They told him the son to whom Hecuba was about to give birth would be responsible for the city's destruction, and so Priam reluctantly ordered that he be exposed as soon as he was born."

"He would have done better to pray to the gods for deliverance," said Teiresias. "The will of the gods cannot be thwarted by human action."

"Well, it certainly wasn't in this case," said Hector. "Paris was left on Mount Ida, where some shepherds found him, one of whom raised Paris as his own son.

"Though Paris lived a simple life, it was a happy one. He grew into a very handsome man and won the love of Oenone, a nymph who became totally devoted to him. Together they had a son, Corythus, who grew up to as handsome as his father was.

"One day Priam decided to have games in honor of the son he had exposed—yes, I know, an odd choice, but Priam had never quite come to terms with having to abandon his son, and the games were perhaps his way of trying to find peace with his choice. In any case, he sent his men out to find a suitable prize, and they found and took a bull belong to Paris's father. When Paris questioned them, he learned about the games, and he decided to enter himself to win the bull back.

"It was a naive move, but the gods were with Paris that day, and he won every event, even though some of his brothers, who had received much more formal training, were also competing. At the end of the games, one of our brothers, Deiphobos, drew his sword against Paris, intending to challenge him. It was an unsportsmanlike act, but before Priam could intervene, Paris, who was unaccustomed to the ways of the royal court and of the city, fled to the altar of Zeus, where he took refuge.

"Our sister, Cassandra, who had the power of prophecy, revealed who Paris really was before the conflict with Deiphobos could go any further. Priam rejoiced at the news and acknowledged Paris as his son, ignoring the earlier prophecy of doom."

"There wasn't much else he could have done at that point," said Achilles. "Despite our society's cruel willingness to cast aside unwanted infants, it would never have tolerated a father murdering an adult son, prophecy or no prophecy."

"No, I don't blame our father for restoring Paris to his place within the family," said Hector. "Paris deserves much blame, though, for the way he handled the task Zeus set before him. Perhaps it was a test, for the gods are fond of testing us, and if so, he failed miserably.

"Mortals never fare well when they judge contests among the gods, and a wise man would have humbly pleaded inability to discern different degrees of beauty among the goddesses. A few Roman authors say Paris tried, but in fact, he embraced the task willingly enough, flattered to have been recognized as a fit judge for such a competition."

"Hubris," mumbled Teiresias.

"Artists love to portray that scene with the three goddesses naked, but that cannot have been what happened," said Hector. "Aphrodite might have been willing enough, but I doubt Hera would have been, and in any case, Zeus would have reduced any mortal who saw her naked to ashes with a thunderbolt, contest or no contest. As for Athena, the myths bear witness to the fact that she would never allow herself to be seen naked by a mortal."

"As I can certainly attest," said Teiresias, "for that sight was my last, accidental though it was."

"While Paris was judging the goddesses, each offered him a gift if he would select her."

"They tried to bribe him?" asked Mateo.

"The practice was actually fairly common among ancient people," said Hector. "However, if my theory is correct, and the contest was really a test of Paris, that part of the story makes much more sense. Had Paris chosen his gift more wisely, he could have become Troy's savior rather than its destroyer.

"Hera offered Paris all of Asia Minor as his kingdom, Athena offered to make him unbeatable in battle, and Aphrodite offered him the most beautiful woman in the world as his wife.

"If Paris had taken Hera's gift, he would have controlled a vast kingdom and could have protected Troy from any conceivable Greek attack. He could have done the same if he had taken Athena's gift, the ability to win every battle. Accepting either offer would have brought safety to Troy as well as glory to him.

"Instead, he chose the one totally selfish gift, the one that would bring ruin upon his city."

"Why would having a beautiful wife bring...oh, I see," said Yasmin.

"Yes," said Helen. "I was the most beautiful woman at that point—and I was already married, as Aphrodite must have known perfectly well. Not only that, but virtually every king in Greece was oath-bound to side with Menelaus in any kind of conflict."

"Which means Paris would have to have been a complete idiot to choose Aphrodite," said Hector. "The choice made war inevitable. Not only that, but it made Hera and Athena mortal enemies of Troy—an especially grave loss in the case of Athena, who had been Troy's patron ever since its founding. It did give us the support of Aphrodite—which we already had—but of what use would that be in a war? Very little!

"As if all of that were not enough, remember that Paris was already married himself. He cast aside his wife and the mother of his son for a woman he had never even seen, let alone known."

"He is not the first who could not resist Helen," said Theseus.

"Your case is different," said Hector. "You and she were both unmarried at the time, so there was no spouse to betray. Nor was any city except Sparta likely to care, so yes, Athens might have faced war because of your act, but at least not war with all of Greece. Besides, you had at least seen Helen. Paris was in love with the idea of Helen at that point, not with the actual woman."

"All the fault does not lie with Paris, though," said Helen. "He did not take me by force; I went with him willingly, abandoning my husband and making war unavoidable."

"Surely, you were bewitched by Aphrodite," suggested Agamemnon.

"I may have been," said Helen, "but I have always wondered if she could so easily have manipulated me if I had truly loved Menelaus. Though our society placed little importance on love as a requirement for marriage, if ours had been built on that foundation, it might have been stronger."

"There is no way to know," said Hector. "At least you weren't bombarded by prophecies predicting the destruction of Troy if you went with Paris. On the other hand, he ran into prophets everywhere he turned. His own wife had prophetic gifts, and she told him he would doom both Troy and himself if he stole Helen from Menelaus. Our sister Cassandra said much the same, as did our brother Helenus.

"Paris might have dismissed Oenone's prophecy as the words of a jealous woman—which in fact they were. As for Cassandra, she had gained her prophetic gift by promising to sleep with Apollo, a promise she then broke. Apollo could not take back his gift, but to it he added a curse that Cassandra would never be believed, so I can't fault Paris for not believing her. Helenus, however, was a different matter. Everyone knew he was a prophet, and he had neither curse nor obvious motive to lie, yet Paris ignored him completely. For that, there can be no excuse.

"Paris went to Sparta and became a guest of Menelaus, making his later theft of Helen also a violation of the host-guest relationship and thus an affront to Zeus, though the king of the gods made a point of not taking sides in the subsequent war when he could avoid it. I have no doubt he would have punished Paris if my brother had survived—"

The ground shook again, and a large chunk of rock barely missed crushing

Hector.

"The question now is whether any of us are going to survive," said Teiresias. "Keep going!"

Chapter 27: Heroes of the Trojan War, Part 2

"The next part perhaps is mine to tell," said Helen, surprisingly unruffled by the disintegration of Elysium all around her.

"I wish with all my heart that I had never loved Paris. To this day, I have no explanation—and certainly no excuse."

"The gods who wished the destruction of Troy would have found some other instrument if they had not been able to use you," said Hector, though his tone was more grim than reassuring.

"As one who was often manipulated by Hera, I'd have to agree," said Heracles. "There are times when humans are not truly responsible for what they do."

Helen sighed. "Often I have run through the same arguments in my head, but if the hand of any goddess was upon me, it was Aphrodite, and she wasn't trying to destroy Troy."

"That doesn't mean she didn't contribute unwittingly," said Hector.

"Regardless of that, I am a daughter of Zeus," said Helen. "I know Aphrodite didn't exert enough influence to crush my conscious mind completely, and I should have had enough willpower to resist what influence she did use. I knew betraying my husband with Paris would be wrong, and I knew it would inevitably lead to war, but I did it anyway. The truth is I had never really loved Menelaus, and at the moment of decision, I thought I did love Paris.

"Centuries later, Stesichorus invented that wild tale about the real me being left in Egypt while only a phantom traveled with Paris to Troy. How I long for that to be what happened, but my memories tell a different story.

"The weather did not favor us, some say because Hera was trying to stop us from reaching Troy, though I do not think that was her motive, for she wanted to see Troy devoured by flames. More likely, she was trying to delay us so that the Greek demand for my return would reach Priam before I had, and so his denial that I was in Troy would be taken as a lie by the Greeks.

"Whatever the reason may be, adverse winds forced us far off course and eventually compelled us to land in Egypt. From there we tried to journey back to Troy but were forced aground near Sidon in Phoenicia. By the time we finally reached Troy, the Greeks had already declared war, though it was to be a long time before the war actually began."

"When Helen fled with Paris, Menelaus had been in Crete for the funeral of Catreus, our maternal grandfather," said Agamemnon. He returned from Crete as quickly as he could, and we called upon all the former suitors who had sworn the oath to Tyndareus to join us in recovering Helen, but actually gathering them together was a long process.

"Menelaus, Nestor, and I had to travel all over Greece, and as Achilles has already told you, we had to hunt for him to ensure our victory. However, our biggest problem was Odysseus."

"To be fair, I had received an oracle that if I went to Troy, it would take me many years longer than anyone else to return, and my family would suffer much in my absence," said a tall, muscular Greek who had to be Odysseus. "I was not concerned for myself, but for the welfare of my wife and child."

"It is not my intent to criticize you," said Agamemnon, "but your pretense of madness did delay us. Yoking an ox and a horse to your plow and then sowing the field with salt made me question your sanity, but my cousin, Palamedes, who was with us, revealed the truth by putting your newborn son, Telemachus, in the way of the plow. When you stopped and rescued him, we knew you were sane."

"Ah, but if I had been as mad as I seemed, Palamedes would have been responsible for the death of my son," Odysseus pointed out.

Agamemnon looked uncomfortable. "One of us would have intervened before it was too late—surely you must know that."

"Of course," said Odysseus, but in a tone that suggested he wasn't fully convinced.

"In any case, once the kings had gathered all of their troops, we met at Aulis to sail to Troy—and our expedition nearly ended before it began.

"Artemis had borne a grudge against our family since the time of Atreus, for which I can hardly blame her, but she picked this particular moment to deny us a favorable wind. When we consulted an oracle, Artemis revealed the horrible condition under which she would allow us to sail: I had to sacrifice my daughter, Iphigenia.

"Excuse me for interrupting, but that doesn't sound like Artemis," said

Yasmin. "Didn't she normally protect young girls?"

"As it turned out, Artemis wasn't demanding a human sacrifice, as I should have known perfectly well," said Agamemnon. "Her goal was to stop us from sailing to Troy, and she assumed I would refuse to sacrifice my daughter, after which the army would be unable to sail.

"Unfortunately, I could see no other way to fulfill the oath I had sworn, and I feared the consequences of allowing Troy to get away with such a brazen attack on our rights. Hard as the decision was for me, at the time I believed the only way to uphold my honor was to do as Artemis had asked. I summoned Iphigenia from Mycenae on the pretense that she was going to be married to Achilles, and while she traveled to Aulis, I prepared for the sacrifice.

"When Achilles found out at the last minute what I was up to, he tried to save Iphigenia, and there was a good possibility that his anger might have obstructed the expedition just as effectively as the lack of wind did. Ironically, it was Iphigenia who saved the expedition by agreeing to be sacrificed for the common good. Her selflessness made me feel even worse about sacrificing her, but I still saw no other choice.

"Artemis, however, did see another choice. When I tried to proceed with the sacrifice, Artemis at the last minute substituted a lamb and whisked Iphigenia away to Tauris, where she became one of the goddess's priestesses.

"Unfortunately, most people didn't know of Artemis's last-minute mercy, and my wife, Clytemnestra, believing I had murdered our daughter, began to plot against me. The curses upon our family were awake once more, though I did not feel the weight of them until I returned from the war.

"The wind was with us then, but good fortune still didn't smile upon us. We stopped briefly on the island of Lemnos, and the archer Philoctetes, the owner of Heracles's bow, was confronted by a love-struck nymph, Chryse. I suspected the hand of Aphrodite in this, for when Philoctetes refused the nymph, she sent a snake to bite him. The creature had an unusual venom that created an unhealable wound. Machaon tried everything he could think and failed to cure poor Philoctetes. Not only would he be incapable of fighting, but his cries of pain and the vile stench of his wound were bound to distract the other warriors, so we had to leave him on Lemnos. That proved to be a mistake, though we didn't learn that until much later.

"However, the incidents with Iphigenia and Philoctetes shook the confidence of some Greek leaders. They had assumed that all the gods, except presumably Aphrodite, would be on their side, but it now seemed as if Olympus might be more evenly divided than anyone had expected. Menelaus offered to forgo any kind of vengeance if he could get Helen back, and so we sent ahead of us Menelaus and Odysseus with an offer of peace in exchange if only the Trojans would return Helen and the treasures stolen by Paris to Menelaus."

"As reasonable as that proposal was, I always had my doubts it would be accepted," said Odysseus. "Though Paris's violation of the laws of hospitality was a grievous one, Priam had seen most of his family slaughtered by Greeks when he was younger, and he also still resented the capture of Hesione, though she had been happy enough with Telamon and had no desire to return to Troy. Thus, the king was not eager to give any Greek satisfaction. However, he did not totally lack wisdom, so he took the unprecedented step of calling an assembly of all Trojans. He knew a war against the armed might of all Greece could be long and would definitely be unwinnable if the people were not behind him."

"After we presented our offer, Antenor, one of the Trojan nobles, spoke strongly on behalf of peace, pointing to the justice of our cause. His words would probably have swayed the assembly, but Antimachus countered them even more forcefully. Though we did not know it at the time, Antimachus had been richly bribed by Paris to promote Paris's cause in the assembly—and Paris got his money's worth. Antimachus stirred by so much anti-Greek sentiment that he very nearly persuaded the assembly, rapidly reduced to a mob, to kill us on the spot. Only Antenor's quick thinking and help enabled us to escape."

Odysseus shook his head sadly. "I'll not deny that violence may sometimes be unavoidable, but that day the entire war could have been averted. Antimachus let himself be twisted by silver—and paid for it in blood, for Agamemnon later killed Antimachus's only two sons on the battlefield. Antimachus had more than enough money to ransom them, but after what their father had done, the king of Mycenae refused to listen to their pleas."

"After that fiasco, we knew there was no prospect of peace any longer," said Agamemnon. "Even the most nervous among us steeled themselves for the inevitable war."

"The Trojans, forewarned of our approach, tried to prevent us from landing. Once again, the expedition was in danger of faltering, for by then we had received a prophecy that the first man who set foot on Trojan soil would die immediately. Brave as our warriors were, there is something about facing certain death that daunted even them."

"Not I," said Achilles. *Even Hades feels pity*

"No," agreed Agamemnon. "You were stopped by your own mother from setting foot on the shore, but it was well she did, for we needed you later.

"Protesilaus, a man who had married only a day before he had to leave with the army, made the sacrifice of jumping ashore. His act was so noble, and his situation so heart-rending, that even Hades was moved and honored his dying wish to be able to visit his wife, Laodameia, one last time. Alas, that led to more tragedy, for the poor woman, believing her husband had been returned to her, was heartbroken when Hermes took him back to the Underworld, so much so that she killed herself. *that's tragic*

"Once the brave Protesilaus had made the ultimate sacrifice, the Greek practically threw themselves from the ships, led by Achilles and his Myrmidons. However, they were almost turned back by Cycnus, a son of Poseidon whose skin couldn't be pierced by any weapons, just like that of Achilles.

"Now you can see how desperate our situation would have been if Achilles had been the one who offered his life before, for only Achilles could defeat Cycnus, who could wound anyone else too badly before they could do him any harm.

"Realizing that Cycnus was immune to the cutting edges of his weapons, Achilles tried to bludgeon him with the hilt of his sword. Cycnus, who could feel the blows, fell back. Achilles threw him to the ground and pushed on him a shield, managing finally to crack his ribs. That slowed Cycnus down enough for Achilles to strangle him with the man's own helmet strap. The Trojans, alarmed by the rapid death of one of their most powerful fighters, retreated as fast as they could to the safety of their high walls, a safety they seldom left for the next nine years."

"That almost sounds like an accusation of cowardice," said Hector, looking as if he itched to hit Agamemnon. *Still tension between Greeks and Trojans*

"I'm accusing you of common sense, not cowardice," said Agamemnon.

"We had the larger force at our disposal. It would have been madness to risk open combat in such circumstances, especially considering the strength of your walls and the size of your garrison. We Greeks could foresee victory only at the end of a long siege, and there was always the prospect that we would tire of the lengthy campaign and go home. Even if there wasn't a general withdrawal, we might have lost enough men to be beatable in the field.

"For nine years the siege dragged on. The Greek forces, unable to breach the walls of Troy, had to settle for campaigning against Troy's allies. We overcame a number of smaller cities in the area, cutting the Trojans off from vital food sources, for that was the one obvious weakness of the Trojan position—their food would eventually run out. All we had to do was make our patience last longer than the Trojan food, and they would be forced to meet us in open combat, where we felt they were sure to lose.

"It was during that period of time that I sealed my own doom," said Achilles, "though I did not know it at the time."

"Are you talking about the murder of Troilus?" asked Hector.

Achilles looked stricken. "You know better than that, though you may not have in life. I never intended any harm to your brother. Aphrodite manipulated me in hopes of getting me killed.

"You see," said Achilles to the students, "Troilus was treated by Priam as a much-loved son, but really he was Apollo's son by Hecuba, as you could probably tell if you saw him. He was the ideal handsome youth, the kind of model any artist would yearn to possess. He was also popular with everyone, in many ways Troy's favorite son. Many men, including Hector here, were far better warriors and much wiser men, but Troilus inspired Trojan morale more than anyone else. Wise men know that beauty by itself is nothing, but beauty, when joined to virtue and to youthful enthusiasm, is hard to resist.

"The gods were so involved in the war with Troy that the city was surrounded by a web of divine interventions as gods friendly to Troy tried to protect it, and those hostile to it tried to destroy it. As a result, the oracles had to work overtime to keep up with all the special conditions Greeks and Trojans needed to meet in order to win. You have already heard the fate of poor Protesilaus, but he was far from the last casualty of this divine manipulation.

"When I first heard the prophecy that Troy would never fall if Troilus lived until his twentieth birthday, my blood ran cold in my veins, for I knew the charming youth would have to die.

"For centuries writers have libeled both me and Troilus. Sophocles, eager to show how barbarous the Trojans were compared to Greeks, wrote that Troilus had an unnatural passion for his sister, Polyxena, and it was that failing that caused his death. Later Roman writers, who believed their society was founded by Trojans, wrote that I loved Troilus and killed him for rejecting me. Lies, all lies—though the truth was in some ways just as horrible, and certainly as painful. *Many Misconceptions*

"Aphrodite needed more allies if her cause was to prevail. She had Artemis because of that goddess's dislike of the house of Atreus, and she knew she could probably win Ares to her side without much trouble, but she needed more, and Apollo would make a fine recruit. That Troilus would be killed by some Greek was certain, but Aphrodite did her best to manipulate circumstances so that I would be the one to kill Troilus, knowing that if I did that, Apollo might kill me and rob the Greeks of victory in the process.

"Killing Troilus was about the last thing I wanted to do, but Aphrodite kindled in my heart a love for Polyxena. It was one of the stupidest emotions I had ever felt. Quite aside from the fact that I had promised to return to Deidamia, there seemed little prospect that Polyxena and I could ever be together. Even if the Trojans won the war or at least managed to achieve a stalemate with the Greeks, was Priam likely to allow a Greek to wed one of his daughters after so many years of war? Hardly. Yet my chances were even worse if the Greeks won, which would almost certainly mean that all the men of Polyxena's family would have been killed by me or some other Greek. Polyxena herself would be given away as a prize of war, and I likely could have possessed her that way, but, smeared with the blood of her family, I could never have won her love.

"Despite the siege, Trojans still sneaked out at times to try to find supplies or to pray in the temple of Apollo, which was regarded as neutral territory. It is said I planned an ambush for Troilus, but what I was really doing was trying to find an opportunity to speak to Polyxena. It was my ill fortune—and his—that he happened to be with her when I found her.

"They were on horseback, and as soon as they saw me, they fled toward the temple of Apollo. They had actually been closer to Troy than to the temple, and if they had only fled back home, they would have been safe.

"I still didn't want to be the one who killed Troilus, and if I had just broken off pursuit, I might have avoided that fate, but I had such an aching longing for Polyxena that I pursued as rapidly as I could.

Even now I can't tell you how I expected this situation to work out well. I think I had some insane notion that Troilus would flee back out once I entered the temple, leaving me to have the meeting with Polyxena that I wanted.

"I reckoned without the youth's virtue. When I entered the temple, he attacked me to defend his sister. He fought with such ferocity I was surprised, but there was really no way he could have harmed me. Still, I knew the war might never end if he lived, and there he was, blocking my path to his sister.

"In what was one of the worst mistakes of my life, I killed him right there in the temple of Apollo. I killed a boy perhaps younger than some of you. Priam ever after called me boy-slayer, and he was right.

"I took Polyxena prisoner, promising she would not be harmed, though, covered in her brother's blood as I was, I doubt she could have found me very reassuring. She looked at me with undisguised hatred, and a little of me died that day along with Troilus.

"Since Troilus had not lived to the age of twenty, his life could not act as a charm to protect Troy, but Aphrodite got what she wanted. Apollo, reluctantly pulled onto the Trojan side by Artemis despite the shabby treatment he had received a generation earlier from Laomedon, now became determined to give the Trojans victory and even more determined to kill me."

"Apollo's support for Troy came at a bad time," said Agamemnon, "for we Greeks had done everything we could to weaken Troy by attacking its allies, but the city was nowhere near surrendering, and Greek morale was shaky at best. Achilles had already persuaded the men to not leave once as it was, and the Troilus incident had done nothing to improve morale, for many realized that Apollo was likely to take the field against us.

"At that very moment, my judgment failed me. We had captured the beautiful Chryseis in one of our raids, and she had been assigned to me as part of my portion of the spoils. When Chryses, priest of Apollo and father of Chryseis, came to offer a ransom for her, I sent him away rudely instead of honoring his request.

"This was a perfect opportunity for Apollo to act, and he began shooting arrows into our camp that brought plague down upon us. It would not take such a tactic long to break the Greek resolve.

"Fortunately, Calchas, our seer, told us we could stop the plague if we returned Chryseis. I grudgingly agreed, but then I found another way to make the situation worse by demanding Briseis, a woman who had been assigned to Achilles, as part of his share.

"In some ways, I erred worse than I had with Iphigenia. Then at least I was making a decision I thought was for the common good. Now I was just satisfying my own ego, abusing my powers as the leader of the Greek forces in the process." *Blaming himself again*

"I could have reacted better to it," said Achilles.

"Yes, but you were young and far less experienced than I," replied Agamemnon. "I put you in a difficult position when there was no need to."

"And I responded in the worst way possible," said Achilles. "As the only Greek leader not oath-bound to help recover Helen, I could withdraw—and I did so, taking my Myrmidons with me. Though I didn't leave right away, as long as I was not willing to fight, I put every Greek at greater risk, for the Trojans would be much more tempted to attack. Not only that, but I prayed to Thetis, my mother, to ask Zeus to ensure that the Greeks lost the next battle as a punishment for Agamemnon's disrespect to me. In doing so, I dishonored myself more than he ever could have.

"It was not long before your prayer was answered," said Hermes. "Zeus, who, behind his facade of neutrality, favored Troy, seized on Thetis's request as a possible way to save the city. To Agamemnon he sent a lying dream in the shape of Nestor, the counselor to whom Agamemnon paid the most attention. The dream told Agamemnon that Hera had won over all the other gods to the Greek cause and that he could now take Troy by direct assault. Believing the dream, Agamemnon woke and prepared for a battle he could not win."

"However, nothing in life is ever simple," said Agamemnon. "Just as Zeus lied to me, so I lied to the men to test their resolve, having first told the other kings my plan. I told the soldiers Zeus had ordered us back to our homelands, leaving Troy undefeated and free to keep Helen.

"To my horror and the horror of the other kings as well, the men neither protested nor questioned, but headed to ships to embark at once."

"Does that really prove lack of resolve?" asked Thanos. "You had just told them Zeus wanted a retreat. Would you have expected them to defy Zeus?"

"I would have expected them to question my words rather than blindly obeying them," said Agamemnon. "Instead, they showed how eager they were to flee back home. If Athena had not inspired Odysseus to get the men back long enough for them to hear the truth and then rallied them behind it, the war would have ended then and there."

"Perhaps it would be better if it had," said Hector.

"But not in such a way," said Agamemnon. "Would not Troy have felt empowered to see us skulk away, disgraced? Would not your city have been tempted to a war of conquest against us by such a display?"

"It might have been better to have saved the lives of all the men lost at the end of the war," said Teiresias. "However, destiny itself would have been undone, and many events that flowed from the fall of Troy, including the founding of Rome, would never have come to pass. I shudder to think of how so many changes might have unsettled the world."

"The world would have been different," agreed Helen, "but perhaps it would also have been better. Not for me, for I had already come to regret my decision to go with Paris, but perhaps for the men whose lives could have been spared."

"Those lives would have been spared anyway, if only the gods had left us alone," said Agamemnon. "That very day as we and the Trojans readied for battle, Paris offered to meet a warrior of our choice in single combat to settle the issue. Menelaus took up the challenge, Priam and I swore oaths to respect the outcome, and it looked as if, one way or the other, the war would end that day.

"Menelaus, clearly the better warrior, wounded Paris with his first spear toss and would have finished him with his sword, had not some freak accident caused it to shatter. Undeterred, Menelaus grabbed Paris by the helmet, intending to end the battle swiftly.

"Calchas told me later that was when Aphrodite interfered, first breaking the chin strap of Paris's helmet so that it came loose, then concealing Paris in a mist and spiriting him back to his own bedroom in Troy.

"At that point, I declared Menelaus the winner and demanded not only Helen and the stolen treasure, but also the tribute Priam had agreed to if Paris lost. The rules had not specified that the loser must die, and in any case, Paris had forfeited by leaving the field."

"Aphrodite carried him away," said Yasmin.

"He didn't come back," Agamemnon pointed out.

"No, and he didn't acknowledge defeat, either," said Helen. "I know because Aphrodite came to take me to him. I would have refused, for by now I hated him as much as I had once loved him, but Aphrodite told me if I did such a thing she would make the Trojans and Greeks universally hate me. I took that for the death threat it was and went back to Paris, though I took no pleasure in it."

"Zeus might have saved Troy then," said Hermes. "He wanted to get Priam to accept Agamemnon's ruling on the trial-by-combat, but Hera demanded that Troy be destroyed, going so far in her fury as to say she would not oppose Zeus if he destroyed all three of her favorite cities, Mycenae, Argos, and Sparta. The king of the gods yielded in the interest of harmony, and Athena in disguise then tempted Pandarus the Trojan to foolishly try to shoot Menelaus. The goddess steered the arrow so that the wound was not fatal, but the truce was broken, and the war resumed.

"The two sides clashed with the gods still interfering at every turn—micromanaging, I think you would call it. First Ares rallied the Trojans while Athena inspired the Greeks. When the Trojan lines nearly broke, and even Hector looked as if he might give way, Apollo did his best to rally them.

"Athena, realizing that the Greeks' greater numbers would allow them to prevail if only the other gods would stop interfering, agreed to withdraw from the field if Ares would as well. Ares, content to watch as long as there was enough bloodshed, agreed. However, before Athena left the action, she placed a great blessing upon Diomedes, who became practically unstoppable until he was wounded.

"Then Diomedes prayed to Athena for help, and she somehow managed to slip away from Ares. She gave the hero even greater agility, and she filled him with bloodlust to make him stronger. Even more, she cleared his eyes so he could see the gods upon the field, but she also gave him a dire warning: he must not oppose any god in battle except Aphrodite.

"Made even more powerful by Athena, Diomedes mowed down any Trojan who came within his reach, fighting so fiercely some of the Trojans became convinced he was a god in disguise. In the ensuing chaos, the hero cornered Aeneas and would have killed him, but Aphrodite intervened to save her son, taking him in her arms and folding her immortal cloak about him.

"Thanks to Athena, Diomedes could see Aphrodite, and he thrust at her with his spear. Athena guided the stroke, and he wounded the love goddess in the hand. She, unaccustomed to such treatment from a mortal—or anyone else—screamed and might have been overpowered, but Apollo swooped down to rescue Aeneas.

"It was then that Diomedes made a costly error by disregarding Athena's advice. As Apollo tried to leave the battlefield with Aeneas, Diomedes three times tried to attack the Trojan prince. On the fourth try, Apollo shouted at the Greek hero to desist, and Diomedes did so, but the damage was done."

"Did Apollo kill him?" asked Mateo.

"No, for the god was more concerned at that point with getting Aeneas to safety. Much later, though, after the war was over, Aphrodite was permitted by Zeus, despite Athena's protests, to make Diomedes's wife unfaithful to him—epically unfaithful, with many lovers. Even more treacherously, she turned Argos against him, forcing him to relinquish the throne and flee into exile. Athena helped him to win a new kingdom in Italy and to found many cities, so in the end his life was not destroyed, though it did take him many years to recover what he had lost. That is the best fate that someone who disregards the commands of the gods could possibly expect.

"As Apollo was carrying Aeneas back to Troy, he called out to Ares, inciting him to avenge Aphrodite on the field of battle, something the war god was perfectly happy to do. Not only that, but Apollo created a phantom double of Aeneas so that the Trojans would rally in an attempt to rescue him.

"Ares had little trouble raising Trojan morale, and standing by Hector's side, he had no difficulty turning the tide of battle. Diomedes, seeing the war god, urged the Greeks to retreat, this time being wise enough to avoid another confrontation with a god.

"Hera, furious that Ares would so disrupt her plans, came down to the battlefield in person, took the form of Stentor, the bellowing herald, and rallied the Greeks as best she could. At the same time, Athena, carefully getting Zeus's permission to deal with Ares, went to Diomedes and told him he could strike the war god—or any other god who interfered—as long as she was with him.

"Athena then climbed into the chariot with Diomedes and put on the helm of darkness, so she would be invisible even to Ares. Then, when Ares saw Diomedes and charged, not only did Athena deflect Ares's spear toss, but she guided Diomedes's hand as he wounded Ares in the stomach.

"The war god screamed so loudly that he terrified both armies, then fled to Olympus to complain to Zeus, who, thanks in part to Athena's good planning, refused to take his side.

"At this point the gods retired from the field for a while, and the mortals battled back and forth, Diomedes doing the best on the Greek side and Hector on the Trojan.

"However, the gods could not keep out of the struggle for long. Apollo, wanting to give the Trojans some rest, proposed to Athena that they arrange a truce, to be followed by another single combat.

"Why Athena would have agreed, even I cannot tell you, for Hector would obviously be the Trojan champion this time, and the one Greek who could hope to beat Hector without divine intervention was Achilles, still nursing his wounded pride in his tent. Nonetheless, Athena did agree, and Helenus, the Trojan prophet, conveyed the news to Hector.

"The Greeks at first were afraid to take up the challenge. The frustrated Menelaus accepted it, though Agamemnon quickly talked him out of it. Even Menelaus had to agree that, though he could easily beat Paris, he was no match for Hector.

"Eventually, Nestor shamed nine of the Greeks into volunteering, including Agamemnon himself, Diomedes, Ajax, and Odysseus. The lots chose mighty Ajax, larger and brawnier than most, though not the special favorite of a god as Diomedes was of Athena. Next to Achilles, he was the strongest warrior the Greeks had when fighting on his own, so perhaps fortune blessed the Greeks by choosing him.

"Ajax proved himself well in battle. Hector could not pierce his mighty shield, but he pierced Hector's, and his cuirass too, wounding the Trojan prince and knocking him to the ground. Apollo had to lift him up so that Ajax could not claim the victory, and then the two warriors battled, more or less evenly, until sunset forced them to call a halt. In contrast to the earlier fight between Paris and Menelaus, this time the two men parted friends, and had their spirit infected their respective ranks, a peaceful solution might have been found.

"Indeed, Ajax's might had awakened enough fear in the Trojans that Antenor tried again to bring peace, suggesting the Trojans offer the return of Helen and the treasure. The selfish Paris managed to convince the assembled Trojans to offer only the return of the treasure, an offer the Greeks firmly rejected. They then set about building a wall and moat in front of the ships, just in case the Trojans should try to attack.

"The next day Zeus ordered all gods to stay out of the battle, on pain of being cast into Tartarus, though Athena did extract the concession that from time to time the gods might give a little advice. She worried that Zeus intended to aid the Trojans—and she had reason to fear that, for it was exactly what Zeus had planned.

"Around midday, Zeus flashed his lighting in the face of the Greeks, terrifying them and sending them fleeing. Nestor alone stood his ground, and he would have died if Diomedes had not turned back in time to rescue him. Still, the Greeks did not cover themselves with glory that day.

"Hector led the Trojan charge, attacking the Greek wall and coming close to being able to burn the ships. He would have succeeded had not Hera heartened the Greeks and given Agamemnon time to pray to Zeus, who took pity on him and gave the Greeks enough inspiration to keep their army from being destroyed and their ships unburnt.

"Even with a little respite from Zeus, the Greeks were still doing far worse than the Trojans. Nor did Zeus complain when Apollo, in defiance of Zeus's edict, redirected an arrow that would have wounded Hector and possibly given the Greeks a better chance.

"Enraged by this turn of events, Hera and Athena both tried to take the field, but Zeus angrily sent them away, later telling them that the Trojans would keep winning until Agamemnon made appropriate apologies to Achilles."

"I did not have that knowledge of the conversations among the gods," said

Agamemnon, "but I would have to have been an even bigger fool than I was not to realize that Zeus was aiding the Trojans and that my own stupid pride was the cause. I called the Greek leaders and told them what I intended to offer Achilles as an apology: a large treasure; seven beautiful captive women from Lesbos; the return of Briseis; if the gods gave us victory, a bigger share of the Trojan treasure than he would otherwise have gotten, including twenty Trojan women; and marriage to one of my daughters without any need to pay a bride price and with a rich dowry, seven cities, all of them prosperous. When the other leaders agreed that this offer was more than fair, I sent Phoenix, who had tutored Odysseus when he was young, along with Odysseus and Ajax, to ask Achilles to put aside his anger."

"If only I had accepted that offer!" said Achilles. "How many Greek lives could I have saved? How much grief could I have spared others—and myself? Alas, I didn't, even though all three envoys argued most eloquently for me to make peace with you, Agamemnon. Instead, I placed my pride above all else, and the discord among us continued."

"But didn't you know you would die if you stayed at Troy?" asked Mateo. "Most guys would take that as reason enough to leave."

"My mother made almost exactly that argument," said Achilles. "However, I had already chosen the short and glorious life over the long and uneventful one. Though I told the envoys I would just go home to Phthia, in truth I had no desire to do so. I was nursing my wounded ego, not trying to save my life."

"The past is the past," said Odysseus. "You were not the only one who erred in those long ten years of war, and no amount of brooding over what you did will ever undo it.

"We Greeks were not idle. Though Agamemnon was much disturbed by the failure of our embassy, he decided to send Diomedes and me to scout the Trojan camp, for instead of returning to the city, they had camped on the plain before us, probably to keep us from regaining the ground we had lost in the day's wretched battle.

"We might not have found much out, except that we spotted the Trojan spy, Dolon, trying to scout our camp. He was disguised in animal hides and walking on all fours, but through the inspiration of Athena, we saw him and managed to catch him before he could run back to the Trojans.

"Dolon had one valuable piece of information: Rhesus of Thrace, the son of the muse Calliope and the river god Strymon, had recently arrived and posed a great danger to the Greeks. Troy's allies had blocked us from a quick victory already, and the last thing we needed was another god-born champion to fight against us.

"It might seem ridiculous to attempt a sneak attack on a king, presumably well-guarded and housed in the middle of the enemy camp, but we were a little desperate, and both of us had the favor of Athena, who I have to think was looking after us that night. Having also heard of Rhesus's arrival, wearing golden armor and riding a chariot of gold and silver drawn by horses whiter than snow, we had reason to suspect him of hubris, and if we were right, the gods would be looking for an opportunity to punish him."

"Though he would have been a valuable ally, I cannot argue about the hubris," said Hector. "As soon as he arrived, he announced he would defeat the Greek army the following day with only the help of his own Thracians. Coming from an ally who took nine years to show up, his words did not sit well with the Trojans."

"Odd that we should have become the instrument the gods used to vindicate Troy's pride," said Odysseus. "After killing Dolon, we used the details he had provided to find Rhesus's tent, where we killed the king and the twelve men with him. There should have been guards, but they and Rhesus's whole party were deep in sleep. Then we managed to smuggle those whiter-than-snow horses out of the Trojan camp and back to our own, bringing the Greeks a much-needed morale boost.

"At first, the following day's battle went well for us, but that good fortune did not stay with us long."

"Zeus had plans," said Hermes. "He had told Hector not to join the battle until Agamemnon was driven from the field. Not long after the king of Mycenae was wounded badly enough that he had to fall back, and when Hector took the field, Zeus ensured that the tide of battle would shift in favor of the Trojans."

"So I have heard since coming to Elysium," said Odysseus. "Once Hector was back in action, we suffered heavy casualties, and Diomedes and I were both badly wounded in the most embarrassing way possible. Diomedes took an arrow shot from the unmanly Paris, and I was so surrounded by Trojans that Menelaus and Ajax had to rescue me. The valiant Ajax then almost succeeding in countering the Trojans—until Zeus filled him with fear and caused him to retreat.

"When the Trojans had driven us all the way back to our wall, they dismounted because of the moat and attacked us on foot."

"Though I pretended to be uninterested in the outcome of the fight, I was watching from my ship," said Achilles. "Seeing Nestor return to camp with the wounded Machaon, I sent my cousin Patroclus to find out what was happening. My resolve to stay out of the battle was weakening, but stubborn pride still blocked my immediate return."

"Zeus encouraged his son, Sarpedon, to lead the Lycians in a charge against the Greek wall, but the Greeks, led by a somewhat recovered Ajax, succeeded in holding the line—barely," said Hermes.

"While Ajax was occupied with Sarpedon, Hector prepared for an attack on one of the other gates, which he succeeded in smashing through," said Agamemnon. "The Greeks came closer to losing at that point than they ever had before."

"Troy would have won but for a momentary distraction of Zeus," said Hermes. "Confident in the Trojan victory, the king of gods turned his eyes to Thrace and other nearby lands. That gave Poseidon a brief opening, and he took it. The lord of the sea inspired Ajax, as well as his namesake, the son of Oileus, to great heights of valor and helped other Greeks as well. With his help the Greeks avoided immediate defeat, though Poseidon did not interfere enough to rout the Trojans, for fear of the wrath of Zeus."

"I thought that was a good moment to prepare the ships and flee from the Trojan shore," said Agamemnon. "Odysseus pointed out that the Trojans could conceivably kill us all while we tried to ready the ships, and I bowed to his wisdom. Wounded as we were, Diomedes, Odysseus, and I all reentered the fight."

"Meanwhile, Hera tricked Aphrodite into helping her become even more desirable to Zeus," said Hermes. "Then the queen of gods occupied her husband in lovemaking while Poseidon rallied the Greeks with a great war cry and helped them drive back the Trojans. Ajax even wounded Hector, though not decisively, and the Trojans were still able to retire in good order.

"Unfortunately for the Greeks, Zeus, who had been sleeping in Hera's arms, awoke and realized how his wife had been manipulating him. He rebuked her, quickly ordered Poseidon to leave the battlefield, and sent Apollo to revive Hector and encourage the Trojans, who surged forward again under the god's guidance. At that point Patroclus, who had been helping treat the wounded, raced back to Achilles to tell him what was happening. By the time he reached Achilles, the Trojans had fought their way back through the wall and gotten close enough to the ships to start burning them."

"The kind-hearted Patroclus, now in tears, begged me to let him wear my armor and lead the Myrmidons into battle before it was too late," said Achilles. "I should mention that Patroclus was more than a cousin to me. My father had raised both of us, and I loved him as I would have loved a brother. I could not bring myself to say no to his request, though I cautioned him to be content with saving the ships and not try to pursue the Trojans back across the plain toward the city. If only he had followed my advice!"

"Patroclus and the Myrmidons came to our aid just in time," said Agamemnon, "for the Trojans had already begun to burn our ships. However, believing Patroclus was Achilles, the Trojans fell back in alarm. Patroclus drove them back beyond our walls, and we were able to save the ships."

"However, brave Sarpedon challenged Patroclus," said Hermes. "The moment was bitter for Zeus, for Sarpedon was destined to die. Zeus actually hesitated, wondering if he should find a way to save Sarpedon. With Hera's help, he realized that he should not defy fate, and so Patroclus killed Sarpedon."

"It is true the gods could defy fate if they wished," said Teiresias. "Zeus could easily have thwarted destiny in this case—but if he had, anarchy would almost certainly have resulted. The king of the gods let his own son die rather than threaten the stability of the universe."

"Unfortunately, it was the death of Sarpedon that got Patroclus carried away," said Achilles. "Instead of following my advice and fighting defensively, he started chasing the Trojans, maybe thinking he could bring down Hector and end the war himself."

"Perhaps he might even have succeeded, but Apollo saw what was happening and intervened," said Hermes. "Moving invisibly up behind Patroclus, Apollo struck him hard enough to stun him, then caused the poor man's armor to fall to the ground. Euphorbus, a reincarnation of my own son, Aethalides, speared Patroclus between the shoulder blades. After that it was easy for Hector to finish him, though with his dying breath Patroclus ridiculed him and predicted his own death.

"Shocked by the fall of Achilles's dear friend, the Greeks did what they could to save his body so that it could be properly buried," said Agamemnon. "Menelaus sent Euphorbus on to his next reincarnation—Pythagoras, or so I've heard, anyway—but then the Spartan king was driven back by Hector and other Trojans. The Trojan prince seized Achilles's armor and put it on, but Menelaus, this time with Ajax, made a valiant effort to grab the body. The fight raged back and forth, with Athena helping the Greeks and Apollo the Trojans, but in the end the Greeks safely carried the body away. Nor did the Trojans capture the immortal horses of Achilles, who overcame their grief over Patroclus in time to get away from Hector and Aeneas.

"When I heard of the death of Patroclus, I cried out so loudly that my mother heard me beneath the sea," said Achilles. "She and other Nereids joined me in mourning, but my mother mourned for me as well as Patroclus, because she now knew I would return to the fight and make my own death inevitable. I knew it as well, but I didn't care at all. Patroclus had died for my folly. Nothing else mattered except avenging him. Death was all I deserved, anyway.

"My mother made me wait a day so that she could bring new armor from Hephaestus. I had no sooner agreed, however, than the Trojans made another attempt to seize poor Patroclus's body. I stepped outside and gave my war cry, which shook the Trojans. To make sure they got the message, Athena caused a flame to hover above my head, and the ominous sign threw the Trojans into confusion, after which all of them, even Hector, were eager enough to withdraw. They might have retreated back inside the walls, but Hector, struck momentarily by hubris, ignored all the signs and believed he could beat the Greeks, even led by me, in open combat.

"What he didn't know was that Zeus's interventions on the Trojan side were almost at an end," said Hermes. "He had been helping the Trojans partly to please Thetis, who now wanted exactly the opposite. Hector also underestimated the strength of Achilles's wrath, never having seen it. He was to find out all too soon how powerful a force Achilles could be when angered."

"My one regret was that I couldn't fight immediately," said Achilles. "Even after my mother brought my new armor, there were hateful delays. I was content to renounce my anger at Agamemnon, but he wanted to give me all the gifts he had promised. I cared nothing for that anymore, and particularly not for Briseis. I cared only to avenge Patroclus as I had sworn to do."

"That you did," said Odysseus. "I had to remind you that the men needed to eat before fighting the Trojans, but you refused food or drink until you had avenged your friend."

"Had not Zeus allowed Thetis to give you nectar and ambrosia, I fear you might have collapsed from hunger," said Hermes. "About that he may have had second thoughts, though, for before the battle began he summoned all the gods, even the lowliest nymph, to Olympus and rescinded his earlier ban on divine intervention. Indeed, though he said he would stay on Olympus this time, he encouraged gods to take what side they pleased. That seemed a very neutral gesture, but from what Zeus said I gathered he was a little afraid you would crush the Trojans single-handedly and perhaps hoped other gods would restrain you.

"As you might have expected, Poseidon, Athena, and Hera went at once to join the Greeks, joined this time by Hephaestus, no doubt irked by Aphrodite's part in the war, and even by me. Most of us had children in the war, and some had children on both sides, but with Euphorbus gone, I felt the closest tie to Odysseus. Besides that, I felt justice was on the Greek side.

"The Trojans, as you might imagine, were not without their allies, though. Apollo, this time joined by Artemis and Leto, let his obsession with the death of Troilus cloud his usually firm commitment to justice. Aphrodite naturally still fought on the Trojan side, and Ares, never the most rational of the gods, fought for Troy as well, even though his much-loved son, Ascalaphus, had been slain by a Trojan. Rounding out their number was the river god Xanthus, tired of the Greeks clogging his channel with Trojan corpses.

"I began to doubt Zeus's wisdom, for instead of working mostly through mortals, as in previous battles, the gods quickly took arms against each other. Athena challenged Ares, and each shouted a war cry that shook the field;

Poseidon, who shook the earth so much he frightened even Hades, faced the determined Apollo; Artemis resolved to test her arrows against Queen Hera; as for me, I squared off against gentle Leto, who on this day fought in support of her children. I did so with misgivings, for gods should not fight gods in such a way. *If he didn't, would fate be changed?*

"Fortunately, we gods became fascinated with what the mortals were doing and refrained from attacking each other just yet. That was a good thing because Achilles nearly killed Aeneas, who unwisely faced the Greek champion. The Trojan prince was not fated to die that day; in fact, a crucial destiny awaited him, so Poseidon, even though he was on the Greek side, whisked Aeneas out of harm's way. Apollo did the same with Hector, though the god knew he could not save that Trojan prince forever. Without the Trojans' strongest fighter interfering, Achilles was able to slaughter one Trojan after another.

"Achilles did nearly meet his match when Xanthus turned on him. The hero had once again filled the river with corpses, one of which was the river god's own son. However, Hephaestus intervened, and with his fire he drove back the angry river, nearly turning him to steam in the process.

"As the gods clashed with each other, their successes and failures anticipated the outcome of the war. Ares made the mistake of challenging Athena, who hurled a boulder at him that hit his neck and injured him badly. As Aphrodite helped him from the field, Athena struck her down as well, for neither war nor love could save the Trojans now.

"Poseidon would have clashed with Apollo, who wisely declined to fight him, but Artemis mocked Apollo for what she supposed was his cowardice. Enraged at this abuse, Hera grabbed Artemis's own quiver and boxed her ears with it. Surprised by such an assault, Artemis, who would normally have fought back against any attack, instead went crying up to Zeus—the first and last time I ever saw her do such a thing.

"Leto would have faced me, but I declined to fight her, partly because I felt it unseemly, partly because I had just been reminded of how powerful an elder goddess such as Hera might be and had no desire to be beaten by a woman, and partly because I could count.

"Xanthus had lost to Hephaestus; Ares and Aphrodite had lost to Athena; Apollo had conceded to Poseidon. Whatever would have happened in a battle

Women are actually strong. Must have made him mad

between Leto and me, the gods supporting Troy had lost or conceded every other fight. Unless Zeus again chose to intervene, the Trojans were finished. In any case, all Leto did after I conceded was to gather up her daughter's bow and arrows and follow her up to Olympus.

"By this point most of the gods had realized the folly of fighting each other, and they retired to Olympus in triumph or defeat. Apollo stayed long enough to help the Trojans get back behind their walls before Achilles could kill them all, but Hector stayed behind, determined to fight Achilles after Apollo had twice before prevented him.

"The truth was that Hector's fated hour of death was almost upon him, and this time Apollo did not try the kind of trickery he had used to save Admetus. Too many other gods had lost children or favorites of theirs for them to tolerate such interference with fate.

"When Hector saw Achilles approaching, his resolve to fight the Greek champion faltered, and he ran. Zeus considered saving him, but Athena successfully persuaded her father not to interfere and even to allow her to aid Achilles.

"Knowing that if Hector kept running, he might eventually decide to run behind the Trojan walls, Athena made herself look like his brother, Deiphobos, and convinced him to stand and face Achilles.

"Hector was a great warrior, but without divine support, he was no match for Achilles, who was finally able to avenge Patroclus."

"It was pure hubris for me to ever think otherwise," Hector admitted.

"We were more evenly matched than most people think," said Achilles. "At the time, my rage over the death of Patroclus would never have allowed me to acknowledge the fact. Nor did it allow me to behave honorably after your death, for I dragged your body behind my chariot all the way back to the Greek camp and pledged never to release it for burial, an affront not only to the Trojans but to the gods.

"I was finally able to bury Patroclus, and the Greek troops held funeral games in his honor, though I did not participate, for my heart was still heavy from his loss."

"The gods do not favor carrying on mortal feuds after death," said Hermes, "and even the ones who hated the Trojans disliked Achilles's refusal to allow Hector to be buried.

"While Apollo preserved the body from Achilles's abuse, Zeus sent down Thetis to let Achilles know how displeased the gods were, and Achilles, to his credit, relented at that point. Zeus sent Iris to tell Priam he should go ask Achilles for the body in person, and he sent me, disguised as one of Achilles's men, to guide Priam to Achilles and ensure that no harm befell the king of Troy while he visited the Greek camp under the protection of a truce.

"It was wise of Zeus to send Priam himself," said Achilles. "He reminded me of my own father, and he dispelled my last resistance to returning the body for burial. Had we not met, I fear I might have been unable to go through with the surrender of the body, and in so doing brought the wrath of the gods upon the Greeks.

"One might have expected that Trojan morale would have collapsed after Hector's death, but the Trojans received aid from unexpected foreign allies, the first of which was Penthesilea, daughter of Ares and Amazon queen, who arrived with a large group of warriors to earn glory in battle. *didnt like batth*

"Once I too sought glory, but by now that desire was dead in me. I fought because I had to, not because I wanted to. Despite that, my desire to see Troy fall kept me going, and I was able to defeat Penthesilea, though she had fought so bravely her death gave me no pleasure. If anything, it only deepened my grief—but worse trials were yet to come.

"An even greater force than Penthesilea commanded was led to the aid of Troy by Memnon, king of the Aethiopians, son of the dawn goddess Eos and Tithonus. Earlier, Memnon had led some of his people to colonize an area near Persia, and from that faraway land he brought an army that might under other circumstances have turned the tide in the Trojans' favor.

"Instead of emerging victorious, Memnon doomed himself, though unlike so many men, not by some act of hubris, but by accident.

"Memnon was a great warrior, perhaps even my equal, and many Greeks lost their lives at his hands. Still distracted by grief, I might have fallen to his sword as well, but by providing me with fresh grief, he roused me to one last great battle.

"Memnon almost caught Nestor when one of his chariot horses had been shot by Paris. Antilochus, Nestor's son and my closest friend now that Patroclus was gone, died saving his father. When I realized I had lost another friend, I made short work of Memnon. His choice of battles sealed his fate. His men fought on bravely after he fell, but to no avail.

"By that time, the Trojans were weary from ten years of war, had no more allies on whom to call, and had lost so many men in battle that they began to realize the end was near. I wanted to bring that end about as a final tribute to Patroclus and Antilochus, but instead I brought about my own.

"Leading the charge against Troy that day, I nearly forced my way into the city as the Trojans tried to retreat through the gate. It was exactly that kind of moment for which Apollo had been waiting. The god still remembered Troilus, and more recently the death of Hector gave the divine archer one more reason to hate me. He guided Paris's hand as the Trojan prince shot a poisoned arrow into my vulnerable heel, and after that my death came quickly.

"The Trojans rejoiced and tried to seize both Achilles's body and his god-forged armor," said Odysseus. "We could not allow that, and so Ajax carried the body back to camp while I fought against the Trojans to keep them from following. *very honored among Greeks*

"We mourned Achilles for seventeen days, and both the Nereids and the Muses joined us in our dirges. Acting on our fallen hero's earlier instructions, after his body had been burned on a funeral pyre, we mixed his ashes with those of Patroclus in an urn fashioned by Hephaestus.

"Well we might have mourned for our faded hopes of victory, for at that moment we could not see how to win without Achilles. Another loss was to befall us very soon—and in that loss I played an unfortunate role.

"Thetis wished that the weapons and armor of Achilles should go to the worthiest warrior on the Greek side. I don't remember exactly how, but it was decided that Athena and the Trojan captives should make the choice."

"Why the Trojan captives?" asked Mateo. "Why not the Greek leaders? That seems as if it would have made more sense."

"And so it would have," said Odysseus, "but the fear was that having the Greeks vote might create discord in the ranks. Even if such a vote did not pit Greek against Greek, it might be unfairly influenced by old rivalries and quarrels."

"The Trojan captives wouldn't be impartial, though," said Keisha.

"Exactly!" said Odysseus. "The theory was that they would vote for the warrior whom they most feared in combat, but what reason did they have to be honest? They could just as easily vote for an inferior warrior out of spite.

"Only two of us decided to compete for the prize, Ajax and I. Diomedes would have had a good claim as well, but he already had armor forged by Hephaestus and graciously declined to compete.

"Would that I had done so as well! In later years, I often looked back on those events and regretted not letting Ajax win by acclamation, for even I knew he was a better warrior than I, our greatest next to Achilles. Instead, my stupid pride prompted me to enter. I had long enjoyed Athena's favor, and as for the Trojans, I think they voted for me to spite Ajax.

"Their strategy could hardly have paid off better. Ajax couldn't believe I had defeated him. The shock drove him mad, and in that state he slaughtered the livestock, thinking the animals were the other Greek leaders. When he recovered from that delusion and realized how close he had come to being a mass murderer, he killed himself in shame. Once again, the Greeks had lost the best man they had.

"In the days that followed, yet another blow fell upon us. I advised Agamemnon that we should try to capture Helenus, Cassandra's prophetic brother, to see if he could tell us how to defeat Troy. We knew the city was fated to fall, yet still it defied our efforts to defeat it.

"We did indeed capture Helenus, but the prophecies he made filled us with dread. There were three more conditions we must meet for Troy to fall, ranging from difficult to seemingly impossible.

"The first was that we needed to possess the bow of Heracles. The problem was that Philoctetes, whom Agamemnon already told you we abandoned on Lemnos, was the owner of the bow, and he was very unlikely to want to help us.

"Since we had no choice, a group of men, including Diomedes and me, went to Lemnos to seek Philoctetes. At the last minute, our mission received a vital boost from Machaon, who had been thinking about Philoctetes's wound and believed he had a cure for it. Once healed, Philoctetes was more than willing to accompany us back to Troy with the bow.

"It was Philoctetes who fatally wounded Paris. The Trojan prince managed to make it back to his first love, Oenone, who had told him to come to her if ever he were dying. Oenone could have healed him, but all those years he had ignored her and made love to Helen had darkened Oenone's heart. She refused to lift a finger, and Paris finally got the death he deserved.

"The second condition we had to meet to defeat Troy was to have Neoptolemus, Achilles's son, fight at our side. We knew that would be difficult to bring about, for Deidamia, once she heard of Achilles's death, was very unlikely to allow her son to go back to Troy with us, and her father, King Lycomedes, would probably support her."

"I would think another problem would be that he could only have been what? Ten? Eleven at most?" asked Thanos.

"We weren't able to leave for Troy for some time after we recruited Achilles," replied Odysseus. "By the time we reached Scyros, Neoptolemus was about your age—old enough to hold a sword by the standards of our time.

"Luckily for us, Neoptolemus was eager to avenge his father, and in the end his desire overrode his mother's objections.

"While we had been fetching Neoptolemus, Priam had somehow managed to find yet another ally: Eurypylus, a grandson of Heracles who came leading a troop of Mysians. Because he was fresh and rested, not worn out by ten years of war, he initially did quite well, killing many Greeks in battle. It was the newly arrived Neoptolemus, equally fresh, who managed to kill him, thereby living up to the prophecy.

"The third condition was the most daunting of all. We had to steal the Palladium, a statue of Athena that supposedly fell from heaven. Ancient prophecy had proclaimed that Troy could not fall as long as it had the Palladium, and naturally the statue was one of the most well-guarded things in the city.

"Direct assault was out of the question—if we could have forced our way into the gates, we wouldn't have needed the Palladium. Diomedes and I disguised ourselves as beggars and managed to get close to it, but we would have failed if not for Helen."

"By that time, I was thoroughly miserable," Helen added. "I wanted nothing more than to return to Sparta and the family I had abandoned, and so I was more than happy to distract the guards long enough for Odysseus and

Diomedes to make off with the Palladium."

"Unfortunately, even with all of the conditions for victory fulfilled, Troy still stubbornly refused to fall," said Odysseus. "Neoptolemus and Philoctetes, not as worn down as the rest of us, were all in favor of continuing the war. However, many of the leaders began to doubt that we would ever overcome Troy, that the gods were playing some kind of game and would keep revealing new conditions for victory until we all gave up or died of old age.

"Knowing that Troy was no longer impregnable, I realized that there must be some worthwhile strategy we had not yet tried, and it was then I hit on the idea for the Trojan horse.

"The horse, a gigantic wooden beast with a hollow space inside in which Greek soldiers could hide, was built by Epeius of Locris using a design inspired by Athena herself. With the goddess's help, creating the Trojan horse was easy. Tricking the Trojans into taking it inside their city so the soldiers hidden within could sneak out and unlock the gates offered a much greater challenge. However, I also had a plan for that.

"After a small group of men and I had hidden inside the horse, my fellow Greeks burned their camp and pretended to sail away, though they stayed just off Tenedos, waiting for our signal to return.

"When the Trojans saw signs that we had abandoned the siege, they naturally came out to investigate and found the horse—which it would have been relatively hard to miss. Some Trojans wanted to drag it into the city as a trophy of their victory, but others mistrusted our intent in leaving it, just as we feared they might. Some wanted to break it open to make sure nothing was inside; others wanted to burn it as a sacrifice to the gods.

"Laocoon led the group that suspected the horse was some kind of trick. That was a lucky break for us, because Laocoon, though a priest of Apollo, had sinned enough to be out of favor with his god. He was also a priest of Poseidon, but that god would not stand up for him if it meant saving Troy. When Laocoon struck the horse with a spear to demonstrate it was hollow, he and his sons were almost immediately devoured by giant serpents sent by Athena.

"The Trojans would likely have interpreted such a gruesome display as a divine repudiation of Laocoon's position, but Sinon, my cousin, was there to help them reach that conclusion. At the risk of his own life, Sinon pretended to have been left behind when we left and claimed very convincingly to hate us. His words by themselves might not have been enough, but when coupled with the grisly death of Laocoon, they were sufficient to persuade the Trojans that the gods wanted them to accept the horse.

"Later that night, the Trojans, weary from celebrating their victory, were mostly slumbering deeply, and we had little difficulty slipping from the horse. We easily killed the guards at the front gate before they could raise the alarm, after which we signaled Sinon and opened the gate. At the tomb of Achilles, Sinon lit the signal fire that alerted the Greeks it was safe to return, and before long the whole Greek army—what was left of it after ten years of fighting, anyway—moved with surprising quietness through the gates. Now even a god would have had difficulty saving Troy. At this point the biggest potential threat came not from hostile gods, but from ourselves.

"We should have been cautious at this point—but cities are seldom sacked cautiously, especially after a ten-year siege, and some of us behaved so barbarically that we lost the favor of the very gods who had been supporting us for ten years.

"The worst offender was Ajax, the son of Oileus, who raped Cassandra in the temple of Athena where she had taken refuge. The statue of Athena averted its eyes at this terrible sacrilege, and the goddess became even more enraged when we failed to punish Ajax for his unforgivable deed. As a result, the goddess who for so long had been our greatest supporter became our greatest enemy— not enough to make her want to save Troy, but certainly enough to delay our return home, sometimes with catastrophic results.

"Neoptolemus made the situation even worse, though at least he had the excuse of youth. He was more than just youthfully impulsive, however, for his soul had been poisoned by the death of the father he had never known. The boy killed Priam at the very altar of Zeus where the Trojan king had sought sanctuary. In so doing, he condemned himself to a much shorter life than he might otherwise have had—not short and glorious like that of his father, just short.

"The male members of the Trojan royal family, including Hector's infant son, were all killed, as were most other Trojan men. A few, like the honorable Antenor, who had tried so hard to get justice for Agamemnon, were spared. As was the custom in our society, the women were considered part of the spoils of war and were distributed among the Greek men."

"With one exception," said Achilles. "The unhappy Polyxena, whose brother Troilus met his death by my hand. In later days my enemies, in one last attempt to blacken my name, claimed my ghost had demanded that Polyxena be sacrificed at my tomb to ensure the Greeks a favorable wind for their departure. Others, trying to slander Polyxena, insisted that she had betrayed the secret of my vulnerable heel to her brothers. Later, supposedly wracked by guilt, she was said to have committed suicide at my tomb. None of those tales were true.

"Keep in mind that I had taken Polyxena prisoner on the ill-fated day when I killed her brother. Even loving her as I did, I thought she could never love me—but I kept her anyway. I treated her as much like a guest and as little like a captive as I could, but I kept my feelings for her to myself, and they silently tortured me until the day of my death.

"If only I had known that, as the months passed, her heart began to soften toward me. It was seeing my grief over Patroclus, and then over Antilochus, that moved her. Though she said nothing to me, she had begun to forgive me for the killing of her brother. What more might have happened if I had lived, I will never know, but I know my death caused more her pain than she would ever admit.

"Of course, the death of brother after brother caused Polyxena even more pain, unendurable amounts. Not only that, but the shadow of a grim fate fell upon her, for she knew that at the end of the war she would inevitably become part of one of the Greek leaders' shares of the spoils.

"Yes, Polyxena killed herself at my tomb, but not out of guilt for betraying me. Instead, she chose a quick death in preference to a long, unhappy life.

"Many years after, we found each other in the Elysian Fields, and we knew in death the love that we had been denied in life. It is said that I married Helen here, or even—unbelievably—Medea, but, in fact, it was my Polyxena I wed. Aphrodite may have tortured me in life, but she blessed me in death."

Keisha and Yasmin both thought about complaining again about the sexism of treating women as property. After all, Achilles had just told them Polyxena had killed herself rather than become the prize of some Greek king—

but would it really have been better if she and the women had been killed the way their kinsmen were? They were too tired to try to solve that dilemma.

They wouldn't have had a chance to argue the point, anyway. Almost as soon as Achilles finished his last sentence, a shadow fell across all of them, followed by a burst of dim light that might have been moonlight. As it faded, so did the inhabitants of Elysium.

Seconds before, the students had been looking at men and women. Suddenly, their hosts' flesh melted away, leaving only dull bone.

Except for Heracles and Helen, the former humans in the group had all been transformed into skeletons, though they somehow remained standing. Behind them, the image of burning Troy reasserted itself, and their bones gleamed as the firelight reflected off of them.

Chapter 28: Heroes of the Trojan War, Part 3

"Don't panic!" commanded Hermes, though whether he was addressing the students or the inhabitants of the Elysian Fields was unclear. It took the god a lot of caduceus waving and an agonizingly long time, but he finally restored both Greeks and Trojans to their normal appearance.

Most of the heroes rushed away to check on their family members and friends, though Mateo had the sneaking suspicion that some of them actually looked frightened of him and his fellow students, as if they believed being close to the students was causing the problem. Agamemnon and Odysseus remained, as did a Trojan who introduced himself as Aeneas, though all three looked shaken. As for their earlier escort, Theseus left, he said to seek out his sons, but Heracles and Teiresias remained.

"What caused that ghastly change?" asked Odysseus.

"The environment in Elysium continues to deteriorate," said Hermes. "To give you a more specific answer, I would need to know who is causing this decay."

"We must be near to finding out," said Teiresias. "Aeneas was the last name on our list, and Agamemnon and Odysseus have the most substantial stories after the fall of Troy. They were fated to stay."

"Let us continue," said Agamemnon, looking nervously at the image of burning Troy that Hermes no longer seemed to be able to banish. "As a result of the sacrilege committed by Ajax and Neoptolemus, capturing Troy was the last fortunate event most of us would experience for a long, long time, though we did not know then the extent of the misfortunes awaiting us.

"Even as we prepared to return home, only Menelaus seemed truly happy, for he was reunited with Helen. He had decided to kill her for her disloyalty, but seeing her again melted his heart, and he took her back gladly. Everyone else was eager to leave, but most didn't get their wish.

"Athena instigated a quarrel between Menelaus and me, with the result that he and I returned by different ways and at different times. Storms blew Menelaus off course and forced him to land in Egypt, where he and Helen were trapped for eight years. Only by wrestling the shapeshifting Proteus and holding onto him regardless of what he turned into was Menelaus finally to learn the right method to appease Athena and reach home again.

"Nestor, a grandson of Poseidon, was able to return to Pylos. Diomedes, one of Athena's special favorites, was also granted a quick homecoming, though as we have already told you, he came home only to lose both wife and crown.

"Neoptolemus, warned by Thetis not to travel by sea, had a long overland trek, but at least he did not face bad weather. In every other respect, however, his luck was foul. The most prominent woman he got as part of his share of the spoils was Andromache, Hector's wife. Sometimes relationships that begin in such an unpromising way grow and prosper. I have known kings who found their dearly loved queens in such a way, but that was not to be Neoptolemus's destiny, for his father had killed Andromache's husband, and the bloodthirsty Neoptolemus had killed Andromache's infant son, Astyanax—and right in front of her eyes. Only her exceptional moral character prevented her from plotting his death.

"Neoptolemus did have a child by Andromache, Molossus, but Neoptolemus did not live to raise him. Achilles's son had set his heart on the beautiful Hermione, the daughter of Menelaus and Helen. At some moment near the end of the war, Menelaus had allowed Neoptolemus to think Hermione would be his bride, and once he organized his kingdom in Epirus, he set off to claim her, but before the war Menelaus had already promised her to my son, Orestes. The two fought, and Neoptolemus died of his wounds from that battle.

"I would never have said this if Achilles were still here, but Neoptolemus grew to a hard, cruel, and bloodthirsty man, as if he were perpetually trying to avenge a father he had already avenged. The only reason the gods kept him alive as long as they did was to father Molossus, one of whose descendants would be Olympias, the mother of Alexander the Great.

"At least Andromache finally had some good fortune," said Aeneas. "With Neoptolemus gone, she was free to marry the Trojan seer, Helenus, who had ended up as Neoptolemus's slave. Together they ruled Epirus and raised Molossus far better than Neoptolemus ever could have."

"I would have to agree," said Agamemnon. "At least Neoptolemus got home, though. Ajax, the rapist, was not allowed to even get that far. His ship was wrecked, but Poseidon decided to save him on some odd whim.

Unfortunately for Ajax, he decided to brag that he had survived without any help from the gods. Poseidon struck the rock on which Ajax was standing. It shattered, and the hubristic hero fell back into the sea, where he drowned.

"Many other men drowned by the malice of Nauplius, who blamed the Greeks for the death of his son, Palamedes. The grieving father set up false beacons that led those who trusted in them to sink their own ships on the jagged rocks to which the beacons led them.

"As for me, by the favor of Hera I got home relatively quickly—but a reception even worse than the one Diomedes got awaited me.

"Clytemnestra had never forgiven me for the supposed death of Iphigenia, and in my absence my queen had formed an adulterous bond with the evil Aegisthus, the incestuous instrument of the vengeance of his father, Thyestes.

"The unhappy Cassandra was part of my share of the spoils, and the poor woman tried to warn me toward what doom I sailed, but because of her curse I did not believe her. Instead, I rushed into the waiting arms of Clytemnestra, who killed me and handed my bloody crown to her lover. The poor Cassandra my murderous wife also killed. The Trojan princess deserved better, for she had done everything in her power to have my brother's wife and treasure returned.

"Menelaus would certainly have avenged me had he not been trapped in Egypt. Because he was, the duty fell to my young son, Orestes, who managed to escape Aegisthus with the help of his sister, Electra. He was taken in by King Strophius of Parnassus, and seven years later he returned to Mycenae with his friend, Pylades, son of Strophius. Again with Electra's help, Orestes killed both Clytemnestra and Aegisthus.

"Unfortunately, by killing his own mother, Orestes had violated an ancient taboo enforced by the Furies, who hounded him unmercifully, giving him not a moment of peace. He was saved only by the aid of Apollo and Athena, who through a trial before the Areopagus in Athens were able to temper the unbending justice of the Furies with reason and mercy. I wept for the suffering of Orestes, but it was through him that our family curse was finally broken.

"I was both more and less fortunate than Agamemnon," said Odysseus. "My wife was always faithful to me, but it took me ten years to return to her, and even then I almost lost my life trying to regain control of my own household and kingdom.

"I started out from Troy with Menelaus's part of the fleet, but we had some silly argument—I don't even remember over what—and I ended up separating my own ships from the rest of the fleet and sailing a different way.

"Our first stop was Ismarus, a town in Thrace where we ended up raiding the Ciconians."

"Had they been Trojan allies?" asked Mateo.

"Perhaps," said Odysseus cautiously. "Some Thracian groups did support Troy, but in truth we had little reason to attack them even if they had fought on Troy's side. The time for such violence was long over, and I fully admit my error in getting involved in a senseless conflict.

"One good thing came out of those battles, however. I protected Maron, a priest of Apollo, and his family. As it turned out, he was no ordinary priest, for he was the grandson of Dionysus and Ariadne. One of the gifts he gave me to show his appreciation was twelve jars of sweet wine, a present that was to save my life and the lives of some of my crew later in our travels.

"Our next landfall was Cape Malea in Greece, and from there it should have been a comparatively easy trip back to Ithaca, but the gods were still angry with us Greeks for the sacrileges after the fall of Troy. The north wind blew us far off course."

"Egypt or Libya?" asked Yong.

"Later writers tried to map this and other parts of my journey, but truly I doubt we were in any natural place, for no one was ever able to find most of the spots we landed."

"Like the way Heracles couldn't find the entrance to the garden of the Hesperides in the west where it was supposed to be?" asked Keisha.

"I believe so," said Odysseus. "Some places are not exactly part of the normal world, and such spots can be found only through the help of strong magic or of the gods. However we got there, we found ourselves in the land of the Lotus Eaters, people who ate a strangely sweet fruit that made them forget everything except the fruit itself. If strangers tried this unusual delicacy, they forget their duty, their homes—everything except the fruit."

"Like addicts?" asked Yasmin.

"Very much like an addict in your society," replied Odysseus. "A few of my crew members were caught in the pleasure of the fruit, and I had to drag

436 A Dream Come True

them back to the ships, but eventually they recovered. Thank the gods we didn't all try the lotus before realizing the danger, or we would never have escaped.

"Next we reached the far more dangerous island of the Cyclopes, though we didn't know at the time who lived there."

"Why were they dangerous?" asked Fatima. "Weren't they the ones who helped Hephaestus at his forge?"

"All Cyclopes look similar, but looks can be deceiving. Hephaestus's Cyclopes were the children of Uranus and Gaia, and they were both gentle and skillful. The Cyclopes of this island were children of Poseidon and the nymph Thoosa, and they were savages without even a drop of respect for the gods.

"While exploring we came upon a cave with large amounts of cheese and lamb meat. My crew favored stealing some supplies and being on our way, but I insisted on waiting for the cave's owner to return. It seemed better to observe the normal customs of the host-guest relationship rather than to become common thieves. Little did I know that our 'host' would spit upon those very customs.

"When the Cyclops Polyphemus returned with his flock of sheep, he treated us not as guests, but as prisoners—no, as less than prisoners. More like food. He ate two of us that evening and another two the next morning.

"Weren't there enough of you to defeat one Cyclops?" asked Mateo. "You must have faced worse odds at Troy some of the time."

"The problem was that when Polyphemus returned, he rolled an enormous boulder over the cave entrance. Since we didn't have Heracles with us, we had no way to move the stone. If we had killed Polyphemus in battle, we would have been trapped in the cave.

"Fortunately for us, Polyphemus had long ago been consumed by his own hubris. His disregard for the will of the gods made that much clear. Because he was too arrogant to see us as any kind of threat, he didn't pay much attention to what we were doing, so I had no trouble fashioning a sharp stake during the day when he was out pasturing his sheep. That evening we got Polyphemus drunk with some of the wine Maron had given me and used the stake to blind his one eye.

"He did shout for help, but because I had told him my name was Nobody, when his fellow Cyclopes came, and he told them Nobody was attacking him, they supposed the gods were tormenting him somehow and went away, for even they knew better than to interfere with divine punishment.

"When morning came, the blind Cyclops believed he could kill us as we tried to leave the cave, but he wasn't very smart about the way he looked for us, and we were able to escape the cave by tying ourselves to the bellies of his large sheep. He felt the fleecy back of each one and let it out of the cave, never suspecting we were strapped underneath.

"Eventually, he did figure out what we had done, but by then we were sailing away. He came after us and tried throwing boulders at the ship, barely missing us even though he was blind.

"Then I made a mistake I will regret forever. My own hubris got the best of me, and I told Polyphemus he had been tricked by Odysseus. Knowing my name, he was able to call on Poseidon to curse me so that I would never return home, or, if that wasn't possible, that I at least would lose all my companions and find disaster awaiting me at home.

"At first it seemed as if Poseidon had not heard Polyphemus's plea, for we found our way to Aeolia, the floating island of Aeolus, the god of the winds. As a former mortal, he was sympathetic to our plight and even tied up all the winds except the gentle west wind in a bag and gave it to us, telling us not to open it until we were safely back at home.

"As we neared home, I fell asleep, and it was then that Poseidon's curse began to grip us. My men, thinking that in the bag I was concealing treasure I didn't want to share with them, opened the bag. The other winds, once released, blew up a storm that drove us all the way back to Aeolia. At that point Aeolus, seeing that his seemingly foolproof plan had failed, concluded that it was not the will of the gods for us to reach home and refused to help us any further.

"From that point our situation deteriorated rapidly. Without any clear idea of where we were or how to get home, we sailed our way to the land of the Laistrygones, a society of man-eating giants equal to the Cyclopes in savagery. Most of my men perished trying to escape, leaving only one ship and its crew.

"We next landed on Aeaea, which superficially looked less threatening. At least there were no giants lurking around! However, the island had its own unique danger: Circe, daughter of Helios and Perseis, aunt and teacher of the sorceress Medea—and not a very hospitable host, to say the least.

"When I sent a search party out to scout the island, they stumbled upon Circe's magnificent home, and her beauty conquered the caution that should have ruled their actions. They accepted a drink from her which turned them into pigs, for it was Circe's habit to transform any uninvited guests into whatever animal form suited her.

"The one man who had remained outside, Eurylochus, realized what had happened and ran to find me. Knowing I had to attempt to rescue my men, I moved toward the house, but I had no idea how to defeat someone who was at the very least a sorceress, perhaps even a goddess.

"At that point, I received the first indication since leaving Troy that Athena had not forgotten me."

"She sent me to Odysseus," said Hermes. "I was eager to help, for Odysseus was my great-grandson. I told him how to overcome Circe and gave him the herb moly, the same one I gave you earlier, for enchantments like those of Circe will fail in the presence of moly."

"When I arrived at her home, I pretended to be taken in by her show of hospitality," said Odysseus. "When her magic failed to change me, I took advantage of her surprise to threaten her with my sword, just as Hermes had advised. I compelled her to swear an oath not to harm me nor any of my men and to change back those touched by her magic, and she agreed. Once the oath was sworn, we made love." *double standards*

"What?" asked Keisha. "I'm sorry to interrupt, but you were married, right? To Penelope, who was *loyally* waiting at home for you."

"Yes," said Odysseus, looking puzzled. Then he added, "Oh, I forgot, your culture is different in that respect. I was loyal to Penelope by the standards of my society, for it was not forbidden for men to sleep with women other than their wives, even on a long-term basis. In my case it didn't matter that I slept with Circe. What mattered was that I came back to Penelope in the end."

"Be patient," he added to the girls, all of whom looked frustrated with his explanation. "The rest of my tale will make clear where my loyalties lie."

Both Keisha and Yasmin wanted to tell him what they really thought of his culture's double standard, but the fires of Troy were crackling more and more loudly in the background, reminding them of how short time was.

"Keep in mind that I didn't know then how much longer I would be away from home," said Odysseus. "My men and I spent some time with Circe on the assumption that the worst was over and that, once we left Circe, we only needed to sail a short distance to be home. If only that had been the case!

"After a year—"   *Keisha doesn't seem to like*

"A year?" asked Keisha, glaring at the hero.   *Odysseus*

"Now is not the time!" snapped Teiresias. "Allow Odysseus to finish his story, for time is frighteningly short." Keisha nodded but didn't trust herself to speak.

"After a year," Odysseus continued, "we realized we had stayed too long and missed our homeland terribly. When I prepared to say goodbye to Circe, she shocked me with the unwelcome news that we needed to visit the Underworld to speak with Teiresias in order to complete our journey.

"I was naturally reluctant to take such a dark journey, but Circe was insistent that our only hope of reaching home lay through the Underworld, and so we made the journey.

"Unlike the route taken by later heroes, we were able to sail from Circe's island to the Underworld. I suppose we were in a magical realm, so the difference in geography should not surprise me.

"Following Circe's instruction, we stayed near the outer edge of the Underworld, just beyond Persephone's Grove. There we dug a pit which we filled with ram's blood. At the time we believed that such a ritual was the only way to communicate with the dead. Much later I learned that we were but communing with their shadows, that their real selves were elsewhere, such as here in Elysium. The shadows used the blood to form enough connection with their true selves to enable them to communicate with us, making it unnecessary to trek further into the Underworld.

"Teiresias told me that my men and I could all reach home if we avoided eating any of the cattle of Helios on the island of Thrinakia, which we would have to visit on the way. If we did not avoid the temptation of the cattle, only I would reach home, and I would find a miserable situation.

"Having delivered that ominous warning, the prophet also told me how to appease Poseidon after I finally got home. The way was not easy, but at least it gave me hope that Poseidon would not be haunting me all the rest of my days. *He's been gone for a very long time*

"While I was in the Underworld, I also saw shadows of my Trojan War comrades and earlier heroes. The one image that shocked me most, however, was that of Anticlea, my own mother, who I had not known was dead until that moment. Seeing her in that gloomy place reminded me of how long I had been away from home and how desperately I wanted to get back. What Anticlea told me about the disasters befalling my household heightened my sense of urgency."

Keisha was tempted to point out that he could have gotten home a year earlier if he hadn't spent that year with Circe, but she kept that idea to herself.

"When we returned to the island of Circe, she gave me advice about other menaces we would face on our way home and how best to deal with them," Odysseus said. "We spent one more night with her and then departed as rapidly as we could.

"The first menace Circe had warned us of were the Sirens, creatures with the heads of beautiful women and the bodies of birds. Their voices were so compelling that sailors who heard them inevitably sailed in their direction, only to sink their ships on the jagged rocks they never noticed. They also didn't notice the piles of bones, a clear sign that the Sirens ate any men who came within their grasp. *Very deadly*

"The Argonauts had escaped this menace with the help of Orpheus, who used his own music to drown out the Sirens' alluring song, but we had no such musician among us, so Circe advised us to plug our ears with wax.

"She also told me that if I wanted to hear the song myself, I could leave my ears unplugged, though I would need to have my men tie me to the mast to ensure that I didn't dive off the boat and try to swim to the Sirens. I would also need to order them not to untie me, no matter how much I threatened or begged."

"That seems like a lot of extra trouble—and risk," said Thanos. "There are a lot of stories in other cultures, like the Celtic stories about encounters with faerie queens, in which the men who have those experiences can never think of anything else for the rest of their lives. Weren't you afraid that something like that could happen if you heard the song of the Sirens?"

"Was I afraid I might long for their music forever once I'd heard it? I suppose such a thing could have happened," said Odysseus. "No man had ever heard the Sirens and lived to tell about it, so who knew what the effects might have been? However, I trusted Circe not to lead me astray. She was bound by oath not to harm me, remember? I figured that would prevent her from making such a suggestion if following it would ruin me. *A lot of trust*

"I did hear their song, and it was like nothing I had ever heard in my life. I would have swum clear across a sea full of monsters just to get closer to it. Fortunately, my men did as I told them—for once—and kept me tied. After I was away from the Sirens, I quickly regained my wits, and my men were able to untie me.

"The next menace presented me with a dilemma I didn't want to face. We needed to pass between Scylla, a six-headed monster with three rows of teeth in each head, and Charybdis, a great whirlpool. To pass through, we had to get too close to either one or the other. Circe told me that if we got too close to Scylla, we would definitely lose some men. If we got too close to Charybdis, we might pass successfully, but there was the risk the whole ship would be sucked down into the sea, in which case the whole crew would perish.

"I did the only thing I could; I chose to move too close to Scylla, sacrificing a few men to avoid the possibility of losing them all."

"That must have been difficult," said Fatima.

"It was," replied Odysseus. "However, leaders often have to face dilemmas of that kind. I knew that years before, when I had first become king.

"After that, we landed on Thrinakia, the island where the cattle of Helios were pastured. I had gotten my men to swear to leave the cattle alone, but we were trapped on the island for a month by unfavorable winds, and so we ran out of provisions. I went a distance away to pray for help, but while I was gone, the men despaired of receiving divine aid and decided to kill some of the cattle without waiting to see what would come of my prayers.

"The winds suddenly became favorable, and I raced back to ready the ship to set sail. I was horrified to discover what the men had done, but there was no undoing their crime, so I decided to leave the island anyway."

"Helios complained to Zeus about the theft," said Hermes. "The king of the gods struck the ship with a thunderbolt soon after it reached the open sea. The ship sank, and everyone on board except Odysseus drowned."

"I only survived because Calypso rescued me," said Odysseus. "I thought I was lucky she had noticed me—but I quickly found out I would have been luckier if anyone else had found me.

"Calypso was a daughter of Atlas confined to the island of Ogygia for giving aid to the Titans when they fought with Zeus. Unfortunately, her long imprisonment had made her lonely, so instead of helping me continue my journey, she made me her prisoner and unwilling lover."

Given how easily Circe had gotten Odysseus into her bed, Keisha doubted Calypso had to use much coercion to get Odysseus into hers, but she kept that idea to herself, just as she had the last one. *"men can't be raped."*

"Seven years Calypso kept me, and I had begun to despair of ever escaping from her. She offered me everything a man would want, and more besides, for she pledged to make me immortal if I would swear to remain with her forever. I won't say the offer wasn't appealing, but I never wavered in my determination to return to my country, my son, and my wife.

"And that," he added, looking at the girls, "is why I would be judged a faithful husband by my society, for I turned down the chance to be a god to return to my wife."

"Unfortunately, all that determination would have done you little good without the aid of Athena, who had been waiting for the right moment to free you from Calypso," said Hermes. "Finally, when Poseidon was away feasting with the Aethiopians, she got Zeus to agree to order Calypso to release you, and I flew as fast as I could to Ogygia to deliver Zeus's decree."

"Calypso was saddened by the order, and as I recall, critical of the gods for forcing her to give me up, but in the end she yielded, even providing me with the supplies to build a raft.

"Alas, even then I was unable to get as far as Ithaca, for Poseidon saw me sailing on my raft as he returned from the Aethiopians and summoned up a storm that smashed my poor raft to bits, nearly drowning me.

"That time the sea goddess Leucothea—you know, the one who used to be the mortal Ino—saved me. She gave me her veil and told me I could not drown if I tied it around my chest.

"Sure enough, buoyed by her veil, I managed to make it to Phaeacia. Though not as threatening as Calypso's island, it wasn't an ideal place to land, either. The Phaeacians disliked strangers, and while they did respect the host-guest relationship, they were not about to accept just anyone as their guest. Worse, the royal family descended from Poseidon, so if the Phaeacians knew who I was, there was virtually no chance they would give me any help."

"I only survived because of Athena's help. It was she who inspired Princess Nausicaa to do laundry on the morning after I washed up on the shore of Phaeacia barely alive. It was also Athena who increased what you would call my charisma so that Nausicaa would be charmed and agree to help me despite the fact that I was a stranger, and she had no reason to trust me.

"Nausicaa advised me to approach her mother, Queen Arete first. She told me that through Arete I would gain the favor of her husband, King Alcinous.

"When I arrived in the city, Athena in the form of a young girl gave me a great deal of information about how to best appeal to the king and queen. Then she wrapped me in a mist and smuggled me into the palace.

"I was skeptical of how well I would be received if I just suddenly appeared, but Athena's wisdom proved itself again. My sudden appearance and my heightened charisma convinced the king and queen that I was probably a god disguised as a human. With that advantage, Arete accepted my appeal at once, as did Alcinous. I was accepted formally as a guest without even having to say my name. Alcinous was so certain I was divine he even offered me marriage to Nausicaa, an offer it took me a while to decline diplomatically.

I did eventually have to reveal who I was, but to their credit the Phaeacians did all that they had promised me, including taking me back to Ithaca, even knowing I was an enemy of their patron. When Poseidon realized what had happened, he turned the Phaeacian ship that had taken me home to stone, and from that day the Phaeacians became even more suspicious of foreigners.

"Athena prevented me from going immediately to my palace—mostly because I would have been killed the moment I arrived.

"The basic problem was that almost everyone thought I was dead, the exceptions being my wife and son. After a few years, suitors had begun appearing in Ithaca—not quite as distinguished a group as that which courted Helen, but what those suitors lacked in dignity they made up in numbers. There were over a hundred!"

"Was that considered typical?" asked Yong.

"No, the number was unusually high, but there were reasons for that," replied Odysseus. "Penelope was considered a great beauty, despite her age, but there were practical reasons why a man might desire marriage with her as well. Keep in mind that the rules of succession in various monarchies were not yet as fixed as they afterward became. You might think that my son, Telemachus, would have automatically succeeded to the throne of Ithaca, but that wasn't necessarily the case. Some early societies had allowed the new husband of the queen to become king, as the ill-fated Oedipus did by marrying Jocasta, for no one realized at the time that he was the son of the previous king. Therefore, Penelope's new husband would have had some kind of claim to the Ithacan throne.

"Nor was that the only throne potentially in play. Penelope's father was the brother of King Tyndareus of Sparta, who had made Menelaus, his son-in-law, his heir. However, Menelaus and Helen were trapped in the east for seven years, remember, so at the time suitors began asking for Penelope's hand, the situation in Sparta was at best unclear. Menelaus had three sons with Helen, none of whom were still alive. He also had two sons by a slave woman after Paris had stolen his wife, but he had not acknowledged either as an heir, and illegitimate sons had no inherent right to succeed to the throne. He also had a legitimate daughter, Hermione, but as you know, Menelaus had promised her to Orestes and to Neoptolemus, neither one of whom therefore had a clear claim either. At the time Neoptolemus was still establishing himself in Epirus, and Orestes had not yet reclaimed his father's throne. By the way, since Penelope was also related to Agamemnon's family by marriage, her husband might even have had some chance of ending up as king of Mycenae, considering the throne was then held by the usurper Aegisthus."

"But wouldn't whoever married Penelope have only a distant claim on Sparta at best?" asked Thanos. "And surely any claim on Mycenae would have been too remote to have been worth worrying about."

"Remember how fluid the succession rules were," said Odysseus. "Remember also that the person with the best claim on Mycenae was in no position to press that claim at the time and that, since no one knew what had happened to Menelaus, Sparta had no one clear claimant.

"I hate to say it, but the situation would have boiled down to who could raise the largest army. The king of Ithaca might easily have mustered a larger force than any of the non-royal claimants to either throne.

"Orestes eventually ended up with both thrones—and Argos too, a vacant throne to which he had no obvious claim. However, at the time the suitors were making plans, no one could have foreseen that outcome. It was just as likely Orestes would end up dead than that he would emerge triumphant.

"Anyway, two generations later, the Heraclids, who had some claim on Mycenae but none at all on Argos or Sparta, ended up with all three thrones and that of Pylos as well. I can't think of any clearer demonstration that armed might overcame succession rights every time.

"What a mess!" said Mateo, shaking his head.

"Indeed, but poor Penelope had to contend with more than just this political tangle. If she had been sure I was dead, she could have picked a new husband relatively easily, but her heart kept telling her I was still alive, and she would not be disloyal to me. However, thinking I was alive also kept her from trying to proclaim Telemachus king. The result was that the kingdom had no suitable male head, at least as far as the outside world was concerned. The suitors became more and more demanding, eventually using Penelope's failure to make a choice as an excuse to become more or less permanent guests and slowly eat up my wealth. They also reduced Penelope, Telemachus, and the few loyal servants who remained to little better than prisoners in their own home. By the time things went that far, Telemachus was no longer in a position to take the crown even if he and Penelope had decided I was truly dead, and if he had tried, he would have been killed. The suitors were actually plotting to kill him anyway, just in case. Athena saved him by inspiring him to seek news of my fate, a clever way of getting him off the island. When he returned, Athena prevented the suitors, some of whom were preparing to ambush him, from catching him."

"I don't understand how a queen could be overcome that way on her own island," said Yasmin. "Couldn't she have had the police…the guards… whoever…throw out the suitors. Didn't she have the right to do that?"

"Rights mean little without the power to enforce them," said Odysseus. "Collectively, the suitors and their retainers were the largest military force on the island. I had taken practically every able-bodied man of my generation with me to Troy, and none of them had come back. There was no regular police force. Typically, families protected their own members, but Penelope's family was mostly on the mainland, and my father was too old to be of much help."

"Wouldn't the suitors have fought with each other rather than becoming allies?" asked Mateo. "After all, only one of them could marry Penelope."

"Ah, but let us not forget hubris," said Odysseus. "Each suitor believed he would be the one Penelope would choose, and each, therefore, believed he was merely using the others for his own purposes. It would have been just as likely the chosen one would have ended up dead in that atmosphere, but each of them saw only what he wanted to see."

"Why didn't Athena kick them out, then?" asked Fatima. "Surely they weren't strong enough to overcome a goddess."

"No, they weren't, but think about the other stories you've heard. The gods did occasionally intervene that directly, but most of the time they preferred to work through mortals, intervening only when their mortal agents couldn't possibly prevail. I think one reason for that was to avoid direct confrontations between gods—though that didn't always work out. Another reason was to give mortals a chance to become heroes. It's pretty difficult to develop as a hero if a god is fighting all your battles for you.

"What Athena did do for me was give me the wise advice to disguise myself as a beggar while I made my plans to defeat the suitors. With her guidance, I was able to find those few servants who had not aligned themselves with the suitors. I was also able to reveal myself to Telemachus, whose help was invaluable.

"The planning also gave me time to see for myself what kind of people the suitors were. Athena was determined to use me as the instrument of divine justice for the suitors' egregious violations of the host-guest relationship as well as for their other crimes, but for that design to work, I couldn't hesitate. I had to know beyond any doubt that the suitors deserved death. It only took me a few days to learn how thoroughly despicable most of them were.

"Once I had what I needed for victory, Athena ensured the suitors would all be present at the same time by inspiring Penelope to propose the contest of the bow: whoever could string my famous bow and shoot an arrow through the loops on the top of ten ax heads would become her husband. No suitor was going to pass up that opportunity."

"But she still thought you were alive, right?" asked Mateo.

"She did, but she was also desperate. The suitors were on the verge of forcing her to choose. The contest, which she assumed none of them could win, was a way of stalling for time. Only I could string that bow, and only an exceptional archer could have shot through all ten ax heads. Looked at in that way, it was a clever way to put off her choice in hopes the gods would save her. As it happened, they did.

"While the suitors were distracted by the preparations for the contest and by Athena, Eumaios, my loyal swineherd, removed the suitors' weapons from the chamber. Still in my beggar disguise, I entered the contest over the protests of the suitors. Telemachus shamed them into allowing it, and then, of course, I both strung the bow and made the shot. At that moment, Athena removed my disguise, shocking the suitors, and Telemachus and I struck.

"Even though we were armed, and the suitors were not, we were still outnumbered by more than fifty to one. Athena made the contest more even by clouding the suitors' wits so that they came at us one by one instead of rushing us all at once."

"Just like a bad action flick," said Mateo.

"It took a while, but we killed all of them, after which we dealt swift justice to the servants who had betrayed Penelope.

"I was finally reunited with Penelope, who could not believe at first that I was really Odysseus and needed a good deal of convincing."

"Then you finally got to live happily?" asked Fatima.

"For a time," said Odysseus. "You've heard enough of these tales by now to know we heroes seldom live 'happily ever after,' and I was no exception.

"Apollodorus includes four or five wild stories about me and Penelope that make either her or me disloyal, but none of those betrayals ever happened. The gods granted our marriage strength despite our long separation. One detail from that mass of stories, however, is true: I was killed by my own son."

"Telemachus killed you?" asked Fatima. "Why would he do that?"

"Telemachus was not my only son," said Odysseus. "Some of you," he added, glancing at the girls, "will perhaps think of it as justice that it was Telegonus, one of the sons I fathered with Circe, who killed me."

A few minutes earlier Keisha and Yasmin would have said exactly that, but they knew Odysseus a little better now, and even though he shouldn't have slept with Circe, neither of them thought he deserved to die for it.

"Unfortunately, when an oracle told me my son would kill me, I also assumed that the son in question was Telemachus, for Circe had never told me of the three sons we had. As a result, I exiled Telemachus. He was crushed by my decision, as was Penelope, but both accepted it, fearing that otherwise Telemachus might kill me by accident.

"Foolish…foolish indeed to think I could change fate. All I did was deprive myself of Telemachus's company near the end of my life.

"Telegonus had ended up as a king among the Etruscans, but he was not satisfied with his life, because he wanted to know who his father was, and Circe had never told him. He went back to her island to see her and demanded she tell him. Deciding her son should know his father, Circe told him all about me, and he immediately went to find me. Knowing how dangerous such trips could be, Circe presented him with a spear tipped with venom from a sting ray, a weapon she had Hephaestus fashion especially for him.

"Unfortunately, the path to and from Circe's island was devious, even for her own son. Though she told him where he could find Ithaca, he became lost. When he finally landed on Ithaca, he didn't realize where he was. Thinking he was an invader, I fought him, and he killed me, only finding out later that he had killed the very father he had been so anxious to see.

"Penelope forgave him, for he looked too much like me for there to be any doubt he was the son fated to kill me through no fault of his own. Athena sent both of them, together with Telemachus, to Circe's island, where they all buried me and mourned together.

"It is said Athena ordered Telemachus to marry Circe and Telegonus to marry Penelope, but what really happened was much different. Circe wished to marry Telemachus, but he declined, for he was already married—to Nausicaa, if you can believe that strange twist of fate. Nausicaa thought she loved me because of Athena's manipulation, but when she met Telemachus, she found she really did love him. By that time I had appeased Poseidon, so the Phaeacians had no objection to such a union.

"As for Telegonus and Penelope, Athena suggested they pretend to be married in order to spare Penelope another mob of unworthy suitors. Telegonus, eager to make amends for killing me, agreed to the arrangement, turned over his share of the Etruscan kingdom to Latinus and Ardeas, his two brothers who already ruled parts of the kingdom, and settled on Ithaca, looking after Penelope as vigilantly as Telemachus did. When the time came, Circe granted all of them immortality.

"So my tale does end happily—just not as happily for me as it could have. Since I ended up in Elysium, though, and so did they, I can hardly complain."

"I suppose I should consider myself fortunate as well," said Aeneas, whose features were reminiscent of Aphrodite's, but who also looked more than capable of winning battles. "I was fated to survive the Trojan War and travel to Italy, where my descendants, Romulus and Remus, would found Rome, and all of those things came to pass, but my life was not free of suffering.

"Though I am called a Trojan prince, I was not Hector's brother. My father was Anchises, Priam's cousin. My family ruled Dardania and was originally intent on staying out of the Trojan War, but when the Greeks began raiding our lands during the long siege, we were pulled into the conflict, and I went to Troy to fight.

"However, I knew the sons of Priam well enough to think of them as brothers, and watching so many of them die filled me with grief. Even worse was the loss of Creusa, my wife and their sister, who perished during the fall of the city. However, with the help of the gods, I did escape from Troy with my father, whom I carried on my back. I also managed to save my infant son, Ascanius, and several close companions.

"It is said the Greeks, after having seen me rescued by gods on more than occasion, decided to allow me to escape rather than risking any more divine wrath than Ajax and Neoptolemus had already brought upon them. It is also said that some of them had seen me carrying my father on my back and were impressed by my moral strength. However, I knew I couldn't settle anywhere nearby. Later generations of Greeks, fearing the revival of Troy, might have reason to attack my descendants, and I had already seen too much of war to wish it on the generations that followed me.

"I traveled first to Thrace, but the ghost of Polydorus, one of Priam's sons, warned me not to settle there. Next I wandered to Delos, where I was hospitably received by the priest-king Anius. He was both wise and powerful, being the son of Apollo, and through his mother, Rhoio, a grandson of Dionysus. Not only did Anius have three daughters who could draw olive oil, wine, and grain from the ground at will, but he was known for his prophetic abilities. I thought that surely he could offer me guidance about where to settle. As it happens, guidance came instead from a divine voice in Apollo's temple—probably the god himself—telling me to settle in the land of my ancestors, where my descendants were destined to rule.

"This was a puzzling prediction since my ancestors had lived in Asia Minor for many generations, and Dardanus, the son of Zeus and Electra who was my ultimate human ancestor, had been born in Samothrace, near where Polydorus had already warned me away.

"Then I realized there was one possibility I had not considered. After Dardanus had settled in Asia Minor, he married Bataie, daughter of Teucer. Though he was the son of Xanthus, the local river god, Teucer had once lived in Crete, so perhaps Crete was our intended destination.

"We tried to settle in Crete, but we were struck by famine and plague. I was on the verge of despair when I received a vision of my household gods, whose idols I had saved from the destruction of Troy. They told me that Dardanus had once lived in Italy, and it was there that I should settle.

"We set out from Crete with hope in our hearts, but the trip to Italy was not so easily accomplished. I did not realize until much later that Hera was still nursing her hatred of the Trojans even though the city had fallen and that she was determined to thwart my efforts to start a new life.

"Bad weather drove us off course after we left Crete, and we found ourselves on the island of the harpies. We successfully defeated them and drove them off, but their leader left us with a chilling prophecy: that we would eat our tables before we ever founded a city in Italy.

"We got more hopeful advice from Helenus in Epirus. He told us the sign that would tell us where to settle was a giant sow nursing thirty piglets. He also suggested visiting the Sibyl of Cumae, who would be able to give us more help.

"On the way to Italy, we landed on Sicily, where Anchises died. It was also there that Hera caught up with us again. When we tried to sail toward Italy, she got Aeolus to raise a storm that again drove us far off course. Poseidon saved us from sinking, but we had to land in North Africa, near the spot where Dido had recently founded Carthage.

"To ensure our safety, my mother, Aphrodite, caused Dido to fall in love with me—but unfortunately, as with Medea, she overdid the effect, making Dido incapable of living without me.

"I found myself falling in love with Dido as well, and I stayed with her in Carthage for several months. It was not long before she offered to make me her king and to rule Carthage jointly with me. I could have been happy there, but that was not where I was fated to settle, and eventually Zeus sent Hermes to remind me of my duty.

"Leaving Dido was as hard as leaving Troy, but I did what Zeus had told me to do. Unfortunately, Dido could not endure separation from me, and she killed herself, cursing my family with her dying breath. Some believe that the later hostilities between Rome and Carthage were the result of Dido's curse, but it was the memory of Dido and how I had to leave her that was much more of a curse to me. Even years later, when I was happily married, that memory still haunted me.

"Once we had finally reached the Sibyl of Cumae, who advised me to visit my father in the Underworld. She also told me how to find the golden bough which you now carry. Though I was reluctant to visit the Underworld, I was eager to see my father again. When I found him, he showed me a vision of the future glories of Rome that encouraged me to keep going, despite the many obstacles that lay ahead.

"When we first made landfall in Italy, we ate meals off flat bread and then ate the bread—thus fulfilling the prophecy of the harpy, for we had figuratively eaten our tables. Not long after, we saw the sow with thirty piglets, and on that site we eventually built Lavinium.

"Of course, to found a new city, we would need the cooperation of the locals. Latinus, a local king, had received an oracle instructing him to marry his daughter to a foreigner, so he willingly welcomed me and gave me Lavinia as a wife. Hera made one last effort to stop me by inspiring Turnus, king of the Rutuli and former suitor of Lavinia, to attack us. He had an impressive collection of allies, including Camilla, queen of the Volsci, a warrior maiden favored by Artemis who could have competed well against any Amazon, as well as Mezentius, a deposed Etruscan king. On our side were some of the Latins and some Arcadians led by Evander.

"Turnus was a fierce opponent, but he sealed his own doom when he killed Pallas, the son of Evander and a good friend of mine. Filled with rage, I would let nothing stop me from avenging Pallas. Much later, when I had Turnus cornered, and he was begging for his life, I almost spared him—until I saw that he was wearing Pallas's sword belt. After that, I killed him without hesitation."

"With Turnus gone, peace was quickly restored. I was able to found Lavinium without further opposition. Eventually, my son Ascanius was able to found Alba Longa and become the first of a long series of kings. The Britons claimed that his grandson, Brutus, emigrated to Britain and became the ancestor of King Arthur. Silvius, my son by Lavinia, became the ancestor of Romulus, who founded Rome and whose descendants were said to include Julius Caesar.

"My life was not as happy as it might have been, but I did my duty and fulfilled my destiny, laying the foundation for two great kingdoms in the process. I can hardly complain about that!"

At that moment another earthquake shook Elysium, knocking both students and heroes to the ground. When it finally ended, flaming Troy had collapsed, but the fire was spreading all around them.

"This place is going to hell—pretty literally," said Yong. "We need to get out of here!"

"I can get us away," said Hermes, "but where should we go? From what I can tell, Elysium is not the only place falling apart right now."

"Someplace quiet, but still in the Underworld," said Keisha. "We have to discuss what we've learned—and I think I know who's causing all of this."

Chapter 29: The Culprit Revealed

Hermes found them a spot in Elysium that at least wasn't burning, though he cautioned them that he had no idea how long it would be before the place was consumed.

"Persephone is still trying to hold everything together, but the task is too much for her alone, and I suspect Hades has become too paranoid to do anything but look over his shoulder," Hermes explained. "If we are to prevent the Underworld, and probably the world above as well, from disintegrating, we had better be quick about it."

"Spill, Keisha," said Mateo. "Who's doing all this?"

"I would never have been able to figure this out without the water of Mnemosyne," said Keisha. "Since I could remember every word of every story, I tried something like a computer search in my head. Apollo had said we had to hear all the stories, I thought at first that there would be a clue in each story, and collectively they all added up to something, but I wasn't getting anywhere thinking in those terms. Then I thought maybe the clues weren't additive; it could just as easily be one clue repeated in each story to make it clear that that's what we were looking for.

"Aside from common words, there is only one word that occurs in every single story: discord." *Eris was behind everything*

"That's a pretty common word too," said Yong.

"Yes, but it's also the English equivalent of Eris," said Thanos. "You think she's the one behind this?"

"Exactly," said Keisha. "She is easily angered: just look at the Trojan War. And she's had millenniums since then to build up petty grievances."

"It is true," said Hermes slowly. "She has remained an outsider in divine society, which I'm sure she resents. However, she lacks the power to create the kind of chaos we have seen."

"But she can influence the minds of other gods, right?" asked Keisha. "She got Athena to care about a beauty contest, for example, and we know that was out of character for the goddess. Could she make the gods mistrust each other?"

"She can do pretty much anything that leads to conflict," said Hermes. "I suppose if she caught enough of them by surprise, she could do what you *had help?*

suggest, but that still doesn't explain the wide range of natural disasters. For instance, Dionysus believed he was under attack by Poseidon because of the earthquake on Naxos, and Eris can't cause earthquakes. Nor could she create the problems in the Underworld that made Hades suspect he was under attack."

"That's true," said Keisha, "but early on she could have recruited an ally who could easily be convinced the other gods were against her. You know, an outsider, someone powerful enough to lend substance to the wave of paranoia and mistrust Eris was trying to create."

"Hecate!" said Thanos.

"She has never really been accepted by the Olympian gods, with the possible exceptions of Demeter and Persephone," Hermes said. "Since she started living in the Underworld, she has become progressively darker and more alienated. It would not have taken much to convince her the other gods were conspiring against her.

"As for the various disasters, yes, I have seen nothing she could not have created, especially if the gods who might have prevented such disruptions were already distracted."

"OK, now we know, but what are we going to do about it?" asked Mateo.

"An excellent question," said Hermes.

"Hecate is obviously the foundation of Eris's plan," said Teiresias. "Remove that foundation, and the plan will crumble quickly."

"Hecate is notoriously hard to find unless she wants to be found," said Hermes. *Plan is to take out Hecate*

"She can be summoned at a crossroads, can she not?" asked Thanos.

"Yes, but if we leave the Underworld at this point, I can't be sure we could get back in easily if Hecate refuses to appear," said Hermes. "The place is too unstable right now."

"There is a crossroads right here in the Underworld," said Thanos. "One road leads to the place of judgment, and then two paths lead from it, one to Elysium, and one to the place where sinful mortals are punished. Ancient Greeks would call that a place where three roads meet—or a crossroads."

"Clever!" said Hermes, patting Thanos on the shoulder. "That just might work. However, we may need to restrain Hecate until we can convince her that no one is conspiring against her, and we already decided that require several gods, at least two of whom are not in the Underworld. Persephone is, and Artemis probably still is, but Selene isn't, and neither is Ceto, and neither of them would be easy to get down here on short notice. Without the right combination of goddesses to restrain the different aspects of Hecate's power, there will be little hope of stopping her long enough to make her listen.

"Selene and Ceto are both here," said Teiresias. "Amphiarus must have advised Persephone to summon them. I also see someone has caused a crack in the earth directly above the crossroads as a way of letting in real moonlight. That must be the way Persephone could get Selene down here so quickly."

"I'll make sure everyone else is where we need them to be," said Hermes. "Heracles, Teiresias, will you see our friends reach the crossroads safely?"

"Either Teiresias can figure out a safe route for us, or I can fight my way through pretty much anything," said Heracles. "We also have Hephaestus's magnificent automatons if we need them. Go ahead."

Hermes flitted off, and Heracles led the way, taking his directions from Teiresias. The students saw many parts of Elysium that had been leveled by earthquakes, but Teiresias steered them successfully around fires, illusionary Telchines, and other potential hazards.

By the time the students and their escort reached the crossroads, Hermes, Persephone, Artemis, Selene, and a stranger they presumed to be Ceto were waiting for them. So was Pan.

The upper part of Ceto was a lovely woman, though her expression was fierce. Her lower body was a long, dark-scaled fish tail, giving her the appearance of a mermaid on steroids. She was balancing awkwardly, making it clear she was seldom on dry land, let alone in the Underworld. Even so, she looked more than formidable enough to face Hecate. The other goddesses looked grim and determined. If the plan failed, it was not going to be for lack of willpower on their part.

"Stay back as far as you can," Hermes told the students. "Your protection against magic won't hold up long against a determined assault by Hecate. Also, we should be able to restrain her—but if we fail, run. At that point, she's likely to be enraged, so anywhere in the universe would be better than right here."

"Good pep talk," muttered Mateo as Hermes hurried over to join the other gods. Teiresias stood with the students, while Ardalos and Patricius stood slightly in front of them.

Persephone, Artemis, and Selene each lit a torch, and then Persephone struck the ground three times and spoke the words of the invocation.

It was clear from what happened next that Hecate must have expected an ambush—and prepared for one. She appeared, looking a little like Demeter, though with a much colder expression, but she stayed that way for only a moment. Then her form flickered, and she seemed to have three heads and six arms, each wielding a sharp spear.

"Triple Hecate," said Thanos. "I never knew the expression was so physical."

"What you see is only part of what is there," said Teiresias, though he had no time to elaborate, for Hecate attacked without waiting for Persephone to speak to her. By now Hecate seemed to be three separate people, one of whom hurled boulders, one of whom sprayed salt water at fire hose intensity, and one of whom shot moonbeams as if they were arrows.

Fierce as her attacks were, at first it looked as if the gods' strategy would work. Ceto raised a hand to fend off the spraying water, Selene did the same to block the lunar attack, and Heracles and Artemis deflected the boulders by club and arrow. Hermes backed them up with his magic as best he could, and the first wave of Hecate's attack did not break through the divine defenses.

Unfortunately, Hecate had not come alone. Suddenly, what looked like an army of ghosts materialized all around her, then came shrieking at the defenders, looking one moment like a flying wall of solid mist studded with soulless faces and the next like a howling tornado. Persephone and Hermes managed to slow their offensive, but then the next wave hit: a mob of lamiae, beautiful and deadly, poured from somewhere—and aimed straight at the students, positioning themselves to prevent the students from trying to escape.

The gods who might have come to their aid dared not stop concentrating on Hecate and the ghosts. The faithful Patricius and Ardalos did what they could, and even Teiresias lashed out with the walking stick Athena had given him, but they were grossly outnumbered, and the students found themselves pressed against the rocky wall. The Lamiae's grasping fingers were only inches away from them.

At that point the real Melinoe came, and from her poured waves of nightmarish, madness-inducing directed against the gods. Pan, who had been trying sneak up on Hecate, jumped at Melinoe, but she dodged, and Pan already looked a little crazed as he got up. He did not look as if he would hold up very well against a continuous barrage of insanity.

Even the students could tell that the odds now favored Hecate. There were too many different forces for the gods to contend with all of them at the same time— and once their defenders faltered, the students were sure they would find out whether dying in a dream meant dying in reality.

"Our amulets!" said Mateo abruptly. "Could we use them as weapons?"

"I...say...yes," said Teiresias, struggling with a lamia who had both hands on his staff. "Don't...let...go...though, or the evil magic will overcome you."

Mateo whipped the chain from around his neck, used the chain to spin the amulet, and, once he had worked enough speed, slammed the amber part right into the face of one of the lamiae, who screamed and fell back, holding her injured cheek. A couple more quick swings, and he had knocked two more away.

The problem was that the lamiae could stay out of reach if Mateo stayed too close to the wall, but if he moved too far out, they could surround him. He needed the help of his friends, but when they tried the same strategy he was using, their results were mixed at best. Thanos and Keisha could make the same attack work, but Yong, Yasmin, and Fatima didn't aim well enough or manage to strike with enough force to do much damage. Weaponizing the amulets might have been a clever idea, but it didn't seem likely to save the day.

However, the students were not alone in trying new strategies. Thanos noticed Hermes's figure flicker as Hecate's had earlier. He was still Hermes, but another image pulsed around him, a figure with the dark head of an ibis. In its hands it held a staff and an ankh rather than a caduceus.

"Thoth, his Egyptian counterpart," whispered Thanos in disbelief. "Hermes was too modest. He's channeling Hermes Thrice-Greatest."

The change made an immediate difference as the figure that was both Hermes and Thoth abandoned a strictly defensive strategy to pound Hecate with wave after wave of powerful magic. She even staggered backward. The tide seemed to be turning—but Hecate had at least one more trick up her sleeve.

Hordes of black dogs suddenly appeared from nowhere and raced toward the students. They proved much more effective than the lamiae had at overwhelming Teiresias, Ardalos, and Patricius, who were immune to the lamiae's charms but could be knocked over by enough dogs hitting them. Patricius put up a good struggle against his nonmetallic brothers, but even he could not fight twenty or thirty of them at a time, and he fell beneath their weight as he had the centaur's hooves earlier.

Even worse, the dogs were not as hurt by the amulets as the lamiae had been. The students had only seconds before the dogs reached them. Their linothoraxes would protect their torsos but not the exposed parts of their bodies.

"Caps!" yelled Yasmin. In all the excitement, they had forgotten them, and they put them on now. But their invisibility came too late. The dogs were close enough to smell them.

Taking advantage of a momentary lull in Hecate's attack to look back in their direction, Hermes Thrice-Greatest gestured at Yong, who felt his inner dragon stir.

"Stand back!" Yong yelled to his friends. Just as the dogs reached them, he was once again a dragon, this time a more Asian version, and the ferocious beasts hesitated. He used the opportunity to sweep several of them aside with a swat from one of his claws. The others didn't back down, but he made short work of them, then turned on the lamiae, most of whom fled. He singed the slower ones with his fiery breath, then roared and turned to face Hecate herself.

Even she looked shocked by his sudden transformation, but she recovered quickly. By now witches were arriving to reinforce her, and they turned their attention to Yong, who in his excitement over being a dragon had forgotten to hold onto his amulet. He was too strong for a physical attack to work, and his willpower had resisted Ares, but it took all he had to fight Melinoe's nightmarish assault. As a result, the witches were able to make him sleepy almost immediately, and his reluctance to rip them apart with his claws or fry them with his fire did the rest. He hit the ground with a resounding crash and almost immediately became human—dangerously close to the witches and their goddess.

"We have to save him!" yelled Mateo, but Teiresias's staff pressed against his chest, preventing him from charging forward.

"You can't save him now," said Teiresias. "Yet there is a way," he added, his blind eyes looking at Fatima.

Surprisingly, Yong didn't get attacked immediately. His fall had jarred all those around him, including Melinoe. The momentary lapse in her attacks gave Pan a moment to realize where he was and what was happening. Taking advantage of that, he let out one of his deafening roars, shaking all of Hecate's allies.

"Great God Pan is on the case!" said Thanos. "Can we help more? Do we all have dragons inside of us like Yong does?" he asked Teiresias.

"All of you have something great within you," said Teiresias. "You don't know how to release it yet, though."

Pan tackled Melinoe, who was no match for him physically, but she managed to slip out from under him and then away before he could stop her. He looked around frantically, but from some hidden spot she lashed out again with madness. His eyes clouded, and he staggered, but then he seemed to shake the madness from him as he drew more and more power from nature. He could probably defeat Melinoe—if he could find her. In the meantime, he turned on the witches, and they started to fall to his rough attacks. The problem was that there were a lot of them, and he could physically attack them only one at a time. The ones out of his immediate reach attacked with magic until the air itself writhed with their foul spells. It wasn't clear whether he could withstand so many attacks long enough to take them down.

At that point the lamiae, realizing there was no dragon to threaten them any longer, regrouped and attacked the students a second time.

Their attack shifted the tide of battle yet again because Persephone tried to hold them back. Unfortunately, she proved unable to restrain both them and the ghosts at the same time, and the dead spirits flooded forward, crashing into her like a tidal wave.

Facing resistance from several directions had been taxing even for Triple Hecate, but as Persephone fell, Hecate smiled, an expression that could have frozen molten lava in its tracks. Even the students could tell she had the strength to win.

The students now found themselves pinned to the wall again, this time by a suffocating wave of ghosts. If not for their amulets, the wave would have drowned them.

In the confusion, Fatima was able to slip away before the lamiae and ghosts made movement impossible. Her friends cried out to her, but she didn't even look in their direction.

Somehow, she made it to Heracles without being intercepted and said something to him. He seemed to argue at first, then nodded.

She took off her amulet and handed it to him, then fell screaming as Melinoe's hellish illusions smashed into her skull.

"What's she doing?" asked Yasmin, looking frantically.

"The only thing she could," said Teiresias.

Taking advantage of a momentary lull in the boulder barrage, Heracles threw the amulet up in the air, then hit it with his club. Having been crafted by Hephaestus, it didn't shatter. Instead, it flew with tremendous force and speed at Hecate.

Under ordinary circumstances, the witch goddess could have warded off such an amulet—but deflecting one driven by the strength of Heracles was a very different situation. It drove itself into her left arm with a burst of sunlight, and she fell, screaming.

With Hecate down, her minions fought on, but without the same frenzied determination. Persephone, whom the ghosts could not truly hurt, got control of them again. Artemis turned her arrows upon the lamiae, with devastating effect, and those who could still flee quickly did so. Pan found Melinoe and this time managed to hold on to her. Hermes made short work of the witches once he no longer needed to focus entirely on Hecate. Heracles raced to the dark goddess, ready to strike if she overcame the power of the amulet, and Ceto managed to waddle over to back him up if needed.

In a few minutes the battle ended. Hecate's allies were all defeated, and she became the prisoner of the other gods. With the various magic attacks now ended, Fatima and Yong quickly recovered, and Hermes assured them that no permanent harm had been done. *Hecate really was really misled and had manipulated*

However, one problem remained: getting Hecate to believe Eris had misled her. The process of convincing her dragged on as long as the battle had without putting a dent in Hecate's belief that the other gods were conspiring against her, even though the pain from the amulet weakened her substantially.

"Isn't defeating her enough?" Keisha quietly asked Teiresias.

"I wish it were," said the old prophet. "However, Eris is still free and may have other allies. Hecate can't reinforce Eris's schemes right now, but that doesn't mean Eris can't do some damage on her own. We need Hecate to help heal the damage she's already done and to denounce Eris so that the other gods will know the truth. Otherwise, I fear war may come even without any more agitation from Hecate."

"Isn't she close to Persephone?" asked Yasmin. "She doesn't act like it."

"Hecate has been too twisted by Eris," said Teiresias. "She no longer trusts Persephone—which means there is probably no one besides Eris and Melinoe she will trust."

"Ares trusted his son, Ascalaphus, enough to listen to him," said Thanos. "Is there one of the blessed dead who might have the same kind of connection with Hecate? Maybe someone Eris wouldn't think to poison her against?"

"I know of no one," said Teiresias.

"What about Orpheus?" asked Thanos. "I remember Dionysus said something about Orpheus charming Hecate—perhaps too much."

"If that story is true, it sounds to me as if Hecate now hates Orpheus," said Yong. "Why would she believe him?"

"The line between hate and love is sometimes thinner than we think," said Teiresias. "What her feelings might be I cannot surely say, for if she has any, she has buried them deeply."

"Regardless of how she feels, perhaps his music could do some good," said Thanos. "He did once bend the Underworld gods to his will, did he not?"

By this time Hermes had overheard part of the conversation and walked over to join it. "If Hecate ever loved Orpheus, she kept that love a closely guarded secret. However, we need to try something. Persephone doesn't want to just consign Hecate to Tartarus, even temporarily, but we have little choice if we can't convince her to trust us. In her current state of mind, we dare not let her free, and keeping her prisoner outside Tartarus would be too taxing for us." *they need Orpheus' help*

"Can we find him?" asked Keisha.

Hermes glanced at Teiresias, who said, "I can't see where he is right now."

"There is so much confusion in the Underworld at the moment that I can't get a clear idea where he is, either," admitted Hermes. "I will have to look around. With Hecate in her current condition, the others can spare me for a few minutes."

"Use the signet ring of Hades," suggested Persephone. "It appears the visitors didn't need it to speak to the blessed dead, but you could use it now, Hermes. Combine your own power with the lingering authority of Hades that the ring possesses, and your vision may clear enough to find Orpheus."

"Excellent thought!" said Hermes. Fatima, who had forgotten she even had the ring, handed it to the messenger of the gods, who flew off even faster than normal. In a surprisingly short time, he was back, leading a handsome but nervous-looking man carrying a lyre.

"You!" said Hecate with surprising vehemence. "Have you come to gloat?" she asked, pointing an accusing finger at him.

"Never to gloat, Goddess," said Orpheus. "Only to put past differences behind us and help you as much as I can."

"Help?" she asked, her tone skeptical. "What help could you possibly give me now?"

"If nothing else, I can lead you to the truth," he replied, strumming his lyre. The students felt the music resonate in their bones.

Hecate tensed as if she could tell what Orpheus was about to do. Though she couldn't break free of whatever magic was restraining her, she started to scream as if to drown out his music.

That scream was shrill enough to break glass, but even it was not powerful enough to entirely drown out Orpheus. No longer looking nervous, he played a calming melody and sang in a voice Fatima couldn't help comparing to an angel's, though she knew there were no angels in Greek mythology.

Though Orpheus's mother had been a goddess, he had been mortal, but the students found it hard to believe as they listened to him play. Somehow the combination of his divine ancestry, a lyre made by Hermes, and music lessons from Apollo had created a whole greater than the sum of its parts.

Orpheus sang the truth so powerfully that the stone floor itself must have believed. Hecate still stared at Orpheus with hatred, but her screams diminished to whispers.

On and on he sang. Hecate was calmer, but she still seemed unconvinced.

Even in her weakened condition, she continued to resist him.

"Maybe she did love him," whispered Fatima. "How could anyone not?"

At last the hatred burning in the goddess's eyes cooled slightly.

"It's working," said Mateo.

"Even a heart as touched by darkness as Hecate's could not resist that music forever," whispered Hermes.

"Stop!" shouted someone behind them. The voice echoed from every piece of rock.

Turning, the students saw a tall goddess whose face was a solid mask of hatred. She wore bloodstained black robes, and two wings dark as midnight stretched out to either side of her.

"Eris," whispered Yong.

The happiness inspired by Orpheus's music shriveled inside of them as they felt the waves of hatred pouring from her. No wonder that, with just a little work, she could turn gods against each other.

Undeterred, Orpheus turned the full force of his music on her. He sang of love and harmony, but the hatred radiating from Eris just kept flowing outward in acidic waves. Orpheus by himself was not strong enough to overcome her.

As if in answer to some unspoken signal, Hermes took out his lyre and started playing. Pan joined with his panpipes, as did Ardalos with his flute.

Eris's assault slowed but did not stop. Even with backup, Orpheus was not going to be able to beat an elder power as strong as discord. He might play for hours, but eventually even he would be overcome.

"I wish there were something we could do," said Keisha, knowing none of them were musical.

"Why don't you club her or something?" Mateo asked Heracles.

"Strife feeds on violence," Heracles replied. "I tried that once, but I just made her stronger."

"Think of those you love," Teiresias told the students. "Violence cannot weaken discord, but love will."

Hard as it was to concentrate when the very air they breathed felt as if it burned with hatred, the students tried their best to follow Teiresias's instructions.

Bit by bit, they made headway. They thought of parents, of brothers and sisters, of friends. Slowly they became less aware of Eris and more aware of Orpheus and his music, until they felt as if that music was their feelings made audible.

Suddenly, the murky darkness around them was pierced by white light. Primal Eros appeared, beautiful as Eris was ugly, his white wings stretching out to an even greater span than her dark ones. He embraced her, and she struggled.

For a moment, Eros's white light became gray, but then it became even more intense than before, a supernova of love. Eris screamed once, though the sound was muted. Then she was gone, and so was the darkness all around them. Eros glanced their way and smiled as brightly as sunlight. Then he too was gone, and the gloom of the Underworld returned.

Well, not quite. The students felt as if they had somehow summoned Eros, as if his light was now within them.

"See that you cherish it," said Teiresias, as if reading their minds. "I told you that you had something great within you. Everyone does—but not everyone realizes it."

"We should have invoked Eros earlier," said Hermes. "The only thing that can beat hatred is love. It has always been so."

"Look at Hecate," whispered Fatima.

Even the witch goddess had been moved by Eros, and the students got a glimpse of her as she must have been before all the centuries of rejection by the other gods and the millenniums of time in the Underworld.

"She...she looks almost like Aphrodite," said Mateo.

"Orpheus, you spoke the truth," said Hecate softly. "I see it now. I don't know how I could ever have been so deceived by Eris."

"You were not alone," said Hermes as he and Persephone helped her up. "No god nor mortal is immune to her corrosive whispering. Were it not for the balancing power of love, we would all have been lost long ago."

Hecate nodded, but there was still a little guilt floating like a shadow in her eyes. "Nonetheless, I must do what I can to make amends."

Hermes had feared the need for a long struggle to get the other gods to stop fighting each other, but with Eris banished for the moment so that not even Hecate could feel her presence, the conflicts among the gods quickly returned to normal levels.

Events moved rapidly after that. With Hecate's help, the group had little trouble finding Patrick, who had been hidden in the Underworld under a web of concealment spells. He was still a dog, but Hermes assured the other students that he could become himself again as soon as they returned him to Hera. They took Hecate up to Olympus as well, so that Asclepius could remove the amulet from her flesh and heal her.

When Patrick did finally get to return to human form, he was a very different person than he had been. He even thanked Hera for changing him back. Then he hugged all the other students, thanking each one for every single thing he or she had done during the hunt for him.

"How do you know about all of that?" asked Yasmin.

"That magic piece of wood you used to communicate with me," Patrick explained. "Even when you weren't trying to talk to me, once you'd made a connection, I was able to listen in on you. Knowing you were trying to help me was the only thing that kept me from dying."

"Dying?" asked Yong.

"I'm not trying to be a drama king, but at first I felt as if my heart was going to explode," Patrick replied. "I don't know if it really would have, but that's what it felt like, and I was alone in the dark, with nobody to tell me it was going to be all right. Without you guys, who knows what would have happened?"

Patrick was not the only one who was grateful. Zeus himself thanked the students for contributing so substantially to thwarting Eris's plans, as did the other gods who were present.

The students, who were only a short time ago wishing they could leave, found it a little unsettling when Olympus suddenly vanished, and they found themselves back in the Demos Oneiroi. Of the gods who had just been surrounding them, only Hermes remained.

"I suspected this would happen soon," said Hermes. "You have accomplished what you were brought here for, and now you are back at the place through which you entered. Any time now, you should be waking up."

"We didn't have a chance to thank Ardalos and Patricius," said Fatima.

"I think they know," said Hermes. A distant mechanical barking seemed to confirm his words.

"Was this really just a dream?" asked Yasmin.

"What do you think?" asked Hermes.

"I think after all we went through, we should get a real answer," said Yong.

Hermes smiled. "How could any of this have been real?" They spent a little longer pestering him for a clear answer instead of another question, but he would say no more, no matter how much they pressed him.

Then Thanos tried a new, unexpected approach. "Am I Aethalides?"

Hermes stared at him, his eyes widening in surprise. "What would make you think that?"

"I know he frequently reincarnated. I know he was once Pythagoras, and I've always liked math, and I've also been crazy about mythology as long as I can remember. Also, during this…adventure I found out I was a pretty good diplomat, and so was he. Then there's the fact that my name means something like *immortal scholar* in Greek. Also, if I were Aethalides, that would account for your interest in this group—and why you called me *son* once."

Hermes laughed heartily. "You know *son* can be used in a general sense. Anyway, what difference would it make if you were Aethalides? Would you want to stay here if you were?

"As you have seen, this world can be beautiful—and terrible. We gods often try to hold mortals to standards we don't meet ourselves, and though we usually don't go to war as we nearly did this time, there is seldom harmony among us. It seems Eris finds a home in our hearts more readily than Eros."

"I…don't really want to stay," said Thanos. "I just couldn't help wondering."

"Then learn what you can from the experience, and move on," said Hermes. "The tales about us gods and the mortals who worshiped us have much to teach, but your real world is capable of being so much greater than the one those tales portrayed. You—all of you—have the potential for greatness. Every single one of you can make your world a better place in ways you cannot even imagine." He glanced around him. "Vivid as your imaginations are!"

Thanos would have said more, but suddenly Hermes vanished into the mist, and Thanos felt himself falling. Moments later he jerked awake. He and the others found themselves around the table where they had been studying—

the one they must have fallen asleep at hours ago.

"Is…is it over?" asked Thanos, touching the table as if he couldn't believe it was real.

"A better question," said Yong, "would be what it was—and that, I fear, we will never know for sure."

Chapter 30: Epilogue

Despite their feeling that they had been in the world of Greek mythology for days, they had really only been asleep for an hour or two. They each shuffled home and slept surprisingly soundly.

Needless to say, they all aced the mythology test. Well, actually Patrick got a B-, but even miracles only stretch so far, and he was more than content with his score. It was the highest one he had ever gotten on a literature test.

At first, they half expected to find themselves back in the realm of Greeks myths when they slept, but that never happened again. Some of them occasionally had dreams with mythic subject matter, but never were they as coherent or as real.

Yong once suggested trying to replicate the circumstances to see what would happen. Surprisingly, Thanos was dead-set against the idea.

"What if it didn't work?" he asked. "I'm not sure...how I'd feel about that."

"What would happen if it did work?" asked Patrick. "After all, I almost got stuck as a dog forever, and all of you almost died. I say leave well enough alone!" For the first time in Patrick's life, people actually took his advice seriously.

That wasn't the only thing that was different. All of them felt different...better. Patrick was the most obviously changed—and not just because for a while he found himself scratching quite a bit, and people said his laugh sometimes sounded like a bark. He was no longer arrogant or mean to other people; in fact, he became one of the nicest people in the class. When the time came to think about community service, he ended up working with a group that tried to find homes for abandoned and abused dogs. He also gave up the idea of becoming a sports hero and began talking about training to be a veterinarian.

The others were different, too, though the changes were subtler. Yong moved and spoke more confidently, Yasmin became less self-absorbed, and Fatima, who had been the quietest student in the whole school, became much more outspoken. Thanos found he had a lot more friends than he realized. Keisha no longer worried that her life had no purpose.

They swore to stay in touch after high school, but as so often happens, they drifted apart over time, though each of them kept enough track of the others to know they had all become successful in their chosen fields.

Many years later, Keisha and Thanos ran into each other by chance, and they ended up having lunch. By that time, Keisha was a bestselling fantasy writer, and Thanos, who returned to the United States after college, had developed revolutionary new methods for teaching math skills to struggling students.

"You know," said Keisha, "Teiresias was right. Each one of us did have something great within us. Probably everyone does, but we were lucky enough to have that…dream…that helped us bring it out."

"Teiresias?" asked Thanos, raising an eyebrow.

"Don't front like you don't remember," said Keisha. "You named your educational solutions company Aethalides. Nobody could figure out why—but we know, don't we?"

Thanos smiled a little. "OK, you know me too well for me to fool you."

They laughed long and hard at their little inside joke.

At least, they thought it was a joke…

This makes zero sense and is a terrible ending sentence

Appendix A: Approach to Mythology Used in This Book

Why do high school students have such a hard time with Greek mythology?

I often asked myself that question during the many years I taught Freshman Honors English at Beverly Hills High School. I had discovered mythology when I was very young and loved it, but once I started teaching it, I quickly discovered that most of my students did not share my enthusiasm.

One of the reasons many of them found mythology daunting was that it developed in a culture very different from their own. Of course, one doesn't need to agree with the morality of the characters—or even the author—in a piece of literature in order to appreciate it. However, it takes time to adjust to that cultural difference, and often students weren't willing to give mythology that time for one simple reason: they didn't find the characters relatable, and not just because their morality was sometimes different.

Beverly Hills High School has a very multicultural student population, so students were generally used to dealing with philosophical and cultural differences. Even students in a much more homogeneous community would still have been pushed by genres like science fiction to consider their responses to other sets of values. For instance, fans of the Star Trek universe would have had to cope with the very different moralities represented by alien races such as Klingons, Romulans, and Ferengi. The Klingons are in some ways reminiscent of ancient civilizations, and the Romulans (whose home planet is Romulus, named after the mythological founder of Rome) are even more obviously connected. If students could embrace such variety in science fiction, why couldn't they treat mythology the same way?

The short answer is that, while modern science fiction and fantasy universes are coherent, Greek mythology is not. Mythology—at least for those of us that appreciate it—is beautiful, but there's no denying it's also messy. It developed over centuries and reflects the often inconsistent ideas and values of dozens of authors. As society changed, authors adapted the work of their earlier peers to reflect the changing audience, but more often than not, the earlier versions also survived. Mythographers like Apollodorus and Hyginus tried to wrestle the mass of stories into a more coherent whole, but their attempts at standardization often just created yet another version to add to the jumble.

This variety can be fascinating, but it's also confusing. Not only that, but the inconsistent stories are filled with inconsistent—and thus unrelatable—characters. Of course, real people are inconsistent, too, but if we know them well enough, we can see reasons for their inconsistencies. It's much harder to understand Greek mythic characters in that way, because their inconsistencies are often not motivated by their personalities or circumstances, but by the differences between authors. For example, Homer's Odysseus is a noble figure, though his morality is not the same as ours. However, the Odysseus of later writers is an opportunist, a coward, and a backstabber. Similarly, Heracles is always strong, but he alternates between being brave and kind in some stories, and savage, perhaps even psychotic, in others. In neither case is there even an attempt to explain these obvious contradictions. Even worse, almost every major character is the same way. That means that, unlike modern literary characters, the gods and mortals of Greek mythology aren't just different from us; they are also hard to get a fix on, because the way they are characterized jumps all over the place.

Is there a way to make mythological characters more accessible to a modern audience without losing their original context? That is the question that prompted me to write this book.

I addressed the differences in values by enclosing the myths in a fantasy frame story in which some high school students find themselves trapped in the world of Greek mythology. While trying to escape, they hear the myths from the mythological characters themselves. The discussions among the student characters about what they hear and experience are designed to help high school students more easily compare and contrast the myths to their own world views.

Of course, just slapping a modern wrapper around the myths wouldn't solve the problem of confusingly inconsistent characters. To address that problem without denaturing the myths, I selected authentic details from ancient sources in such a way that I could build each character a coherent personality. Such an approach does risk creating characters that are too much a product of my own imagination, but I tried to minimize that risk by not throwing out inconsistent details. Instead, I kept them as different viewpoints among the mythological characters, misunderstandings, rumors, or even deliberate attacks on some of the characters—which is how some of the myths may have originated. For instance, Robert Graves argues that the more negative portrayals of Heracles may spring from a desire of Greeks to discredit the Dorian invaders, whose leaders claimed descent from Heracles.

Aside from favoring details that fit together into a unified whole, I tried to keep the myths as genuine as possible. In a few cases I needed to fill gaps (particularly when the motives of characters weren't clear), and occasionally I created details to make one of the stories hang together better, but even in such cases I tried to extrapolate from elements in the the original literature to do so. (By the way, ancient mythographers used exactly the same approach at times.) These exceptional cases are often identified clearly in the text, but to avoid confusion, I have also noted all of them in Appendix B.

If you are a high school student—or even if you're not—I hope you find this book both enjoyable and educational.

Appendix B: Adaptation of Ancient Sources

Below is a list by chapter of those places in which I used details not explicitly provided by ancient writers.

Chapter 1: The Demos Oneiroi is never described as foggy. Actually, it's never described, and foggy seemed as appropriate as anything.

Chapter 8: There are no talking mechanical dogs in the myths. However, Hephaestus did fashion gold and silver guard dogs for the palace of Alcinous, and he also made singing maidens for the temple of Apollo at Delphi. If he could make dogs, and if he could make automatons capable of verbal activity, it's no great stretch to assume he could make talking dogs.

There is only one invisibility cap in the original myths, but since the Cyclopes are supposed to have made the original, there's really no reason why they or Hephaestus couldn't have copied it. Some stories, such as Perseus getting the cap from Stygian nymphs works better if there is more than one. After all, why wouldn't Hades have kept the cap always near him, instead of storing it some distance away?

Chapter 10: No Greek or Roman author explicitly says that the afterlife evolved over time, but certain details suggest that it did. For example, the sons of Zeus who serve as judges were not the first men; there must have been a time when they were not judges in the Underworld. In the same way, a few mortals become gods or are resurrected to continue their old lives. However, Aethalides is the first mortal, who was permitted to return to life after dying by being born into a new life rather than being resurrected to continue his old one. Later his pattern was identified with reincarnation, which was eventually considered a universal phenomenon. For those reasons, I felt justified in describing the afterlife as the product of a process of evolution.

Chapter 13: The resolution of the Endymion story is different from that of any ancient writer. However, ancient writers agreed on very little in the story.

Endymion's parents and wife vary. He may live near Olympia or near Mount Latmus in Asia Minor. He is either a king, a shepherd, or an astronomer. (I made him all three, since in early Greek society kings were not afraid to get their hands dirty.) The divine being who loves Endymion is usually Selene, but sometimes Artemis, and once the god Hypnos. Sometimes Selene wishes for eternal sleep; sometimes Endymion does; once Zeus imposes it as a punishment because Endymion was gazing inappropriately at Hera. Under those circumstances, I thought creating an ending that preserved the tragic element without making either Selene or Endymion seem like an idiot was warranted.

Chapter 14: The version of the Callisto myth in which Zeus is disguised as Artemis seems to imply he had sex with her in that form, which makes it a little difficult to believe Callisto didn't catch on that she wasn't dealing with Artemis. Another version said Zeus was disguised as Apollo, and Hesiod apparently had a version in which there was no disguise, just an ordinary seduction. I have blended the Artemis version with the Hesiod one, making the disguise part of the seduction.

Chapter 15: Iasion is usually regarded as a mortal and as having been killed by Zeus, though some versions do vary as to how he died, and the connection with Demeter's cult in Samothrace, combined with Iasion's parentage, makes the assumption that he could have been a minor god more reasonable.

Chapter 18: The Melinoe story doesn't provide much motivation for the characters, so I have tried to provide some based on other stories about Zeus and Persephone.

The idea that there were two Cronuses doesn't appear in any ancient source but is a logical way to account for the inconsistencies in the way Cronus's fate is presented. It is sometimes assumed that other gods, such as Eros and Pan, are more than one person, and Hesiod explicitly says that of Eris, so though the specific detail is my own invention, it is not without precedent.

The idea that most gods cannot easily communicate with the inhabitants of

Elysium doesn't have any obvious precedent, but it is a reasonable way of explaining why the gods mourn when their mortal favorites die.

Chapter 21: The sources on the family of Sisyphus express horror that Salmoneus slept with his niece Tyro but don't seem to have a problem with Cretheus doing the same thing with the same unfortunate girl, even though Cretheus was the girl's guardian at the time. It seemed more logical to assume that Cretheus had a son, Cretheus II, who married Tyro, especially since ancient storytellers frequently did confuse men of the same name.

The story of Chrysippus ends in different ways in the several versions which exist, and I ended up blending two of them rather than following just one. Given the character of Atreus and Thyestes, it was logical for them to kill him, less logical for them or their mother to follow him to Thebes and kill him as he lay beside Laius. That version of the story also presupposed that Chrysippus was in love with Laius, which would have reduced the motivation for Hera to punish the Theban king. Consequently, I followed the version in which Chrysippus escaped from Laius but had him killed by his half-brothers instead of committing suicide from shame.

Chapter 23: No ancient source refers to rivers only accessible by magic, but it is a good way to explain some of the geographically unsound travels in the *Argonautica*, and a similar approach could account for some of the contradictory accounts about the location of particular mythological places.

Teiresias's discussion of gay relationships in the myths is a fair representation of the confusion and inconsistency present in the original sources. Ignoring the issue completely would have been misleading, but finding a reasonable way to reconcile the differing viewpoints eluded me. In the end, the best choice seemed to be to acknowledge the possibility that some of the relationships may have been gay and allow readers to make up their own minds.

Chapter 27: The Troilus story had many variations, so I felt justified in blending them in such a way that they supported Homer's portrayal of Achilles rather than working against it. I added the idea that Aphrodite was manipulating Achilles to explain his seemingly random actions and used his feelings for Polyxena, frequently noted in the ancient sources, as a way of explaining the killing of Troilus. I also blended the various stories of Polyxena's death, again in a way that would support Homer's characterization.

Chapter 28: The explanation of using blood to communicate with the dead is much more involved than the one in the *Odyssey*. I made some changes to reconcile the story with later versions of the Underworld.

Chapter 29: Later Greeks identified Hermes with Thoth, but there are no myths in which Hermes "channels" Thoth in the way he does in this chapter.

General Observation on Character Development: As I've noted in Appendix A, several characters vary enormously from one source to another. No one is completely good or bad, and everyone changes over time, but sometimes the variations in these characters are too great to fit into a realistic psychological framework. To bridge that kind of gap, I took the prevailing view and selected the details to fit it. In other words, if the character was supposed to be heroic, I used details appropriate for a hero, presenting the other details as rumors or deliberate slander. The heroes still have their flaws, as real people do, but understandable flaws rather than completely incomprehensible lapses. In some cases, I've also softened the rough edges a little by having the characters reflect on their past failings. The myths themselves sometimes show a similar process, as with Oedipus, for example, so I felt justified in assuming that other characters might have done so as well if they had had the chance.

Observations Regarding Rape in the Original Myths: This is the one area in which I threw the idea of being as true as possible to the original sources out the window. In addition to the usual problem of different authors having tremendously different views, there is no getting around the fact that the general Graeco-Roman attitudes toward rape are so different from our own—and so repugnant to us—that there is no way to make them understandable to modern readers. Frankly, since the primary audience is high school students, I wouldn't even want to try to make the Graeco-Roman view understandable. There are simply too many possibilities for misunderstanding.

As with so many other issues, the myths are not consistent, either in their attitudes toward rape or even about whether or not particular characters were guilty of that crime. There is no denying that ancient writers sometimes treat the subject in a way that to us seems repulsive. For instance, some Roman writers, like Terence, used rape as a subject of humor, and Greek New Comedy, from which he drew his subject matter, in some cases must have done the same. On the other hand, some stories treat rape with almost modern sensitivity. For instance, Ares is acquitted of the crime of murdering Poseidon's son, Halirrhothius, because the war god is able to prove that Halirrhothius raped Alcippe. Considering that murder was often punished by exile, the notion that death is an appropriate punishment for rape says quite a bit about how seriously at least one storyteller regarded the crime.

As I reviewed the myths, I couldn't help noticing the number of times what one storyteller called seduction, another called rape. Some writers didn't seem to differentiate at all. Part of the reason for this inconsistency is that is that, as Edward M. Harris points out, in ancient Greece there was no single word that encompassed everything we mean by rape, and the words that are used can also be used to describe other kinds of crimes. In addition, rape was not a question of whether or not a woman consented. In contrast to our society, women had few rights. Hence, it was the right of the male in charge of the woman (her father initially, and if she married, her husband) to determine with whom she had sex. Consequently, women in at least some of the myths could have been willing participants in the acts described as rape, but since the male who had authority over them had not given consent, those acts were still deemed unlawful. In one case, Chione is described as bragging about her encounters with Apollo and Hermes—hardly the behavior of a typical rape victim, then or now. In another, preserved only in Statius's *Achilleid*, Deidamia makes it clear she has long been attracted to Achilles and loves him after their first sexual encounter, even though he is described as taking her by force. Though confused—she had only just learned for sure he was a boy and not a girl—she seems willing enough. Her attitude raises the question of whether the one reference to force really relates to her own state of mind or whether it is inspired by the fact that Achilles does not have her father's consent to marry her. Similarly, Paris's taking of Helen is often described, by Herodotus for instance, as an abduction, even though Herodotus makes it clear that Helen has feelings for Paris, suggesting she consents to run away with him. From Herodotus's point of view, whether she consented or not, her husband Menelaus did not consent, which made Paris's act an abduction. By the way, *abduction* is a word sometimes used interchangeably with *rape*, just as *seduction* is. Hades abducts (or rapes) Persephone, but no writer suggests a sexual relationship between them until after they are married.

Some of the reactions of the female characters may stem from the fact that the stories were written by male authors who didn't understand how a rape victim would feel. Nonetheless, both myth and history furnish numerous examples of women who commit suicide following a rape, providing a grim clue that at least some people understood the miserable state a rape victim might be in. Given that flicker of awareness, I think it at least possible that women who seem willing and/or content with the situation in the myths might not be victims of rape in the modern sense. Instead, their fathers or husbands were the ones regarded as the victims. Harris points out a number of examples in which, whether the woman seems a victim as we would think about it or not, the offense is described from the point of view of the father or husband, not the woman.

The issue is further complicated by the fact that women could not choose their own husbands for most of the classical period. The prevalence of arranged marriages illustrates how little control women had over their own lives. So does the distribution of women as part of the spoils of war. In fact, a man who married a woman with her consent but without her father's would quite often have been considered a criminal. A man marrying a woman without her consent but with her father's would never have been regarded as a criminal.

Obviously, both the ambiguities in ancient Greek attitudes and the chasm between their beliefs and ours creates problems for the approach of being as faithful as possible to the originals, and there is no easy solution to those problems.

Even in a text intended for high school students, I didn't want to adopt the neo-Victorian, just-don't-talk-about-it position. That might create the false impression, particularly among students who do additional reading and find the original stories, that rape is something to be hidden away, perhaps even that rape is something victims should be ashamed of. Clearly, neither of those are attitudes I want to promote. Horrific as rape is, unpleasant as it is to think about, burying conversation about it has not reduced its likelihood, and high school students are not too young to understand the realities of rape; in fact, their safety requires that they be aware of those realities. With the U.S. Department of Justice reporting that 35.8% of rape victims are between the ages of twelve and seventeen and that 20% of female high school students are physically or sexually abused by a dating partner, some knowledge of the potential dangers is necessary for the safety and wellbeing of students.

On the other hand, calling every act rape that is so described by any storyteller would make almost all the male characters, both mortal and divine, rapists. In its own way, that creates just as distorted a picture as ignoring rape altogether. Many of the acts described as rape would probably not be considered that way by today's standards, and in any case, the myths often disagree about the way they characterize specific acts. For example, our earliest sources, Homer and Hesiod, do not usually describe the sexual relations between gods and mortal women as rapes. Instead, a woman lays in the arms of a god, a pattern we see both in the fragments from Hesiod's *Catalog of Women* and in the *Odyssey*. Later storytellers, perhaps trying to preserve the image of some of the women as dutiful daughters and faithful wives, came up with the bad solution of making the gods and heroes involved rapists. Shocking as it sounds to us, storytellers were willing to give the gods and at least some of the heroes a free pass. They did this partly because of the widespread belief that the gods were above human law. Besides that, for many ancient Greeks believed a man taking a woman by force, particularly if he had some kind of "good" reason, such as allegedly being in love with her, was a far less serious offense than a woman defying her father or cheating on her husband—about as big a double standard as one could imagine. It never seemed to occur to anybody that, if destiny or divine purpose require a woman and a god or hero to produce a son, the woman should be as considered as blameless as the man.

In this text I tried to take the position I wish the ancient storytellers had taken, neither assuming that the male characters are rapists nor that the female characters are guilty of adultery or other offenses. This approach does at least conform with the general attitude of Homer and Hesiod, and it also preserves their attitude that the gods, despite their acknowledged flaws, are still worthy of worship, and that the mortal heroes are often worthy of praise. Neither attitude would be comprehensible to modern readers if most of the gods and heroes were rapists. Other storytellers do take a tiny step toward a no-fault approach by praising the husbands who know their wives have slept with gods but who choose not to criticize those wives and to raise the children of the god as their own, the implication being that the relationship between their wives and the gods is not adultery in the normal sense. By contrast, men who mistreat their wives who have become mothers of divine offspring are almost always condemned rather than supported in their actions.

I assumed lack of consent and reserved the label of rape for situations in which punishment, particularly divine retribution, occurs (Orion, Halirrhothius, Laius, the lesser Ajax). In all of these stories except that of Laius, the male character is clearly guilty of rape in the modern sense in the most common version of the myths. I included the Laius story because Hera's actions against Laius make more sense in the version in which he is a rapist, and because the shame of Chrysippus in that version gave me a good opportunity to remind readers that the victim is never the one at fault. I mentioned the possibility of rape in a couple of other stories, where the evidence was a little less clear, and in such circumstances, the characters discuss the issues involved. In no case do I intend this kind of discussion as an attempt to minimize or justify rape. Rather, it is just an acknowledgment of the fact that the Greeks were still struggling toward a coherent definition of rape, and so most of the stories leave far more room for argument than a modern rape case would.

I'm aware my approach is an imperfect one, but it does seem preferable to ignoring the issue or to presenting all the male characters as rapists. The second option doesn't really do justice to how they were perceived by the original writers and audiences, nor to the numerous ambiguities created by those writers.

The truth is that the ancient Greeks, though they contributed much to our society, still struggled with a number of issues. At times they condoned violence when we would not. They accepted slavery as part of life. At least part of the time, they tolerated the exposure of unwanted infants. And by denying women more control of their own lives, they institutionalized practices we would today regard as rape.

I've tried to acknowledge such realities in the text. At the same time, I've tried to point out that they were moving toward more humane attitudes, and I've tried to acknowledge that effort as well. Homer may relish portraying scenes of violence, but he also raises questions about the desirability of war and makes its costs frighteningly clear. Eumaios, Odysseus's loyal swineherd, is a slave, but he was raised as a member of the family and is unfailingly loyal to it, and his story is perhaps intended to hint at the way slaves ought to be treated—just like everyone else. Many of the myths include exposure of infants, but in almost every one, that exposure backfires on the people who commit it, sealing their own fates. As for the role of women, while they are commonly treated like property in the myths, just as they were in life, many characters, including Atalanta, Athena, and Artemis demonstrate that women can be just as strong and independent as men. The love stories often show men treating women as far more than just property, in some cases even being willing to give up their lives for them.

Appendix C: Genealogies

The plots of a number of myths are driven by family relationships, so having a clear idea of how the characters are connected can be helpful. The following genealogies are intended as an easy visual reminder of the relationships among the characters.

If someone wanted to chart all the relationships in Greek mythology, the job could easily take a whole classroom wall. There's no way such a chart could fit a book page or be readable on a mobile device screen. Consequently, I had to use many small charts to display the relationships most relevant to the myths in this book. The size of each chart determined whether it was oriented top-down or left-to-right.

The genealogy template in SmartDraw was designed for modern family trees, not Greek mythological ones in which siblings frequently had children together. SmartDraw also allows for only one spouse (or sexual partner), though in the myths the same person or god often had children with multiple partners. The paragraphs below indicate how I used the software to portray the mythological relationships accurately.

SmartDraw represents spouses with lines connecting the two people involved. The box these lines form connects back to the parent(s), with the assumption being that the left name on a top-down chart or the bottom name on a left-right chart is the child of those parents, while the other name is the spouse. For purposes of this book, assume that both spouses are children of those parents if you are using one of the god charts. Exceptions are marked with parenthetical notes, *d. of X* or *s. of X* to distinguish the spouse's parentage. For example, Genealogy 1 shows that Erebus and Nyx are both children of Chaos and have two children together. In contrast, Typhoeus and Echidna also have children together but are not both children of Tartarus and Gaia, so Echidna's parentage is shown.

In the human charts you don't need to worry about sibling relationships, though I retained the parenthetical notes to make clear which member of the couple was the child of the parents listed above them. For instance, in Genealogy 12, Eurymede is labeled as the daughter of Nisus. Such labeling can also be useful to distinguish characters with the same name.

On both the god charts and the human charts, if the parentage of the spouse was unknown, I used an asterisk instead of a parenthetical note. Also, I didn't bother with parenthetical notes where the character's parentage was listed on the same chart or where the character was a god or well-known mortal whose parentage would be obvious.)

In both the god and mortal charts, I used certain abbreviations for parents whose names often occur. *Oceanid* refers to a daughter of Oceanus and Tethys. *River god* refers to a son of Oceanus and Tethys. *Nymph* may refer to a minor goddess of unknown parentage but is usually a Naiad, daughter of a river god and thus a granddaughter of Oceanus and Tethys. *Nereid* refers to a daughter of Nereus and Doris. *Pleiade* refers to a daughter of Atlas and Pleione. *Spartoi* (sown men) refers to one of the men born from the dragon's teeth in the Cadmus story.

To get around the single spouse limit, I normally listed the character's name more than once. If you see that in a chart, it never means that parents had two children of the same name. Althaea in Genealogy 17 is a good example of listing someone twice to show children with two different partners. In situations in which there wasn't room to list the name twice or in which there wasn't room for a spouse's name, I used parenthetical notes like *w. X* (with X) to indicate the other parent's name in each case. Chione's two sons by different fathers in Genealogy 14 are good examples of this situation.

If you see no spouse indicated on one of the god charts, it means the children were produced by only one parent. On one of the human charts, the omission of a spouse typically means that the spouse is unknown or uncertain.

For space reasons, members of the same generation don't always line up exactly with each other. There are also cases, such as Genealogies 8 and 26, in which short, related genealogies may appear on the same page; in that situation, the fact that a genealogy is farther down on the page doesn't necessarily mean it is later chronologically.

If you are using a mobile device and want to avoid a lot of scrolling by printing the charts out, you can download a PDF version at http://wp.me/P4QtX8-AI.

Genealogy 1: Primal Forces, Children of Erebus and Nyx, Children of Gaia and Tartarus

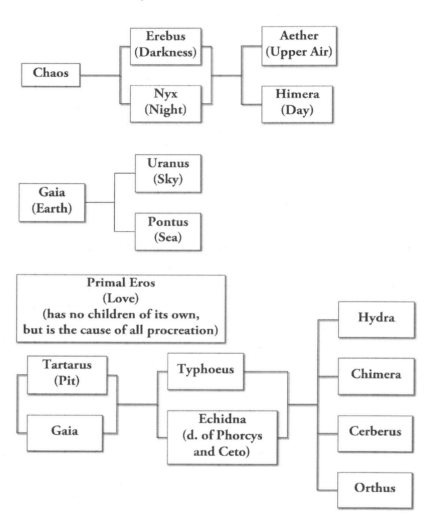

Genealogy 2: Children of the Night

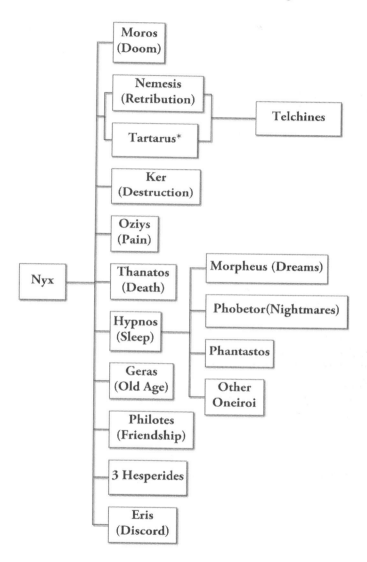

Genealogy 3: Children of Earth and Sky A (Cronus, Rhea, Cyclopes, Hecatoncheires, Uranus's "Flesh and Blood")

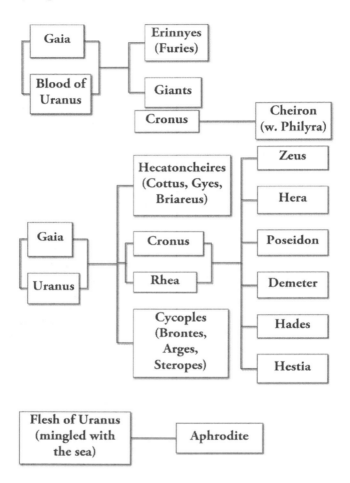

Genealogy 4: Children of Earth and Sky B (Titans of Water and Mind)

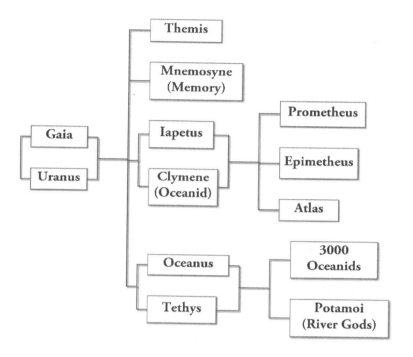

Genealogy 5: Children of Earth and Sky C (Titans of Sky)

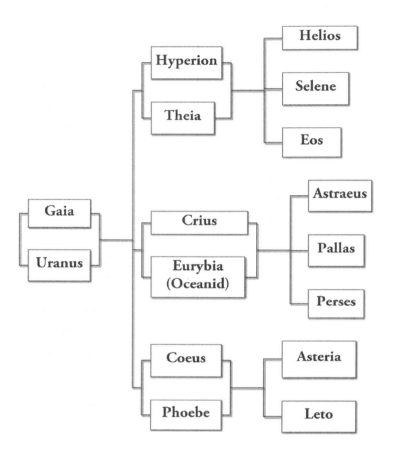

Genealogy 6: Children of Earth and Sea

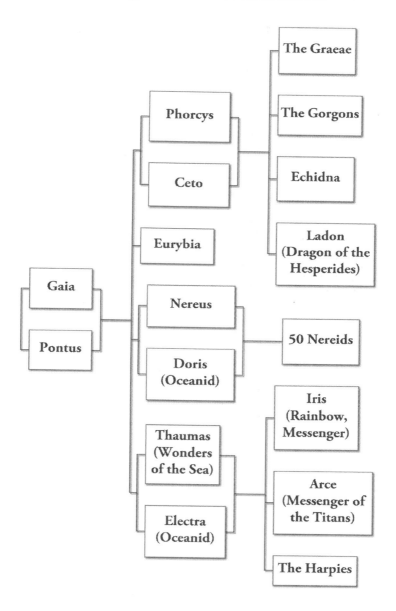

Genealogy 7: Later Titans

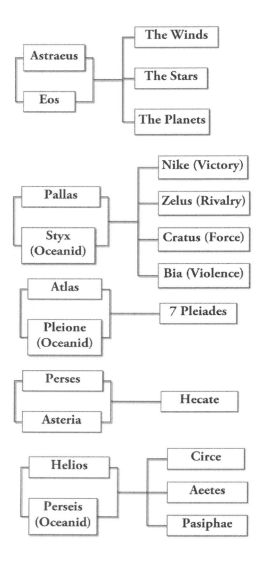

Genealogy 8: Divine Children of Zeus A

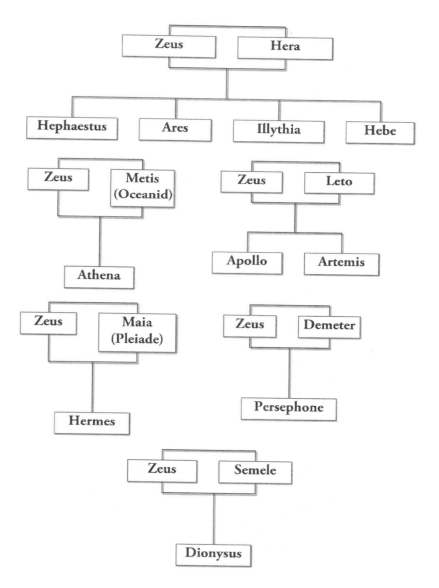

Genealogy 9: Divine Children of Zeus B

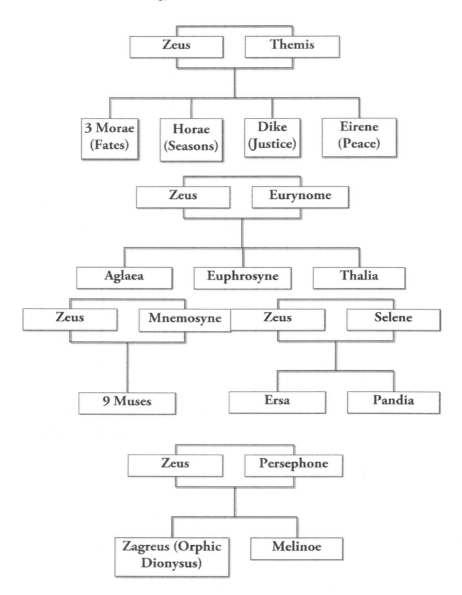

Genealogy 10: Divine Children of Other Gods (Selected)

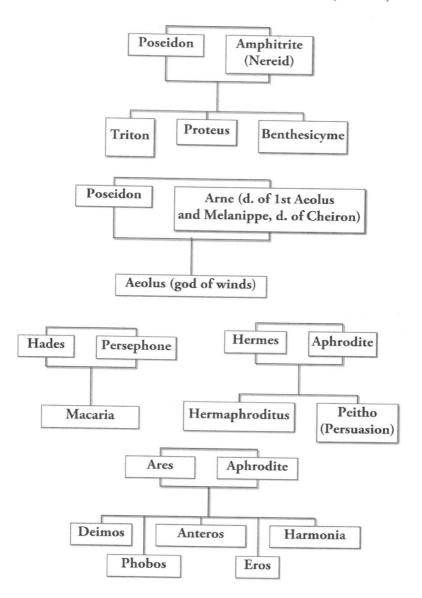

Genealogy 11: Family of Deucalion, Xuthus Branch

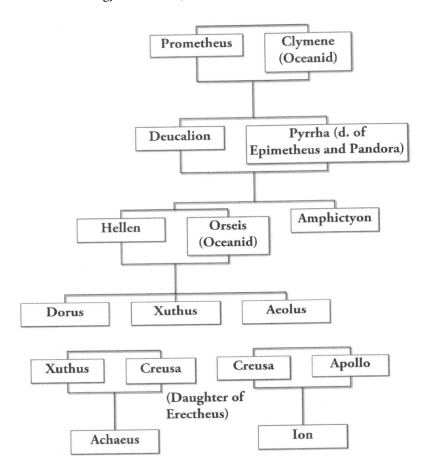

Genealogy 12: Family of Deucalion, Aeolus Branch, Sisyphus's Family

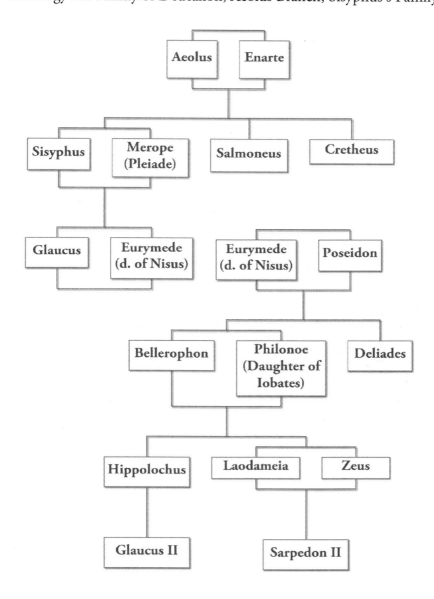

Genealogy 13: Family of Deucalion, Aeolus Branch, Families of Cretheus and Salmoneus

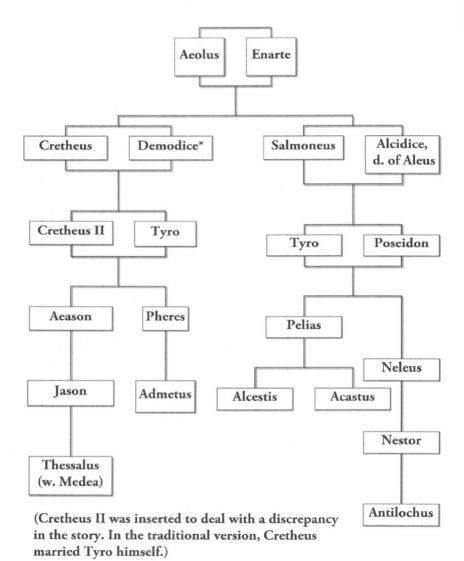

(Cretheus II was inserted to deal with a discrepancy in the story. In the traditional version, Cretheus married Tyro himself.)

Genealogy 14: Jason's (and Odysseus's) Maternal Descent

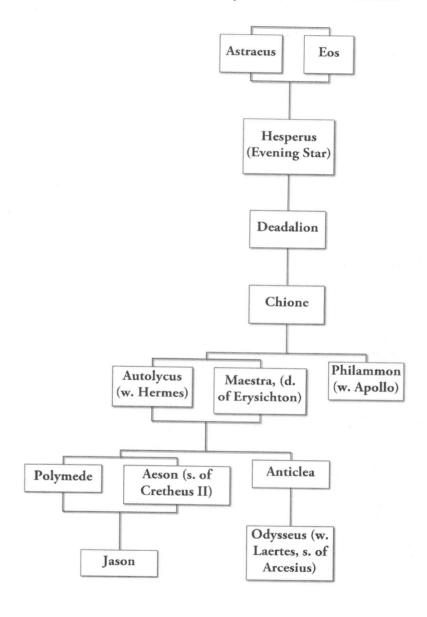

Genealogy 15: Family of Deucalion, Aeolus Branch, Family of Calyce
(royal family of Elis, beginnings of Calydon)

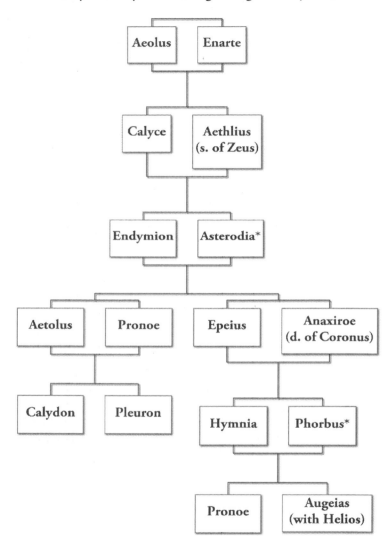

Genealogy 16: House of Calydon to Diomedes

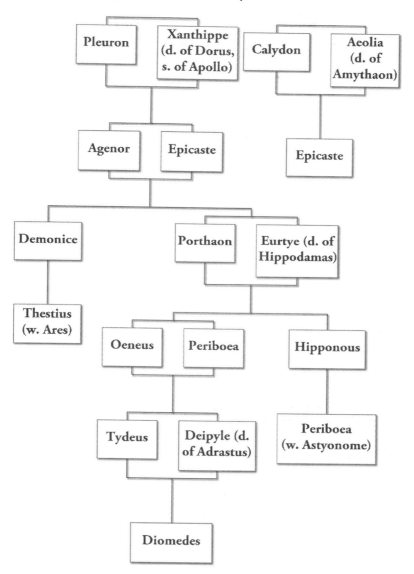

Genealogy 17: House of Calydon, Children of Thestius A

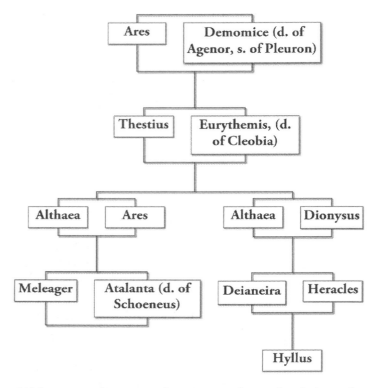

(Althaea was also married to Oeneus, king of Calydon. They
had children together, and Oeneus was the legal father of
Meleager and Deianeira as well.)

Genealogy 18: House of Calydon, Children of Thestius B

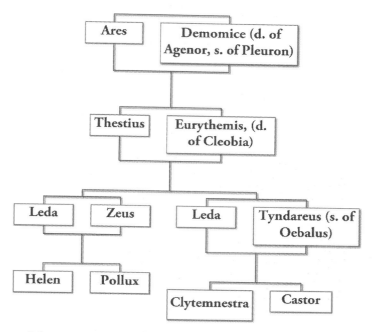

(Thestius also had Hypermenestra, who married Oicles and was the mother of Amphiarus, the seer.)

Genealogy 19: Early Inachids

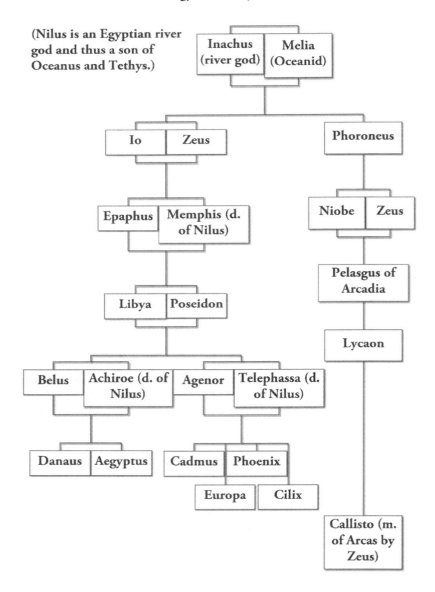

Genealogy 20: Later Inachids to Perseus

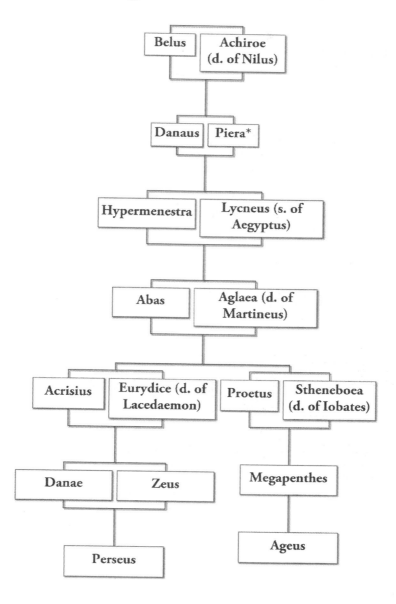

Genealogy 21: Later Inachids, Perseus to Heracles

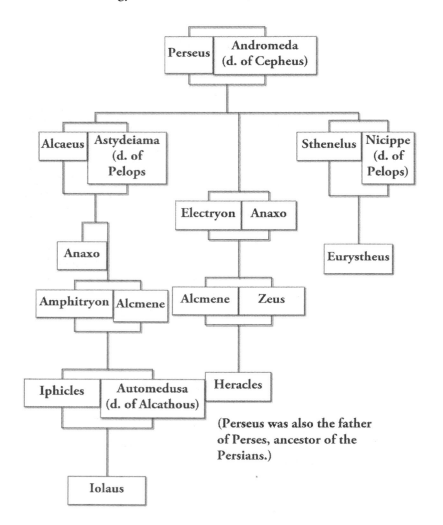

(Perseus was also the father
of Perses, ancestor of the
Persians.)

Genealogy 22: Later Inachids, House of Thebes A

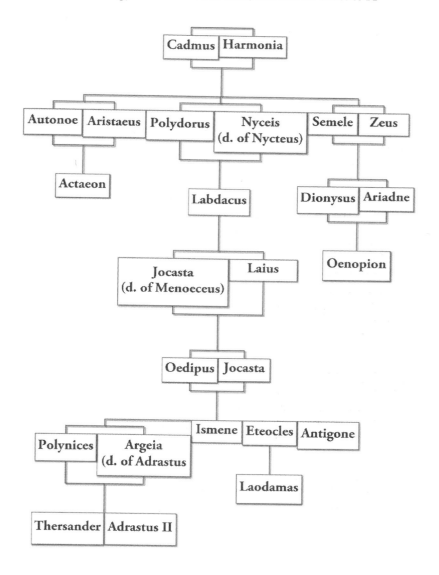

Genealogy 23: Later Inachids, House of Thebes B

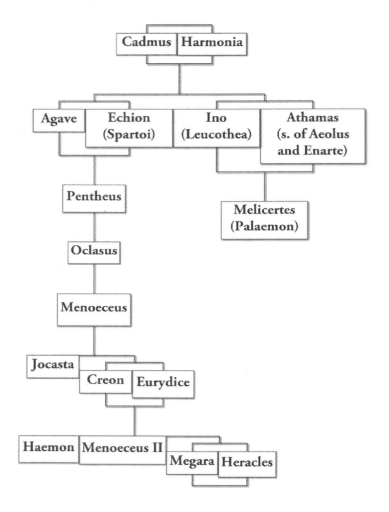

Genealogy 24: House of Thebes C (usurpers)

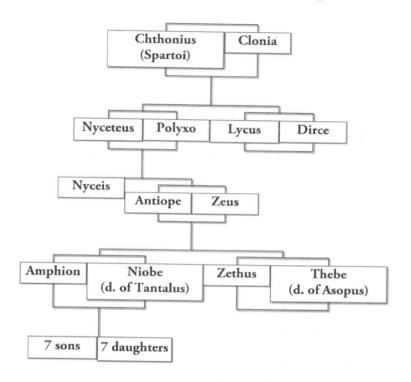

Genealogy 25: House of Athens A, Hephaestus to Pandion II

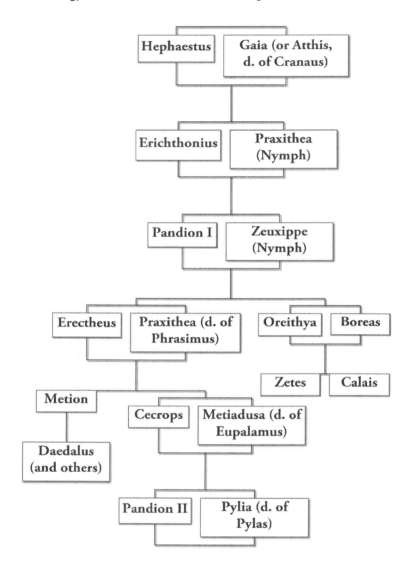

Genealogy 26: Royal House of Athens B, Pandion II to Demophon (Including Theseus)

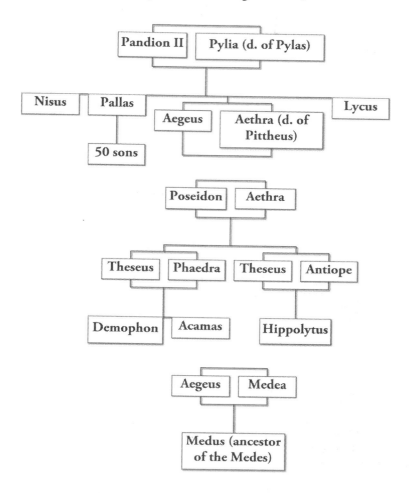

Genealogy 27: Royal House of Crete

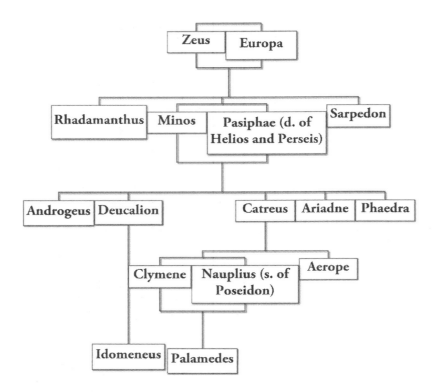

Genealogy 28: Family of Tantalus, Alcathous Branch

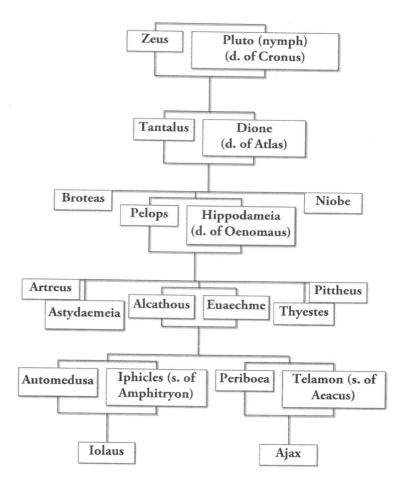

Genealogy 29: Family of Tantalus,
House of Atreus (Mycenae) and Thyestes

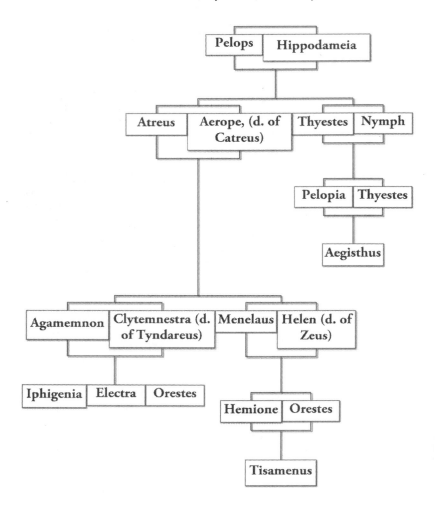

Genealogy 30: Family of Achilles

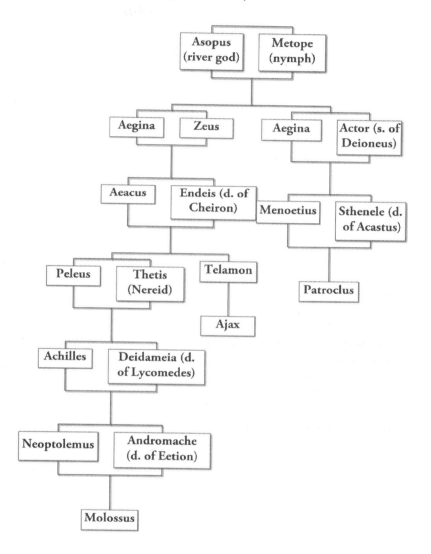

Genealogy 31: Family of Odysseus (Including House of Sparta)

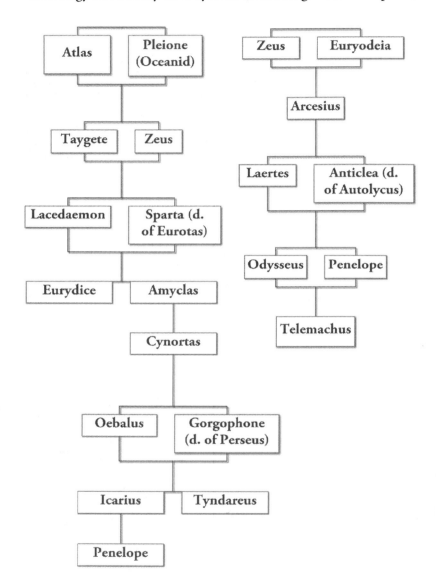

Genealogy 32: House of Troy A,
from beginning to Laomedon and Capys

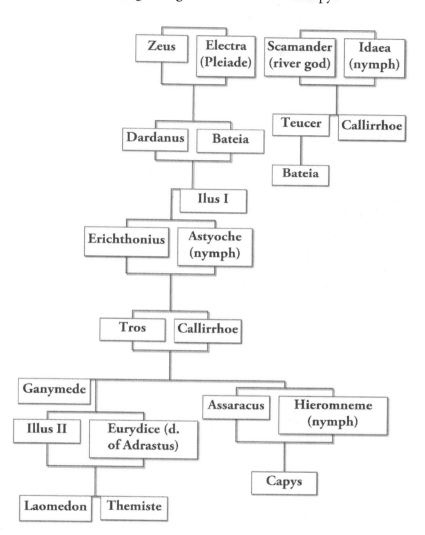

Genealogy 33: House of Troy B (Main Royal Line)

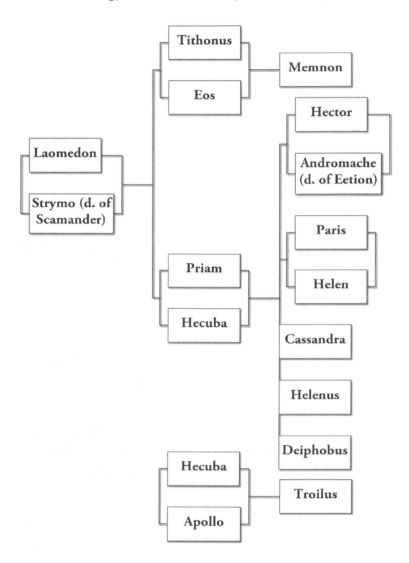

Genealogy 34: House of Troy C (Aeneas's Line)

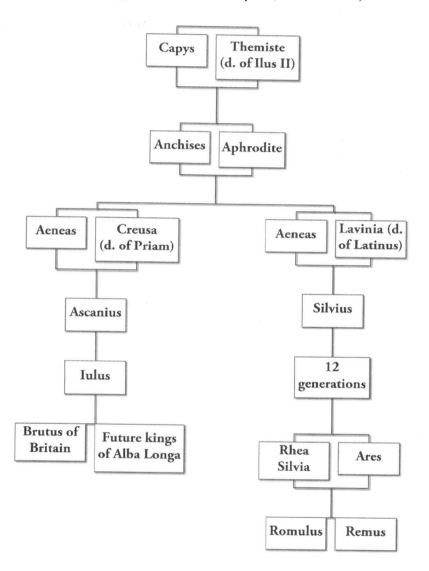

Appendix D: Roman Names

Romans already had a religion before they encountered the Greeks, but Roman gods did not have personalities in the same way the Greek gods did, so when Romans adopted some aspects of Greek culture, they tried to identify their gods with the Greek ones. The table below shows these some of these relationships.

Greek God	Roman God
Amphitrite	Salacia
Aphrodite	Venus
Apollo	Apollo
Ares	Mars
Artemis	Diana
Athena	Minerva
Cronus	Saturn
Demeter	Ceres
Dionysus	Bacchus
Eos	Aurora
Eris	Discordia
Eros	Cupid
Gaia	Tellus or Terra Mater
Hades	Pluto
Hecate	Trivia (sometimes)
Helios	Sol
Hephaestus	Vulcan
Hera	Juno
Hermes	Mercury
Hestia	Vesta
Hypnos	Somnus
Nike	Victoria
Pan	Faunus
Persephone	Proserpine

Greek God	Roman God
Phobos	Timor
Poseidon	Neptune
Rhea	Ops
Selene	Luna
Themis	Justitia
Tyche	Fortuna
Uranus	Uranus
Zeus	Jupiter

Appendix E: Sources, Suggestions for Further Study

For the high school students reading this book, I'll remind you that sources always need to be acknowledged in some way. However, this text is in the form of a novel, which normally would not require formal citation. In any case, parenthetical notes citing the specific source of each piece of information would be cumbersome. Even footnotes would interfere with the reading flow for some high school students. Because of the genre, purpose, and intended audience, I've adopted a somewhat less formal acknowledgment of sources than I would have if this work had been an exposition of the myths intended for more scholarly use. Any reader interested in the exact locations of particular myths or details can easily find them in some of the secondary sources mentioned below.

By the way, in this context primary sources are the ancient works from which the myths come originally. Secondary sources are more recent works that retell and/or analyze those myths. The mythic content in this book generally comes from primary sources, but I often used secondary sources to help me locate the relevant ancient texts, alert me to different versions, give me an idea of which versions were the most widely known, and in general keep me on the right track by making the overall context of each myth clear. I'll discuss these secondary sources first, indicating the value they might have for those of you who want to pursue your study of mythology further. Then I'll indicate which material in the book comes from which primary sources.

I found three secondary sources so valuable that I referred to them constantly: *The Routledge Handbook of Greek Mythology* by Robin Hand (2004); *The Greek Myths* by Robert Graves (2011 edition, based on Graves's 1960 text); *Theoi* (http://www.theoi.com/) by Aaron Atsma (based on research at the universities of Auckland and Leiden).

Hand's book is a very thorough scholarly introduction to the myths. It's hard to find a single story or character of any importance that isn't included. In addition, Hand's notes make it easy to trace myths back to their ancient sources.

Graves pursues a scholarly approach as well, but since he is also a noted novelist and poet, his version is more suitable for pleasure reading. Like Hand, he includes references to the ancient sources he uses. When reading Graves, it's important to keep in mind that he has very distinct theories about the myths which are *his* and not always representative of the scholarly consensus. However, he keeps his ideas separate from his retelling of the stories, so it's easy to tell which parts are ancient and which parts are Graves.

Atsma provides handy summaries of Greek gods, heroes, and monsters, so his site is a high-quality quick reference. However, it also goes beyond that by providing a great genealogy of the gods all in one place (as opposed to the ten small charts I used to cover some of the same material!) Also of great value is his classical texts library, which includes sixty-nine ancient Greek and Roman works in good public domain translations. Actually, the summary pages also include extensive quotations from ancient sources, a handy way of spotting differences in the way different authors tell each story. Finally, there is a large image collection, so you can also see how ancient artists portrayed the myths.

In the context of online collections of ancient literature, I should also mention *Perseus Digital Library*, sponsored by Tufts University, under the direction of Gregory R. Crane, editor-in-chief: http://www.perseus.tufts.edu/hopper/collection?collection=Perseus:collection:Greco-Roman. The collection includes a number of texts in their original languages, but it also has a fairly extensive selection of English translations of both primary and secondary works.

A good, well-organized source for summaries, as well as perhaps the best online source for the mortal genealogies, is *Timeless Myths*, created by Jimmy Joe (presumably a pseudonym: http://www.timelessmyths.com/classical/genealogy.html. (If you want to consult a few larger family trees instead of relying on the much smaller ones in this book, then that site would be a good resource for you.)

I should also mention I found *Wikipedia* handy for quick look-ups —who someone's father was, for example. I also found it informative with regard to Orphic versions of myths, on which writers like Hand and Graves did not spend much time. Of course, with a source involving so much public contribution, it is always a good idea to check an article's sources to ensure the material is being presented correctly, but I generally found no problems.

As far as primary sources are concerned, I had read most of them over the years—I loved mythology from a very young age—but I reread large portions in preparation for this book and relied upon them heavily. (The names in parentheses are the translators. In some cases I consulted more than one translation, as I was more familiar with the one I had in print, but the online and/or ebook versions were faster to search for information.)

Hesiod's *Theogony* (Lattimore, though the quotations in the text are from Evelyn-White) is the principal source for the creation story, the genealogy of the gods (with a few exceptions), the functions of many of the lesser gods, some details of the gods' personalities, the battles with the Titans, giants, and Typhoeus, and the story of Prometheus—in other words, the first four chapters, as well as considerable material after that. The Pandora story comes from Hesiod's *Works and Days*.

The two epics ascribed to Homer, the *Iliad* (Fitzgerald, Lattimore) and the *Odyssey* (Lattimore), are one source for several of the shorter myths. However, their primary contribution is to the story of the Trojan War and its aftermath. The *Iliad* is the primary source for the wrath of Achilles during the Trojan War (chapter 27), while the *Odyssey* is the primary source for the wanderings of Odysseus (chapter 28). Both epics are also rich sources for the personalities of the gods and particularly the ways in which they interact with each other. My portrayal of Zeus as a politician is particularly indebted to Homer, and I generally followed him in the way I characterized the heroes about which he writes.

The only ancient Greek mythographer whose work survived (though partially in the form of summaries by later writers) is Apollodorus, whose *Library* (Simpson, Smith) has left its mark on practically every chapter. In some cases, such as baby Hermes's cattle raid (chapter 5), the life of Perseus (chapter 23) and the life of Heracles (chapter 25), the *Library* is the primary source, but in many other stories, Apollodorus supplies some detail.

The *Homeric Hymns* (Athanassakis) provide descriptive detail for many of the gods, as well as some important narratives, such as Hades's kidnapping of Persephone (chapter 15) some of Apollo's deeds (chapter 10) and the love of Aphrodite and Anchises (chapter 9).

Pindar, the author of several collections of odes (Lattimore, Verity) frequently provides detail, as well as being the primary source for some stories (such as the early life of Jason (chapter 23) and parts of the Tantalus story (chapter 6)

The *Argonautica* by Apollonius of Rhodes is the primary source for Jason's adventures on the *Argo* (chapter 23). As with Homer, Apollonius also weaves other myths into the story.

The three Greek tragedians whose works survive (Aeschylus, Sophocles, and Euripides, for whom I read versions by various translators in Complete Greek Tragedies series published by University of Chicago Press) are primary sources for a large number of myths, including the beginning of the Io story (Aeschylus's *Prometheus Bound,* Chapter 20), the Ion story (Euripides's *Ion,* Chapter 20), Oedipus and his family (Sophocles's Theban Plays, Chapter 21), Jason's later life (Euripides's *Medea,* Chapter 23) Orestes and his family (Aeschylus's *Oresteia,* Chapter 28), as well as several other, smaller stories and details for a few others.

The listing below shows a more detailed breakdown of sources by chapter and includes some sources used less extensively than those above. In the interest of clarity (and brevity), it includes only major sources for particular stories, not sources that might have contributed only a detail or two. It does not include other possible versions of the same story, though in many cases stories do appear in several places. Hymns mentioned only by the name of a god refers to the Homeric Hymn(s) for that god.

Chapter 1: Homer, *Odyssey*, Ovid, *Metamorphoses* (Demos Oneiroi).

Chapter 2: Hesiod, *Theogony.*

Chapter 3: Hesiod, *Theogony*; Apollodorus, *Library* (Gigantomachy).

Chapter 4: Hesiod, *Theogony,* (Prometheus); Hesiod, *Works and Days,* (Pandora).

Chapter 5: Apollodorus, *Library*; *Hymn to Hermes.*

Chapter 6: Pindar, *Odes*; Euripides, *Orestes* (Tantalus), Diodorus Siculus, *Library of History* (Ixion); Hesiod, *Theogony* (lovers of Zeus, Iris); Homer, *Iliad* (revolt against Zeus); Apollodorus, *Library* (Semele).

Chapter 7: Hesiod, *Shield of Heracles* (Cycnus); Homer, *Iliad* (Ascalaphus); Pindar, *Odes*, *Hymn to Apollo*, *Hymn to Asclepius* (Asclepius).

Chapter 8: Pausanias, *Description of Greece* (Ardalos); Apollodorus, *Library* (Melampus); Hesiod, *Theogony* (Metis, birth of Athena)

Chapter 9: Ovid, *Metamorphoses* (Hermaphroditus); Apollodorus, *Library*, Hyginus, *Fabulae* (Erichthonius); Ovid, *Metamorphoses* (Pygmalion and Galatea); Apollodorus, *Library*, Ovid, *Metamorphoses* (Adonis).

Chapter 10: Herodotus, *Histories*, Pindar, *Odes*, Diodorus Siculus, *Library of History* (Hyperborea); Diodorus Siculus, Apollonius, *Argonautica*, Pausanias, *Description of Greece*, Ovid, *Metamorphoses* (Phaethon); Ovid, Pausanias (Daphne); Apollonius, Diodorus Siculus (Aristaeus); Ovid, Hyginus, *Fabulae* (Actaeon); Hesiod, *Theogony*, *Hymn to Demeter* (Hecate).

Chapter 11: Diodorus Siculus, *Library of History* (Aex, origin of aegis); Apollodorus, *Library* (contest between Athena and Poseidon, Halirrhothius); Ovid, *Metamorphoses* (Arachne, Herse, and her sisters); Apollonius, *Argonautica* (prow of the *Argo*).

Chapter 12: *Hymn to Artemis*; Callimachus, *Hymn to Artemis*; Eratosthenes, *Placings among the Stars* (summarizing a lost work of Hesiod) (Orion); Euripides, *Hippolytus*, Ovid, *Metamorphoses*, Virgil, *Aeneid* (Hippolytus).

Chapter 13: Apollodorus, *Library*, Lucian, *Dialogues of the Dead* (Endymion).

Chapter 14: *Hymn to Pan* (birth); Ovid, *Metamorphoses* (Syrinx, Pan's competition with Apollo); Apuleius, *Metamorphoses* (Cupid and Psyche); Ovid, *Metamorphoses* (Callisto); Ovid, Hyginus, *Fabulae*, Apollodorus, *Library* (Lycaon).

Chapter 15: *Hymn to Demeter*, Hesiod, *Theogony*, Hyginus, *Fabulae*, Apollodorus, *Library* (abduction of Persephone); *Suda* (Macaria); Virgil, *Aeneid* (golden bough); Hesiod, *Theogony* (Iasion); Hesiod, Pausanias, *Description of Greece* (Demeter's relationship with Poseidon); Callimachus, *Hymn to Demeter,* Ovid, *Metamorphoses* (Erysichthon).

Chapter 16: Apollodorus, *Library*; Seneca, *Oedipus*; *Hymn to Dionysus*; Nonnus, *Dionysiaca*; Apollodorus, *Library*, Ovid, *Metamorphoses* (Calydonian Boar Hunt); Euripides, *Bacchae* (Pentheus); Apollodorus, Pindar, *Odes*, Ovid, *Metamorphoses*, Virgil, *Georgics, Orphic Hymns* (Orpheus); Diodorus Siculus, *Library of History* (Ariadne)

Chapter 17: Hyginus, *Astronomica* (marriage of Poseidon and Amphitrite); Apollodorus, *Library* (children of Poseidon); Homer, *Odyssey* (Cyclopes); Plato, *Timaeus* and *Critias* (Atlantis); Homer, *Odyssey*, Apollodorus, *Library* (Otus and Ephialtes); Ovid, *Metamorphoses* (Caenis/Caeneus); Homer, *Odyssey* (Poseidon and Aethiopians, Poseidon's palace); Hesiod, *Theogony* (penalty for breaking oaths sworn on the Styx); Pindar, *Odes*; Strabo, *Geography*, Ovid, *Metamorphoses* (Telchines); Aelian, *On Animals* (Nerites); *Orphic Hymns* (Mnemosyne's spring).

Chapter 18: Homer, *Odyssey*; Virgil, *Aeneid* (description of the Underworld, Charon); Hesiod, *Theogony*; Virgil, *Aeneid* (Cerberus); Servius on *Virgil's Eclogues* (Leuce); Strabo, *Geography*, Ovid, *Metamorphoses* (Minthe); *Orphic Hymns*, Nonnus, *Dionysiaca* (Melinoe); Philostratus, *Life of Apollonius of Tyana* (Lamiae); Pausanias, *Description of Greece* (Eurynomus); Homer, *Odyssey*, Pindar, *Odes*, Virgil, *Aeneid* (Elysian Fields).

Chapter 19: Apollodorus, *Library*, Hesiod, *Theogony* (Deucalion, flood); Hesiod, *Catalog of Women* (Hellen and his sons); Euripides, *Ion* (Ion).

Chapter 20: Apollodorus, *Library,* Hyginus, *Fabulae* (Phoroneus); Pausanias, *Description of Greece*, Aeschylus, *Prometheus Bound* (Io); Apollodorus, *Library* (Argus Panoptes); Apollodorus, Hyginus (descendants of Io in general, Danaus and Aegyptus); Apollodorus, Ovid, *Metamorphoses* (Europa).

Chapter 21: Apollodorus, *Library* (Cadmus, Athamas and Ino); Hesiod, *Theogony* (Aristaeus and Autonoe); Apollodorus (Sisyphus); Ovid, *Metamorphoses*, Hyginus *Fabulae* (Chione, Autolycus); Apollodorus, Diodorus Siculus *Library of History* (Salmoneus); Apollodorus, Hyginus (Tyro, Pelias); Apollodorus (Amphion and Zethus); Apollodorus, Hyginus (Chrysippus); Sophocles, *Oedipus the King, Oedipus at Colonus, Antigone* (Laius, Jocasta, Creon, Oedipus, Antigone, Eteocles, Polynices, Ismene); Aeschylus, *Seven against Thebes* (war between Polynices and Eteocles); Apollodorus (Amphiarus, last members of Cadmus's line)

Chapter 22: Hesiod, *Theogony*, Homer, *Iliad*; Pindar, *Odes* (Bellerophon); Apollodorus, *Library*, Pausanias, *Description of Greece*, Ovid, *Metamorphoses*(Perseus)

Chapter 23: Pindar, *Odes* (Jason's early life); Apollonius, *Argonautica* (Jason's quest); Apollodorus, *Library*; Ovid, *Metamorphoses* (Jason's fall from grace); Euripides, *Medea* (Jason's downfall).

Chapter 24: Apollodorus, *Library*; Ovid, *Metamorphoses*; Euripides, *Hippolytus*; Plutarch, *Lives*.

Chapter 25: Apollodorus, *Library*, Diodorus Siculus, *Library of History*; Hesiod, *Shield of Heracles* (birth, family, battle with Cycnus); Euripides, *Heracles* (murder of his family); Euripides, *Alcestis* (Admetus and Alcestis); Herodotus, *Histories* (Scythes); Sophocles, *Women of Trachis* (death); Euripides, *Children of Heracles* (battle between his sons and Eurystheus).

Chapter 26: Apollodorus, *Library* (Pelops, Atreus, and Thyestes); Aeschylus, *Oresteia*; Hyginus, *Fabulae* (Atreus and Thyestes, Aegisthus); Euripides, *Helen*; Apollodorus, *Library* (Helen, birth, and marriage); Statius, *Achilleid* (Achilles, early life)

Chapter 27: Proclus, summary of *Cypria*; Homer, *Iliad*; Proclus, summary of Aethiopis, *Little Iliad* and *Iliupersis*

Chapter 28: Aeschylus, Oresteia (Agamemnon and Orestes); Homer, *Odyssey* (Odysseus, lesser Ajax, Menelaus); Proclus's summary of *Telegony* (Odysseus); Virgil, *Aeneid* (Aeneas).

Chapter 29: Robert Graves in *Greek Myths* extrapolated from Greek artwork the idea that Orpheus charmed Hecate at some point.

For background material, I used the following sources:

Chapter 7: Details of ancient Greek weapons came from https://learnodo-newtonic.com/ancient-greek-weapons. And from *Greece and Rome at War* by Peter Connolly.

Chapter 8: Details of the linothorax came from the *New Yorker* (http://www.newyorker.com/books/joshua-rothman/how-to-make-your-own-greek-armor). (The experiences mentioned in the article became the basis for a book, *Reconstructing Ancient Linen Body Armor*, by Gregory S. Aldrete, Scott Bartell, and Alex Aldrete.)

Chapter 9: The descriptions of Aphrodite's Rock and other details of Cyprus come from images available through Google Earth, a downloadable program invaluable for digital tourism and certain kinds of research (https://www.google.com/earth/).

Chapter 10: The details of Greek temple architecture come from (http://www.crystalinks.com/greekarchitecture.html) and from *The Earth, the Temple, and the Gods: Greek Sacred Architecture*, by Vincent Scully. The magical lore of amber comes from the J. Paul Getty Museum website (http://museumcatalogues.getty.edu/amber/intro/3/).

Chapter 11: The Parthenon details come from *The Earth, the Temple, and the Gods: Greek Sacred Architecture*, by Vincent Scully. Details of the topography of ancient Athens come from (http://www.ancientgreece.com/MapOfAthens/).

Chapter 15: Eleusis and Telesterion details come from *The Earth, the Temple, and the Gods: Greek Sacred Architecture*, by Vincent Scully, and from the University of Warwick's website, Classics and History section (http://www2.warwick.ac.uk/fac/arts/classics/students/modules/greekreligion/databas e/hypaaq/)

Chapter 16: Details about the Melanes Valley come from Naxos Dreams (http://www.naxosdream.com/en/around-naxos/regions/melanes-valley.html). The information about sea grape wine comes from https://www.leaf.tv/articles/how-to-make-sea-grape-wine/.

Chapter 17: The information on Freudian psychology comes from S. E. McLeod's "Id, Ego, and Superego" (https://www.simplypsychology.org/psyche.html). The information on the use of terms like *Apollonian* and *Dionysian* comes from Chris Baldick's *Oxford Dictionary of Literary Terms*, Nancy A. Taylor's online discussion outline at http://www.csun.edu/nancytaylor/ad.html and from *Wikipedia*, "Apollonian and Dionysian" (https://en.wikipedia.org/wiki/Apollonian_and_Dionysian)

Chapter 21: Details of the topography of ancient Thebes come from a map in Wikipedia, but originally from William Smith's *A Dictionary of Greek and Roman Geography* (https://en.wikipedia.org/wiki/Thebes,_Greece#/media/File:Plan_of_Thebes.jpg).

Chapter 23: Details about the Greek and Roman attitudes toward gay relationships came from John Boswell's *Same-Sex Unions in Premodern Europe*, John F. Dwyer's *Those 7 References: Study of 7 References to Homosexuality in the Bible* (which is obviously much more focus on Israelite society, but the analysis of Paul's references do give some insight into Graeco-Roman society), and James Davidson's article in the *The Guardian*, "Mad about the Boy" (https://www.theguardian.com/books/2007/nov/10/history.society), based on his book, *The Greeks and Greek Love*.

Chapter 24: The details about Cape Sounion and its temple to Poseidon come from http://ancient-greece.org/architecture/temple-poseidon-sounio.html.

Appendix B: The information about rape in ancient Greece comes from Edward M. Harris's "Did Rape Exist in Classical Athens? Further Reflections on the Laws about Sexual Violence" available at http://www.ledonline.it/Dike/allegati/dike7_harris.pdf. The statistics come from the U.S. Department of Justice (https://www.nsopw.gov/en-US/Education/FactsStatistics?AspxAuto DetectCookieSupport=1

About the Author

Bill Hiatt taught for thirty-six years. Thirty-four of those years he spent teaching English at Beverly Hills High School. He also served in a number of other capacities at Beverly, including Director of Forensics, English Department Chairperson, Honors English Coordinator, School Site Council Chairperson, member of the Superintendent's Advisory Council, and member of the District Technology Committee. He was a recipient of the Beverly Hills Education Foundation's Apple Award, The Beverly Hills Chamber of Commerce's Teacher of the Year Award, and the PTSA Honorary Service Award.

Beginning in 2012, Bill became a writer, both of fantasy fiction and of education-related works. You can find a list of his current titles in the next section.

Other Books and Booklets by Bill Hiatt

Spell Weaver Series
(Shorts set in the Spell Weaver universe are inserted where they belong in the storyline but are not numbered.)

"Echoes of My Past Lives" (0)
Living with Your Past Selves (1)
Divided against Yourselves (2)
Hidden among Yourselves (3)
"Destiny or Madness"
"Angel Feather"
Evil within Yourselves (4)
We Walk in Darkness (5)
Separated from Yourselves (6)

Different Dragons Series

Different Lee (1)

Soul Salvager Series

The Devil Hath the Power (0)

Anthologies
[The names of the piece(s) by Bill Hiatt are in parentheses following the anthology title.]

Anthologies of the Heart, Book 1: Where Dreams and Visions Live
("The Sea of Dreams")
Flash Flood 2: Monster Maelstrom, A Flash Fiction Halloween Anthology
("In the Eye of the Beholder")
Flash Flood 3: Christmas in Love, A Flash Fiction Anthology
("Naughty or Nice?" and "Entertaining Unawares")

Hidden Worlds, Volume 1: Unknown, a Sci-Fi and Fantasy Anthology
("The Worm Turns" and "Abandoned")
[Summer of 2017]
Great Tomes Series, Book 6: The Great Tome of Magicians, Necromancers, and Mystics
("Green Wounds")

Education-related Titles

"A Parent's Guide to Parent-Teacher Communications"
"A Teacher's Survival Guide for Writing College Recommendations"
"Poisoned by Politics: What's Wrong with
Education Reform and How To Fix It"

Index

The index includes characters and places related to Greek mythology, as well as some literary terms. It does not include items less relevant to the purpose of the book. Please note that, because of the way the indexing software operates, characters with the same name are indexed together.

91472240R00312

Made in the USA
Lexington, KY
22 June 2018